# THE ESSENTIAL MAILER

# THE ESSENTIAL
## MAILER
### Norman Mailer

NEW ENGLISH LIBRARY

*Acknowledgments:* The author gratefully acknowledges permission to include the following previously copyrighted works in this collection:

'King of the Hill.' Copyright © 1971 by Norman Mailer. First published in *Life*, March 19, 1971. Also published by New American Library, Inc.

'Homage to El Loco.' Copyright © CBS Records, 1967. Published by the CBS Legacy Collection.

'The Playwright as Critic.' Copyright © 1967 by Norman Mailer. A portion of the introduction was first published in the *New York Times Book Review* in 1967. The entire piece was first published as an introduction to *The Deer Park*, published by the Dial Press in 1967.

'Some Dirt in the Talk.' Copyright © 1967 by Norman Mailer. First published in *Esquire*, December 1967.

'A Course in Film-Making.' Copyright © 1971 by Norman Mailer. First published in *New American Review #12*.

'Up the Family Tree.' Copyright © 1968 by Norman Mailer. First published in *Partisan Review*, Spring 1968.

'Introduction to *The End of Obscenity*.' Copyright © 1969 by Norman Mailer. First published in the British edition of the book, published by André Deutsch Ltd. in 1969. Not published in the American edition.

'An Imaginary Interview.' Copyright © 1967 by Norman Mailer. First published in the *New York Times Book Review*, September 17, 1967.

'Lament for Ignacio Sánchez Mejías.' Copyright © 1955 by New Directions Publishing Corp. Translation copyright © 1967 by Norman Mailer. Translation first published in *The Poetry Bag*, Volume 1, Number 6, Winter 1967–68.

'Excerpts from *Playboy*.' Copyright © 1967 by *Playboy*. First published in *Playboy*, January 1968.

'To the *New York Review of Books*.' Copyright © 1966 by Norman Mailer. First published in the *New York Review of Books*, April 28, 1966.

'To the *Saturday Review*'. Copyright © 1971 by Norman Mailer. First published in the *Saturday Review*, April 20, 1971.

'To the *New York Times*.' Copyright © 1971 by Norman Mailer. First published in the *New York Times Book Review*, June 20, 1971.

'An Appreciation of Henry Miller.' Copyright © 1966 by the Delacorte Press. First published as a contribution to *Double Exposure* by Roddy McDowall, published by Delacorte Press in 1966.

'An Appreciation of Cassius Clay.' Copyright © 1967 by Norman Mailer. First published in the *Partisan Review*, Summer 1967.

'Two Oddments from *Esquire*.' Copyright © 1963 by Norman Mailer. First published in the October and November 1963 issues of *Esquire*.

'*Rush to Judgment* by Mark Lane.' Copyright © 1966 by Norman Mailer. First published in the *Village Voice*, September 1, 1966.

'Looking for the Meat and Potatoes.' Copyright © 1969 by Norman Mailer.

First published in *Look*, January 7, 1969.
'Contribution to a *Partisan Review* symposium on Black Power and a following exchange.' Copyright © 1968 by Norman Mailer. First published in *Partisan Review*, Spring, Summer, Fall, 1968.
'An Open Letter to Richard Nixon.' Copyright © 1968 by Norman Mailer. First published in *Newsweek*, December 9, 1968.
'An Instrument for the City.' Copyright © 1969 by Norman Mailer. First published in the *New York Times* Magazine, May 18, 1969.
'Two mayoralty speeches.' Copyright © 1969 by Norman Mailer. First published by Doubleday & Co., Inc. in *Running Against the Machine*, edited by Peter Manso, in 1969.

Parts One to Eight first published in the United States of America by Dell Publishing Co. Reprinted by arrangement with the author by Howard Fertig Inc., New York, in 1980

Parts Nine to Eleven first published in the United States of America by Little, Brown & Company

This collection first published in Great Britain in 1982 by New English Library

First NEL Paperback Edition August 1983

NEL Books are published by
New English Library,
Mill Road, Dunton Green,
Sevenoaks, Kent.
Editorial office: 47 Bedford Square, London WC1B 3DP

Typeset by Rowland Phototypesetting Ltd,
Bury St Edmunds, Suffolk
Printed in Great Britain by Collins, Glasgow

0 450 05609 0

# Contents

# Introduction

It has been remarked that the short fiction of this author is neither splendid, unforgettable, nor distinguished, and I hasten hereby to join such consensus. A man may go his way, look for his education, grow cultivated, even become superb, yet he need never come in contact with a short story of mine. He will still seem almost perfect. Nay, he will be almost perfect. Of course one would not want to chance this of a man ignorant of *An American Dream, The Deer Park, Barbary Shore*, or *The Naked and the Dead* – no, they should not be avoided. Why, others in fact might go on so far as to insist this highly cultivated fellow was directly hurting his appreciation of American rackets and letters by not catching up on the journalism, politics, essays, and general nonfiction of the author under examination. But, one place, there is agreement. The friends of the author, and his detractors, may argue over his position as novelist, philosopher, essayist, journalist, personality, cathartic, spark, or demiurge, but they hold hands on the short fiction. He's a journeyman there. And he agrees. The author agrees now twice. He does not have the gift to write great short stories, or perhaps even very good ones. In fact, he will confess he does not have the interest, the respect, or the proper awe. The short story bores him a little. He will admit he rarely reads them. He is, in secret, not fond of writers who work at short stories. Nor are they often, he suspects, fond of him. He has a private sneer for the reputations they have amassed. There is a terrible confession to make: he thinks the short story is relatively easy to write. You have only to be good for a day or a week – there is none of that arduous collaboration between character and passion, inspiration and asceticism, which goes into keeping one's balance on the teeter-totter of a novel where work goes on day after day through many a season into the years. Anyone can be good for a week, but who can be good for a year, or two, or three? So, while there may be admiration or affection for a few writers of the short story, for Chekhov, for Hemingway, for

Isaac Bashevis Singer, for James T. Farrell – the list is really not that long. One does not really want to include de Maupassant, Steinbeck, or Katherine Anne Porter, or Katherine Mansfield. If Maugham always gave pleasure, and A. Conan Doyle and Edgar Allan Poe, Hawthorne seemed unreadable. While Joyce was admittedly a master in *Dubliners*, no one cared less, Katherine Anne Porter was an avatar of the art but dependably left you flat. Mary McCarthy – yes, that lady wrote very good short stories, and there was Truman Capote, and one story by Paul Bowles, but: Eudora Welty – couldn't read her, Flannery O'Connor – somehow never did read her, John Cheever and John Updike – old Prince and young Prince of good old maggie, *The New Yorker* – why push on with the list? It is evident we are confronting the taste of a mucker. He obviously doesn't care about the short story. The man is telling the truth. His short stories show it. They have little in common. They do not give us a great many different facets and situations and glimpses of people in a very specific milieu as Isaac Babel's stories about the Red Cossacks did, nor do they have that private vision of the whole you can find in the short fiction of Hemingway, Singer, Farrell, Sholem Aleichem, or Scott Fitzgerald – another favourite, Fitzgerald. When one thinks of the charm which resides in even the worst of his quick commercial stories, it is painful to push one's own plain efforts so far forward. Yet we do it. Yes, for the bucks first, paperback reader! For the good wives and good kids; for the ego – that snake who won't die no matter how we beat it on the head – that ego is a *muscle*. Finally, it is done for a legitimate motive – to keep Renaissance man alive. Yes. You see every one of these stories is different from every other one. They are all excursions and experiments. We might just as well be in at the birth of science – Renaissance man is looking for his experimental method, which he encounters, let us suspect, by dramatic contrast.

Should we explain? Then shift the metaphor this round. The real short story writer is a jeweler. Like most such craftsmen, he does not – unless knighted by genius, as Hemingway or Faulkner – do much else. No, he stays in his shop, he polishes those jewels, he collects craft, lore, confirms gossip, assays jeweler's rouge, looks to steal the tricks of the arcane, and generally disports like a medieval alchemist who's got a little furnace, a small retort, a cave, a handful of fool's gold, and a mad monk's will. With such qualifications, one in a hundred becomes an extraordinary writer, but on the other hand, the worst of this guild makes a life from kissing spiders.

Now consider the hearty protagonist who has collected his short fiction for your pleasure, entertainment and approval; here is a big, brawny nineteenth-century version of Renaissance man – a prospector, son. He's not looking for jewels, no, he's digging up buckets of ore, he's panning by all various vigours and methods. The truth is that he is seduced more by method than by gold or gem. He is, you see, possessed of extraordinary greed. He is a modern man like all nihilists. So he does not wish to pick up a nugget or two and reduce it to its proper wealth, its full sheen; rather he's impatient, ambitious, and obsessed with one idea – move on fast. Keep looking for the biggest mine of them all. He doesn't want to get caught in the refining and polishing. So he sticks in a shovel here, sets off dynamite there, diverts a fast stream, builds up a dam, slap dash, bang and boom, move on fast. Look to learn a little about everything. That is the instinct of the Renaissance – it speaks not only of the energies and techniques of that twentieth century which will eventually issue out of it, but gives a hint as well of the wastes which are also to follow.

Yes, these short stories are imperfect artifacts – various drillings, diggings, tests, and explosions on the way to finding a certain giant mine, well-advertised over the years by the prospector. If some show too little evidence of the craftsman, others are even overpolished. There is in fact a spectrum, nay, a panoply of fictional techniques: we can go all the way over from the total solid conventionality of the three war stories to the experiments in style of *Truth and Being, Nothing and Time*; or *Advertisements for Myself on the Way Out*. We can travel on the scale of literary merit from the precisions of *Ministers of Taste* down to the casual, even slovenly, prose which mars the narrative tension of *The Last Night*. The point to this collection is found in its contrast. It is therefore not without value to the young college writer of the short story, for an exploration to a given fictional point is often done more than once, but by opposite means. So, for example, *Truth and Being, Nothing and Time*, and *The Killer* are both about the slow deadening of the self, and that is their last resemblance, for *The Killer* is vastly impersonal – one could not determine the author from the style – while the other could have been written by no one but the servant of letters here in the stocks. Yet both stories were done within a month of each other.

Look further: *A Calculus at Heaven* and *Advertisements for Myself on the Way Out* are about the deaths of two men, both murdered – it is just that the deaths are very different, for one is killed in war, and the other is slain criminally, although we do not know how. Also – they are written sixteen years apart.

Continue: *The Greatest Thing in the World* and *Maybe Next Year* are stories composed in college, so predictably are about people in trouble because they have no money. But the styles are searching for their object in opposite directions.

See here: three war stories, *The Paper House, The Language of Men*, and *The Dead Gook*, all complete with sturdy construction of atmosphere are presented alternately with three humorous stories – one dry, *The Notebook* – one episodic, *The Patron Saint of Macdougal Alley* – one arch, *Great in the Hay*. The first five of these six stories were written in the same few weeks.

Now consider that *Great in the Hay* is followed by *The Last Night*, a treatment for a projected movie which bears no relation to *Great in the Hay*. No relation but the most umbilical one – guys like Bert are the guys who make movies like *The Last Night*, that is if you are lucky. From what I hear, guys like Bert are getting rare. Next, two extraordinarily short stories, *It* and *The Shortest Novel of Them All*, are set side by side for instant examination. (One dare not say more or the comment will be longer than the stories.) They are followed by two ventures in mixed genre. Short stories full of resonance, evocation, style, mood, horror, outrage, etc., which began nonetheless as something else – *Ministers of Taste* as a letter, then two letters; *The Locust Cry* as a commentary on *The Early Masters* by Martin Buber.

Finally, we have *The Time of Her Time* and *The Man Who Studied Yoga* – two subtle ways are here presented by which love may be made to women. Since, however, no bad taste is so seductive as to write about oneself with iron objectivity – we will not go on to talk of what is very good or even – now it is confessed – superior in *The Time of Her Time* and *The Man Who Studied Yoga*. It is enough to say they are superior to most good short fiction. (But then these last two are also short novels and were written with the idea that they were the beginnings of real, full-length novels, so the dedication was deeper. Which proves a previous point.) But, at this stage, resolutely we turn the book over to the reader. May he consider the introduction modest, too modest by far.

NORMAN MAILER

## PART ONE

# The Disappearance of the Ego

# The Killer: A Story

'Now,' he said to me, 'do you think you're going to bear up under the discipline of parole?'

'Yessir,' I said.

He had white hair even though he was not more than fifty-two. His face was red. He had blue eyes. He was red, white, and blue. It was a fact I noticed before. They had this coloring. Maybe that was why they identified with the nation.

'In effect you're swearing that you won't take a drink for eight months.'

'I know, sir, but I haven't had a drink inside for four years.' Which was a lie. Three times I had come in with my cellmate on part of a bottle. The first time I was sick. The second time we had a fight, a quiet fight which I lost. He banged my head on the floor. Without noise. The third time we had sex. Democratic sex. We did each other.

'You understand that parole is not freedom.'

'Yessir.'

They asked these questions. They always asked the same questions, and they always got the same answers. It had nothing to do with what you said. It had nothing to do with how you shaved or how you combed your hair because you combed your hair the way everybody else did, and the day you went up to Board you shaved twice. Maybe, it had to do with how many shaving cuts you had, but I didn't have any. I had taken care, wow. Suppose it had to do with the way you moved. If two of the three men on the parole board liked the way you moved, you were all right, provided they didn't like the way you moved too much. Sex. No matter who I'm with, man or woman, always get a feeling off them. At least I used to. I always could tell if they were moving inside or moving away, and I could tell if anything was going on inside. If we ever touched, I could tell better. Once I was in a streetcar and a girl sat down next to me. She was a full barrel. A very fat girl. Pretty face. I don't like fat. Very fat people have no quick. They can always stop. They can stop from doing a lot of things.

This girl and me had a future however. Her hip touched. I could feel what I did to her. From side of my leg, through my pants, and her dress, through some kind of corset, cheap plastic corset, something bad, through that, through her panties, right into her, some current went out of me, and I could feel it in her, opening up future. She didn't do a thing, didn't move. Fixed.

Well, five minutes, before I got off at my stop. In those minutes I was occupied by a project with that girl where we projected five years. I knew what I could do to her. I say without exaggeration I could take her weight down from one hundred eighty to one-eighteen in a year and it would have been a pleasure because all that fat was stored-up sugar she was saving. For somebody. She was stingy, congealed like lard, but I had the current to melt that. I knew it would not be hard to pick her up. If I did, the rest would happen. I would spend a year with her. It is difficult to pick up a fat girl, but I would have used shock treatment. For example, I would have coughed, and dropped an oyster on her skirt. I think it is revolting to do something like that, but it would have worked with this fat girl because disgust would have woke her up. That's the kind of dirt sex is, in the mind of somebody fat and soft and clammy. Sex to them is spit and mucus. It would have given me the opportunity to wipe it off. I could trust my fingers to give a touch of something. The point to the entire operation (people watching in the streetcar, me standing with my handkerchief, apologizing) would be that my fingers would be doing two things at once, proper and respectful in the part of my hand everybody else could see, flame through the handkerchief on her lap. I would have begun right there. For the least I would get her name. At the end of the five minutes I turned to take a look at her, and under that fat face, in the pretty face which could be very attractive, I could see there was a dumb look in her eyes that nothing was going to improve. That stopped me. Putting in a year on a girl like that would be bad unless she was all for me at the end. Stupidity is for nothing, not even itself. I detest stupidity in women – it sets me off. So I got off the car. Didn't even look at the girl. After she gets married to somebody fat and stupid like herself she will hate any man who looks like me because of that five minutes. Her plastic corset must have had a drug-store smell after I got off the trolley car. Think of plastic trying to smell.

I tell this as an example. On the outside it used to be that I never sat down next to anybody that I didn't feel them even when we didn't touch and two or three times a week, or even a day, I would be close to the possibilities of somebody like the fat girl. I know about certain things. I know with all policemen, detectives, correction officers, turnkeys, hacks, parole-board officials, that sex is the problem with them. Smartest cellmate I had said one time like a philosopher, 'Why, man, a judge will forgive any crime he is incapable of committing himself.' My friend put it right. Sex is a bitch. With police. They can't keep their hands off. They do, but then it builds tension. For some it's bad. They can get ready to kill. That's why you comb your hair. Why you must look neat. You have to be clean. About sex. Then a cop can like you. They ask you those questions knowing how you will answer. Often they know you are lying. For example they know that you will take a drink in the next six months. What is important is not that you are lying, but the kind of lie they hear in your voice. Are you afraid of them? Are you afraid they will see down into your lying throat? Then you are okay. They will pass you. If you are afraid of them, you're a good risk. But if you think they are stupid, faintest trace of such a thought in yourself, it comes through. Always one of them will be sensitive to condescension. It gets them ready to kill. A policeman never forgives you when you get him ready to kill. Obviously he can't do it, especially in a room performing official duty with a stenographer at the side. But the adrenalin goes through him. It is bad to take a flush of adrenalin for nothing. All that murder and nowhere to go. For example when you're standing up talking to a parole board it's important the way you stand, how tight your pants are. Good to be slim, trim, ship-shape, built the way I am, provided you are modest. Do not project your groin forward or your hips back. It is best if your pants are not tight-fit. Younger juvenile delinquents actually make this sort of mistake. It is not that they are crazy so much as egotistical. They think older men will like them so much they will give them parole in order to look them up. A mistake. Once read in the newspapers about a Russian soldier who picked up a

German baby and said, 'It's beautiful,' but then he got angry because he remembered the baby's father had been shooting his children, so he killed the baby. That's a cop. If you strut, even in good taste and subtle, they will start to get a glow where it is verboten, and they will like you, they will get a little rosy until they sense it goes nowhere, and wow the sex turns. Gets ready to kill you. If cops have an adrenalin wash for their trouble, you are remembered badly. It is much better to be slim, trim, shipshape, and a little peaked-looking, so they can see you as a thrifty son, which is the way they must have seen me because they gave me parole that day, and I was out of there in a week. Out of prison. Out of the can. I think I would have died another year. Liver sickness or go berserk.

Now you may ask can police be so dumb as to let me go on an armed-robbery sentence, six years unserved out of ten. Well, they saw me as thrifty. I was careful that day with voice and posture. But how can police be so stupid as to think in categories like thrifty? That's easy, I can answer. Police are pent up, they're apes, they're bulls. Bulls think in categories.

2

Well, I've been feeling small for four years now. Prison is a bitch for people like me. It cuts your – I don't want to use doubtful language. It's a habit you build up inside. Some do use language that way. Some lifers. Spades. People who don't give a damn. They're playing prison as if it is their life, the only one they are going to have. But I am conservative in temperament. I comb my hair every morning, I comb it the same way. Minor matter you may say, but it isn't for me. I like to comb my hair when I feel like it. Animal of the woods. I have the suspicion – some would call it superstition – that combing my hair can spoil some good ideas. I would never say this to a hack but why is it not possible that some ideas live in your hair, the way the hair curls. I have very wavy hair when it is left to itself. Whenever I get a haircut, I have the feeling I'm losing possibilities I never got around to taking care of. Put it this way: when I comb my hair, it changes my mood. So naturally I prefer to comb it when I want to. In prison forget that. Comb your hair the same time same way every day. Look the same. If you're smart, keep your mood the same way. No ups. Nor downs. Don't be friendly. Don't be sullen. Don't offer company. Don't keep too quiet. If you stay safe, in the middle, and are the same thing every day you get a good report. The reason I get parole first time out, six years off a ten-year sentence is that I was a model prisoner which means just this: you are the same thing every day. Authorities like you if you are dependable. Be almost boring. I think what it may be about is that any man in authority finds his sleep important to him. People in authority can't stand the night. If you wear a uniform and you go to bed to sleep and a certain prisoner never bothers your dreams, you'll say a good word for him when it comes time to making out reports.

Of course you are not popular. Necessarily. My bunky shakes my hand when I get this good news, but I can see he is not happy in every way. So I complain about details. I am not to possess liquor at home, nor am I to frequent any bar even once, even at Christmas. Moreover, I am not to eat in any restaurant which serves liquor.

'What if you don't drink? But just eat there?'

'I'm not to go into any premises having a liquor license.'

'A restaurant that don't serve liquor is a tearoom or a hash house.'

'Crazy,' I say. I don't like such expressions, but this is perfect to express my sentiments.

'Well, good luck.'

It is possible we are thinking of the same things, which is the three times he got a bottle into the cell and we drank it together. The first time sick, second time we had a fight, third time sex. I remember I almost yelled in pain when my rocks got off, because they wouldn't stop. I was afraid I'd hurt myself. It had been so long. It seemed each time I took liquor something started in me that was different from my normal personality. By normal I mean normal in prison, no more. You wouldn't want a personality like that on the outside any more than you would want to smell like a laundry bag. But so far as inside personality went, I couldn't take liquor and keep the same. So if I started drinking on the secret when outside, I was in trouble. Because my style of personality would try to go back to what it was before, and too many eyes would be on me. My parole officer, people in the neighborhood. The parole board was getting me a job. They just about picked out the room where you lived. They would hear about it even if I didn't get into a rumble when I was drunk. If I kept a bottle in my room, I would have to hide it good. The parole officer has been known to come around and pay a friendly visit which is to say a sneak visit. Who could enjoy the idea of him sniffing the air in my room to see was there liquor on the breeze? If they caught me drinking in the eight months, back I would be sent to here. A gamble, this parole. But I was glad to take it, I needed out. Very much. Because there was a monotony in me. It had been coming in day after day. I didn't have the feeling of a current in me any more, of anything going. I had the feeling if I sat down next to a girl like the fat girl now, and our legs touched, she would move away cause there was a blank in me which would pass into her. Something repulsive. There was something bad in me, something very dull. It wasn't in my body, it wasn't even in my mind, it was somewhere. I'm not religious, but it was somewhere. I mean I didn't know if I could keep control or not. Still, I couldn't have done it the other way. Eight more months. I might have flipped. Talking back to a hack, a fight. I'd have lost good time. There is only one nightmare in prison. It's that you don't get out, that you never get out because each time you come close the tension has built up in you so that you have to let it break out, and then your bad time is increased. So it's like being on the wrong escalator.

'Take it slow, take it easy,' said my bunky. 'Eight months goes by if you get yourself some sun.'

'Yeah, I'm going to sleep in the sun,' I said. 'I'm going to drink it.'

'Get a good burn your first day out, ha-ha. Burn the prison crap out of your pores.'

Maybe the sun would burn the dullness away. That's what I was thinking.

*December 1960*

# Truth and Being: Nothing and Time

Now that there is no doubt I am going to die, and my death will be by that worst of diseases (for it is other than disease), I think the time may be here to tell the story of the revolution which came to New York in the second half of the Twentieth Century, of its outrageous internal history, of my part in it, and the style of my mind. If I do not offer my name, it is because I am one of the actors in the mystery, a principal of the revolution, and I would not like to detract from any excitement attached to my actions by linking all of my person in this first breath with the four consonants and two vowels of cancer. For it is indeed just that rebellion of the cells from which I am dying . . . at the rate . . . it is curious that I do not know the rate. Might it not tell us something of the impulse within the disease if we were to measure this rate of growth from day to day of the malignancy of the cells? I am certain the formula would belong to one of those exquisite curves of increase or deterioration which lit my adolescent comprehension of mathematics, as for example some equation to determine an exponential expansion, or the curve of the logarithm. (Even the terms are no longer secure to my memory; but as meaning dissipates, sound presents its attractions.) Since I mention these curves, however, best it is for me to admit that there is only one curve I expect to be found in the graph of the rate of growth of my mutinous cells – it would have, I suspect, some relation to the formula for the rate of increase in the decomposition of radium to lead. For this is not merely a scientific image to me, but the precise metaphor to describe the possessions and dissipations of my Self over these years, it is exactly the measure – this transit from radium to lead – of certain beauties of love, sex, flesh, and other sweetmeats of Being, which were transmuted by the intensity of my ambition into purposeful and more or less lost radiations of consciousness. Radium emits that which it will radiate and in

giving of itself to whatever matter surrounds it, or is brought
before it, radium diminishes to lead. One can feel little pity for
it: radium has never learned to receive. So its history among the
elements must present an irony or two: among themselves (that
is to say, among the elements) do they speak of radium as the
royal fool, the King Lear of the atoms? They do not dare, I
think. Radium is too dangerous. It alters wherever it reaches.
But in fact I am close to indulging an unwise vice because
metaphors live for me with the power of mechanical laws. It is
an evil philosopher who cannot mourn his own passing, and if
that art work – a tear of pure compassion for oneself – were to
emerge in my eye, it would be for the loss of my sensitivity to the
dialect, a sensitivity which was perhaps as exquisite in me at my
best as any mind in this century. There were others who
possessed the dialectic with greater power; the Frenchman
Jean-Paul . . . Sartre I remember now was his last name had a
dialectical mind good as a machine for cybernetics, immense in
its way, he could peel a nuance like an onion, but he had no
sense of evil, the anguish of God, and the possible existence of
Satan. That was left for me, to return the rootless disordered
mind of our Twentieth Century to the kiss *sub cauda* and the
Weltanschauung of the Medieval witch. The kiss *sub cauda*: if I
had not come to recognize over the years of my career that
nobility of form and aristocracy of manner are the last hope of
man, I would not explain that *sub cauda* means beneath the tail,
the hole in the highness of the cat, the place the witch would kiss
when out she voyaged to visit the Demon (or is it in?), cats being
classified by Medieval logic as the trinity of the Devil shaped
into One. Naturally. But to give a taste of what I offer, to prove
that there are dreams, essays, baths of flesh I never found
behind each word and curious phrase, let me hold for a moment
all disquisition on the character of my compassion for myself
and offer instead a nugget of new ore. The hole, the royal hole
(forgive my gentility, but I do not wish to jar the ghosts of the
Time whose style I inhabit for this writing), the hole, the brown
one, rich as purple in some, withered to dun-green for others,
flower, weed, perfume, ill-fumed, cathedral and shanty, pleasure, pustule, muscle, orifice, avatar, pile and grave, is the final
executor of that will within us to assign value to all which passes

through. Do we bite into an apple? It is not perfect, not often. Good cells and poor, tastes, monotonies, and taints mill in the vaults of our digestion; the needs, desires, snobberies, and fashions of our will devil one's sense of selection, twist our taste: good cells of the apple, tart let us say, brave in the way the cell of an apple can be brave – I think such a bravery might exist, might it not? (the tart cell could maintain its taste against a bland environment for the years of its life) and yet brave or bland could be ignored, could be flushed away, good mistaken for bad, nourishment lost, because the form of *our* character was too insensitive to absorb the most particular character of my brave cell in the apple. So out it goes, pushed into the Styx by the body, buried with the foulest hoodlums and lowest slime, the dullest scum and deadest skin of those fecal molecules, ejected already into the journey to the end of the hole. What rich possibilities and poor wastes are shit into the vast bare lands of sanitation by the middle-class mind. So it is that some of the best and some of the worst of us are drawn to worship at the congregation of the last cells. (Why is their colour brown? – I have pondered this question for years.)

Yes, there are those of us who worship our own, there are all too many who prostrate themselves before another, and there were even a few like our revolutionary leader who was drawn toward his own and rarely repelled by others. It is characteristic of revolutionaries, passionate lovers, the very ambitious, the greedy, the stingy, and dogs, to fix on what is excreted by others; it is typical of Narcissists, children, nuns, spinsters, misers, bankers, conservative statesmen, dictators, compulsive talkers, bores, and World War I generals accomplished at trench warfare, to be forever sniffing their own. But the intelligent and conservative among you are annoyed already for there is a tendency to my remarks which you detect with unease, you fear I lead the argument into the alp of the high immoral. I do; but perhaps my aim is to rescue morality. To be conservative does not mean to be cowardly: follow my argument, for you quit it at a loss – I am not necessarily archbishop of the New Royal Scatological in our society.

Good. We are drawn to shit because we are imperfect in our uses of the good. If all we eliminated was noxious, hopeless,

used up or never-intended, it would be a pervert or a maniac
who found the subject attractive. But not all of what we give
away is useless. There is a spirit to nourishment, an élan to food,
a dash of the existence of an Other – who among you would
presume to argue that the flesh of a brave animal is the same in
flavor, substance, or final effect upon us as the meat of a
contented cow? Each cell in each existence labours like all of life
to make the most of what it is or can be, each cell is different,
perhaps even so different as one of us from another. So perhaps
we do not digest all that is good for us. Indeed, some is lost
because it is too good for us, we do not deserve it, the guilt in the
enzymes of our stomach prevents the process. (Who among
you? scientists? chemists? doctors of organism? can prove that
guilt is *in*capable of entering an enzyme?) Yet other riches elude
the peristalsis – the best of us cannot absorb a nutrient which is
beyond the possibility of our style: particles of food which urge
us to be generous are disagreeable to the stingy; spices which
gratify our sense of the precise are lost and refused by thicket-
witted minds. The dung of the brave is filled with riches for the
fearful: precisely those subtleties, reservations, and cautions
the courageous dislike are grace and wit for the coward; the offal
of the fool has sweets to accelerate a genius – a dull mind must
reject those goods for fear the head would hemorrhage from
unexpected and indisposable enthusiasms. All the mineral
riches of stone, the essence of earth, the spirits of the Wind,
creativities of the Sun, omens and intimations of the moon,
scalding and compassionate courses of rain, pass upward into
the aristocracies of nature, into the nutrient offered us by plant
and animal. The wealth of our ground enters us – we digest a
million insinuations a day, and fail to digest perhaps a million
more, for all of us are too narrow for the wealth we devour, and
expel the exquisite in time with the despised.

But if excrement is the enforced marriage of Tragic Beauty
and Filth, why then did God desert it, and leave our hole to the
Devil, unless it is because God has hegemony over us only as we
create each other. God owns the creation, but the Devil has
power over all we waste – how natural for him to lay siege
where the body ends and weak tragic air begins. Out of the
asshole pour the riches of Satan – these souls of nutrient, these

lost cells spurned by the universe of the body they traversed, their being about to be cast into the lower existence of Chance. For you see, and do not be altogether nervous (since the explanation, if given in haste, will be amplified at leisure), there are three possibilities of Being. There is Culture when one exists in a milieu, when one's life is obedient to a style – the peasant in his village lives in Culture like bacteria in a petri dish. There is History, the highest form of life; it has the turns and starts, the surprises, the speed of change and the fires of courage an animal knows on a long trip to search for food. And there is Chance. That is the life of an organism which has been deprived of the possibility to organize itself – it is the lowest form of active life, it is entropy. (A word to remember.) With Chance we can depend no longer upon ourselves (which is the grace that History offers) nor can we even depend on growth in obedience to the shape of the culture which conceived us, no, we are cast loose, we are blown, we are transported, we are shifted, pushed, we are carried by forces larger than ourselves toward fates of elimination which inspire terror. Those freight trains dense with the bodies of victims moving from a camp of concentration to a camp of extermination (small intestine and colon of German Idealism), these souls so soon to die by gas in a room as bleak as the lavatory of a men's penitentiary, they were souls ripped from Culture or defeated in History, and so linked into the purposeful streamings of Chance as she went toward the abyss. Yes, it was I who first demonstrated to the world by the rigor of philosophical argument (a Herculean labor) that the state of Being in the Twentieth Century was close to the extinction of itself because of the diseases and disasters of soul over the centuries, the victories of the Devil. Being was now warped. History, Culture, and Chance – that choice offered to Being from the beginning of our existence was turning into the contrary of itself. History was now made by cowards who gave no shape to History even as they blurred the shape of what we saw (those modern buildings without faces). Culture was un-timely ripped – the foods of Being and the maintenance of Being grown thick, anomalous, and bland with hybrid growths from the field, antibiotics, and a technological jargon for the cure of the body. Only Chance prospered in the Twentieth

Century. The circuits of the circuitless turned to purpose. One had only to rip one's root free from Culture, relinquish one's dreams of authority, one's sense of self, one's love of adventure, one's desire to make a History, relinquish oneself to Chance, and all was planned. One's life, emptied of novelty, organized, cleansed, plotted, secure, unpursued, could then proceed in the monotonies of welfare from the cradle to the tomb. Chance was a purposeful stream moving the bodies of all millions of us away from roots, below history, out of grace. The progression was from man to *merde*, the Twentieth Century was the rush of all souls to search out shit, to kiss the Devil, to rescue a molecule of the brown from its extinction. For think: we began all this (and disturb yourself not unduly if you have comprehended but little, for we return again and again) but we began with the kiss *sub cauda*, the kiss to the hole of the cat. The cat – that marriage of grace and cruelty, self-centered, alien, alone, what can the cat use in its food of tender cells, compassionate meats, philosophical greens? It cannot – the drop of the cat is rich in royal and generous affections; one has only to absorb, and one will love with grace. Yes, such waste has all the darting odors of fish-meat and love. The witches knew it; they were burned for no less than the addition of this dung to their cakes-for-the-encouragement-of-love and more than one saint was present, the rack of hagflesh burning in his nose, his legs twisted with the ache of a witch's soul being returned finally to her separate masters. St. Exquisitas of Odometamo, that unpredictable and much despised saint of the Twelfth Century, almost excommunicated three times for heresy (that rare and only saint admired to my knowledge by the Marquis de Sade), was the first I know to suggest that the witch was the finest jewel of the Devil because she was a woman originally of noble soul much beloved by God, who had been rifled by Satan in the womb, which is to say that witches generally are born of evil mothers, God investing the cruel placenta with the spirit of a rare soul, as if God wished to steal – if one may speak this way (for St. Exquisitas of course could not) – one human of evil back from the Devil. What the Devil owns, he generally cares for, although he is not perfect as a custodian any more than God is all foreseeing as a lover, but as a rule of thumb (since one is hardly so divine oneself as to speak with authority of the Divine Economy) God must raid upon evil to recover it, even as the Devil lusts to capture love. So St. Exquisitas gave his formula for the creation of a witch: God anoints the womb of an evil creature in the moment of her conception and in turn is tricked of his effort by the Devil who is so alert that this particular one of his creatures might be lost (for God being wealthy and a snob never chooses any ordinary lady of evil) that Satan follows behind God and poisons the anointment with his tongue.

Thus, at last, a hint of my style and the character of my mind.

*December 1960*

## PART TWO

# The Air of the Dying

# A Calculus at Heaven

*He will not be a part-time thing.*

Sometimes they all were running, sometimes walking running crawling. All of them, Rice the Indian, Father Meary, the captain, cursing and stumbling; thirty men, gouging, elbowing, crawling through their narrow increment in space. 'Come on,' the captain shouted, 'Come on, come on,' and Father Meary looking back at him, stumbled and fell. In the distance, he could hear the guns debating still, fiercely as if they were intolerant of each other, and the sounds were breaking and bursting in his head. He rolled over on the ground, feeling the captain tugging at his shoulder, swearing at him. 'Come on, we got to get to the house.' He saw men passing him, running isolated from each other, and although the panic was in him too, he felt separated from them. Not understanding, he stumbled to his feet. Jogging after the retreating men, feeling the captain by him, motivating him through space by his presence, he told himself that the man should not have sworn at him, he was an officer of God.

He did not understand, everything had suddenly mixed inside him, burbled like the running mass of men, and what had happened back in the second trench line he did not know. For two days they had been holding back the Japanese, and then suddenly the trench line had broken, had gone, and he was running with the men. 'Oh, Heavenly Father,' automatically he began, and then the harshness of the machine gun, the mechanical signpost to death, had sounded behind him, and feeling a hand against his back, he had prostrated himself before the earth only to hear the enemy's cry of victory, pulsing behind him, working its way up from the beach. Then they were up again, running all the time now, dropping whenever a gun sounded, stumbling up the leisurely pitted street of Tinde. His prayers lost their logical sequence, became jumbled. 'Hail Mary, Pax est. . . .'

Then himself, once more a part of the struggling ill-formed matrix of men running hoarse-breathed to . . . to where? He needed assurance, his plump hands wavering uncertainly away from his body as he tripped, and caught up and tripped, trying desperately not to fall behind the men running . . . running to where? The captain was leading them, the captain must know, he thought. The captain was a military man.

Under him, he felt his thin legs bend together once more, felt himself breathing in the dirt, the city of Tinde flowing into his material self as the sounds from the arena – the Roman arena, he thought – as the sounds came closer and closer, became embodied in the intolerance of the machine gun. He didn't have to fall, he thought, he was already on the ground. But the gun had stopped, and then he felt the earth careening away from him. After a moment he realized that someone had picked him up, carrying him with his head down, his face near the man's back. He watched the cross on his shoulder, swaying from his uniform, jerkily in an unholy rhythm, and when it fell off, he found himself gazing after it, as if it were a bird disappearing in the sky. When he could see it no more, he still kept his eyes focused for it, seeing the ground twist and recede under him. He was terrified; his head upside down felt heavy and uncomfortable, the back carrying him was not broad – he felt an augment of his fear. The men running beside him, was there terror at their faces too? The lines had broken, he kept telling himself, but how, but when; he felt his absolute sense of time leaving him. He didn't understand such affairs, he was a godly man, he did not know of such matters, but the Japanese had come through, their faces yellow with lust. The pagan men, they would not understand, they would not respect a man of God. He had lost his cross, they would shoot him with the rest. The smoke of death was over the city.

The gun came back, hovered about him; the man carrying him made a sound, lurched and fell. Father Meary fell with him, the two tangled in the dirt. He felt blood on his face, and turning his head on the ground, realized that none of the men were running any more, that they all lay in random prostration on the ground, while the gun and then another gun spoke angrily over them. Hearing screams, he could no longer feel that men were dying, but their souls . . . it meant . . . he thought of Conditional Absolution for them. There was blood on his face but he felt no pain. . . .

*Once in San Francisco an unhappiness had come to him and had remained for many months. One evening in the winter, he had been traveling through the city and, feeling hunger, had entered unthinking the first restaurant he passed. The food was not expensive, and feeling his unhappiness more pointedly, he had ordered the highest priced dinner. The meal had been excellent, the waitress attractive. She had seemed to him a little bit like a Madonna from the school of Florence, and after the meal had been over, he had given her the dollar for the meal, and happy with her face, had added half of it again for the tip. He had noted the surprise on her face, and feeling happy he had said, 'If there is anything I like, it is a well-prepared meal, well served, by a pretty young waitress like yourself.' Embarrassed by the effort he had made to keep his voice deep, he left before she could thank him. Outside, he had suddenly felt more unhappy than before.*

. . . The machine gun came back, licking at the bodies of the men about him. Overhead, a few planes distorted the sky. 'It's a death trap, it's a death trap,' he heard someone muttering beside him. The terror had worked its way into his finger tips; every muscle seemed to have sprung free, quivering loosely. The fact of his probable death came to him, and it loosed a new type of fear. Already, in the road, the *tap-tap-tap* of men's souls changing existences had begun. He was afraid, he had lived his life for the moment of meeting his death, and he was afraid. He did not understand – but why? And then all thought in his mind trailed out along the ground, and he could only feel his fear. After that, only the sun, warm on his back. The machine gun, indecent, angry again; God taking His inscrutable will.

Were they all to die here, lying in a road, while a machine gun worked from body to body, seemingly never satisfying itself that the body it was striking was dead? He saw a man beside him waver to his feet, throw a hand grenade at the machine gun.

Somewhere he heard a shout, and then the grenade fulfilling itself. The machine gun did not sound any more. Then the men about him, on their feet again, running on hands and knees he saw himself counting them, guessing they were ten or twelve, until abruptly he realized that in their run down the road he was being left behind. On his feet, laboring after them, shouting, 'Captain Hilliard, Captain, Captain,' shouting, and then he fell. Someone had run back, was dragging him; he felt dirt forcing against his face, abrading his plump white flesh. He was trying to hold back his groan, but then the pain ceased, the rough dirt changing to mud, becoming actually wet. He remembered. They were going into the stone house by the edge of the swamp. The sounds about him seemed to be changing, perhaps he heard a cheer. The man let him go, he saw it was the Indian, Thomas Rice; he must thank him. Another machine gun ripped at them from a hill, men falling about him again. Dirt was in his eyes, he could not see; in the terrible moment, he felt a hand pulling him; half crouching, he felt himself led to the cellar window, felt its rough stone sides scraping against his flanks as he crawled through, fell suddenly for two or three feet onto a pile of sandbags. Men kept coming over him, he crawled away. Still dazed, he was able to see a little out of his eyes. Someone had kicked him angrily. Looking up, he saw it had been DaLucci, but he could feel no anger. Was the man Catholic and godless? . . . Ahh . . . these Italians.

His situation came back more clearly. He remembered now that the house had been prepared as a defense three days before. On the edge of the swamp . . . it was cool here, if only it didn't become too wet. He felt himself drifting away again . . . the cellar walls seemed sandbagged . . . that meant less splinters, he imagined, it was functional, he was certain. . . . If only his wrist weren't so painful. He must have sprained it when he fell through the window. Were they safe from a cannonading, he wondered, and then abruptly, he sat up, panic catching at him. How many men left? He counted four, counted again, there were only four besides himself – Captain Hilliard, DaLucci, Rice and a blond soldier he did not know. Did it mean he was to die after all? He could see the Indian firing the gun, the blond soldier feeding. He heard him say, 'That's it, Sergeant, give it back to 'em, Sergeant, give it to those bastards.' The priest noted it numbly, long conditioning having accustomed him to the sound of the profanity. He wondered how safe they were, could the brick house really shut out the Japanese? Fascinated, he watched the sunlight glancing through the window, leaving the cellar almost completely dark. . . .

*For months, Sister Vittoria had been treating him with especial attention, complimenting him on his lessons when he had prepared them well; looking sad and unhappy rather than angry, when he had played ball out on the street too long the day before. He noticed, even, that she spoke of him to Sister Josette and pointed to him often, as the best student in the class. He liked it; the kids used to call him 'teacher's pet', but it didn't bother him as much as it had used to, because somehow, he had always liked studying a little better than fighting the kids on the block. So that when she called him over one day and pinched his cheek, and gave him a letter to his mother, he was not surprised.*

His mother had read it slowly several times; he feeling shame for her at the unease with which she read. He kept thinking of how his mother didn't smell as cool and starchy as Sister Vittoria. But then his mother had looked up at him, from her chair, and smiled at him very happily. They talked a long while. 'Be a priest, be a priest, Timothy,' she kept saying, 'and God will always be with you.' He kept feeling how uncomfortable she was with the words. 'It's an honor, do you know, it's an honor.' Then later . . . 'God will not be a part-time thing to be shared with a woman, and sure with a pay check, but He will stay.' And he, the boy, after a long while, 'But I do not want to be a priest, Mother, I do not feel a vocation.' She had sighed. 'You will be the most important man of all your friends, you will be more important than any rich man; do you know what that means for a poor man?' He had shook his head, unhappy. 'Think of it,' she had said.

Then two weeks later, Sister Vittoria had called him into her private little study room. She had talked to him in her beautiful soft voice, and he had been unsure beneath it. At last when she asked, 'Do you not feel a vocation stirring within you?' he had tried, contracting his stomach forcibly to feel some inner tenseness or emotion, as he was to squeeze it in later years when he looked at *religious paintings. 'I think, Sister, I think I do feel a small vocation within me.' She had smiled. 'You are fortunate, Timothy, you will feel it grow and grow, there are very few men who are godly enough to feel even the beginnings of one.' As he had been about to go out the door, he had turned to her and said, 'Sister Vittoria, I feel, I think I feel it growing a little more already.'*

Light red dust was filtering across the column of sunlight in the cellar. He saw the Indian firing every now and then, saw the captain speaking beside him. 'We're going to save the mortar until they bring one up; just keep firing the gun. We're protected here, we'll be able to knock their mortar out first. Now look, we've got to hold the road out there, there's only one other way to the coastal road, and that's being defended by a house like this one . . . only with more men probably.'

Father Meary forced himself into devotion. Oh, my God, I am ready to meet you, he thought desperately. But a piece of plaster broke from the ceiling, its fragments landing on his chest, and he felt death with it. Once, he had said, in speaking to the men, 'There are no atheists in foxholes. All of you do not have the same faith I do, but all of you believe in the supremacy of God.' 'But, Father Meary,' someone had interrupted him. He had stared back coldly. 'When you meet your Maker, you believe. . . . You must believe. . . .' Then why this persistent fear? His tired mind fought against relaxing, fought against the temptings of Hell. But the words sounded ornate to him for a moment. Almost crying, he demanded all the resolution within him. The men must not see him crying, they would have their faith weakened if they did. And they would have need of him in the house when the Japanese threatened even more. He got to his feet; he would comfort them.

In the semi-gloom of the cellar, they were crouched against the wall or under the window, firing the machine gun irregularly, being answered irregularly. They did not seem to know he was with them. He slumped, feeling his resolution ebb. Three days before, in preparing the house they had dug a slit trench against one of the side walls. It would be better if he were to remain in it, where a chance bullet could not reach him. After all, he could not do the men any good if he were dead. And then mockingly, he felt his fear disappearing, as he dropped into the greater safety of the trench. He shut his eyes. Why, why had he been afraid; it disturbed the order of things, the certainties were not so . . . well, not so certain. But he believed, he was certain he believed more than ever. For with the horrors he had seen, well of necessity God existed, for men could not bear up under the horrors they saw, if it were not for God. He kept thinking of this, trying to strengthen it in his mind.

The silence disturbed him; he realized that the guns had stopped for a moment. Crouching in the darkness, he wished for them to start again, so that he could think about it and reinforce it even more in his mind. . . .

THE CAPTAIN, 1926–1930

> *Two tight kids on a red silk coverlet. . . .*

He spent his college life with the creative clique; surrealist poetry was in vogue. He drank a lot, he would be very happy for a while, and then very unhappy, but in back of it all, he felt a certain integrity within him, a certain feeling which made him know that he would paint, that he would slap the lie of America across a thousand canvases, that he would shove beauty into a million people who had never felt it before, that he would shake people up, stamp on them, blast their smugness away, and say, 'Here, here is your graft, here is your marriage morality (a picture of a businessman sleeping with a prostitute, with a little locket on the canvas entitled 'Sister') here is your democracy (a portrait of a syphilitic Negro), and finally, here is your life (which was a triptych of a motion picture, a clerk, and a plain woman to represent the clerk's wife).' Only . . . in hating all this, he was reaffirming himself, for like all college men who stop believing, he was at the particular point where he was the only person who had ever realized a slum or recognized the lie in a politician's voice.

He had come to this endowed university, wondering, already beginning to disbelieve, but he was young and enthusiastic. (Later he was to say, 'You stop believing in God at seventeen, in communism at twenty-seven.') Breaking from his family, he was to paint (it was not a new sitution, he had read it in several books), but his father was an army colonel, and he had been allowed to go to this university only on the agreement with his father that he, Bowen Hilliard, was to join the R.O.T.C. and to remain in it until after graduation when he would have attained a reserve commission. So that in 1926, when of the class of '30, he was one of the forty-one freshmen out of eight hundred to sport the khaki uniform with the blue lapels, it was to be to him a sign of disparity as painful and unique as the soda jerker who from some outside compulsion had been forced to grow a beard.

Bowen Hilliard, not believing, made the university's literary magazine; Bowen Hilliard, not believing, was known as the best artist in college. Bowen Hilliard went up to Boston and picketed the streets before Sacco and Vanzetti were killed, and came back to write an editorial in the magazine which was to suspend it for a half-year, 'Listen, America, listen to your shame. . . .'

He defended nothing intellectually, almost everything emotionally. He said, 'The only thing infinite about man is his vanity,' but he liked to walk in the streets, to feel people about him. He painted a great deal, read a great many books of art criticism, so that his painting was always conscious, articulate; he was one of the few artists who could explain his work clearly, and what it made him feel. He said he believed in nothing, and he enjoyed it, for he found that believing in nothing meant believing in himself, and at that time he was capable of it. Certainly, he was growing as an artist, his line (always his weak point) was becoming more certain; he had always had an acute sense of texture, but beyond that his canvases had a measure of structural feeling, unusual for a college painter. During this time he painted a discordant abstraction in which the color did not coincide with the line area, very much like a badly printed comic in a newspaper – and he had termed this his masterpiece and called it 'Society Out of Whack.' . . .

He was to believe in someone else by his senior year. . . . At a party, he met a girl named Cova – there was to be a lot of drinking – and somehow at the end, he was to sleep the night with her. Eventually they were to know each other very well, but in the darkness only the crudest attempts were to be made.

'What color are your eyes?' she had asked, and when he had told her brown, she sighed. 'I thought they were blue, some-how,' she said. Then she laughed. 'Of course it doesn't mat-ter. . . .'

The intellectual's passion is ramified by its implications; the artist's is augmented. Cova became an absolute to him, and, in many ways, since she was beautiful and intense and clever, and therefore was like his image of himself (the image of the artist), he was to become an absolute for her. In the last year of college, they had their unhappinesses, but they felt them more healthy, for they came from acute realizations rather than from a doubt-ing of themselves.

They came to a certain understanding early, for she had other lovers besides Bowen Hilliard. 'I can't paint,' she had said, 'and I can't write music, and I don't write nearly so well as I should like to. You must see it; when I take a man, and I may take him for a lot of reasons, in back of it all is the feeling that that is when I'm making something, and that that is something I can do better than any other woman. I don't envy you your paintings, Bowen, you can't envy mine. Some women are born to have a lot of men.'

In a measure he understood, and by the time they were out of college and married, it even made sense to him. For he had found that she might take a man for a variety of reasons, because (although this was not often), he attracted her, or because the situation warranted it, or because she was sorry for him. (He once said, 'You like any man who is under five feet four and has acne,') or in many cases because it was necessary in the evolu-tion of the friendship, but always she had come back to him, loving him more, taking him more fiercely, reaffirming and even re-evaluating their absolute. She said to him once after a long silence, 'We're like two tight kids on a red silk coverlet,' and that was what they went by. That was what they believed in. . . .

THE MEN, APRIL 1924, FIRST DAY

*There was a dame once. . . .*

Heavy with morning and the tenseness of the night before, the men lay encrusted in their double line of trenches, gazing out to sea. Tight and uncomfortable with a fear of butterflies and leadenness in their bellies, gazing nervously out to sea, out between the two arms of the harbor of Tinde. All through the night, polishing the weapons, preparing themselves, cleansing themselves with furtive finalities in every motion. Anxiously, eyes at sea, waiting, who will see the first boat? Looking with dry eyes and throat, tongues licking at the backs of dry and sticky teeth. What will it be like, what will it be like, Jesus Christ . . . Jesus Christ. . . .

The major in command of the three companies at Tinde had written a dispatch for his men that morning. It read:—

THE JAPANESE ATTACKED AT OTEI 0623. THE FORCE CONSISTED OF A FLEET OF ARMORED BARGES. WE HAVE RECEIVED A REPORT THAT HALF OF THE BARGES HAVE CONTINUED ON TOWARD TINDE. ANALOW ISLAND IS SURROUNDED BY IMPASSABLE CLIFFS ON THIS SIDE. THE ONLY POSSIBLE LANDING PLACES ARE AT HANSON BEACH, OTEI, AND TINDE. SINCE THEY HAVE ALREADY ATTACKED THE OTHER TWO POINTS IT IS A CERTAINTY THAT THEY WILL PROCEED ON TO HERE.

I knew this dame once, it was back in Albany. She was saying to me I know your kind, bud, they come twenty to the dozen, so I say to her, you count a funny dozen sister, why don't you come here and play dozen with me? Funny, she says, aren't you. I wasn't going to take that from any dame, I tell her, listen, after they made me, they threw the mold away, it was cracked from laughing so hard at my line. Well, she took it a little easier after that, but . . . I dunno, it was still no deal. . . . When the hell are they gonna come? . . .

WE ARE DEFENDING ONE ISLAND IN A CHAIN OF ISLANDS. THE JAPANESE DO NOT CONSIDER THIS ISLAND IMPORTANT ENOUGH TO SEND ANY NAVAL UNITS ALONG. WE ARE GOING TO SHOW THEM THEY HAVE MADE A MISTAKE. THEIR MOTORBOAT FLEETS ARE PROGRESSING FROM ISLAND TO ISLAND. IF WE HOLD THEM HERE,

THEY WILL HAVE TO REVISE THEIR PLAN OF ATTACK. CONTROL OF
THE CHAIN DEPENDS ON THE CONTROL OF ANY SINGLE ISLAND.
CONTROL OF THIS ISLAND DEPENDS ON CONTROL OF THE COASTAL
ROAD WHICH RUNS ALONG THE NORTHERN SIDE OF THE ISLAND,
FROM HANSON BEACH TO OTEI TO TINDE. OUR MAIN FORCE IS AT
HANSON BEACH AND WILL HOLD THE JAPANESE UNLESS THEY ARE
ABLE TO SEND REINFORCEMENTS FROM OTEI OR TINDE. WE MUST
HOLD THE CITY, BUT MORE IMPORTANT, WE MUST MAINTAIN
CONTROL OF THE COASTAL ROAD.

There was this movie, Jimmie Cagney, I think. Did you see it
when it played in town? 'Cause I saw it you know at the Strand
in New York. They had a band there . . . I can't remember the
name, only the vocalist with them was all right, I can still
remember her. But anyway, the movie was all about war, only it
was in France; there was no little island fighting in the last one
ya know, and this guy Jimmie Cagney is yellow, it gave me quite
a jump 'cause you know Cagney, but then I figured that it's
anybody's turn to be yella maybe when it all starts happening.
Have you got any idea of the time? . . . That picture gave me
quite a smack, I ain't forgetting it in a hurry. . . .

IF OUR LINES SHOULD CRACK, WE MUST STILL KEEP THEM FROM
TAKING THE COASTAL ROAD WHICH IS ABOUT TWO MILES INLAND
FROM THE CITY AT THIS POINT. THERE ARE TWO STREETS LEADING
OUT TO IT, AND WE HAVE CONSTRUCTED FORTRESSES IN A SEPA-
RATE HOUSE COMMANDING EACH ROAD. FOR THE RIGHT FLANK
WINDOWS COMMAND EVERY DIRECTION. THE HOUSE ON THE LEFT
FLANK IS THE OLD BANKERS STONE HOUSE, SITUATED IN THE
SWAMP WITH ONLY ONE SIDE ON SOLID GROUND. ALL WINDOWS
HAVE BEEN SEALED WITH THE EXCEPTION OF ONE CELLAR WIN-
DOW WHICH COMMANDS THE ROAD. IF BY ANY CHANCE YOUR
LINES CRACK, YOU MUST TRY TO REACH ONE OF THE HOUSES, THAT
IS ESSENTIAL.

Tamping rifle butts slowly on the ground, snapping
cigarettes nervously against thumbnails, waiting, waiting for
the attack, I dunno, I never saw action before. The end of his
heel delicately clicking against the other, waiting for the fall of a
little clod of mud. It kinda gets ya waitin', doesn't it? I wish
there was somethin' to do sort of. Fingering at a button, moving
the hat back and forth. These cigarettes taste kinda good, I

mean, you know, you smoke 'em all, and they taste the same, and then maybe ya find one ya like . . . I dunno, you know what I mean.

IT IS NOW APRIL, FOUR MONTHS AFTER WAR HAS STARTED, YOU ALL KNOW THAT WE ARE UNEQUIPPED, WITHOUT TANKS AND AIRCRAFT. INSTALLATIONS ARE NOT EVEN A WEEK OLD ON THE ISLAND. HOWEVER, THE JAPANESE HAVE TO MAKE A LANDING, AND THAT ADVANTAGE RESTS WITH US. YOU WILL FIGHT FOR YOUR COUNTRY, THE GREATEST IN THE WORLD. GOOD LUCK.

Just where do ya think ya're shovin' that rifle? Get it out of my face.

Take it easy bud, take it easy.

Well, I like my face, see, I don't like it ruined, there're girls back home, got to go for this face.

I said I was sorry, what the hell were ya blockin' the path?

Listen, bud, you ain't talkin' to Joe Crap, see; you watch what you say with me.

Aaaaah, save it for the Japs.

Well where are they, well when the hell are they comin'? The goddam yellow bastards, what are they, afraid to fight? . . .


THE CAPTAIN: 1931–1936

*Something soothing, yet jolly. . . .*

The year Bowen Hilliard married Cova Reynolds was the year of the unemployment march on Washington. They were not to do very well. His art was still improving, still powerful, still better than competent in execution, but it was not the year to sell paintings. Their friends bought a few, but their friends had no money either, and Bowen, hating the talk of price, had valued his paintings low, so that when his friends bought them, they said, 'I'm sorry as hell, Bowen,' and he took to snarling back, 'It's all right, goddam you, it's all right.' Cova had a small income from her family, which she increased with her earnings as a twelve-dollar-a-week shop girl, but he hadn't seen his family since college, and there was no money in them anyway.

After a while, when the country didn't come to see his work, and he knocked no people down with it, he began to get a little tighter. Occasionally he compromised with some mantlepiece art, but even that wasn't selling very well. The galleries were closing down everywhere. Once, in one of the back galleries in the fifties, a dealer had agreed to put on a two-week exhibition of his work. . . .

For three days they sat around, Cova by him (she had lost her job), and they would not speak very much until a friend came in. Then they all started chattering very violently, becoming satirical or enthusiastic in turn over painters, screaming platitudes on Munch and Beckmann and Marin, and then abruptly going quiet. The dealer, Mr. Loestler, was taking three hours for lunch by this time. They all knew it was a mistake. Hilliard looked at his fourteen canvases, at the grey carpeting of the dealer's office, and then muttered something about the light being bad. 'It's killing them,' he said slowly. 'It's killing them, I tell you.' Cova was pacing around. She turned to his friends, who were polite, sympathetic and enthusiastic to the best degree of taste, and said, 'I still can't learn anything about when they're good or not, but they are good, they are good, aren't they?'

'Cova!' he said.

He watched her coming towards him, making the most of her red dress. It fitted with the carpet he thought. 'I'm sorry, Bowen,' she said. He gained control of himself. 'It's all right, I'm sorry, too,' he said.

Their friends left. Another batch would be coming in soon, he knew. The dealer's shop was dry smelling. 'They *are* good,' he whispered desperately to himself. He thought of their two-room flat. If only they would let him do something for the walls he thought. A mural perhaps, 'The Artist Out of Whack'.

Then the terrible event occurred. A woman came in to buy something. She was forty, had dark hair, and was growing fat. She wanted a picture for her children's room. 'Something soothing, yet happy-looking. In good taste, of course.' How many jokes had he heard like that. How many long tedious artist's jokes. She looked about for a while. 'I'd like that,' she said. It was an experiment with a Barbizon Landscape. Something about the composition of the field he had been in reminded him of a bad Corot, but beyond that, the entire view had been a little too rich, a little too green, a little too much foliage, almost as if any brown cow that had strayed into the field would have had its flanks of a deep purple to maintain the color order. 'What is it called?' she asked. 'Whore in a Green Negligee,' he said. Cova looked at him in horror, a protest of poverty in her eyes. The woman recovered, 'Well, I don't have to call it that, I suppose,' she said. He held his anger, 'No, of course not.' Afterwards, she bargained with him for the painting, making the final bit of bad taste in the artist–patron breach of etiquette, he decided. She got it for thirty-five dollars. He had spent two weeks on it. After that, when he could not sell a painting right away, he gave it to somebody, be it a boy roller skating, or a shopkeeper, or a laborer in a ditch. (He once said, 'I have more paintings in delicatessens than any other representative artist in America.')

For four years he held on, working with the WPA for a while, but Cova and he were losing something. People no longer thought them clever and talented; men were not so interested in making love to Cova any more. As for him, she became the last outpost. Over and over through the bad years, he took her with a terrible kind of fury, performing almost every time, it seemed, a lover's last entrance. But they were depending on each other too much, trying to draw everything, able to believe in nothing else.

Once, when his depression had lasted for months, he started to write his autobiography. As a book, it was amorphous, but since he added to it from time to time, the brunt of his thought began to fill it. He would write; 'Malraux says that all that men are willing to die for tends to justify their fate by giving it a foundation in dignity. Perhaps, everywhere, this is felt. But in America, men live, work and die without even the rudest conception of a dignity. At their death . . . well then they wonder what the odds are on a heaven, and perhaps they make futile desperate bets on it, adding up their crude moral calculus, so that if the big team, heaven, comes through, and wins and therefore exists, they will be able to collect their bets that evening. . . .'

He was to surrender at last. Cova's family had been architects for several generations, and in 1936 he gave up, accepting a job with them as a draftsman. After a year, by studying on the side, he was an architect of sorts. They were living much better (they could afford to live in the Village now), but he found very little desire to paint. . . . To make up for it, he worked on his book quite steadily. . . .

DALUCCI, APRIL 1942, FIRST, SECOND, THIRD DAYS

*it's cheap . . . it's cheap. . . .*

After the boats had come into sight around the end of the harbor, DaLucci hadn't known what he was doing for two days. Every now and then, though, he could remember them coming nearer, coming nearer, he wishing there was a cannon around somewhere, any lousy bit of fieldpiece to keep them away, but they just kept coming. A coupla Jap planes had started fighting with an American one and they had whipped all around the sky, going out to sea and then coming back. When they started to strafe the beach and the trenches he just sort of ducked automatically, going up and down with the rest like he was a goddam jack-in-the-box, or something, but he didn't know, Jesus, they kept actin' like they was out to get him first. He wished he could shoot something, but the Jap boats were too far away, although he could see them keep coming and coming.

His sergeant, the Indian, kept bending over the machine gun, waiting for them, whistling something, lining it up this way and that, firing it short, just a little *ta-ta-ta*, to see how it was working, but all DaLucci knew was that he felt just like puking.

Holding on to his Garand, he didn't know what to do with it. After a while, with them moving in all the time, he had picked it up, and started shooting, until someone pushed him down. Then the Jap boats started beaching, and the machine guns on each side of him started going, there was more noise than he'd ever heard in his life before, he didn't know, he just kept emptying and loading his rifle, shooting at them but not taking aim. When he looked up, he could see that with all their boats coming in at once, they'd been able to sneak one up on the shore. First thing, before their men tried to come out, they started lobbing with a field mortar from the boat, but then the machine guns on each side of him and all over the place had started cutting that boat to pieces, and even a coupla their own mortars started cracking down. It mighta been Fourth of July if it wasn't for all that black smoke.

Only during all this, the Japs got a coupla other boats on the shore, and they were shooting for all hell from the guns they had mounted in the front part of the barge. He ducked down for a second, scared, and when he looked up again, and started shooting, he could see that there was four boats on the beach now, with their guns all going, and mortars – he heard a whistle, someone shoved him down, and then there was a guy screaming his yap off next to him, falling down, holding his face. For a second, he thought the guy's blood was his own, 'cause it was all over him, but then he knew he was standing, and there was nothing hurting him. The guy was grabbing at his feet and looking up at him. He couldn't look at the guy's face, there was so much blood, so goddam much noise. 'What the hell,' he said, 'what the hell, whatthehell,' and then another mortar came, and he had to duck again. . . .

*In Terre Haute where he lived in the poor part of town, the people used to have their coalbins under the sidewalk, with big metal plates, like sewer covers, over them. When the coal trucks came along, they would unscrew a plate, and dump as much coal in as they ordered. The metal covers were to keep the coal from getting wet.*

*When they first moved in, there was no cover for their bin. A few years before, a cover had broken, and after that, whenever a family moved out, the house without the cover would take the one that was left.*

*He was too young to know this when they started living there, but the first thing in his whole life that he did remember was when the family next to him moved out, and they had gotten a coal cover for their house at last. Everybody in the family was very happy, and they kept showing it to him, saying, 'Here, Tony, look, look, see the cover,' but he was too young and hadn't understood. Not knowing why, he had struck at the cover, and started crying. When they*

*laughed at him for this, he had a temper fit, and Mama DaLucci had
to give him a little wine.*

For two days the whole thing kept up. The Japs kept losing
men, and coming in, and where they had gotten four boats in at
one point, they caused a lot of trouble. Everybody was working
on them (and it was hard to hit them because only the machine
gunner showed, and the Japs crouched behind the steel front of
the barge), and while they were trying to take care of the four
boats, another two had landed on the other side of his flank, and
had gone over the barbed wire with mattresses, piling into a
front trench and going like mad there. They couldn't fire any
mortars into the trench, because the men were fighting too close
together there, and then when another part of the front trenches
half emptied to send men over to where the Japs had gotten in,
the first Japs, waiting in the four boats, had emptied out, and
captured almost a hundred yards of front trenches. From there
they set up a fire so hot that DaLucci didn't even stick his head up
for five minutes. But while this was going on, all the other Jap
boats, or most of them, were able to land behind the part of the
trench that the Japs held. All the rest of the afternoon, the Japs
kept fighting in the front trenches, and along toward night, he
heard a guy say that they had control of the front trenches down
the whole line. After that, it got so he couldn't stick his head up
without going to lose it too, and the two trenches, not seventy
yards apart, had kept firing up and down at each other. For two
days, he had been ducking into the dugout, catching a bit of
sleep that kept being interrupted, choking down a chocolate
bar, and standing around under a trench, not knowing what to
do, afraid to stand up and aim that gun of his, but even more
afraid of the sergeant who kept yelling at him to get up and
shoot. So every now and then, he just had to close his eyes
almost, stand up, just fire his gun, three or four times as fast as
he could, and then drop back in the trench. He never saw
anyone long enough to take aim on him like they taught him at
target school. The three planes that had been fighting the day it
all started, had crashed, he thought, but every now and then an
American or a Jap plane would come out and take shots until
another plane came to fight it, and then the two of them would

lace it up all over the sky, sometimes twisting all the way out to sea, or maybe getting lost on the jungle side of the island. Once, he heard that a Jap plane had crashed in the swamp, but he didn't know about that.

After two days though, it seemed as if both sides were all finished, and everything let up on the morning of the third day. The lieutenant came along, and told them that half of them could get sleep. The sergeant had picked him out as one of them, saying it looked like he wasn't any use anyway, and he might as well sleep so the sergeant could have him off his mind. He didn't like that at all, but he figured it would be awful good to get out of that goddam noise and heat.

But after he got down to the dugout, he found that he just lay on his bed going tense all over. After a while, he turned over, and that seemed to loosen him a little bit, but all the while he could feel this anger growing in him, and not knowing why, he kept murmuring, 'It's cheap, it's cheap.' He kept thinking of his house and his job back in Terre Haute, and somehow that made him get angrier. He kept seeing the porch with the railing in the place where it had come off, and how through the years each of the vertical sticks that held it up were pulled off to fight with, or had worked off in the rain and wind. Even when the guns sounded every now and then, he was so excited he couldn't listen to them, but kept thinking of his old man, the fat . . . and here he started cursing him, sobbing a little between the words, which he pulled out one at a time from his stomach. He remembered the old man sitting on the porch of the house that was coming apart in Terre Haute, not even a drinking Italian, goddam him, sitting there all pooped out after work . . . after working twelve hours a day, breaking a length of railroad track in, making sixteen a week, sitting on the porch in his shirt sleeves, reading a newspaper . . . turning to the sports page, and reading it slo ly, talking to his friends, telling old riddles to the kids, pinching Mama's bottom, with a huh, haw, huh, not even playing cards with his friends, just sitting there on the porch, all pooped out, just a fat hunk of flesh, talking about Italy. Frig him, frig him, frig the old man, he kept saying to himself.

A shell from a mortar cracked apart ten or fifteen yards away.

Some dirt came flying down the dugout steps, and all through it he heard a guy give out a bunch of yelps that died slowly, like a dog he had once heard after a car ran over it. He kept thinking that maybe some of the guy was mixed up with the earth that was blowing in the dugout, and his stomach felt like it was trying to move.

He sat up on the bunk sweating, and for a couple of minutes he couldn't get to relax at all. He lit a cigarette, and then after the first couple of inhales, he felt the anger coming back in him, only he started crying. A guy across from him in the next bunk sat up too. 'Take it easy, bud,' he heard him say, 'let's have a cigarette.'

'Shut up, you goddam bastard,' he yelled. He tossed over the pack. He felt all funny inside, he kept thinking of the lousy jobs he'd had, first blacking shoes, smelling the stink of people's feet, smelling the stink of shoe polish, he could still smell it, it made him sick even now, being laughed at in school because he had the smell on him. (His fingers came up to his nose, he sniffed at them automatically.) Then, older, another job after another; washing dishes, balancing them on his finger tips when they came out of the machine and were too hot to grab hold of, picking up two-foot piles of plates and lugging them to hell and gone, working at a gas station, best pay to start thirteen a week, he'd worked there for two years, they gave him fifteen, Mary wet against him in the park, 'Why don't we get married, Tony?' he getting angry and tight, 'Aaaah, go frig yourself, I play it the lone way. Whata you got that I can't get for a buck fifty?' the guys hanging out on the corner, not enough money to go to a whorehouse, sometimes enough to play pool, what I say, you bastards, is get yourselves a trade, that's the way to make dough, stay off the railroads, they bleed ya dry, looka your old man, what I say is, 'Tony, for crise-sakes, whena you gonn' fix that porch railing . . . ?' He sat up again, his head was whirling. 'What the hell's it all about?' he kept saying to himself softly. 'What the hell . . . ?' Only very softly now.

A soldier stuck his head in. 'Come on, they're starting again. Get up here.' Numbly he reached for his helmet, slung the pack up, grabbed his gun, and lurched out into the sky that was like the Fourth of July only blacker. The Japs were coming over, he kept hearing, and then he began to see it a little. They were doing it the way they had with the boats, charging first at one stretch of trench, and then while all the guns were working there, setting off at another, until there weren't enough guns to cover them all. Then finally, when they did get into a trench, and waited for the reinforcements to come at them, the Japs in the second trenches really charged over with all they had wherever the reinforcements had left.

An order passed down to his platoon to march on to another section, but before they were halfway over, the Japs started racing for the part of trench he was in. Just before this, his head still whirling, he had asked of himself furiously, 'What the hell am I in it for, what for, what for?' and then while the Japs came over, he kept screaming, it's cheap, it's cheap, and something musta changed in him, because when the Japs started pouring into the trench not more than forty yards away, he hadn't given a damn about the sergeant or anything, he'd just hurdled out of the trench, and started running for the city. And pretty soon it seemed to him as if the whole goddam army was running with him. . . .


THE CAPTAIN, 1936–1941

> *'I don't know, Bowen; we're rotten.'*

To believe in nothing was no longer a source of comfort to him. At the architect's office, the days passed slowly. He who used to argue that to analyze the relation of line to line without considering texture was an artistic affectation, now placed line on line, inserted textures where they were necessary, only now instead of painting cement-rubble, or reinforced concrete, he sketched in the cross-sectional symbols for them. In the drafting office, the men worked with their sleeves held up by little bicep garters, bending over the long stools, their heads lower than their shoulders. Several of the draftsmen sported spats. He considered this worth a generalization, and said, 'Draftsmen are not happy unless they wear spats,' but since the people he told it to had never been in a drafting office, they did not consider this particularly profound.

On most mornings when he woke up, he made a grimace. For a short while he was to spend the rest of his working day transcribing one symbol into another, but he had not invented the symbols. A day at the introverts convention, he used to say to Cova in the mornings, but she rarely smiled at it. He realized that Cova held it against him, considered that he had sold out, and for a while remembering that she had wanted him to take the job, had talked her family into it, he was angry and hurt; but later, he realized that she had felt they were at an impasse, that more money was necessary, and that the opportunity had to be made so that they could refuse it, and reaffirm each other. She had told him to take the job because that was part of the balancing factor; he was to make his decision with the scales even. He knew now that she had wanted him to say, 'We'll stick it, we'll keep the WPA job, I will not sell out,' which was not to say that she was not tired of living without money, for she was, but the art, he realized too late, was what kept the two tight kids on the red silk coverlet.

One evening, they were out drinking in a bar with a friend, Henry, who had several parallels with Bowen Hilliard. They had all gotten quietly drunk on sidecars, until Henry had broken the silence by chanting over and over, 'We are the people of the death-urge, we are the people of the death-urge.' 'Shut up,' Cova had said, but he kept talking. 'We are the people of the death-urge. . . . Sounds like Eliot, doesn't it, Bowen?' Then Cova had done something unexpected, reaching over and slapping Henry's face.

'No don't, Cova, don't hit him,' he had shouted, and then all three had become conscious of the place they were in. Cova looked at him for just a moment, and then she was crying. 'Come on, let's go,' he said. 'I'll be late at the office tomorrow, I'll be late. I gotta put in fifteen johns on the third floor of the apartment house we're planning.' Henry had started laughing. 'Sounds like Eliot, doesn't it, Cova? The artist putting fifteen johns on a blueprint.' He had gotten up then. 'All right, Cova, let's go. . . . I'm not an artist any more, Henry. You can't paint when you're dead, can you?' He sucked in his breath. Henry looked up. 'I'm sorry,' Henry said.

'Forget it.'

'No, I said I'm sorry. . . . *Don't* forget it.'

After that, when Cova Hilliard slept with a man it was not because it was her act of creation, but because her husband had nothing left to give her. And he, knowing that, had worked harder at the plans for the tan brick apartment house, or had found a passing woman, or even had tried to paint, feeling the rage growing in him as the paint built up on the canvas, until the moment when what he had wanted to do would not superimpose over what he had done, and he had destroyed the painting.

They were reaching a point where they would give the last hard veer away from each other. Already they had broken up several times, but every time, frightened of the step from sensualism to irrevocable cynicism, they had stopped and come together. In one of these rightings, one of the unexplainables happened, and something of the old certainty had come back. It could not remain, however. There was nothing to hold it any longer. One night, very embarrassingly, he had come home too early. Even in the pain it reminded him of the triteness of the dark-haired woman in the art gallery. When they were alone, he had tried to talk.

'What's the matter, Cova?'

'Oh, go to hell, Bowen, I don't want any sharing of our mutual troubles.'

He lit a cigarette. It was very necessary to maintain whatever existed of the situation. 'You're not feeling very good, Cova, are you?'

'I don't know, Bowen, we're rotten.'

How many times had he asked himself that? 'People like us can't afford to go in for labels.'

'Listen, Bowen, I'm not afraid of them, I don't mind the words. All right I'm not creative, I'm a bitch. That's still perfectly all right. So I'm a bitch.'

He let some ash drop on his pants. Abstractedly, his finger rubbed it in. 'I didn't mean that, Cova. I still don't think we're rotten. Maybe we had just a little too much to buck. Maybe two people do suck each other dry.'

She had worked one of her shoes off irritably. 'Look, Bowen, that's been on the wall for a long time.'

He stood up slowly. 'And after I leave?'

'I'm sure we'll be even more pointless than ever. . . .'

He did a lot at once after that; he left his job, he moved in with Henry (feeling the symbolism of it, but he didn't have to pay Henry any rent), and he finished his book, which in one of his recurring moments of anger, he entitled *The Artist in Transit Inglorious*. It was an angry book. Published by a wildcat liberal firm, it made him very little money, but it served as meat for more than a few of the family-newspaper critics. He thought of painting some more, but it seemed a little like a dirty joke to start all over again. He spent a year working from job to job.

A good deal of his time now, he tried to re-evaluate his life. He felt that somewhere along the line he had missed not a turn so much as perhaps a flubbed traffic signal, stopping when he should have moved forward. It seemed to him that in college he had been talented, clever, and even sincere within the limits of his life that he had defined. And it seemed to him that Cova had been that, too. They had not been mismated, and yet they had broken up, because in not believing they had had to expect too much of each other. If they had believed in something outside themselves, it would have been all right, but everything they had been told for the first twenty years of their lives had become on examination a piece of disjunctivity. The form and the matter had not coincided. So that having no end for their life, they had tried to get by on style.

It seemed to him that his life could be compared to the friendly quarrel over an after-dinner bill; that when for some reason two people wanted to pay a bill, the battle was always fought out by jockeying, so that very rarely would two people both reach at the same time and tear the bill. It was like two trucks entering a one-lane junction at the same time. Inch by inch they might try to ride the other out, but unless the stakes were very high, there was never a collision.

Since in his life he had believed in nothing external, he had never found the stakes high enough to collide. By the time he had broken with Cova this had been so ingrained in them that even then', no great wreckage had occurred. It seemed to him that he had gotten quite far away from anything direct, and that the lack of meaning in his life might be explained by that.

In early 1941 he wrote to his father that he would like to take advantage of his reserve commission to enter the army. A half-year later, he was made (after reinduction school) a captain, by virtue of his age. He thought that the United States would be at war within a short time, indeed, that was why he had entered. He told himself that he had no real illusions about the war to come, that his stake was personal.

He had entered the army, because at the end of his recapitulation of himself, he had come to the conclusion that to justify his life, to find some meaning in it would be possible only when he faced death. He remembered Malraux's foundation in dignity. It might be necessary for him to die to find that dignity. Certainly, he thought, life and death and violent action were the fundamentals, and he would find no lie there. He had decided that it was time for him to clutch at the bill, even if it were to tear apart in his hands. He had traveled the bridge from sensualism to mysticism, but he preferred it to cynicism. And in the meantime, he wondered like the rest what the feel and sound of actual bullets was like. . . .

WEXLER, APRIL 1942, THIRD NIGHT

*He could just see it in the Freehold papers. . . .*

Jewboy, blond Jewboy Wexler perched by the cellar window, tackling Japs with machine-guns bullets, tackling them dead, for the University of Minnesota. Swearing to himself, blond Jewboy Wexler, the farmer from Freehold, New Jersey, the big blond tackle for the Golden Gophers firing machine-gun bullets, blocking tackling the dirty yellow team from across the tracks in Trenton, doing it for the big football team. The gun bucked away from his hand. Tearing after it, he caught the elusive runner, ran his sights on the incoming interference, hit them low with machine-gun bullets for hands, and got the ball carrier. They were a little team holding off the big team he said to himself, they were a little team, and the big team couldn't get to score.

'Take it easy,' Rice, the sergeant, said to him. 'You're wastin' your shots.'

'Listen, Sergeant, I'm firing this gun.'

A grenade splattered unsuccessfully against the outside wall. He started firing again. No half-Indian sergeant was going to tell him how to fight, he was born fighting, playing football for the University of – but he had to correct himself – for the Freehold High football team.

Outside, it had become dark, and the Japs looked like bushes, or like tackling dummies in the evening when practice was over. They were a little team, they were Brooklyn College standing off the University of Minnesota, they were Minnesota standing off the world. 'Come on, you Japs, come on, you yellow-shirted bastards,' he muttered. 'Stop holdin', come on, start tryin' to nail me.'

Every now and then he could get to see them, especially when they tried to cross the flat football field in front of the house; that was when the moon coming over the house's shoulder guard played him okay, that was when he could see the faces, that was when he could see death slapping them. It was just a spray, he was holding the garden hose on them, giving feed to the hens on the farm, making butter of the Japs. The Indian next to him, feeding, fighting quiet, not talking, he didn't like the Indian, dark, whistling, doing it like it was his business. It wasn't a business, it was a game, the most it was a business was a professional football team. Come on, you Chicago Bears, this is the Philadelphia Eagles, this is the Pittsburgh Steelers, and they're holdin' you on the three-yard line. A gun behind the other goal post tried to put his fingers in his eye. He ducked down, feeling the bullets pouring through the window, smacking against the opposite wall back of him. In the distance, he could hear guns going off, this was big, this was being fought all over the island. The machine gun kept chopping at the back wall.

'I tell you not to fire so much,' the Indian said. 'You spot them the window.'

'Don't fire, Wexler, unless they come within a hundred yards, we can't have them hitting the gun.' The captain came out of the trench, wiggled over to the window. 'DaLucci, you relieve at the gun in five minutes.' A sound of consent came from the dugout. 'I don't like the way DaLucci's actin', Captain,' the Indian said, 'he's too quiet.' 'You're quiet yourself, Sergeant,' Wexler let himself say. 'Me?' Rice grunted, 'I'm an Indian.' The captain smiled slowly. 'How many do you think are out there?' he asked. 'There ain't many, Cap'n, there's just a coupla platoons.' 'There's more, Captain,' Wexler said. He must have killed thirty of them already.

The captain looked worried. 'They need this road, there ought to be more.' 'Yessir,' the Indian said. The guns outside had become quiet, the moon making divots on the field whereever a body lay. Wexler felt caught. At home he had his field, he had the hens and the butter and eggs, he had the place outside Freehold where they played football on Sunday afternoon, the biggest toughest blond Jewboy ever to play football for Freehold High. The cellar was too small, he didn't like bein' caught here. 'Yessir, it's a tough war,' he said to himself. The captain took out a chocolate bar, broke it in three. They chewed slowly on it. 'DaLucci,' the captain said, 'come up here.' The Italian came up slowly, bellied over. The guns of the Japs were still quiet. They were scared quiet, Wexler thought. He focused on a few broken trees at the end of the moonlit plain. He said to himself that they looked like tackling dummies too, but they didn't. He thought they were too ragged to get away with that.

'I'm afraid the other house may be taken, men,' the captain said. He separated a piece of silver foil from his teeth, and dropped it to the ground. 'I need the sergeant,' he said. 'Father Meary obviously cannot be considered. I want one of you men to make a reconnaissance over to it. If you can get in, which I doubt, tell them we need more men. If you can't, come back, and tell me how they're making out. The most important thing is that you get back. The radio here is shot out. Does one of you want to go?'

DaLucci scowled in the darkness. 'Naw,' he said. Wexler spat softly on his hands, 'Why not?' he asked. 'I'll make it, Captain.' 'But get back.' He grinned: 'You bet, Captain, that's one thing I'm gonna do.' The Jewboy running broken-field, the Freehold papers carrying the story.

He was starting out the window, when the Indian held his

arm. 'Wait,' he said. 'They're quiet now, they're looking. Stay back yet.' Rice fired a few random bursts. The other gun answered, crawling along the outside wall, becoming quiet after a while. 'All right, now,' Rice said. 'Keep to the shadow of the wall as long as you can. When you come to the end, I'll start firing, then run.' Jewboy inched his way through the window. The air felt looser outside, and the field seemed enormous as he crawled near the wall, his face close to the ground. He felt excited, this was tough stuff. The air of Tinde was cold suddenly, he could see the trees shivering a little. He shivered too. Hell, he didn't want to be in the papers dead.

Creeping along in the shadow, the wall seemed to go for fifty yards. It was so damn light outside, why couldn't the Japs see him, he could see them. He glanced back at the house. From his angle the window was foreshortened so that he couldn't see inside. It felt very lonely out here, no interference, no tacklers, just the Japs. 'This is no damn football game,' he muttered to himself.

Coming to the end of the shadow, he paused, crouched into a halfback's position, waiting for the ball. If that Jap machine gunner ever saw him now, by Jesus. Jewboy Wexler alone in the dark, playing games for keeps. The machine gun sounded abruptly from the house, cutting white lines into the darkness. The Jap gun answered, both of them throwing blocks; he started running, there was forty yards in the clear, if they ever saw him, it would be like stepping on stunned bugs. He ran. The darkness of the bushes forty yards to the side of the house's shadow came towards him, whipped into his face. He sprawled in them, resting, feeling scared. To be putting eggs in crates now, that was all he asked.

The other house was a mile away, he had to keep off the road. What if all the men, including the captain, were killed back there while he was away, what then? He would be killed with them if he hadn't gone away, he thought. Was Vera making out the invoices for the eggs now, he wondered, was Vera worried about the butter?

On the other side of the bushes, the ground rose and fell in gentle slopes, with enough trees sticking out of it to make it okay for him. He had to cut in back of the town somehow, he'd be caught going through it. Running quickly, from tree to tree, he headed inland. A patrol was coming by, and he stiffened behind a branch. After they passed, he felt the tightness pulsing through his legs. He had to relax; you broke a leg taking back a kick unless you were loose. If he coulda gotten to the University of Minnesota like he'd wanted, then he'd be a captain too, sittin' on his tail sendin' out the privates to see this and to see that. He crawled through some bushes. When he poked his head out the other end, it seemed like a tree was standing with its back to him, only it was no tree, it was a sentry. He lay there waiting for the man to move, but he didn't. Slowly the Jap turned around, then showed his back again. Jewboy Wexler caught in a trap. He waited there, wondering if he should make a sudden tackle. Could he get the guy before he yelled? But he couldn't get himself to do it, the legs gave out first, every good athlete got it in the legs first. Slowly, holding his body an inch from the ground, he began to edge away on hands and toes, one foot back, one hand back, the other foot back. When he was thirty yards away, he stood up in a crouch, and backed into the shadow of a tree. He wanted a cigarette. How the hell was he expected to go over a mile like this and back? In the hills, away from the ocean, a couple of machine guns were going like all hell. That must be the jungle already, he thought. The coastal road was at his right, but he'd never make it that way, that was where the Japs were fighting.

After a while he started going again, running, crawling at times, gliding from tree to tree. He felt better; this was the longest damn run any man ever made. No Minnesota back ever did this. If only they woulda given him that football scholarship, he'd be back in the cellar now, and DaLucci would be sweatin' here. The hell with the Freehold newspaper, what the hell good would that do Vera and him? They could use that Freehold newspaper for toilet paper. And he almost started giggling. It was soft paper.

He came to the top of a hill, worked his way through the tall grass, afraid to stick his head up. From the next hill, maybe, he could see the other house. It had oughta be away from the town, like the cellar was. He heard Japs laughing, slid on his belly away from them. Something, maybe it was a snake slicked across his face. He almost yelled. When the sound of the Japs came too near, he stopped, wondering how he was to breathe. He didn't have a big Jewish nose, that was one help, and he blew his nose that was another. Minnesota hadn't given him the scholarship 'cause he was Jewish, but for crise-sakes what was in a name? He had blond hair, didn't he? He was five feet eleven, fast, and weighed one-ninety before a shower. Jewish, hell, in Freehold they said he played like a big Swede. Swede Wexler, he thought, holding his breath. The Japs were passing. Swede Wexler waited, and then ran, duckwaddling through the tall grass. At the bottom of the hill he had to cross a stream, and his shoes started squishing. After a while, he took them off, and held them in his hand, while he worked his way up the hill. A butter-and-egg farmer, what the hell kind of a life was that for Swede Wexler, he woulda been a pro footballer by now. They'd heard of him all around Freehold, Asbury, Long Branch, he bet Point Pleasant even.

When he came near the top of the other hill, he got excited, he was gonna make it after all. The road and the house oughta be on the other side, but it worried him 'cause there was no shooting. At the top, he felt his way around some rocks, looked down. The Japs were marching along the road, the house seemed broken in two, he could see a little fire in places from it.

Jewboy Wexler put his shoes on, turned around, and started back. There wouldn't be anything for the papers now, they paid off on touchdowns. There wouldn't be any ads to sign and get money so the mortgage could be paid off in ten years instead of the twenty it was amortized at. It was easier going back, somehow. He kept telling himself not to get sloppy, to keep blocking, or his head'd be off, and they'd be fryin' the fat from it. He wondered what it meant now that the other house was gone. The captain'd know, he guessed, although the captain didn't look on the ball either, but he supposed it was important. He kept tellin' himself to think of Vera 'cause he might as well think of the best friend a man had which was no dog, you could bet your life on that, but he felt all free and easy now, not scared of being killed, and he didn't need to think of her.

Before he knew it, he was sticking his head out of the bushes, and looking at the house with its windows all filled in, and the cellar under it, where the gun still was firing. He didn't know how to get back in there, he'd have to cross the part where the moon was, and he couldn't signal them to keep the Japs' minds off him. He guessed he'd just have to wait. The guns stopped tangling with each other, and then started again. He remembered that the Japs would be busy firing. There might be a coupla them stickin' out away from the guns, and they might spot him, but he'd have to chance it. He darted across the field in the moonlight. A couple of rifles started banging at him, and then just as he hit the shadow, the machine gun changed over toward him. He scrabbled for the wall, burrowed into the right angle it made with the ground, hunching his body up, hoping they couldn't see him. He didn't have time to be scared. The damned gun kept spraying around him. They didn't know where he was. The cellar machine gun wasn't going now. They wouldn't know where the window was. He ran along the wall, dived through the window, almost knocking the gun over, and landed on the ground. The gun started going again, and he crawled up against the wall, breathing as noisy as he felt now, sort of snug against the sandbags.

'Nice goin', kid,' Rice said to him. DaLucci was firing now, the captain feeding. The captain made a sign, and Rice took over the feeding. 'I wonder they haven't gotten a trench mortar up yet,' the captain said. Rice grunted. 'They ain't many of them, they just seem to be wantin' to hold us here.'

The captain kneeled beside him. 'Can you talk yet?'

'Yeah,' he said, trying to get control of his heaves, feeling kind of weak and tired all over.

'What happened, what's at the other house?'

'They took it, there's Japs all around, they're marchin' along the road.' The captain nodded, whistling tunelessly. 'That's the answer, Cap'n,' Sergeant Rice said. The captain nodded again. He bent down beside him. 'Oh, and say . . . Wexler, ahh . . . what was it like?'

'What?'

'Out there.'

'Oh,' he shrugged. 'All right, I guess. Kinda tough, maybe.'

It looked like the captain was going to ask him something else, but he stopped. After a while he asked, 'You're sure about the house?' 'Yessir,' he said. He was getting control of his breath.

All of a sudden he realized that the captain had bellied over to the dugout in the middle of the floor. He was coming back with Father Meary, the two of them crawling up to the wall near the gun. 'Keep firing as usual,' the captain said, 'there's something we have to talk over.' They were all huddling around the gun emplacement. 'The other house fell, and the Japs are going through on the road. They don't need this house any more. Do you all understand me?' The priest stirred a little. 'Do you mean, Captain, that this is no longer an important objective?' The captain seemed to be smiling. 'Yes, that's right . . . Now, they're not going to let us stay here. They don't want any little pockets left. So sooner or later they're going to bring up some small fieldpieces and blast us out of here. There's really no point in staying. We might be fighting them on the other road, but I doubt it.'

'They didn't look like they was fighting,' Wexler said.

'All right. Now I . . . for personal reasons,' he halted. 'I'm going to stay here. But since I have no right to ask your lives, any of you that wish may surrender. There's no point in heroics in all this. I will not consider it cowardice. Now which of you wants to surrender?'

The priest spoke a little nervously. 'You say there's absolutely no point in remaining.'

'Too doubtful a one to demand it of any of you.'

Rice made a sound of impatience. 'I been in tougher spots than this.' The priest made a soft sound of indecision. 'There will be a lot of captured men, no doubt?'

'Yes,' the captain said.

'The hell with it,' DaLucci said suddenly, standing up. 'I'm going. You can frig this goddam war.'

'You, Wexler?' the captain asked.

He didn't want to be out in the open again. If they held, maybe he'd be in the papers, maybe. . . . He didn't know what the hell to do. 'I'll stay,' he said slowly, before he knew it.

'All right, and you, Chaplain?'

Meary got to his feet. 'The captured men will have need of me. Captured men need God perhaps . . . more.' His lips were trembling. 'Are any of you Catholic?' he asked. . . . 'Well, God be with you anyway.' DaLucci and Meary knelt by the window. 'Go out with your hands up,' the captain said. 'Don't yell, because they won't understand you, and they may think it's a charge.' The priest crossed himself. Slipping the gun to the side, Rice put his back to the wall. 'So long, you bastard, DaLucci,' he said. 'Frig yourself,' DaLucci said, his short squat form heavy with anger. They went out.

All of them watched from the window. Wexler didn't know how to figure it. He saw them pass into the light, start walking to the Japs. The moon kept catching a piece of their hands. For a moment the priest stumbled, and then went on. They had separated from each other, and walked about ten yards apart. There wasn't any sound from the Japs. They had walked across the entire field almost when the Jap gun started. DaLucci went down first, then the priest. The gun kept playing over them for a few moments.

The first thing Wexler heard was the captain saying slowly, 'I never thought of that, I just didn't think of it.' A yell of derision came from the Japs. Wexler grabbed the gun. 'Let me at those goddam bastards, let me at them, I'll cut their goddam hides off.' Rice pushed him away. 'Shut up, they had it comin' to them.'

'Why, you goddam Indian,' Wexler said.

'Shut up, both of you!' It was the captain.

Wexler stopped. The funny thing he kept telling himself was that he didn't really feel sore, he didn't feel much at all.

A Jap soldier came crawling forward cautiously to see if any men were left. Rice bent over the gun, sighting it carefully. He pulled the trigger for just a few bursts, then ran it back and forth on the fallen soldier. He catcalled across to the Japs. 'Jeez, they haven't got anything, not even flares. This ain't so bad.'

The captain was silent for a few minutes. After a long while he said, 'What did DaLucci do before he joined the army?'

'He was a gas-station attendant, I think,' Wexler said. 'I didn't get to know him very well.'

'Yes, I see,' the captain said.

'Huh, why sure, sir?'

'All right, start feeding the gun,' the captain said to him.

The Japs were holding back now. There just wasn't anything doing. He wondered how long they had been there, maybe three hours, that was pretty long for a little team to hold off a big one. But as he thought it, there kept running something else, and he couldn't keep it back. He didn't know why it was, but he kept thinking that it was more like they were the big team and they were gettin' pushed around by the little one. He didn't know if he believed it or not, but he wasn't sure of anything. He didn't know what to think. . . .

THE CAPTAIN, APRIL 1942, FOURTH DAY 4 A.M.

*. . . like men standing in line, naked, waiting to be examined.* . . .

He had seen death in many forms during those three days and nights. And to the captain, waiting in the cellar now beside Wexler and the Indian, waiting for the final irrevocable attack, it seemed to him that all his life he had been waiting for his death, and now that it was approaching, there might not be any meaning extracted from it. All day and night, for three days and nights he had been seeing men fighting and dying, and perhaps it had all happened too quickly, but all he knew was that it had no emotion or meaning to him. He remembered the burnt body of a man that he had looked at for quite a time. It had seemed a terrible degradation, as if the man in burning to death had reverted to a prehistoric type. He had been blackened all over, his flesh in shriveling had given the appearance of black fur, and his features, almost burnt off, had been snubbed and shrunken, so that the man's face in death had only registered a black circle of mouth with the teeth grimacing whitely and out of place in the blackness of the ape.

It was not inconceivable to him that his own death could produce a similar violation of his flesh, and yet he felt no emotion from it. It seemed as if for the past three days, he had been numb, numb, not so much from fear, as from a voidity of sensation. Lying in the cellar, his back against a wall, he wondered how long it would be until morning when the Japanese would be able to see the window, and could release a fire through it that would kill any of them trying to answer it. Under that morning fire, he knew, would come Japanese, bellying forward across the plain outside. He wished for a cigarette, knowing he could not smoke one till morning when its light would no longer be dangerous. About him, the Indian and Wexler crouched on either side of the gun, only a small part of their helmets turning the angle of the window. 'Stop moving around so much,' he heard the sergeant say, then Wexler answering, 'I feel itchy.'

Now that the forces of his life were approaching this final result, he tried to imagine what his death would feel like, and whether at the very end there would be some all-encompassing sensation. Feeling the night throbbing about him in the dampness of the cellar he was trying to find some resonating quality, some bit of beauty that would have meaning before the final result enacted itself. In this darkness, he was trying, as desperately as his mind would allow, to plumb the content of it, and throw it up against the form of his life. His hand reached out tensely in the night. To achieve the ultimate in his death, to reach out and catch it and pin it up against himself in death – his arm relaxed. It would not be that way. Nor would it be, he thought, in terms of a common denominator, it would be no more and no less of one than a group of men standing in line naked, waiting to be examined.

Wexler stood up and walked away from the machine gun. In the darkness, the captain could only hear him, but it seemed as if he had felt his confinement, and wanted some sudden release. 'Listen,' Wexler said, 'Sergeant! Did I ever tellya how I got to throw a pass in the Red Bank game one year?' A grunt came from the window. 'You know I played guard, you don't even get to handle a football that way, but we had this play see? . . .' The sergeant flexed his feet, 'Get away from the window. You never can tell when I can fire this gun.'

The captain counted three cigarettes in his pocket. In two hours it might be light enough outside to smoke. Wexler was ranging the blackness with his large feet. He stumbled over something and swore indistinctly. 'You see the thing was I could pass. They ain't many guards can do anything with a ball, but ya see I got these big hands. . . .' He reached the other end of the cellar, and headed back for the window, talking slowly. The captain felt a desire to make him stop. 'Well, they had this play built around me, where I shift into the backfield' – he moved a few steps sideward in the dark – 'making me eligible to hold the ball, see, only it don't go to me, it looks just like I'm protection for the ball carrier, like I pulled out of the line for it, so they ain't worryin' about me.' His body moved tensely now – 'and then after I miss a block purposely, the ball's whipped over to me, I'm eligible, see? . . .' The machine gun started suddenly from the window. 'Got him,' the Indian said.

'So then I pull back, hold the ball up,' his arm cocked, 'set to throw and . . .' The Japanese gun answered through the window. Wexler folded slowly, his arm reared back almost to the last.

The captain stood up and, then, knowing the man was dead, sat down more slowly. 'I told him, the dumb bastard,' the Indian muttered.

'Do you want me to feed the gun for you?' the captain asked.

'It's okay, I can handle it myself. It's kinda quiet now.'

They sat there silently. By turning his head and leaning forward a little, the captain could see out the window, and he suddenly understood, now that Wexler had died, a little more what his own death would be like. He doubted if he would feel anything. It would be as casual as Wexler's, with no emotion for him. Too late, it seemed to him ridiculously clear that emotion could only come from the connotations of experience, and not from the experience itself. Things like first sex experience, if it were unexpected, violent action, death that did not come after a slow sickness, would all give no emotion when they happened. The captain, having experienced the first two, remembered that they had left him numb; the emotion was to come later in tiny quanta until a week or a year later, the remembrance of the experience would arouse a surcharge of feeling in him; at the origin, however, was only the numbness. So that his death, he knew at that moment, would come in casual form without the death orgasm, the instinct for ultimate ecstasy never to be gratified. And to anyone else, his death would be meaningless. To Cova it would be a shock, to his friends, a jar that would merely titillate them because it was expected, perhaps would mean an extra drink at some late hour. To his nation it would be a line in some newspaper, far less interesting than the line about a murdered prostitute. To anyone else . . . he couldn't think of anyone else. Perhaps someone would discover his paintings. He smiled wryly. . . .

He kept coming back to Cova. Little by little a scene was building up for him. And because he could see so much of his own shadow in it, so much of what he might have been if the war hadn't come, he let himself amplify it, not paying any attention to the scattering sounds of battle outside. . . .

*He didn't know how she would find out; he supposed, he preferred to have his father called because his father would be ill-equipped for it, and because Cova listening to his stumbling would feel compelled to exhibit some emotion while listening. After she would have cradled the phone, she would go upstairs to her room and lie down to think. She would be living, he thought, in a private house, perhaps a suburb by now, sharing the rent and fornications with a woman perhaps three years older than herself.*

*Lying in her room, her bed would begin to feel lumpy, and in shifting her position she would begin to cry. There was so much of herself in Bowen; she would feel a little bit as if she had died too. And crying, she would begin to whisper to herself, 'I feel rocky as hell, I feel rocky as hell. . . .'*

*There would be a ring downstairs, and she would remember that she had an appointment that night. The first impulse would be not to answer, but she didn't want to be alone; the second would be to call the date off, but that would be just too damned ostentatious. After a while, she would run downstairs, and catch the man just as he was about to go away.*

*'I'm sorry,' she would say, 'I . . . I was just sleeping a little. . . . Come in.'*

*He would be a man of medium height with a dark sensitive face. This would be – let this be his first date with her. He would be very interested in sleeping with her. They had met at a party.*

*'You've . . .' but he would not say, 'You've been crying.' He would smile sympathetically, leaving the admission or rejection to her.*

*She would throw her head back as if to balance the tears on her eyeballs, preparatory to absorbing them. 'Oh . . . it's too stupid,' she would say. 'I just found out that a man I was married to died on some damn island. I used to love him.'*

*He would say, 'You must be very unhappy.' His voice would be low, in good taste, calculated to serve for emergencies such as this one. Also, he would not have declared himself by the question. He would be finding out more about this woman, and if she held her husband's death in war against his civilian's bed-courtship, he would be turning her thoughts away from himself.*

*She would smile a little. 'Oh, I've got a bad case of nostalgics,' (she had coined the word once), 'but they always dissolve in cointreau.'*

*'It's difficult to get cointreau, nowadays,' he would say. 'Perhaps you would prefer to remain at home; our evening can wait for a week or two.' He would be thinking that for this evening she would be loving her husband again.*

*'Oh, no, we must go out,' she would say, but the false gaiety in her voice would be misunderstood by him to mean that she wanted to be alone with her rewarmed love, whereas she had made the gaiety false so that he would be indebted to her, and if during the evening she felt a let-down, no compulsion to be witty and entertaining would exist.*

*The man would make his fatal error here. He would say, 'I know how you feel, we would hate each other. After all, while it may be a convention to mourn and stay at home, it is also one to keep one's engagements, and since you must be conventional tonight, it would be better to do what you want, which is, I think, to stay home.' He would be thinking that she would remember the kindness, but even more, the insight, so that he could enact his seduction a week later when it would have a certain logical sequence, whereas on this night it would smack too much of a perversion.*

*She would recognize then that all protestations would only convince him the more, and so she would acquiesce, chat for a few minutes, and then close the door to go back to the empty house. Only now, wanting perhaps a little more to cry, she would not be able to, for the moment had passed, and the situation no longer would warrant it. . . .*

He swallowed slowly. There was a painful saltiness in his nose, and he felt a sudden hatred for himself. It was occurring to him that he was emotionally convinced of his death, and he wondered at how far he had come to feel like this, amazed that he felt no fear for it seemed to him that the fear of death must be stronger than anything else in a man's life, and that few were the men who surmounted it. Perhaps, he thought, a few that were really religious or that believed in something hard enough to clamp down on all the other feelings, but he did not know. Perhaps to die for your country, but here the captain felt a rebellion in himself. For a long time, in his moments of reaction against his fate, he had postulated, rather than believed in, he had postulated a something to rail against. And that 'something' had most often been the word America; he would feel sometimes, America has cheated me, but the phrase was uncomfortable; it sounded alien to him, made up perhaps of a self-pity he was not wise enough to realize. For although it might have been true, it was too large a word to attack; it sounded awkward, and perhaps a little cheap in the language of his logic. And yet now, he hated the word America for a moment; he felt that the wreck of his life had come out of himself to a great extent, but he felt also that America had cheated him, had taught him all the wrong things, and had offered him nothing in return. He felt that it had not been strong enough to admit its faults, that when it had made a mistake or was ashamed of something, it had yelled a little louder, and had waved the flag about a little too hard. He did not know, he wanted to believe in her, but he knew that was impossible in the hour or two that remained to him. But for some little part of him, he hoped idly that others would find something there in the next few years . . . that something would come out of the country, and that it wouldn't go hard and selfish as it always had before. But he was very doubtful of this, for he had never learned anything from America to make him feel that anything worth while would come after him. He had been told to love God, but to love God beyond the mechanical emotion of the religious ritual was for very few people; he had been told of an equality, but it was only a frame; he had been told of a morality, but finally it was not of the context of its people. . . .

*When his book had come out, years before, all the critics had attacked it; they had called it cynical, and cheap, filled with an undue proportion of self-pity and glory, and he, months later, had had to agree with them that in most ways it was.*

*But one review hurt him terribly. There had been one part in the book that he had written honestly and sincerely; centering about one sentence that had been a summation to him of the futility about him. He was thinking of the war to come when he wrote it, and he had wondered that everybody had not seen it.*

*Only this review noticed it. He remembered holding it in his hand for a long time. It had read:*

There have been cynics, I suppose, less witty, bitterer and less unepigrammatically epigrammatic than Bowen Hilliard. It would be very easy to dismiss Hilliard as another misanthrope, if it were not that the man advertises himself as a sage. After deciphering his key sentence . . . which is . . . 'To die in terms of a subsequent humanity is a form of emotional sophistication that may be achieved only by the people of that nation which puts its philosophy in action' . . . I have been compelled to believe that Bowen Hilliard's book would have been more accurately entitled, *The Artist in Belly-Ache Inglorious*. We have had enough rot these days. . . .

Soon he could smoke a cigarette, a last futile cigarette of distaste. And yet, amused with himself, there was a hope remaining that it would taste a little better than all the thousands preceding it. He was waiting for the dawn, wanting to see a last day, hoping too that he would feel this dawn more intensely than any that had come before. He heard the Japanese outside, firing, then the Indian answering, then silence once more. The Indian with his neat efficient motions at the gun aroused his interest. For a short while he thought of the Indian and himself in terms of 'they' but he could not feel it. At last he compromised by bellying over to the window, and relieving him of the gun. . . .

THE INDIAN, APRIL 1942, FOURTH DAY 5:30 A.M.

> *Some guys are born to go to whorehouses. . . .*

The trouble with Rice started when he was adding up his accounts. Perched by the window, his knees bent, feeling the tight roll of his bottom against the backs of his heels, he had just picked off a Jap who was trying to sneak down the side bushes, and in relaxing had thought to himself that that made fourteen he had bagged. Rice knew what he knew, he always used to think that. He knew when he had to hit a guy, and when talking would get him out of it; he knew how to tell when a whore was tired, and if you felt like talking (which wasn't often with Rice) how to pick out the right tired whore. He also knew not to think when thinking made you crazy, which is what made his thinking now so unusual.

He'd been trading bursts with the Japs every ten minutes or so, feeling it was the slack season. Naturally, he'd been fighting so long in so many places, he had gotten to the point where if he wanted to think he could do it while he fired a gun. And he had been telling himself with pride that of the Japs that had been killed, he had knocked off thirteen out of fifteen as near as he could tell. He had to admit that he'd been firing the gun more than Wexler or DaLucci, but then they'd gotten killed which'd meant no one spelled him at the gun. And he knew that your accuracy went down when you were tired. So it all balanced out, except that he couldn't figure what percentage thirteen out of fifteen was. He tried for a while to work that out, but he quit school too early at the Indian reservation in Oklahoma ('Where whores were born,' he used to say sometimes), and he didn't have much luck. He was also thinking that they'd held out for pretty long, although the Japs only had one machine gun and no flares. The thing was they hadn't gotten any more guns because the main body was probably halfway to Tinde by now, he guessed.

He was estimating about how, for an afternoon and a night, they had killed off fifteen Japs to only three of theirs, and how at the very worst the last profit-and-loss would be fifteen to five. This was where the trouble came in. He stopped. He realized he'd been figuring himself in the five. That meant they got him, the Indian. It hit him that way, he hadn't figured on being killed since . . . since, Jesus, since the first World War. He'd been eighteen, and it had been in Belleau, or wasn't it? . . . All he remembered was that he'd been sick and scared, and now although there was something in his stomach, it wasn't anything like that. He felt kinda surprised almost, he just never figured it that way. With the things he'd done, the Marines in Nicaragua, Bolivia on his own, rumrunning in New Orleans, somehow he'd kinda forgotten that you stood a chance of dying too. . . . He kept wondering what it would be like.

*He had felt like talking; it had been a tired whore that night. Except that when he'd been in the room with her, sitting on the soiled blanket, batting his eyes against the glare from the bulb naked-looking in that room, he hadn't been able to say much at all.*

*They smoked a couple of cigarettes. It wasn't that she was pretty, he hadn't found many pretty whores, but there was something about her that moved him back three years, or up ahead to what he would do if they gave him a grand out of nowhere one day, no strings attached.*

*Finally she said: 'You're a funny guy' (one thing was she didn't use 'dearie'), 'you never talk much.'*

*He blew his smoke out. 'I'll tell ya somethin'.' He paused. She nodded at him to go on. He felt queer. 'I had a lot of girls in my day, for a long time, but none of them was amateurs. I paid on the line every time.'*

*She still nodded, still receptive. 'I tried to think it out once. I ain't a good-lookin' guy, but I'm awright. I finally figured it out that I started too late. The first time was at twenty-two, New Orleans, I think.'*

*She lay back on the bed. 'That could be it, of course,' she said, 'but I dunno, darling, the way I see it is just that some guys are born to go to whorehouses.'*

*He felt dumb for talkin'. 'Yeah, that's it,' he said, and left soon after.*

For a while he was busy shooting the gun off, and that took his mind off his troubles, as shooting a gun always did, but there was something uncomfortable in the back of his head all this while, and the first lull there was, it popped back again to him that he was going to get his, come two three four hours. That was all right, of course, you didn't live forever, but at the same time, he had the damn craziest feeling thinking about death, because he just couldn't guess what it was like. He knew you didn't think any more, that was obvious, but, you . . . you just didn't do anything after that. It was just the end. He fired his gun viciously, ducking down as the return came back. That meant . . . no more. It was like wrestling trying to figure that out, only with your head.

He wanted suddenly to know why the hell he was gonna get his. He just wanted to know what it was all about. They called him Creepy Joe around the army camps, and said he knew all the answers 'cause he never asked questions. But he had to ask questions now, because he was buying something that cost a lot. He'd never asked what the fightin' was about; fightin' was his business, and you didn't ask questions if business was good, but now he kinda liked to know. The papers said Freedom, and he guessed maybe they were right because that was something they knew about, just like he knew about whores, but Freedom . . . ? Did it figure with a slug in the belly . . . he didn't know . . . and by now, he was damn sure he wanted to know. He wanted it put in words. He wasn't scared of dying, but he wanted it down on paper, some of the reasons anyway. Anyway, he wanted, that in the fifteen-to-five ledger, there would be a remark after his name. He'd never thought that way before, but he could see it now, a business ledger, all written in, like the mess sergeant used, with something after his name. THOMAS RICE, THE INDIAN.

He felt a hand tugging at his shoulder. It was the captain: 'I'll take over the gun now.' He crawled away, propping his back against the wall. For about ten minutes, he just sat there thinking. He shoulda known enough not to think when thinking didn't do any good, but he couldn't keep from it this time. After a while he crawled back to the machine gun. The captain hadn't fired in a long time. He fingered a couple of bullets in their jackets before he spoke to him. 'It's getting light out, Captain.' He felt funny, he was talking just for the talking. The captain turned towards him. 'They've brought another machine gun up. They're not moving, so I haven't fired.' He felt himself nodding, feeling more like talking than he had in a long time. The captain said, 'I think they'll wait till it's light out, they only have twenty minutes, and they can take it safe.' He saw the captain slap his breast pocket. 'We'll be able to have a cigarette soon,' he was saying. The Indian felt uncomfortable. 'Of course, there's a chance,' he said, 'we might have knocked them back; maybe we got a patrol coming up or something.' 'Yeah, there's always a chance,' the captain said to him. They were silent. He felt himself having to speak, and he couldn't understand it.

'Think they'll win this island?' he asked.

'I never thought we had a chance to keep them from winning here. They had more time to get ready.'

He nodded. He could have answered that himself . . . but . . . 'Do ya think we'll win the war?' he muttered suddenly.

The captain took so long in answering, he wished he hadn't asked it. 'I think so,' he said finally. 'We're taking a licking now, but we've only been fighting four months.' He went silent again. 'Yes, I think so,' he repeated. 'We have more men and materials, and you know, our allies are pretty good.'

'Yeah,' Rice said. He felt balked somehow. Not knowing what to do he took out his pistol. 'Well, what are we . . .' but the question was too damn lousy. 'We *gotta* win, don't we?' he asked. 'Yes, that's the thing,' the captain said, 'we're fighting because we can't lose.'

He felt at his buckle. 'That's all?' he asked. 'Just because we can't lose? Isn't there anything else?' He felt just too damn dumb, but the questions hurt him until he got them out.

'I don't know; it's too early in the war yet,' the captain said.

'Well, what about us, we're goin' to have to die, because we can't lose. . . . I don't know, I want more than that.'

'That's all there is,' the captain shouted, his voice going hard. 'Now shut up!'

It didn't matter any more whether he talked. He saw the captain's face pulsing, and he didn't want to hear him speak. The captain got control of himself. 'We're dying alone, Sergeant, that's all.'

'I'm sorry, sir,' he said.

They could see each other's faces by now. Across from them the bushes were beginning to change from black to green. 'They'll be over very soon, Captain,' he said. He just felt tired, that was all. 'The trouble with you, Sergeant,' the captain said, his voice drawn out thin, 'is that you think it is one of man's inalienable rights to have a little idealism with his death. You wouldn't mind that, would you, Sergeant?'

'No, I don't know what. I'd like a cigarette, sir.'

They lit them away from the window, cupping their hands. The captain came back and felt at the gun. 'The sun's starting to show,' he said. 'We really ought to get the trench mortar out.' As he spoke, the Jap gun fired at them again, and they both ducked. The captain peered around the side of the window. 'It's going to be one hell of a sun,' he said.

'Yes,' the Indian answered slowly, 'sometimes you want to look pretty carefully at it.'

*October 1942*

# Advertisements for Myself
## on the Way Out

*Prologue to a Long Novel*

I

To be forced to admire what one instinctively hates, and to hate all which one would naturally love is the condition of our lives in these bad years, and so is the cause beneath other causes for our sickness and our death. If some of you will understand immediately what I mean, I still must think of the others who are to take the trip with me: that mob of readers whose experience of life is as narrow as it is poor, and worse if the truth be told – they are picking up this book because they have heard it is good for the bathroom and so may palliate their depression; this book! my tale of heroes and villains, murderers and suicides, orgy-masters, perverts, and passionate lovers, my lust to capture Time.

For those readers courage is required. My passion is to destroy innocence, and any of you who wish to hold to some part of that warm, almost fleshly tissue of lies, sentimentality, affectation and ignorance which the innocent consider love must be prepared instead for a dissection of the extreme, the obscene and the unsayable.

The mark of a philosopher is that he puts his name to his work, he wants his ideas to carry the connotation of the syllables (those primitive sounds) which make up the armature of his character. So, properly, I should introduce myself here, and indeed I would, if I were able, but my name eludes me and at present would slip by without meaning to you – I am virtually married to Time unless she has already divorced me (of which indigestible statement, more explanation later) and so my name alters as Time turns away from me, and it is not all that natural to explain who I am. Let it go. Only a dreary mind cannot bear mystery.

Yet I do not know if I should evade your questions. The most murderous emotions are aroused when we cannot find the word to fit the particle, and murder (in favor of which I will find some arguments) still has the disadvantage of distracting the attention. Since I wish the various intelligences who take the trip with me to finish with stimulation to their brains and sweet for their bodies, I must necessarily take into account that the duller minds among you cannot support the luxury of listening to a voice without a face unless you are handed some first approximation to my state. I will therefore suggest it is possible I am a kind of ghost, the ghost of exhausted passion – but I prefer to believe this is completely untrue. How much less disagreeable to be some breath in the caverns of the unconscious of one of the figures in this unnatural mystery, or indeed to be the consciousness brought into being by the relations and mutilations of the exceptional characters I will introduce.

Only to say this is to deny it, for if I am the creature of relationship, I must be not so much consciousness as corporeal, containing a blastopore whose nucleic proteins limn a signature, the given first half of my destiny. Yes, I must be the breath of the present-present, a point of size swimming in my unglimpsed mother's first freshets of amniotic fluid, an embryonic two-cell, me, engaging no less than the fluid consciousness of a God, His comprehension still in mine, as I believe is true of all beings not yet born but budding in the belly. So I could be an embryo eight instants old, a work of gestation away from light and noise and pain, and yet knowing more than I will ever know again because I am part of Him. (Or is it Her?)

But to step without benefit of clergy onto the moot worms of theology is to lose our ground. The dock of our embarkation is the mystery of my eye and to whom or what it belongs: am I ghost, embryo, intellect, wind of the unconscious, or some part of Him or Her or Hem or Hir? – but there it is – Hem or Hir – a bona fide clue; only the Devil would ever boast of being thus intimate with the Divinity. So, through this work, at the best of times between us, when we are even laughing together, there should remain a reservation, a polite terror that the illumination is furnished by the Prince of Darkness, and the colour of my light is satanic.

Of course, I could be as easily the old house in which the end of this story takes place (what resonances are contained in the studs, the joists, and the bowed floor planks of an old house). I could be a tree – there is a tree outside this house, an unusual maple whose bole divides into four trunks only a few hands from the ground, and whose branches in the leafless winter articulate the noble forms of the nerve paths of a brain as one might see them in the surgically drafted plates of one of those sturdy grisly nineteenth-century handbooks on medical practice. There is even a garden, a most delicate garden – we are near the sea – and the flowers in summer have that rare electric vivaciousness which comes from salt air, sandy soil, and fertilizer laced up overrich with artificial nectar and mead. Flowers have always been sinister to me when they are lovely – they seem to share the elusive promise of a woman who is beautiful and whose voice is too perfect – one never knows if she is the avatar of a dream or some masterwork of treachery, she is so different from ourselves.

If I make such a comparison, it is obviously quite unnatural to me that I should share my existence with a flower, yet I advance the hypothesis in the interest of being comprehensive, and because the possibility is perversely appealing: where better could a demon hide himself than in the vulva of a garden bloom – if some pleasure-snatcher plucks the stem (have you ever heard *that* cry of pain?) the ex-flower can poison the house before it withers away. Yes, one does well to fear plants – once, out of an ill-timed overabundance of energy and boredom I kicked over a giant mushroom. It was five inches across the head, and I could have sworn it gave a venomous cry of rage as death came to it – 'You bastard,' I heard it say; such a vile fate for that exceptional mushroom, skull-like in its proportions and bold in size. I was sorry. Not every mushroom grows with such lust, and I had violated a process perhaps centuries in the chain. So from fear I mention the flower as well as the tree, and while whispering that vegetative life repels me more than not, I would add my bow to nature – I could be of the ocean and the sand dunes, that primal marriage of the little stones and the vast water – I could be of them, but I hope not; certain embraces are too monumental and so become dull. To say that the oceans of the world are but one tear of God's compassion is a metaphor so excruciatingly empty that the flatulence of a celibate must have been its first wind. But to believe that God like man can suffer occasionally from diarrhea is an infectious thought which stimulates all but the churchly and the vicious.

I will leave the oceans then, I will leave the flowers and the bees and the trees, reminding you that the extraordinary can hide in the meanest maggot, and will reduce myself as an interesting speculation to the dimensions of a dog. There is a hound in this book, brought to a climactic party we are soon to talk about, a poodle dog, Standard, pedigree, A.K.C., descended by his dam from a line of Westchester champions, his sire merely certified, and like all large poodles who have gained the attention due a rich pervert, he is an incredible dog. I know him so well that I cannot evade the last hypothesis – I could be that dog, for the vision of our life which is soon to disrupt your brain is in part a dog's view: a dog has no more than to meet another dog on the street, smell the hindquarters, and know whether friendship is possible, which well may be why dogs are invariably gloomy.

Enough. It would be unseductive to boast of how I will probably travel from the consciousness of one being to the emotions of another – a house, a tree, a dog, a cop, a cannibal, all equal to my hunter's eye and promiscuous ear.


2


There is a master pimp in our presence who is a candidate for the role of hero (his rivals for your vote, a television celebrity and a psychoanalyst) and for a time some years ago, this pimp, whose name is Marion Faye, dabbled at the edges of painting (giving for excuse the observation that such study might enrich his conception of the pornographic photography by which he then was making his living). Faye was a poor painter, but he had a love affair which went on for several weeks with the form of the spiral, and it was a matter of no mean significance to him that the valve of a snail shell as seen through his microscope (Zeiss, 2,000 Deutschmarks, oil immersion, binocular eyepiece) was a spiral galaxy of horny cells whose pigmentation had the deep orange of a twilight sun. Staring into the eye of the snail valve, he would wonder what heats of emotion had breathed into its red – he was of course on drugs at the time – and afterwards, giving his marijuana-refreshed eyes to the whorls on the ball of his thumb and the tips of his fingers, he found the spiral again, and he had that thrill of fright so common to medieval alchemists, psychics, drug addicts, and perhaps available to a few of you: that exquisite terror of sensing oneself at the edge of secrets no other being has been brave enough to invade. For there it was: the tips of the fingers were for touch, as indeed was the snail valve (obliged to close at the lick of danger) and so for touch were all the other natural spirals he knew – he was by profession an accomplished familiar to the intricate double helix in the vaginal expansion, and the other holes of women, and for that matter, men; so he accepted the logic of his intuition: the natural spiral, wherever it appeared, was the mark for a complex of feeling, and if parts of the night sky disported in a spiral, there was sensation behind them, light years of space vibrating with sensuality and anguish, desiring . . . ? But this was another question, too vast. Temporarily he gave up the investigation – in truth the form of his thought was also spiral: he would have to make that all but circular voyage through experience before he would come back to contemplate the spiral again.

Which perhaps is why I have chosen this way to introduce so active a man as a master pimp. If one is interested to begin to understand one's own life, the first of the useful axioms is that genius appears in all occupations, and as a pimp, Marion Faye was a genius. The proof is that he made a million dollars in a few years. Just how is a matter of such interest that it will later concern us in great detail, for one can explore such minutiae only by discovering the psychic anatomy of our republic.

Good. He was a millionaire, and still young, and he owned several houses in different parts of the country and one in Acapulco, and he had his private plane which he flew himself, and various cars, accoutrements, servants, jewelries, larders, and investments. Not to mention several going businesses and the two endowed lovers who attended him, man and woman.

He had done this all in a few years, after coming out of prison without a penny, and he was of course not nearly satisfied, at least not at the moment I describe. Like all men who are Napoleonic in their ambitions and wide as the Renaissance in their talents, he had instincts about the nature of growth, a lover's sense of the moment of crisis, and he knew, perhaps as well as anyone alive, how costly is defeat when it is not soothed by greater consciousness, and how wasteful is the profit of victory when there is not the courage to employ it. So he knew the danger of inertia (if one does not grow, one must pay more for remaining the same), and for months there had been a decision he was unable to make: as had happened before, he felt his powers leaving him. His strength came from decision and action, he was religious (in a most special way to be sure), he was superstitious with the most sophisticated of superstitions, but as a practical matter he believed in the reality of Hell, and he had come to the point in his life, as he had foreseen in terror many a time, when the flux of his development, the discovery of the new beauties of his self-expression, depended on murdering a man, a particular man, perhaps as exceptional as he, a man who could hardly fail to be aware that his own development, as opposed to Marion's was also at an impasse which could be breached equally, if in the opposite direction, by the murder of Marion Faye who once had been his friend.

It was a problem, then, and one of no mean proportions. The tension to murder is as excruciating as the temptations to confess when on a torture rack. So long as one holds one's tongue the destruction of the body continues, the limbs and organs under question may be passing the last answer by which they can still recover, and if one is going to confess eventually it is wiser to do it soon, do it now, before the damage is irrevocable. So with the desire to murder. Each day we contain it a little of that murder is visited upon our bodies, the ulcers seat themselves more firmly, the liver sickens, the lungs wither, the brain bursts the most artful of our mental circuits, the heart is sapped of stamina and the testicles of juice – who knows? this may be indeed the day when the first of the exploited cells takes that independent and mysterious flip from one life into another – from the social, purposive, impoverished, and unspeakably depressing daily life of an obedient cell, to the other life, wild-life, the life of the weed or hired gun, rebel cell growing by its own laws, highwayman upon the senses, in siege to the organs, rife with orgiastic speed, the call of the beat drumming its appeal to the millions of cells, for if other-life is short, it is wild as well, and without work. Yes, to hold murder too long is to lose the body, hasten that irreversible instant when the first cell leaps upon the habit of stale intelligence and gives itself as volunteer to the unformed cadres in the future legions of barbarian and bohemian.

Of course, murder is never simple for old thieves. Old thieves have tired balls, and if Marion Faye often thought with distant pride that he was one of the few to have climbed beyond the killing precipice of manners, morals, the sense of sin and the fear of germs, he knew how much he had paid – yes, he had lost a part of his gift, he had drained the more extraordinary pleasures of his balls, dulled the finer knives of his brain, and left himself prey to such inertias of exhaustion as he was experiencing in these weeks before he sent out the invitation to the party in the old house at Provincetown, the party which was properly to come off in calculated murder.

### 3

It is time now to say a little about this house and where it is situated. The peninsula of Cape Cod is perhaps eighty miles long, and bent in its middle like the knotty, no longer agreeable arm of an old man who once was strong. To the forearm and hand of this coast is given the name of The Upper Cape, and it is pleasant land if one's humor is mournful – wind-swept, with barren moors, lonely dunes, deserted ponds and stunted trees; its colours are gray and dun and the foliage is a dull green. Off the arterial highway with its savage excremental architecture of gas stations, chromium-paneled diners, souvenir traps, fruit stands, motels, blinker lights, salt-eroded billboards, all in cruel vision-blunting pigments, in contrast to this arterial highway garish in its petrifactions of the overextended American will, the side roads are quiet, hardly more than lanes, with

small mouse-gray salt-box houses inhabited for the most part by
retired Protestants, decent, lean, spare and stingy, gray themselves for the most part with a mouse gray.

There is no excess of life in the fall and winter, and it is
country which can be recommended for the solitary – the
lonely walks on sandy trails pass by cranberry bogs whose
thorny undergrowth is violet in color against the lavender hues
of the dunes when the sky is gray. Near Provincetown there are
a few miles of empty sand between the bay and the ocean which
have the sweep of the desert – the dunes rise into small hills and
fall away to valleys where one could believe oneself lost in the
Sahara – I have heard of people who wandered about in circles
over one dune and down another, never reaching the ocean and
never finding the bay, at least not for hours. There are few
places on the eastern seaboard where one could bury a man as
easily and leave one's chances so to nature, for the wind could
leave the corpse under twenty feet of fill, or as easily could
discover the cadaver before the cells were cold.

Beyond this desert, at the tip of the Cape, in the palm of the
almost closed hand, is one of the last great fishing villages of the
world, the place called Provincetown, in winter 3,000 population I suppose, its situation one of the most easterly promon-
tories of the Atlantic coast. Three miles long and two streets
wide, the town curls around the bay on the skin of the palm, a
gaudy run with Mediterranean slashes of color, crowded
steep-pitched roofs, fishing piers and fishing boats whose
stench of mackerel and gasoline is as aphrodisiac to the sensuous nose as the clean bar-whisky smell of a nightclub where
call girls congregate.

It was in Provincetown the Puritans landed and held to a
starving bivouac for three months before they broke the en-
campment and moved on to Plymouth Rock. They were without food and besides there was the spiral to wear them down:
the Cape from the wrist to the fingers curls like a snail shell, the
harbor an eye of water in the center, and one's sense of
direction is forever confused. Without looking at the sun one
could not point across the bay in the proper direction to Boston,
Portugal, or the shores of Barbary. It is a place which defies
one's nose for longitude and latitude, a cartographer's despair

and a Puritan's as well. (The character of narrow intense faith is rectilinear in conception, which is why the clitorine cove in the façade of most New England churches is triangular or ice-pick steeple in its form rather than obeying the feminine Catholic arch of almost equally narrow Gothic faiths.)

The house Marion purchased was on a sand dune behind the last hill overlooking the town, and it was isolated, especially in fall and winter, reached by a sandy road which dipped down one dune and up another to give a view of rolling furze, rain water ponds, and the ocean and beach of the back shore. In bad weather the wind was a phenomenon, a New England wind of the lost narrow faiths which slashed through open doors, tempted shutters loose from their catch and banged them through the night, vibrated every small pane in every Cape Cod window and came soughing out of the sky with the cries of storm water in its vaults – on such nights the hundred years of the house were alive with every murderous sleep it had ever suffered: it was the kind of house in which the dogs barked insanely in bad weather, and the nurse could not rest, and the baby awoke in hysterical terror at one in the morning while the mother would feel dread at the hundred rages of her husband restless beside her in marriage sleep, and the house shifted and swayed to the wind like a ship in North Atlantic seas, yes it seemed to contain every emotion which had died a frustrated death in its rooms and walls through a hundred New England winters, each ghost of emotion waiting to seize the storm feelings of the present; it was a house which had the capacity to set free, one upon the other, dank sore-rotted assassins in the dungeons of a family's character. A storm at the wrong time came on with the horror that this was the night – and indeed there had been one killing there, an unexplained nineteenth-century crime, an old ship captain's widow who had worn a rectangular trough in the planks in the widow's walk at the ridgepole centre of the steep roof. She was found dead on a late February night after three days of rain, the wind howling like a wounded shrew.

Now I know it is not in the mode of our pompous oblitera-tion-haunted years to encourage such pathetic fallacies as the animism of the wind and an old house, but since (be I ghost, *geist*, demiurge, dog, bud, flower, tree, house, or some lost way-station of the divine, looking for my mooring in the labial tortures and languors of words) be I whatever, it must be evident that I am existentialist and would propose that when the wind carries a cry which is meaningful to human ears, it is simpler to believe the wind shares with us some part of the emotion of Being than that the mysteries of a hurricane's rising murmur reduce to no more than the random collision of insensate molecules. Yes, if I were to meet that saint with the body of an ox, St. Thomas Aquinas, a gentleman with whom I agree about very little, I would still be obliged to nod in obligation to his exceptional phrase, 'the authority of the senses,' exactly because I now feel the frustration of a wind which knows so much and can tell your ears so little. As our century moves towards its death, and the death of all of us, so our senses die first, and who has ears to hear the wind when the smoke of mutual hatred is thick on commuter trains, and the subway rails of an evening's television batter into stupidity the sense of the sensual, leaving us null and dumb to the almost ineffable sounds which touch beyond the vanity, the will, the force and the imprisonment of the ego, grim and God-murdering ego, champion of the practical, peasant divinity of the Reformation, that Faustian burgher who built our mills of steel on the stern, the palpable, and the self-evident notion that through a point only one line can be drawn parallel to a given line, when already we are traveling through the non-Euclidean present of space-time. Sooner than we think, lo, the line parallel to the given line will prove to be nothing other than the same line once around the route in the expanding spiral of Being.

And as yet I have said hardly a word about Time.

## 4

But if through a given point, a line is drawn parallel to a given line, and proves to be nothing other than the same line, why then we have abstracted a first theorem on the nature of Time: that lines in parallel represent a function of the natural unwind-

ing of Time (its onanistic tracings) when Time left to its own
resources is excited into action neither by murder nor love, and
so remains in step to the twitching of a clock. Such is passive
Time, Time on its way to death; but Time as growth, Time as
the excitations and chilling stimulations of murder, Time as the
tropical envelopments of love (even if murder is lusty in the
chest and love a cold sweat on the hip), Time is then the hard of
a hoodlum or the bitch on her back looking for the lover whose
rhythm will move her to the future.

But this conjunction is too soon complex and blurs the
attention – let us leave it, let us fall away again to the cold
palpable house of Marion Faye in the back sands of Provincetown, this sea-salted building which first gave me the thesis that
houses are polar in their nature, tending to be boudoirs or
churches. This purchase, if we are to agree in what we see, was a
church of a house with an enormous two-story cathedral of a
living room in dark overstained walnut, the dining room,
kitchen, pantry and servant quarters built into what had been
the cellar, and the bedrooms, studies, studios, and sun rooms
clustered like white-guanoed barnacles, cubicles of rooms all
over the top sides of this two-story chapel with its Gothic
arched windows and sombre light. Marion Faye bought it in the
hour he saw it – it was a bargain – so big, so chill, so impractical – one had to go down to the cellar to make a sandwich – so gloomy, so sonorous, so sepulchral that it was church
for him, and all his other houses (with the exception of the town
house, a complex affair) were no more than boudoirs for his
pleasure, doll houses in liege to the attractive childhood he had
never spent except for some rare bitch-perfumed hours with his
mother.

Yes, this was a house for rare occasions, and he visited it
seldom, and never in summer when Provincetown was a
whore's trunk of frying hot dogs, boat excursionists from
Boston, battalions of the gay and regiments of the hip – he
saved it for rare weekends in fall and winter, and so far as most
people knew, it was not even his house – he had given it on
virtually permanent loan to the most extraordinary of his
former call girls, a tall dignified Negress with a velvet sensuality
who had made her fortune in company with Marion, and

now – her various investments concealed – was a rich hostess of no small reputation in many parts of New York, her parties indeed so well run that her net of fine jazz captured the best of intellectual stimulation – what little there was in that dying electric city. This Negress, who had through her career a series of names (the last, by which people now knew her, being Cara Beauchamp) had found in herself a set of exquisitely parallel personalities like hand-worked nesting tables, and so had avoided the hermetic fate of many call girls and almost all prostitutes – she had dissolved that cyst of character, that prison of nonperceptive muscles which maroons even a high-grade whore in self-pity, hysteria, and loathing for her material. No, this one was fluid, she had a touch of accommodation for all perverse duties, blown into a not uncool flame by her fortune in studying with a master. So she was capable of using her encyclopedic knowledge of the colliding congesting rhythms in the bodies of the strangers she met; and the shyest poor parcel of a man, distinguished physicist let us say, ashy, halfway to the grave, with a dull gray suit and black scuffed shoes dulled to gray, and a pallor of face whose equivocal good health was yellow, and whose oncoming death was gray, was capable still of appealing to her: somewhere in his habit-haunted body and far-departed mind, somewhere in his racked frame which had all the animal magnetism of a catatonic worm (chill and bitter-smelling in its parts) there was a piston of will which would (all whore-patience and art properly applied) give her a memorable night even if the poor will-driven gentleman were half into the grave afterwards with the outrage to his sedentary heart. So here was a man who could give her a furious pleasure, for an evening at least, and therefore meeting him at the door to her party, accepting the introduction from her good friend and favourite psychoanalyst (who will become for us a figure of obsessive interest later on) (he had introduced the physicist as an old college friend), she dipped into her enormous reserves of relaxed sensuous attention, took an immediate plot of the physicist's clang-riddled nerves, and came back with a tight formal smile and the suggestion of a feminine will-driven tic at the corner of her own eye (if she thus momentarily debased her beauty, she was seizing the opportunity to relax the muscles of her eye and make a friend – on the whole a profit for our hostess). Indeed she succeeded; the physicist liked her – he liked her even more when late in the evening and pleasantly if quietly – in his way – hysterically drunk with the blending of the tongues, the reentrate cool jazz of the combination for the night – four homosexual Negroes in horn-rimmed glasses – and the murderous ambiguities of such varied honey-wild pussy as paraded at that party, the physicist had the fair opportunity to discuss physics with the remarkable knife-eyed intelligence of the face in *café au lait* who had greeted him at the door. I choose their conversation to repeat because it is essential to our mystery, and if you find it bizarre you must recognize that we hover at the edge of an orgy of language, the nihilism of meaning fair upon us.

'Isn't modern physics to the square side?' she asked of him.

A true language of indeterminate functions, he was thinking, an expression of the off-phase waves of the Negro masses. 'Oh, no not at all, not really,' he said. 'After all, Einstein was no square.'

'I could die that he is dead – so hoped to meet that man,' Cara Beauchamp said, 'he was hip – a funny man.' She sighed for the dead. 'But, like I mean, *procedurally* – aren't you physicists nowhere with Time?'

'Nowhere – the philosophical groundwork is lacking I suppose.'

'Yes, you don't make the scene.' She restrained her force and added softly, 'Like Time is when you connect.'

'It doesn't exist in between?' He had answered easily, pleased at how well he had picked up his contextual field, but then he repeated it, 'Time does not exist when it makes no . . . connections?' Perhaps he was too drunk, but there was an old physicist's terror in the beauty of the thought. My God, maybe she's on to something, he was thinking.

'Well, it don't exist, and yet it does.'

'Time rests as potential?' he asked, excitement in his dry sad voice, 'rests there until the gap is jumped to Time dynamic.'

'Yeah – potential and dynamic – that's Time. It dies if it don't connect,' and for an instant she was as fond of him as a mother learning from her child. For the rest of her life she had two new words, and what words they were. Through all her unconscious were flexings of cellular pleasure – so much of her experience was rushing to the higher plateau of more precise language.

Actually she had been not altogether inspired in this conversation. She still had the masculine mind of a whore or a hostess – she was a businessman – she searched for synthesis, the big view, and her ideas on Time had come from Marion. Finally she was a salesman – she cannibalized the salvageable from the junk of old conversations to put together some speed for the pitch in her conversation.

She could hardly have done otherwise. She came from a poor Harlem family, late-migrated to New York from the North Georgia line, and her mother had run a cheap Georgia brothel (three girls) and sold heroin in New York until the arithmetic of cutting the ounces wore her down. Cara was the first child in the family to be able to read and write with less difficulty than it took to load a trailer truck. Yet she now had the pride that they all came to her parties, the hothouse haul from Madison Avenue, advertising men and television people laughing at homey house jokes about the sick, curling themselves around a Martini or a model like ivy which slides over ubiquitously from vertical support to vertical support; there was the subtle cream of Negro entertainers from certain particular bistros at the moment not out of favor with Cara Beauchamp, there was a sprinkling from the theatre (those flamboyant timid people), there was a gossip columnist who exercised the discipline not to print a word of what he saw, one or two of the most overrated and/or berated young writers in America would be there, and one fashion photographer, not to mention the pads of Harlem and the cellars of the Village, painters (a growing collection of Abstract Expressionists on her walls), pimps and pushers (those who had proved the most talented of her childhood companions), musicians, a labor leader (yes, there was one) and a banker. It had taken her months but a lawyer who was a friend had induced him to come, and Cara found enough in common to draw him back – her ideas about the personality of those investors with some credit rating whom an exurban bank,

proud of its personal touch, might allow to kite a check for
twenty-four hours so intrigued the banker as a merger of
psychological nuance with fiduciary practice that he returned
once or twice. Yes, there was a horde: movie stars who left
early, promoters, producers, occasional professional athletes,
surgeons, psychiatrists, councillors, pot-heads (discreet to be
sure), hoodlums (who could contain themselves), college girls,
poetesses . . . the apocryphal story was of her middle-aged Irish
elevator operator who became so used to her odd visitors that
even a plump Episcopalian prep school instructor, wearing his
go-to-New-York homburg, hand in hand with a sloe-eyed Arab
boy who looked like an untamed pet on the prowl from the
Casbah gave the elevator man no pause: only a brace of bull-
dykers ever did him in – a famous actress in a sailor's peajacket
and a gargantuan blonde in pink mink went up together sipping
away from long platinum cigarette holders at sticks of Turkish
hashish until the smell of sugar and death made the elevator
operator so high with the smoke of contact that he was as stone
on the return down, and for the first time in thirteen years he
dug into the hanging of his cage and floated it on loverly skill to
the lobby with the awesome anticipatory joy of the first lunar
explorer to kiss the tail of his rocket onto the acned skin of the
moon.

So, there it was, the home of Cara Beauchamp, a ten-room
co-operative apartment and circus overlooking the East River of
the fifties, with a collection of guests almost every Saturday
night whose intellectual and physical connections were
accelerating Time, and weighting the charge of future acceleration. No wonder that Cara gave it up for a month each year and
disappeared into Provincetown where she had nothing more
than a few close friends and entertainers to visit out the nights in
Marion Faye's private church. Yes, she needed her *schule* as she
called it, and she liked the surf-soothing hurdy-gurdy of this
fishing town so poorly considered for even her social purposes
that hardly anyone she knew was found there.

But I must interrupt, for one pretense I can maintain no
longer. I notice that I wander back and forth, speak of the pages
which follow, and yet, even as I have the illusion that I put
words together at a desk, and the little actions I describe have

already happened to me, or to others, still I do not know who I
am nor where I am, nor even if literally I write. Yet, just so soon
as I suggest that I am without particular embodiment I feel
bubbles of laughter at the peculiar present tense of my consciousness which sees into the past, is recovering the future, and
yet does neither, for perhaps I scramble the order of Time in
order to retrieve the order of form from what is formless and yet
over-real. Like the easily distractible feather of attention in the
gales of infancy, I move from dread to light amusement to
metaphysical certainty, and yet away again as if no one is so real
to me as the consciousness which leads me now, but for a
moment probably, to the breath of my narrative, and I feel
certain – I know not exactly why – that it was after this party,
after the conversation between Cara Beauchamp and the physicist, that Marion called for the proper tuition to his instruction
and made his demand: Cara was to give a weekend party in
Provincetown for a select two dozen from their acquaintance,
the guests to be flown up and back by chartered plane, and this
in the middle of November when the New York season
was on, and the weather in Provincetown was bound to
be bad.

'Marion,' she had answered, 'explain what you're doing.'

His extraordinary face (one of the handsomest cleanest most
sensual faces ever cut from a block of boyish ice) smiled back in
arch thought at her. 'I feel in the mood for a party that will go on
for a while.' Then he yawned, and his groin in remonstrance for
this thespian's triumph of the casual, gave him a cruel pinch of a
grip. He was empty again, the charge was down, he was moving
into the late middle-age of some men's middle-thirties, a Dorian
Gray whose secret portrait was fleshed within, painted by the
outrages he had exacted of a hundred thousand nerves. He
knew the prescription to reverse the process on the portrait, it
was the last of the nostrums and it had worked once before; it
was murder. Brave murder. Brave murder gave the charge of
the man one killed. Time potential and Time dynamic – it was
the grand connection, and the dead man's Time became one's
own Time, his energies regenerated the dead circuits of one's
own empty-balled Time, and one moved away with greater
strength, new nerves and a heavier burden. For the balance

(that natural grasp of moral justice which the old murder-tempted God still retained – should one hope so?) would be laden even more on the side of Hell, and Marion knew what would await him in Hell, the onanisms of connectionless Time, the misery of the lone chance in one out of the billion of billions to be born again. Hell, where his nerves (those advance intimations of a flesh-terrifying fire, electric in its cold) would unwind their unspeakable tension with the infinite slowness of nerves become Time in its death, the spiral spinning a blind spider's path, the dreams collapsed, the empire lost, and the fate of the world as well. That was the worst; that was his vanity; that he alone held the vision to save the world – if he failed, his agony would be all the greater for what a rage would be the rage of God. 'Am I ready to die?' he asked, listening to the answer the portrait might give him, and the portrait said *no* with a murmur of dread. The balance of his deeds was dark to Marion, and from the God-like eye with which he contemplated himself he knew he was still not Godly enough – it was beyond his vision whether the force of his life upon others had accelerated new love into the agonized fatigues of Time, or had worn Time closer to her hag-ridden dreams of the destiny that failed because it arrived too late, of the new conception which never reached the womb.

5

The invitations went out, were accepted by almost everyone, the plane was chartered – two flights proved necessary – and the party took place. It is with some hesitation, and the awareness I have betrayed certain premises of your interest, that I must now confess I will not be able to describe this party in rousing detail until we have taken a wide and still unforeseeable circuit of the past. Indeed, it would probably be a disservice of the first order to insert ourselves too brusquely into the dance of deceptions, seductions, perversions and passions which the party whipped into being, the riot of new relationship an unlashed acceleration of the Time of the ladies and gentlemen present. To be successful a party must become more than was intended for it, and I can give you the mean contentment that by my measurement the party was not boring: it had an artist's assortment of those contradictory and varied categories of people who made up the obdurate materials of new sociological alloy in the heat-forge of a ball at Cara Beauchamp's. What gave this party an added attraction, an unconscious verve, was that there were guests who were not altogether what they appeared to be, a Russian spy for one, avid to snap up the friendship of our physicist, a spy of such importance that an agent of the FBI was also present, each of these gentlemen carefully furnished with a false life which was not his own. To complicate matters, there were two other operators with portfolio from the police: one, a narcotics agent, unfortunately addicted himself; another from the vice squad of New York City – what completed the circle was that the detective from the vice squad believed himself close on the proof that Marion Faye had murdered another detective from the vice squad some years before, which in fact was true, but what was unknown to any of these policemen (although the agent from the FBI smelled hints of the possibility) was that the Russian spy, suffering from the mitotic tension latent in the psyche of all spies, had not been content with a double life, but indeed had divided a part of himself again; certain of his more desperate and unprofessional activities in this country had spilled him into the broth of blackmail which nourished the vice squad detective who had been killed; Marion, in taking care of this precise act, had discovered the profession of the spy and so was able to use him for purposes which were by now related to this program for the party – if all of this seems complicated, I can only say that it is but a superficial counterfeit of the real complexities which involved a dozen other guests as well, including Shawn Sergius (born perhaps as Sergius O'Shaugnessy), the only creative personality ever to dominate television, and Dr. Joyce, the psychoanalyst, who had become so overextended beyond his humane means, and had so compromised his career, his profession, and his intimate honor that he was contemplating suicide long before he came to the party.

Indeed a suicide did take place (I do not yet know whether it was the doctor), it was followed by murder, a murder inflamed into fury by exactly that suicide, the suicide preceded by an orgy, the orgy by a series of communions in the act of coitus, both natural and illegal, by sodomists who dictated their characters upon weaker flesh, and copulations which failed as well as fornications which captured pure smell of the fact and left the lovers fluxed with the rhythms and reflexes of one another. It was a ball. There were two dead bodies when all was done, and on one of them the town police found a notebook which contained a list, a peculiar list, for it included everyone, and yet there were more items on the list than people present, and titles applicable to more than one, as if some of the guests contained several categories within themselves. I give it as it was scribbled down, a most appetizing menu:

a queer
a cop
a crook

a Negro
a war hero
a movie star

an athlete
a dope addict
a socialite

a fisherman
an analyst
a call girl

a whore
a businessman
a mother
a father

a child
a sibling
a television entertainer
a politician

E.M.–D

a writer
a painter
a jazzman
a rapist

a Timeless wonder (originally a man but altered to a
facsimile of woman)

---

(There was a line drawn here)

a physicist
a doctor

a taxicab driver
an assembly-line worker
a poodle

a police dog
a boxer
servants

---

(and another line drawn here)

a ghost (God?) (from the hole – he?)
a house
a tree
a pact
a cemetery

a bug
a flower
a rat
a cow
a horse

an insane man

a storm
a plane
an executioner

a bullfighter

One could do worse than to read this list again. I wonder if in the history of our republic there has been a party equal in montage: a movie star and a rat, a rapist and a war hero, a psychoanalyst and a call girl, poodle and assembly-line worker, child and sibling, an executioner and a ghost, a cemetery and a television entertainer; yes, it is like one of those new games which trap psychology and sociology in a three-dollar cardboard box – 'Theatre' it could be called, for one chooses one's role: be a whore, a physicist, a jazz musician, a queer – how dreary is our republic that so few people would buy the game.

A bloody aye! What is to be said of the dead body? How extraordinary a man – if it was a man – to compile such a schedule of personality when he must have known how close he was himself to being taken to the cleaners' – that quick phrase which contains the notion that death purifies.

But death does not purify says my Reason, death dissipates: our consciousness radiates away from ourselves as the cellves deteriorate (forgive the pun, but we speak of death), we slip away – wastefully, unheard but for the night air, our emotions, sneaks, smells, terrors, titillations, thoughts, projects, plans, and – if we have died too late – the dull blanketing gas of our boredom all enter the air, are breathed by others and exhaled away again – perhaps we have influenced the million light years of their imagination by a millimeter. The fats, the blood, the muscles and the bone sink into the earth again (if we are so fortunate as not to stifle in a deluxe hermetic crypt) yes, with the pores of a pinewood box, we give of our poor soured flesh to the wistful cemetery grass – in a century or two perhaps they will let the cows enter there to eat and make the milk and give the meat which will permit one distant relative of a molecule, ten hundred dynasties of family removed, to slip into a human body again. A few of our cells may make the transmigration from our body, which is gone, to the body of another – all that was us reduced to a molecule whose minor deviations from the classical form of the giant protein chain recapture (as do all deviations from classical form) some wry shrunken ion's head of the contradictions and possibilities which were once a man, general of the armies of his cells, Deus to his body-universe.

And is that all? a sacred cow ('I dig the Hindu bit,' said Marion once) our best poor bridge to make it back, no matter how cruelly reduced, to the life of those beings who have the power – all too unconsciously – to shift the changing beat of Time? Or is there more?

And if I say I think there is, I turn the key into the category of my own secret, for as some of you may have sensed by now, the list I offered up to your amusement is from me, and I am, oh yes, now I know who I am or was, I am the dead man on the floor, for so I am, yes (what a pure moment of grief at all that has not been done), I am in the endless deliberate instant of the vision given by death, the million dying spasms of the radiating consciousness of words, this last of me, wailing within, turbulent with the terror that I no longer know where I am, nor if there are voices to hear me and answer back. I am off finally, departed on the demented journey whose first echoes I knew in those overpromiscuous moments of malice, license, promise and horror at the heart of a cocktail party when, too drunk with the knowledge of what courage was demanded of me, and what little I had, I used to close my eyes, sitting in the saviorship of a chair, and I would give up the ghost of ego-erect will, and let the vertigo of the liquors suck me away, a far long way in those few instances when I was spinning out with a rapidity to match the salacious pace of our revolving earth, and I was one with something other until the wife or the mistress or whichever latest embodiment of the royal bitch was at my elbow, nudging me back, feminine fingers of fury at spineless disappearing man wrenching me with procreative determination clean up to the living so I would hear:

'Are you all right?'

'I was thinking of something,' I would say, 'and I like to think with my eyes closed,' but that was the lie of appearances to share between us, a bread of false flour, forcibly refreshing me back to my determinations, back to the party after the long swoon away.

But now I go, the vortex does not stop, the winds of the whirlpool – God's gyre again? – are heavy with consequence, and I sink or do I fly? all vectors gone, while in my center, clear as the icy eye of cocaine, I race towards a point of judgment, my courage and cowardice (my masculine thrust and retreat from the avaricious energy-plucking hairy old grotto of Time) trailing behind me in that comet of connotations which is the past topologically reversed by the vision of *now*, as if in recovering the past I am chasing after the future, so that the past, the net of the name-giving surface-perceiving past, is my future again, and I go out into the past, into the trail of the cold eye of past relationship, the eye of my I at home in the object-filled chaos of any ego I choose, at least for this short while between the stirrup and the ground, for in an instant – will it be eternally long? like some cell at the crisis of its cellvish destiny, I race into the midnight mind, the dream-haunted determinations of that God of whom I was a part, and will He choose me to be born again? have I proven one of his best? am I embryo in some belly of the divisible feminine Time, or is the journey yet to make? Or worst of all am I? – and the cry which is without sound shrieks in my ears – am I already on the way out? a fetor of God's brown sausage in His time of diarrhea, oozing and sucking and bleating like a fecal puppy about to pass away past the last pinch of the divine sphincter with only the toilet of Time, oldest hag of them all, to spin me away into the spiral of star-lit empty waters.

So I approach Him, if I have not already lost Him, God, in His destiny, in which He may succeed, or tragically fail, for God like Us suffers the ambition to make a destiny more extraordinary than we conceived for Him, yes God is like Me, only more so.

Unless – spinning instead through the dark of some inner Space – the winds are icy here – I do no more than delude myself, fall back into that hopeless odyssey where libido never lingers, and my nature is nothing other than to search for the Devil while I carry with me the minds of some of you.

## PART THREE

# Poor Kids

# The Greatest Thing in the World

Inside, out of the rain, the lunch wagon was hot and sticky. Al Groot stopped in front of the doorway, wiped his hands and wrung his hat out, and scuffed his shoes against the dirt-brown mat. He stood there, a small, old, wrinkled boy of eighteen or nineteen, with round beady eyes that seemed incapable of looking at you unless you were in the back of him. He stopped at the door and waited, not sure of his reception, examining the place carefully, as if he might have need of this knowledge soon after. It was a little fancier than the ordinary lunchroom, having dark, old wood booths at the left that fronted the sharp, glittering stools and counter of well-polished chromium. A clock on the wall showed that it was after ten, which might have explained why the place was almost empty. There was no one at the counter and the few truck drivers, sprawled out on two adjoining booths to catch a late dinner, were tired, and very quiet, engrossed only in their sandwiches and hamburgers. Only one man was left behind the counter, and he was carefully cleaning the grease from the frankfurter griddle, with the slow motions of a man who has a great deal of time on his hands and is desperately afraid of finishing his work, to face the prospect of empty tables and silent people. He looked at Al, uncertain for a moment how to take him, and then he turned back to the griddle and gave it a last studious wipe. He spoke, without looking up, but his tone was friendly.

'Hi,' he said.

Al said hello, watching the man scrape some crumblings off.

'It's a hell of a night, ain't it?' the counterman asked.

'Lousy.'

'It sure is. Guess we needed it,' he said. 'The crops are hit bad when it don't rain enough.'

'Sure,' said Al. 'Look, what does coffee and doughnuts cost?'

'Ten.'

'Two doughnuts?'

'That's it.'

'Uh-huh,' said Al. 'Could you let me have one doughnut and half a cup of coffee for five cents? I ain't got but a nickel.'

'I don't know,' he said. 'I could, but why should I?'

'I ain't had nothing to eat today,' Al pleaded. 'Come on.'

The man looked up. Al sucked expertly on his cheeks, just pulling them enough to make it look good.

'I guess you could stand it. Only, pay me now.'

Al reached into his pocket, and tenderly extracted a nickel from two halves of a dollar bill. He finished over one-third of the doughnut in the first bite, and realizing how extravagant he had been, he took a small begrudging sip of the coffee.

'Nice place,' he said.

'I like it,' the man said.

'You own it?'

'You're damn right, buddy. I worked to get this place. It's all mine. You don't find me giving anything away on it. Every cup of coffee a guy drinks feeds me too.'

'Top of the world,' Al said.

'Nyahr,' he answered bitterly. 'Lot of good it does me. You see anybody in here? You see me clicking the cash register? The hell you do.'

Al was thinking of how tough his luck was that the truck drivers should be uniformed, which was as good as a NO RIDER sign. He grinned sympathetically at the owner, trying to look as wet as he could.

'Boy,' he said. 'I sure am stuck.'

'Been hitching, huh?'

'Yeah, walked the last three miles, ever since it started to rain.'

'Must be kind of tough.'

'Sure, I figure I won't be able to sleep if it don't stop raining. That was my last nickel. Say, look, you wouldn't have a job for me?' he said stupidly.

'What'll I do, watch you work?'

'Then let me sleep here tonight. It won't cost you nothing.'

'I don't run a flophouse.'

'Skip it, forget it,' Al said. 'Only let me stay here a while to dry off. When somebody comes in, maybe they'll give me a ride.'

'Stay,' he said. 'I have such a fancy trade. New chromium, brass fixtures. Ahhhhr.'

Al slipped off the stool and sat down at a table in the rear, out of sight of the counterman. He slouched down against the side of the booth and picked up a menu, supported between the salt and pepper shakers, looking at it interestedly, but past all craving or desire. He thought that it had been almost a year since he had had a steak. He tried to remember what it tasted like, but his memory failed, and to distract him from that tantalizing picture he started examining the spelling on the sheet, guessing at a word first, then seeing how close he had been. Another company truck driver had come in, and Al shot a quick look back to see where the owner was. Finding him up front, almost out of sight, he quickly picked up the ketchup bottle and shook large gobs of it into his mouth as fast as he could get it out. It burned and stung inside his stomach, and he kept blowing, trying to cool his mouth. Noticing a few drops on the table, he took a paper napkin, and squeezed them over to the edge, where they hung, ready to fall. He ran his little finger along underneath, gathering them up, and catching the drops in his mouth as they dripped off.

He felt for the split dollar bill, and fingered it. This time, he thought, it was really his last. Once, three months ago, he had five dollars. He thought back and tried to remember how he had gotten it. It was very vague, and he wondered whether he had stolen it or not. The image of five separate bills, and all that he could do with them, hit him then with all its beauty and impossibility. He thought of cigarettes, and a meal, and a clean woman in a good place, and new soles to his shoes, but most of all he thought of the soft leathery feel of money, and the tight wad it made in his pants. 'By God,' he said thickly, 'there's nothing like it. You can't beat it. If I just had five dollars again.'

He withdrew his hand, taking the two pieces out, smoothing them lovingly on the table. He considered breaking the bill for another doughnut, but he knew he couldn't. It was the last thing between him and . . . He stopped, realizing that he had passed the last thing – there was no 'and'. Still, he did not think any more of spending this last bill. Tomorrow or tonight he would be in Chicago, and he could find something to eat for a day or two. He might even pick up half a buck by mooching. In the meantime he felt hungry. He stayed in the booth, staring at the end wall, and dreaming of his one-time hoard.

Three men came in to eat. Al saw them hesitate at the door, wondering whether to eat in a booth or at the counter.

'Take a booth,' one said.

Al looked at them. This might be a ride, he thought. He waited until they had started eating, and then he went over to them, hitching at his faded gray-blue dungarees.

'Hi, sports,' he said.

'Hello, sweet-face,' one of them said.

'They call me Al Groot.'

'His father's name was Groot,' said one of them turning to the others.

'I ain't asking for any dough.'

They eased up a little. 'Boy, you sure ain't, sweet-face,' one of them said. 'Sit down, sit down,' he said. 'My name's Cataract, account of my eye, it's no good, and this here is Pickles, and this is Cousin.'

They all looked alike.

'I guess you know what I want,' Al said.

'Ride?'

'Yeah, where you going?'

'Chicago.'

'Start warming the seat up for me,' Al said.

They grinned, and continued eating. Al watched Cataract go to work on a hamburger. He held it between thick, greased-stained fingers that dug into it, much as they might have sunk into a woman. He swallowed a large piece, slobbering a little, and slapping his tongue noisily against the roof of his mouth as he ate. Al watched him, fascinated. Wild thoughts of seizing the hamburger, and fighting the man for it, devilled him. He moved his head, in time to Cataract's jaws, and he felt madly frustrated as Cataract dropped the last bit into his mouth. Cataract lit a cigarette, and exhaled noisily, with a little belch of content.

'Jesus Christ,' Al whispered.

He turned his attention to the other two, and watched them

eat each piece down to the very bitter end. He hated them, and felt sick.

'Let's go,' shouted Pickles. 'Come on, sweet-face.'

The car was an old Auburn sedan, with a short, humped-up body. Al sat in back with Cataract; Cousin was driving. Cataract took out a pack of Luckies, and passed them around. Al took the pack, and fumbled with it, acting as if he were having trouble extracting a cigarette. When he handed it back, he had a bonus of two more cuddled next to his dollar bill.

'Where you from?' Pickles asked.

'Easton,' Al said. 'It's in Pennsy.'

Cararact rolled his tongue around. 'Good town,' he said, extending his arm, fist closed, twisting it in little circles at the wrist.

'Yeh,' Al said. 'One of the best. I ain't been there in four, no three, years. Been on the road since.'

'Hitching?'

'Hell, no,' Al exploded with contempt. 'It's a sucker's game hitching. I work the trains; you know, "Ride the rails in comfort with Pullman".'

'Yeahr. How're the hobo camps?' Cousin asked.

It was Al's turn to extend his arm.

They all started laughing with wise, knowing, lewd laughs.

'What do you boys do?' Al asked.

They laughed again.

'We're partners in business,' Cataract said.

Al looked at them, discarding one thing after another, trying to narrow down the possibilities. He decided they were sucker players of some sort.

'You guys know of any jobs in Chicago?' Al asked.

'How much you want?'

'About twenty a week. I'm in now. Got thirty-four bucks.'

Pickles whistled. 'What're you mooching meals for, then?'

'Who's mooching?' Al demanded. 'Did I ask you guys for anything besides a ride?'

'Noooo.'

'Awright, then don't go around being a wise guy.'

Pickles looked out the window, grinning. 'Sorry, bud.'

'Well, awright then,' Al said, acting sore.

'Well, awright then, dig, dig, dig, well awright,' Cousin mimicked.

Cataract laughed, trying to be friendly. 'They're funny boys, you know, just smart. They wish they had your thirty-four, that's all.'

It worked, Al thought. He let himself grin. 'It's okay,' he said.

He looked out the window. They weren't in Chicago yet, but the lights shining from the houses on the side of the road were more frequent, making a steady yellow glare against the wet windows, and he knew that they must be almost at the outskirts by now. Just then, he saw a CITY LIMITS and WELCOME sign flash past. Cousin turned off the highway, and went along for a way on a dirt road that in time turned onto an old oil-stained asphalt street. They passed a few factories, and Al thought of dropping off, but he wondered if it might not pay him to stay with the men for a while.

Cataract yawned. 'What about a game of pool now, boys?' he asked.

So that's what they are, Al thought.

'Say,' he said, 'I'd like to play too. I ain't very good, but I like the game.' He had played exactly three times in his life. Pickles assured him. 'We're no good either, that is, I'm no good. You and me can play.'

'Yeah,' Al said, 'it ought to be fun.'

Cousin was driving up Milwaukee Avenue now. He turned left, slowing down very carefully as he did so, although there were no cars in sight.

'That Cousin drives like an old woman,' Pickles commented. 'I could drive faster going backwards.'

Cousin jeered at him. 'You couldn't drive my aunt's wheel-barrow. I'm the only guy left who hasn't lost his license,' he said speaking to Al. 'It's because I take it easy when I drive a car.'

Al said he didn't know much about cars, but he guessed maybe Cousin was right.

The car pulled up in front of a dark gray building on the corner of a long row of old brownstone homes. It was a dark street, and the only evidence that people lived on it were the overflowing garbage and ash cans spaced at irregular intervals in front of the houses. The poolroom itself was down in the cellar, underneath a beauty parlor and a secretarial school. On the steps going down, Al could see pencilled scribblings on the walls: some hasty calculation of odds, a woman's telephone number with a comment underneath it, a few bits of profanity, and one very well-drawn nude woman.

The foot of the stairs opened right on to the tables, which were strung out in one long narrow line of five. The place was almost dark, only the first table being used, and no lights were on in the back. Pickles stepped over to the counter and started talking to the boss, calling him familiarly, and for some reason annoyingly, by the name Nick. Nick was a short, very broad and sweaty Italian. He and Pickles looked up at Al at the same time, and Pickles motioned to him.

'Nick, this is a pal of mine. I want you to treat him nice if he ever comes in again. Tell thick Nick your name, sweet-face.'

'Call me sweet-face,' Al said.

'H'lo,' Nick said. 'Pleased to meet you.'

'Where we play?' Al asked. He noticed that Cataract and Cousin had not come down yet.

'Take number four.'

'Sweet-face and me on number four,' Pickles said. 'Got it.'

He walked down turning on a few lights. He stopped at the cue rack, and picked one at random. Al followed him, selected one carefully, sighting along it to see if there was any warp, and sprinkling some talc over it. 'Should we play a rack for table?' he asked.

'Sure,' said Pickles. 'You mind if we play straight? I don't know any fancy stuff.'

'Me neither.'

They tossed a coin, and Al had to break. He shot poorly, hit the wrong ball and scratched. Pickles overshot and splattered balls all over the table. Al sunk two, shooting as well as he could, knowing that Pickles would notice any attempts at faking. They both played sloppily and it took fifteen minutes to clear the table. Al won, eight balls to seven.

'We're pretty close,' Pickles said. 'What about playing for a couple of bucks this next table?'

He watched Cataract and Cousin, who had just come in and were starting to play.

Al could feel the sweat starting up in the small of his back and on his thighs. I can still get out of it, he thought. At least I'll have my buck. The thought of another five dollars, however, was too strong for him. He tried to think of what would happen to him if he didn't get away with it, but he kept remembering how it felt to have money in his hand. He heard himself speaking, feeling that it was not he but someone right in back, or on top of him.

'Make it a buck,' he said.

Pickles broke, again shooting too hard. Al watched him flub balls all over the table, slightly overdoing it this time. They finished the rack, Al getting a run of three at the end, to win, ten to five. Pickles handed him a dollar, and placed another on the side of the table. Al covered it with the one he had won. I wonder when he starts winning, Al thought. If I can only quit then. They played for a dollar twice more, Al winning both times. A first drop of perspiration drew together, and raced down his back. He saw Cataract watching them play, juggling two balls in his hand. They played for three dollars, Al winning, after being behind, five to two.

He straightened up, making an almost visible effort to relax. 'That makes six bucks,' he said.

'Sure,' said Pickles. 'Let's make it five this time. I want to win my dough back.'

This time Pickles won. Al handed him five dollars, separating the bills with difficulty, and handing them over painfully.

'Another one for five,' Pickles said.

Al looked around him desperately, wondering if he could get out. 'Five,' he croaked. Cataract was still juggling the balls.

It was the longest game he ever played. After every shot he stopped to wipe his hands. In the middle, he realized that this game was going to be given to him. He couldn't relax, however, because he knew the showdown would merely be delayed for another game or so.

He won, as he knew he would, but immediately the pressure was on again. They played once more for five, and he won. After it was over, he didn't trust himself to stand, and he leaned against the cue rack, trying to draw satisfaction from the money in his pocket. He dreamed of getting out, and having it all to do as he pleased, until he saw Pickles and Cataract looking at each other. Cataract threw a ball up, and closed his fingers too soon, missing it. It came down with a loud shattering crack that made Nick look up from his counter. That's the signal, Al thought.

They were the only ones in the place now.

Pickles stroked his cue, grinning. 'Your luck's been too good, sweet-face. I think this is going to be my game. I got twenty bucks left. I'm laying it down.'

'No,' said Al. 'I don't want to.'

'Listen, I been losing dough. You're playing.'

They all looked at him menacingly.

'I want to quit,' Al said.

'I wouldn't try it,' Cousin said.

Al looked about him, trapped, thoughts of fighting them mixing with mad ideas of flight.

Cataract stepped towards him, holding a cue in his hand.

'All right,' Al said, 'I'll play.'

Pickles broke, making a very beautiful 'safe', leaving Al helpless. He bent over his stick to shoot. The balls wavered in front of him, and he could see the tip of the cue shaking up and down. He wiped his face and looked around to loosen his muscles. When he tried again, it was useless. He laid his cue on the table and walked to the back.

'Where you going?' asked Pickles.

'To the can. Want to come along?' He forced a laugh from the very bottom of his throat.

He passed through a small littered room, where old soda boxes were stored. The bathroom was small and filthy; the ceiling higher than the distance from wall to wall. Once inside he bolted the door, and sank down on the floor, whimpering softly.

After a while he quieted and looked around. The only other possible exit was a window, high up on the wall facing the door. He looked at it, not realizing its significance, until a chance sound from outside made him realize where he was and what was happening to him. He got up, and looked at the wall, examining its surface for some possible boost. He saw there was none, crouched down, and jumped. His hands just grasped the edge, clung for a fraction of a second, and then scraped off. He knelt again, as close to the wall as he could possibly get, flexed himself, and leaped up. This time his palms grasped hold. He pressed his finger tips against the stone surface and chinned up enough to work his elbows over. He rested a moment, and then squeezed his stomach in and hung there on the ledge against the window, his legs dangling behind. He inched the window open noiselessly and, forgetting he was in the cellar, looked down into blackness. For a moment he was panic-stricken, until he remembered he was in the cellar, and had to look up. He shifted his position, and raised his head. There was a grating at right angles to the window, fixed above a dump heap, much like the one beneath a subway grille. It was very dark outside, but he could make out that it opened into an alley. Overjoyed, he took his money out, almost falling off in the act, kissed it, put it back, and tried to open the grating. He placed his hands under it and pushed up as hard as he could in his cramped position. The grille didn't move. He stuck one foot through the open window, and straddled the ledge, one foot in, one foot out. Bracing himself, he pushed calmly against the grating, trying to dislodge it from the grime imbedded in it. Finding his efforts useless, he pushed harder and harder until his arms were almost pushed into his chest and his back and crotch felt as if they would crack. Breathing heavily, he stopped and stared up past the grating. Suddenly, with a cry of desperation, he flung himself up, beating against it with his hands and arms, until the blood ran down them. Half crazy, he gripped the bars and shook, with impassioned groans. His fingers slipped against a little obstruction on one of the end bars. His hand felt it, caressed it, hoping to find some lever point, and discovered it to be a rivet between the foundation and the grille. He sat there, huge sobs torn from him, his eyes gazing hungrily at the sky above. After a bit, he withdrew his leg, wormed his body in again, closed the window, and dropped heavily to the floor, lying in a heap, as he had fallen, his face to the wall. I'll just wait till they come for me, he thought. He could hear someone coming towards the door. Pickles knocked. 'Hey kid,' he yelled from the other side of the partition, 'hurry up'.

Al stood up, a mad flare of hope running through him as he

thought of the money he still had. He held his hand to his throat, and struggled to control his voice. 'Be right out,' he said, managing to hold it through to the end. He heard Pickles walk away, and felt a little stronger. He started to wash himself, to get the blood off. His hands were still bleeding dully, the blood oozing out thickly and sluggishly, but he was able to stop the flow somewhat. He backed away, glanced out the window once more, and took his money out. He held it in his hands, and let the bills slip through his fingers. Gathering them up, he kissed them feverishly, rubbing the paper against his face and arms. He folded them tenderly, let down his pants and slipped the cash into a little secret pocket, just under the crotch. He flattened out the bump it made, and unlocked the door to go out. His heart was still pounding, but he felt calmer, and more determined.

They were waiting for him impatiently, smoking nervously. Al took out one of Cataract's cigarettes and asked for a match. He lit it, sucking deeply and gratefully from it. They glared at him, their nerves almost as tight as his.

'Come on,' said Pickles, 'it's your turn to shoot.'

Al picked up his cue, gripping it hard to make his hand bleed faster. He bent over, made a pretense of sighting, and then laid his cue down, exposing the place where his hand had stained it.

'What's the matter?' Cousin snapped.

'I can't hold a cue,' Al said. 'I cut my hand in there.'

'What do you mean you can't play?' Pickles shouted. 'My money's up. You got to play.'

'You can't force me. I'm not going to play. It's my money, it's mine see, and you can't make me. You guys can't pull this on me; you're just trying to work a sucker game.'

It was the wrong thing to say. Cataract caught him by the shirt, and shook him. 'Grab ahold of that stick,' he said.

Al wrenched loose. 'Go to hell,' he said. 'I'm quitting.'

He picked up his hat, and started walking down past the tables to go out. He had to pass three tables and the counter to get to the stairs. He walked slowly, hoping to bluff his way out. He knew he had no chance if he ran. He could feel the sweat starting up much faster this time. His shoulders were twitching, and he was very conscious of the effort of forming each step, expecting something to hit him at every second. His face was wet, and he fought down an agonizing desire to turn and look at them. Behind him, they were silent. He could see Nick at the entrance, watching him walk towards him, his face expressionless. Fascinated, he hung on to Nick's eyes, pleading silently with him. A slight smile grew on Nick's face. It broke into a high unnatural laugh, squeaking off abruptly. Terrified, Al threw a quick glance back, and promptly threw himself on his face. A cue whizzed by, shattering on the far wall with a terrific smash. Before he could get up, they were on him. Cataract turned him on his back, and knelt over him. He brought the heel of his hand down hard on Al's face, knocking his head on the floor. He saw them swirl around him, the pool tables mixed in somewhere, and he shook his head furiously, to keep from going out. Cataract hit him again.

Al struck out with his foot, and hit him in the shin.

'You dirty little bastard,' Cataract said. 'I'll teach you.'

He slammed his knee down into Al's stomach. Al choked and writhed, the fight out of him for a moment. They turned him over, and stripped his pockets, looking for his money. They shook him. 'Where is it, sweet-face?' Pickles asked.

Al choked for breath.

'I lost it,' he said mockingly.

'It's in his pants somewhere,' Cousin said. 'These rats always got a secret pocket.' They tried to open his pants. He fought crazily, kicking, biting, screaming, using his elbows and knees.

'Come on,' Cataract commanded, 'get it off him.'

Al yelled as loud as he could. Nick came over. 'Get him out,' he said. 'The cops'll be dropping in soon. I don't want trouble.'

'What'll we do with him?'

'Take him out on the road where no one will hear you. After that, it's your imagination.' He squealed with laughter again.

They picked him up, and forced him out. He went with them peacefully, too dazed to care. They shoved him in the car, and Cousin turned it around. Al was in front, Cataract in the back seat, holding his wrist so he couldn't break loose before they started.

Al sat there silently, his head clearing, remembering how slowly Cousin drove. He looked out, watching the ground shoot by, and thought of jumping out. Hopelessly, he looked at the speedometer. They were going around a turn, and Cousin had slowed down to less than twenty miles an hour. He had jumped off freight trains going faster than that, but there had been no door in the way, and no one had been holding him. Discouraged, he gave up the idea.

Cousin taunted him. 'See that white sign, sweet-face? We turn left there, just around it, and after that it won't be long.'

Anger and rebellion surged through him. They were taking away something that he had earned dangerously, and they were going to beat him up, because they had not been as smart as he. It was not fair. He wanted the money more than they did. In a fury, he decided to jump at the turn. The sign was about a hundred yards away; it would be his last chance. He figured it would take seven seconds to reach it.

He turned around to face Cataract, his left elbow resting loosely against the door handle. He had turned the way his wrist was twisted, holding it steadily, so that Cataract would not realize the pressure was slackened. One, he counted to himself, 'Look,' he begged Cataract, 'let me off. I ain't got the money, let me off.' Maybe thirty yards gone by. Cataract was talking. 'Oh, you're a funny boy, sweet-face. I like you sweet-face.' Another twenty. 'Yeh, sure I'm funny, I'm a scream,' he said. 'Oh, I'm so funny.' The sign, where is it? We should have reached it. Oh please God, show me the sign, you got to, it's my money, not theirs, oh please. 'Goddam you, please,' he shouted. 'What?' Cataract yelled. Cousin slowed down. The sign slipped by. They started to turn. Al spat full in Cataract's face, and lashed out with his wrist against the thumb. His elbow kicked the door open, and he yanked his hand loose, whirled about, and leaped out, the door just missing him in its swing back.

His feet were pumping wildly as he hit the ground. He staggered in a broken run for a few steps, before his knees crumpled under him, he went sprawling in the dust. His face went grinding into it, the dirt mashing up into his cheeks and hands. He lay there stunned for a very long second, and then he pushed hard with his hands against the ground, forcing himself up. The car had continued around the turn, and in the confusion had gone at least a hundred feet before it stopped. Al threw a stone at the men scrambling out, and plunged off into a field.

It had stopped raining, but the sky was black, and he knew they would never catch him. He heard them in the distance, yelling to each other, and he kept running, his legs dead, his head lolling sideways, his breath coming in long ripping bursts. He stumbled over a weed and fell, his body spreading out on soft wet grass. Exhausted, he lay there, his ear close to the ground, but no longer hearing them, he sat up, plucking weakly at bits of grass, saying over and over again. 'Oh, those suckers, those big, dumb, suckers. Oh, those dopes, those suckers. . . .'

At two-thirty, Al Groot, his stomach full, swung off a streetcar near Madison Street, and went into a flophouse. He gave the night man a new dollar bill, and tied the eighty-five cents change in a rag that he fastened to his wrist. He stood over his bed, and lit some matches, moving them slowly over the surface of his mattress. A few bedbugs started out of their burrows, and crept across the bed. He picked them up, and squashed them methodically. The last one he held in his hand, watching it squirm. He felt uneasy for a moment, and impulsively let it escape, whirling his hand in a circle to throw it away from the bed. He stretched himself out, and looked off in the distance for a while, thinking of women, and hamburgers, and billiard balls, and ketchup bottles, and shoes and, most of all, of the thrill of breaking a five-dollar bill. Lighting the last of Cataract's cigarettes, he thought of how different things had been, when he had first palmed them. He smoked openly, not caring if someone should see him, for it was his last. Al smoked happily, tremendously excited, letting each little ache and pain well into the bed. When the cigarette was finished he tried to fall asleep. He felt wide awake, though, and after some time he propped himself on an elbow, and thought of what he would do the next day. First he would buy a pack of cigarettes, and then he would have a breakfast, and then a clean woman; he would pay a buck if he had to, and then a dinner and another woman. He stopped suddenly, unable to continue, so great was his ecstasy. He lay over his pillow and addressed it.

'By God,' Al Groot said, about to say something he had never uttered before, 'by God, this is the happiest moment of my life.'

*1940*

# Maybe Next Year

The trains used to go by, used to go by very fast in the field past the road on the other side of my house. I used to go down there and walk and walk through the fields whenever Mom and Pop were fighting, fighting about money like they always were, and after I'd listen awhile, I'd blow air into my ears so I couldn't hear them, then I'd go out in the field, across the road from my house and slide down the steep part of the grass where it was slippery like dogs had been dirty there, and then I used to climb up the other side, up the big hill on the other side, and walk through the fat high grass until I would come to the railroad tracks where I'd just keep going and going and going.

*Why don't we have any money, we never have any money, what kind of man did I marry, what good is he, what good is he, look at him, look at his boy there, look at your boy there, look at him, he takes after you, look at him walk away like he never hears us, look at him, no good like you, why don't you ever get any money?*

The grass sticks would be rough and sharp sort of, like sharp pages in a book, and I had to walk with my hands in my pockets so I wouldn't cut my fingers. They were tall, the grasses, and sometimes they would hit me in the face, but I would hit them back, only that used to cut my fingers, and I'd start crying, but I stopped soon, because there was nobody around, and I knew that when there was nobody to hear me, I always stopped soon, although I never could figure it out, because I always could cry for a long time, and say I was going to run away and die if people were around.

*I can't help it if I'm not making money, my God there's limits to what a man can do, nag, nag, nag, all the time. My God I can't help it, there's limits, there's a depression, everybody's losing money, just worry about keeping the house, and don't compare the child to me, the God-damn child is splitting us up the middle, I can't help it if he's a stupid kid, he's only mine, maybe he'll get smarter yet, I can't help it if he's dumb, there's a depression going on I tell you, everybody's losing money, there just isn't any money around.*

The railroad tracks made a funny kind of a mirror. I could see myself in them, one of me on each side, I was so tall in them, but I was awfully short, as short as my arm, but I was awful tall, I looked as tall as Pop, except as tall as if I was to see Pop all the way in the distance coming up the hill to our house, when he looked as tall as my arm, but I knew anyway that he was oh ten times bigger than me.

*Why is the boy always disappearing, why don't you find him, you haven't a job, you just sit around, you might keep him near you, you might teach him to be like you, and sit around all day, and make it easier for me so at least I wouldn't have to look for him, but you can't even teach him that, I never saw such a man like you, they didn't make my father out of men like you.*

If I walked and walked along the tracks, there was a spot where I could get a place where all the big slow trains came into town. If I was careful I could sneak up in the grass near to where the men who jumped off the big trains camped in the fields.

They were dirty old men, they just sat around, and smoked pipes and washed their dirty old shirts in the yellow water spot where I used to go swimming before Mom started yell yell yell about the dirty old men and wouldn't let me swim there.

*They're filthy old things, you'll get sick and die, they're diseased, they're diseased, why did the town let them camp and flop in a meadow like that, right on the town limits, what's the good of living out of town when our only neighbors are bums, what's the good, what's the town mean, why aren't they put in the coop where they belong, why should they be flopping so near our house in a meadow?*

I didn't like the men, they used to talk and laugh to themselves all the time, sometimes they would sing songs. I knew they were dirty men 'cause Mom said they would give me diseases, but one time I came up and talked to them, when I went out Mom and Pop were shouting, and the men looked at me, one of the old ones who was sitting on his old stork bundle bag sort of, got up and looked at me, he made fun of me, he said sonny got a dime for a poor old man to have some coffee, and then all the men started laughing, haw haw haw kind of laughing. The other men came around me, one of them said he was going to take my shirt and use it for a snot-rag, and they all laughed again, the big man in the middle of them making believe he was going to throw dirt at me only I didn't know he was going to fool me until I started crying, and he laughed too, and dropped the dirt.

*That boy is going to get in trouble, why don't you take care of him, keep him around you, he goes off into the meadow, and God knows what those bums are going to do to him, they're all vile, they don't live like men, they're not men I heard, they're no more men than you are, both of you are, why don't you take care of him, he'll turn out weak in everything like you, those bums will get him in trouble.*

Pop came over, grab-me picked me up, and carried me upstairs, and licked me, and locked the door on me, and then he went downstairs, and he and Mom yelled and yelled right through my crying. I waited and waited for them to hear me, but I must have fallen asleep because the next thing it was morning, and I didn't remember stopping and rubbing my hands on my nose to wipe off the crying. They unlocked the door before I sneaked downstairs, the front door was open and Mom and Pop were sitting around front, not saying anything, I hated them, I ran out the door between them, and hid around the side of the house. Pop and Mom came running out, they ran the wrong way calling to me, they were looking for me, and they weren't smiling, but they were talking nice the way they did when they didn't mean it, just like when they wanted to catch our dog, and that made me feel sad, and oh I felt just terrible, and then when they started coming back I didn't want to get another licking so I ran away without their seeing me, and sneaked across the road further down, into the field, and up the slippery hill, run run running away off until I got to the railroad tracks. I sneaked along them to where the dirty men with the diseases were, and I hid down in the grass, and hid behind some to look at them, but they were all gone, there weren't any of them, but the old man who had made fun of me the day before, and he was lying on the ground crying and yowling like he was hurt or dead.

I walked over to him, he looked at me, he started crawling to me. I could see it was his foot that was hurt 'cause it was all bloody like, and bleeding near the knee. Help me kid, help me kid, he kept yelling.

*Go ahead, hit the child, hit it, hit it, it deserves it, playing with*

*dirty old men, hit it, it's a terrible child, it never listens to us, there's*
*something wrong with it.*

The old man looked like a snake, and I stepped back to run away from him, but he kept crawling after me, yelling don't go away kid, I won't hurt you, please don't go away kid, but he looked like a snake, only bleeding. I yelled at him, I said go away, you're a dirty old man, but he wouldn't stop, and I picked up a rock, and threw it at him, it missed him, but I threw another rock, and it hit him in the head, he stopped moving to me, he was crying something terrible, there was a lot of blood all over his face.

Why kid, why kid, why kid, why hit me?

You're a dirty old man, leave me alone, I don't like you, you're a dirty old man.

Kid for God's sakes help me, I'm going crazy kid, don't leave me here, it's hot here kid, it's hot here kid.

Then I picked up a stone, and threw it at him again, only I didn't see if it hit him because I was running away. I heard him crying, screaming, and I was scared, but I kept running and then I said I hate them, I hate them, the grass kept cutting at me, I couldn't run with my hands in my pockets, kept cutting at me and cutting at me, I fell down, and then I got up and kept running home.

I walked down the last part of the hill, and across the road, and when I got back Mom and Pop were sitting around again, and I started crying. I cried and cried, they asked me what's the matter, what's the matter with you, why are you crying, but I just kept saying the dirty old man, the dirty old man.

And Mom said I thought they all were kicked out of town, I don't know how any of them were left, you're not lying?

I'm not lying, I'm not lying.

And Pop got up, and said to Mom I told you not to do it, you get an idea in your head, and you can't stop, those men were beaten, I don't know how any were left in the dark, we had flashlights, but there might have been, it's the boy's own fault, he had no business going around there today, and anyway he wasn't hurt, he didn't start crying until he saw us, I saw him before he saw me.

And Mom said, if you were a man you'd go over there now,

and finish them off, you wouldn't even go last night without any help, if I were a man I'd thrash the man that touched my boy, but you just sit there and talk talk talk that it's the boy's fault.

Pop got up, and walked around and around, and he said it isn't the boy's fault, but it isn't the man's either, and then he stood up, and said I'm not going to do anything about it, what with the boy between us, and the job ruined, and everything God-damned else, I might be one of them myself, maybe next year, and then Pop stood up and walked off down the road only farther out of town, not the way the old man was. I could see that Pop's shoulders were screwed up around his neck, and then I was happy, because all I could think of was that I'd seen two big men cry that day, and maybe that meant I was getting bigger too, and that was an awful good feeling.

*1941*

## PART FOUR

# Sobrieties, Impieties

# The Paper House

Friendship in the army is so often an accident. If Hayes and I were friends, it was due above all else to the fact that we were cooks on the same shift, and so saw more of one another than of anyone else. I suppose if I really consider it seriously, I did not even like him, but for months we went along on the tacit assumption that we were buddies, and we did a great many things together. We got drunk together, we visited the local geisha house together, and we even told each other some of our troubles.

It was not a bad time. The war was over, and we were stationed with the understrength company of men in a small Japanese city. We were the only American troops for perhaps fifty miles around, and therefore discipline was easy, and everyone could do pretty much what he wished. The kitchen was staffed by four cooks and a mess sergeant, and we had as many Japanese K.P.s to assist us. The work was seldom heavy, and duty hours passed quickly. I never liked the army so much as I did during those months.

Hayes saw to it that we had our recreation. He was more aggressive than me, older and stronger, much more certain of his ideas. I had no illusions that I was anything other than the tail to his kite. He was one of those big gregarious men who need company and an uncritical ear, and I could furnish both. It also pleased him that I had finished two years of college before I entered the army, and yet he knew so much more than me, at least so far as the army was concerned. He would ride me often about that. 'You're the one who's cracked the books,' he would say as he slammed a pot around, 'but it seems none of those books ever taught you how to boil water. What a cook!' His humor was heavy, small doubt about it. 'Nicholson,' he would yell at me, 'I hear there's a correspondence course in short-arms inspections. Why don't you advance yourself? You too can earn seventy-eight bucks a month.'

He was often in a savage mood. He had troubles at home, and

he was bitter about them. It seems his wife had begun to live with another man a few months after he entered the army. He had now divorced her, but there were money settlements still to be arranged, and his vanity hurt him. He professed to hate women. 'They're tramps, every one of them,' he would announce. 'They're tramps and I can tell you it's a goddam tramp's world, and don't forget that, sonny.' He would shift a boiler from one stove to another with a quick jerk-and-lift of his powerful shoulders, and would call back to me, 'The only honest ones are the honest-to-God pros.'

I would argue with him, or at least attempt to. I used to write a letter every day to a girl I liked in my home town, and the more time went by and the more letters I wrote, the more I liked her. He used to scoff at me. 'That's the kind I really go for,' he would jeer. 'The literary ones. How they love to keep a guy on the string by writing letters. That's the kind that always has ten men right in her own back yard.'

'I know she dates other fellows,' I would say, 'but what is she supposed to do? And look at us, we're over at the geisha house almost every night.'

'Yeah, that's a fine comparison. We're spending our money at this end, and she's coining it at the other. Is that what you're trying to say?'

I would swear at him, and he would laugh. At such moments I disliked him intensely.

There was, however, quite another side to him. Many evenings after finishing work he would spend an hour washing and dressing, trimming his black mustache, and inspecting critically the press in his best uniform. We would have a drink or two, and then walk along the narrow muddy streets to the geisha house. He would usually be in a fine mood. As we turned in the lane which led to the house, and sat in the vestibule taking off our boots, or more exactly, waiting luxuriously while a geisha or a maid removed them for us, he would begin to hum. The moment we entered the clean pretty little room where the geishas greeted the soldiers, his good mood would begin to flood him. I heard him be even poetic once as he looked at the girls in their dress kimonos, all pretty, all petite, all chirping beneath the soft lights, all treading in dress slippers upon the bright woven straw mats. 'I tell you, Nicholson,' he said, 'it looks like a goddamn Christmas tree.' He loved to sing at the geisha house, and since he had a pleasant baritone voice, the geishas would crowd about him, and clap their hands. Once or twice he would attempt to sing a Japanese song, and the errors he made in pitch and in language would be so amusing that the geishas would giggle with delight. He made, altogether, an attractive picture at such times, his blue eyes and healthy red face contrasting vigorously with his black mustache and his well-set body in its clean uniform. He seemed full of strength and merriment. He would clap two geishas to him, and call across the room with loud good cheer to another soldier. 'Hey, Brown,' he would shout, 'ain't this a rug-cutter?' And to the answer, 'You never had it so good,' he would chuckle. 'Say that again, Jack,' he might roar. He was always charming the geishas. He spoke a burlesque Japanese to their great amusement, he fondled them, his admiration for them seemed to twinkle in his eyes. He was always hearty. Like many men who hate women, he knew how to give the impression that he adored them.

After several months he settled upon a particular girl. Her name was Yuriko, and she was easily the best of the geishas in that house. She was quite appealing with her tiny cat-face, and she carried herself with considerable charm, discernible even among the collective charm all geishas seemed to possess. She was clever, she was witty, and by the use of a few English words and the dramatic facility to express complex thoughts in panto-mime, she was quite capable of carrying on extended conversations. It was hardly surprising that the other girls deferred to her, and she acted as their leader.

Since I always seemed to follow in Hayes's shadow, I also had a steady girl, and I suspect that Mimiko, whom I chose, had actually been selected for me by the artifice of Yuriko. Mimiko was Yuriko's best friend, and since Hayes and I were always together, it made things cosy. Those alternate Sundays when we were not on duty in the kitchen we would pay for the girls' time, and Hayes would use his influence, established by the judicious bribes of cans of food and pounds of butter to the motor pool sergeant, to borrow a jeep. We would take the girls out into the country, drive our jeep through back roads or mountain trails, and then descend to the sea where we would wander along the beach. The terrain was beautiful. Everything seemed to be manicured, and we would pass from a small pine forest into a tiny valley, go through little villages or little fishing towns, nestled on the rocks, would picnic, would talk, and then towards evening would return the girls to the house. It was very pleasant.

They had other clients besides us, but they refused to spend the night with any other soldier if they knew we were coming, and the moment we entered the place, word was sent to Yuriko or Mimiko if they were occupied. Without a long wait, they would come to join us. Mimiko would slip her hand into mine and smile politely and sweetly, and Yuriko would throw her arms about Hayes and kiss him upon the mouth in the American style of greeting. We would all go together to one of the upper rooms and talk for an hour or two while sake was drunk. Then we would separate for the night, Yuriko with Hayes, and Mimiko with me.

Mimiko was not particularly attractive, and she had the placid disposition of a draught animal. I liked her mildly, but I would hardly have continued with her if it had not been for Yuriko. I really liked Yuriko. She seemed more bright and charming with every day, and I envied Hayes for his possession of her.

I used to love to listen to her speak. Yuriko would tell long stories about her childhood and her parents, and although the subject was hardly calculated to interest Hayes, he would listen to her with his mouth open, and hug her when she was done. 'This baby ought to be on the stage,' he would say to me. Once, I remember, I asked her how she had become a geisha, and she told about it in detail. 'Papa-san, sick sick,' she began, and with her hands, created her father for us, an old Japanese peasant whose back was bent and whose labor was long. 'Mama-san sad.' Her mother wept for us, wept prettily, like a Japanese geisha girl, with hands together in prayer and her nose touching the tip of her fingers. There was money owed on the land, the crops were bad, and Papa-san and Mama-san had talked together, and cried, and had known that they must sell Yuriko, now fourteen, as geisha. So she had been sold and she had been trained, and in a few moments by the aid of a montage which came instinctively to her, she showed us herself in transition from a crude fourteen-year-old peasant to a charming geisha of sixteen trained in the tea ceremony, her diction improved, her limbs taught to dance, her voice to sing. 'I, first-class geisha,' she told us, and went on to convey the prestige of being a geisha of the first class. She had entertained only the wealthy men of the town, she had had no lovers unless she had felt the flutterings of weakness in her heart, her hands busy fluttering at her breast, her arms going out to an imaginary lover, her eyes darting from one of us to the other to see if we comprehended. In ten years she would have saved money enough to buy her freedom and to make an impressive marriage.

But, boom-boom, the war had ended, the Americans had come, and only they had money enough for geisha girls. And they did not want geisha girls. They wanted a *joro*, a common whore. And so first-class geishas became second-class geishas and third-class geishas, and here was Yuriko, a third-class geisha, humiliated and unhappy, or at least she would be if she did not love Hayes-san and he did not love her.

She was moody when she finished. 'Hayes-san love Yuriko?' she asked, her legs folded beneath her, her small firm buttocks perched upon the straw mat while she handed him a sake cup, and extended her hand to the charcoal brazier.

'Sure, I love you, baby,' Hayes said.

'I, first-class geisha,' she repeated a little fiercely.

'Don't I know it,' Hayes boomed.

Early the next morning as we walked back to the dormitory where the company was installed, Hayes was talking about it. 'She jabbered at me all night,' he said. 'I got a hangover. That Jap sake.'

'The story Yuriko told was sad,' I murmured.

He stopped in the middle of the street, and put his hands on his hips. 'Listen, Nicholson, wise up,' he said angrily. 'It's crap, it's all crap. They'd have you bleed your eyes out for them with those stories. Poor papa-san. They're all whores, you understand? A whore's a whore, and they're whores cause they want to be whores and don't know nothing better.'

'It's not true,' I protested. I felt sorry for the geishas. They seemed so unlike the few prostitutes I had known in the United States. There was one girl at the house who had been sold when she was thirteen, and had entered service a virgin. After her first night of work, she had wept for three days, and even now many of the soldiers selected her shame-facedly. 'What about Susiko?' I said.

'I don't believe it, it's a gag,' Hayes shouted. He gripped me by the shoulder and made a speech. 'I'll wise you up. I don't say I'm Superman, but I know the score. Do you understand that? I know the score. I don't say I'm any better than anybody else, but I don't kid myself that I am. And it drives me nuts when people want to make me swallow bull.' He released my shoulder as suddenly as he had gripped it. His red face was very red, and I sensed what rage he had felt.

'All right,' I muttered.

'All right.'

In time he came to treat Yuriko the way he treated anyone with whom he was familiar. He indulged his moods. If he were surly, he did not bother to hide it; if he were aggressive, he would swear at her; if he were happy, he would sing for her or become roisteringly drunk or kiss her many times before Mimiko and myself, telling her that he loved her in a loud voice which often seemed close to choler. Once he abused her drunkenly, and I had to pull him away. The next day he brought Yuriko a present, a model of a wooden shrine which he had purchased from a Japanese cabinet maker. All the while it was evident to me that Yuriko was in love with him.

I used to think of the rooms upstairs as paper rooms. They were made of straw and light wood and parchment glued to wooden frames, and when one lay on the pallet in the center of the floor, it seemed as if all the sounds in all the adjoining rooms flowed without hindrance through the sliding doors. Mimiko and I could often hear them talking in the next cubicle, and long after Mimiko would be asleep, I would lie beside her and listen to Yuriko's voice as it floated, breathlike and soft, through the frail partitions. She would be telling him about her day and the events which had passed in the house. She had had a fight with Mama-san, the wrinkled old lady who was her madame, and

Tasawa had heard from her brother whose wife had just given him a child. There was a new girl coming in two days, and Katai who had left the day before had proven to be sick. Mama-san was limiting the charcoal for the braziers, she was stingy without a doubt. So it went, a pageant of domesticity. She had resewn the buttons on his battle jacket, he looked good, he was gaining weight, she would have to buy a new kimono for the number two kimono had become shabby, and the number three was hopeless. She was worried about Henderson-san who had become drunk two nights in a row and had struck Kukoma. What should she do about him?

And Hayes listened to her, his head in her lap no doubt, and mumbled gentle answers, relaxed and tender as she caressed the bitterness from his face, drawing it out with her finger tips while her childlike laugh echoed softly through the rooms. There were other sounds of men snoring, girls giggling, two soldiers in a quarrel, and the soft muted whisper of a geisha crying somewhere in one of the rooms. So it washed over me in this little house with its thirty paper cells in the middle of a small Japanese city while the Japanese night cast an artist's moon over the rice paddies and the pine forests where the trees grew in aisles. I envied Hayes, envied him with the touch of Mimiko's inert body against mine, envied him Yuriko's tenderness which she gave him so warmly.

He told her one night that he loved her. He loved her so much that he would re-enlist and remain in this Japanese city for at least another year. I overheard him through the parchment walls, and I would have asked him about it next morning if he had not mentioned it himself. 'I told her that, and I was lying,' he said.

'Well, why did you tell her?'

'You lie to a dame. That's my advice to you. You get them in closer and closer, you feed them whatever you want, and the only trick is never to believe it yourself. Do you understand, Nicholson?'

'No, I don't.'

'It's the only way to handle them, I've got Yuriko around my finger.' And he insisted on giving me a detailed account of how they made love until by the sheer energy of his account, I realized what he wished to destroy. He had been sincere when he spoke to Yuriko. With her hands on his face, and the night drifting in fog against the windows, he had wanted to re-enlist for another year, had wanted to suspend her fingers upon his face, and freeze time so it could be retained. It must have all seemed possible the night before, he must have believed it and wanted it, seen himself signing the papers in the morning. Instead, he had seen me, had seen the olive-drab color of my uniform, and had known it was not possible, was not at all possible within the gamut of his nature.

He was drunk the following night when he went to see her, moody and silent, and Yuriko was without diversion to him. I think she sensed that something was wrong. She sighed frequently, she chatted in Japanese with Mimiko, and threw quick looks at him to see whether his mood was changing. Then – it must have meant so much to her – she inquired timidly, 'You re-enlist one year?'

He stared back at her, was about to nod, and then laughed shortly. 'I'm going home, Yuriko. I'm due to go home in one month.'

'You repeat, please?'

'I'm getting out of here. In one month. I'm not re-enlisting.'

She turned away and looked at the wall. When she turned around, it was to pinch his arm.

'Hayes-san, you marry me, yes?' she said in a voice sharp with its hurt.

He shoved her away. 'I don't marry you. Get away. You skibby with too many men.'

She drew in her breath and her eyes were bright for a moment. 'Yes. You marry skibby-girl.' Yuriko threw her arms around his neck. 'American soldier marry skibby-girl.'

This time he pushed her away forcefully enough to hurt her. 'You just go blow,' he shouted at her.

She was quite angry. 'American soldier marry skibby-girl,' she taunted.

I had never seen him quite as furious. What frightened me was that he contained it all and did not raise his voice. 'Marry you?' he asked. I have an idea what engaged him was that the thought had already occurred to him, and it seemed outrageous to hear it repeated in what was, after all, the mouth of a prostitute. Hayes picked up his bottle and drank from it. 'You and me are going to skibby, that's what,' he said to Yuriko.

She held her ground. 'No skibby tonight.'

'What do you mean, "no skibby tonight"? You'll skibby tonight. You're nothing but a *joro*.'

Yuriko turned her back. Her little head was bent forward. 'I, first-class geisha,' she whispered in so low a voice we almost did not hear her.

He struck her. I tried to intervene, and with a blow he knocked me away. Yuriko fled the room. Like a bull, Hayes was after her. He caught her once, just long enough to rip away half her kimono, caught her again to rip away most of what was left. The poor girl was finally trapped, screaming, and more naked than not, in the room where the geishas met the soliders. There must have been a dozen girls and at least as many soldiers for an audience. Hayes gripped her hairdress, he ripped it down, he threw her up in the air, he dropped her on the floor, he laughed drunkenly, and among the screams of the girls and the startled laughter of the soldiers, I got him out to the street. I could hear Yuriko wailing hysterically behind us.

I guided him home to his cot, and he dropped into a drunken sleep. In the morning, he was contrite. Through the dull headache of awakening, he certainly did not love her, and so he regretted his brutality. 'She's a good girl, Nicholson,' he said to me, 'she's a good girl, and I shouldn't have treated her that way.'

'You ripped her kimono,' I told him.

'Yeah, I got to buy her another.'

It turned out to be a bad day. At breakfast, everybody who passed on the chow line seemed to have heard what had happened, and Hayes was kidded endlessly. It developed that Yuriko had been put to bed with fever after we left, and all the girls were shocked. Almost everything had halted for the night at the geisha house.

'You dishonoured her in public,' said one of Hayes's buddies with a grin. 'Man, how they carried on.'

Hayes turned to me. 'I'm going to buy her a good kimono.' He spent the morning selecting articles of food to sell on the black market. He had to make enough to amass the price of a good kimono, and it worried him that the supplies might be too depleted. The afternoon was taken up with selling his goods, and at dinner we were two weary cooks.

Hayes changed in a hurry. 'Come on, let's get over there.' He hustled me along, did not even stop to buy a bottle. We were the first clients of the evening to appear at the geisha house. 'Mama-san,' he roared at the old madame, 'where's Yuriko?'

Mama-san pointed upstairs. Her expression was wary. Hayes, however, did not bother to study it. He bounded up the stairs, knocked on Yuriko's door, and entered.

Yuriko was sweet and demure. She accepted his present with a deep bow, touching her forehead to the floor. She was friendly, she was polite, and she was quite distant. She poured us sake with even more ceremony than was her custom. Mimiko entered after a few minutes, and her face was troubled. Yet it was she who talked to us. Yuriko was quiet for a long time. It was only when Mimiko lapsed into silence that Yuriko began to speak.

She informed us in her mixture of English, Japanese and pantomime that in two weeks she was going to take a trip. She was very formal about it.

'A trip?' Hayes asked.

It was to be a long trip. Yuriko smiled sadly.

Hayes fingered his hat. She was leaving the geisha house?

Yes, she was leaving it forever.

She was going perhaps to get married?

No, she was not getting married. She was dishonored and no one would have her.

Hayes began to twist his hat. She had a *musume*? She was going away with a *musume*?

No, there was no *musume*. Hayes was the only *musume* in her life.

Well, where was she going?

Yuriko sighed. She could not tell him. She hoped, however, since she would be leaving before Hayes, that he would come to see her often in the next few weeks.

'Goddammit, where are you going?' Hayes shouted.

At this point, Mimiko began to weep. She wept loudly, her

hand upon her face, her head averted. Yuriko leaped up to comfort her. Yuriko patted her head, and sighed in unison with Mimiko.

'Where are you going?' Hayes asked her again.

Yuriko shrugged her shoulders.

It continued like this for an hour. Hayes badgered her, and Yuriko smiled. Hayes pleaded and Yuriko looked sad. Finally, as we were about to leave, Yuriko told us. In two weeks, at two o'clock on Sunday afternoon, she was going to her little room, and there she would commit hari-kari. She was dishonored, and there was nothing else to be done about it. Hayes-san was very kind to apologize, and the jewels of her tears were the only fit present for his kindness, but apologies could never erase dishonor and so she would be obliged to commit hari-kari.

Mimiko began to weep again.

'You mean in two weeks you're going to kill yourself?' Hayes blurted.

'Yes, Hayes-san.'

He threw up his arms. 'It's crap, it's all crap, you understand?'

'Yes, Crap-crap,' Yuriko said.

'You're throwing the bull, Yuriko.'

'Yes. Hayes-san. Crap-crap.'

'Let's get out of here, Nicholson.' He turned in the doorway and laughed. 'You almost had me for a minute, Yuriko.'

She bowed her head.

Hayes went to see her three times in the week which followed. Yuriko remained the same. She was quiet, she was friendly, she was quite removed. And Mimiko wept every night on my pallet. Hayes forbore as long as was possible, and then at the end of the week, he spoke about it again. 'You were kidding me, weren't you, Yuriko?'

Yuriko begged Hayes-san not to speak of it again. It was rude on her part. She did not wish to cause him unnecessary pain. If she had spoken, it was only because the dearer sentiments of her heart were in liege to him, and she wished to see him often in the week which remained.

He snorted with frustration. 'Now, look you . . . cut . . . this . . . out. Do you understand?'

'Yes, Hayes-san. No more talk-talk.' She would not mention it again, she told us. She realized how it offended him. Death was an unpleasant topic of conversation in a geisha house. She would attempt to be entertaining, and she begged us to forgive her if the knowledge of her own fate might cause her to be sad at certain moments.

That morning, on the walk back to the schoolhouse, Hayes was quiet. He worked all day with great rapidity, and bawled me out several times for not following his cooking directions more accurately. That night we slept in our barrack, and in the early hours of the morning, he woke me up.

'Look, Nicholson, I can't sleep. Do you think that crazy honey is really serious?'

I was wide awake. I had not been sleeping well myself. 'I don't know,' I said. 'I don't think she means it.'

'I know she doesn't mean it.' He swore.

'Yeah.' I started to light a cigarette, and then I put it out. 'Hayes, I was just thinking though. You know the Oriental mind is different.'

'The Oriental mind! Goddammit, Nicholson, a whore is a whore. They're all the same I tell you. She's kidding.'

'If you say so.'

'I'm not even going to mention it to her.'

All through the second week, Hayes kept his promise. More than once, he would be about to ask her again, and would force himself into silence. It was very difficult. As the days passed, Mimiko wept more and more openly, and Yuriko's eyes would fill with tears as she looked at Hayes. She would kiss him tenderly, sigh, and then by an effort of will, or so it seemed, would force herself to be gay. Once she surprised us with some flowers she had found, and wove them in our hair. The week passed day by day. I kept waiting for the other men in the company to hear the news, but Hayes said not a word and the geishas did not either. Still, one could sense that the atmosphere in the house was different. The geishas were extremely respectful to Yuriko, and quite frequently would touch her garments as she passed.

By Saturday Hayes could stand it no longer. He insisted that we leave the geisha house for the night, and he made Yuriko accompany us to the boot vestibule. While she was lacing our shoes, he raised her head and said to her, 'I work tomorrow. I'll see you Monday.'

She smiled vaguely, and continued tying the laces.

'Yuriko, I said I'd see you Monday.'

'No, Hayes-san. Better tomorrow. No here, Monday. Gone, bye-bye. You come tomorrow before two o'clock.'

'Yuriko, I'm on duty tomorrow. I said I'll see you Monday.'

'Say good-bye now. Never see me again.' She kissed us on the cheek. 'Good-bye, Nick-san. Good-bye, Hayes-san.' A single tear rolled down each cheek. She fingered Hayes's jacket and fled.

That night Hayes and I did not sleep at all. He came over to my cot, and sat there in silence. 'What do you think?' he asked after a long while.

'I don't know.'

'I don't know either.' He began to swear. He kept drinking from a bottle, but it had no effect. He was quite sober. 'I'm damned if I'm going over there tomorrow,' he said.

'Do what you think is best.'

He swore loudly.

The morning went on and on. Hayes worked rapidly and was left with nothing to do. The meal was ready fifteen minutes early. He called chow at eleven-thirty. By one o'clock the K.P.s were almost finished with the pots.

'Hey, Koto,' Hayes asked one of the K.P.s, a middle-aged man who had been an exporter and spoke English, 'hey, Koto, what do you know about hari-kari?'

Koto grinned. He was always very polite and very colorless. 'Oh, hari-kari. Japanese national custom,' he said.

'Come on,' Hayes said to me, 'we've got till three o'clock before we put supper on.' He was changing into his dress clothes by the time I followed him to the dormitory. He had neglected to hang them up the night before, and for once they were bedraggled. 'What time is it?' he asked me.

'A quarter past one.'

'Come on, hurry up.'

He ran almost all the way to the geisha house, and I ran with him. As we approached, the house seemed quiet. There was nobody in the vestibule, and there was nobody in the receiving room. Hayes and I stood there in empty silence.

'*Yuriko!*' he bawled.

We heard her feet patter on the stairs. She was dressed in a white kimono, without ornament, and without make-up. 'You do come,' she whispered. She kissed him. 'Bye-bye, Hayes-san. I go upstairs now.'

He caught her arm. 'Yuriko, you can't do it.'

She attempted to free herself, and he held her with frenzy. 'I won't let you go,' he shouted. 'Yuriko, you got to stop this. It's crap.'

'Crap-crap,' she said, and suddenly she began to giggle.

'Crap-crap,' we heard all around. 'Crap-crap, crap-crap, crap-crap.'

Squealing with laughter, every geisha in the house entered the room. They encircled us, their voices going 'crap-crap' like a flock of geese.

Yuriko was laughing at us. Mimiko was laughing at us, they were all laughing. Hayes shouldered his way to the door. 'Let's get out of here.' We pushed on to the street, but the geishas followed. As we retreated across the town, they flowed out from the geisha house and marched behind us, their kimonos brilliant with color, their black hair shining in the sunlight. While the townspeople looked and giggled, we walked home, and the geishas followed us, shouting insults in English, Japanese and pantomime. Beneath their individual voices, with the regularity of marching feet, I could hear their cadence, 'Crap-crap, crap-crap.'

After a week, Hayes and I went back to the house for a last visit before we sailed for home. We were received politely, but neither Yuriko nor Mimiko would sleep with us. They suggested that we hire Susiko, the thirteen-year-old ex-virgin.

*1951*

# The Notebook

The writer was having a fight with his young lady. They were walking toward her home, and as the argument continued, they walked with their bodies farther and farther apart.

The young lady was obviously providing the energy for the quarrel. Her voice would rise a little bit, her head and shoulders would move toward him as though to add weight to her words, and then she would turn away in disgust, her heels tapping the pavement in an even precise rhythm which was quite furious.

The writer was suffering with some dignity. He placed one leg in front of the other, he looked straight ahead, his face was sad, he would smile sadly from time to time and nod his head to every word she uttered.

'I'm sick and tired of you,' the young lady exclaimed. 'I'm sick and tired of you being so superior. What do you have to be superior about?'

'Nothing,' the writer said in so quiet a voice, so gentle a tone that his answer might as well have been, 'I have my saintliness to be superior about.'

'Do you ever give me anything?' the young lady asked, and provided the response herself. 'You don't even give me the time of day. You're the coldest man I've ever known.'

'Oh, that's not true,' the writer suggested softly.

'Isn't it? Everybody thinks you're so nice and friendly, everybody except anybody who knows you at all. Anybody who knows you, knows better.'

The writer was actually not unmoved. He liked this young lady very much, and he did not want to see her unhappy. If with another part of his mind he was noticing the way she constructed her sentences, the last word of one phrase seeming to provide the impetus for the next, he was nonetheless paying attention to everything she said.

'Are you being completely fair?' he asked.

'I've finally come to understand you,' she said angrily. 'You don't want to be in love. You just want to say the things you're supposed to say and watch the things you're supposed to feel.'

'I love you. I know you don't believe me,' the writer said.

'You're a mummy. You're nothing but a . . . an Egyptian mummy.'

The writer was thinking that when the young lady became angry, her imagery was at best somewhat uninspired. 'All right, I'm a mummy,' he said softly.

They waited for a traffic light to change. He stood at the curb, smiling sadly, and the sadness on his face was so complete, so patient and so perfect, that the young lady with a little cry darted out into the street and trotted across on her high heels. The writer was obliged to run a step or two to catch up with her.

'Your attitude is different now,' she continued. 'You don't care about me. Maybe you used to, but you don't care any more. When you look at me, you're not really looking at all. I don't exist for you.'

'You know you do.'

'You wish you were somewhere else right now. You don't like me when I'm nasty. You think I'm vulgar. Very well, then, I'm vulgar. I'm too vulgar for your refined senses. Isn't that a pity? Do you think the world begins and ends with you?'

'No.'

'No, what?' she cried.

'Why are you angry? Is it because you feel I didn't pay enough attention to you tonight? I'm sorry if I didn't. I didn't realize I didn't. I do love you.'

'Oh, you love me; oh, you certainly do,' the young lady said in a voice so heavy with sarcasm that she was almost weeping. 'Perhaps I'd like to think so, but I know better.' Her figure leaned towards his as they walked. 'There's one thing I will tell you,' she went on bitterly. 'You hurt people more than the cruellest person in the world could. And why? I'll tell you why. It's because you never feel anything and you make believe that you do.' She could see he was not listening, and she asked in exasperation, 'What are you thinking about now?'

'Nothing. I'm listening to you, and I wish you weren't so upset.'

Actually the writer had become quite uneasy. He had just thought of an idea to put into his notebook, and it made him anxious to think that if he did not remove his notebook from his vest pocket and jot down the thought, he was likely to forget it. He tried repeating the idea to himself several times to fix it in his memory, but this procedure was never certain.

'I'm upset,' the young lady said. 'Of course, I'm upset. Only a mummy isn't upset, only a mummy can always be reasonable and polite because they don't feel anything.' If they had not been walking so quickly she would have stamped her foot. 'What are you thinking about?'

'It's not important,' he said. He was thinking that if he removed the notebook from his pocket, and held it in the palm of his hand, he might be able to scribble in it while they walked. Perhaps she would not notice.

It turned out to be too difficult. He was obliged to come to a halt beneath a street light. His pencil worked rapidly in nervous elliptic script while he felt beside him the pressure of her presence. *Emotional situation deepened by notebook*, he wrote. *Young writer, girl friend. Writer accused of being observer, not participant in life by girl. Gets idea he must put in notebook. Does so, and brings the quarrel to a head. Girl breaks relationship over this.*

'You have an idea now,' the young lady murmured.

'Mmm,' he answered.

'That notebook. I knew you'd pull out that notebook.' She began to cry. 'Why, you're nothing but a notebook,' she shrieked, and ran away from him down the street, her high heels mocking her misery in their bright tattoo upon the sidewalk.

'No, wait,' he called after her. 'Wait, I'll explain.'

It occurred to the writer that if he were to do such a vignette, the nuances could be altered. Perhaps the point of the piece should be that the young man takes out his notebook because he senses that this would be the best way to destroy what was left of the relationship. It was a nice idea.

Abruptly, it also occurred to him that maybe this was what he had done. Had he wished to end his own relationship with his own young lady? He considered this, priding himself on the fact that he would conceal no motive from himself, no matter how unpleasant.

Somehow, this did not seem to be true. He did like the young lady, he liked her very much, and he did not wish the relationship to end yet. With some surprise, he realized that she was almost a block away. Therefore, he began to run after her. 'No, wait,' he called out. 'I'll explain it to you, I promise I will.' And as he ran the notebook jiggled warmly against his side, a puppy of a playmate, always faithful, always affectionate.

*1951*

# The Language of Men

In the beginning, Sanford Carter was ashamed of becoming an army cook. This was not from snobbery, at least not from snobbery of the most direct sort. During the two and a half years Carter had been in the army he had come to hate cooks more and more. They existed for him as a symbol of all that was corrupt, overbearing, stupid, and privileged in army life. The image which came to mind was a fat cook with an enormous sandwich in one hand, and a bottle of beer in the other, sweat pouring down a porcine face, foot on a flour barrel, shouting at the K.P.s, 'Hurry up, you men, I ain't got all day.' More than once in those two and a half years, driven to exasperation, Carter had been on the verge of throwing his food into a cook's face as he passed on the serving line. His anger often derived from nothing: the set of a pair of fat lips, the casual heavy thump of the serving spoon into his plate, or the resentful conviction that the cook was not serving him enough. Since life in the army was in most aspects a marriage, this rage over apparently harmless details was not a sign of unbalance. Every soldier found some particular habit of the army spouse impossible to support.

Yet Sanford Carter became a cook and, to elaborate the irony, did better as a cook than he had done as anything else. In a few months he rose from a private to a first cook with the rank of Sergeant, Technician. After the fact, it was easy to understand. He had suffered through all his army career from an excess of eagerness. He had cared too much, he had wanted to do well, and so he had often been tense at moments when he would better have been relaxed. He was very young, twenty-one, had lived the comparatively gentle life of a middle-class boy, and needed some success in the army to prove to himself that he was not completely worthless.

In succession, he had failed as a surveyor in field artillery, a clerk in an infantry headquarters, a telephone wireman, and finally a rifleman. When the war ended, and his regiment went to Japan, Carter was still a rifleman; he had been a rifleman for

eight months. What was more to the point, he had been in the
platoon as long as any of its members; the skilled hard-bitten
nucleus of veterans who had run his squad had gone home one
by one, and it seemed to him that through seniority he was
entitled to at least a corporal's rating. Through seniority he was
so entitled, but on no other ground. Whenever responsibility
had been handed to him, he had discharged it miserably,
tensely, overconscientiously. He had always asked too many
questions, he had worried the task too severely, he had conveyed his nervousness to the men he was supposed to lead.
Since he was also sensitive enough and proud enough never to
curry favor with the noncoms in the platoons, he was in no
position to sit in on their occasional discussions about who was
to succeed them. In a vacuum of ignorance, he had allowed
himself to dream that he would be given a squad to lead, and his
hurt was sharp when the squad was given to a replacement who
had joined the platoon months after him.

The war was over, Carter had a bride in the States (he had
lived with her for only two months), he was lonely, he was
obsessed with going home. As one week dragged into the next,
and the regiment, the company, and his own platoon continued
the same sort of training which they had been doing ever since
he had entered the army, he thought he would snap. There were
months to wait until he would be discharged and meanwhile it
was intolerable to him to be taught for the fifth time the
nomenclature of the machine gun, to stand a retreat parade
three evenings a week. He wanted some niche where he could
lick his wounds, some army job with so many hours of work and
so many hours of complete freedom, where he could be alone by
himself. He hated the army, the huge army which had proved to
him that he was good at no work, and incapable of succeeding at
anything. He wrote long, aching letters to his wife, he talked
less and less to the men around him, and he was close to violent
attacks of anger during the most casual phases of training –
during close-order drill or cleaning his rifle for inspection. He
knew that if he did not find his niche it was possible that he
would crack.

So he took an opening in the kitchen. It promised him
nothing except a day of work, and a day of leisure which would

be completely at his disposal. He found that he liked it. He was given at first the job of baking the bread for the company, and every other night he worked till early in the morning, kneading and shaping his fifty-pound mix of dough. At two or three he would be done, and for his work there would be the tangible reward of fifty loaves of bread, all fresh from the oven, all clean and smelling of fertile accomplished creativity. He had the rare and therefore intensely satisfying emotion of seeing at the end of an army chore the product of his labor.

A month after he became a cook the regiment was disbanded, and those men who did not have enough points to go home were sent to other outfits. Carter ended at an ordnance company in another Japanese city. He had by now given up all thought of getting a noncom's rating before he was discharged, and was merely content to work each alternate day. He took his work for granted and so he succeeded at it. He had begun as a baker in the new company kitchen; before long he was the first cook. It all happened quickly. One cook went home on points, another caught a skin disease, a third was transferred from the kitchen after contracting a venereal infection. On the shift which Carter worked there were left only himself and a man who was illiterate. Carter was put nominally in charge, and was soon actively in charge. He looked up each menu in an army recipe book, collected the items, combined them in the order indicated, and after the proper time had elapsed, took them from the stove. His product tasted neither better nor worse than the product of all other army cooks. But the mess sergeant was impressed. Carter had filled a gap. The next time ratings were given out Carter jumped at a bound from Private to Sergeant T/4.

On the surface he was happy; beneath the surface he was overjoyed. It took him several weeks to realize how grateful and delighted he felt. The promotion coincided with his assignment to a detachment working in a small seaport up the coast. Carter arrived there to discover that he was in charge of cooking for thirty men, and would act as mess sergeant. There was another cook, and there were four permanent Japanese K.P.s, all of them good workers. He still cooked every other day, but there was always time between meals to take a break of at least an hour and often two; he shared a room with the other cook and lived in comparative privacy for the first time in several years; the seaport was beautiful; there was only one officer, and he left the men alone; supplies were plentiful due to a clerical error which assigned rations for forty men rather than thirty; and in general everything was fine. The niche had become a sinecure.

This was the happiest period of Carter's life in the army. He came to like his Japanese K.P.s. He studied their language, he visited their homes, he gave them gifts of food from time to time. They worshipped him because he was kind to them and generous, because he never shouted, because his good humor bubbled over into games, and made the work in the kitchen seem pleasant. All the while he grew in confidence. He was not a big man, but his body filled out from the heavy work; he was likely to sing a great deal, he cracked jokes with the men on the chow line. The kitchen became his property, it became his domain, and since it was a warm room, filled with sunlight, he came to take pleasure in the very sight of it. Before long his good humor expanded into a series of efforts to improve the food. He began to take little pains and make little extra efforts which would have been impossible if he had been obliged to cook for more than thirty men. In the morning he would serve the men fresh eggs scrambled or fried to their desire in fresh butter. Instead of cooking sixty eggs in one large pot he cooked two eggs at a time in a frying pan, turning them to the taste of each soldier. He baked like a housewife satisfying her young husband; at lunch and dinner there was pie or cake, and often both. He went to great lengths. He taught the K.P.s how to make the toast come out right. He traded excess food for spices in Japanese stores. He rubbed paprika and garlic on the chickens. He even made pastries to cover such staples as corn beef hash and meat and vegetable stew.

It all seemed to be wasted. In the beginning the men might have noticed these improvements, but after a period they took them for granted. It did not matter how he worked to satisfy them; they trudged through the chow line with their heads down, nodding coolly at him, and they ate without comment. He would hang around the tables after the meal, noticing how much they consumed, and what they discarded; he would wait for compliments, but the soldiers seemed indifferent. They seemed to eat without tasting the food. In their faces he saw mirrored the distaste with which he had once stared at cooks.

The honeymoon was ended. The pleasure he took in the kitchen and himself curdled. He became aware again of his painful desire to please people, to discharge responsibility, to be a man. When he had been a child, tears had come into his eyes at a cross word, and he had lived in an atmosphere where his smallest accomplishment was warmly praised. He was the sort of young man, he often thought bitterly, who was accustomed to the attention and the protection of women. He would have thrown away all he possessed – the love of his wife, the love of his mother, the benefits of his education, the assured financial security of entering his father's business – if he had been able just once to dig a ditch as well as the most ignorant farmer.

Instead, he was back in the painful unprotected days of his first entrance into the army. Once again the most casual actions became the most painful, the events which were most to be taken for granted grew into the most significant, and the feeding of the men at each meal turned progressively more unbearable.

So Sanford Carter came full circle. If he had once hated the cooks, he now hated the troops. At mealtimes his face soured into the belligerent scowl with which he had once believed cooks to be born. And to himself he muttered the age-old laments of the housewife; how little they appreciated what he did.

Finally there was an explosion. He was approached one day by Corporal Taylor, and he had come to hate Taylor, because Taylor was the natural leader of the detachment and kept the other men endlessly amused with his jokes. Taylor had the ability to present himself as inefficient, shiftless, and incapable, in such a manner as to convey that really the opposite was true. He had the lightest touch, he had the greatest facility, he could charm a geisha in two minutes and obtain anything he wanted from a supply sergeant in five. Carter envied him, envied his grace, his charmed indifference; then grew to hate him.

Taylor teased Carter about his cooking, and he had the knack of knowing where to put the knife. 'Hey, Carter,' he would shout across the mess hall while breakfast was being served, 'you turned my eggs twice, and I asked for them raw.' The men would shout with laughter. Somehow Taylor had succeeded in conveying all of the situation, or so it seemed to Carter, insinuating everything, how Carter worked and how it meant nothing, how Carter labored to gain their affection and earned their contempt. Carter would scowl, Carter would answer in a rough voice, 'Next time I'll crack them over your head.' 'You crack 'em, I'll eat 'em,' Taylor would pipe back, 'but just don't put your fingers in 'em.' And there would be another laugh. He hated the sight of Taylor.

It was Taylor who came to him to get the salad oil. About twenty of the soldiers were going to have a fish fry at the geisha house; they had bought the fish at the local market but they could not buy oil, so Taylor was sent as the deputy to Carter. He was charming to Carter, he complimented him on the meal, he clapped him on the back, he dissolved Carter to warmth, to private delight in the attention, and the thought that he had misjudged Taylor. Then Taylor asked for the oil.

Carter was sick with anger. Twenty men out of the thirty in the detachment were going on the fish fry. It meant only that Carter was considered one of the ten undesirables. It was something he had known, but the proof of knowledge is always more painful than the acquisition of it. If he had been alone his eyes would have clouded. And he was outraged at Taylor's deception. He could imagine Taylor saying ten minutes later, 'You should have seen the grease job I gave to Carter. I'm dumb, but man, he's dumber.'

Carter was close enough to giving him the oil. He had a sense of what it would mean to refuse Taylor, he was on the very edge of mild acquiescence. But he also had a sense of how he would despise himself afterward.

'No,' he said abruptly, his teeth gritted, 'you can't have it.'

'What do you mean we can't have it?'

'I won't give it to you.' Carter could almost feel the rage which Taylor generated at being refused.

'You won't give away a lousy five gallons of oil to a bunch of G.I.s having a party?'

'I'm sick and tired –' Carter began.

'So am I.' Taylor walked away.

Carter knew he would pay for it. He left the K.P.s and went to change his sweat-soaked work shirt, and as he passed the large dormitory in which most of the detachment slept he could hear Taylor's high-pitched voice.

Carter did not bother to take off his shirt. He returned instead to the kitchen, and listened to the sound of men going back and forth through the hall and of a man shouting with rage. That was Hobbs, a Southerner, a big man with a big bellowing voice.

There was a formal knock on the kitchen door. Taylor came in. His face was pale and his eyes showed a cold satisfaction. 'Carter,' he said, 'the men want to see you in the big room.'

Carter heard his voice answer huskily. 'If they want to see me, they can come into the kitchen.'

He knew he would conduct himself with more courage in his own kitchen than anywhere else. 'I'll be here for a while.'

Taylor closed the door, and Carter picked up a writing board to which was clamped the menu for the following day. Then he made a pretense of examining the food supplies in the pantry closet. It was his habit to check the stocks before deciding what to serve the next day, but on this night his eyes ranged thoughtlessly over the canned goods. In a corner were seven five-gallon tins of salad oil, easily enough cooking oil to last a month. Carter came out of the pantry and shut the door behind him.

He kept his head down and pretended to be writing the menu when the soldiers came in. Somehow there were even more of them than he had expected. Out of the twenty men who were going to the party, all but two or three had crowded through the door.

Carter took his time, looking up slowly. 'You men want to see me?' he asked flatly.

They were angry. For the first time in his life he faced the hostile expressions of many men. It was the most painful and anxious moment he had ever known.

'Taylor says you won't give us the oil,' someone burst out.

'That's right, I won't,' said Carter. He tapped his pencil

against the scratchboard, tapping it slowly and, he hoped, with an appearance of calm.

'What a stink deal,' said Porfirio, a little Cuban whom Carter had always considered his friend.

Hobbs, the big Southerner, stared down at Carter. 'Would you mind telling the men why you've decided not to give us the oil?' he asked quietly.

'Cause I'm blowed if I'm going to cater to you men. I've catered enough,' Carter said. His voice was close to cracking with the outrage he had suppressed for so long, and he knew that if he continued he might cry. 'I'm the acting mess sergeant,' he said as coldly as he could, 'and I decide what goes out of this kitchen.' He stared at each one in turn, trying to stare them down, feeling mired in the rut of his own failure. They would never have dared this approach to another mess sergeant.

'What crud,' someone muttered.

'You won't give a lousy five-gallon can of oil for a G.I. party,' Hobbs said more loudly.

'I won't. That's definite. You men can get out of here.'

'Why, you lousy little snot,' Hobbs burst out, 'how many five-gallon cans of oil have you sold on the black market?'

'I've never sold any.' Carter might have been slapped with the flat of a sword. He told himself bitterly, numbly, that this was the reward he received for being perhaps the single honest cook in the whole United States Army. And he even had time to wonder at the obscure prejudice which had kept him from selling food for his own profit.

'Man, I've seen you take it out,' Hobbs exclaimed. 'I've seen you take it to the market.'

'I took food to trade for spices,' Carter said hotly.

There was an ugly snicker from the men.

'I don't mind if a cook sells,' Hobbs said, 'every man has his own deal in this army. But a cook ought to give a little food to a G.I. if he wants it.'

'Tell him,' someone said.

'It's bull,' Taylor screeched. 'I've seen Carter take butter, eggs, every damn thing to the market.'

Their faces were red, they circled him.

'I never sold a thing,' Carter said doggedly.

'And I'm telling you,' Hobbs said, 'that you're a two-bit crook. You been raiding that kitchen, and that's why you don't give to us now.'

Carter knew there was only one way he could possibly answer if he hoped to live among these men again. 'That's a goddam lie,' Carter said to Hobbs. He laid down the scratchboard, he flipped his pencil slowly and deliberately to one corner of the room, and with his heart aching he lunged toward Hobbs. He had no hope of beating him. He merely intended to fight until he was pounded unconscious, advancing the pain and bruises he would collect as collateral for his self-respect.

To his indescribable relief Porfirio darted between them, held them apart, with the pleased ferocity of a small man breaking up a fight. 'Now, stop this! Now, stop this!' he cried out.

Carter allowed himself to be pushed back, and he knew that he had gained a point. He even glimpsed a solution with some honor.

He shrugged violently to free himself from Porfirio. He was in a rage, and yet it was a rage he could have ended at any instant. 'All right, you men,' he swore. 'I'll give you the oil, but now that we're at it, I'm going to tell you a thing or two.' His face red, his body perspiring, he was in the pantry and out again with a five-gallon tin. 'Here,' he said, 'you better have a good fish fry, 'cause it's the last good meal you're going to have for quite a while. I'm sick of trying to please you. You think I have to work' – he was about to say, my fingers to the bone – 'well, I don't. From now on, you'll see what chow in the army is supposed to be like.' He was almost hysterical. 'Take that oil. Have your fish fry.' The fact that they wanted to cook for themselves was the greatest insult of all. 'Tomorrow I'll give you real army cooking.'

His voice was so intense that they backed away from him. 'Get out of this kitchen,' he said. 'None of you has any business here.'

They filed out quietly and they looked a little sheepish.

Carter felt weary, he felt ashamed of himself, he knew he had not meant what he said. But half an hour later, when he left the kitchen and passed the large dormitory, he heard shouts of raucous laughter, and he heard his name mentioned and then more laughter.

He slept badly that night, he was awake at four, he was in the kitchen by five, and he stood there white-faced and nervous, waiting for the K.P.s to arrive. Breakfast that morning landed on the men like a lead bomb. Carter rummaged in the back of the pantry and found a tin of dehydrated eggs covered with dust, memento of a time when fresh eggs were never on the ration list. The K.P.s looked at him in amazement as he stirred the lumpy powder into a pan of water. While it was still half-dissolved he put it on the fire. While it was still wet, he took it off. The coffee was cold, the toast was burned, the oatmeal stuck to the pot. The men dipped forks into their food, took cautious sips of their coffee, and spoke in whispers. Sullenness drifted like vapors through the kitchen.

At noontime Carter opened cans of meat-and-vegetable stew. He dumped them into a pan and heated them slightly. He served the stew with burned string beans and dehydrated potatoes which tasted like straw. For dessert the men had a single lukewarm canned peach and cold coffee.

So the meals continued. For three days Carter cooked slop, and suffered even more than the men. When mealtime came he left the chow line to the K.P.s and sat in his room, perspiring with shame, determined not to yield and sick with the determination.

Carter won. On the fourth day a delegation of men came to see him. They told him that indeed they had appreciated his cooking in the past, they told him that they were sorry they had hurt his feelings, they listened to his remonstrances, they listened to his grievances, and with delight Carter forgave them. That night, for supper, the detachment celebrated. There was roast chicken with stuffing, lemon meringue pie and chocolate cake. The coffee burned their lips. More than half the men made it a point to compliment Carter on the meal.

In the weeks which followed the compliments diminished, but they never stopped completely. Carter became ashamed at last. He realized the men were trying to humor him, and he wished to tell them it was no longer necessary.

Harmony settled over the kitchen. Carter even became friends with Hobbs, the big Southerner. Hobbs approached him one day, and in the manner of a farmer talked obliquely for an hour. He spoke about his father, he spoke about his girl friends, he alluded indirectly to the night they had almost fought, and finally with the courtesy of a Southerner he said to Carter, 'You know, I'm sorry about shooting off my mouth. You were right to want to fight me, and if you're still mad I'll fight you to give you satisfaction, although I just as soon would not.'

'No, I don't want to fight with you now,' Carter said warmly. They smiled at each other. They were friends.

Carter knew he had gained Hobbs' respect. Hobbs respected him because he had been willing to fight. That made sense to a man like Hobbs. Carter liked him so much at this moment that he wished the friendship to be more intimate.

'You know,' he said to Hobbs, 'it's a funny thing. You know I really never did sell anything on the black market. Not that I'm proud of it, but I just didn't.'

Hobbs frowned. He seemed to be saying that Carter did not have to lie. 'I don't hold it against a man,' Hobbs said, 'if he makes a little money in something that's his own proper work. Hell, I sell gas from the motor pool. It's just I also give gas if one of the G.I.s wants to take the jeep out for a joy ride, kind of.'

'No, but I never did sell anything.' Carter had to explain. 'If I ever had sold on the black market, I would have given the salad oil without question.'

Hobbs frowned again, and Carter realized he still did not believe him. Carter did not want to lose the friendship which was forming. He thought he could save it only by some further admission. 'You know,' he said again, 'remembering when Porfirio broke up our fight? I was awful glad when I didn't have to fight you.' Carter laughed, expecting Hobbs to laugh with him, but a shadow passed across Hobbs' face.

'Funny way of putting it,' Hobbs said.

He was always friendly thereafter, but Carter knew that Hobbs would never consider him a friend. Carter thought about it often, and began to wonder about the things which made him different. He was no longer so worried about becoming a man; he felt that to an extent he had become one. But in his heart he wondered if he would ever learn the language of men.

*1951*

# The Patron Saint of MacDougal Alley

How can one describe Pierrot? It is impossible to understand him; one may only tell stories about him. Yet with every move he makes, he creates another story, so one cannot keep up. Pierrot is an original; he is unlike anyone else on the face of the earth.

I can describe how he looks. He is now nineteen, and of average height. He has dark hair, regular features, and a very pleasant smile. There are times when he grows a mustache, and there are times when he shaves it off. During those periods when he sports a few hairs beneath his nose, he looks a year or two younger; when he strips it, he is nineteen again. I suspect he will look nineteen a decade from now; what is worse I often have the suspicion that he looked the same when he was born. Pierrot will never change. He is absolutely predictable in the most unforeseen situations.

He is the son of my friend Jacques Battigny, who is a professor of Romance languages at a university in New York, and never were a father and son more related and less alike. Jacques is a gentleman of considerable culture; as a representative French intellectual it is somewhat intolerable to him to pass through experience without comprehending it rationally. He demands order in every corner of his life. It is his cross that Pierrot is the eternal flux.

Father and son are thesis and antithesis. Put another way, Pierrot is Jacques turned inside out, the clothes-dummy of an intellectual. He has all the attributes of the French mind except its erudition; his greatest joy is to approach logically large bodies of experience about which he knows nothing. The first time I met him, Pierrot spoke to me for hours; he mentioned in passing, Marx, Freud, and Darwin; Heidegger, Kierkegaard, and Sartre; Lawrence and Henry Miller; Nietzsche and Spengler; Vico and Edmund Wilson; Jean Genet and Simone de Beauvoir; Leon Trotsky and Max Schachtman; Wilhelm Reich, Gregory Zilboorg, and Karen Horney. There were two hundred other names of varied importance, and I do not believe he used a word which had less than four syllables. Therefore, it took some time for me to realize that Pierrot was an idiot.

In the hours between, he husked my brains. What did I think of Mr. Aldous Huxley? Pierrot would inquire, and long before I had reconstituted my recollections of Huxley's work and delivered them in some organized form, Pierrot was wondering how I evaluated Mr. Thomas Stearns Eliot. It seemed to me that I had never met an adolescent who was more intelligent: the breadth of his queries, the energy of his curiosity, and the quick reception which shone in his brown eyes, were quite impressive. Chaplin and Griffiths, Jackson Pollack and Hans Hofman, did I like Berlioz and had I heard Benjamin Britten? Pierrot was tireless. Only when the afternoon had passed and my wife felt obliged to invite him for dinner, did I begin to suspect that Pierrot did not contribute as much as I.

A few minutes later in response to a discreet inquiry or two, Pierrot confessed to me with relish that he had never seen a single one of the pictures he mentioned, nor read one of the authors we spoke about. 'You understand,' he said to me, 'it is so depressing. I want to amass the totality of knowledge, and consequently I don't know where to begin.' He sighed. 'I look at the books on my father's shelf. I say to myself, "Is it in these books that I will find the termination, or even the beginning, of my philosophical quest?" You understand? What is the meaning to life? That is what obsesses me. And will these books give the answer? I look at them. They are paper, they are cardboard. Is it possible that the essence of truth can be communicated to paper and ink?' He paused and smiled. 'Reality and illusion. I think about history, and I wonder, "Does Marxism take proper account of history?" Someone was telling me to read Engel's *Marriage and the Family*. Would you recommend it? I am very interested in the subject.'

He was absolutely tireless. As dinner progressed, as the dishes were washed, the brunt of conversation shifted from my tongue to Pierrot's. He sat with my wife and me through the evening, he discussed his ambitions, his depressions, his victories, his defeats. What did I think of his parents, he wanted to know, and immediately proceeded to tell me. Pierrot's mother had died, and his father had married again. Georgette was ten years younger than Jacques, and Pierrot found this disturbing. 'You understand,' he said to me cheerfully, 'I look for love. I search for it in the midst of my family, and I do not find it. Between Georgette and me there is an attraction, I ask myself whether it is maternal or physical? I should like to bring matters to a head, but I am a virgin, and I should detest it if I could not satisfy her. Is it true that one must serve the apprenticeship of love?' Long before I could have turned an answer, he had forgotten his question. 'And then I wonder in the privacy of my thoughts if what I really seek is the conquest of Georgette, or if I am looking for her only to be my mother. I should like her to hold me close. You understand, I am masochistic. I feel so many things.' He held his breast. 'I am an infant and I am a lover. Which is my nature? Which do I desire to satisfy? You realize, I want to be close to my father, and yet I am repelled by him. It is like psycho-analysis. I think sometimes I wish to live *ménage à trois*, but then I decide I am destructive and desire to live in isolation. Is it man's nature to live in isolation? I feel so lonely at times. I wish to communicate. Communication is a problem which interests me. Does it you?'

At one o'clock in the morning, after numerous hints had failed, I was obliged to tell Pierrot that he must go home. He looked at me sadly, he told me that he knew he bored me, he left with an air of such dejection that my wife and I were ashamed of ourselves, and felt we had turned a waif into the streets. The next time I saw his father, I apologized for this, and was cut short.

'Apologize for nothing,' Jacques shouted. 'The boy is a monster. He has no conception whatsoever of time. If you had not put him out, he would have stayed for a week.' Jacques held his head. 'I shall certainly go mad. There is nothing to do with him but to be completely rude. Listen to what has happened.'

The story Jacques told was indeed painful. Battigny the senior is a lover of books. He loves to read, he declaims on the art of reading, he loves bindings, he loves type, he loves books separately and together. It seems that Pierrot was once talking to a friend of Jacques's, a somewhat distinguished professor. The professor, taken with the boy, loaned him a copy of Florio's translation of Montaigne's essays. It was not a first edition, but it was an old one, and of some value, beautifully tooled in leather, and handsomely printed. 'Do you know how long ago that was?' Jacques demanded of me. 'It was two years ago. Pierrot has kept it in his brief case for two years. Has he ever read a page?' The answer was that he had not. He had merely kept it, and in the course of keeping it, the cover-board had been sheared and the spine exposed. 'I screamed at him,' Jacques said softly, 'it was indecent. I told him it was two years he had kept it, and he told me no, it was only a short period. He cannot comprehend the passage of time. He is always about to dip into the book, to study it here and smell it there. It is shameful.

'It is intolerable,' Jacques cried. 'He torments me. I have talked to his English teacher at high school. He asks her if he should study *Beowulf*, and he cannot even pass the examinations. I do not care if he does not go to college, I am not a snob about it, but the boy is incapable of doing anything with his hands. He cannot even learn a trade.'

I was to discover that Pierrot could not even learn to say yes or no. He was quite incapable of it, no matter to what brutal lengths I pursued him. Once in eating at my house, I asked him if he wished some bread and butter.

'I do not know,' Pierrot said, 'I ask myself.'

'Pierrot, do you want bread and butter?' I cried out.

'Why do you wish me to eat?' he asked dreamily, as if my motive were sinister. 'One eats to live, which supposes that life is worth while. But I ask myself: is life worth while?'

'Pierrot! Do you want bread and butter? Answer yes or no!'

Pierrot smiled sheepishly. 'Why do you ask me a yes-and-no question?'

One could say anything to him, and he enjoyed it immensely. He had been making advances to my wife for quite some time. No matter how she teased him, scolded him, or ignored him, he persisted. Yet once, when I took a walk with him, he launched into a long description of my virtues. I was handsome, I was attractive, he was stirred by me. And with that he pinched my bicep and said, 'You are so strong.'

'My God, Pierrot,' I said in exasperation. 'First you try to make love to my wife, and then you try to make love to me.'

'Yes,' he said morosely, 'and I succeed with neither.'

His father finally drove him from the house. He gave Pierrot two hundred dollars, and told him he was to find a job in the city and learn to live by his own labor. Jacques was penitent. 'I am so cruel to the boy. But what is there to do? I cannot bear the sight of him. Have you ever watched him work? If he picks up a hammer, he smashes his thumb. He lays down the hammer, he sucks his finger, he loses the hammer, he forgets why he needed it in the first place, he tries to remember, he ends by falling asleep.' Jacques groaned. 'I dread to think of him out in the world. He is completely impractical. He will spend the two hundred dollars in a night on his bohemian friends.'

Only a father could have been so wrong. Pierrot had the blood of a French peasant. The two hundred dollars lasted for six months. He lived with one friend, he lived with another; he lunched with an acquaintance and stayed for dinner. He drank beer in the Village; he was always to be found at Louis's, at Minetta's, at the San Remo, but no one remembered when he had paid for a drink. He was pretty enough to be courted, and he had frequent adventures with homosexuals. They were always finding him in a bar, they would talk to him, he would talk to them. He would tell them his troubles, he would confide, he would admit warmly that he had never discovered anyone who understood him so well. He would end by going to the other's apartment. There Pierrot would drink, he would continue to talk, he would talk even as the friend removed his shirt and apologized for the heat. It was only at the penultimate moment that Pierrot would leave. 'You understand,' he would say, 'I want to know you. But I am so confused. Do we have a basis to find a foundation of things in common?' And out he would skip through the door.

'Why do they always approach me?' he would ask in an innocent voice.

I would make the mistake of being severe. 'Because you solicit, Pierrot.'

He would smile. 'Ah, that is an interesting interpretation. I hope it is true. I would love to make my living in an antisocial manner. Society is so evil.'

He lived with a girl who was a fair mate for him. She had a tic at one corner of her mouth, and she was a follower of Buddha. The girl was trying to start a Buddhist colony in America. It was all mixed somehow with a theory about the birth trauma which she explained to me one night at a party. The reason armies functioned in combat was because the noise of battle returned the ordinary soldier to the primal state of birth. At such a moment his officers came to represent the protecting mother, and the soldier would obey their will even if it meant death. She was proud of the theory, and snapped at Pierrot when he would attempt to discuss it with her.

'A wonderful girl,' he told me once. 'It is a most exciting affair. She is absolutely frigid.'

It seemed that if he dropped his shoes upon the floor, she would not allow him to approach her. 'There is such uncertainty. It recaptures the uncertainty of life. I think about it. People meet. Lives intersect. It is points on a plane. Would you say this is a fit topic for philosophical investigation?'

In the course of events the Buddhist threw him out. At any rate, metaphorically she threw him out. The affair ended, but since Pierrot had no place to live, he continued to stay with her while he looked for another friend to give him a bed. During this period he came to me to ask if I would put him up, but I refused. After making these requests, he would look so forlorn that I hated myself.

'I understand,' he said. 'One of my friends who is analyzing me by hypnosis has made me see that I exploit everyone. It is the influence of the culture, I would think. I have become very interested in the movements of political bodies. I see that previously I adopted too personal an attitude. What is your opinion of my new political approach?'

'We'll discuss it another time, Pierrot. I'm awfully sorry I can't put you up for the night.'

'It is all right,' he said sweetly. 'I do not know where I shall sleep tonight, but it does not matter. I am an exploiter, and it is only proper that people should recognize this in me.' He left with a meek forgiving look. 'I shall sleep. Do not worry about me,' he said as the door closed.

Five minutes later I was still trying to put the matter from my mind when the doorbell rang. Pierrot was back. All night he had had a problem he wanted to discuss with me, but in the interest of our conversation, it had completely slipped his mind.

'What is it?' I asked coldly, annoyed at having been taken in.

He answered me in French. *'Tu sais, j'ai la chaude-pisse.'*

'Oh, Christ!'

He nodded. He had been to see a doctor, and it would be cleared up. There would be a wonder drug employed.

'Not by one of your friends, I hope?'

No, this was a bona-fide doctor. But he had another problem. The ailment had been provoked by the Buddhist. Of this, he was certain. At the moment, however, he was engaged in an affair with a young married woman, and he was curious to know whether he should tell her.

'You certainly should.' I grasped him by the shoulder. 'Pierrot, you have to tell her.'

His brown eyes clouded. 'You understand, it would be very difficult. It would destroy so much rapport between us. I would prefer to say nothing. Why should I speak? I am absolutely without morality,' he declared with passion.

'Morality be damned,' I said. 'Do you realize that if you don't tell the girl, you will have to see the doctor again and again? Do you know how expensive that is?'

He sighed. This is what he had been afraid of. Like the peasant brought slowly and stubbornly to face some new and detestable reality, he agreed dourly. 'In that case, I shall tell her. It is too bad.'

Lately, I have hardly seen Pierrot. His two hundred dollars has run out, and he is now obliged to work. He has had eleven jobs in four months. I could not hope to describe them all. He has been let go, fired, dismissed, and has resigned. He was an office boy for two days, and on the second day, pausing to take a drink, he placed his letter basket on the lip of the water cooler. Somehow – he is convinced it is the fault of the cooler – the water ran over the papers. In attempting to wipe them, he dropped the basket, and the wet paper became dirty. Signatures ran, names became illegible, and to the fury of the office manager, Pierrot did not attempt to excuse himself but asked instead why Americans were so compulsive about business correspondence.

He also worked in a factory. He was very depressed after the first day of work had ended, and called me up in such a mournful voice that I felt obliged to see him. He was tired, he was disgusted. 'I hold a piece of metal in my hand,' he said to me, 'and I touch it to an abrasive agent. Slowly square corners become round. Eight hours of such work I suffer. Can this be the meaning of existence?' His voice conveyed that he expected to continue the job until the end of time. 'I search for my identity. It is lost. I am merely Agent 48.'

At this point I rose upon him in wrath. I told him that he had two choices. He could work in order to live, or he could die. If he wished to die, I would not attempt to discourage him. In fact, I would abet him. 'If you come to me, Pierrot, and ask for a gun, I will attempt to find you a gun. Until then, stop complaining.' He listened to me with an enormous smile. His eyes shone at the vigor of my language. 'You are marvelous,' he said with admiration.

The very last I've heard is that Pierrot is soon to be drafted. Some of my friends are very upset about this. They say that the boy will be a mental case in a few weeks. Others insist that the army will be good for him. I am at odds with both of them.

I see Pierrot in the army. He will sleep late, curled in a little ball beneath his blankets. He will be certain to miss reveille. About eight o'clock in the morning he will stumble drowsily to the mess hall, his mess gear falling from his hand, and will look stupidly at the cook.

'Oh,' he will say, 'oh, I am late for breakfast.'

'Get out of here,' the cook will say.

'Oh, I go,' Pierrot will nod. 'I deserve to miss a meal. I have been negligent. Of course, I will be out all day on a march, and I will be very hungry, but it is my fault. And it does not matter. What is food?' He will be so unhappy that the cook no matter how he curses will scramble him some eggs. Pierrot will suggest toast, he will induce the cook to heat the coffee, he will engage him in a philosophical discussion. At eleven o'clock, Pierrot will leave to join his training platoon, and at two in the afternoon he will find them. Hours later, at retreat parade, the inspecting officer will discover that Pierrot has lost his rifle.

That will be the beginning of the end. Pierrot will be assigned to K.P. for three days in a row. By the first morning he will so have misplaced and mis-washed the pots that the cooks will be forced to assist him, and will work harder than they have ever worked. By evening the mess sergeant will be begging the first sergeant never to put Pierrot on K.P. again.

The army cannot recover from such a blow. K.P. is its foundation, and when cooks ask to remove men from that duty, it can take only a few days before every soldier in the army will follow the trail blazed by Pierre Battigny. I see the army collapsing two months after Pierrot enters it.

At that moment I hope to influence the course of history. Together with such responsible individuals as I may find, I will raise a subscription to send Pierrot to the Soviet Union. Once he is there, the world is saved. He will be put in the army immediately, and before his first day is over, the Russians will have him up before a firing squad. Then Pierrot will rise to his true stature.

'I ask myself,' he will say to the Russian soldiers, 'Am I not miserable? Is life not sad? Shoot me.'

At this point the Russians will throw down their arms and begin to weep. 'We do not enjoy ourselves either,' they will sob. 'Shoot us, too.' In the grand Russian manner, the news will spread across the steppes. Soldiers everywhere will cast away their weapons. America and Russia will be disarmed in a night, and peace will come over the earth.

They will build a statue to Pierrot at the corner of Eighth Street and MacDougal. New generations will pass and spit at him. 'He was Square,' they will say.

*1951*

# The Dead Gook

The regiment was dispersed over an area twenty miles wide and more than ten miles deep. In the conventional sense it could hardly be called a front. Here could be found an outpost of ten men; there, one mile away, a platoon of thirty or forty men; somewhere to the rear was Hq and Hq company, somewhere to the flank another unit. Through all the foothills and mountains of this portion of the Philippines, a few thousand American soldiers in groups of ten and twenty and fifty faced approximately as many Japanese, established like themselves along the summits of advantageous heights or bedded in ambush in the tropical growth of the valleys and streams. There was almost no contact. If either army had wished to advance, and had added so much as another regiment, progress would have been rapid, but the fate of the campaign was being determined elsewhere. For a month and then another, as the mild winter ended and the tropical rains of spring began, the outposts and detachments of these isolated forces made long patrols against one another, tramped for miles over rice paddies, up small mountains, along narrow rivers, and through jungle forests – patrols which covered ten or fifteen or as many as twenty miles in a single day, and more often than not were entirely without incident. Instead of a front there was a mingling of isolated positions, with Japanese units between Americans, and Americans between Japanese. The patrols were as often to the rear as to the front, and small groups of men brushed one another with rotary maneuvers, each detachment sweeping its own area in a circle.

It was not the worst of situations. Casualties were very few, and supply was regular. Many of the outposts had hot food brought from the rear, and some of the detachments were stationed in Filipino villages and slept beneath a roof. Still, it was not the best of situations. There were patrols almost every day for every man, and though they were invariably uneventful, they were nonetheless hard work. A squad would leave at eight in the morning; it would be fortunate to return by the end of the afternoon. The morning sun would beat upon the men, the midday rain would drench them, mud would cake upon their boots. They went nowhere, they patrolled in circles, up mountains and down cliffs, and yet each of them was obliged to carry an assortment of gear which never weighed less than twenty-five pounds. They carried their rifles, they carried two grenades hooked to the load of their cartridge belts. Over their shoulders were slung two bandoliers of ammunition, at their hips tugged the sluggish weight of water canteens, in their breast pockets chafed the cardboard corners of a food ration. None of these items was heavy in itself; taken together they were hardly to be disregarded. It was a reasonable load for a healthy man upon a hunting trip; these were unhealthy men burdened by a chronic residue of such diseases as malaria and yellow jaundice, and such discomforts as foot ulcers, diarrhea, and fungus rot.

It was dreary. There was danger, but it was remote; there was diversion, but it was rare. For the most part it was work, and work of the most distasteful character, work which was mean and long. The men, most often, did not complain. There were better things to do, but there were certainly worse, and for those who had been overseas for several years and had participated in more than this campaign, it was certainly not the most odious way in which to serve their time. They were satisfied to let events pass in the most quiet manner possible.

On a particular spring morning, the third squad of the first platoon of B Company was preparing to go out on patrol. Because of illness and a single casualty, their numbers had been reduced in the last two months from twelve men to seven, and since two men had to be left behind on the knoll of the hill where they had dug their outpost to serve as guard and answer the telephone, only five men were left to satisfy the requirements of a patrol which counted theoretically upon a strength of ten. This fact, which in a more arduous campaign would be considered a dangerous injustice, was here accepted merely as an annoyance. There was always the possibility that something could happen where their lack of numbers might be disastrous, but inasmuch as they had been operating with five men for quite some time and nothing had as yet occurred, the main source of their grievance was that they almost never received any rest. If in one of the sudden and seemingly arbitrary disposals of replacements, they had been brought up to strength, it is likely that they would have continued to patrol with five men, and gained the advantage of an alternate day of inactivity.

This morning four Filipinos were apparently joining them. They appeared in the valley which lay beneath the knoll and strolled towards the outpost. Visible from quite a distance with their loose white shirts and bright blue pants, they advanced without caution as if expecting to be recognized. Lucas, the buck sergeant in command of the squad, had been on the phone earlier in the morning, and now he said quietly, 'Well, here they are. Let's get ready.' He had already named the men who were to go out, and they were strapping on their equipment. In a few minutes, he and the four other men weaved down through the grass of the hill and moved towards the Filipinos in the rice paddy.

'What's up, we got the Gooks today?' Brody, a thin hard-bitten private, asked of Lucas.

'Seems like we do.' Lucas was a big relaxed man who spoke slowly and thought slowly. He was not very intelligent and did not pretend to be, but perhaps for this reason he was not a bad soldier as sergeants go. Events rarely ruffled him. He had small sensitivity to distinguish between the extraordinary and the commonplace, and so he took his orders, acted upon that portion of them he understood, and was never agitated if things turned out different than had been expected.

Private Brody was nervous, he was high-strung, he was often angry. 'Well, what the hell are the Gooks here for?' he asked, pointing to the Filipinos.

'Shoot if I know,' Lucas drawled. He was readjusting a grenade in his belt. 'There was some kind of fuss over the telephone. The Gooks are from Panazagay, some such place. They went to headquarters this morning, and then head-quarters decided to send them here.'

The squad approached the Filipinos. They were small brown men with the lithe bodies of Oriental peasants, and they all smiled in unison at the soldiers.

'Sergeant Lucas, sair?' one of them inquired. By the way he

stood forward from the others it was apparent that he was the only one who spoke English.

'How do,' Lucas said mildly. He was courteous and bored.

The Filipino who spoke English began to talk to Lucas. He spoke at great length in a stammering mixture of what was English and of what he thought was English. The other men in the squad did not bother to listen. They squatted on their heels in the muddy turf of the rice paddy, and looked dispassionately at the Filipinos who squatted in a line, facing them, about ten yards away. From time to time one of the Filipinos would smile, and in response one of the Americans would nod. Off to one side, Lucas stood heavily, his ear inclined to catch a detail here and there in the seemingly endless story.

'Let me get this straight,' he asked quietly. 'The guerrillas ambushed the Japs?'

'No, sair, no don't know. Maybe Jap, maybe guerrilla, big ambush maybe. Lot of shooting. Guerrilla no come back. Now, American soldiers ambush Jap maybe.'

Lucas nodded. It was obvious he knew no more than before, and as he continued to listen, it became equally obvious that he no longer bothered to distinguish the words. When the Filipino had exhausted his account, Lucas yawned.

'All right. What's your name? Miguel?'

'Yes, sair.'

'Okay, Miguel, you lead us. You take us where you want. Only nice and slow, you understand? We're in no hurry, and it's a hot day.'

Miguel said something to the other Filipinos in the Tagalog language, and they answered curtly. They stood up, and began to move across the paddy at a half-trot.

'That's what I meant,' Lucas said to Miguel. 'Tell them to slow up.'

Reluctantly, he conveyed this message to the other three Filipinos, who seemed to obey it just as reluctantly.

'Man, they're always in a hurry,' Lucas drawled aloud.

The other four soldiers fell into line behind their sergeant. The Filipinos moved in a group which was bunched close together, and about thirty yards in front of the Americans, who moved in a leisurely file with some distance between them.

None of the soldiers knew what the patrol was about, and they did not bother to ask. There was only so much variety to a patrol, and it had long been exhausted. There seemed no reason now to inquire. If all went well, they would find out in due time. They did not even bother to watch the direction in which they moved; they had been over these hills and paddies so often that it was almost impossible for them to get lost. They trudged along behind Lucas, their guns slung, their heads drooped forward to examine the footing before them. Not even the thought of an ambush caused them much concern. In such a large area there was a small likelihood that at any given moment enemy troops might blunder into one another. To attempt to be constantly on the alert seemed a little ridiculous. Each followed the man in front of him, daydreamed a little, looked about him a little, and tried not to think too exclusively of the heat or the sores upon his legs or the familiar small distress of his chronic diarrhea.

Only Brody was an exception. Brody worried. Brody was irritable. Brody saw all kinds of possibilities. 'Where are we going?' he panted as he walked behind Lucas.

'Oh, I don't know,' Lucas said. 'We're just following the Gooks.'

Brody trotted for a few steps and caught up to the sergeant. 'Well, why?'

Lucas shrugged. 'I guess they sold the Old Man a bill of goods. He told me to go along with 'em.'

'What did the Gooks say?' Brody persisted.

'Miguel, he said a lot, but I just can't follow that Gook talk. It's something about an ambush, and guerrillas and Japs. It's all a mess and I bet it's a false alarm. You know these Gooks, how excited they get.'

'Me, I know them,' Brody said with ferocity. 'I hate the Gooks.' He tripped in a hole the hoof of a carabao had made and jarred his ankle. 'They're always laughing at us. They're dirty, you see, they're two-faced.' As abruptly as he had spoken, he lapsed into a frustrated silence.

Lucas made no answer. He had pouched a cut of tobacco in his cheek, and he moved with the long lazy pace of a big man, holding his rifle in one hand and allowing it to swing in rhythm to his steps. 'Oh, there're good Gooks and bad Gooks,' Lucas said after a while.

Brody cursed. 'Look at them with their white shirts. They can be seen from ten miles away.' His body quivered with pent emotion.

Lucas reddened. The truth was that he had not paid attention to this detail. 'That don't make much difference,' he muttered.

'It does to me.' Lucas's dismissal of everything he had said fretted Brody. Perspiration ran into his eyes. 'Hey, you,' Brody shrieked at the Filipinos ahead, 'hey, you Gooks, take off those shirts. You want to get us ambushed?'

They looked at him stupidly, they smiled, they tried to understand. Blindly, Brody ran towards them, his canteens, his ration, his bandolier and grenades jouncing with leaden metallic sounds as he trotted. He shoved the first Filipino in his path with force enough to send him almost to the ground. 'Your shirt,' Brody said apoplectically, 'get it off.'

They comprehended at last. They smiled again, they murmured apologies, they stripped their shirts to expose their brown chests and wrapped the white cotton about their waists like a belt.

'That's better,' Brody grunted. He slowed his pace and fell into line behind Lucas who did not look at him. Lucas merely shifted the plug from one side of his mouth to the other.

Brody was in a state which all the men in the squad could recognize. It visited each of them at different times. A man's normal manner might be friendly or distant or casual, but there were periods when he seemed to consist of nothing but rage, when his outraged nerves would snap surly responses to the most insignificant questions, and everything he did expressed a generalized hatred towards the most astonishing people and objects – his best friend or a stone he might kick with his foot. Brody was experiencing such a period.

It started with a letter from his girl friend that told him she was to marry someone else. She had waited for four years, but she was waiting no longer. In a sense the letter hardly bothered him. His girl friend had become as remote to Brody as the moon. But the letter had nonetheless served to remind Brody of how he lived, and that was unbearable. He had seen a great deal of combat, he had gone through all the stages. He had had the excitement of the untested soldier, and the competence of the veteran; he had passed from the notion that he would never be killed to the gloomy and then indifferent acceptance of the idea that he probably would be killed. He had never come to the point where it no longer mattered particularly. Like the other men, his senses diminished, his thoughts slowed, and time was a neutral vacuum in which neutral experience was spent. Life passed in a mild and colorless depression.

The letter destroyed his armor. It reminded him of a world in which people cared enough about themselves to take such actions as getting married. It awakened in him a feeling that it might not be unpleasant to live, and that feeling made much intolerable. It made death vivid to him again, and worse than that, it made him conscious of himself. It did the worst thing which could befall a soldier in combat, it made Brody wonder who he was, and what it would mean if he would die. There was no way to find out, there was no way even to think about it connectedly. The result was that every sleeping nerve in Brody's body had become alive and asked its question. The only answer, considering conditions, was a grass-fire of hatred which smoldered within him, and rasped into flame at anything which crossed his path. On this particular day it was the Filipinos. For the moment Brody considered them as directly responsible for everything which had happened to him.

Slowly, the patrol moved on. The men crossed rice paddies and swamps, they traversed trails through bamboo groves, and climbed hills with tall grass and scattered trees. The heat increased as the sun moved towards its zenith, and gnats, mosquitoes, and flies plagued the exposed surfaces of their skin. After an hour had passed they took a break and then moved on again. It was hot and the faded green fatigues of the soldiers began to turn black with their perspiration. They were thirsty. The sun beat upon their heads.

The hills were now covered with brush. Soon the brush thickened, the ground became softer, more muddy, and the trees grew higher. Their foliage met overhead and dimmed the light of the day. It was still hot, but it was dark now, it was steamy, and the air had the stagnant expectancy of a thunderstorm. The men sweated even more profusely.

The Filipinos came to a small brook which they forded. On the other side the trail split into two forks. Miguel came back to talk to Lucas.

'Sair, is very dangerous from here, Jahpanese, many Jahpanese.'

Lucas nodded. 'Okay, let's watch our step.' He gathered his men about him, and informed them of what Miguel had said. 'Seems to me,' he mumbled softly, 'I was over this trail a couple of weeks ago and nothing was here. But maybe the Gooks know something. Let's keep our eyes open.'

This warning from Lucas changed the character of the patrol. Now, every man was alert. It was often like this. After hours of dull marching all the men in the squad would seem to awaken at once, as if the fear or readiness of one had been communicated to all.

The trail contributed to their caution. It was very narrow, and permitted only one man to pass at a time. Moreover, it took a turn to the left or right every few yards, and each soldier had the unpleasant sensation of watching the man in front disappear around each bend. Sweat dripped from their eyes, fell from their noses, ran into their mouths. They breathed heavily, and with each step they examined the foliage on either side of them, looking for a possible sniper. Each time a man blundered over a root or made some small noise, the others winced in unison. After ten minutes of working along the trail, they were more tired than they had been at any time that day, they were hotter, they were wetter, they were more oppressed.

Lucas whistled to Miguel. 'Stop your men.' Miguel looked as if he wished to continue, but Lucas had sat down already. 'We're taking a break. Pass it down,' he whispered to the man behind him.

Quietly, each man whispered the same message to his neighbor. They all remained standing for a moment, their damp shirts collapsed wetly upon their bodies, their mouths puffing at damp cigarettes whose paper was brown where sweat had reached it. They seated themselves cautiously, each soldier facing alternately an opposite side of the trail. Although they rested their backs against tree trunks, and draped their rifles

over their knees, they were not exactly in repose. Their heads
were turned upward, their eyes studied the foliage before them,
and the muscles in their forearms were tense to grasp their rifles
if it were necessary. Nonetheless they smoked their cigarettes.

Up ahead came a dull thumping sound. Each of the men
started and then relaxed. It was the blade of a machete chopping
into something – a wet branch, a mass of pulpy fruit – they did
not know. A minute later the sounds ceased, and each man was
rewarded with an unexpected comfort. Pieces of ripe pineapple
cut from a pineapple bush by the Filipinos were passed back.
They ate the fruit greedily, and watched for snipers. Their legs
were tired, their eyes hurt from staring into the jungle, their
throats were parched and reacted with delight to the sweet tart
juices, their stomachs accepted the food with lust, and their
arms trembled with the tension of holding a rifle, a piece of
fruit, and a cigarette. There was both the blissful satisfaction of
thirst as each mouthful was gorged from a shaking hand, and
the anxious heavy knowledge that to rest on a trail like this was
dangerous, in the gloom of the jungle each minute seemed more
ominous, and yet the deliciousness of the feast was increased by
the situation.

After some minutes, Lucas sent another message down the
trail. One hoarse whisper generated the next. 'Let's get going.
Let's get going.'

As they moved on, it became evident to Lucas that the
Filipinos were heading towards a particular place. Their tension increased with every step, and they proceeded with more
and more caution. Now, there were halts along the trail of a
minute or more, while one Filipino would work ahead, would
study the trail, and then come back to wave them forward. Half
an hour passed with less ground covered every moment. The
pauses increased the irritation, the fatigue, and the tension. The
men would stand in the narrow trail, foliage tickling the back of
their necks, insects plaguing their motionless bodies. To stand
still became more onerous than to move. They were able to
think of nothing but the heat, the humidity, and the smart of
the sores upon their feet. They could hear sounds more intensely than when they marched. They could sense danger

more acutely than if they were in motion. Altogether they felt more vulnerable and it made them cranky.

Brody fretted the most. 'Tell them to get a move on, Lucas,' he would whisper. Or else he would wipe his chin of its sweat. 'Leave it to the Gooks,' he would moan.

These protests seemed to leave Lucas quite indifferent. He stood placidly at the point, watching the Filipinos dart ahead and then work their way back, nodded solemnly each time they waved for him to come ahead, and then remained still while they reconnoitered the next few hundred feet of trail. 'They're taking us into a trap,' Brody hissed furiously, and Lucas shrugged. 'I don't think so,' he whispered back.

Traveling no more than a few hundred yards every quarter of an hour, the patrol inched forward along the trail. They crossed another brook, and while they waited several of the men quietly filled their canteens and inserted one of the pills they kept to disinfect their drinking water. A little further on, they passed the corpse of a Japanese soldier who was lying near the trail, and they took pains to keep as far away from him as possible, more from their repugnance of the feeding maggots than from the novelty of seeing a dead man.

They were soon to see another. It developed that the objective of the patrol was reached before they had even learned the objective. The trail rose for a few hundred feet, and then dipped into an empty draw. In the middle of the draw, lying behind a Japanese machine gun, lay a dead Filipino. Miguel and the three peasants stood at the top of the draw, and looked sadly upon him. One by one the soldiers reached them, until a group of nine men, five in uniform, and four in blue pants and white shirts wrapped about their middle, collected on one bank of the small ravine and stared into the quiet buzzing sunlight which glinted upon the skin of the dead guerrilla and reflected the tropical yellow-green of the grass in the draw.

'Oh, sair,' Miguel said softly to Lucas, 'he brave mahn. He kill three Jahpanese last month. He come here every night.'

'He came here alone every night?' Brody asked.

Miguel nodded. 'Last night in village we hear shooting. Jahpanese grenade. Luiz no possess Jahpanese grenade. They kill him, we think, last night.'

'What'd he want to set up for in the middle of the draw?' Lucas asked. 'He's a sitting duck there.'

'Oh,' Miguel said, 'Luiz only amateur soldier.'

Lucas looked at him sharply, but Miguel's expression was impassive. Lucas yawned. 'Let's scout around, men, there might still be Japs here.'

The fragment of the squad divided into two men and three men. Lucas and Brody circled the draw from one side, and joined the others on the continuation of the trail. The draw seemed deserted. 'Cover me,' Lucas said, and darted into the open grass.

He approached the dead man cautiously to make certain no wires connected him to a booby trap. After a moment he waved to Brody to join him.

'We might as well take the gun back,' he said. 'That's a nice Jap machine gun.' He looked at it with the professional curiosity of a hobbyist. 'Man, that's a funny old gun,' Lucas said.

Miguel joined them at the bottom of the draw. 'Sair, we go back now?'

'I guess we found what we came for,' Lucas shrugged.

'Sair. Four Filipinos. We carry back body. You come with Filipinos?'

Brody shouldered his way between them. 'It's going to slow us up. Let them do it on their own.'

'Sair, very dangerous without American soldiers.'

Lucas was working the bolt on the Japanese weapon. 'This is a real light machine gun. It's sort of like our BAR,' he announced. Miguel touched him tentatively on the sleeve, and Lucas looked up. 'I guess we can go along with them,' he said to Brody half-apologetically.

Brody felt as if an injustice were being perpetrated. 'They tricked us into coming out here,' he swore. 'All they wanted us for was to pick up one of their lousy men. They could have done this whole patrol themselves.'

'I dunno,' Lucas murmured. 'I mean a man deserves a funeral. We'll escort them, I suppose.' He looked away from Brody, and patted the gun. 'We ought to take this, too.'

'What for?' Brody demanded. 'It's heavy.'

'Oh, just because.' Lucas was thinking with pleasure of stripping the gun when he returned to the outpost. He intended to take it completely apart, and then put it back together again. The thought of this gave him a feeling of anticipation for the first time in months.

Brody was angrier than ever. Everything Lucas did seemed outrageous. Like a man who wishes to strike a woman and frustrates the impulse, Brody now effectively begged the woman to strike him. With passion he picked up the Japanese machine gun. 'You want to take it back?' he asked rhetorically of Lucas. 'Well, I'll carry the bugger.'

'That's right, Brody, you carry it all the way back.' Brody realized he had gone too far. 'And I don't want to hear any griping,' Lucas added.

The patrol started back. It was hotter than ever, it was wetter than ever, it began to rain again. The soldiers plodded forward through a gumbo muck, and the Filipinos staggered behind them, carrying the body of Luiz, the dead guerrilla, lashed to a pole. Now, it was the Americans who wanted to go fast, who wished to quit the contaminated area as quickly as possible, and it was the Filipinos mired in the labor of carrying a dead man on a heavy pole who time and again were forced to stop.

Brody stepped along in a rage. The Japanese machine gun must have weighed at least twenty pounds; added to the load of his own gear, it was a cruel increment. There seemed no way to hold the gun properly. No matter how he slung it, over a shoulder, upon his back, in front of his belly, the gun seemed all knobs, protuberances, points and edges. Either the stock, the muzzle, or the handle of the bolt was always pressing into his ribs, his arms, his shoulder blades. Worst of all the gun had a detestable odor. There was the smell of Japanese fish oil, and the smell of Luiz who had acquired the gun, a smell of Filipino peasant which to Brody meant carabao flop and Philippine dust and Filipino food, an amalgam not unlike stale soya sauce. Worst of all, there was the odor of Luiz's blood, a particularly sweet and intimate smell, fetid and suggesting to his nostrils that it was not completely dry. It was the smell of a man who had died, and it mingled with the fish oil and the soya sauce and the considerable stench of Brody's own body and Brody's own

work-sweated clothes, until he thought he would gag. The
odor was everywhere; it stuck to his lungs and eddied in his
nostrils. As he perspired, his sweat touched the gun, seemed to
dissolve from it newer, more unpleasant odors. Brody
traveled on his anger. It was his luck, he thought incoherently,
to have a man like Lucas for a sergeant; it was his luck to be in a
squad so stupid that the stupidest of Filipinos and the most
cunning could take them in, or more properly, could take them
anywhere, take them on a five-mile hike, for what, for nothing,
to serve as escort so they could bring one of their own men back,
a man stupid enough to go out at night and get himself killed.
Brody began to think it was a plot. It had all been calculated to
make him carry the machine gun. The smell became Luiz to
him, and he cursed the gun as he walked, talking to Luiz and
telling him what a no-good Gook he thought him to be,
spanking the gun away as it thudded upon his ribs and jabbed
his sternum. Trust the Gooks, trust the Gooks, trust the blasted
Gooks, he kept repeating to himself, saying it faster and faster
like a talisman to protect him in his exasperation and
growing exhaustion from bursting into tears of childish
frenzy.

The walk back was exceptionally long. The Filipinos jogged
and panted from their exertion, dropped the pole when the
Americans would rest, and picked it up to run in their Oriental
half-trot each time the Americans would start again. When they
came out of the jungle, the patrol set across the fields towards
the Filipino village, towards Panazagay. The sun broiled them,
the rain wet them, the sun dried them again. Heat drenched
their clothing with body moisture. Brody staggered, the Filipinos staggered, the others trudged, and the sun fried the bowl
of earth over which they traveled. How the gun stank!

Brody would hardly have cared if they had been ambushed by
Japanese. He would have flopped to the ground, and let the
others worry about it. He did not bother to look ahead of him.
He merely wavered along for thirty or forty steps, and then
outraged his lungs by running for ten or fifteen yards to catch up
with the last American. To the Filipinos behind him, he paid no
attention. He was thinking of all kinds of things. Through the
stupor of the march, he could not rid himself of the idea that he

was carrying a dead man in his arms. A man who was completely dead. He had seen dead men whole and dead men in fractions and mutilations, but this was the first dead man who was completely dead to Brody, and it filled him with fright. He was not too far from delirium. It seemed almost possible that Luiz was carrying him, and he was the one who had died. What did it mean? He had seen so much death that death was the one thing absolutely without meaning to him. Except for now. It filled his pores. To the hot sweat of the sun he added the cold sweat of his thoughts. Brody's tortured nerves could have been relieved only by a scream.

'Pigs, the Gooks are pigs,' he muttered aloud. 'They live like pigs.' And the gun hugged him, a dancing skeleton, jiggling its death's head in his face.

The patrol came at last to Panazagay, a village of bamboo houses upon stilts with a muddy lane between the houses, and no street at all, no stores at all. The Filipino carriers brought the body of Luiz to his home. It was a small bamboo house and stood in front of the village pump. The soldiers sprawled by the pump, bathed their heads and bodies with water, and lay around heavily, too fatigued to eat.

From the house came screams. A woman's scream, then a child's wail, then the cries of several women and children. People began to emerge from all the houses of the village, they converged upon the houses in front of the village pump, they climbed the bamboo ladder which led into the bamboo house. A concert of grief spread in volume from moment to moment. The soldiers lay on the ground and hardly heard these cries.

They were far too weary. The sounds of bereavement seemed as remote as Oriental music with its unfamiliar scale. Women wept, children wept, grief washed from the bamboo house with the regularity and monotony of surf. After a while the soldiers were rested enough to eat, and they plugged languidly at their hard cheese, their cardboard biscuits, and sipped indifferently at their antiseptic water.

When they had finished and their siesta was run, they were fresh enough to look with some curiosity at the tear-stained faces of the male and female peasants who left the bamboo house. Lucas decided it was time to return. The five men of the squad hooked up their cartridge belts, slung their bandoliers, grasped their rifles, and prepared to move out. Miguel intercepted them.

In his broken speech of English and its facsimile, he thanked the members of the patrol in the name of Luiz's widow, he expressed to them her gratitude for returning her husband, and conveyed her apologies for not inviting them to eat. Lucas accepted this like a courtier, and told Miguel to tell her that the American soldiers were happy to have been of aid. The two men shook hands and Lucas slapped the stock of his rifle to cover his embarrassment.

'Say, Miguel,' he said.

'Sair?'

'What made this fellow Luiz' – he pronounced it *Louise* – 'go out like that?'

'Do not know, sair, very brave mahn. His son killed by Jahpanese. Luiz go out every night for month.'

Lucas whistled. 'Well, what do you know.'

'Yes, sair.'

'Yeah, I guess he was all right,' Lucas said. He waved a hand at Miguel, and strolled his men out of the village.

There was a three-mile walk back to the outpost. It ran along the ridges of bare grass-covered hills, and the men climbed up, and then down, and then around the flank of endless wells of earth. Brody walked with his head down, sucking air, his chest heaving helplessly. It was one of the longest three miles he had ever walked and he had walked some which were long indeed. When they reached the outpost, he flung himself on the ground beside the machine gun he had carried, and lay there panting. The two men who had been on guard through the day came over to examine the gun, but Brody snarled at them like an animal.

'What do you think, you own it?' one complained.

'I carried that gun, see? I get to look at it first.'

While the other members of the squad were washing themselves in water which they poured from five-gallon jerricans into their helmets, or were writing letters, or were sleeping in their holes, Brody stared at the gun. He was preparing to clean it when Lucas came over to claim the prize. Brody was too tired to argue. Passively, he relinquished the gun to Lucas, and dropped into his hole to rest.

Brody fell asleep, was awakened for the evening meal which was brought up in a jeep. It consisted of hot stew in an insulated pot and heated coffee. He munched it down and fell asleep again, slumbering like a drunk drugged with his alcohol. Even when he was awakened for guard in the middle of the night, he was still tired. He sat in the machine-gun emplacement, and stared into the valley below. Illuminated by a full moon, the grass rustled in swells of silver light and shadow. There was a period of fifteen minutes when he sat with his hand on the bolt of the machine gun, convinced that he could see two men standing close to one another in the field. It turned out to be a horse which had somehow wandered there, and though Brody did not even know if the guerrilla Luiz had possessed a horse, he was nonetheless certain that the horse belonged to the dead Filipino.

Luiz had waited alone in a moonlit draw, waiting for Japanese to come so he could ambush them. Luiz had carried the machine gun in darkness down the trail where they had stopped to eat the pineapple, and he had sat alone to wait on a silver night with nothing for company but the slithering of animals and the torment of insects. It seemed impossible; it seemed . . . enormous. The force of this entered Brody's recognition like an iron spike.

For the first time Brody really heard the weeping of the Filipino women. They had all been crying for the dead Gook. In the security of his machine-gun emplacement, Brody shivered. It made him terribly uneasy. If he were killed at this moment, the men in the squad would stand around and look at him. Eventually the news would reach the few men he knew in other squads of other platoons. They would say, 'Tough, wasn't it, about Brody?' or perhaps they would say no more than, 'Brody, was he the guy who . . .?' Who did what? Brody had the uncomfortable sensation of wondering what in his life had he ever done?

He felt a million miles from anyone else on the face of the earth. He had never done a thing in his life which he could consider the least bit exceptional, he could not think of anything to do. He only felt that somehow before he died he must do something. He must be remembered.

He thought of his parents. They would cry for him, but he no longer knew what they were like. He no longer believed in them. He was isolated on a little hill beneath a vast tropic night, and no one nor nothing cared for him. The family of Luiz had wept, they had wept over a dead Gook. But who would weep for Brody?

It was unfair. He was stripped of the casual monotony, the dull work, and the saving depression which had wrapped him like a bandage. He was naked, and it was one of the most terrifying experiences of his life. When his hour of guard was over, Brody lay on his back and shuddered with dread. The sky above his head was infinite and black – like death it could absorb him.

Yet somehow, in the morning, the crisis was past. His nerves had gone to sleep. Brody took up again his anonymous place in the squad. He was just another of the seven men, one who talked no more and talked no less, who wrote his letters, and played his cards, and went out laconically for the daily patrols. It was soon the turn of another to sulk, to be moody, and to spit furious answers to well-intentioned questions.

Brody, however, did not forget completely. Out of all the patrols he had made, and out of all the patrols he was to make in the months ahead, he always remembered the patrol which had found Luiz. When the campaign ended, and the regiment went into garrison to train for the coming invasion of Japan, Brody found himself thinking of the bamboo house and the village water pump at the most extraordinary times. He would remember it when he was drunk, or in the midst of a training class, and once even at the climax of a poker game when he had won a big hand. The night the war ended, he remembered the patrol in the most peculiar way of all.

He and Lucas had gone out to get drunk. They had drifted through the small Filipino city where the regiment had been garrisoned, and they had listened to the celebration of small-arms fire being shot off into the sky. They had wandered and wandered, drunk yet numb, unable to talk to one another. They each felt frozen.

At the end of town they came to a little street which had been razed in the course of the battle for the city. All the wooden and concrete homes had been destroyed, and in their place, drawn from the junkyard of war's familiar passage, were tiny shacks built from cartons and packing crates and rusted corrugated roofing. Filipinos were living in the cabins, and from several the light of a candle guttered in its holder, throwing a warm glow upon the burlap curtains which hung limply in the cool of the August evening. The shacks reminded Brody of a street of shanties at the edge of the American town where he lived, and he recalled a time when he had walked there with a girl on a warm night of summer. He kicked aside a bit of rubble, and said, 'Remember the Gook with the Jap machine gun?'

'Yeah,' said Lucas as if both of them had known him well, 'he was a funny guy.'

'Yeah.'

The thaw had come. 'Remember Newman, and how he got it at Aitape?' Lucas asked.

'Yeah, and Benton.'

'That's right, Benton,' Lucas said.

They walked, they reminisced. To Brody the two years and a fraction of harsh empty time he had spent on islands of the Pacific began to fill with the accumulation of small detail which made memory supportable. He thought it was the liquor, but he was beginning to feel very sad. He had a picture of all the men who had been killed on all the beaches, under all the coconut trees, in all the swamps and jungles and paddies of all the alien land they had traversed, and he could have wept for them if Lucas were not there. He wished that they could be present to smell the Philippine twilight on the day the war ended.

They talked, and night deepened over the rubble of a Philippine city, and they went at last to join the line of soldiers waiting to see a movie under the big tent in the tent city of the regiment. No one could sit still, and long before the movie was over, Brody and Lucas went out into the night and walked away. They bought a bottle from a Filipino dealer, and Brody drank more liquor, Brody staggered back to his cot.

As he fell asleep on the night of victory, he discovered himself weeping for Luiz, weeping as hard as the old women in the bamboo house. He wept for Luiz with all his heart because now it was no longer unbearably necessary that he find someone to weep for him.

*1951*

## PART FIVE

# Dark to Dawn, Dawn to Dark

# Great in the Hay

Once there were two producers named Al and Bert. They were both short, they were both bald, they were both married, and they both produced pictures. They even had offices next to one another. Everything about them was so similar that they might have been considered twins if it were not for a difference so great that one never thought of them as being the least alike.

The difference was that the one named Al had the reputation of being great in the hay. In every other respect he was much the same as Bert, whose only reputation for want of something better was that he made a great deal of money.

This irritated Bert. He would call people in, he would talk to them, he would say: 'I've known Al for twenty years. We got married within three months of each other, we make the same salary, we've had approximately the same number of big box-office grossers and box-office duds, we're the same height, we're almost the same weight, our looks are similar, and yet Al has the reputation of being great in the hay. Why should he have that reputation?'

It came to bother Bert, it came to bother him colossally. He would ask everyone, and no one would tell him the answer. He came at last to approach it as a business problem. He called in a private detective.

To the detective, he said, 'I want you to find out the reason. I don't care how low-down and dirty. The man has a secret, there's a reason why Al is an expert and I'm an unknown. I want you to find that reason.'

The detective went out, he scouted around, he compiled a list of names, he ended with a duplicate of the little black book which Al was keeping. To each of the addresses listed went the detective. As he obtained his answers he filed his reports, and when he was done he returned to Bert.

'Your report is wasted money,' Bert cried. 'You've taught me nothing. You've merely confused me. Let me read to you what they say. It's disgusting.'

Bert read from the report. He read what Claudia Jane had to say, and Dianthe, and Emeline, and Fay, and Georgia, and Hortense, and all the others.

'He's the best lover I've ever used,' said Claudia Jane, 'because he is floppy and lets me throw him around.'

'He is magnificent,' murmured Dianthe, 'he melts my ice. He rides over me, disdains me, leaves me convinced I am a woman.'

'He is cute,' wrote Emeline, 'and all my own.'

'A master at sexpertease,' stated Hortense, 'because I tell you, buster, I'm bored with less.'

'Pure,' dictated Fay, 'and not addicted to the nasty. Love for him is a communion of purity and simplicity which intensifies my hard-won religious conversion.'

'He likes to spend money,' lisped Georgia, 'and I think that's everything, don't you?'

Bert was enraged. 'You call this a report?' he shouted at the detective. 'It is nothing but a mish-mosh.' He threw the sheets into the air. 'You go find his secret.'

The detective pounded a weary scented beat. His flat shoes trod through boudoirs while he attempted to elicit a gimmick from the mish-mosh. At last the case was closed. There came a morning when to everyone's surprise, Al left a note which read *Every year I have been getting more and more depressed*, and blew out his brains.

Bert could never understand it. When he discharged the detective, he complained with a sigh, 'I still don't understand why Al was so great. It's aggravating. I've lived a full life, and I can tell you. All women are the same in the dark. I ought to know.'

So the moral of this story may well be: People who live in the dark live longest of all.

*1950*

# The Last Night: A Story

NOTE TO THE READER: *Obviously a movie must be based on a novel, a story, a play, or an original idea. I suppose it could even derive from a poem. 'Let's do* The Wasteland,' *said a character of mine named Collie Munshin. The novel may be as much as a thousand pages long, the play a hundred, the story ten, the original idea might be stated in a paragraph. Yet each in its turn must be converted into an art form (a low art form) called a treatment. The treatment usually runs anywhere from twenty to a hundred pages in length. It is a bed of Procrustes. Long stories have their limbs lopped off. Too brief tales are stretched. The idea is to present for the attention of a producer, a director, or a script reader, in readable but modest form, the line of story, the gallery of characters, the pith and gist of your tale.*

*But one's duty is to do this without much attempt at style and no attempt at high style. The language must be functional, even cliché, and since one's writing prepares the ground for a movie script, too much introspection in the characters is not encouraged. 'Joey was thinking for the first time that Alice was maybe in love with him' is barely acceptable. An actor on contract could probably manage to register that emotion in a closeup. Whereas,*

> *. . . the little phrase, as soon as it struck his ear, had the power to liberate in him the room that was needed to contain it; the proportions of Swann's soul were altered; a margin was left for a form of enjoyment which corresponded no more than his love for Odette to any external object, and yet was not, like his enjoyment of that love, purely individual, but assumed for him an objective reality superior to that of other concrete things,*

*would bake the clay of a producer's face a little closer to stone. A producer is interested in the meat and bone of a story. His question as he reads a treatment is whether he should go on to assign a writer to do a screenplay of this story with specific dialogue and most specific situations added, or whether he should ask for another treatment with new characters and plot, or whether indeed he should write off the loss and quit right now. So a treatment bears the same relation to a finished screenplay as the model for a wind tunnel does to the airplane. Since a treatment is functional, any excellence must be unobtrusive. In fact, a good director (George Stevens) once told me that good writing in a treatment was a form of cheating because it introduced emotional effects through language which he might not as a director be able to repeat on film.*

*So, thus modestly, I present here a treatment of a movie. It is based on an original idea. It is a short treatment. Only a few of the scenes are indicated. As an example of the art of the treatment, it is not characteristic, for it is written in somewhat formal prose, but it may have the virtue of suggesting a motion picture to your imagination.*

*Best wishes. See you in the morning after this last night. – N.M.*

We're going to describe a movie which will take place twenty years from now, forty years from now, or is it one hundred years from now? One cannot locate the date to a certainty. The world has gone on just about the way we all expected it would go on. It has had large and dramatic confrontations by heads of state, cold wars galore, economic crises resolved and unresolved, good investment, bad investment, decent management and a witch's bag full of other complexities much too numerous ever to bring into a movie. The result has been a catastrophe which all of us have dreaded, all of us expected, and none of us has been able to forestall. The world in twenty or forty years – let us say it is thirty-six – has come to the point where without an atomic war, without even a hard or furious shooting war, it has given birth nonetheless to a fearful condition. The world has succeeded in poisoning itself. It is no longer fit to inhabit. The prevalent condition is fallout radiation, anomalous crops, monstrous babies who grow eyes in their navels and die screaming with hatred at the age of six weeks, plastics which emit cancerous fumes, buildings which collapse like camphor flakes, weather which is excruciatingly psychological because it is always too hot or too cold. Governments fall with the regularity of pendulums. The earth is doomed. The number of atom bombs detonated by the Americans, Russians, English,

French, the Algerians, Africans, the Israelis and the Chinese, not to mention the Turks, Hindus and Yugoslavians, have so poisoned existence that even the apples on the trees turn malignant in the stomach. Life is being burned out by a bleak fire within, a plague upon the secrets of our existence which stultifies the air. People who govern the nations have come to a modest and simple conclusion. The mistakes of the past have condemned the future. There is no time left to discuss mankind's guilt. No one is innocent of the charge that all have blighted the rose. In fact, the last President to be elected in the United States has come to office precisely by making this the center of his plank: that no one is innocent. The political reactions have been exceptional. Earlier in the century the most fundamental political notion was that guilt could be laid always at the door of one nation and one nation only. Now a man had been elected to one of the two most powerful offices in the world on the premise that the profound illness of mankind was the fault of all, and this victory had prepared the world for cooperative action.

Shortly after the election of this last of the American Presidents, the cold war was finally ended. Russia and America were ready to collaborate, as were Algeria and France, China, England, Western Europe, India and Africa. The fact had finally been faced. Man had succeeded in so polluting the atmosphere that he was doomed to expire himself. Not one in fifty of the most responsible government scientists would now admit that there were more than twenty years left to life. It was calculated that three-quarters of the living population would be gone in five years from the various diseases of fallout. It was further calculated that of the one-quarter remaining women and men, another three-quarters would be dead in the two following years. What a perspective – three-quarters of the people dead in five years, another three-quarters lost in two, one in sixteen left after seven years to watch the slow extinction of the rest. In the face of this fact, led by a President who was exceptional, who was not only the last but perhaps the greatest of America's leaders, the people of the world had come together to stare into the grim alternatives of their fate. All men and women who continued to live on earth would expire. Five hundred thousand at least could survive if they were moved to Mars, perhaps even as many as one million people could be saved, together with various animals, vegetables, minerals and transportable plants. For the rocketeers had made fine advances. Their arts and sciences had developed enormously. They had managed to establish a company of astronauts on Mars. Nearly one thousand had perished earlier on the Moon, but on Mars over a hundred had managed to live; they had succeeded in building a camp out of native vegetation found on the surface. Dwellings had been fabricated from it and, in triumph, a vehicle constructed entirely from materials found on Mars had been sent back to earth, where men and women received it with extravagant hope.

No space here, or for that matter in the movie, to talk of the endless and difficult negotiations which had gone on. The movie could begin perhaps with the ratification of the most astounding piece of legislation ever to be passed in any country. In this case the piece of legislation had been passed by every nation in the world. It was a covenant which declared that every citizen in each nation was going to devote himself to sending a fleet of rocket ships to Mars. This effort would be herculean. It would demand that the heart of each nation's economy be turned over completely to building and equipping ships, selecting the people, training them, and having the moral fortitude to bid them goodbye. In a sense, this universal operation would be equivalent to the evacuation of Dunkirk but with one exception: three-quarters of the British Expeditionary Force was removed safely from the beach. In this case, the world could hope to send up to Mars no more than one million of its people, conceivably less.

It was calculated that the operation must be accomplished in eighteen months – the spread of plague dictated this haste, for half of the remaining members of mankind might be dead in this time and it was felt that to wait too long would be tantamount to populating the ships with human beings too sick, too weak, too plague-ridden to meet the rigors of life on Mars.

It was indeed a heroic piece of legislation, for the people on earth had had the vision to see that all of them were doomed, and so the majority had consented to accept a minority from within themselves to go out further across space and continue the species. Of course, those who were left would make some further effort to build new rocket ships and follow the wave of the first million pioneers, but the chances of this were unlikely. Not only would the resources of the world be used at an unprecedented rate to build a fleet of ten thousand rocket ships capable of carrying one hundred persons each out so far as Mars, but, in fact, as everyone knew, the earth would be stripped of its most exceptional people, its most brilliant technicians, artists, scientists, athletes and executives, plus their families. Those who were left could hardly hope to form a nucleus or a new cadre brilliant enough to repeat the effort. Besides, it was calculated that the ravages of the plague would already be extreme by the time the fleet departed. The heroism of this legislation resided therefore in the fact that man was capable of regarding his fate and determining to do something exceptional about it.

Now the President of the United States, as indicated earlier, was an unusual man. It was a situation right for a dictator, but he was perhaps not only the most brilliant but the most democratic of American presidents. And one of the reasons the separate nations of the world had been able to agree on this legislation, and the Americans in particular had voted for it, was that the President had succeeded in engaging the imagination of the world's citizens with his project, much as Churchill had brought an incandescence to the morale of the English by the famous speech where he told them he could offer them nothing but blood, sweat, toil and tears. So this President had spared no detail in bringing the citizens of America face to face with the doom of their condition. There were still one hundred million people alive in America. Of that number, one hundred thousand would voyage to Mars. One person in a thousand then could hope to go. Yet there were no riots in the streets. The reason was curious but simple. The President had promised to stay behind and make every effort to train and rally new technicians for the construction of a second fleet. This decision to remain behind had come from many motives: he had recognized the political impossibility of leaving himself – there was moreover sufficient selflessness in the man to make such a

course tasteless to him – and, what was also to the point, his
wife, whom he loved, was now incurably sick. It had been
agreed that the first of the criteria for selection to the fleet was
good physical condition, or at least some reasonable suggestion
of health, since everyone on earth was now ill in varying degree.

In the first six months after the worldwide ratification of what
had already become known as the Legislation For A Fleet, an
atmosphere of cooperation, indeed almost of Christian sanctity
and good will, came over the earth. Never before in the memory
of anyone living had so many people seemed in so good a mood.
There was physical suffering everywhere – as has been mentioned, nearly everyone was ill, usually of distressing internal
diseases – but the pain now possessed a certain logic, for at least
one-half the working force of the world was engaged directly or
indirectly in the construction of the Fleet or the preparations
surrounding it. Those who were to travel to Mars had a
profound sense of mission, of duty and humility. Those who
knew they would be left behind felt for the first time in years a
sensation of moral weightlessness which was recognized finally
as the absence of guilt. Man was at peace with himself. He could
even feel hope, because it was, after all, not known to a certainty
that those who were left behind must inevitably perish. Some
still believed in the possibility of new medical discoveries which
could save them. Others devoted themselves to their President's vow that the construction of the second fleet would begin
upon the departure of the first. And, with it all, there was in
nearly everyone a sense of personal abnegation, of cooperation,
of identification with the community.

It was part of the President's political wisdom that the people
who were chosen for the American Fleet had also been selected
geographically. Every town of ten thousand inhabitants had ten
heroes to make the trip. Not a county of five thousand people
scattered over ten thousand square miles of ranches was without
its five men, women, and children, all ready. And, of course, for
each person chosen there were another ten ready to back them
up in case the first man turned ill, or the second, or the third.
Behind these ten were one hundred, directly involved in the
development, training and morale of each voyager and his ten
substitutes. So participation in the flight reached into all the

corners of the country, and rare was the family which had nothing to do with it. Historians, writing wistfully about the end of history, had come to the conclusion that man was never so close to finding his soul as in this period when it was generally agreed he was soon to lose his body.

Now, calculate what a blow it was to morality, to courage, and the heart of mankind when it was discovered that life on Mars was not supportable, that the company of a hundred who had been camping on its surface had begun to die, and that their disease was similar to the plague which had begun to visit everyone on earth, but was more virulent in its symptoms and more rapid in its results. The scientific news was overwhelming. Fallout and radiation had poisoned not only the earth but the entire solar system. There was no escape for man to any of the planets. The first solar voyagers to have journeyed so far away as Jupiter had sent back the same tragic news. Belts of radiation incalculably fierce in their intensity now surrounded all the planets.

The President was, of course, the first to receive this news and, in coordination with agreements already arrived at, communicated it to the Premier of the Soviet Union. The two men were already firm friends. They had succeeded, two and a half years before, in forming an alliance to end the Cold War, and by thus acting in concert had encouraged the world to pass the Legislation For A Fleet. Now the Premier informed the President that he had heard the bad news himself: ten of the one hundred men on Mars were, after all, Russians. The two leaders met immediately in Paris for a conference which was brief and critical in its effect. The President was for declaring the news immediately. He had an intimation that to conceal such an apocalyptic fact might invite an unnameable disaster. The Premier of Russia begged him to wait a week at least before announcing this fact. His most cogent argument was that the scientists were entitled to a week to explore the remote possibility of some other solution.

'What other could there possibly be?' asked the President.

'How can I know?' answered the Premier. 'Perhaps we shall find a way to drive a tunnel into the center of the earth in order to burn all impurities out of ourselves.'

The President was adamant. The tragic condition of the world today was precisely the product, he declared, of ten thousand little abuses of power, ten thousand moments in history when the leaders had decided that the news they held was too unpleasant or too paralyzing for the masses to bear. A new era in history, a heroic if tragic era, had begun precisely because the political leaders of the world now invited the citizens into their confidence. The President and the Premier were at an impasse. The only possible compromise was to wait another twenty-four hours and invite the leaders of Europe, Asia, South America and Africa to an overnight conference which would determine the fate of the news.

The second conference affected the history of everything which was to follow, because all the nations were determined to keep the new and disastrous news a secret. The President's most trusted technical adviser, Anderson Stevens, argued that the general despair would be too great and would paralyze the best efforts of his own men to find another solution. The President and Stevens were old friends. They had come to power together. It was Stevens who had been responsible for some of the most critical scientific discoveries and advances in the rocketry of the last ten years. The Legislation For A Fleet had come, to a great extent, out of his work. He was known as the President's greatest single friend, his most trusted adviser. If he now disagreed with the President at this international conference, the President was obliged to listen to him. Anderson Stevens argued that while the solar system was now poisoned and uninhabitable, it might still be possible to travel to some other part of our galaxy and transfer human life to a more hospitable star. For several days, scientists discussed the possibilities. It was admitted that no fuel or system of booster propulsion was sufficiently powerful to take a rocket ship beyond the solar system. Not even by connecting to booster rockets already in orbit. But then it was also argued that no supreme attempt had yet been made and if the best scientific minds on earth applied themselves to this problem the intellectual results were unforseeable. In the meantime, absolute silence was to be observed. The program to construct the Martian Fleet was to continue as if nothing had happened. The

President acceded to this majority decision of the other leaders, but informed them that he would hold the silence for no more than another week.

By the end of the week, Anderson Stevens returned with an exceptional suggestion: a tunnel ten miles long was to be constructed in all haste in Siberia or the American desert. Pitched at an angle, so that its entrance was on the surface and its base a mile below the earth, the tunnel would act like the muzzle of a rifle and fire the rocket as if it were a shell. Calculated properly, taking advantage of the earth's rotation about its own axis and the greater speed of its rotation about the sun, it was estimated that the rocket ship might then possess sufficient escape velocity to quit the gravitational pull of the sun and so move out to the stars. Since some of the rocket ships were already close to completion and could be adapted quickly to the new scheme, the decision was taken to fire a trial shot in three months, with a picked crew of international experts. If the ship succeeded in escaping the pull of the sun, its crew could then explore out to the nearest stars and send back the essential information necessary for the others who would follow.

Again the question of secrecy was debated. Now Stevens argued that it would be equally irresponsible to give people hope if none would later exist. So, suffering his deepest misgivings, the President consented to a period of silence for three months while the tunnel was completed. In this period, the character of his administration began to change. Hundreds and then thousands of men were keeping two great secrets: the impossibility of life on Mars, and the construction of the giant cannon which would fire an exploratory ship to the stars. So an atmosphere of secrecy and evasion began to circle about the capital, and the mood of the nation was affected. There were rumors everywhere; few of them were accurate. People whispered that the Russians were no longer in cooperation with us, but engaged in a contest to see who could get first to Mars. It was said that the climate of Mars had driven the colonists mad, that the spaceships being built would not hold together because the parts were weakened by atomic radiation. It was then rumored – for the existence of the tunnel could not be hidden altogether – that the government was planning to construct an entire state beneath the surface of the earth, in which people could live free of radiation and fallout. For the first time in three or four years, the rates of the sociological diseases – crime, delinquency, divorce and addiction – began again to increase.

The day for the secret test arrived. The rocket was fired. It left the earth's atmosphere at a rate greater than any projectile had yet traveled, a rate so great that the first fear of the scientists was substantiated. The metal out of which the rocket was made, the finest, most heat-resistant alloy yet devised by metallurgists, was still insufficient to withstand the heat of its velocity. As it rose through the air, with the dignitaries of fifty countries gathered to watch its departure, it burst out of the earth, its metal skin glowing with the incandescence of a welding torch, traced a path of incredible velocity across the night sky, so fast that it looked like a bolt of lightning reversed, leaping lividly from the earth into the melancholy night, and burned itself out thirty miles up in the air, burned itself out as completely as a dead meteor. No metal existed which could withstand the heat of the excessive friction created by the extreme velocity necessary to blast a ship through the atmosphere and out beyond the gravitational attractions of the sun and its planets. On the other hand, a rocket ship which rose slowly through the earth's atmosphere and so did not overheat could not then generate enough power to overcome the pull of the sun. It seemed now conclusive that man was trapped within his solar system.

The President declared that the people must finally be informed, and in an historic address he did so inform them of the futility of going to Mars and of the impossibility of escape in any other way. There was nothing left for man, he declared, but to prepare himself for his end, to recognize that his soul might have a life beyond his death and so might communicate the best of himself to the stars. There was thus the opportunity to die well, in dignity, with grace, and the hope that the spirit might prove more miraculous and mighty than the wonders man had extracted from matter. It was a great speech. Commentators declared it was perhaps the greatest speech ever delivered by a political leader. It suffered from one irrevocable flaw: it had been delivered three months too late. The ultimate reaction was cynical. 'If all that is left to us is our spirit,' commented a German newspaper, 'why then did the President deny us three useful months in which to begin to develop it?'

Like the leaden-green airless evening before an electrical storm, an atmosphere of depression, bitterness, wildness, violence and madness rose from the echoes of this speech. Productivity began to founder. People refused to work. Teachers taught in classrooms which were empty and left the schools themselves. Windows began to be broken everywhere, a most minor activity, but it took on accelerated proportions, as if many found a huge satisfaction in throwing rocks through windows much as though they would proclaim that this was what the city would look like when they were gone. Funerals began to take on a bizarre attraction. Since ten to twenty times as many people were dying each day as had died even five years before, funeral processions took up much of the traffic, and many of the people who were idle enjoyed marching through the streets in front of and behind the limousines. The effect was sometimes medieval, for impromptu carnivals began to set themselves up on the road to the cemetery. There were speeches in Congress to impeach the President and, as might conventionally be expected, some of the particular advisers who had counseled him to keep silence were now most forward in their condemnation of his act.

The President himself seemed to be going through an exceptional experience. That speech in which he had suggested to mankind that its best hope was to cultivate its spirit before it died seemed to have had the most profound effect upon him. His appearance had begun to alter: his hair was subtly longer, his face more gaunt, his eyes feverish. He had always been unorthodox as a President, but now his clothing was often rumpled and he would appear unexpectedly to address meetings or to say a few words on television. His resemblance to Lincoln, which had in the beginning been slight, now became more pronounced. The wits were quick to suggest that he spent hours each day with a makeup expert. In the midst of this, the President's wife died, and in great pain. They had been close for twenty years. Over the last month, he had encouraged her not to take any drugs to dull the pain. The pain was meaningful, he informed her. The choice might be one of suffering now in the present or later in eternity. In anguish she expired. On her deathbed she seared him with a cruel confession. It was that no matter how she had loved him for twenty years, she had always felt there was a part of him never to be trusted, a part which was implacable, inhuman and ruthless. 'You would destroy the world for a principle,' she told him as she died. 'There is something diabolical about you.'

On the return from her funeral, people came out to stand silently in tribute. It was the first spontaneous sign of respect paid to him in some months, and riding alone in the rear of an open limousine, he wept. Yet, before the ride was over, someone in the crowd threw a stone through the windshield. In his mind, as he rode, was the face of his wife, saying to him some months before, 'I tell you, people cannot bear suffering. I know that I cannot. You will force me to destroy a part of your heart if you do not let me have the drugs.'

That night the chief of America's Intelligence Service came to see the President. The Russians were engaged in a curious act. They were building a tunnel in Siberia, a tunnel even larger than the American one, and at an impossible angle; it went almost directly into the earth and then took a jog at right angles to itself. The President put through a call to Moscow to speak to the Premier. The Premier told the President that he had already made preparations to see him. There was a matter of the most extreme importance to be discussed: the Russians had found a way to get a rocket ship out of the solar system.

So, the two men met in London in a secret conference. Alone in a room, the Premier explained the new project and his peculiar position. Slowly, insidiously, he had been losing control in his country, just as the President had become progressively more powerless in America. Against the Premier's wishes, some atomic and rocket scientists had come together on a fearsome scheme which the Army was now supporting. It had been calculated that if an ordinary rocket ship, of the sort which belonged to the Martian Fleet, were fired out from the earth, it would be possible to blast it into the furthest reaches of our own galaxy, provided – and this was most important – a planet were exploded at the proper moment. It would be like the impetus a breaking wave could give to a surfboard rider. With proper timing the force released by blowing up the planet would more than counteract the gravitational pull of the sun. Moreover, the rocket ship could be a great distance away from the planet at the moment it was exploded, and so the metal of its skin would not have to undergo any excessive heat.

'But which planet could we use?' asked the President.

The two men looked at one another. The communication passed silently from one's mind to the other. It was obvious. With the techniques available to them there was only one planet: the earth.

That was what the Russian tunnel was for. A tunnel going deep into the earth, loaded with fissionable material, and exploded by a radio wave sent out from a rocket ship already one million miles away. The detonation of the earth would hurl the rocket ship like a pebble across a chasm of space.

'Well,' says the President, after a long pause, 'it may be possible for the Fleet to take a trip after all.'

'No,' the Premier assured him, 'not the Fleet.' For the earth would be detonated by an atomic chain reaction which would spew radioactive material across one hundred million miles of the heavens. The alloy vuranel was the only alloy which could protect a rocket ship against the electronic hurricane which would follow the explosion. There was on earth enough vuranel to create a satisfactory shield for only one ship. 'Not a million men, women, and children, but a hundred, a hundred people and a few animals will take the trip to a star.'

'Who will go?' asks the President.

'Some of your people,' answers the Premier, 'some of mine. You and me.'

'I won't go,' says the President.

'Of course you will,' says the Premier. 'Because if you don't go, I don't go, and we've been through too much already. You see, my dear friend, you're the only equal I have on earth. It would be much too depressing to move through those idiotic stars without you.'

But the President is overcome by the proportions of the adventure. 'You mean we will blow up the entire world in order that a hundred people have some small chance – one chance in five, one chance in ten, one chance in a hundred, or less – to reach some star and live upon it. The odds are too brutal. The cost is incalculable.'

'We lose nothing but a few years,' says the Premier. 'We'll all be dead anyway.'

'No,' says the President, 'it's not the same. We don't know what we destroy. It may be that after life ceases on the earth, life will generate itself again, if only we leave the earth alone. To destroy it is monstrous. We may destroy the spirit of something far larger than ourselves.'

The Premier taps him on the shoulder. 'Look, my friend, do you believe that God is found in a cockroach? I don't. God is found inside you, and inside me. When all of us are gone, God is also gone.'

'I don't know if I believe that,' answers the President.

Well, the Premier tells him, religious discussion has always fascinated him, but politics are more pressing. The question is whether they are at liberty to discuss this matter on its moral merits alone. The tunnel in Siberia had been built without his permission. It might interest the President to know that a tunnel equally secret is being constructed near the site of the old Arizona tunnel. There were Russian technicians working on that, just as American technicians had been working in Siberia. The sad political fact is that the technicians had acquired enormous political force, and if it were a question of a show-down tomorrow, it is quite likely they could seize power in the Soviet Union and in America as well.

'You, sir,' says the Premier, 'have been searching your soul for the last year in order to discover reasons for still governing. I have been studying Machiavelli because I have found, to my amusement, that when all else is gone, when life is gone, when the promise of future life is gone, and the meaning of power, then what remains for one is the game. I want the game to go on. I do not want to lose power in my country. I do not want you to lose it in yours. I want, if necessary, to take the game clear up into the stars. You deserve to be on that rocket ship, and I deserve to be on it. It is possible we have given as much as anyone alive to brooding over the problems of mankind in these last few years. It is your right and my right to look for a continuation of the species. Perhaps it is even our duty.'

'No,' says the President. 'They're holding a gun to our heads. One cannot speak of the pleasures of the game or of honor or of duty when there is no choice.'

He will not consent to destroying the earth unless the people of earth choose that course, with a full knowledge of the consequences. What is he going to do, asks the Premier. He is going to tell the world, says the President. There must be a general worldwide election to determine the decision.

'Your own people will arrest you first,' says the Premier. He then discloses that the concept of exploding the earth to boost the power of the rocket had been Anderson Stevens' idea.

The President picks up the phone and makes a call to his press chief. He tells him to prepare the television networks for an address he will deliver that night. The press chief asks him the subject. The President tells him he will discuss it upon his return. The press chief says that the network cannot be cleared unless the President informs him now of the subject. It will be a religious address, says the President.

'The networks may not give us the time,' says the press chief. 'Frankly, sir, they are not certain which audiences share your spiritual fire.'

The President hangs up. 'You are right,' he tells the Premier. 'They will not let me make the speech. I have to make it here in London. Will you stand beside me?'

'No, my friend,' says the Russian, 'I will not. They will put you in jail for making that speech, and you will have need of me on the outside to liberate your skin.'

The President makes the address in London to the citizens of the world. He explains the alternatives, outlines his doubts, discusses the fact that there are technicians ready to seize power, determined to commit themselves to the terrestrial explosion. No one but the people of the earth, by democratic procedure, have the right to make this decision, he declares, and recommends that as a first step the people march on the tunnel sites and hold them. He concludes his address by saying he is flying immediately back to Washington and will be there within two hours.

The message has been delivered on the network devoted to

international television. It reaches a modest percentage of all
listeners in the world. But in America, from the President's
point of view the program took place at an unfortunate time,
for it was the early hours of the morning. When he lands in
Washington at dawn, he is met by his Cabinet and a platoon of
M.P.s, who arrest him. Television in America is devoted that
morning to the announcement that the President has had a
psychotic breakdown and is at present under observation by
psychiatrists.

For a week, the atmosphere is unbearable. A small percentage of the people in America have listened to the President's
speech. Many more have heard him in other countries. Political
tensions are acute, and increase when the Premier of the Soviet
Union announces in reply to a question from a reporter that in
his opinion the President of the United States is perfectly sane.
Committees of citizens form everywhere to demand an open
investigation of the charges against the President. It becomes a
rallying cry that the President be shown to the public. A
condition close to civil war exists in America.

At this point, the President is paid a visit by Anderson
Stevens, the scientist in charge of the rocket program, the
man who has lately done more than any other to lead the
Cabinet against the President. Now they have a conversation
behind the barred windows of the hospital room where the
President is imprisoned. Anderson Stevens tells the President
that the first tunnel which had been built for the star shot was,
from his point of view, a ruse. He had never expected that
rocket ship, which was fired like a bullet, to escape from the
earth's atmosphere without burning to a cinder. All of his
experience had told him it would be destroyed. But he had
advanced the program for that shot because he wished to test
something else – the tunnel. It had been essential to discover
how deeply one could dig into the crust of the earth before the
heat became insupportable for an atomic bomb. In effect, the
tunnel had been dug as a test to determine the feasibility of
detonating the earth. And so that shot which had burned up a
rocket ship had been, from Stevens' point of view, a success,
because he had learned that the tunnel could be dug deep
enough to enable a superior hydrogen bomb to set off a chain

reaction in the fiery core of the earth. The fact that one hundred rocketeers and astronauts, men who had been his friends for decades, had died in an experiment he had known to be all but hopeless was an indication of how serious he was about the earth bomb shot. The President must not think for a moment that Stevens would hesitate to keep him in captivity, man the ship himself, and blow up the earth.

Why, then, asks the President, does Stevens bother to speak to him? Because, answers Stevens, he wants the President to command the ship. Why? Because in some way the fate of the ship might be affected by the emotions of everybody on earth at the moment the earth was exploded. This sounded like madness to some of his scientific colleagues, but to him it was feasible that if life had a spirit and all life ceased to exist at the same moment, then that spirit, at the instant of death, might have a force of liberation or deterrence which could be felt as a physical force across the heavens.

'You mean,' says the President, 'that even in the ruthless circuits of your heart there is terror, a moral terror, at the consequence of your act. And it is me you wish to bear the moral consequence of that act, and not you.'

'You are the only man great enough, sir,' says Anderson Stevens, bowing his head.

'But I think the act is wrong,' says the President.

'I know it is right,' says Stevens. 'I spent a thousand days and a thousand nights living with the terror that I might be wrong, and still believe I am right. There is something in me which knows that two things are true – that we have destroyed this earth not only because we were not worthy of it, but because it may have been too cruel for us. I tell you, we do not know. Man may have been mismated with earth. In some fantastic way, perhaps we voyaged here some millions of years ago and fell into a stupidity equal to the apes. That I don't know. But I do know, if I know anything at all, because my mind imprisoned in each and every one of my cells tells me so, that we must go on, that we as men are different from the earth, we are visitors upon it. We cannot suffer ourselves to sit here and be extinguished, not when the beauty which first gave speech to our tongues commands us to go out and find another world, another earth, where we may strive, where we may win, where we may find the right to live again. For that dream I will kill everyone on earth. I will kill my children. In fact I must, for they will not accompany me on the trip. And you,' he says to the President, 'you must accompany us. You must help to make this trip. For we as men may finally achieve greatness if we survive this, the most profound of our perils.'

'I do not trust myself,' said the President. 'I do not know if my motive is good. Too many men go to their death with a hatred deep beyond words, wishing with their last breath that they could find the power to destroy God. I do not know – I may be one of those men.'

'You have no choice,' says Anderson Stevens. 'There are people trying to liberate you now. I shall be here to shoot you myself before they succeed. Unless you agree to command the ship.'

'Why should I agree?' says the President. 'Shoot me now.'

'No,' says Stevens, 'you will agree, because I will make one critical concession to you. I do it not from choice, but from desperation. My dreams tell me we are doomed unless you command us. So I will let you give the people their one last opportunity. I will let you speak to them. I will put my power behind you, so that they may vote.'

'No,' says the President, 'not yet. Because if such an election were lost, if the people said, "Let us stay here and die together, and leave the earth to mend itself, without the sound of human speech or our machines," then you would betray me. I know it. You would betray everyone. Some night, in some desert, a rocket ship would be fired up into the sky, and twenty hours later, deep in some secret tunnel, all of us would be awakened by the last explosion of them all. No, I will wait for the people to free me first. Of necessity, my first act then will be to imprison you.'

After this interview between Stevens and the President, the ruling coalition of Cabinet officers and technicians refused, of course, to let the people see the President. The response was a virtually spontaneous trek of Americans by airplane, helicopter, automobile, by animal, by motorcycle, and on foot, toward the tunnel site the President had named. The Army was quickly deployed to prevent them, but the soldiers refused to protect the approaches to the tunnel. They also asked for the right to see the President. The Cabinet capitulated. The President was presented on television. He announced that the only justification for the star ship was a worldwide general election.

The most brilliant, anguished, closely debated election in the history of the world now took place. For two months, argument licked like flame at the problem. In a last crucial speech the night before the election, the President declared that it was the words of a man now in prison, Anderson Stevens, which convinced him how he would vote. For he, the President, had indeed come to believe that man rising out of the fiery grave of earth, out of the loss of his past, his history, and his roots, might finally achieve the greatness and the goodness expected of him precisely because he had survived this, the last and the most excruciating of his trials. 'If even a few of us manage to live, our seed will be changed forever by the self-sacrifice of nobility, the courage and the loss engraved on our memory of that earth-doomed man who was our ancestor and who offered us life. Man may become human at last.' The President concluded his speech by announcing that if the people considered him deserving of the honor, he would be the first to enter the ship, he would take upon himself the act of pressing that button which would blow up the earth.

The answer to this speech was a solemn vote taken in favour of destroying the world, and giving the spaceship its opportunity to reach the stars.

The beginning of the last sequence in the movie might show the President and the Premier saying goodbye. The Premier has discovered he is now hopelessly ill, and so will stay behind.

The Premier smiles as he says goodbye. 'You see, I am really too fat for a brand-new game. It is you fanatics who always take the longest trips.'

One hundred men and women file into the ship behind the President. The rocket is fired and rises slowly, monumentally. Soon it is out of sight. In the navigation tower within the rocket the President stares back at earth. It is seen on a color television screen, magnified enormously. The hours go by and the time is approaching for the explosion. The radio which will send out the wave of detonation is warmed up. Over it the President speaks to the people who are left behind on earth. All work has of course ceased, and people waiting through the last few hours collect, many of them, in public places, listening to the President's voice on loudspeakers. Others hear it on radios in their rooms, or sprawled on the grass in city parks. People listen in cars on country crossroads, at the beach, watching the surf break. Quietly, a few still buy tickets for their children on the pony rides. One or two old scholars sit by themselves at desks in the public library, reading books. Some drink in bars. Others sit quietly on the edge of pavements, their feet in the street. One man takes his shoes off. The mood is not too different from the mood of a big city late at night when the weather is warm. There is the same air of expectation, of quiet, brooding concentration.

'Pray for us,' says the President to them, speaking into his microphone on that rocket ship one million miles away. 'Pray for us. Pray that our purpose is good and not evil. Pray that we are true and not false. Pray that it is part of our mission to bring the life we know to other stars.' And in his ears he hears the voice of his wife, saying through her pain, 'You will end by destroying everything.'

'Forgive me, all of you,' says the President. 'May I be an honest man and not first deluded physician to the Devil.' Then he presses the button.

The earth detonates into the dark spaces. A flame leaps across the solar system. A scream of anguish, jubilation, desperation, terror, ecstasy, vaults across the heavens. The tortured heart of the earth has finally found its voice. We have a glimpse of the spaceship, a silver minnow of light, streaming into the oceans of mystery, and the darkness beyond.

*1962*

## PART SIX

# Microbes

## It

We were going through the barbed-wire when a machine gun started. I kept walking until I saw my head lying on the ground.

'My God, I'm dead,' my head said.

And my body fell over.

*1939*

# The Shortest Novel of Them All

At first she thought she could kill him in three days.

She did nearly. His heart proved nearly unequal to her compliments.

Then she thought it would take three weeks. But he survived.

So she revised her tables and calculated three months.

After three years, he was still alive. So they got married.

Now they've been married for thirty years. People speak warmly of them. They are known as the best marriage in town.

It's just that their children keep dying.

*1963*

## PART SEVEN

# Mutants

# Ministers of Taste: A Story

*A very short story in the form of two real letters written by Norman Mailer to Robert B. Silvers, editor of* The New York Review of Books *with copies directed to associate editors, publishers, and several interested observers.*

February 22, 1965

Dear Bob,

Your letter, January 26, invites me to an 'essay' of eighteen hundred words on the new Hubert Humphrey. In the last year you have also asked me to review biographies of Johnson (Jack) and George Patton. Since it is not easy to think of three books which could attract me less, I expect I must make my position clear. Forgive me for digging in old ground.

A year and a half ago, you asked me to review *The Group*. Said you had offered the novel to seven people – all seven were afraid to review it. You appealed to my manhood, my fierce eschatological sword. St. Mary's wrath (according to you) was limned with brimfire. Would I do it, you begged, as a most special favor to you. Perhaps, you suggested, I was the only man in New York who had the guts to do it. A shrewd appeal. I did it. Two months later my book (*The Presidential Papers*) came out. You had given the copy to Midge Decter for review. Her submitted piece was, in your opinion – I quote your label – 'overinflated'. That is to say, it was favorable. Changes were requested. The reviewer refused to make them. The review was not printed. No review of *The Presidential Papers* appeared in *The New York Review of Books*. Only a parody. By a mystery guest. Now, we have my new book, *An American Dream*. I hear you have picked Philip Rahv to review it, Philip Rahv whose detestation of my work has been thundering these

last two years into the gravy stains of every literary table on the
Eastern Seaboard.

In the name therefore of the sweet gracious Jesus, why expect
me to do eight words on your subject? To the contrary,
experience now suspects that a state of cordial relations with
*The Review* is congruent to a lack of cordial relations with *The
Review*, and marks you, Bob, on this note: negotiations with
your Editorship are, by open measure, inching, tedious, and
impoverished as spit. But cheer up, dear Silvers. The letter is
for publication, and so should enliven the literary history of
your unbloodied rag.

Yours in trust,

*Norman Mailer*

cc: Barbara Epstein      Samuel N. Antupit
    Elizabeth Hardwick    George Plimpton
    Eve Auchincloss      Jason Epstein
    Alexandra T. Emmet    Midge Decter
    A. Whitney Ellsworth   Malcolm Muggeridge
    Terry Ehrich

April 4, 1965

Dear Bob,

I have decided to use again our particular method of correspondence by copy. All reports say you enjoy it.

Now, your last letter informs me the *Review* has no intention
of publishing my previous letter because you feel the disclo-
sures are inappropriate. That your methods (which inspired my
letter) may not be any more appropriate seems not to have
entered your grasp of the issue.

In any case I want to make one more effort to change your
decision. The alternative is, after all, disagreeable. I will be
forced to publish the letter somewhere else: that small communication which in your pages might leaven the *Review*'s
worthy academic yeastings will, printed in another place, take

on a literary history larger than its merits. Furthermore, it will be out of our hands. We will both look like fools. That is disagreeable, but I have habits for playing the fool; it will bother me less, it is expected of me. Whereas – it bruises sensibility to point this out – most Americans don't know old Bob Silvers, they don't know what a marvelous and complicated fellow he is. They won't know his private reputation among his devoted friends is rich and various. No, you will be inserted most unfairly into literary history as the editor who wouldn't print an entertaining letter about himself and so gave the letter twenty times its natural publicity. That would be awful. I fear you must now face the unendurable, and make up your mind. Print or do not print my letter. Still, be of good cheer. It is these difficult decisions which make field marshals or tycoons of us all, kid.

Your devoted friend,

*Norman Mailer*

cc: Barbara Epstein          Samuel N. Antupit
    Elizabeth Hardwick       George Plimpton
    Eve Auchincloss          Jason Epstein
    Alexandra T. Emmet        Midge Decter
    A. Whitney Ellsworth     Malcolm Muggeridge
    Terry Ehrich

# The Locust Cry

On p. 293 of *The Early Masters*[1] is a short story.

## The Test

It is told:

When Prince Adam Czartoryski, the friend and counselor of Czar Alexander, had been married for many years and still had no children, he went to the maggid of Koznitz and asked him to pray for him and because of his prayer the princess bore a son. At the baptism, the father told of the maggid's intercession with God. His brother who, with his young son, was among the guests, made fun of what he called the prince's superstition. 'Let us go to your wonder-worker together,' he said, 'and I shall show you that he can't tell the difference between left and right.'

Together they journeyed to Koznitz, which was close to where they lived. 'I beg of you,' Adam's brother said to the maggid, 'to pray for my sick son.'

The maggid bowed his head in silence. 'Will you do this for me?' the other urged.

The maggid raised his head. 'Go,' he said, and Adam saw that he only managed to speak with a great effort. 'Go quickly, and perhaps you will still see him alive.'

'Well, what did I tell you?' Adam's brother said laughingly as they got into their carriage. Adam was silent during the ride. When they drove into the court of his house, they found the boy dead.

What is suggested by the story is an underworld of real events whose connection is never absurd. Consider, in parallel, this Haiku:[2]

[1] From Martin Buber's *Tales of the Hasidim*. Published by Schocken Books. Volume I: *The Early Masters*, Volume II: *The Later Masters*.

So soon to die
and no sign of it showing –
locust cry.

The sense of stillness and approaching death is occupied by the cry of the locust. Its metallic note becomes the exact equal of an oncoming death. Much of Haiku can best be understood as a set of equations in mood. Man inserting himself into a mood extracts an answer from nature which is not only the reaction of the man upon the mood, but is a supernatural equivalent to the quality of the experience, almost as if a key is given up from the underworld to unlock the surface of reality.

Here for example is an intimation of the architecture concealed beneath:

## Upsetting the Bowl[3]

It is told:
Once Rabbi Elimelekh was eating the Sabbath meal with his disciples. The servant set the soup bowl down before him. Rabbi Elimelekh raised it and upset it, so that the soup poured over the table. All at once young Mendel, later the rabbi of Rymanov, cried out: 'Rabbi, what are you doing? They will put us all in jail!' The other disciples smiled at these foolish words. They would have laughed out loud, had not the presence of their teacher restrained them. He, however, did not smile. He nodded to young Mendel and said: 'Do not be afraid, my son!'

Some time after this, it became known that on that day an edict directed against the Jews of the whole country had been presented to the emperor for his signature. Time after time he took up his pen, but something always happened to interrupt him. Finally he signed the paper. Then he reached

[2]*An Introduction to Haiku* by Harold G. Henderson, p. 43. The poem is by Matsuo Basho, translated by Henderson.

*Yagate shinu
keshiki wa mei-zo
semi-no koe*

[3]*The Early Masters*, p. 259.

for the sand-container but took the inkwell instead and upset it on the document. Hereupon he tore it up and forbade them to put the edict before him again.

A magical action in one part of the world creates its historical action in another – we are dealing with no less than totem and taboo. Psychoanalysis intrudes itself. One of the last, may it be one of the best approaches to modern neurosis is by way of the phenomenological apparatus of anxiety. As we sink into the apathetic bog of our possible extinction, so a breath of the Satanic seems to rise from the swamp. The magic of materials lifts into consciousness, proceeds to dominate us, is even enthroned into a usurpation of consciousness. The protagonists of *Last Year at Marienbad* are not so much people as halls and chandeliers, gaming tables, cigarettes in their pyramid of 1, 3, 5, and 7. The human characters are ghosts, disembodied servants, attendants who cast their shadows on the material. It is no longer significant that a man carries a silver cigarette case; rather it is the cigarette case which is significant. The man becomes an instrument to transport the case from the breast pocket of a suit into the air; like a building crane, a hand conducts the cigarette case to an angle with the light, fingers open the catch and thus elicit a muted sound of boredom, a silver groan from the throat of the case, which now offers up a cigarette, snaps its satisfaction at being shut, and seems to guide the hand back to the breast pocket. The man, on leave until he is called again, goes through a pantomime of small empty activities – without the illumination of his case he is like all dull servants who cannot use their liberty.

That, one may suppose, is a proper portrait of Hell. It is certainly the air of the phenomenological novel. It is as well the neurotic in slavery to the material objects which make up the locks and keys of his compulsion.

But allow me a quick portrait of a neurotic. He is a sociologist, let us say, working for a progressive foundation, a disenchanted atheist ('Who knows – God may exist as some kind of thwarted benevolence'), a liberal, a social planner, a member of SANE, a logical positivist, a collector of jokes about fags and beatniks, a lover of that large suburban land between art and the documentary. He smokes two packs of cigarettes a day: he drinks – *when* he drinks – eight or ten tots of blended whiskey in a night. He does not get drunk, merely cerebral, amusing, and happy. Once when he came home thus drunk, he bowed to his door and then touched his doorknob three times. After this, he went to bed and slept like a thief.

Two years later he is in slavery to the doorknob. He must wipe it with his fingertips three times each morning before he goes out. If he forgets to do this and only remembers later at work, his day is shattered. Anxiety bursts his concentration. His psyche has the air of a bombed city. In an extreme case, he may even have to return to his home. His first question to himself is whether someone has touched the knob since he left. He makes inquiries. To his horror he discovers the servant has gone out shopping already. She has therefore touched the knob and it has lost its magical property. Stratagems are now necessary. He must devote the rest of the day to encouraging the servant to go out in such a manner that he can open the door for her, and thus remove the prior touch of her hand.

Is he mad? the man asks himself. Later he will ask his analyst the same question. But he is too aware of the absurdity of his activities. He suffers at the thought of the work he is not accomplishing, he hates himself for being attached to the doorknob, he tries to extirpate its dominance. One morning he makes an effort to move out briskly. He does not touch the brass a second and third time. But his feet come to a halt, his body turns around as if a gyroscope were revolving him, his arm turns to the knob and pats it twice. He no longer feels his psyche is to be torn in two. Consummate relief.

Of course his analysis discloses wonders. He has been an only son. His mother, his father, and himself make three. He and his wife (a naturally not very happy marriage) have one child. The value of the trinities is considered dubious by the analyst but is insisted upon by the patient. He has found that he need touch the doorknob only once if he repeats to himself, 'I was born, I live, and I die.' After a time he finds that he does not have to touch the knob at all, or upon occasion, can use his left hand for the purpose. There is a penalty, however. He is obliged to be concerned with the number nine for the rest of the day. Nine sips of water from a glass. A porterhouse steak consumed in nine bites. His wife to be kissed nine times between supper and bed. 'I've kicked over an ant hill,' he confesses to his analyst. 'I'm going bugs.'

They work in his cause. Two testes and one penis makes three. Two eyes and one nose; two nostrils and one mouth; the throat, the tongue, and the teeth. His job, his family, and himself. The door, the doorknob, and the act of opening it.

Then he has a revelation. He wakes up one morning and does not reach for a cigarette. There is a tension in him to wait. He suffers agonies – the brightest and most impatient of his cells seem to be expiring without nicotine – still he has intimations of later morning bliss, he hangs on. Like an infantryman coming up alive from a forty-eight-hour shelling, he gets to his hat, his attaché case, and the doorknob. As he touches it, a current flows into his hand. 'Stick with me, pal,' says the message. 'One and two keep you from three.'

Traveling to the office in the last half hour of the subway rush, he is happy for the first time in years. As he holds to the baked enamel loop of the subway strap, his fingers curl up a little higher and touch the green painted metal above the loop. A current returns to him again. Through his fingertips he feels a psychic topography which has dimensions, avenues, signals, buildings. From the metal of the subway strap through the metal of the subway car, down along the rails, into the tunnels of the city, back to the sewer pipes and electric cables which surround the subway station from which he left, back to his house, and up the plumbing, up the steam pipe, up the hall, a leap through the air, and he has come back to the doorknob again. He pats the subway strap three times. The ship of his body will sink no further. 'Today,' thinks the sociologist, 'I signed my armistice. The flag of Faust has been planted here.'

But in his office he has palpitations. He believes he will have a heart attack. He needs air. He opens the window, leans out from the waist. By God, he almost jumped!

The force which drew him to touch the knob now seems to want to pull his chest through the window. Or is it a force opposed to the force which made him touch the doorknob? He does not know. He thinks God may be telling him to jump. That thwarted benevolent God. 'You are swearing allegiance to materials,' says a voice. 'Come back, son. It is better to be dead.'

Poor man. He is not bold enough to be Faust. He calls his analyst.

'Now, for God's sake, don't do anything,' says the analyst. 'This is not uncommon. Blocked material is rising to the surface. It's premature, but since we've gotten into it, repetition compulsions have to do with omnipotence fantasies which of course always involve Almighty figures and totemic Satanistic contracts. The urge to suicide is not bona fide in your case – it's merely a symbolic contraction of the anxiety.'

'But I tell you I almost went through the window. I felt my feet start to leave the floor.'

'Well, come by my office then. I can't see you right now – trust me on this – I've got a girl who will feel I've denied her her real chance to bear children if I cut into her hour, she's had too many abortions. You know, she's touchy' – rare is the analyst who won't gossip a *little* about his patients, it seems to calm the other patients – 'but I'll leave an envelope of tranquilizers for you on the desk. They're a new formula. They're good. Take two right away. Then two more this afternoon. Forget the nausea if it comes. Just side-effect. We'll get together this evening.'

'Mind if I touch your doorknob three times?'

'Great. You've got your sense of humor back. Yes, by all means, touch it.'

> So soon to die
> and no sign of it is showing –
> locust cry.

*1963*

# PART EIGHT

# Clues to Love

# The Time of Her Time

I was living in a room one hundred feet long and twenty-five feet wide, and it had nineteen windows staring at me from three of the walls and part of the fourth. The floor planks were worn below the level of the nails which held them down, except for the southern half of the room where I had laid a rough linoleum which gave a hint of sprinkled sand, conceivably an aid to the footwork of my pupils. For one hundred dollars I had the place whitewashed; everything: the checkerboard of tin ceiling plates one foot square with their fleur-de-lis stamped into the metal, the rotted sashes on the window frames (it took twelve hours to scrape the calcimine from the glass), even part of the floor had white drippings (although that was scuffed into dust as time went on) and yet it was worth it. When I took the loft it stank of old machinery and the paint was a liverish brown – I had tried living with that color for a week, my old furniture which had been moved by a mover friend from the Village and me, showed the scars of being humped and dragged and flung up six flights of stairs, and the view of it sprawled over twenty-five hundred feet of living space, three beat old day beds, some dusty cushions, a broken-armed easy chair, a cigarette-scarred coffee table made from a door, a kitchen table, some peeled enamel chairs which thumped like a wooden-legged pirate when one sat in them, the bookshelves of unfinished pine butted by bricks, yes all of this, my purview, this grand vista, the New York sunlight greeting me in the morning through the double filter of the smog-yellow sky and the nineteen dirt-frosted windows, inspired me with so much content, especially those liver-brown walls, that I fled my pad like the plague, and in the first week, after a day of setting the furniture to rights, I was there for four hours of sleep a night, from five in the morning when I maneuvered in from the last closed Village bar and the last coffee-klatsch of my philosopher friends for the night to let us say nine in the morning when I awoke with a partially destroyed

brain and the certainty that the sore vicious growl of my
stomach was at least the onset of an ulcer and more likely the
first gone cells of a thoroughgoing cancer of the duodenum. So I
lived it that way for a week, and then following the advice of a
bar-type who was the friend of a friend, I got myself up on the
eighth morning, boiled my coffee on a hot-plate while I shivered
in the October air (neither the stove nor the gas heaters had yet
been bought) and then I went downstairs and out the front door
of the warehouse onto Monroe Street, picking my way through
the garbage-littered gutter which always made me think of the
gangs on this street, the Negroes on the east end of the block,
the Puerto Ricans next to them, and the Italians and Jews to the
west – those gangs were going to figure a little in my life, I
suspected that, I was anticipating those moments with no quiet
bravery considering how hung was my head in the morning, for
the worst clue to the gangs was the six-year-olds. They were the
defilers of the garbage, knights of the ordure, and here, in this
province of a capital Manhattan, at the southern tip of the
island, with the overhead girders of the Manhattan and Brooklyn bridges the only noble structures for a mile of tenement
jungle, yes here the barbarians ate their young, and any type
who reached the age of six without being altogether mangled by
father, mother, family or friends, was a pint of iron man, so
tough, so ferocious, so sharp in the teeth that the wildest alley
cat would have surrendered a freshly caught rat rather than
contest the meal. They were charming, these six-year-olds, as I
told my uptown friends, and they used to topple the overloaded
garbage cans, strew them through the street, have summer
snowball fights with orange peel, coffee grounds, soup bones,
slop, they threw the discus by scaling the raw tin rounds from
the tops of cans, their pillow fights were with loaded socks of
scum, and a debauch was for two of them to scrub a third
around the inside of a twenty-gallon pail still warm with the heat
of its emptied treasures. I heard that the Olympics took place in
summer when they were out of school and the streets were so
thick with the gum of old detritus, alluvium and dross that the
mash made by passing car tires fermented in the sun. Then the
parents and the hoods and the debs and the grandmother
dowagers cheered them on and promised them murder and the

garbage flew all day, but I was there in fall and the scene was quiet from nine to three. So I picked my way through last night's stew of rubble on this eighth morning of my hiatus on Monroe Street, and went half down the block to a tenement on the boundary between those two bandit republics of the Negroes and the Puerto Ricans, and with a history or two of knocking on the wrong door, and with a nose full of smells of the sick overpeppered bowels of the poor which seeped and oozed out of every leaking pipe in every communal crapper (only as one goes north does the word take on the Protestant propriety of john), I was able finally to find my man, and I was an hour ahead of him – he was still sleeping off his last night's drunk. So I spoke to his wife, a fat masculine Negress with the face and charity of a Japanese wrestler, and when she understood that I was neither a junk-peddler nor fuzz, that I sold no numbers, carried no bills, and was most certainly not a detective (though my Irish face left her dubious of that) but instead had come to offer her husband a job of work, I was admitted to the first of three dark rooms, face to face with the gray luminescent eye of the television set going its way in the dark room on a bright morning, and through the hall curtains I could hear them talking in the bedroom.

'Get up, you son of a bitch,' she said to him.

He came to work for me, hating my largesse, lugging his air compressor up my six flights of stairs, and after a discussion in which his price came down from two hundred to one, and mine rose from fifty dollars to meet his, he left with one of my twenty-dollar bills, the air compressor on the floor as security, and returned in an hour with so many sacks of whitewash that I had to help him up the stairs. We worked together that day, Charlie Thompson his name was, a small lean Negro maybe forty years old, and conceivably sixty, with a scar or two on his face, one a gouge on the cheek, the other a hairline along the bridge of his nose, and we got along not too badly, working in sullen silence until the hangover was sweated out, and then starting to talk over coffee in the Negro hashhouse on the corner where the bucks bridled a little when I came in, and then ignored me. Once the atmosphere had become neutral again, Thompson was willing to talk.

'Man,' he said to me, 'what you want all that space for?'

'To make money.'

'Out of which?'

I debated not very long. The people on the block would know my business sooner or later – the reward of living in a slum is that everyone knows everything which is within reach of the senses – and since I would be nailing a sign over my mailbox downstairs for the pupils to know which floor they would find me on, and the downstairs door would have to be open since I had no bell, the information would be just as open. But for that matter I was born to attract attention; given my height and my blond hair, the barbarians would notice me, they noticed everything, and so it was wiser to come on strong than try to sidle in.

'Ever hear of an *Escuela de Torear*?' I asked him without a smile.

He laughed with delight at the sound of the words, not even bothering to answer.

'That's a bullfighter's school,' I told him. 'I teach bull-fighting.'

'You know that?'

'I used to do it in Mexico.'

'Man, you can get killed.'

'Some do.' I let the exaggeration of a cooled nuance come into my voice. It was true after all; some do get killed. But not so many as I was suggesting, maybe one in fifty of the successful, and one in five hundred of the amateurs like me who fought a few bulls, received a few wounds, and drifted away.

Charlie Thompson was impressed. So were others – the conversation was being overheard after all, and I had become a cardinal piece on the chaotic chessboard of Monroe Street's sociology – I felt the clear bell-like adrenalins of clean anxiety, untainted by weakness, self-interest, neurotic habit, or the pure yellows of the liver. For I had put my poker money on the table, I was the new gun in a frontier saloon, and so I was asking for it, not today, not tomorrow, but come sooner, come later, something was likely to follow from this. The weak would leave me alone, the strong would have respect, but be it winter or summer, sunlight or dark, there would come an hour so cold or so hot that someone, somebody, some sexed-up head, very strong and very weak, would be drawn to discover a new large truth about himself and the mysteries of his own courage or the lack of it. I knew. A year before, when I had first come to New York, there was a particular cat I kept running across in the bars of the Village, an expert with a knife, or indeed to maintain the salts of accuracy, an expert with two knives. He carried them everywhere – he had been some sort of hophead instructor in the Marines on the art of fighting with the knife, and he used to demonstrate nice fluid poses, his elbows in, the knives out, the points of those blades capering free of one another – he could feint in my direction with either hand, he was an artist, he believed he was better with a knife than any man in all of New York, and night after night in bar after bar he sang the love-song of his own prowess, begging for the brave type who would take on his boast, and leave him confirmed or dead.

It is mad to take on the city of New York, there is too much talent waiting on line; this cat was calling for every hoodlum in every crack gang and clique who fancied himself with the blade, and one night, drunk and on the way home, he was greeted by another knife, a Puerto Rican cat who was defective in school and spent his afternoons and nights shadow-knifing in the cellar club-house of his clique, a real contender, long-armed for a Latin, thin as a Lehmbruck, and fast as a hungry wolf; he had practiced for two months to meet the knife of New York.

So they went into an alley, the champion drunk, a fog of vanity blanketing the point of all his artistic reflexes, and it turned out to be not too much of a fight: the Puerto Rican caught it on the knuckles, the lip, and above the knee, but they were only nicks, and the champion was left in bad shape, bleeding from the forearm, the belly, the chest, the neck, and the face: once he was down, the Puerto Rican had engraved a double oval, labium majorum and minorum on the skin of the cheek, and left him there, having the subsequent consideration or fright to make a telephone call to the bar in which our loser had been drinking. The ex-champion, a bloody cat, was carried to his pad which was not far away (a bit of belated luck) and in an hour, without undue difficulty the brother-in-law doctor of somebody or other was good enough to take care of him. There were police reports, and as our patois goes, the details were a drag, but what makes my story sad is that our ex-champion was through. He mended by sorts and shifts, and he still bragged in the Village bars, and talked of finding the Puerto Rican when he was sober and in good shape, but the truth was that he was on the alcoholic way, and the odds were that he would stay there. He had been one of those gamblers who saw his life as a single bet, and he had lost. I often thought that he had been counting on a victory to put some charge below his belt and drain his mouth of all the desperate labial libido.

Now I was following a modest parallel, and as Thompson kept asking me some reasonable if openly ignorant questions about the nature of the bullfight, I found myself shaping every answer as carefully as if I were writing dialogue, and I was speaking practically for the black-alerted senses of three Negroes who were sitting behind me, each of them big in his way (I had taken my glimpse as I came in) with a dull, almost Chinese, sullenness of face. They could have been anything. I had seen faces like theirs on boxers and ditch diggers, and I had seen such faces by threes and fours riding around in Cadillacs through the Harlem of the early-morning hours. I was warning myself to play it carefully, and yet I pushed myself a little further than I should, for I became ashamed of my caution and therefore was obliged to brag just the wrong bit. Thompson, of course, was encouraging me – he was a sly old bastard – and he knew even better than me the character of our audience.

'Man, you can take care of yourself,' he said with glee.

'I don't know about that,' I answered, obeying the formal minuet of the *macho*. 'I don't like to mess with anybody,' I told him. 'But a man messes with me – well, I wouldn't want him to go away feeling better than he started.'

'Oh, yeah, ain't that a fact. I hears just what you hear.' He talked like an old-fashioned Negro – probably Southern. 'What if four or five of them comes on and gangs you?'

We had come a distance from the art of the *corrida*. 'That doesn't happen to me,' I said. 'I like to be careful about having some friends.' And part for legitimate emphasis, and part to fulfil my image of the movie male lead – that blond union of the rugged and the clean-cut (which would after all be *their* image as well) – I added, 'Good friends, you know.'

There we left it. My coffee cup was empty, and in the slop of the saucer a fly was drowning. I was thinking idly and with no great compassion that wherever this fly had been born it had certainly not expected to die in a tan syrupy ring-shaped pond, struggling for the greasy hot-dogged air of a cheap Negro hashhouse. But Thompson rescued it with a deft little flip of his fingers.

'I always save,' he told me seriously. 'I wouldn't let nothing be killed. I'm a preacher.'

'Real preacher?'

'Was one. Church and devoted congregation.' He said no more. He had the dignified sadness of a man remembering the major failure of his life.

As we got up to go, I managed to turn around and get another look at the three spades in the next booth. Two of them were facing me. Their eyes were flat, the whites were yellow and flogged with red – they stared back with no love. The anxiety came over me again, almost nice – I had been so aware of them, and they had been so aware of me.

2

That was in October, and for no reason I could easily discover, I found myself thinking of that day as I woke on a spring morning more than half a year later with a strong light coming through my nineteen windows. I had fixed the place up since then, added a few more pieces of furniture, connected a kitchen sink and a metal stall shower to the clean water outlets in the john, and most noticeably I had built a wall between the bullfight studio and the half in which I lived. That was more necessary than one might guess – I had painted the new wall red; after Thompson's job of whitewash I used to feel as if I were going snowblind; it was no easy pleasure to get up each morning in a white space so blue with cold that the chill of a mountain peak was in my blood. Now, and when I opened my eyes, I could choose the blood of the wall in preference to the ice slopes of Mt.

O'Shaugnessy, where the sun was always glinting on the glaciers of the windows.

But on this particular morning, when I turned over a little more, there was a girl propped on one elbow in the bed beside me, no great surprise, because this was the year of all the years in my life when I was scoring three and four times a week, literally combing the pussy out of my hair, which was no great feat if one knew the Village and the scientific temperament of the Greenwich Village mind. I do not want to give the false impression that I was one of the lustiest to come adventuring down the pike – I was cold, maybe by birth, certainly by environment: I grew up in a Catholic orphanage – and I had had my little kinks and cramps, difficulties enough just a few years ago, but I had passed through that, and I was going now on a kind of disinterested but developed competence; what it came down to was that I could go an hour with the average girl without destroying more of the vital substance than a good night's sleep could repair, and since that sort of stamina seems to get advertised, and I had my good looks, my blond hair, my height, build, and bullfighting school, I suppose I became one of the Village equivalents of an Eagle Scout badge for the girls. I was one of the credits needed for a diploma in the sexual humanities, I was par for a good course, and more than one of the girls and ladies would try me on an off-evening like comparison-shoppers to shop the value of the boy friend, lover, mate, or husband against the certified professionalism of Sergius O'Shaugnessy.

Now if I make this sound bloodless, I am exaggerating a bit – even an old habit is livened once in a while with color, and there were girls I worked to get and really wanted, and nights when the bull was far from dead in me. I even had two women I saw at least once a week, each of them, but what I am trying to emphasize is that when you screw too much and nothing is at stake, you begin to feel like a saint. It was a hell of a thing to be holding a nineteen-year-old girl's ass in my hands, hefting those young kneadables of future power, while all the while the laboratory technician in my brain was deciding that the experiment was a routine success – routine because her cheeks looked and felt just about the way I had thought they would while I was sitting beside her in the bar earlier in the evening, and so I still had come no closer to understanding my scientific compulsion to verify in the retort of the bed how accurately I had predicted the form, texture, rhythm and surprise of any woman who caught my eye.

Only an ex-Catholic can achieve some of the rarer amalgams of guilt, and the saint in me deserves to be recorded. I always felt an obligation – some noblesse oblige of the kindly cocksman – to send my women away with no great wounds to their esteem, feeling at best a little better than when they came in, I wanted it to be friendly (what vanity of the saint!). I was the messiah of the one-night stand, and so I rarely acted like a pig in bed, I wasn't greedy, I didn't grind all my tastes into their mouths, I even abstained from springing too good a lay when I felt the girl was really in love with her man, and was using me only to give love the benefit of a new perspective. Yes, I was a good sort, I probably gave more than I got back, and the only real pains for all those months in the loft, for my bullfighting classes, my surprisingly quiet time (it had been winter after all) on Monroe Street, my bulging portfolio of experiments – there must have been fifty girls who spent at least one night in the loft – my dull but doggedly advancing scientific data, even the cold wan joys of my saintliness demanded for their payment only one variety of the dead hour: when I woke in the morning, I could hardly wait to get the latest mouse out of my bed and out of my lair. I didn't know why, but I would awaken with the deadliest of depressions, the smell of the woman had gone very stale for me, and the armpits, the ammonias and dead sea life of old semen and old snatch, the sour fry of last night's sweat, the whore scent of overexercised perfume, became an essence of the odious, all the more remarkable because I clung to women in my sleep, I was one Don John who hated to sleep alone, I used to feel as if my pores were breathing all the maternal (because sleeping) sweets of the lady, wet or dry, firm or flaccid, plump, baggy, or lean who was handled by me while we dreamed. But on awakening, hung with my head – did I make love three times that year without being drunk? – the saint was given his hour of temptation, for I would have liked nothing more than to kick the friendly ass out of bed, and dispense with the coffee,

the good form, my depression and often hers, and start the new
day by lowering her in a basket out of my monk-ruined retreat
six floors down to the garbage pile (now blooming again in the
freshets of spring), wave my hand at her safe landing and get in
again myself to the blessed isolations of the man alone.

But of course that was not possible. While it is usually a creep
who generalizes about women, I think I will come on so heavy as
to say that the cordial tone of the morning after is equally
important to the gymkhana of the night before – at least if the
profit made by a nice encounter is not to be lost. I had given my
working hours of the early morning to dissolving a few of the
inhibitions, chilled reflexes and dampened rhythms of the
corpus before me, but there is not a restraint in the world which
does not have to be taken twice – once at night on a steam-head
of booze, and once in daylight with the grace of a social tea. To
open a girl up to the point where she loves you or It or some
tremor of her sexual baggage, and then to close her in the morning is to do the disservice which the hateful side of women loves
most – you have fed their cold satisfied distrust of a man. Therefore my saint fought his private churl, and suffering all the
detail of abusing the sympathetic nervous system, I made with
the charm in the daylight and was more of a dear than most.

It was to be a little different this morning, however. As I said,
I turned over in my bed, and looked at the girl propped on her
elbow beside me. In her eyes there was a flat hatred which gave
no ground – she must have been staring like this at my back for
several minutes, and when I turned, it made no difference – she
continued to examine my face with no embarrassment and no
delight.

That was sufficient to roll me around again, my shoulder
blades bare to her inspection, and I pretended that the opening
of my eyes had been a false awakening. I felt deadened then with
all the diseases of the dull – making love to her the night before
had been a little too much of a marathon. She was a Jewish
girl and she was in her third year at New York University, one of those harsh alloys of self-made bohemian from a
middle-class home (her father was a hardware wholesaler), and
I was remembering how her voice had irritated me each time I
had seen her, an ugly New York accent with a cultured overlay.

Since she was still far from formed, there had been all sorts of Lesbian hysterias in her shrieking laugh and they warred with that excess of strength, complacency and deprecation which I found in many Jewish women – a sort of 'Ech' of disgust at the romantic and mysterious All. This one was medium in size and she had dark long hair which she wore like a Village witch in two extended braids which came down over her flat breasts, and she had a long thin nose, dark eyes, and a kind of lean force, her arms and square shoulders had shown the flat thin muscles of a wiry boy. All the same, she was not bad, she had a kind of Village chic, a certain snotty elegance of superiority, and when I first came to New York I had dug girls like her – Jewesses were strange to me – and I had even gone with one for a few months. But this new chick had been a mistake – I had met her two weeks ago at a party, she was on leave from her boy friend, and we had had an argument about T. S. Eliot, a routine which for me had become the quintessence of corn, but she said that Eliot was the apotheosis of manner, he embodied the ecclesiasticism of classical and now futureless form, she adored him she said, and I was tempted to tell her how little Eliot would adore the mannerless yeasts of the Brooklyn from which she came, and how he might prefer to allow her to appreciate his poetry only in step to the transmigration of her voice from all urgent Yiddish nasalities to the few high English analities of relinquished desire. No, she would not make the other world so fast – nice society was not cutting her crumpets thus quickly because she was gone on Thomas Stearns Eeeee. Her college-girl snobbery, the pith for me of eighty-five other honey-pots of the Village aesthetic whose smell I knew all too well, so inflamed the avenger of my crotch, that I wanted to prong her then and there, right on the floor of the party, I was a primitive for a prime minute, a gorged gouge of a working-class phallus, eager to ram into all her nasty little tensions. I had the message again, I was one of the millions on the bottom who had the muscles to move the sex which kept the world alive, and I would grind it into her, the healthy hearty inches and the sweat of the cost of acquired culture when you started low and you wanted to go high. She was a woman, what! she sensed that moment, she didn't know if she could handle me, and she had the guts to decide to find out.

So we left the party and we drank and (leave it to a Jewish girl to hedge the bet) she drained the best half of my desire in conversation because she was being psychoanalyzed, what a predictable pisser! and she was in that stage where the jargon had the totalitarian force of all vocabularies of mechanism, and she could only speak of her infantile relations to men, and the fixations and resistances of unassimilated penis-envy with all the smug gusto of a female commissar. She was enthusiastic about her analyst, he was also Jewish (they were working now on Jewish self-hatred), he was really an integrated guy, Stanford Joyce, he belonged on the same mountain as Eliot, she loved the doers and the healers of life who built on the foundationless prevalence of the void those islands of proud endeavor.

'You must get good marks in school,' I said to her.

'Of course.'

How I envied the jazzed-up brain of the Jews. I was hot for her again, I wanted the salts of her perspiration in my mouth. They would be acrid perhaps, but I would digest them, and those intellectual molecules would rise to my brain.

'I know a girl who went to your bullfighting school,' she said to me. She gave her harsh laugh. 'My friend thought you were afraid of her. She said you were full of narcissistic anxieties.'

'Well, we'll find out,' I said.

'Oh, you don't want me. I'm very inadequate as a lover.' Her dark hard New York eyes, bright with appetite, considered my head as if I were a delicious and particularly sour pickle.

I paid the bill then, and we walked over to my loft. As I had expected, she made no great fuss over the back-and-forth of being seduced – to the contrary. Once we were upstairs, she prowled the length of my loft twice, looked at the hand-made bullfighting equipment I had set up along one wall of the studio, asked me a question or two about the killing machine, studied the swords, asked another question about the cross-guard on the descabellar, and then came back to the living-room-bedroom-dining-room-kitchen of the other room, and made a face at the blood-red wall. When I kissed her she answered with a grinding insistence of her mouth upon mine, and a muscular thrust of her tongue into my throat, as direct and unfeminine as the harsh force of her voice.

'I'd like to hang my clothes up,' she said.

It was not all that matter-of-fact when we got to bed. There was nothing very fleshy about the way she made love, no sense of the skin, nor smell, nor touch, just anger, anger at her being there, and another anger which was good for my own, that rage to achieve . . . just what, one cannot say. She made love as if she were running up an inclined wall so steep that to stop for an instant would slide her back to disaster. She hammered her rhythm at me, a hard driving rhythm, an all but monotonous drum, pound into pound against pound into pound until that moment when my anger found its way back again to that delayed and now recovered Time when I wanted to prong her at the party. I had been frustrated, had waited, had lost the anger, and so been taken by her. That finally got me – all through the talk about T. S. Eliot I had been calculating how I would lay waste to her little independence, and now she was alone, with me astride her, going through her paces, teeth biting the pillow, head turned away, using me as the dildoe of a private gallop. So my rage came back, and my rhythm no longer depended upon her drive, but found its own life, and we made love like two club fighters in an open exchange, neither giving ground, rhythm to rhythm, even to even, hypnotic, knowing neither the pain of punishment nor the pride of pleasure, and the equality of this, as hollow as the beat of the drum, seemed to carry her into some better deep of desire, and I had broken through, she was following me, her muscular body writhed all about me with an impersonal abandon, the wanton whip-thrash of a wounded snake, she was on fire and frozen at the same time, and then her mouth was kissing me with a rubbery greedy compulsion so avid to see all there was of me, that to my distant surprise, not in character for the saint to slip into the brutal, my hand came up and clipped her mean and openhanded across the face which brought a cry from her and broke the piston of her hard speed into something softer, wetter, more sly, more warm, I felt as if her belly were opening finally to receive me, and when her mouth kissed me again with a passing tender heat, warm-odored with flesh, and her body sweetened into some feminine embrace of my determination driving its way into her, well, I was gone, it was too late, I had driven right past her in that moment she turned, and I had begun to come, I was coming from all the confluences of my body towards that bud of sweetness I had plucked from her, and for a moment she was making it, she was a move back and surging to overtake me, and then it was gone, she made a mistake, her will ordered all temptings and rhythms to mobilize their march, she drove into the hard stupidities of a marching-band's step, and as I was going off in the best of many a month, she was merely going away, she had lost it again. As I ebbed into what should have been the contentments of fine after-pleasure, warm and fine, there was one little part of me remaining cold and murderous because she had deprived me, she had fled the domination which was liberty for her, and the rest of the night was bound to be hell.

Her face was ugly. 'You're a bastard, do you know that?' she asked of me.

'Let it go. I feel good.'

'Of course you feel good. Couldn't you have waited one minute?'

I disliked this kind of thing. My duty was reminding me of how her awakened sweets were souring now in the belly, and her nerves were sharpening into the gone electric of being just nowhere.

'I hate inept men,' she said.

'Cool it.' She could, at least, be a lady. Because if she didn't stop, I would give her back a word or two.

'You did that on purpose,' she nagged at me, and I was struck with the intimacy of her rancor – we might as well have been married for ten years to dislike each other so much at this moment.

'Why,' I said, 'you talk as if this were something unusual for you.'

'It is.'

'Come on,' I told her, 'you never made it in your life.'

'How little you know,' she said. 'This is the first time I've missed in months.'

If she had chosen to get my message, I could have been preparing now for a good sleep. Instead I would have to pump myself up again – and as if some ghost of the future laid the squeak of a tickle on my back, I felt an odd dread, not for tonight so much as for some ills of the next ten years whose first life was stirring tonight. But I lay beside her, drew her body against mine, feeling her trapped and irritable heats jangle me as much as they aroused me, and while I had no fear that the avenger would remain asleep, still he stirred in pain and in protest, he had supposed his work to be done, and he would claim the wages of overtime from my reserve. That was the way I thought it would go, but Junior from New York University, with her hard body and her passion for proper poetry, gave a lewd angry old grin as her face stared boldly into mine, and with the practical bawdiness of the Jew she took one straight utilitarian finger, smiled a deceptive girlish pride, and then she jabbed, fingernail and all, into the tight defended core of my clenched buttocks. One wiggle of her knuckle and I threw her off, grunting a sound between rage and surprise, to which she laughed and lay back and waited for me.

Well, she had been right, that finger tipped the balance, and three-quarters with it, and one-quarter hung with the mysteries of sexual ambition, I worked on her like a beaver for forty-odd minutes or more, slapping my tail to build her nest, and she worked along while we made the round of positions, her breath sobbing the exertions, her body as alive as a charged wire and as far from rest.

I gave her all the Time I had in me and more besides, I was weary of her, and the smell which rose from her had so little of the sea and so much of the armpit, that I breathed the stubborn wills of the gymnasium where the tight-muscled search for grace, and it was like that, a hard punishing session with pulley weights, stationary bicycle sprints, and ten breath-seared laps around the track. Yes, when I caught that smell, I knew she would not make it, and so I kept on just long enough to know she was exhausted in body, exhausted beyond the place where a ten-minute rest would have her jabbing that finger into me again, and hating her, hating women who could not take their exercise alone, I lunged up over the hill with my heart pounding past all pleasure, and I came, but with hatred, tight, electric and empty, the spasms powerful but centered in my heart and not from the hip, the avenger taking its punishment even at the end, jolted clear to the seat of my semen by the succession of rhythmic blows which my heart drummed back to my feet.

For her, getting it from me, it must have been impressive, a convoluted, smashing, and protracted spasm, a hint of the death throe in the animal male which cannot but please the feminine taste for the mortal wound. 'Oh, you're lucky,' she whispered in my ear as I lay all collapsed beside her, alone in my athlete's absorption upon the whisperings of damage in the unlit complexities of my inner body. I was indeed an athlete, I knew my body was my future, and I had damaged it a bit tonight by most certainly doing it no good. I disliked her for it with the simple dislike we know for the stupid.

'Want a cigarette?' she asked.

I could wait, my heart would have preferred its rest, but there was something tired in her voice beyond the fatigue of what she had done. She too had lost after all. So I came out of my second rest to look at her, and her face had the sad relaxation (and serenity) of a young whore who has finished a hard night's work with the expected lack of issue for herself, content with no more than the money and the professional sense of the hard job dutifully done.

'I'm sorry you didn't make it,' I said to her.

She shrugged. There was a Jewish tolerance for the expected failures of the flesh. 'Oh, well, I lied to you before,' she said.

'You never have been able to, have you?'

'No.' She was fingering the muscles of my shoulder, as if in unconscious competition with my strength. 'You're pretty good,' she said grudgingly.

'Not really inept?' I asked.

'*Sans façons,*' said the poetess in an arch change of mood which irritated me. 'Sandy has been illuminating those areas where my habits make for destructive impulses.'

'Sandy is Doctor Joyce?' She nodded. 'You make him sound like your navigator,' I told her.

'Isn't it a little obvious to be hostile to psychoanalysis?'

Three minutes ago we had been belaboring each other in the nightmare of the last round, and now we were close to cozy. I put the sole of my foot on her sharp little knee.

'You know the first one we had?' she asked of me. 'Well, I

wanted to tell you. I came close – I guess I came as close as I ever came.'

'You'll come closer. You're only nineteen.'

'Yes, but this evening has been disturbing to me. You see I get more from you than I get from my lover.'

Her lover was twenty-one, a senior at Columbia, also Jewish – which lessened interest, she confessed readily. Besides, Arthur was too passive – 'Basically, it's very comprehensible,' said the commissar, 'an aggressive female and a passive male – we complement one another, and that's no good.' Of course it was easy to find satisfaction with Arthur, 'via the oral perversions. That's because, vaginally, I'm anesthetized – a good phallic narcissist like you doesn't do enough for me.'

In the absence of learned credentials, she was setting out to bully again. So I thought to surprise her. 'Aren't you mixing your language a little?' I began. 'The phallic narcissist is one of Wilhelm Reich's categories.'

'Therefore?'

'Aren't you a Freudian?'

'It would be presumptuous of me to say,' she said like a seminar student working for his pee-aitch-dee. 'But Sandy is an eclectic. He accepts a lot of Reich – you see, he's very ambitious, he wants to arrive at his own synthesis.' She exhaled some smoke in my face, and gave a nice tough little grin which turned her long serious young witch's face into something indeed less presumptuous. 'Besides,' she said, 'you are a phallic narcissist. There's an element of the sensual which is lacking in you.'

'But Arthur possesses it?'

'Yes, he does. And you . . . you're not very juicy.'

'I wouldn't know what you mean.'

'I mean this.' With the rich cruel look of a conquistador finding a new chest of Indian gold, she bent her head and gave one fleeting satiric half-moon of a lick to the conjugation of my balls. 'That's what I mean,' she said, and was out of bed even as I was recognizing that she was finally not without art. 'Come back,' I said.

But she was putting her clothes on in a hurry. 'Shut up. Just don't give me your goddamned superiority.'

I knew what it was: she had been about to gamble the reserves which belonged to Arthur, and the thought of possibly wasting them on a twenty-seven-year-old connoisseur like myself was too infuriating to take the risk.

So I lay in bed and laughed at her while she dressed – I did not really want to go at things again – and besides, the more I laughed, the angrier she would be, but the anger would work to the surface, and beneath it would be resting the pain that the evening had ended on so little.

She took her leisure going to the door, and I got up in time to tell her to wait – I would walk her to the subway. The dawn had come, however, and she wanted to go alone, she had had a bellyful of me, she could tell me that.

My brain was lusting its own private futures of how interesting it would be to have this proud, aggressive, vulgar, tense, stiff and arrogant Jewess going wild on my bottom – I had turned more than one girl on, but never a one of quite this type. I suppose she had succeeded instead of me; I was ready to see her again and improve the message.

She turned down all dates, but compromised by giving me her address and the number of her telephone. And then glaring at me from the open door, she said, 'I owe you a slap in the face.'

'Don't go away feeling unequal.'

I might have known she would have a natural punch. My jaw felt it for half an hour after she was gone and it took another thirty minutes before I could bring myself back to concluding that she was one funny kid.

All of that added up to the first night with the commissar, and I saw her two more times over this stretch, the last on the night when she finally agreed to sleep over with me, and I came awake in the morning to see her glaring at my head. So often in sex, when the second night wound itself up with nothing better in view than the memory of the first night, I was reminded of Kafka's *Castle*, the tale of the search of a man for his apocalyptic orgasm: in the easy optimism of a young man, he almost captures the castle on the first day, and is never to come so close again. Yes, that was the saga of the nervous system of a man as it was bogged into the defeats, complications, and frustrations of middle age. I still had my future before me of course – the full engagement of my will in some go-for-broke I considered worthy of myself was yet to come, but there were times in that loft when I knew the psychology of an old man, and my second night with Denise – for Denise Gondelman was indeed her name – left me racked for it amounted to so little that we could not even leave it there – the hangover would have been too great for both of us – and so we made a date for a third night. Over and over in those days I used to compare the bed to the bullfight, sometimes seeing myself as the matador and sometimes as the bull, and this second appearance, if it had taken place, in the Plaza Mexico, would have been a *fracaso* with kapok seat cushions jeering down on the ring, and a stubborn cowardly bull staying in *querencia* before the doubtful prissy overtures, the gloomy trim technique of a veteran and mediocre *torero* on the worst of days when he is forced to wonder if he has even his *pundonor* to sustain him. It was a gloomy deal. Each of us knew it was possible to be badly worked by the other, and this seemed so likely that neither of us would gamble a finger. Although we got into bed and had a perfunctory ten minutes, it was as long as an hour in a coffee shop when two friends are done with one another.

By the third night we were ready for complexities again; to see a woman three times is to call on the dialectic of an affair. If the waves we were making belonged less to the viper of passion than the worm of inquiry, still it was obvious from the beginning that we had surprises for one another. The second night we had been hoping for more, and so got less; this third night, we each came on with the notion to wind it up, and so got involved in more.

For one thing, Denise called me in the afternoon. There was studying she had to do, and she wondered if it would be all right to come to my place at eleven instead of meeting me for drinks and dinner. Since that would save me ten dollars she saw no reason why I should complain. It was a down conversation. I had been planning to lay siege to her, dispense a bit of elixir from my vast reservoirs of charm, and instead she was going to keep it *in camera*. There was a quality about her I could not locate, something independent – abruptly, right there, I knew what it was. In a year she would have no memory of me, I would not exist for her unless . . . and then it was clear . . . unless I could be the first to carry her stone of no-orgasm up the cliff, all the way, over and out into the sea. That was the kick I could find, that a year from now, five years from now, down all the seasons to the hours of her old age, I would be the one she would be forced to remember, and it would nourish me a little over the years, thinking of that grudged souvenir which would not die in her, my blond hair, my blue eyes, my small broken nose, my clean mouth and chin, my height, my boxer's body, my parts – yes, I was getting excited at the naked image of me in the young-old mind of that sour sexed-up dynamo of black-pussied frustration.

A phallic narcissist she had called me. Well, I was phallic enough, a Village stickman who could muster enough of the divine It on the head of his will to call forth more than one becoming out of the womb of feminine Time, yes a good deal more than one from my fifty new girls a year, and when I failed before various prisons of frigidity, it mattered little. Experience gave the cue that there were ladies who would not be moved an inch by a year of the best and so I looked for other things in them, but this one, this Den-of-Ease, she was ready, she was entering the time of her Time, and if not me, it would be another – I was sick in advance at the picture of some bearded Negro cat who would score where I had missed and thus cuckold me in spirit, deprive me of those telepathic waves of longing (in which I obviously believed) speeding away to me from her over the years to balm the hours when I was beat, because I had been her psychic bridegroom, had plucked her ideational diddle, had led her down the walk of her real wedding night. Since she did not like me, what a feat to pull it off.

In the hours I waited after dinner, alone, I had the sense – which I always trusted – that tonight this little victory or defeat would be full of leverage, magnified beyond its emotional matter because I had decided to bet on myself that I would win, and a defeat would bring me closer to a general depression, a fog bank of dissatisfaction with myself which I knew could last for months or more. Whereas a victory would add to the panoplies of my ego some peculiar (but for me, valid) ingestion of her arrogance, her stubbornness, and her will – those necessary ingredients of which I could not yet have enough for my own ambition.

When she came in she was wearing a sweater and dungarees which I had been expecting, but there was a surprise for me. Her braids had been clipped, and a short cropped curled Italian haircut decorated her head, moving her severe young face half across the spectrum from the austerities of a poetess to a hint of all those practical and promiscuous European girls who sold their holy hump to the Germans and had been subsequently punished by shaved heads – how attractive the new hair proved; once punished, they were now free, free to be wild, the worst had happened and they were still alive with the taste of the first victor's flesh enriching the sensual curl of the mouth.

Did I like her this way? Denise was interested to know. Well, it was a shock, I admitted, a pleasant shock. If it takes you so long to decide, you must be rigid, she let me know. Well, yes, as a matter of fact I was rigid, rigid for her with waiting.

The nun of severity passed a shade over her. She hated men who were uncool, she thought she would tell me.

'Did your analyst tell you it's bad to be uncool?'

She had taken off her coat, but now she gave me a look as if she were ready to put it on again. 'No, he did not tell me that.' She laughed spitefully. 'But he told me a couple of revealing things about you.'

'Which you won't repeat.'

'Of course not.'

'I'll never know,' I said, and gave her the first kiss of the evening. Her mouth was heated – it was the best kiss I had received from her, and it brought me on too quickly – 'My fruit is ready to be plucked,' said the odors of her mouth, betraying that perfume of the ducts which, against her will no doubt, had been plumping for me. She was changed tonight. From the skin of her face and the glen of her neck came a new smell, sweet, sweaty, and tender, the smell of a body which had been used and had enjoyed its uses. It came to me nicely, one of the nicest smells in quite some time, so different from the usual exudations of her dissatisfied salts that it opened a chain of reflexes in me, and I was off in all good speed on what Denise would probably have called the vertical foreplay. I suppose I went at her like a necrophiliac let loose upon a still-warm subject, and as I gripped her, grasped her, groped her, my breath a bellows to blow her into my own flame, her body remained unmoving, only her mouth answering my call, those lips bridling hot adolescent kisses back upon my face, the smell almost carrying me away – such a fine sweet sweat.

Naturally she clipped the rhythm. As I started to slip up her sweater, she got away and said a little huskily, 'I'll take my own clothes off.' Once again I could have hit her. My third eye, that athlete's inner eye which probed its vision into all the corners, happy and distressed of my body whole, was glumly cautioning the congestion of the spirits in the coils of each teste. They would have to wait, turn rancid, maybe die of delay.

Off came the sweater and the needless brassière, her economical breasts swelled just a trifle tonight, enough to take on the convexities of an Amazon's armor. Open came the belt and the zipper of her dungarees, zipped from the front which pleased her not a little. Only her ass, a small masterpiece, and her strong thighs, justified this theatre. She stood there naked, quite psychically clothed, and lit a cigarette.

If a stiff prick has no conscience, it has also no common sense. I stood there like a clown, trying to coax her to take a ride with me on the bawdy car, she out of her clothes, I in all of mine, a muscular little mermaid to melt on my knee. She laughed, one harsh banker's snort – she was giving no loans on my idiot's collateral.

'You didn't even ask me,' Denise thought to say, 'of how my studying went tonight.'

'What did you study?'

'I didn't. I didn't study.' She gave me a lovely smile, girlish and bright. 'I just spent the last three hours with Arthur.'

'You're a dainty type,' I told her.

But she gave me a bad moment. That lovely fresh-spent smell, scent of the well used and the tender, that avatar of the feminine my senses had accepted so greedily, came down now to no more than the rubbings and the sweats of what was probably a very nice guy, passive Arthur with his Jewish bonanzas of mouth-love.

The worst of it was that it quickened me more. I had the

selfish wisdom to throw such evidence upon the mercy of my own court. For the smell of Arthur was the smell of love, at least for me, and so from man or woman, it did not matter – the smell of love was always feminine – and if the man in Denise was melted by the woman in Arthur, so Arthur might have flowered that woman in himself from the arts of a real woman, his mother? –·it did not matter – that voiceless message which passed from the sword of the man into the cavern of the woman was carried along from body to body, and if it was not the woman in Denise I was going to find tonight, at least I would be warmed by the previous trace of another.

But that was a tone poem to quiet the toads of my doubt. When Denise – it took five more minutes – finally decided to expose herself on my clumped old mattress, the sight of her black pubic hair, the feel of the foreign but brother liquids in her unembarrassed maw, turned me into a jackrabbit of pissy tumescence, the quicks of my excitement beheaded from the resonances of my body, and I wasn't with her a half-minute before I was over, gone, and off. I rode not with the strength to reap the harem of her and her lover, but spit like a pinched little boy up into black forested hills of motherly contempt, a passing picture of the nuns of my childhood to drench my piddle spurtings with failures of gloom. She it was who proved stronger than me, she the he to my silly she.

All considered, Denise was nice about it. Her harsh laugh did not crackle over my head, her hand in passing me the after-cigarette settled for no more than a nudge of my nose, and if it were not for the contempt of her tough grin, I would have been left with no more than the alarm to the sweepers of my brain to sweep this failure away.

'Hasn't happened in years,' I said to her, the confession coming out of me with the cost of the hardest cash.

'Oh, shut up. Just rest.' And she began to hum a mocking little song. I lay there in a state, parts of me jangled for forty-eight hours to come, and yet not altogether lost to peace. I knew what it was. Years ago in the air force, as an enlisted man, I had reached the light-heavyweight finals on my air base. For two weeks I trained for the championship, afraid of the other man all the way because I had seen him fight and felt he was better than me; when my night came, he took me out with a left hook to the liver which had me conscious on the canvas but unable to move, and as the referee was counting, which I could hear all too clearly, I knew the same kind of peace, a swooning peace, a clue to that kind of death in which an old man slips away – nothing mattered except that my flesh was vulnerable and I had a dim revery, lying there with the yells of the air force crowd in my ears, there was some far-off vision of green fields and me lying in them, giving up all ambitions to go back instead to another, younger life of the senses, and I remember at that moment I watered the cup of my boxer's jock, and then I must have slipped into something new, for as they picked me off the canvas the floor seemed to recede from me at a great rate as if I were climbing in an airplane.

A few minutes later, the nauseas of the blow to my liver had me retching into my hands, and the tension of three weeks of preparation for that fight came back. I knew through the fading vistas of my peace, and the oncoming spasms of my nausea, that the worst was yet to come, and it would take me weeks to unwind, and then years, and maybe never to overcome the knowledge that I had failed completely at a moment when I wanted very much to win.

A ghost of this peace, trailing intimations of a new nausea, was passing over me again, and I sat up in bed abruptly, as if to drive these weaknesses back into me. My groin had been simmering for hours waiting for Denise, and it was swollen still, but the avenger was limp, he had deserted my cause, I was in a spot if she did not co-operate.

Co-operate she did. 'My God, lie down again, will you,' she said, 'I was thinking that finally I had seen you relax.'

And then I could sense that the woman in her was about to betray her victory. She sat over me, her little breasts budding with their own desire, her short hair alive and flowering, her mouth ready to taste her gentleman's defeat. I had only to raise my hand, and push her body in the direction she wished it to go, and then her face was rooting in me, her angry tongue and voracious mouth going wild finally as I had wished it, and I knew the sadness of sour timing, because this was a prize I could not enjoy as I would have on first night, and yet it was good enough – not art, not the tease and languor of love on a soft mouth, but therapy, therapy for her, the quick exhaustions of the tension in a harsh throat, the beseechment of an ugly voice going down into the expiation which would be its beauty. Still it was good, practically it was good, my ego could bank the hard cash that this snotty head was searching me, the act served its purpose, anger traveled from her body into mine, the avenger came to attention, cold and furious, indifferent to the trapped doomed pleasure left behind in my body on that initial and grim piddle spurt, and I was ready, not with any joy nor softness nor warmth nor care, but I was ready finally to take her tonight, I was going to beat new Time out of her if beat her I must, I was going to teach her that she was only a child, because if at last I could not take care of a nineteen-year-old, then I was gone indeed. And so I took her with a cold calculation, the rhythms of my body corresponding to no more than a metronome in my mind, tonight the driving mechanical beat would come from me, and blind to nerve-raddlings in my body, and blood pressures in my brain, I worked on her like a riveter, knowing her resistances were made of steel, I threw her a fuck the equivalent of a fifteen-round fight, I wearied her, I brought her back, I drove my fingers into her shoulders and my knees into her hips. I went, and I went, and I went, I bore her high and thumped her hard, I sprinted, I paced, I lay low, eyes all closed, under sexual water, like a submarine listening for the distant sound of her ship's motors, hoping to steal up close and trick her rhythms away.

And she was close. Oh, she was close so much of the time. Like a child on a merry-go-round the touch of the colored ring just evaded the tips of her touch, and she heaved and she hurdled, arched and cried, clawed me, kissed me, even gave of a shriek once, and then her sweats running down and her will weak, exhausted even more than me, she felt me leave and lie beside her. Yes, I did that with a tactician's cunning, I let the depression of her failure poison what was left of her will never to let me succeed, I gave her slack to mourn the lost freedoms and hate the final virginity for which she fought, I even allowed her baffled heat to take its rest and attack her nerves once more, and then, just as she was beginning to fret against me in a new and unwilling appeal, I turned her over suddenly on her belly, my avenger wild with the mania of the madman, and giving her no chance, holding her prone against the mattress with the strength of my weight, I drove into the seat of all stubbornness, tight as a vice, and I wounded her, I knew it, she thrashed beneath me like a trapped little animal, making not a sound, but fierce not to allow me this last of the liberties, and yet caught, forced to give up millimeter by millimeter the bridal ground of her symbolic and therefore real vagina. So I made it, I made it all the way – it took ten minutes and maybe more, but as the avenger rode down to his hilt and tunneled the threshold of sexual home all those inches closer into the bypass of the womb, she gave at last a little cry of farewell, and I could feel a new shudder which began as a ripple and rolled into a wave, and then it rolled over her, carrying her along, me hardly moving for fear of damping this quake from her earth, and then it was gone, but she was left alive with a larger one to follow.

So I turned her once again on her back, and moved by impulse to love's first hole. There was an odor coming up, hers at last, the smell of the sea, and none of the armpit or a dirty sock, and I took her mouth and kissed it, but she was away, following the wake of her own waves which mounted, fell back, and in new momentum mounted higher and should have gone over, and then she was about to hang again, I could feel it, that moment of hesitation between the past and the present, the habit and the adventure, and I said into her ear, 'You dirty little Jew.'

That whipped over her. A first wave kissed, a second spilled, and a third and a fourth and a fifth came breaking over, and finally she was away, she was loose in the water for the first time in her life, and I would have liked to go with her, but I was blood-throttled and numb, and as she had the first big moment in her life, I was nothing but a set of aching balls and a congested cock, and I rode with her wistfully, looking at the contortion of her face and listening to her sobbing sound of 'Oh, Jesus, I made it, oh Jesus, I made it.'

'Compliments of T. S. Eliot,' I whispered to myself, and my head was aching, my body was shot. She curled against me, she kissed my sweat, she nuzzled my eyes and murmured in my ear, and then she was slipping away into the nicest of weary sweet sleep.

'Was it good for you too?' she whispered half-awake, having likewise read the works of The Hemingway, and I said, 'Yeah, fine,' and after she was asleep, I disengaged myself carefully, and prowled the loft, accepting the hours it would take for my roiled sack to clean its fatigues and know a little sleep. But I had abused myself too far, and it took till dawn and half a fifth of whisky before I dropped into an unblessed stupor. When I awoke, in that moment before I moved to look at her, and saw her glaring at me, I was off on a sluggish masculine debate as to whether the kick of studying this Denise for another few nights – now that I had turned the key – would be worth the danger of deepening into some small real feeling. But through my hangover and the knowledge of the day and the week and the month it would take the different parts of all of me to repair, I was also knowing the taste of a reinforced will – finally, I had won. At no matter what cost, and with what luck, and with a piece of charity from her, I had won nonetheless, and since all real pay came from victory, it was more likely that I would win the next time I gambled my stake on something more appropriate for my ambition.

Then I turned, saw the hatred in her eyes, turned over again, and made believe I was asleep while a dread of the next few minutes weighed a leaden breath over the new skin of my ego.

'You're awake, aren't you?' she said.

I made no answer.

'All right, I'm going then. I'm getting dressed.' She whipped out of bed, grabbed her clothes, and began to put them on with all the fury of waiting for me to get the pronouncement. 'That was a lousy thing you did last night,' she said by way of a start.

In truth she looked better than she ever had. The severe lady and the tough little girl of yesterday's face had put forth the first agreements on which would yet be a bold chick.

'I gave you what you could use,' I made the mistake of saying.

'Just didn't you,' she said, and was on her way to the door. 'Well, cool it. You don't do anything to me.' Then she smiled. 'You're so impressed with what you think was such a marvelous notch you made in me, listen, Buster, I came here last night thinking of what Sandy Joyce told me about you, and he's right, oh man is he right.' Standing in the open doorway, she started to light a cigarette, and then threw the matches to the floor. From thirty feet away I could see the look in her eyes, that unmistakable point for the kill that you find in the eyes of very few bullfighters, and then having created her pause, she came on for her moment of truth by saying, 'He told me your whole life is a lie, and you do nothing but run away from the homosexual that is you.'

And like a real killer, she did not look back, and was out the door before I could rise to tell her that she was a hero fit for me.

*1958*

# The Man Who Studied Yoga

## I

I would introduce myself if it were not useless. The name I had last night will not be the same as the name I have tonight. For the moment, then, let me say that I am thinking of Sam Slovoda. Obligatorily, I study him, Sam Slovoda, who is neither ordinary nor extraordinary, who is not young nor yet old, not tall nor short. He is sleeping, and it is fit to describe him now, for like most humans he prefers sleeping to not sleeping. He is a mild pleasant-looking man who has just turned forty. If the crown of his head reveals a little bald spot, he has nourished in compensation the vanity of a mustache. He has generally when he is awake an agreeable manner, at least with strangers; he appears friendly, tolerant, and genial. The fact is that like most of us, he is full of envy, full of spite, a gossip, a man who is pleased to find others are as unhappy as he, and yet – this is the worst to be said – he is a decent man. He is better than most. He would prefer to see a more equitable world, he scorns prejudice and privilege, he tries to hurt no one, he wishes to be liked. I will go even further. He has one serious virtue – he is not fond of himself, he wishes he were better. He would like to free himself of envy, of the annoying necessity to talk about his friends, he would like to love people more; specifically, he would like to love his wife more, and to love his two daughters without the tormenting if nonetheless irremediable vexation that they closet his life in the dusty web of domestic responsibilities and drudging for money.

How often he tells himself with contempt that he has the cruelty of a kind weak man.

May I state that I do not dislike Sam Slovoda; it is just that I am disappointed in him. He has tried too many things and never with a whole heart. He has wanted to be a serious novelist and now merely indulges the ambition; he wished to be of consequence in the world, and has ended, temporarily perhaps, as an overworked writer of continuity for comic magazines; when he

was young he tried to be a bohemian and instead acquired a wife
and family. Of his appetite for a variety of new experience I may
say that it is matched only by his fear of new people and novel
situations.

I will give an instance. Yesterday, Sam was walking along the
street and a bum approached him for money. Sam did not see
the man until too late; lost in some inconsequential thought, he
looked up only in time to see a huge wretch of a fellow with a red
twisted face and an outstretched hand. Sam is like so many;
each time a derelict asks for a dime, he feels a coward if he pays
the money, and is ashamed of himself if he doesn't. This once,
Sam happened to think, I will not be bullied, and hurried past.
But the bum was not to be lost so easily. 'Have a heart, Jack,' he
called after in a whisky voice, 'I need a drink bad.' Sam
stopped, Sam began to laugh. 'Just so it isn't for coffee, here's a
quarter,' he said, and he laughed, and the bum laughed.
'You're a man's man,' the bum said. Sam went away pleased
with himself, thinking about such things as the community
which existed between all people. It was cheap of Sam. He
should know better. He should know he was merely relieved the
situation had turned out so well. Although he thinks he is sorry
for bums, Sam really hates them. Who knows what violence
they can offer?

At this time, there is a powerful interest in Sam's life, but
many would ridicule it. He is in the process of being
psychoanalyzed. Myself, I do not jeer. It has created the most
unusual situation between Sam and me. I could go into details
but they are perhaps premature. It would be better to watch
Sam awaken.

His wife, Eleanor, has been up for an hour, and she has shut
the window and neglected to turn off the radiator. The room is
stifling. Sam groans in a stupor which is neither sleep nor
refreshment, opens one eye, yawns, groans again, and lies
twisted, strangled and trussed in pyjamas which are too large
for him. How painful it is for him to rise. Last night there was a
party, and this morning, Sunday morning, he is awakening
with a hangover. Invariably, he is depressed in the morning,
and it is no different today. He finds himself in the flat and
familiar dispirit of nearly all days.

It is snowing outside. Sam finally lurches to the window, and opens it for air. With the oxygen of a winter morning clearing his brain, he looks down six stories into the giant quadrangle of the Queens housing development in which he lives, staring morosely at the inch of slush which covers the monotonous artificial park that separates his apartment building from an identical structure not two hundred feet away. The walks are black where the snow has melted, and in the children's playground, all but deserted, one swing oscillates back and forth, pushed by an irritable little boy who plays by himself among the empty benches, swaddled in galoshes, muffler, and overcoat. The snow falls sluggishly, a wet snow which probably will turn to rain. The little boy in the playground gives one last disgusted shove to the swing and trudges away gloomily, his overshoes leaving a small animal track behind him. Back of Sam, in the four-room apartment he knows like a blind man, there is only the sound of Eleanor making breakfast.

Well, thinks Sam, depression in the morning is a stage of his analysis, Dr. Sergius has said.

This is the way Sam often phrases his thoughts. It is not altogether his fault. Most of the people he knows think that way and talk that way, and Sam is not the strongest of men. His language is doomed to the fashion of the moment. I have heard him remark mildly, almost apologetically, about his daughters: 'My relation with them still suffers because I haven't worked through all my feminine identifications.' The saddest thing is that the sentence has meaning to Sam even if it will not have meaning to you. A great many ruminations, discoveries, and memories contribute their connotation to Sam. It has the significance of a cherished line of poetry to him.

Although Eleanor is not being analyzed, she talks in a similar way. I have heard her remark in company, 'Oh, you know Sam, he not only thinks I'm his mother, he blames me for being born.' Like most women, Eleanor can be depended upon to employ the idiom of her husband.

What amuses me is that Sam is critical of the way others speak. At the party last night he was talking to a Hollywood writer, a young man with a great deal of energy and enthusiasm. The young man spoke something like this: 'You see, boychick,

I can spike any script with yaks, but the thing I can't do is heartbreak. My wife says she's gonna give me heartbreak. The trouble is I've had a real solid-type life. I mean I've had my ups and downs like all of humanity, but there's never been a shriek in my life. I don't know how to write shrieks.'

On the trip home, Sam had said to Eleanor, 'It was disgraceful. A writer should have some respect for language.'

Eleanor answered with a burlesque of Sam's indignation. 'Listen, I'm a real artist-type. Culture is for comic-strip writers.'

Generally, I find Eleanor attractive. In the ten years they have been married she has grown plump, and her dark hair which once was long is now cropped in a mannish cut of the prevailing mode. But, this is quibbling. She still possesses her best quality, a healthy exuberance which glows in her dark eyes and beams in her smile. She has beautiful teeth. She seems aware of her body and pleased with it. Sam tells himself he would do well to realize how much he needs her. Since he has been in analysis he has come to discover that he remains with Eleanor for more essential reasons than mere responsibility. Even if there were no children, he would probably cleave to her.

Unhappily, it is more complicated than that. She is always – to use their phrase – competing with him. At those times when I do not like Eleanor, I am irritated by her lack of honesty. She is too sharp-tongued, and she does not often give Sam what he needs most, a steady flow of uncritical encouragement to counteract the harshness with which he views himself. Like so many who are articulate on the subject, Eleanor will tell you that she resents being a woman. As Sam is disappointed in life, so is Eleanor. She feels Sam has cheated her from a proper development of her potentialities and talent, even as Sam feels cheated. I call her dishonest because she is not so ready as Sam to put the blame on herself.

Sam, of course, can say all this himself. It is just that he experiences it in a somewhat different way. Like most men who have been married for ten years, Eleanor is not quite real to him. Last night at the party, there were perhaps half a dozen people whom he met for the first time, and he talked animatedly with them, sensing their reactions, feeling their responses, aware of the life in them, as they were aware of the life in him. Eleanor, however, exists in his nerves. She is a rather vague embodiment, he thinks of her as 'she' most of the time, someone to conceal things from. Invariably, he feels uneasy with her. It is too bad. No matter how inevitable, I am always sorry when love melts into that pomade of affection, resentment, boredom and occasional compassion which is the best we may expect of a man and woman who have lived together a long time. So often, it is worse, so often no more than hatred.

They are eating breakfast now, and Eleanor is chatting about the party. She is pretending to be jealous about a young girl in a strapless evening gown, and indeed, she does not have to pretend altogether. Sam, with liquor inside him, had been leaning over the girl; obviously he had coveted her. Yet, this morning, when Eleanor begins to talk about her, Sam tries to be puzzled.

'Which girl was it now?' he asks a second time.

'Oh, you know, the hysteric,' Eleanor says, 'the one who was parading her bazooms in your face.' Eleanor has ways of impressing certain notions upon Sam. 'She's Charlie's new girl.'

'I didn't know that,' Sam mutters. 'He didn't seem to be near her all evening.'

Eleanor spreads marmalade over her toast and takes a bite with evident enjoyment. 'Apparently, they're all involved. Charles was funny about it. He said he's come to the conclusion that the great affairs of history are between hysterical women and detached men.'

'Charles hates women,' Sam says smugly. 'If you notice, almost everything he says about them is a discharge of aggression.' Sam has the best of reasons for not liking Charles. It takes more than ordinary character for a middle-aged husband to approve of a friend who moves easily from woman to woman.

'At least Charles discharges his aggression,' Eleanor remarks.

'He's almost a classic example of the Don Juan complex. You notice how masochistic his women are?'

'I know a man or two who's just as masochistic.'

Sam sips his coffee. 'What made you say the girl was an hysteric?'

Eleanor shrugs. 'She's an actress. And I could see she was a tease.'

'You can't jump to conclusions,' Sam lectures. 'I had the impression she was a compulsive. Don't forget you've got to distinguish between the outer defenses, and the more deeply rooted conflicts.'

I must confess that this conversation bores me. As a sample it is representative of the way Sam and Eleanor talk to each other. In Sam's defense I can say nothing; he has always been too partial to jargon.

I am often struck by how eager we are to reveal all sorts of supposedly ugly secrets about ourselves. We can explain the hatred we feel for our parents, we are rather pleased with the perversions to which we are prone. We seem determinedly proud to be superior to ourselves. No motive is too terrible for our inspection. Let someone hint, however, that we have bad table manners and we fly into a rage. Sam will agree to anything you may say about him, provided it is sufficiently serious – he will be the first to agree he has fantasies of murdering his wife. But tell him that he is afraid of waiters, or imply to Eleanor that she is a nag, and they will be quite annoyed.

Sam has noticed this himself. There are times when he can hear the jargon in his voice, and it offends him. Yet, he seems powerless to change his habits.

An example: He is sitting in an armchair now, brooding upon his breakfast, while Eleanor does the dishes. The two daughters are not home; they have gone to visit their grandmother for the weekend. Sam had encouraged the visit. He had looked forward to the liberty Eleanor and himself would enjoy. For the past few weeks the children had seemed to make the most impossible demands upon his attention. Yet now they are gone and he misses them, he even misses their noise. Sam, however, cannot accept the notion that many people are dissatisfied with the present, and either dream of the past or anticipate the future. Sam must call this 'ambivalence over possessions.' Once he even felt obliged to ask his analyst, Dr. Sergius, if ambivalence over possessions did not characterize him almost perfectly, and Sergius whom I always picture with the flat precision of a coin's head – bald skull and horn-rimmed glasses – answered in his

German accent, 'But, my dear Mr. Slovoda, as I have told you, it would make me happiest if you did not include in your reading, these psychoanalytical text-works.'

At such rebukes, Sam can only wince. It is so right, he tells himself, he is exactly the sort of ambitious fool who uses big words when small ones would do.

2

While Sam sits in the armchair, gray winter light is entering the windows, snow falls outside. He sits alone in a modern seat, staring at the grey, green, and beige décor of their living room. Eleanor was a painter before they were married, and she has arranged this room. It is very pleasant, but like many husbands, Sam resents it, resents the reproductions of modern painters upon the wall, the slender coffee table, a free-form poised like a spider on wire legs, its feet set onto a straw rug. In the corner, most odious of all, is the playmate of his children, a hippopotamus of a television-radio-and-phonograph cabinet with the blind monstrous snout of the video tube.

Eleanor has set the Sunday paper near his hand. Soon, Sam intends to go to work. For a year, he has been giving a day once or twice a month to a bit of thought and a little writing on a novel he hopes to begin sometime. Last night, he told himself he would work today. But he has little enthusiasm now. He is tired, he is too depressed. Writing for the comic strips seems to exhaust his imagination.

Sam reads the paper as if he were peeling an enormous banana. Flap after flap of newsprint is stripped away and cast upon the straw rug until only the Magazine Section is left. Sam glances through it with restless irritability. A biography of a political figure runs its flatulent prose into the giant crossword puzzle at the back. An account of a picturesque corner of the city becomes lost in statistics and exhortations on juvenile delinquency, finally to emerge with photographs about the new style of living which desert architecture provides. Sam looks at a wall of windows in rotogravure with a yucca tree framing the pool.

There is an article about a workingman. His wife and his family are described, his apartment, his salary and his budget. Sam reads a description of what the worker has every evening for dinner, and how he spends each night of the week. The essay makes its point; the typical American workingman must watch his pennies, but he is nonetheless secure and serene. He would not exchange his life for another.

Sam is indignant. A year ago he had written a similar article in an attempt to earn some extra money. Subtly, or so he thought, he had suggested that the average workingman was raddled with insecurity. Naturally, the article had been rejected.

Sam throws the Magazine Section away. Moments of such anger torment him frequently. Despite himself, Sam is enraged at editorial dishonesty, at the smooth strifeless world which such articles present. How angry he is – how angry and how helpless. 'It is the actions of men and not their sentiments which make history,' he thinks to himself, and smiles wryly. In his living room he would go out to tilt the windmills of a vast, powerful, and hypocritical society; in his week of work he labors in an editorial cubicle to create spaceships, violent death, women with golden tresses and wanton breasts, men who act with their fists and speak with patriotic slogans.

I know what Sam feels. As he sits in the armchair, the Sunday papers are strewn around him, carrying their war news, their murders, their parleys, their entertainments, mummery of a real world which no one can grasp. It is terribly frustrating. One does not know where to begin.

Today, Sam considers himself half a fool for having been a radical. There is no longer much consolation in the thought that the majority of men who succeed in a corrupt society are themselves obligatorily corrupt, and one's failure is therefore the price of one's idealism. Sam cannot recapture the pleasurable bitterness which resides in the notion that one has suffered for one's principles. Sergius is too hard on him for that.

They have done a lot of work on the subject. Sergius feels that Sam's concern with world affairs has always been spurious. For example, they have uncovered in analysis that Sam wrote his article about the worker in such a way as to make certain it would be refused. Sam, after all, hates editors; to have such a piece accepted would mean he is no better than they, that he is a mediocrity. So long as he fails he is not obliged to measure himself. Sam, therefore, is being unrealistic. He rejects the world with his intellect, and this enables him not to face the more direct realities of his present life.

Sam will argue with Sergius but it is very difficult. He will say, 'Perhaps you sneer at radicals because it is more comfortable to ignore such ideas. Once you became interested it might introduce certain unpleasant changes in your life.'

'Why,' says Sergius, 'do you feel it so necessary to assume that I am a bourgeois interested only in my comfort?'

'How can I discuss these things,' says Sam, 'if you insist that my opinions are the expression of neurotic needs, and your opinions are merely dispassionate medical advice?'

'You are so anxious to defeat me in an argument,' Sergius will reply. 'Would you admit it is painful to relinquish the sense of importance which intellectual discussion provides you?'

I believe Sergius has his effect. Sam often has thoughts these days which would have been repellent to him years ago. For instance, at the moment, Sam is thinking it might be better to live the life of a worker, a simple life, to be completely absorbed with such necessities as food and money. Then one could believe that to be happy it was necessary only to have more money, more goods, less worries. It would be nice, Sam thinks wistfully, to believe that the source of one's unhappiness comes not from oneself, but from the fault of the boss, or the world, or bad luck.

Sam has these casual daydreams frequently. He likes to think about other lives he might have led, and he envies the most astonishing variety of occupations. It is easy enough to see why he should wish for the life of an executive with the power and sense of command it may offer, but virtually from the same impulse Sam will wish himself a bohemian living in an unheated loft, his life a catch-as-catch-can from day to day. Once, after reading an article, Sam even wished himself a priest. For about ten minutes it seemed beautiful to him to surrender his life to God. Such fancies are common, I know. It is just that I, far better than Sam, know how serious he really is, how fanciful, how elaborate, his imagination can be.

The phone is ringing. Sam can hear Eleanor shouting at him to answer. He picks up the receiver with a start. It is Marvin Rossman, who is an old friend, and Marvin has an unusual request. They talk for several minutes, and Sam squirms a little in his seat. As he is about to hang up, he laughs. 'Why, no, Marvin, it gives me a sense of adventure,' he says.

Eleanor has come into the room toward the end of his conversation. 'What is it all about?' she asks.

Sam is obviously a bit agitated. Whenever he attempts to be most casual, Eleanor can well suspect him. 'It seems,' he says slowly, 'that Marvin has acquired a pornographic movie.'

'From whom?' Eleanor asks.

'He said something about an old boy friend of Louise's.'

Eleanor laughs. 'I can't imagine Louise having an old boy friend with a dirty movie.'

'Well, people are full of surprises,' Sam says mildly.

'Look, here,' says Eleanor suddenly. 'Why did he call us?'

'It was about our projector.'

'They want to use it?' Eleanor asks.

'That's right.' Sam hesitates. 'I invited them over.'

'Did it ever occur to you I might want to spend my Sunday some other way?' Eleanor asks crossly.

'We're not doing anything,' Sam mumbles. Like most men, he feels obliged to act quite nonchalantly about pornography. 'I'll tell you, I am sort of curious about the film. I've never seen one, you know.'

'Try anything once, is that it?'

'Something of the sort.' Sam is trying to conceal his excitement. The truth is that in common with most of us, he is fascinated by pornography. It is a minor preoccupation, but more from lack of opportunity than anything else. Once or twice, Sam has bought the sets of nude photographs which are sold in marginal bookstores, and with guilty excitement has hidden them in the apartment.

'Oh, this is silly,' Eleanor says. 'You were going to work today.'

'I'm just not in the mood.'

'I'll have to feed them,' Eleanor complains. 'Do we have enough liquor?'

'We can get beer.' Sam pauses. 'Alan Sperber and his wife are coming too.'

'Sam, you're a child.'

'Look, Eleanor,' says Sam, controlling his voice, 'if it's too much trouble, I can take the projector over there.'

'I ought to make you do that.'

'Am I such an idiot that I must consult you before I invite friends to the house?'

Eleanor has the intuition that Sam, if he allowed himself, could well drown in pornography. She is quite annoyed at him, but she would never dream of allowing Sam to take the projector over to Marvin Rossman's where he could view the movie without her – that seems indefinably dangerous. Besides she would like to see it, too. The mother in Eleanor is certain it cannot hurt her.

'All right, Sam,' she says, 'but you are a child.'

More exactly, an adolescent, Sam decides. Ever since Marvin phoned, Sam has felt the nervous glee of an adolescent locking himself in the bathroom. Anal fixation, Sam thinks automatically.

While Eleanor goes down to buy beer and cold cuts in a delicatessen, Sam gets out the projector and begins to clean it. He is far from methodical in this. He knows the machine is all right, he has shown movies of Eleanor and his daughters only a few weeks ago, but from the moment Eleanor left the apartment, Sam has been consumed by an anxiety that the projection bulb is burned out. Once he has examined it, he begins to fret about the motor. He wonders if it needs oiling, he blunders through a drawer of household tools looking for an oilcan. It is ridiculous. Sam knows that what he is trying to keep out of his mind are the reactions Sergius will have. Sergius will want to 'work through' all of Sam's reasons for seeing the movie. Well, Sam tells himself, he knows in advance what will be discovered: detachment, not wanting to accept Eleanor as a sexual partner, evasion of responsibility, etc. etc. The devil with Sergius. Sam has never seen a dirty movie, and he certainly wants to.

He feels obliged to laugh at himself. He could not be more nervous, he knows, if he were about to make love to a woman he had never touched before. It is really disgraceful.

When Eleanor comes back, Sam hovers about her. He is uncomfortable with her silence. 'I suppose they'll be here soon,' Sam says.

'Probably.'

Sam does not know if he is angry at Eleanor or apprehensive that she is angry at him. Much to his surprise he catches her by the waist and hears himself saying, 'You know, maybe tonight when they're gone . . . I mean, we do have the apartment to ourselves.' Eleanor moves neither toward him nor away from him. 'Darling, it's not because of the movie,' Sam goes on, 'I swear. Don't you think maybe we could . . .'

'Maybe,' says Eleanor.


3


The company has arrived, and it may be well to say a word or two about them. Marvin Rossman, who has brought the film, is a dentist, although it might be more accurate to describe him as a frustrated doctor. Rossman is full of statistics and items of odd information about the malpractice of physicians, and he will tell these things in his habitually gloomy voice, a voice so slow, so sad, that it almost conceals the humor of his remarks. Or, perhaps, that is what creates his humor. In his spare time, he is a sculptor, and if Eleanor may be trusted, he is not without talent. I often picture him working in the studio loft he has rented, his tall bony frame the image of dejection. He will pat a piece of clay to the armature, he will rub it sadly with his thumb, he will shrug, he does not believe that anything of merit could come from him. When he talked to Sam over the phone, he was pessimistic about the film they were to see. 'It can't be any good,' he said in his melancholy voice. 'I know it'll be a disappointment.' Like Sam, he has a mustache, but Rossman's will droop at the corners.

Alan Sperber, who has come with Rossman, is the subject of some curiosity for the Slovodas. He is not precisely womanish; in fact, he is a large plump man, but his voice is too soft, his manners too precise. He is genial, yet he is finicky; waspish, yet bland; he is fond of telling long rather affected stories, he is always prepared with a new one, but to general conversation he contributes little. As a lawyer, he seems miscast. One cannot imagine him inspiring a client to confidence. He is the sort of heavy florid man who seems boyish at forty, and the bow ties and gray flannel suits he wears do not make him appear more mature.

Roslyn Sperber, his wife, used to be a schoolteacher, and she is a quiet nervous woman who talks a great deal when she is drunk. She is normally quite pleasant, and has only one habit which is annoying to any degree. It is a little flaw, but social life is not unlike marriage in that habit determines far more than vice or virtue. This mannerism which has become so offensive to the friends of the Sperbers is Roslyn's social pretension. Perhaps I should say intellectual pretension. She entertains people as if she were conducting a salon, and in her birdlike voice is forever forcing her guests to accept still another intellectual canapé. 'You must hear Sam's view of the world market,' she will say, or 'Has Louise told you her statistics on divorce?' It is quite pathetic for she is so eager to please. I have seen her eyes fill with tears at a sharp word from Alan.

Marvin Rossman's wife, Louise, is a touch grim and definite in her opinions. She is a social welfare worker, and will declare herself with force whenever conversation impinges on those matters where she is expert. She is quite opposed to psychoanalysis, and will say without quarter, 'It's all very well for people in the upper-middle area' – she is referring to the upper middle class – 'but, it takes more than a couch to solve the problems of . . .' and she will list narcotics, juvenile delinquency, psychosis, relief distribution, slum housing, and other descriptions of our period. She recites these categories with an odd anticipation. One would guess she was ordering a meal.

Sam is fond of Marvin but he cannot abide Louise. 'You'd think she discovered poverty,' he will complain to Eleanor.

The Slovodas do feel superior to the Rossmans and the Sperbers. If pressed, they could not offer the most convincing explanation why. I suppose what it comes down to is that Sam and Eleanor do not think of themselves as really belonging to a class, and they feel that the Sperbers and Rossmans are petit-bourgeois. I find it hard to explain their attitude. Their company feels as much discomfort and will apologize as often as the Slovodas for the money they have, and the money they hope to earn. They are all of them equally concerned with progressive education and the methods of raising children to be well adjusted – indeed, they are discussing that now – they consider themselves relatively free of sexual taboo, or put more properly, Sam and Eleanor are no less possessive than the others. The Slovodas' culture is not more profound; I should be hard put to say that Sam is more widely read, more seriously informed, than Marvin or Alan, or for that matter, Louise. Probably, it comes to this: Sam, in his heart, thinks himself a rebel, and there are few rebels who do not claim an original mind. Eleanor has been a bohemian and considers herself more sophisticated than her friends who merely went to college and got married. Louise Rossman could express it most soundly. 'Artists, writers, and people of the creative layer have in their occupational ideology the belief that they are classless.'

One thing I might remark about the company. They are all being the most unconscionable hypocrites. They have rushed across half the city of New York to see a pornographic film, and they are not at all interested in each other at the moment. The women are giggling like tickled children at remarks which cannot possibly be so funny. Yet, they are all determined to talk for a respectable period of time. No less, it must be serious talk. Roslyn has said once, 'I feel so funny at the thought of seeing such a movie,' and the others have passed her statement by.

At the moment, Sam is talking about value. I might note that Sam loves conversation and thrives when he can expound an idea.

'What are our values today?' he asks. 'It's really fantastic when you stop to think of it. Take any bright talented kid who's getting out of college now.'

'My kid brother, for example,' Marvin interposes morosely. He passes his bony hand over his sad mustache, and somehow the remark has become amusing, much as if Marvin had said, 'Oh, yes, you have reminded me of the trials, the worries, and the cares which my fabulous younger brother heaps upon me.'

'All right, take him,' Sam says. 'What does he want to be?'

'He doesn't want to be anything,' says Marvin.

'That's my point,' Sam says excitedly. 'Rather than work at certain occupations, the best of these kids would rather do nothing at all.'

'Alan has a cousin,' Roslyn says, 'who swears he'll wash dishes before he becomes a businessman.'

'I wish that were true,' Eleanor interrupts. 'It seems to me everybody is conforming more and more these days.'

They argue about this. Sam and Eleanor claim the country is suffering from hysteria; Alan Sperber disagrees and says it's merely a reflection of the headlines; Louise says no adequate criteria exist to measure hysteria; Marvin says he doesn't know anything at all.

'More solid liberal gains are being made in this period,' says Alan, 'than you would believe. Consider the Negro –'

'Is the Negro any less maladjusted?' Eleanor shouts with passion.

Sam maneuvers the conversation back to his thesis. 'The values of the young today, and by the young, I mean the cream of the kids, the ones with ideas, are a reaction of indifference to the culture crisis. It really is despair. All they know is what they don't want to do.'

'That is easier,' Alan says genially.

'It's not altogether unhealthy,' Sam says. 'It's a corrective for smugness and the false value of the past, but it has created new false value.' He thinks it worth emphasizing. 'False value seems always to beget further false value.'

'Define your terms,' says Louise, the scientist.

'No, look,' Sam says, 'there's no revolt, there's no acceptance. Kids today don't want to get married, and –'

Eleanor interrupts. 'Why should a girl rush to get married? She loses all chance for developing herself.'

Sam shrugs. They are all talking at once. 'Kids don't want to get married,' he repeats, 'and they don't want not to get married. They merely drift.'

'It's a problem we'll all have to face with our own kids in ten years,' Alan says, 'although I think you make too much of it, Sam.'

'My daughter,' Marvin states. 'She's embarrassed I'm a

dentist. Even more embarrassed than I am.' They laugh.

Sam tells a story about his youngest, Carol Ann. It seems he had a fight with her, and she went to her room. Sam followed, he called through the door.

'No answer,' Sam says. 'I called her again, "Carol Ann." I was a little worried you understand, because she seemed so upset, so I said to her, "Carol Ann, you know I love you." What do you think she answered?'

'What?' asks Rosyln.

'She said, "Daddy, why are you so anxious?"'

They all laugh again. There are murmurs about what a clever thing it was to say. In the silence which follows, Roslyn leans forward and says quickly in her high voice, 'You must get Alan to tell you his wonderful story about the man who studied yogi.'

'Yoga,' Alan corrects. 'It's too long to tell.'

The company prevails on him.

'Well,' says Alan, in his genial courtroom voice, 'it concerns a friend of mine named Cassius O'Shaugnessy.'

'You don't mean Jerry O'Shaugnessy, do you?' asks Sam.

Alan does not know Jerry O'Shaugnessy. 'No, no, this is Cassius O'Shaugnessy,' he says. 'He's really quite an extraordinary fellow.' Alan sits plumply in his chair, fingering his bow tie. They are all used to his stories, which are told in a formal style and exhibit the attempt to recapture a certain note of urbanity, wit, and *élan* which Alan has probably copied from someone else. Sam and Eleanor respect his ability to tell these stories, but they resent the fact that he talks *at* them.

'You'd think we were a jury of his inferiors,' Eleanor has said. 'I hate being talked down to.' What she resents is Alan's quiet implication that his antecedents, his social position, in total his life outside the room is superior to the life within. Eleanor now takes the promise from Alan's story by remarking, 'Yes, and let's see the movie when Alan has finished.'

'Sssh,' Roslyn says.

'Cassius was at college a good while before me,' says Alan, 'but I knew him while I was an undergraduate. He would drop in and visit from time to time. An absolutely extraordinary fellow. The most amazing career. You see, he's done about everything.'

'I love the way Alan tells it,' Roslyn pipes nervously.

'Cassius was in France with Dos Passos and Cummings, he was even arrested with e.e. After the war, he was one of the founders of the Dadaist school, and for a while I understand he was Fitzgerald's guide to the gold of the Côte d'Azur. He knew everybody, he did everything. Do you realize that before the twenties had ended, Cassius had managed his father's business and then entered a monastery? It is said he influenced T. S. Eliot.'

'Today, we'd call Cassius a psychopath,' Marvin observes.

'Cassius called himself a great dilettante,' Alan answers, 'although perhaps the nineteenth-century Russian conception of the great sinner would be more appropriate. What do you say if I tell you this was only the beginning of his career?'

'What's the point?' Louise asks.

'Not yet,' says Alan, holding up a hand. His manner seems to say that if his audience cannot appreciate the story, he does not feel obliged to continue. 'Cassius studied Marx in the monastery. He broke his vows, quit the Church and became a Communist. All through the thirties he was a figure in the Party, going to Moscow, involved in all the party struggles. He left only during the Moscow trials.'

Alan's manner while he relates such stories is somewhat effeminate. He talks with little caresses of his hand, he mentions names and places with a lingering ease as if to suggest that his audience and he are aware, above all, of nuance. The story as Alan tells it is drawn overlong. Suffice it that the man about whom he is talking, Cassius O'Shaugnessy, becomes a Trotskyist, becomes an anarchist, is a pacifist during the second World War, and suffers it from a prison cell.

'I may say,' Alan goes on, 'that I worked for his defense, and was successful in getting him acquitted. Imagine my dolor when I learned that he had turned his back on his anarchist friends and was living with gangsters.'

'This is weird,' Eleanor says.

'Weird, it is,' Alan agrees. 'Cassius got into some scrape, and disappeared. What could you do with him? I learned only recently that he had gone to India and was studying yoga. In fact, I learned it from Cassius himself. I asked him of his experiences at Brahnaputh-thar, and he told me the following story.'

Now Alan's voice alters, he assumes the part of Cassius and speaks in a tone weary of experience, wise and sad in its knowledge. '"I was sitting on my haunches contemplating my navel," Cassius said to me, "when of a sudden I discovered my navel under a different aspect. It seemed to me that if I were to give a counterclockwise twist, my navel would unscrew."'

Alan looks up, he surveys his audience which is now rapt and uneasy, not certain as yet whether a joke is to come. Alan's thumb and forefinger pluck at the middle of his ample belly, his feet are crossed upon the carpet in symbolic suggestion of Cassius upon his haunches.

'"Taking a deep breath, I turned, and the abysses of Vishtarni loomed beneath. My navel had begun to unscrew. I knew I was about to accept the reward of three years of contemplation. So," said Cassius, "I turned again, and my navel unscrewed a little more. I turned and I turned,"' Alan's fingers now revolving upon his belly, '"and after a period I knew that with one more turn my navel would unscrew itself forever. At the edge of revelation, I took one sweet breath, and turned my navel free."'

Alan looks up at his audience.

'"Damn," said Cassius, "if my ass didn't fall off."'

4

The story has left the audience in an exasperated mood. It has been a most untypical story for Alan to tell, a little out of place, not offensive exactly, but irritating and inconsequential. Sam is the only one to laugh with more than bewildered courtesy, and his mirth seems excessive to everyone but Alan, and of course, Roslyn, who feels as if she has been the producer. I suppose what it reduces to, is a lack of taste. Perhaps that is why Alan is not the lawyer one would expect. He does not have that appreciation – as necessary in his trade as for an actor – of what is desired at any moment, of that which will encourage as opposed to that which does not encourage a stimulating but smooth progression of logic and sentiment. Only a fool would tell so long a story when everyone is awaiting the movie.

Now, they are preparing. The men shift armchairs to correspond with the couch, the projector is set up, the screen is unfolded. Sam attempts to talk while he is threading the film, but no one listens. They seem to realize suddenly that a frightful demand has been placed upon them. One does not study pornography in a living room with a beer glass in one's hand, and friends at the elbow. It is the most unsatisfactory of compromises; one can draw neither the benefits of solitary contemplation nor of social exchange. There is, at bottom, the same exasperated fright which one experiences in turning the shower tap and receiving cold water when the flesh has been prepared for heat. Perhaps that is why they are laughing so much now that the movie is begun.

A title, *The Evil Act*, twitches on the screen, shot with scars, holes, and the dust lines of age. A man and woman are sitting on a couch, they are having coffee. They chat. What they say is conveyed by printed words upon an ornately flowered card, interjected between glimpses of their casual gestures, a cup to the mouth, a smile, a cigarette being lit. The man's name, it seems, is Frankie Idell; he is talking to his wife, Magnolia. Frank is dark, he is sinister, he confides in Magnolia, his dark counterpart, with a grimace of his brows, black from make-up pencil.

This is what the title read:

FRANKIE: She will be here soon.
MAGNOLIA: This time the little vixen will not escape.
FRANKIE: No, my dear, this time we are prepared.
(*He looks at his watch.*)
FRANKIE: Listen, she knocks!

There is a shot of a tall blonde woman knocking on the door. She is probably over thirty, but by her short dress and ribboned hat it is suggested that she is a girl of fifteen.

FRANKIE: Come in, Eleanor.

As may be expected, the audience laughs hysterically at this. It is so wonderful a coincidence. 'How I remember Frankie,' says Eleanor Slovoda, and Roslyn Sperber is the only one not amused. In the midst of the others' laughter, she says in a worried tone, obviously adrift upon her own concerns, 'Do you think we'll have to stop the film in the middle to let the bulb cool off?' The others hoot, they giggle, they are weak from the combination of their own remarks and the action of the plot.

Frankie and Magnolia have sat down on either side of the heroine, Eleanor. A moment passes. Suddenly, stiffly, they attack. Magnolia from her side kisses Eleanor, and Frankie commits an indecent caress.

ELEANOR: How dare you? Stop!

MAGNOLIA: Scream, my little one. It will do you no good. The walls are soundproofed.

FRANKIE: We've fixed a way to make you come across.

ELEANOR: This is hideous. I am hitherto undefiled. Do not touch me!

The captions fade away. A new title takes their place. It says, *But There Is No Escape From The Determined Pair*. On the fade-in, we discover Eleanor in the most distressing situation. Her hands are tied to loops running from the ceiling, and she can only writhe in helpless perturbation before the deliberate and progressive advances of Frankie and Magnolia. Slowly they humiliate her, with relish they probe her.

The audience laughs no longer. A hush has come upon them. Eyes unblinking they devour the images upon Sam Slovoda's screen.

Eleanor is without clothing. As the last piece is pulled away, Frankie and Magnolia circle about her in a grotesque of panto-mime, a leering of lips, limbs in a distortion of desire. Eleanor faints. Adroitly, Magnolia cuts her bonds. We see Frankie carrying her inert body.

Now, Eleanor is trussed to a bed, and the husband and wife are tormenting her with feathers. Bodies curl upon the bed in postures so complicated, in combinations so advanced, that the audience leans forward, Sperbers, Rossmans, and Slovodas, as if tempted to embrace the moving images. The hands trace abstract circles upon the screen, passes and recoveries upon a white background so illumined that hollows and swells, limb to belly and mouth to undescribables, tip of a nipple, orb of a navel, swim in giant magnification, flow and slide in a lurching yawing fall, blotting out the camera eye.

A little murmur, all unconscious, passes from their lips. The audience sways, each now finally lost in himself, communing hungrily with shadows, violated or violating, fantasy triumphant.

At picture's end, Eleanor the virgin whore is released from the bed. She kisses Frankie, she kisses Magnolia. 'You dears,' she says, 'let's do it again.' The projector lamp burns empty light, the machine keeps turning, the tag of film goes *slap-tap*, *slap-tap*, *slap-tap*, *slap-tap*, *slap-tap*, *slap-tap*.

'Sam, turn it off,' says Eleanor.

But when the room lights are on, they cannot look at one another. 'Can we see it again?' someone mutters. So, again, Eleanor knocks on the door, is tied, defiled, ravished, and made rapturous. They watch it soberly now, the room hot with the heat of their bodies, the darkness a balm for orgiastic vision. To the Deer Park, Sam is thinking, to the Deer Park of Louis XV were brought the most beautiful maidens of France, and there they stayed, dressed in fabulous silks, perfumed and wigged, the mole drawn upon their cheek, ladies of pleasure awaiting the pleasure of the king. So Louis had stripped an empire, bankrupt a treasury, prepared a deluge, while in his garden on summer evenings the maidens performed their pageants, eighteenth-century tableau of the evil act, beauteous instruments of one man's desire, lewd translation of a king's power. That century men sought wealth so they might use its fruits; this epoch men lusted for power in order to amass more power, a compounding of power into pyramids of abstraction whose yield are cannon and wire enclosure, pillars of statistics to the men who are the kings of this century and do no more in power's leisure time than go to church, claim to love their wives, and eat vegetables.

Is it possible, Sam wonders, that each of them here, two

Rossmans, two Sperbers, two Slovodas, will cast off their clothes when the movie is done and perform the orgy which tickles at the heart of their desire? They will not, he knows, they will make jokes when the projector is put away, they will gorge the plate of delicatessen Eleanor provides, and swallow more beer, he among them. He will be the first to make jokes.

Sam is right. The movie has made him extraordinarily alive to the limits of them all. While they sit with red faces, eyes bugged, glutting sandwiches of ham, salami, and tongue, he begins the teasing.

'Roslyn,' he calls out, 'is the bulb cooled off yet?'

She cannot answer him. She chokes on beer, her face glazes, she is helpless with self-protecting laughter.

'Why are you so anxious, Daddy?' Eleanor says quickly.

They begin to discuss the film. As intelligent people they must dominate it. Someone wonders about the actors in the piece, and discussion begins afresh. 'I fail to see,' says Louise, 'why they should be hard to classify. Pornography is a job to the criminal and prostitute element.'

'No, you won't find an ordinary prostitute doing this,' Sam insists. 'It requires a particular kind of personality.'

'They have to be exhibitionists,' says Eleanor.

'It's all economic,' Louise maintains.

'I wonder what those girls felt?' Roslyn asks. 'I feel sorry for them.'

'I'd like to be the cameraman,' says Alan.

'I'd like to be Frankie,' says Marvin sadly.

There is a limit to how long such a conversation may continue. The jokes lapse into silence. They are all busy eating. When they begin to talk again, it is of other things. Each dollop of food sops the agitation which the movie has spilled. They gossip about the party the night before, they discuss which single men were interested in which women, who got drunk, who got sick, who said the wrong thing, who went home with someone else's date. When this is exhausted, one of them mentions a play the others have not seen. Soon they are talking about books, a concert, a one-man show by an artist who is a friend. Dependably, conversation will voyage its orbit. While the men talk of politics, the women are discussing fashions, progressive schools, and recipes they have attempted. Sam is uncomfortable with the division; he knows Eleanor will resent it, he knows she will complain later of the insularity of men and the basic contempt they feel for women's intelligence.

'But you collaborated,' Sam will argue. 'No one forced you to be with the women.'

'Was I to leave them alone?' Eleanor will answer.

'Well, why do the women always have to go off by themselves?'

'Because the men aren't interested in what we have to say.'

Sam sighs. He has been talking with interest, but really he is bored. These are nice pleasant people, he thinks, but they are ordinary people, exactly the sort he has spent so many years with, making little jokes, little gossip, living little everyday events, a close circle where everyone mothers the other by his presence. The womb of middle-class life, Sam decides heavily. He is in a bad mood indeed. Everything is laden with dissatisfaction.

Alan has joined the women. He delights in preparing odd dishes when friends visit the Sperbers, and he is describing to Eleanor how he makes blueberry pancakes. Marvin draws closer to Sam.

'I wanted to tell you,' he says, 'Alan's story reminded me. I saw Jerry O'Shaugnessy the other day.'

'Where was he?'

Marvin is hesitant. 'It was a shock, Sam. He's on the Bowery. I guess he's become a wino.'

'He always drank a lot,' says Sam.

'Yeah.' Marvin cracks his bony knuckles. 'What a stinking time this is, Sam.'

'It's probably like the years after 1905 in Russia,' Sam says.

'No revolutionary party will come out of this.'

'No,' Sam says, 'nothing will come.'

He is thinking of Jerry O'Shaugnessy. What did he look like? what did he say? Sam asks Marvin, and clucks his tongue at the dispiriting answer. It is a shock to him. He draws closer to Marvin, he feels a bond. They have, after all, been through some years together. In the thirties they have been in the

Communist Party, they have quit together, they are both weary of politics today, still radicals out of habit, but without enthusiasm and without a cause. 'Jerry was a hero to me,' Sam says.

'To all of us,' says Marvin.

The fabulous Jerry O'Shaugnessy, thinks Sam. In the old days, in the Party, they had made a legend of him. All of them with their middle-class origins and their desire to know a worker-hero.

I may say that I was never as fond of Jerry O'Shaugnessy as was Sam. I thought him a showman and too pleased with himself. Sam, however, with his timidity, his desire to travel, to have adventure and know many women, was obliged to adore O'Shaugnessy. At least he was enraptured with his career.

Poor Jerry who ends as a bum. He has been everything else. He has been a trapper in Alaska, a chauffeur for gangsters, an officer in the Foreign Legion, a labor organizer. His nose was broken, there were scars on his chin. When he would talk about his years at sea or his experiences in Spain, the stenographers and garment workers, the radio writers and unemployed actors would listen to his speeches as if he were the prophet of new romance, and their blood would be charged with the magic of revolutionary vision. A man with tremendous charm. In those days it had been easy to confuse his love for himself with his love for all underprivileged workingmen.

'I thought he was still in the Party,' Sam says.

'No,' says Marvin, 'I remember they kicked him out a couple of years ago. He was supposed to have piddled some funds, that's what they say.'

'I wish he'd taken the treasury,' Sam remarks bitterly. 'The Party used him for years.'

Marvin shrugs. 'They used each other.' His mustache droops. 'Let me tell you about Sonderson. You know he's still in the Party. The most progressive dentist in New York.' They laugh.

While Marvin tells the story, Sam is thinking of other things. Since he has quit Party work, he has studied a great deal. He can tell you about prison camps and the secret police, political murders, the Moscow trials, the exploitation of Soviet labor, the privileges of the bureaucracy; it is all painful to him. He is straddled between the loss of a country he has never seen, and his repudiation of the country in which he lives. 'Doesn't the Party seem a horror now?' he bursts out.

Marvin nods. They are trying to comprehend the distance between Party members they have known, people by turn pathetic, likable, or annoying – people not unlike themselves – and in contrast the immensity of historic logic which deploys along statistics of the dead.

'It's all schizoid,' Sam says. 'Modern life is schizoid.'

Marvin agrees. They have agreed on this many times, bored with the petulance of their small voices, yet needing the comfort of such complaints. Marvin asks Sam if he has given up his novel, and Sam says, 'Temporarily.' He cannot find a form, he explains. He does not want to write a realistic novel, because reality is no longer realistic. 'I don't know what it is,' says Sam. 'To tell you the truth, I think I'm kidding myself. I'll never finish this book. I just like to entertain the idea I'll do something good some day.' They sit there in friendly depression. Conversation has cooled. Alan and the women are no longer talking.

'Marvin,' asks Louise, 'what time is it?'

They are ready to go. Sam must say directly what he had hoped to approach by suggestion. 'I was wondering,' he whispers to Rossman, 'would you mind if I held onto the film for a day or two?'

Marvin looks at him. 'Oh, why of course, Sam,' he says in his morose voice. 'I know how it is.' He pats Sam on the shoulder as if, symbolically, to convey the exchange of ownership. They are fellow conspirators.

'If you ever want to borrow the projector,' Sam suggests.

'Nah,' says Marvin, 'I don't know that it would make much difference.'

5

It has been, when all is said, a most annoying day. As Sam and Eleanor tidy the apartment, emptying ash trays and washing the few dishes, they are fond neither of themselves nor each other.

'What a waste today has been,' Eleanor remarks, and Sam can only agree. He has done no writing, he has not been outdoors, and still it is late in the evening, and he has talked too much, eaten too much, is nervous from the movie they have seen. He knows that he will catch it again with Eleanor before they go to sleep; she has given her assent to that. But as is so often the case with Sam these days, he cannot await their embrace with any sure anticipation. Eleanor may be in the mood or Eleanor may not; there is no way he can control the issue. It is depressing; Sam knows that he circles about Eleanor at such times with the guilty maneuvers of a sad hound. Resent her as he must, be furious with himself as he will, there is not very much he can do about it. Often, after they have made love, they will lie beside each other in silence, each offended, each certain the other is to blame. At such times, memory tickles them with a cruel feather. Not always has it been like this. When they were first married, and indeed for the six months they lived together before marriage, everything was quite different. Their affair was very exciting to them; each told the other with some hyperbole but no real mistruth that no one in the past had ever been comparable as lover.

I suppose I am a romantic. I always feel that this is the best time in people's lives. There is, after all, so little we accomplish, and that short period when we are beloved and triumph as lovers is sweet with power. Rarely are we concerned then with our lack of importance; we are too important. In Sam's case, disillusion means even more. Like so many young men, he entertained the secret conceit that he was an extraordinary lover. One cannot really believe this without supporting at the same time the equally secret conviction that one is fundamentally inept. It is – no matter what Sergius would say – a more dramatic and therefore more attractive view of oneself than the sober notion which Sam now accepts with grudging wisdom, that the man as lover is dependent upon the bounty of the woman. As I say, he accepts the notion, it is one of the lineaments of maturity, but there is a part of him which, no matter how harried by analysis, cannot relinquish the antagonism he feels that Eleanor has respected his private talent so poorly, and has not allowed him to confer its benefits upon more women. I mock Sam, but he would mock himself on this. It hardly matters; mockery cannot accomplish everything, and Sam seethes with that most private and tender pain: even worse than being unattractive to the world is to be unattractive to one's mate; or, what is the same and describes Sam's case more accurately, never to know in advance when he shall be undesirable to Eleanor.

I make perhaps too much of the subject, but that is only because it is so important to Sam. Relations between Eleanor and him are not really that bad – I know other couples who have much less or nothing at all. But comparisons are poor comfort to Sam; his standards are so high. So are Eleanor's. I am convinced the most unfortunate people are those who would make an art of love. It sours other effort. Of all artists, they are certainly the most wretched.

Shall I furnish a model? Sam and Eleanor are on the couch, and the projector, adjusted to its slowest speed, is retracing the elaborate pantomime of the three principals. If one could allow these shadows a life . . . but indeed such life has been given them. Sam and Eleanor are no more than an itch, a smart, a threshold of satisfaction; the important share of themselves has steeped itself in Frankie-, Magnolia-, Eleanor-of-the-film. Indeed the variations are beyond telling. It is the most outrageous orgy performed by five ghosts.

Self-critical Sam! He makes love in front of a movie, and one cannot say that it is unsatisfactory any more than one can say it is pleasant. It is dirty, downright porno dirty, it is a lewd slop-brush slapped through the middle of domestic exasperations and breakfast eggs. It is so dirty that only half of Sam – he is quite divisible into fractions – can be exercised at all. The part that is his brain worries along like a cuckolded burgher. He is taking the pulse of his anxiety. Will he last long enough to satisfy Eleanor? Will the children come back tonight? He cannot help it. In the midst of the circus, he is suddenly convinced the children will walk through the door. 'Why are you so anxious, Daddy?'

So it goes. Sam the lover is conscious of exertion. One moment he is Frankie Idell, destroyer of virgins – take that! you whore! – the next, body moving, hands caressing, he is no

more than some lines from a psychoanalytical text. He is
thinking about the sensitivity of his scrotum. He has read that
this is a portent of femininity in a male. How strong is his latent
homosexuality worries Sam, thrusting stiffly, warm sweat running cold. Does he identify with Eleanor-of-the-film?

Technically, the climax is satisfactory. They lie together in
the dark, the film ended, the projector humming its lonely
revolutions in the quiet room. Sam gets up to turn it off; he
comes back and kisses Eleanor upon the mouth. Apparently,
she has enjoyed herself more than he; she is tender and fondles
the tip of his nose.

'You know, Sam,' she says from her space beside him, 'I
think I saw this picture before.'

'When?'

'Oh, you know when. That time.'

Sam thinks dully that women are always most loving when
they can reminisce about infidelity.

'That time!' he repeats.

'I think so.'

Racing forward from memory like the approaching star
which begins as a point on the mind and swells to explode the
eyeball with its odious image, Sam remembers, and is weak in
the dark. It is ten years, eleven perhaps, before they were
married, yet after they were lovers. Eleanor has told him, but
she has always been vague about details. There had been two
men it seemed, and another girl, and all had been drunk. They
had seen movie after movie. With reluctant fascination, Sam
can conceive the rest. How it had pained him, how excited him.
It is years now since he has remembered, but he remembers. In
the darkness he wonders at the unreasonableness of jealous
pain. That night was impossible to imagine any longer – therefore it is more real; Eleanor his plump wife who presses a
pigeon's shape against her housecoat, forgotten heroine of black
orgies. It had been meaningless, Eleanor claimed; it was Sam
she loved, and the other had been no more than a fancy of which
she wished to rid herself. Would it be the same today, thinks
Sam, or had Eleanor been loved by Frankie, by Frankie of the
other movies, by Frankie of the two men she never saw again on
that night so long ago?

The pleasure I get from this pain, Sam thinks furiously.

It is not altogether perverse. If Eleanor causes him pain, it means after all that she is alive for him. I have often observed that the reality of a person depends upon his ability to hurt us; Eleanor as the vague accusing embodiment of the wife is different, altogether different, from Eleanor who lies warmly in Sam's bed, an attractive Eleanor who may wound his flesh. Thus, brother to the pleasure of pain, is the sweeter pleasure which follows pain. Sam, tired, lies in Eleanor's arms, and they talk with the cozy trade words of old professionals, agreeing that they will not make love again before a movie, that it was exciting but also not without detachment, that all in all it has been good but not quite right, that she had loved this action he had done, and was uncertain about another. It is their old familiar critique, a sign that they are intimate and well disposed. They do not talk about the act when it has failed to fire; then they go silently to sleep. But now, Eleanor's enjoyment having mollified Sam's sense of no enjoyment, they talk with the apologetics and encomiums of familiar mates. Eleanor falls asleep, and Sam falls almost asleep, curling next to her warm body, his hand over her round belly with the satisfaction of a sculptor. He is drowsy, and he thinks drowsily that these few moments of creature-pleasure, this brief compassion he can feel for the body that trusts itself to sleep beside him, his comfort in its warmth, is perhaps all the meaning he may ask for his life. That out of disappointment, frustration, and the passage of dreary years come these few moments when he is close to her, and their years together possess a connotation more rewarding than the sum of all which has gone into them.

But then he thinks of the novel he wants to write, and he is wide-awake again. Like the sleeping pill which fails to work and leaves one warped in an exaggeration of the ills which sought the drug, Sam passes through the promise of sex-emptied sleep, and is left with nervous loins, swollen jealousy of an act ten years dead, and sweating irritable resentment of the woman's body which hinders his limbs. He has wasted the day, he tells himself, he has wasted the day as he has wasted so many days of his life, and tomorrow in the office he will be no more than his ten fingers typing plot and words for Bramba the Venusian and

Lee-Lee Deeds, Hollywood Star, while that huge work with which he has cheated himself, holding it before him as a covenant of his worth, that enormous novel which would lift him at a bound from the impasse in which he stifles, whose dozens of characters would develop a vision of life in bountiful complexity, lies foundered, rotting on a beach of purposeless effort. Notes here, pages there, it sprawls through a formless wreck of incidental ideas and half-episodes, utterly without shape. He is not even a hero for it.

One could not have a hero today, Sam thinks, a man of action and contemplation, capable of sin, large enough for good, a man immense. There is only a modern hero damned by no more than the ugliness of wishes whose satisfaction he will never know. One needs a man who could walk the stage, someone who – no matter who, not himself. Someone, Sam thinks, who reasonably could not exist.

The novelist, thinks Sam, perspiring beneath blankets, must live in paranoia and seek to be one with the world; he must be terrified of experience and hungry for it; he must think himself nothing and believe he is superior to all. The feminine in his nature cries for proof he is a man; he dreams of power and is without capacity to gain it; he loves himself above all and therefore despises all that he is.

He is that, thinks Sam, he is part of the perfect prescription, and yet he is not a novelist. He lacks energy and belief. It is left for him to write an article some day about the temperament of the ideal novelist.

In the darkness, memories rise, yeast-swells of apprehension. Out of bohemian days so long ago, comes the friend of Eleanor, a girl who had been sick and was committed to an institution. They visited her, Sam and Eleanor, they took the suburban train and sat on the lawn of the asylum grounds while patients circled about intoning a private litany, or shuddering in boob-blundering fright from an insect that crossed their skin. The friend had been silent. She had smiled, she had answered their questions with the fewest words, and had turned again to her study of sunlight and blue sky. As they were about to leave, the girl had taken Sam aside. 'They violate me,' she said in a whisper. 'Every night when the doors are locked, they come to my room and they make the movie. I am the heroine and am subjected to all variety of sexual viciousness. Tell them to leave me alone so I may enter the convent.' And while she talked, in a horror of her body, one arm scrubbed the other. Poor tortured friend. They had seen her again, and she babbled, her face had coarsened into an idiot leer.

Sam sweats. There is so little he knows, and so much to know. Youth of the depression with its economic terms, what can he know of madness or religion? They are both so alien to him. He is the mongrel, Sam thinks, brought up without religion from a mother half Protestant and half Catholic, and a father half Catholic and half Jew. He is the quarter-Jew, and yet he is a Jew, or so he feels himself, knowing nothing of Gospel, tabernacle, or Mass, the Jew through accident, through state of mind. What . . . whatever did he know of penance? self-sacrifice? mortification of the flesh? the love of his fellow man? Am I concerned with my relation to God? ponders Sam, and smiles sourly in the darkness. No, that has never concerned him, he thinks, not for better nor for worse. 'They are making the movie,' says the girl into the ear of memory, 'and so I cannot enter the convent.'

How hideous was the mental hospital. A concentration camp, decides Sam. Perhaps it would be the world some day, or was that only his projection of feelings of hopelessness? 'Do not try to solve the problems of the world,' he hears from Sergius, and pounds a lumpy pillow.

However could he organize his novel? What form to give it? It is so complex. Too loose, thinks Sam, too scattered. Will he ever fall asleep? Wearily, limbs tense, his stomach too keen, he plays again the game of putting himself to sleep. 'I do not feel my toes,' Sam says to himself, 'my toes are dead, my calves are asleep, my calves are sleeping . . .'

In the middle from wakefulness to slumber, in the torpor which floats beneath blankets, I give an idea to Sam. 'Destroy time, and chaos may be ordered,' I say to him.

'Destroy time, and chaos may be ordered,' he repeats after me, and in desperation to seek his coma, mutters back, 'I do not feel my nose, my nose is numb, my eyes are heavy, my eyes are heavy.'

So Sam enters the universe of sleep, a man who seeks to live in such a way as to avoid pain, and succeeds merely in avoiding pleasure. What a dreary compromise is our life!

*1952*

# Existential Errands

# Preface

## Existential Errands

This collection covers pieces written almost entirely in the last five years, a period in which *The Deer Park* as a play was given its last draft and then produced, *Why Are We in Vietnam?* was written and then *The Armies of the Night*, *Miami and the Siege of Chicago*, *Of a Fire on the Moon* and *The Prisoner of Sex*. Three movies were also made. So it is a period when, with every thought of beginning a certain big novel which had been promised for a long time, the moot desire to have one's immediate say on contemporary matters kept diverting the novelistic impulse into journalism. Such passing books began to include many of the themes of the big novel. On the way, shorter pieces were also written for a variety of motives and occasions, written in a general state of recognition that if one had a philosophy it was being put together in many pieces. Still a view of life was expressed in those books and those years. Perhaps it was also expressed in the movies which were made and in the campaign to get the Democratic nomination for Mayor of New York. In any case, it was reasonable to think that people who liked my work might be interested in this collection since many a passing remark in the longer books became a chapter of investigation here, and more than one empty space in the high winds of other rhetoric settled into a serious discussion in these pages. So the merit of this assembly may be in the main for people who are sufficiently intrigued with a few of my ideas to try out a few more. If the emphasis is then less personal than *Advertisements for Myself*, *The Presidential Papers*, or *Cannibals and Christians*, it ought also to be said before too many apologies are upon us that this book may have a particular merit the others do not possess. Its parts are more even. It is more coherent. The ends of one piece are likely to buttress the ideas in the next. What is said about film has its relation to boxing, and to theatre and to bullfight; the pieces side by side offer elucidation of one another – besides, what is said about politics comes out of much obsession and some unfiltered experience. Even what is said about literature in the middle of this book is related to the rest, for the remarks on the Establishment and the put-on in 'Up the Family Tree' have their reflection in every piece which follows, and carry by extension into the sinister even vertiginous notions of politics and Establishment which the work, and lack of work, of the Warren Commission aroused in us. The put-on is perhaps the spirit elixir of technology. In that future world where children will be raised by professional nurses who will be guided by directives determined in the main by the ruminative processes of computers, the notion of mother and father itself will take on the same aspects of High Camp we used to recognize in politicians' voices when they spoke of fighting for freedom in Southeast Asia. It is one thing to think of an Establishment as evil (it is equivalent in its sense of bitter tragic security to the gloom of the theologian who decides God is not good), but to come to that slippery slope where one knows that the Establishment is not good, not evil, but a put-on even to itself is to cross that plastic curtain which separates the world of the past from the futures of technology. So these pieces, one may suppose, are the abstract journal of a trip from the relative certainty of boxing and bullfighting to that cubist state of the psyche where one runs for mayor with one's heart in one's mouth and is congratulated for the éclat in the put-on. It is no wonder this is a miscellany of writings on existential themes. For in our world of gesture, role, costume, supposition, and borrowed manner which is all of the air that is left to the graces of our city, in that perpetual transformation of moral axes which is the inner life of the drug, there is except for attrition no way out but by way of that moment which proves deeper than any of our pretenses, that stricken existential moment in which Camp is stripped of its marks of quotation, and put-ons shrivel in the livid air. What better way then to begin than by a description of a fight between heavyweight champions for fifteen rounds?

## PART NINE

# Clues to the
# Aesthetic of The Arena

# Boxing

## King of the Hill

Ego! It is the great word of the twentieth century. If there is a single word our century has added to the potentiality of language, it is ego. Everything we have done in this century, from monumental feats to nightmares of human destruction, has been a function of that extraordinary state of the psyche which gives us authority to declare we are sure of ourselves when we are not.

Muhammad Ali begins with the most unsettling ego of all. Having commanded the stage, he never pretends to step back and relinquish his place to other actors – like a six-foot parrot, he keeps screaming at you that he is the center of the stage. 'Come here and get me, fool,' he says. 'You can't, 'cause you don't know who I am. You don't know *where* I am. I'm human intelligence and you don't even know if I'm good or evil.' This has been his essential message to America all these years. It is intolerable to our American mentality that the figure who is probably most prominent to us after the President is simply not comprehensible, for he could be a demon or a saint. Or both! Richard Nixon, at least, appears comprehensible. We can hate him or we can vote for him, but at least we disagree with each other about him. What kills us about Cassius Clay is that the disagreement is inside us. He is *fascinating* – attraction and repulsion must be in the same package. So, he is obsessive. The more we don't want to think about him, the more we are obliged to. There is a reason for it. He is America's Greatest Ego. He is also, as I am going to try to show, the swiftest embodiment of human intelligence we have had yet, he is the very spirit of the twentieth century, he is the prince of mass man and the media. Now, perhaps temporarily, he is the fallen prince. But there still may be one holocaust of an urge to understand him, or try to, for obsession is a disease. Twenty little obsessions are twenty leeches on the mind, and one big obsession can become one big operation if we refuse to live with it. If Muhammad Ali defeats Frazier in the return bout, then he'll become the national obsession and we'll elect him President yet – you may indeed have to vote for any man who could defeat a fighter as great as Joe Frazier and still be Muhammed Ali. That's a combination!

Yes, ego – that officious and sometimes efficient exercise of ignorance-as-authority – must be the central phenomenon of the twentieth century, even if patriotic Americans like to pretend it does not exist in their heroes. Which, of course, is part of the holy American horseball. The most monstrous exhibition of ego by a brave man in many a year was Alan Shepard's three whacks at a golf ball while standing on the moon. There, in a space suit, hardly able to stand, he put a club head on an omnipurpose tool shaft and, restricted to swinging with one arm, dibbled his golf ball on the second try. On the third it went maybe half a mile – a nonphenomenal distance in the low gravitational field of the lunar sphere.

'What's so unpleasant about that?' asked a pleasant young jet-setter.

Aquarius, of the old book, loftily replied, 'Would you take a golf ball into St. Patrick's and see how far you can hit it?'

The kid nodded his head. 'Now that you put it that way, I guess I wouldn't, but I was excited when it happened. I said to my wife, "Honey, we're playing golf on the moon."'

Well, to the average fight fan, Cassius Clay has been golf on the moon. Who can comprehend the immensity of ego involved? Every fighter is in a whirligig with his ego. The fight game, for example, is filled with legends of fighters who found a girl in an elevator purposefully stalled between floors for two minutes on the afternoon of a main-event fight. Later, after he blew the fight, his irate manager blew his ears. 'Were you crazy?' the manager asked. 'Why did you do it?'

'Because,' said the fighter, 'I get these terrible headaches every afternoon, and only a chick who knows how, can relieve them.'

Ego is driving a point through to a conclusion you are obliged to reach without knowing too much about the ground you cross between. You suffer for a larger point. Every good prizefighter must have a large ego, then, because he is trying to demolish a man he doesn't know too much about, he is unfeeling – which is the ground floor of ego; and he is full of techniques – which are the wings of ego. What separates the noble ego of the prizefighters from the lesser ego of authors is that the fighter goes through experiences in the ring which are occasionally immense, incommunicable except to fighters who have been as good, or to women who have gone through every minute of an anguish-filled birth, experiences which are finally mysterious. Like men who climb mountains, it is an exercise of ego which becomes something like soul – just as technology may have begun to have transcended itself when we reached to the moon. So, two great fighters in a great fight travel down subterranean rivers of exhaustion and cross mountain peaks of agony, stare at the light of their own death in the eye of the man they are fighting, travel into the crossroads of the most excruciating choice of karma as they get up from the floor against all the appeal of the sweet swooning catacombs of oblivion – it is just that we do not see them this way, because they are not primarily men of words, and this is the century of words, numbers, and symbols. Enough.

We have come to the point. There are languages other than words, languages of symbol and languages of nature. There are languages of the body. And prizefighting is one of them. There is no attempting to comprehend a prizefighter unless we are willing to recognize that he speaks with a command of the body which is as detached, subtle, and comprehensive in its intelligence as any exercise of mind by such social engineers as Herman Kahn or Henry Kissinger. Of course, a man like Herman Kahn is by report gifted with a bulk of three hundred pounds. He does not move around with a light foot. So many a good average prizefighter, just a little punchy, does not speak with any particular éclat. That doesn't mean he is incapable of expressing himself with wit, style, and an aesthetic flair for surprise when he boxes with his body, any more than Kahn's obesity would keep us from recognizing that his mind can work with strength. Boxing is a dialogue between bodies. Ignorant men, usually black, and usually next to illiterate, address one another in a set of *conversational* exchanges which go deep into the heart of each other's matter. It is just that they converse with their physiques. But unless you believe that you cannot receive a mortal wound from an incisive remark, you may be forced to accept the novel idea that men doing friendly boxing have a conversation on which they can often thrive. William Buckley and I in a discussion in a living room for an evening will score points on one another, but enjoy it. On television, where the stakes may be more, we may still both enjoy it. But put us in a debating hall with an argument to go on without cease for twenty-four hours, every encouragement present to humiliate each other, and months of preparation for such a debate, hooplas and howlers of publicity, our tongues stuck out at one another on TV, and repercussions in Vietnam depending on which one of us should win, then add the fatigue of harsh lights, and a moderator who keeps interrupting us, and we are at the beginning of a conversation in which at least one of us will be hurt, and maybe both. Even hurt seriously. The example is picayune, however, in relation to the demands of a fifteen-round fight – perhaps we should have to debate nonstop for weeks under those conditions before one of us was carried away comatose. Now the example becomes clearer: Boxing is a rapid debate between two sets of intelligence. It takes place rapidly because it is conducted with the body rather than the mind. If this seems extreme, let us look for a connection. Picasso could never do arithmetic when he was young because the number 7 looked to him like a nose upside down. So to learn arithmetic would slow him up. He was a future painter – his intelligence resided somewhere in the coordination of the body and the mind. He was not going to cut off his body from his mind by learning numbers. But most of us do. We have minds which work fairly well and bodies which sometimes don't. But if we are white and want to be comfortable we put our emphasis on learning to talk with the mind. Ghetto cultures, Black, Puerto Rican and Chicano cultures, having less expectation of comfort, tend to stick with the wit their bodies provide. They speak to each other with their bodies, they signal with their clothes. They talk with many a silent telepathic intelligence. And doubtless feel the frustration of being unable to express the subtleties of their states in words, just as the average middle-class white will feel unable to carry out his dreams of glory by the uses of his body. If Black people are also beginning to speak our mixture of formal English and jargon-polluted American with real force, so white corporate America is getting more sexual and more athletic. Yet to begin to talk about Ali and Frazier, their psyches, their styles, their honour, their character, their greatness and their flaws, we had to recognize that there is no way to comprehend them as men like ourselves – we can only guess at their insides by a real jump of our imagination into the science Ali invented – he was the first psychologist of the body.

Okay. There are fighters who are men's men. Rocky Marciano was one of them. Oscar Bonavena and Jerry Quarry and George Chuvalo and Gene Fullmer and Carmen Basilio, to name a few, have faces which would give a Marine sergeant pause in a bar fight. They look like they could take you out with the knob of bone they have left for a nose. They are all, incidentally, white fighters. They have a code – it is to fight until they are licked, and if they have to take a punch for every punch they give, well, they figure they can win. Their ego and their body intelligence are both connected to the same source of juice – it is male pride. They are substances close to rock. They work on clumsy skills to hone them finer, knowing if they can obtain parity, blow for blow with any opponent, they will win. They have more guts. Up to a far-gone point, pain is their pleasure, for their character in combat is their strength to trade pain for pain, loss of faculty for loss of faculty.

One can cite Black fighters like them. Henry Hank and Reuben Carter, Emile Griffith and Benny Paret. Joe Frazier would be the best of them. But Black fighters tend to be complex. They have veins of unsuspected strength and streaks when they feel as spooked as wild horses. Any fight promoter in the world knew he had a good fight if Fullmer went against Basilio, it was a proposition as certain as the wages for the week. But Black fighters were artists, they were relatively moody, they were full of the surprises of Patterson or Liston, the virtuosities of Archie Moore and Sugar Ray, the speed, savagery, and curious lack of substance in Jimmy Ellis, the vertiginous neuroses of giants like Buster Mathis. Even Joe

Louis, recognized by a majority in the years of his own championship as the greatest heavyweight of all time, was surprisingly inconsistent with minor fighters like Buddy Baer. Part of the unpredictability of their performances was due to the fact that all but Moore and Robinson were heavyweights. Indeed, white champions in the top division were equally out of form from fight to fight. It can, in fact, be said that heavyweights are always the most lunatic of prizefighters. The closer a heavyweight comes to the championship, the more natural it is for him to be a little bit insane, secretly insane, for the heavyweight champion of the world is either the toughest man in the world or he is not, but there is a real possibility he is. It is like being the big toe of God. You have nothing to measure yourself by. Lightweights, welterweights, middleweights can all be exceptionally good, fantastically talented -- they are still very much in their place. The best lightweight in the world knows that an unranked middleweight can defeat him on most nights, and the best middleweight in the world will kill him every night. He knows that the biggest strongman in a tough bar could handle him by sitting on him, since the power to punch seems to increase quickly with weight. A fighter who weighs two-forty will punch more than twice as hard as a fighter who weighs one-twenty. The figures have no real basis, of course, they are only there to indicate the law of the ring: a good big man beats a good little man. So the notion of prizefighters as hardworking craftsmen is most likely to be true in the light and middle divisions. Since they are fighters who know their limitations, they are likely to strive for excellence in their category. The better they get, the closer they have come to sanity, at least if we are ready to assume that the average fighter is a buried artist, which is to say a *body* artist with an extreme amount of violence in him. Obviously the better and more successful they get, the more they have been able to transmute violence into craft, discipline, even body art. That is human alchemy. We respect them and they deserve to be respected.

But the heavyweights never have such simple sanity. If they become champions they begin to have inner lives like Hemingway or Dostoyevsky, Tolstoy or Faulkner, Joyce or Melville or Conrad or Lawrence or Proust. Hemingway is the example above all. Because he wished to be the greatest writer in the history of literature and still be a hero with all the body arts age would yet grant him, he was alone and he knew it. So are heavyweight champions alone. Dempsey was alone and Tunney could never explain himself and Sharkey could never believe himself nor Schmeling nor Braddock, and Carnera was sad and Baer an indecipherable clown; great heavyweights like Louis had the loneliness of the ages in their silence, and men like Marciano were mystified by a power which seemed to have been granted them. With the advent, however, of the great modern Black heavyweights, Patterson, Liston, then Clay and Frazier, perhaps the loneliness gave way to what it had been protecting itself against – a surrealistic situation unstable beyond belief. Being a Black heavyweight champion in the second half of the twentieth century (with Black revolutions opening all over the world) was now not unlike being Jack Johnson, Malcolm X and Frank Costello all in one. Going down the aisle and into the ring in Chicago was conceivably more frightening for Sonny Liston than facing Patterson that night – he was raw as uncoated wire with his sense of retribution awaiting him for years of prison pleasures and underworld jobs. Pools of paranoia must have reached him like different washes of color from different sides of the arena. He was a man who had barely learned to read and write – he had none of the impacted and mediocre misinformation of all the world of daily dull reading to clot the antenna of his senses – so he was keen to every hatred against him. He knew killers were waiting in that mob, they always were, he had been on speaking terms with just such subjects himself – now he dared to be king – any assassin could strike for his revenge upon acts Liston had long forgot; no wonder Liston was in fear going into the ring, and happier once within it.

And Patterson was exhausted before the fight began. Lonely as a monk for years, his daily gym work the stuff of his meditation, he was the first of the Black fighters to be considered, then used, as a political force. He was one of the liberal elite, an Eleanor Roosevelt darling, he was political mileage for the NAACP. Violent, conceivably, to the point of murder if he had not been a fighter, he was a gentleman in public, more, he was a man of the nicest, quietest, most private good manners.

But monastic by inclination. Now, all but uneducated, he was appealed to by political Blacks to win the Liston fight for the image of the Negro. Responsibility sat upon him like a comic cutback in a silent film where we return now and again to one poor man who has been left to hold a beam across his shoulders. There he stands, hardly able to move. At the end of the film he collapses. That was the weight put on Patterson. The responsibility to beat Liston was too great to bear. Patterson, a fighter of incorruptible honesty, was knocked out by punches hardly anybody saw. He fell in open air as if seized by a stroke. The age of surrealistic battles had begun. In the second fight with Liston, Patterson, obviously more afraid of a repetition of the first nightmare than anything else, simply charged his opponent with his hands low and was knocked down three times and out in the first round. The age of body psychology had begun and Clay was there to conceive it.

A kid as wild and dapper and jaybird as the president of a down-home college fraternity, bow tie, brown-and-white shoes, sweet, happy-go-lucky, *raucous*, he descended on Vegas for the second Patterson-Liston fight. He was like a beautiful boy surrounded by doting aunts. The classiest-looking middle-aged Negro ladies were always flanking him in Vegas as if to set up a female field of repulsion against any evil black magnetic forces in the offing. And from the sanctuary of his ability to move around crap tables like a kitten on the frisk, he taunted black majestic king-size Liston before the fight and after the fight. 'You're so ugly,' he would jeer, crap table safely between them, 'that I don't know how you can get any uglier.'

'Why don't you sit on my knee and I'll feed you your orange juice,' Liston would rumble back.

'Don't insult me, or you'll be sorry. 'Cause you're just an ugly slow bear.'

They would pretend to rush at one another. Smaller men would hold them back without effort. They were building the gate for the next fight. And Liston was secretly fond of Clay. He would chuckle when he talked about him. It was years since Liston had failed to knock out his opponent in the first round. His charisma was majestic with menace. One held one's breath when near him. He looked forward with obvious amusement to

the happy seconds when he would take Clay apart and see the
expression on that silly face. In Miami he trained for a three-
round fight. In the famous fifth round when Clay came out with
caustic in his eyes and could not see, he waved his gloves at
Liston, a look of abject horror on his face, as if to say, 'Your
younger brother is now an old blind beggar. Do not strike him.'
And did it with a peculiar authority. For Clay looked like a
ghost with his eyes closed, tears streaming, his extended gloves
waving in front of him like a widow's entreaties. Liston drew
back in doubt, in bewilderment, conceivably in concern for his
new great reputation as an ex-bully; yes, Liston reacted like a
gentleman, and Clay was home free. His eyes watered out the
caustic, his sight came back. He cut Liston up in the sixth. He
left him beaten and exhausted. Liston did not stand up for the
bell to the seventh. Maybe Clay had even defeated him earlier
that day at the weigh-in when he had harangued and screamed
and shouted and whistled and stuck his tongue out at Liston.
The Champ had been bewildered. No one had been able ever to
stare him in the eyes these last four years. Now a boy was
screaming at him, a boy reported to belong to Black Muslims,
no, stronger than that, a boy favored by Malcolm X who was
braver by reputation than the brave, for he could stop a bullet
any day. Liston, afraid only, as he put it, of crazy men, was
afraid of the Muslims for he could not contend with their
allegiance to one another in prison, their puritanism, their
discipline, their martial ranks. The combination was too complex, too unfamiliar. Now, their boy, in a pain of terror or in a
mania of courage, was screaming at him at the weigh-in. Liston
sat down and shook his head, and looked at the press, the press
now become his friend, and wound his fingers in circles around
his ear, as if saying, Whitey to Whitey, 'That Black boy is nuts.'
So Clay made Liston Tom it, and when Liston missed the first
jab he threw in the fight by a foot and a half, one knew the night
would not be ordinary in the offing.

   For their return bout in Boston, Liston trained as he had
never before. Clay got a hernia. Liston trained again. Hard
training as a fighter grows older seems to speak of the dull
deaths of the brightest cells in all the favorite organs; old
fighters react to training like beautiful women to washing floors.

But Liston did it twice, once for Clay's hernia, and again for their actual fight in Maine, and the second time he trained, he aged as a fighter, for he had a sparring partner, Amos Lincoln, who was one of the better heavyweights in the country. They had wars with one another every afternoon in the gym. By the day before the fight, Liston was as relaxed and sleepy and dopey as a man in a steam bath. He had fought his heart out in training, had done it under constant pressure from Clay who kept telling the world that Liston was old and slow and could not possibly win. And their fight created a scandal, for Liston ran into a short punch in the first round and was counted out, unable to hear the count. The referee and timekeeper missed signals with one another while Clay stood over fallen Liston screaming, 'Get up and fight!' It was no night for the fight game, and a tragedy for Clay since he had trained for a long and arduous fight. He had developed his technique for a major encounter with Liston and was left with a horde of unanswered questions including the one he could never admit – which was whether there had been the magic of a real knockout in his punch or if Liston had made – for what variety of reasons! – a conscious decision to stay on the floor. It did him no good.

He had taken all the lessons of his curious life and the out-rageously deep comprehension he had of the motivations of his own people – indeed, one could even approach the beginnings of a Psychology of the Blacks by studying his encounters with fighters who were Black – and had elaborated that into a technique for boxing which was almost without compare. A most cultivated technique. For he was no child of the slums. His mother was a gracious pale-skinned lady, his father a bitter wit pride-oriented on the family name of Clay – they were descendants of Henry Clay, the orator, on the white side of the family, nothing less, and Cassius began boxing at twelve in a police gym, and from the beginning was a phenomenon of style and the absence of pain, for he knew how to use his physical endowment. Tall, relatively light, with an exceptionally long reach even for his size, he developed defensive skills which made the best use of his body. Working apparently on the premise that there was something obscene about being hit, he

boxed with his head back and drew it further back when attacked like a kid who is shy of punches in a street fight, but because he had a waist which was more supple than the average fighter's neck, he was able to box with his arms low, surveying the fighter in front of him, avoiding punches by the speed of his feet, the reflexes of his waist, the long spoiling deployment of his arms which were always tipping other fighters off-balance. Added to this was his psychological comprehension of the vanity and confusion of other fighters. A man in the ring is a performer as well as a gladiator. Elaborating his technique from the age of twelve, Clay knew how to work on the vanity of other performers, knew how to make them feel ridiculous and so force them into crucial mistakes, knew how to set such a tone from the first round – later he was to know how to begin it a year before he would even meet the man. Clay knew that a fighter who had been put in psychological knots before he got near the ring had already lost half, three-quarters, no, all of the fight could be lost before the first punch. That was the psychology of the body.

Now, add his curious ability as a puncher. He knew that the heaviest punches, systematically delivered, meant little. There are club fighters who look like armadillos and alligators – you can bounce punches off them forever and they never go down. You can break them down only if they are in a profound state of confusion, and the bombardment of another fighter's fists is never their confusion but their expectation. So Clay punched with a greater variety of mixed intensities than anyone around, he played with punches, was tender with them, laid them on as delicately as you put a postage stamp on an envelope, then cracked them in like a riding crop across your face, stuck a cruel jab like a baseball bat held head on into your mouth, next waltzed you in a clinch with a tender arm around your neck, winged away out of reach on flying legs, dug a hook with the full swing of a baseball bat hard into your ribs, hard pokes of a jab into the face, a mocking soft flurry of pillows and gloves, a mean forearm cutting you off from coming up on him, a cruel wrestling of your neck in a clinch, then elusive again, gloves snakelicking your face like a whip. By the time Clay defeated Liston once and was training for the second fight, by the time

Clay, now champion and renamed Muhammad Ali, and bigger, grown up quickly and not so mysteriously (after the potent ego-soups and marrows of his trip through Muslim Africa) into a Black Prince, Potentate of his people, new Poombah of Polemic, yes, by this time, Clay – we will find it more natural to call him Ali from here on out (for the Prince will behave much like a young god) – yes, Muhammad Ali, Heavyweight Champion of the World, having come back with an amazing commitment to be leader of his people, proceeded to go into training for the second Liston fight with a commitment and then a genius of comprehension for the true intricacies of the science of Sock. He alternated the best of sparring partners and the most ordinary, worked rounds of dazzling speed with Jimmy Ellis – later, of course, to be champion himself before Frazier knocked him out – rounds which displayed the high aesthetic of boxing at its best, then lay against the ropes with other sparring partners, hands at his sides as if it were the eleventh or thirteenth round of an excruciating and exhausting fight with Liston where Ali was now so tired he could not hold his hands up, could just manage to take punches to the stomach, rolling with them, smothering them with his stomach, absorbing them with backward moves, sliding along the ropes, steering his sparring partner with passive but off-setting moves of his limp arms. For a minute, for two minutes, the sparring partner – Shotgun Sheldon was his name – would bomb away on Ali's stomach much as if Liston were tearing him apart in later rounds, and Ali weaving languidly, sliding his neck for the occasional overhead punch to his face, bouncing from the rope into the punches, bouncing back away from punches, as if his torso had become one huge boxing glove to absorb punishment, had penetrated through into some further conception of pain, as if pain were not pain if you accepted it with a relaxed heart, yes, Ali let himself be bombarded on the ropes by the powerful bull-like swings of Shotgun Sheldon, the expression on his face as remote and as searching for the last routes into the nerves of each punch going in as a man hanging on a subway strap will search into the meaning of the market quotations he has just read on the activities of a curious stock. So Ali relaxed on the ropes and took punches to the belly with a faint disdain, as if,

curious punches, they did not go deep enough and after a
minute of this, or two minutes, having offered his body like the
hide of a drum for a mad drummer's solo, he would snap out of
his communion with himself and flash a tattoo of light and
slashing punches, mocking as the lights on water, he would
dazzle his sparring partner, who, arm-weary and punched out,
would look at him with eyes of love, complete with his admiration. And if people were ever going to cry watching a boxer in
training, those were the moments, for Ali had the far-off
concentration and disdain of an artist who simply cannot find
anyone near enough or good enough to keep him and his art
engaged, and all the while was perfecting the essence of his art
which was to make the other fighter fall secretly, helplessly, in
love with him. Bundini, a special trainer, an alter ego with the
same harsh, demoniac, witty, nonstop powers of oration as Ali
himself – he even looked a little like Ali – used to weep openly
as he watched the workouts.

Training session over, Ali would lecture the press, instruct
them – looking beyond his Liston defense to what he would do
to Patterson, mocking Patterson, calling him a rabbit, a white
man's rabbit, knowing he was putting a new beam on Patterson's shoulders, an outrageously helpless and heavy beam of
rage, fear, hopeless anger and secret Black admiration for the
all-out force of Ali's effrontery. And in the next instant Ali
would be charming as a movie star on the make speaking
tenderly to a child. If he were Narcissus, so he was as well the
play of mood in the water which served as mirror to Narcissus.
It was as if he knew he had disposed of Patterson already, that
the precise attack of calling him a rabbit would work on the
weakest link – wherever it was – in Patterson's tense and tortured psyche and Patterson would crack, as indeed, unendurably for himself, he did, when their fight took place. Patterson's
back gave way in the early rounds, and he fought twisted and in
pain, half crippled like a man with a sacroiliac for eleven brave
and most miserable rounds before the referee would call it and
Ali, breaking up with his first wife then, was unpleasant in the
ring that night, his face ugly and contemptuous, himself well on
the way to becoming America's most unpopular major American. That, too, was part of the art – to get a public to the point

of hating him so much the burden on the other fighter approached the metaphysical – which is where Ali wanted it. White fighters with faces like rock embedded in cement would trade punch for punch, Ali liked to get the boxing where it belonged – he would trade metaphysic for metaphysic with anyone.

So he went on winning his fights and growing forever more unpopular. How he inflamed the temper of boxing's White Establishment, for they were for most part a gaggle of avuncular drunks and hard-bitten hacks who were ready to fight over every slime-slicked penny, and squared a few of their slippery crimes by getting fighters to show up semblance-of-sober at any available parish men's rally and charity church breakfast – 'Everything I am I owe to boxing,' the fighter would mumble through his dentures while elements of gin, garlic, and goddess-of-a-girlie from the night before came off in the bright morning fumes.

Ali had them psyched. He cut through moribund coruscated dirty business corridors, cut through cigar smoke and bush-wah, hypocrisy and well-aimed kicks to the back of the neck, cut through crooked politicians and patriotic pus, cut like a laser, point of the point, light and impersonal, cut to the heart of the rottenest meat in boxing, and boxing was always the buried South Vietnam of America, buried for fifty years in our hide before we went there, yes, Ali cut through the flag-dragooned salutes of drunken dawns and said, 'I got no fight with those Vietcongs,' and they cut him down, thrust him into the three and a half years of his martyrdom. Where he grew. Grew to have a little fat around his middle and a little of the complacent muscle of the clam to his world-ego. And grew sharper in the mind as well, and deepened and broadened physically. Looked no longer like a boy, but a sullen man, almost heavy, with the beginnings of a huge expanse across his shoulders. And developed the patience to survive, the wisdom to contemplate future nights in jail, grew to cultivate the suspension of belief and the avoidance of disbelief – what a rack for a young man! As the years of hope for reinstatement, or avoidance of prison, came up and waned in him, Ali walked the tightrope between bitterness and apathy, and had enough left to beat Quarry and beat Bonavena, beat Quarry in the flurry of a missed hundred punches, ho! how his timing was off! beat him with a calculated whip, snake-lick whip, to the corrugated sponge of dead flesh over Quarry's Irish eyes – they stopped it after the third on cuts – then knocked out Bonavena, the indestructible, never stopped before, by working the art of crazy mixing in the punches he threw at the rugged – some of the punches Ali threw that night would not have hurt a little boy – the punch he let go in the fifteenth came in like a wrecking ball from outer space. Bonavena went sprawling across the ring. He was a house coming down.

Yet it may have been the blow which would defeat him later. For Ali had been tired with Bonavena, lack-luster, winded, sluggish, far ahead on points but in need of the most serious work if he were to beat Frazier. The punch in the last round was obliged, therefore, to inflame his belief that the forces of magic were his, there to be called upon when most in need, that the silent leagues of Black support for his cause – since their cause was as his own – were like some cloak of midnight velvet, there to protect him by Black blood, by Black sense of tragedy, by the Black consciousness that the guilt of the world had become the hinge of a door that they would open. So they would open the way to Frazier's chin, the Blacks would open the aisle for his trip to the gods.

Therefore he did not train for Frazier as perhaps he had to. He worked, he ran three miles a day when he could have run five, he boxed some days and let a day and perhaps another day go, he was relaxed, he was confident, he basked in the undemanding winter sun of Miami, and skipped his rope in a gym crowded with fighters, stuffed now with working fighters looking to be seen, Ali comfortable and relaxed like the greatest of movie stars, he played a young fighter working out in a corner on a heavy bag – for of course every eye was on him – and afterward doing sit-ups in the back room and having his stomach rubbed with liniment, he would talk to reporters. He was filled with confidence there was no Black fighter he did not comprehend to the root of the valve in the hard-pumping heart, and yes, Frazier, he assured everybody, would be easier than they realized. Like a little boy who had grown up to take on a mountain of responsibility, he spoke in the deep relaxation of the wise, and teased two of the reporters who were present and fat. 'You want to drink a lot of water,' he said, 'good cold water instead of all that liquor rot-your-gut,' and gave the smile of a man who had been able to intoxicate himself on water (although he was, by repute, a fiend for soft sweet drinks), 'and fruit and good clean vegetables you want to eat and chicken and steak. You lose weight then,' he advised out of kind secret smiling thoughts, and went on to talk of the impact of the fight upon the world. 'Yes,' he said, 'you just think of a stadium with a million people, ten million people, you could get them all in to watch, they would all pay to see it live, but then you think of the hundreds of millions and the billions who are going to see this fight, and if you could sit them all down in one place, and fly a jet plane over them, why that plane would have to fly for an hour before it would reach the end of all the people who will see this fight. It's the greatest event in the history of the world, and you take a man like Frazier, a good fighter, but a simple hard-working fellow, he's not built for this kind of pressure, the eyes,' Ali said softly, 'of that many people upon him. There's an experience to pressure which I have had, fighting a man like Liston in Miami the first time, which he has not. He will cave in under the pressure. No, I do not see any way a man like Frazier can whup me, he can't reach me, my arms are too long, and if he does get in and knock me down I'll never make the mistake of Quarry and Foster or Ellis of rushing back at him, I'll stay away until my head clears, then I begin to pop him again, pop! pop!' – a few jabs – 'no there is no way this man can beat me, this fight will be easier than you think.'

There was one way in which boxing was still like a street fight and that was in the need to be confident you would win. A man walking out of a bar to fight with another man is seeking to compose his head into the confidence that he will certainly triumph – it is the most mysterious faculty of the ego. For that confidence is a sedative against the pain of punches and yet is the sanction to punch your own best. The logic of the spirit would suggest that you win only if you deserve to win: the logic of the ego lays down the axiom that if you don't think you will win, you don't deserve to. And, in fact, usually don't; it is as if

not believing you will win opens you to the guilt that perhaps
you have not the right, you are too guilty.

So training camps are small factories for the production of
one rare psychological item – an ego able to bear huge pain and
administer drastic punishment. The flow of Ali's ego poured
over the rock of every distraction, it was an ego like the flow of a
river of constant energy fed by a hundred tributaries of Black
love and the love of the white left. The construction of the ego of
Joe Frazier was of another variety. His manager, Yancey 'Yank'
Durham, a canny foxy light-skinned Negro with a dignified
mien, a gray head of hair, gray moustache and a small but
conservative worthy's paunch, plus the quick-witted look of
eyes which could spot from a half-mile away any man coming
toward him with a criminal thought, was indeed the face of a
consummate jeweler who had worked for years upon a diamond
in the rough until he was now and at last a diamond, hard as the
transmutation of black carbon from the black earth into the
brilliant sky-blue shadow of the rarest shining rock. What a
fighter was Frazier, what a diamond of an ego had he, and what
a manager was Durham. Let us look.

Sooner or later, fight metaphors, like fight managers, go sentimental. They go military. But there is no choice here. Frazier
was the human equivalent of a war machine. He had
tremendous firepower. He had a great left hook, a left hook
frightening even to watch when it missed, for it seemed to
whistle; he had a powerful right. He could knock a man out
with either hand – not all fighters can, not even very good
fighters. Usually, however, he clubbed opponents to death,
took a punch, gave a punch, took three punches, gave two, took
a punch, gave a punch, high speed all the way, always working,
pushing his body and arms, short for a heavyweight, up
through the middle, bombing through on force, reminiscent of
Jimmy Brown knocking down tacklers, Frazier kept on coming, hard and fast, a hang-in, hang-on, go-and-get-him, got-
him, got-him, slip and punch, take a punch, wing a punch,
whap a punch, never was Frazier happier than with his heart up
on the line against some other man's heart, let the bullets
fly – his heart was there to stand up at the last. Sooner or later,

the others almost all fell down. Undefeated like Ali, winner of twenty-three out of twenty-six fights by knock-out, he was a human force, certainly the greatest heavyweight force to come along since Rocky Marciano. (If those two men had ever met, it would have been like two Mack trucks hitting each other head on, then backing up to hit each other again – they would have kept it up until the wheels were off the axles and the engines off the chassis.) But this would be a different kind of fight. Ali would run, Ali would keep hitting Frazier with long jabs, quick hooks and rights while backing up, backing up, staying out of reach unless Frazier could take the punishment and get in. That was where the military problem began. For getting in against the punishment he would take was a question of morale, and there was a unique situation in this fight – Frazier had become the white man's fighter, Mr. Charley was rooting for Frazier, and that meant Blacks were boycotting him in their heart. That could be poison to Frazier's morale, for he was twice as black as Clay and half as handsome, he had the rugged decent life-worked face of a man who had labored in the pits all his life, he looked like the deserving modest son of one of those Negro cleaning women of a bygone age who worked from six in the morning to midnight every day, raised a family, endured and occasionally elicited the exasperated admiration of white ladies who would kindly remark, 'That woman deserves something better in her life.' Frazier had the mien of the son, one of many, of such a woman, and he was the hardest-working fighter in training many a man had ever seen, he was conceivably the hardest-working man alive in the world, and as he went through his regimen, first boxing four rounds with a sparring partner, Kenny Norton, a talented heavyweight from the coast with an almost unbeaten record, then working on the heavy bag, then the light bag, then skipping rope, ten to twelve rounds of sparring and exercise on a light day, Frazier went on with the doggedness, the concentration, and the pumped-up fury of a man who has had so little in his life that he can endure torments to get everything, he pushed the total of his energy and force into an absolute abstract exercise of will so it did not matter if he fought a sparring partner or the heavy bag, he lunged at each equally as if the exhaustions of his own heart and the clangor of his lungs were his only enemies, and the head of a fighter or the leather of the bag as it rolled against his own head was nothing but some abstract thunk of material, not a thing, not a man, but thunk! thunk! something of an obstacle, thunk! thunk! thunk! to beat into thunk! oblivion. And his breath came in rips and sobs as he smashed into the bag as if it were real, just that heavy big torso-sized bag hanging from its chain – but he attacked it as if it were a bear, as if it were a great fighter and they were in the mortal embrace of a killing set of exchanges of punches in the middle of the eighth round, and rounds of exercise later, skipping rope to an inhumanly fast beat for this late round in the training day, sweat pouring like jets of blood from an artery, he kept swinging his rope, muttering, 'Two-million-dollars-and-change, two-million-dollars-and-change,' railroad train chugging into the terminals of exhaustion. And it was obvious that Durham, jeweler to his diamond, was working to make the fight as abstract as he could for Frazier, to keep Clay out of it – for they would not call him Ali in their camp – yes, Frazier was fortifying his ego by depersonalizing his opponent, Clay was, thunk! the heavy bag, thunk! and thunk! – Frazier was looking to get no messages from that cavern of velvet when Black people sent their good wishes to Ali at midnight, no, Frazier would insulate himself with prodigies of work, hardest-working man in the hell-hole of the world, and on and on he drove himself into the depressions each day of killing daily exhaustion.

That was one half of the strategy to isolate Frazier from Ali, hard work and thinking of thunking on inanimate Clay; the other half was up to Durham who was running front relations with the Blacks of North Philly who wandered into the gym, paid their dollar, and were ready to heckle on Frazier. In the four rounds he boxed with Norton, Frazier did not look too good for a while. It was ten days before the fight and he was in a bad mood when he came in, for the word was through the gym that they had discovered one of his favorite sparring partners, just fired that morning, was a Black Muslim and had been calling Ali every night with reports, that was the rumor, and Frazier, sullen and cold at the start, was bopped and tapped, then walloped by Norton moving fast with the big training gloves in imitation of Ali, and Frazier looked very easy to hit until the middle of the third round when Norton, proud of his something like twenty wins and one loss, beginning to get some ideas himself about how to fight champions, came driving in to mix it with Frazier, have it out man to man and caught a right which dropped him, left him looking limp with that half-silly smile sparring partners get when they have been hit too hard to justify any experience or any money they are going to take away. Up till then the crowd had been with Norton. Restricted to one end of the Cloverlay gym, a street-level storefront room which could have been used originally by an automobile dealer, there on that empty, immaculate Lysol-soaked floor, designed when Frazier was there for only Frazier and his partners (as opposed to Miami where Ali would rub elbows with the people) the people, since they were here kept to the end off the street, jeered whenever Norton hit Frazier, they laughed when Norton made him look silly, they called out, 'Drop the mother', until Durham held up a gentlemanly but admonishing finger in request for silence. Afterward, however, training completed, Durham approached them to answer questions, rolled with their sallies, jived the people back, subtly enlisted their sympathy for Frazier by saying, 'When I fight Clay, I'm going to get him somewhere in the middle rounds,' until the Blacks quipping back said angrily, 'You ain't fighting him, Frazier is.'

'Why you call him Clay?' another asked. 'He Ali.'

'His name is Cassius Clay to me,' said Durham.

'What you say against his religion?'

'I don't say nothing about his religion and he doesn't say anything about mine. I'm a Baptist.'

'You going to make money on this?'

'Of course,' said Durham, 'I got to make money. You don't think I work up this sweat for nothing.'

They loved him. He was happy with them. A short fat man in a purple suit wearing his revival of the wide-brim bebop hat said to Durham, 'Why don't you get Norton to manage? He was beating up on your fighter,' and the fat man cackled for he had scored and could elaborate the tale for his ladies later how he had put down Yank who was working the daily rite on the edge of the Black street for his fighter, while upstairs, dressed, and sucking an orange, sweat still pouring, gloom of excessive fatigue upon him, Frazier was sitting through his two-hundredth or two-thousandth interview for his fight, reluctant indeed to give it at all. 'Some get it, some don't,' he had said for refusal, but relented when a white friend who had done road-work with him interceded, so he sat there now against a leather sofa, dark blue suit, dark T-shirt, mopping his brow with a pink-red towel, and spoke dispiritedly of being ready too early for the fight. He was waking up an hour too early for roadwork each morning now. 'I'd go back to sleep but it doesn't feel good when I do run.'

'I guess the air is better that hour of the morning.'

He nodded sadly. 'There's a limit to how good the air in Philly can get.'

'Where'd you begin to sing?' was a question asked.

'I sang in church first,' he replied, but it was not the day to talk about singing. The loneliness of hitting the bag still seemed upon him as if in his exhaustion now, and in the thoughts of that small insomnia which woke him an hour too early every day was something of the loneliness of all Blacks who work very hard and are isolated from fun and must wonder in the just-awakened night how large and pervasive was the curse of a people. 'The countdown's begun,' said Frazier, 'I get impatient about now.'


For the fight, Ali was wearing red velvet trunks, Frazier had green. Before they began, even before they were called together by the referee for instructions, Ali went dancing around the ring and glided past Frazier with a sweet little-boy smile, as if to say, 'You're my new playmate. We're going to have fun.' Ali was laughing. Frazier was having nothing of this and turned his neck to embargo him away. Ali, having alerted the crowd by this big first move, came prancing in again. When Frazier looked ready to block him, Ali went around, evading a contact, gave another sweet smile, shook his head at the lack of high spirit. 'Poor Frazier,' he seemed to say.

At the weigh-in early that afternoon Ali looked physically resplendent; the night before in Harlem, crowds had cheered him; he was coming to claim his victory on the confluence of two mighty tides – he was the mightiest victim of injustice in

America and he was also – the twentieth century was nothing if not a tangle of opposition – he was also the mightiest narcissist in the land. Every beard, dropout, homosexual, junkie, freak, swinger, and plain simple individualist adored him. Every pedantic liberal soul who had once loved Patterson now paid homage to Ali. The mightiest of the Black psyches and the most filigreed of the white psyches were ready to roar him home, as well as every family-loving hardworking square American who genuinely hated the war in Vietnam. What a tangle of ribbons he carried on his lance, enough cross-purposes to be the knight-resplendent of television, the fell hero of the medium, and he had a look of unique happiness on television when presenting his program for the course of the fight, and his inevitable victory. He would be as content then as an infant splashing the waters of the bathinette. If he was at once a saint and a monster to any mind which looked for category, any mind unwilling to encounter the thoroughly dread-filled fact that the twentieth-century breed of man now in birth might be no longer half good and half evil – generous and greedy by turns – but a mutation with Cassius Muhammad for the first son – then that mind was not ready to think about Twentieth-Century Man. (And indeed Muhammad Ali had twin poodles he called Angel and Demon.) So now the ambiguity of his presence filled the Garden before the fight was fairly begun, it was as if he had announced to that plural billion-footed crowd assembled under the shadow of the jet which would fly over them that the first enigma of the fight would be the way he would win it, that he would initiate his triumph by getting the crowd to laugh at Frazier, yes, first premise tonight was that the poor Black man in Frazier's soul would go berserk if made a figure of roll-off-your-seat amusement.

The referee gave his instructions. The bell rang. The first fifteen seconds of a fight can be the fight. It is equivalent to the first kiss in a love affair. The fighters each missed the other. Ali blocked Frazier's first punches easily, but Ali then missed Frazier's head. That head was bobbing as fast as a third fist. Frazier would come rushing in, head moving like a fist, fists bobbing too, his head working above and below his forearm, he was trying to get through Ali's jab, get through fast and sear Ali early with the terror of a long fight and punches harder than he had ever taken to the stomach, and Ali in turn, backing up, and throwing fast punches, aimed just a trifle, and was therefore a trifle too slow, but it was obvious Ali was trying to shiver Frazier's synapses from the start, set waves of depression stirring which would reach his heart in later rounds and make him slow, deaden nerve, deaden nerve went Ali's jab flicking a snake tongue, whoo-eet! whoo-eet! but Frazier's head was bobbing too fast, he was moving faster than he had ever moved before in that bobbing nonstop never-a-backward step of his, slogging and bouncing forward, that huge left hook flaunting the air with the confidence it was enough of a club to split a tree, and Ali, having missed his jabs, stepped nimbly inside the hook and wrestled Frazier in the clinch. Ali looked stronger here. So by the first forty-five seconds of the fight, they had each surprised the other profoundly. Frazier was fast enough to slip through Ali's punches. A pattern had begun. Because Ali was missing often, Frazier was in under his shots like a police dog's muzzle on your arm, Ali could not slide from side to side, he was boxed in, then obliged to go backward, and would end on the ropes again and again with Frazier belabouring him. Yet Frazier could not reach him. Like a prestidigitator Ali would tie the other's punches into odd knots, not even blocking them yet on his elbows or his arms, rather throwing his own punches as defensive moves, for even as they missed, he would brush Frazier to the side with his forearm, or hold him off, or clinch and wrestle a little of the will out of Frazier's neck. Once or twice in the round a long left hook by Frazier just touched the surface of Ali's chin, and Ali waved his head in placid contempt to the billions watching as if to say, 'This man has not been able to hurt me at all.'

The first round set a pattern for the fight. Ali won it and would win the next. His jab was landing from time to time and rights and lefts of no great consequence. Frazier was hardly reaching him at all. Yet it looked like Frazier had established that he was fast enough to get in on Ali and so drive him to the ropes and to the corners, and that spoke of a fight which would be determined by the man in better condition, in better physical condition rather than in better psychic condition, the kind of fight Ali could hardly want for his strength was in his pauses, his nature passed along the curve of every dialectic, he liked, in short, to fight in flurries, and then move out, move away, assess, take his time, fight again. Frazier would not let him. Frazier moved in with the snarl of a wolf, his teeth seemed to show through his mouthpiece, he made Ali work. Ali won the first two rounds but it was obvious he could not continue to win if he had to work all the way. And in the third round Frazier began to get to him, caught Ali with a powerful blow to the face at the bell. That was the first moment where it was clear to all that Frazier had won a round. Then he won the next. Ali looked tired and a little depressed. He was moving less and less and calling upon a skill not seen since the fight with Chuvalo when he had showed his old ability, worked on all those years ago with Shotgun Sheldon, to lie on the ropes and take a beating to the stomach. He had exhausted Chuvalo by welcoming attacks on the stomach but Frazier was too incommensurable a force to allow such total attack. So Ali lay on the ropes and wrestled him off, and moved his arms and waist, blocking punches, slipping punches, countering with punches – it began to look as if the fight would be written on the ropes, but Ali was getting very tired. At the beginning of the fifth round, he got up slowly from his stool, very slowly. Frazier was beginning to feel that the fight was his. He moved in on Ali jeering, his hands at his side in mimicry of Ali, a street fighter mocking his opponent, and Ali tapped him with long light jabs to which Frazier stuck out his mouthpiece, a jeer of derision as if to suggest that the mouthpiece was all Ali would reach all night.

There is an extortion of the will beyond any of our measure in the exhaustion which comes upon a fighter in early rounds when he is already too tired to lift his arms or take advantage of openings there before him, yet the fight is not a third over, there are all those rounds to go, contractions of torture, the lungs screaming into the dungeons of the soul, washing the throat with a hot bile that once belonged to the liver, the legs are going dead, the arms move but their motion is limp, one is straining into another will, breathing into the breath of another will as agonized as one's own. As the fight moved through the fifth, the sixth and the seventh, then into the eighth, it was obvious that Ali was into the longest night of his career, and yet with that skill, that research into the pits of every miserable contingency in boxing, he came up with odd somnambulistic variations, holding Frazier off, riding around Frazier with his arm about his neck, almost entreating Frazier with his arms extended, and Frazier leaning on him, each of them slowed to a pit-a-pat of light punches back and forth until one of them was goaded up from exhaustion to whip and stick, then hook and hammer and into the belly and out, and out of the clinch and both looking exhausted, and then Frazier, mouth bared again like a wolf, going in and Ali waltzing him, tying him, tapping him lightly as if he were a speed bag, just little flicks, until Frazier, like an exhausted horse finally feeling the crop, would push up into a trot and try to run up the hill. It was indeed as if they were both running up a hill. As if Frazier's offensive was so great and so great was Ali's defense that the fight could only be decided by who could take the steepest pitch of the hill. So Frazier, driving, driving, trying to drive the heart out of Ali, put the pitch of that hill up and up until they were ascending an unendurable slope. And moved like somnambulists slowly working and rubbing one another, almost embracing, next to locked in the slow moves of lovers after the act until, reaching into the stores of energy reaching them from cells never before so used, one man or the other would work up a contractive spasm of skills and throw punches at the other in the straining slow-motion hypnosis of a deepening act. And so the first eight rounds went by. The two judges scored six for Frazier, two for Ali. The referee had it even. Some of the press had Ali ahead – it was not easy to score. For if it were an alley fight, Frazier would win. Clay was by now hardly more than the heavy bag to Frazier. Frazier was dealing with a man, not a demon. He was not respectful of that man. But still! It was Ali who was landing the majority of the punches. They were light, they were usually weary, but some had snap, some were quick, he was landing two punches to Frazier's one. Yet Frazier's were hardest. And Ali often looked as tender as if he were making love. It was as if he could now feel the whole absence of that real second fight with Liston, that fight for which he had trained so

long and so hard, the fight which might have rolled over his
laurels from the greatest artist of pugilism to the greatest
brawler of them all – maybe he had been prepared on that night
to beat Liston at his own, be more of a slugger, more of a man
crude to crude than Liston. Yes, Ali had never been a street
fighter and never a whorehouse knock-it-down stud, no, it was
more as if a man with the exquisite reflexes of Nureyev had
learned to throw a knockout punch with either hand and so had
become champion of the world without knowing if he were the
man of all men or the most delicate of the delicate with special
privilege endowed by God. Now with Frazier, he was in a sweat
bath (a mud pile, a knee, elbow, and death-thumping chute of a
pit) having in this late year the fight he had sorely needed for his
true greatness as a fighter six and seven years ago, and so
whether ahead, behind or even, terror sat in the rooting instinct
of all those who were for Ali for it was obviously Frazier's fight
to win, and what if Ali, weaknesses of character now flickering
to the surface in a hundred little moves, should enter the vale of
a prizefighting's deepest humiliation, should fall out half-
conscious on the floor and not want to get up. What a death to
his followers.

   The ninth began. Frazier mounted his largest body attack of
the night. It was preparations-for-Liston-with-Shotgun-
Sheldon, it was the virtuosity of the gym all over again, and
Ali, like a catcher handling a fast-ball pitcher, took Frazier's
punches, one steamer, another steamer, wing! went with a
screamer, a steamer, warded them, blocked them, slithered
them, winced from them, absorbed them, took them in and
blew them out and came off the ropes and was Ali the Magnificent for the next minute and thirty seconds. The fight turned.
The troops of Ali's second corps of energy had arrived, the
energy for which he had been waiting long agonizing heartsore
vomit-mean rounds. Now he jabbed Frazier, he snake-licked
his face with jabs faster than he had thrown before, he antici-
pated each attempt of Frazier at counterattack and threw it
back, he danced on his toes for the first time in rounds, he
popped in rights, he hurt him with hooks, it was his biggest
round of the night, it was the best round yet of the fight, and
Frazier was beginning to move into that odd petulant concen-

tration on other rituals besides the punches, tappings of the gloves, stares of the eye, that species of mouthpiece-chewing which is the prelude to fun-strut in the knees, then Queer Street, then waggle on out, drop like a steer.

It looked like Ali had turned the fight, looked more like the same in the tenth, now reporters were writing another story in their mind where Ali was not the magical untried Prince who had come apart under the first real pressure of his life but was rather the greatest heavyweight champion of all time for he had weathered the purgatory of Joe Frazier.

But in the eleventh, that story also broke. Frazier caught him, caught him again and again, and Ali was near to knocked out and swayed and slid on Queer Street himself, then spent the rest of the eleventh and the longest round of the twelfth working another bottom of Hell, holding off Frazier who came on and on, sobbing, wild, a wild hermit of a beast, man of will reduced to the common denominator of the will of all of us back in that land of the animal where the idea of man as a tool-wielding beast was first conceived. Frazier looked to get Ali forever in the eleventh and the twelfth, and Ali, his legs slapped and slashed on the thighs between each round by Angelo Dundee, came out for the thirteenth and incredibly was dancing. Everybody's story switched again. For if Ali won this round, the fourteenth and the fifteenth, who could know if he could not win the fight? . . . He won the first half of the thirteenth, then spent the second half on the ropes with Frazier. They were now like crazy death-march-maddened mateys coming up the hill and on to home, and yet Ali won the fourteenth, Ali looked good, he came out dancing for the fifteenth, while Frazier, his own armies of energy finally caught up, his courage ready to spit into the eye of any devil black or white who would steal the work of his life, had equal madness to steal the bolt from Ali. So Frazier reached out to snatch the magic punch from the air, the punch with which Ali topped Bonavena, and found it and hit Ali a hell and a heaven of a shot which dumped Muhammad into fifty thousand newspaper photographs – Ali on the floor! Great Ali on the floor was out there flat singing to the sirens in the mistiest fogs of Queer Street (same look of death and widowhood on his fargone face as one had seen in the fifth blind round with Liston) yet Ali got up, Ali came sliding through the last two minutes and thirty-five seconds of this heathen holocaust in some last exercise of the will, some iron fundament of the ego not to be knocked out, and it was then as if the spirit of Harlem finally spoke and came to rescue and the ghosts of the dead in Vietnam, something held him up before arm-weary triumphant near-crazy Frazier who had just hit him the hardest punch ever thrown in his life and they went down to the last few seconds of a great fight, Ali still standing and Frazier had won.

The world was talking instantly of a rematch. For Ali had shown America what we all had hoped was secretly true. He was a man. He could bear moral and physical torture and he could stand. And if he could beat Frazier in the rematch we would have at last a national hero who was hero of the world as well, and who could bear to wait for the next fight? Joe Frazier, still the champion, and a great champion, said to the press, 'Fellows, have a heart – I got to live a little. I've been working for ten years.' And Ali, through the agency of alter-ego Bundini, said – for Ali was now in the hospital to check on the possible fracture of a jaw – Ali was reported to have said, 'Get the gun ready – we're going to set traps.' Oh, wow. Could America wait for something so great as the Second Ali-Frazier?

# Bullfighting

## Homage to El Loco

The mind returns to the comedy and the religious dedication of the bullfight. Late afternoons of color – hues of lavender, silver, pink, orange silk and gold in the *traje de luces* – now begin to play in one's mind against the small sharp impact on the eyes of horseballs falling like eggs between the frightened legs of the horse, and the flanks of the bull glistening with the sheen of a dark wet wood. And the blood. The bullfight always gets back to the blood. It pours in gouts down the forequarters of the bull, it wells from the hump of his *morrillo*, and moves in waves of bright red along the muscles of his chest and the heaving of his sides. If he has been killed poorly and the sword goes through his lung, then the animal dies in vomiting of blood. If the matador is working close to the animal, the suit of lights becomes stained – the dark bloodstain is honorable, it is also steeped in horror. Should the taste of your favorite herb come from the death of some rare love, so the life of the bright red blood of an animal river pouring forth becomes some other life as it darkens down to the melancholy hues of an old dried blood which speaks in some lost primitive tongue about the mysteries of death, color, and corruption. The dried blood reminds you of the sordid glory of the bullfight, its hint of the Renaissance when noble figures stated their presence as they paraded through the marketplace and passed by cripples with stumps for legs, a stump for a tongue, and the lewdest grin of the day. Yes, the spectrum of the bullfight goes from courage to gangrene.

In Mexico, the hour before the fight is always the best hour of the week. It would be memorable not to sound like Hemingway, but in fact you would get happy the night before just thinking of that hour next day. Outside the Plaza Mexico, cheap cafés open only on Sunday, and huge as beer gardens, filled with the public (us tourists, hoodlums, pimps, pickpurses and molls, Mexican variety – which is to say the whores had headdresses and hindquarters not to be seen elsewhere on earth, for their hair rose vertically twelve inches from the head, and their posteriors projected horizontally twelve inches back into that space the rest of the whore had just marched through). The mariachis were out with their romantic haunting caterwauling of guitar, violin, songs of carnival and trumpet, their song told of hearts which were true and hearts which were broken, and the wail of the broken heart went right into the trumpet until there were times when drunk the right way on tequila or Mexican rum, it was perhaps the best sound heard this side of Miles Davis. You hear a hint of all that in the Tijuana Brass.

You see, my friends, the wild hour was approaching. The horrors of the week in Mexico were coming to term. Indeed, no week in Mexico is without its horrors for every last Mexican alive – it is a city and a country where the bones of the dead seem to give the smell of their char to every desert wind and auto exhaust and frying tortilla. The mournfulness of unrequited injustice hangs a shroud across the centuries. Every Mexican is gloomy until the instant he becomes happy, and then he is a maniac. He howls, he whistles, smoke of murder passes off his pores, he bullies, he beseeches friendship, he is a clown, a brigand, a tragic figure suddenly merry. The intellectuals and the technicians of Mexico abominate their national character because it is always in the way. It puts the cracks in the plaster of new buildings, it forgets to cement the tiles, it leaves rags in the new pipes of new office buildings and forgets to put the gas cap back on the tank. So the intellectuals and the technicians hate the bullfight as well. You cannot meet a socialist in Mexico who approves of the running of the bulls. They are trying to turn Mexico into a modern country, and thus the same war goes on there that goes on in three-quarters of the world – battlefront is the new highways to the suburbs, and the corporation's office buildings, the walls of hospital white, and the myopic sheets of glass. In Mexico, like everywhere else, it is getting harder and harder to breathe in a mood through the pores of the city because more and more of the city is being covered with corporation architecture, with surgical dressing. To the vampires and banshees and dried blood on the curses of the cactus in the desert is added the horror of the new technology in an old murder-ridden land. And four o'clock on Sunday is the beginning of release for some of the horrors of the week. If many come close to feeling the truth only by telling a lie, so Mexicans come close to love by watching the flow of blood on an animal's flanks and the certain death of the bull before the bravery and/or humiliation of the bullfighter.

I could never have understood it if someone tried to explain ahead of time, and in fact, I came to love the bullfight long before I comprehended the first thing about why I did. That was very much to the good. There are not too many experiences a radical American intellectual could encounter in those days (when the youngest generation was called the silent generation) which invaded his sure sense of his own intellectual categories. I did not like the first bullfights I saw, the formality of the ritual bored me, the fights appeared poor (indeed they were) and the human content of the spectacle came out atrocious. Narcissistic matadors, vain when they made a move, pouting like a girl stood up on Saturday night when the crowd turned on them, clumsy at killing, and the crowd, brutal to a man. In the Plaza Mexico, the Indians in the cheap seats buy a paper cup of beer and when they are done drinking, the walk to the W.C. is *miles* away, and besides they are usually feeling sullen, so they urinate in their paper cup and hurl it down in a cascade of harvest gold, Indian piss. If you are an American escorting an American girl who has blond hair, and you have tickets in *Sol*, you buy your girl a cheap sombrero at the gate, for otherwise she will be a prime target of attention. Indeed, you do well not to sit near an American escorting a blond whose head is uncovered, for the aim of a drunken Indian is no better than you when your aim is drunk. So no surprise if one's early detestation of the bullfight was fortified in kidney brew, Azteca.

Members of a minority group are always ready to take punishment, however, and I was damned if I was going to be excluded from still another cult. So I persisted in going to bullfights, and they were a series of lousy bullfights, and then the third or fourth time I got religion. It was a windy afternoon, with threats of rain, and now and then again ten minutes of rain, poisonous black clouds overhead, the chill gloom of a black sky on Sundays in Mexico, and the particular torero (whose name I could not recall for anything) was a clod. He had a nasty build. Little spindly legs, too big a chest, a butt which was broad and stolid, real peasant ass, and a vulgar worried face with a gold tooth. He was engaged with an ugly bull who kept chopping at the muleta with his horns, and occasionally the bull would catch the muleta and fling it in the air and trample it and wonder why the object was either dead or not dead, the bull smelling a hint of his own blood (or the blood of some cousin) on the blood of the muleta, and the crowd would hoot, and the torero would go over to his sword handler at the barrera, and shake his head and come out with a new muleta, and the bull would chop, and the wind would zig the muleta out of control, and then the matador would drop it and scamper back to the barrera, and the crowd would jeer and the piss would fly in yellow arcs of rainbow through the rain all the way down from the cheap seats, and the whores would make farting sounds with their spoiled knowledgeable mouths, while the aficionados would roll their eyes, and the sound of Mexican laughter, that operative definition of the echo of total disgust, would shake along like jelly-gasoline through the crowd.

I got a look at the bullfighter who was the center of all this. He was not a man I could feel something for. He had a cheap pimp's face and a dull, thoroughgoing vanity. His face, however, was now in despair. There was something going on for him more humiliating than humiliation – as if his life were going to take a turn into something more dreadful than anything it had encountered until now. He was in trouble. The dead dull fight he was giving was going to be death for certain hopes in his psyche. Somehow it was going to be more final than the average dead dull fight to which he was obviously all too accustomed. I was watching the despair of a profoundly mediocre man.

Well, he finally gave up any attempt to pass the bull, and he worked the animal forward with jerks of his muleta to left and right, a competent rather than a beautiful technique at best, and even to my untutored eye he was a mechanic at this, and more whistles, and then desperation all over that vain incompetent pimp's face, he profiled with his sword, and got it halfway in, and the animal took a few steps to one side and the other and fell over quickly.

The art of killing is the last skill you learn to judge in bullfighting, and the kill on this rainy afternoon left me less impressed than the crowd. Their jeers were replaced by applause (later I learned the crowd would always applaud a kill in the lung – all audiences are Broadway audiences) and the approbation continued sufficiently for the torero to take a tour of the ring. He got no ears, he certainly didn't deserve them, but he had his tour and he was happy, and in his happiness there was something suddenly likeable about him, and I sensed that I was passing through some interesting emotions since I had felt contempt for a stranger and then a secret and most unsocialistic desire to see this type I did not like humiliated a little further, and then in turn I was quietly but most certainly overcome by his last-minute success sufficiently to find myself liking a kind of man I had never considered near to human before. So this bad bullfight in the rain had given a drop of humanity to a very dry area of my heart, and now I knew a little more and had something to think about which was no longer altogether in category.

We have presented the beginning of a history then – no, say it better – the origin of an addiction. For a drug's first appeal is always existential – our sense of life (once it is made alert by the sensation of its absence) is thereupon so full of need as the desire for a breath of air. The sense of life comes alive in the happy days when the addict first encounters his drug. But all histories of addiction are the same – particularly in the beginning. They fall into the larger category of the history of a passion. So I will spare each and every one of us the titles of the books I read on the running of the bulls, save to mention the climactic purchase of a three-volume set in leather for fifty 1954 dollars (now doubtless in value one hundred) of *Los Toros* by Cossió. Since it was entirely in Spanish, a language I read with about as much ease and pleasure as Very Old English, *Los Toros* remains in my library as a cornerstone of my largest mental department – *The Bureau of Abandoned Projects*: I was going to write *the* novel about bullfight, dig!

Nor will I reminisce about the great bullfighters I saw, of the majesties of Arruza and the *machismo* of Procuna, the liquidities of Silverio and the solemnity of César Girón, no, we will not micturate the last of such memory to tell a later generation about El Ranchero and Ortiz of the Orticina, and Angel Peralta the Rejoneador, nor of Manolete, for he was dead long before I could with confidence distinguish a bull from a heifer or a steer, and no more can I talk of Luis Miguel and Antonio, for neither of them have I seen in a fight, so that all I know of Ordóñez is his reputation, and of Dominguín his style, for I caught his work in a movie once and it was not work the way he made it look. No, enough of these qualifications for *afición*. The fact is that I do not dwell on Arruza and Procuna and Silverio and Girón and Peralta and Ranchero because I did not see them that often and in fact most of them I saw but once. I was always in Mexico in the summer, you see, and the summer is the *temporada de novillos*, which is to say it is the time when the *novilladas* are held, which is to say it is the time of the novices.

Now the fellow who is pushing up this preface for you is a great lover of the bullfight – make on it no mistake. For a great bullfight he would give up just about any other athletic or religious spectacle – the World Series in a minute, a pro football championship, a mass at the Vatican, perhaps even a great heavyweight championship – which, kids, is really saying it. No love like the love for four in the afternoon at the Plaza Mexico. Yet all the great matadors he saw were seen only at special festivals when they fought very small bulls for charity. The novillada is, after all, the time of the novilleros, and a novillero is a bullfighter approximately equal in rank to a Golden Gloves fighter. A very good novillero is like a very good Golden Gloves finalist. The Sugar Ray Robinsons and the Rocky Marcianos of the bullfighting world were glimpsed by me only when they came out of retirement long enough to give the equivalent of a snappy two-round exhibition. My love of bullfighting, and my experience of it as a spectator, was founded then by watching novilleros week after week over two separate summers in Mexico City. So I know as much about bullfighting as a man would know about boxing if he read a lot and heard a lot about great fighters and saw a few movies of them and one or two exhibitions, and also had the intense, if partial, fortune to follow two Golden Gloves tournaments all the way and to follow them with some lively if not always dependable instinct for discerning what was good and what was not so good in the talent before him.

After a while I got good at seeing the flaws and virtues in novilleros, and in fact I began to see so much of their character in their style, and began to learn so much about style by comprehending their character (for nearly everything good or bad about a novice bullfighter is revealed at a great rate) that I began to take the same furious interest and partisanship in the triumph of one style over another that is usually reserved for literary matters (is Philip Roth better than John Updike? – you know) or what indeed average Americans and some not so average might take over political figures. To watch a bullfighter have an undeserved triumph on Sunday afternoon when you detest his style is not the worst preparation for listening to Everett Dirksen nominate Barry Goldwater or hearing Lyndon Johnson give a lecture on TV about Amurrican commitments to the free universe. Everything bad and God-awful about the style of life got into the style of bullfighters, as well as everything light, delightful, honorable and good.

At any rate, about the time I knew a lot about bullfighting, or as much as you could know watching nothing but novilleros week after week, I fell in love with a bullfighter. I never even met this bullfighter, I rush to tell you. I would not have wanted to meet him. Meeting him could only have spoiled the perfection of my love, so pure was my affection. And his name – not one in a thousand of you out there, dear general readers, can have heard of him – his name was El Loco. El Loco, the Crazy One. It is not a term of endearment in Mexico, where half the populace is crazy. To amplify the power of nomenclature, El Loco came from the provinces, he was God's own hick, and his real name was Amado Ramírez, which is like being a boy from Hicksville, Georgia, with a name like Beloved Remington. Yet there was a time when I thought Beloved Remington, which is to say Amado Ramírez, would become the greatest bullfighter in the whole world, and there were critics in Mexico City hoary with *afición* who held the same opinion (if not always in print). He came up one summer a dozen years ago like a rocket, but a rocket with one tube hot and one tube wet and he spun in circles all over the bullfighting world of Mexico City all through the summer and fall.

But we must tell more of what it is like to watch novilleros. You see, novice bullfighters fight bulls who are called *novillos*, and these bulls are a year younger and two to four hundred pounds lighter than the big fighting bulls up around a thousand pounds which matadors must face. So they are less dangerous. They can still kill a man, but not often does that happen – they are more likely to pound and stomp and wound and bruise a novillero than to catch him and play him in the air and stab him up high on the horns the way a terrible full-grown fighting bull can do. In consequence, the analogy to the Golden Gloves is imperfect, for a talented novillero can at his best look as exciting as, or more exciting than, a talented matador – the novice's beast is smaller and less dangerous, so his lack of experience is compensated for by his relative comfort – he is in less danger of getting killed. (Indeed, to watch a consummate matador like Carlos Arruza work with a new young bull is like watching Norman Mailer box with his three-year-old son – absolute mastery is in the air.)

Novilleros possess another virtue. Nobody can contest their *afición*. For every novillero who has a manager, and a rich man to house and feed him, and influential critics to bring him along on the sweet of a bribe or two, there are a hundred devoted all but unknown novilleros who hitch from *poblado* to *poblado* on back dirt roads for the hint of a chance to fight at some fiesta so small the results are not even phoned to Mexico City. Some of these kids spend years in the provinces living on nothing, half-starved in the desire to spend a life fighting bulls and they will fight anything – bulls who are overweight, calves who are under the legal limit, beasts who have fought before and so are sophisticated and dangerous. These provincial novilleros get hurt badly by wounds which show no blood, deep bruises in the liver and kidney from the flat of a horn, deep internal bleedings in the gut, something lively taken off the groin – a number of them die years later from malnutrition and chronic malfunctions of some number of those organs – their deaths get into no statistics on the fatalities of the bullfight.

A few of these provincial novilleros get enough fights and

enough experience and develop enough talent, however, to pick up a reputation of sorts. If they are very lucky and likable, or have connections, or hump themselves – as some will – to rich homosexuals in the capital, then they get their shot. Listen to this. At the beginning of the novillada, six new bullfighters are brought in every Sunday to fight one bull each in the Plaza Mexico. For six or eight weeks this goes on. Perhaps fifty fighters never seen before in Mexico City have their chance. Maybe ten will be seen again. The tension is enormous for each novillero. If he fails to have a triumph or attract outstanding attention, then his years in the provinces went for nothing. Back again he will go to the provinces as a punishment for failing to be superb. Perhaps he will never fight again in the Plaza Mexico. His entire life depends on this one fight. And even this fight depends on luck. For any novillero can catch a poor bull, a dull mediocre cowardly bull. When the animal does not charge, the bullfighter, unless possessed of genius, cannot look good.

Once a novillero came into the Plaza on such an occasion, was hit by the bull while making his first pass, a veronica, and the boy and cape sailed into the air and came down together in such a way that when the boy rolled over, the cape wrapped around him like a tortilla, and one wit in *Sol*, full of the harsh wine of Mexico's harsh grapes, yelled out, '*Suerte de Enchiladas.*' The young bullfighter was named The Pass of the Enchiladas. His career could never be the same. He went on to fight that bull, did a decent honorable job – the crowd never stopped laughing. Suerte de Enchiladas. He was branded. He walked off in disgrace. The one thing you cannot be in any land where Spanish is spoken is a clown. I laughed with the rest. The bullfight is nine-tenths cruelty. The bullfight brews one's cruelty out of one's pores – it makes an elixir of cruelty. But it does something else. It reflects the proportions of life in Latin lands. For in Mexico it does not seem unreasonable that a man should spend years learning a dangerous trade, be rapped once by a bull, and end up ruined, a Suerte de Enchiladas. It is unfair, but then life is monstrously unfair, one knows that, one of the few gleams in the muck of all this dubious Mexican majesty called existence is that one can on occasion laugh bitterly with the gods. In the Spanish-Indian blood, the substance of one's dignity is found in sharing the cruel vision of the gods. In fact, dignity can be found nowhere else. For courage is seen as the servant of the gods' cruel vision.

On to Beloved Remington. He arrived in Mexico City at the end of the beginning of the novillada in the summer of 1954. He was there, I think, on the next to last of the early Sundays when six bulls were there for six novilleros. (In the full season of the novillada, when the best new young men have been chosen, there are six bulls for only three toreros – each kid then has two bulls, two chances.) I was not yet in Mexico for Amado Ramírez's first Sunday, but I heard nothing else from my bullfighting friends from the day I got in. He had appeared as the last of six novilleros. It had been a terrible day. All of the novilleros had been bad. He apparently had been the last and the worst, and had looked so clumsy that the crowd in derision had begun to applaud him. There is no sign of displeasure greater among the Mexican bullfighting public than to turn their ovations upside down. But Ramírez had taken bows. Serious solemn bows. He had bowed so much he had hardly fought the bull. The Plaza Mexico had rung with merriment. It took him forever to kill the beast – he received a tumultuous ovation. He took a turn of the ring. A wit shouted '*Ole, El Loco.*' He was named. When they cheer incompetence they are ready to set fire to the stadium.

El Loco was the sensation of the week. A clown had fought a bull in the Plaza Mexico and gotten out alive. The promotors put him on the following week as a seventh bullfighter, an extra added attraction. He was not considered worth the dignity of appearing on the regular card. For the first time that season, the Plaza was sold out. It was also the first fight I was to see of my second season.

Six young novilleros fought six mediocre bulls that day, and gave six mediocre fights. The crowd grew more and more sullen. When there is no good bullfight, there is no catharsis. One's money has been spent, the drinks are wearing down, and there has been no illumination, no moment to burn away all that spiritual sewer gas from the horrors of the week. Dull violence breeds, and with it, contempt for all bullfighters. An ugly

Mexican bullfighting crowd has the temper of an old-fashioned street corner in Harlem after the police wagon has rounded up the nearest five studs and hauled them away.

Out came the clown, El Loco. The special seventh bull-fighter. He was an apparition. He had a skinny body and a funny ugly face with little eyes set close together, a big nose, and a little mouth. He had very black Indian hair, and a tuft in the rear of his head stood up like the spike of an antenna. He had very skinny legs and they were bent at the knee so that he gave the impression of trudging along with a lunchbox in his hand. He had a comic ass. It went straight back like a duck's tail feathers. His suit fit poorly. He was some sort of grafting between Ray Bolger and Charlie Chaplin. And he had the sense of self-importance to come out before the bull, he was indeed given a turn of the ring before he even saw the bull. An honor granted him for his appearance the week before. He was altogether solemn. It did not seem comic to him. He had the kind of somber extravagant ceremoniousness of a village mayor in a mountain town come out to greet the highest officials in the government. His knees stuck out in front and his buttocks in back. The Plaza rocked and rocked. Much applause followed by circulating zephyrs of laughter. And under it all, like a croaking of frogs, the beginnings of the biggest thickest Bronx raspberry anybody living ever heard.

Amado Ramírez went out to receive the bull. His first pass was a yard away from the animal, his second was six feet. He looked like a fifty-five-year-old peon ready to retire. The third pass caught his cape, and as it flew away on the horns, El Loco loped over to the barrera with a gait like a kangaroo. A thunderstorm of boos was on its way. He held out his arm horizontally, an injunction to the crowd, fingers spread, palm down, a mild deprecatory peasant gesture, as if to say, 'Wait, you haven't seen nothing yet.' The lip-farters began to smack. Amado went back out. He botched one pass, looked poor on a basic veronica. Boos, laughter, even the cops in the aisle were laughing. *Que payaso*!

His next pass had a name, but few even of the *afición* knew it, for it was an old-fashioned pass of great intricacy which spoke of the era of Belmonte and El Gallo and Joselito. It was a pass of considerable danger, plus much formal content (for a flash it looked like he was inclining to kiss a lady's hand, his cape draped over his back, while the bull went roaring by his unprotected ass). If I remember, it was called a *gallicina*, and no one had seen it in five years. It consisted of whirling in a reverse *serpentina* counterclockwise into the bull, so that the cape was wrapped around your body just like the Suerte de Enchiladas, except you were vertical, but the timing was such that the bull went by at the moment your back was to him and you could not see his horns. Then the whirling continued, and the cape flared out again. Amado was clumsy in his approach and stepped on his cape when he was done, but there was one moment of lightning in the middle when you saw clear sky after days of fog and smelled the ozone, there was an instant of heaven – finest thing I had yet seen in the bullfight – and in a sob of torture and release, 'Olé' came in a panic of disbelief from one parched Mexican throat near to me. El Loco did the same pass one more time and then again. On the second pass, a thousand cried 'Olé', and on the third, the Plaza exploded and fifty thousand men and women gave up the word at the same time. Something merry and corny as a gypsy violin flowed out of his cape.

After that, nothing but comedy again. He tried a dozen fancy passes, none worked well. They were all wild, solemn, courtly, and he was there with his peasant bump of an ass and his knobby knees. The crowd laughed with tears in their eyes. With the muleta he looked absurd, a man about to miss a train and so running with his suitcase. It took him forever to kill and he stood out like an old lady talking to a barking dog, but he could do no wrong now for this crowd – they laughed, they applauded, they gave him a tour of the ring. For something had happened in those three passes which no one could comprehend. It was as if someone like me had gotten in the ring with Cassius Clay and for twenty seconds had clearly outboxed him. The only explanation was divine intervention. So El Loco was back to fight two bulls next week.

If I remember, he did little with either bull, and killed the second one just before the third *aviso*. In a good season, his career would have been over. But it was a dreadful season. A couple of weeks of uneventful bullfights and El Loco was invited back. He looked awful in his first fight, green of face, timid, unbelievably awkward with the cape, morose and abominably prudent with the muleta. He killed badly. So badly in fact that he was still killing the bull when the third *aviso* sounded. The bull was let out alive. A dull sullen silence riddled with Mexican whistles. The crowd had had a bellyful of laughs with him. They were now getting very bored with the joke.

But the second bull he liked. Those crazy formal courtly passes, the *gallicinas*, whirled out again, and the horns went by his back six inches away. Olé. He went to put the banderillas in himself and botched the job, had to run very fast on the last pair to escape the bull and looked like a chicken as he ran. The catcalls tuned up again. The crowd was like a bored lion uncertain whether to eat entrails or lick a face. Then he came out with the muleta and did a fine series of *derechazos*, the best seen in several weeks, and to everyone's amazement, he killed on the first *estocada*. They gave him an ear. He was the *triunfador* of the day.

This was the afternoon which confirmed the beginning of a career. After that, most of the fights are mixed in memory because he had so many, and they were never without incident, and they took place years ago. All through the summer of 1954, he fought just about every week, and every week something happened which shattered the comprehension of the most veteran bullfighting critic. They decided after this first triumph that he was a mediocre novillero with nothing particular to recommend him except a mysterious flair for the *gallicina*, and a competence with the *derechazo*. Otherwise, he was uninspired with the cape and weak with the muleta. So the following week he gave an exhibition with muleta. He did four *pases de pecho* so close and luminous (a pass is luminous when your body seems to lift with breath as it goes by) that the horns flirted with his heart. He did *derechazos* better than the week before, and finished with *manoletinas*. Again he killed well. They gave him two ears. Then his second bull went out alive. A *fracaso*.

Now the critics said he was promising with the muleta, but weak with the cape. He could not do a veronica of any value. So in one of the following weeks he gave five of the slowest, most luminous, most soaring veronicas anyone had ever seen.

Yet, for three weeks in a row, if he cut ears on one bull, he let the other go out alive. A bullfighter is not supposed to let his animal outlive three avisos. Indeed if the animal is not killed before the first aviso, the torero is in disgrace already. Two avisos is like the sound of the knell of the bell in the poorhouse, and a bullfighter who hears the third aviso and has to let his bull go out alive is properly ready for hara-kiri. No sight, you see, is worse. It takes something like three to five minutes from the first aviso to the last, and in that time the kill becomes a pigsticking. Because the torero has tried two, three, four, five times, even more to go in over the horns, and he has hit bone, and he has left the sword half in but in some abominable place like the middle of the back or the flank, or he has had a perfect thrust and the bull does not die and minutes go by waiting for it to die and the peons run up with their capes and try to flick the sword out by swirling cloth around the pommel guard and giving a crude Latin yank – nothing is cruder than a peon in a sweat for his boss. Sometimes they kick the bull in the nuts in the hope it will go down, and the crowd hoots. Sometimes the bull sinks to its knees and the puntillero comes in to sever its neck with a thrust of his dagger, but the stab is off-center, the spinal cord is not severed. Instead it is stimulated by the shock and the dying bull gets up and wanders all over the ring looking for its *querencia* while blood drains and drips from its wounds and the bullfighter, looking ready to cry, trots along like a farmer accompanying his mule down the road. And the next aviso blows. Such scenes are a nightmare for the torero. He will awaken from dreams where he is stabbing and stabbing over the horns with the *descabellar* and the bull does not drop but keeps jerking his head. Well, you receive this communication, I'm sure. A bull going out alive because the torero was not able to kill him in the allotted time is a sight about as bloody and attractive as a victim getting out of a smashed car and stumbling down the road, and the matador is about as popular as the man who caused the accident. The average torero can afford less than one occasion a year when three avisos are heard. El Loco was allowing an average of one bull a week to go out unkilled. One may get an idea of how good he was when he was good, if you appreciate a prizefighter who is so good that he is forgiven even if every other fight he decides to climb out of the ring and quit.

For a period, criticism of El Loco solidified. He had brilliant details, he was able on occasion to kill with inspiration, he had huge talent, but he lacked the indispensable ingredient of the bullfighter, he did not know how to get a good performance out of a bad bull. He lacked tenacity. So Ramírez created the most bizarre *faena* in anyone's memory, a fight which came near to shattering the rules of bullfighting. For on a given Sunday, he caught a very bad bull, and worked with him in all the dull, technical, unaesthetic ways a bullfighter has to work with an unpromising beast, and chopped him to left and to right, and kept going into the bull's querencia and coaxing him out and this went on for minutes, while the public demonstrated its displeasure. And El Loco paid no attention and kept working with the bull, and then finally got the bull to charge and he made a few fine passes. But then the first aviso sounded and everyone groaned. Because finally the bull was going good, and yet Amado would have to kill him now. But Amado had his bull in shape and he was not going to give him up yet, and so with everyone on the scent of the loss of each second, he made derechazos and the pass with the muleta which looks like the *gaonera* with the cape, and he did a deliberate *adorno* or two and the second aviso sounded and he made an effort to kill and failed, but stayed very cool and built up the crowd again by taking the bull through a series of *naturales*, and with twenty seconds left before the third aviso and the Plaza in pandemonium he went in to kill and had a perfect estocada and the bull moved around softly and with dignity and died about ten seconds after the third aviso, but no one could hear the trumpet for the crowd was in delirium of thunder, and every white handkerchief in the place was out. And Amado was smiling, which is why you could love him, because his pinched ugly little peasant face was full of a kid's decent happiness when he smiled. And a minute later there was almost a riot against the judges for they were not going to give him tail or two ears or even an ear – how could they if the bull had died after the third aviso? – and yet the tension of fighting the bull on the very edge of his time had given a quality to this fight which had more than a hint of the historic, for new emotions had been felt. The bullfighting public has a taste for new emotions equaled only by the lust of a lady for new pleasures.

This record of triumphs is in danger of becoming as predictable as any record of triumphs since Caesar. Let us keep it alive with an account of the fiascos. Amado was simply unlike any bullfighter who had ever come along. When he had a great fight, or even a great pass, it was unlike the passes of other fine novilleros – the passes of El Loco were better than anything you had ever seen. It was as if you were looking at the sky and suddenly a bird materialized in the air. And a moment later disappeared again. His work was frightening. It was simple, lyrical, light, illumined, but it came from nowhere and then was gone. When El Loco was bad, he was not mediocre or dull, he was simply the worst, most inept, and most comical bullfighter anyone had ever seen. He seemed to have no technique to fall back on. He would hold his cape like a shroud, his legs would bend at the knees, his sad ass seemed to have an eye for the exit, his expression was morose as Fernandel, and his feet kept tripping. He looked like a praying mantis on its hind legs. And when he was afraid, he had a nerveless incapacity to kill which was so hopeless that the moment he stepped out to face his animal you knew he could not go near this particular bull. Yet when he was good, the comic body suddenly straightened, indeed took on the camber of the best back any Spanish aristocrat chose to display, the buttocks retired into themselves like a masterpiece of poise, and the cape and the muleta moved slowly as full sails, or whirled like the wing of that mysterious bird. It was as if El Loco came to be every comic Mexican who ever breathed the finest Spanish grace into his pores. For five odd minutes he was as completely transformed as Charlie Chaplin's tramp doing a consummate impersonation of the one and only Valentino, long-lost Rudolph.

Let me tell then of Amado's best fight. It came past the middle of that fine summer when he had an adventure every week in the Plaza and we had adventures watching nim, for he had fights so mysterious that the gods of the bulls and the ghosts of dead matadors must have come with the mothers and the witches of the centuries, homage to Lorca! to see the miracles he performed. Listen! One day he had a sweet little bull with nice horns, regular, pleasantly curved, and the bull ran with gaiety, even abandon. Now we have to stop off here for an imperative explanation. I beg your attention, but it is essential to discuss the attitudes of *afición* to the natural. To them the natural is the equivalent of the full parallel turn in skiing or a scrambling T-formation quarterback or a hook off a jab – it cannot be done well by all athletes no matter how good they are in other ways, and the natural is, as well, a dangerous pass, perhaps the most dangerous there is. The cloth of the muleta has no sword to extend its width. Now the cloth is held in the left hand, the sword in the right, and so the target of the muleta which is presented for the bull's attraction is half as large as it was before and the bullfighter's body is thus so much bigger and so much more worthy of curiosity to the beast – besides the bull is wiser now, he may be ready to suspect it is the man who torments him and not the swirling sinister chaos of the cloth in which he would bury his head. Moreover – and here is the mystique of the natural – the bullfighter has a psychic communion with the bull. Obviously. People who are not psychic do not conceive of fighting bulls. So the torero fights the bull from his psyche first. And with the muleta he fights him usually with his right hand from a position of authority. Switching the cloth to the left hand exposes his psyche as well as his body. He feels less authority – in compensation his instinct plays closer to the bull. But he is so vulnerable! So a natural inspires a bullfighting public to hold their breath, for danger and beauty come closest to meeting right here.

It was naturales Amado chose to perform with this bull. He had not done many this season. The last refuge of his detractors was that he could not do naturales well. So here on this day he gave his demonstration. Watch if you can.

He began his faena by making no exploratory pass, no *pase de muerte*, no derechazos, he never chopped, no, he went up to this sweet bull and started his faena with a series of naturales, with a series of five naturales which were all linked and all beautiful and had the Plaza in pandemonium because where could he go from there? And Amado came up sweetly to the bull, and did five more naturales as good as the first five, and then did five more without moving from his spot – they were superb – and then furled his muleta until it was the size of this page and he passed the bull five more times in the same way, the horns going around his left wrist. The man and the bull looked in love with each other. And then after these twenty naturales, Amado did five more with almost no muleta at all, five series of five naturales had he performed, twenty-five naturales – it is not much easier than making love twenty-five times in a row – and then he knelt and kissed the bull on the forehead he was so happy, and got up delicately, and went to the barrera for his sword, came back, profiled to get ready for the kill. Everyone was sitting on a collective fuse. If he managed to kill on the first estocada this could well be the best faena anyone had ever seen a novillero perform, who knew, it was all near to unbelievable, and then just as he profiled, the bull charged prematurely, and Amado, determined to get the kill, did not skip away but held ground, received the charge, stood there with the sword, turned the bull's head with the muleta, and the bull impaled himself on the point of the torero's blade which went right into the proper space between the shoulders, and the bull ran right up on it into his death, took several steps to the side, gave a toss of his head at heaven, and fell. Amado had killed *recibiendo*. He had killed standing still, receiving the bull while the bull charged. No one had seen that in years. So they gave him everything that day, ears, tail, *vueltas* without limit – they were ready to give him the bull.

He concluded the summer in a burst of honors. He had more great fights. Afterward they gave him a day where he fought six bulls all by himself, and he went on to take his *alternativa* and become a full fledged matador. But he was a Mexican down to the bones. The honors all turned damp for him. I was not there the day he fought six bulls, I had had to go back to America and never saw him fight again. I heard about him only in letters and in bullfighting newspapers. But the day he took on the six bulls I was told he did not have a single good fight, and the day he took his alternativa to become a matador, both his bulls went out alive, a disgrace too great even for Amado. He fought a seventh bull. Gypsy magic might save him again. But the bull was big and dull and El Loco had no luck and no magic and just succeeded in killing him in a bad difficult dull fight. It was obvious he was afraid of the big bulls. So he relinquished his alternativa and went back to the provinces to try to regain his reputation and his nerve. And no one ever heard much of him again. Or at least I never did, but then I have not been back to Mexico. Now I suspect I'm one of the very few who remember the happiness of seeing him fight. He was so bad when he was bad that he gave the impression you could fight a bull yourself and do no worse. So when he was good, you felt as if you were good too, and that was something no other torero ever gave me, for when they were good they looked impenetrable, they were like gods, but when Beloved Remington was good, the whole human race was good – he spoke of the great distance a man can go from the worst in himself to the best, and that finally is what the bullfight might be all about, for in dark bloody tropical lands possessed of poverty and desert and swamp, filth and treachery, slovenliness, and the fat lizards of all the worst lust, the excretory lust to shove one's own poison into others, the one thing which can keep the sweet nerve of life alive is the knowledge that a man cannot be judged by what he is every day, but only in his greatest moment, for that is the moment when he shows what he was intended to be. It is a romantic self-pitying impractical approach to the twentieth century's demand for predictable ethics, high production, dependability of function, and categorization of impulse, but it is the Latin approach. Their allegiance is to the genius of the blood. So they judge a man by what he is at his best.

By that logic, I will always have love for El Loco because he taught me how to love the bullfight, and how to penetrate some of its secrets. And finally he taught me something about the mystery of form. He gave me the clue that form is the record of a war. Because he never had the ability most bullfighters, like most artists, possess to be false with their art, tasty yet phony, he taught something about life with every move he made, including the paradox that courage can be found in men whose conflict is caught between their ambition and their cowardice. He even taught me how to look for form in other places. Do you see the curve of a beautiful breast? It is not necessarily a gift of God – it may be the record life left on a lady of the balance of forces between her desire, her modesty, her ambition, her timidity, her maternity, and her sense of an impulse which cannot be denied. If we were wise enough, bold enough, and scholars from head to motorcyclist's boot, we could extract the real history of Europe from the form elucidated between man and beast that we glimpse again in recall of the bullfight. Indeed where is a writer or a lover without a knowledge of what goes on behind that cloth where shapes are born? *Olé*, Amado!

# Theatre

## The Playwright as Critic

Not so very long ago the National Foundation on the Arts and Humanities had a symposium for an invited audience of newspaper critics. Conducted by Roger Stevens and Carolyn Kizer, the symposium was given the formal title of 'What's Wrong with Criticism in the Performing Arts', and Session One took place in a conference room of the Whitney, with Arthur Schlesinger, Gerald Weales, Clive Barnes, William Phillips, Michael Smith of the *Village Voice*, and myself.

Now, it would be nice (and doubtless out of character) for me to describe which opinions were held by the others, and what shape was taken by colloquies between the speakers and the invited audience, but I cannot, for *The Deer Park* was already in rehearsal that day, and I rushed up to the Whitney for a half hour, said my piece somewhere toward the end of that three-hour conference, and was out again, on the way back to Christopher Street downtown in the Village and rehearsals at the DeLys. So I had only an inkling of what had gone before, but it was enough to improvise ten minutes of talk. Because what came through the echo of completed conversations was the old and essential antagonism of the artist in the theatre (the playwright, actor, director, yea, often the producer!) toward the cruel, rigorous, even unreasonable demand of the opening-night reviews, that cry of protest because all the years of writing, the months of preparation, and the repetitive soul-killing weeks of rehearsal must still come to down to the electric hour when the drama reviewer sprints from the theatre, snatches his opening lead from the well-tuned bag of his wit, and is off to his desk, say, say, his guillotine. Three times out of four, nine times out of ten, the work is doomed. If it is an exciting, difficult play, imperfectly presented (as, for example, might be said of *Slow Dance on the Killing Ground*), then the odds are nineteen out of twenty that the critic, the two or three or four good men inhabiting those nerve-festooned portals between the theatre and the public, will do the job in, and the play does not live.

We are all familiar with this profound plaint. But the correctives and/or the preventatives lack salt. Invariably they suggest that the critic see the play after it opens, that he take his time, that he brood upon the nature of what he has seen. All this, while sensible, is nonetheless depressing. That, in fact, is what I began to say at the symposium in the Whitney. For it seemed to me that the opening-night review with all its inequities, yaws of judgment, its surrealistic surgeries upon aesthetic value, is nonetheless indispensable to the theatre, and I would not enjoy writing a play and seeing it produced if I could not have an opening night before a full posse of critics. For that is also a part of the play. That is its dramatic edge, its confrontation with the history it will or will not make. Those opening-night reviews, written to the demand of fever speed, are a ritual at the heart of the drama. A professional theatre without the sense of crisis provided by opening night is like a marriage in city hall.

Yet what a huge price is paid for the excitement of the opening-night review. The desire for success lucubrates secret prostitutions in the soul. Some are not so secret. A theatre whose economic foundations are built on the opinions of five or six men (now reduced to four men, or three men, or two, can it be even one man?) is a theatre whose aesthetics must be built on the most anomalous mechanical principles – the intake pipe is on the outlet valve: the theatre becomes geared to the taste of the newspaper critic, which is to say – not his taste, but his need. And his need – we can make no mistake here – is for simple plays.

A drama critic is a man of some integrity and discipline – he could not otherwise fulfill the professional rigors of his work. Like all men of integrity, he prefers to do a good job. A simple play offers just that opportunity. Its moral situations may be novel but they must be clearcut (go back to *The Moon is Blue*), its characters are happiest when amusing or worthy of our compassion, but they cannot be too contradictory or complex. In a play with five characters, four preferably must be comfortable to the mind so that the play may concentrate on the fifth – perhaps I am thinking of *Come Back, Little Sheba*. It does not matter. Fifty plays a season, good, bad, magnificent, or atrocious, fulfill this formula. The simple play enables the reviewer to make his assessment on the evidence before him. He can mark the play precisely on the scale of his accumulated experience. The simple play – all else equal – inspires the critic therefore with a benevolent sensation; he can feel like a good man doing a good work of appraisal.

The only difficulty is that the simple play alienates the theatre from life, for in life, moral situations are rarely novel, but invariably overloaded with counterpoint, and the people who surround you are not always comfortable to the concepts of the mind; indeed, they often prove most depressing just at the moment when they are presumably most worthy of compassion. In contrast, the simple play provides a wish fulfillment – it extracts a neat pattern from the flux of the unruly: it has, in consequence, as much to do with life, this simple play, as a hairpin has to do with jewelry, but the hairpin is what prospers, the hairpin becomes nine-tenths of the stock in the jewelry store. The theatre roots itself in the simple. Actors learn to look for precise results, directors look for moments – call them tricks – since a simple play depends for its success on offering, let us say, one hundred moments of pleasure rather than fifty, and playwrights develop an eye for linear mechanisms of plot which will lift them from the moral bogs of their theme.

It comes down to one thundering, if matter-of-fact difficulty: You cannot predict success for a play once it is sufficiently complex to need a night's sleep for comprehending it. Any dramatic theme which requires an audience to return to their unconscious later that night, in order to evaluate the depth of what is being said in the theatre, is carrying a most ambitious monkey on its back, for the drama reviewer does not have the time to put the play together in his sleep and write about it in the morning. He must take it as it is, all confusion to the fore, deal with it in the same partial terms of comprehension that we feel when we meet a gallery of dazzlers, freaks, heroes, and creeps at a party and can't begin to divine what is going on until the morning after, not until our sleep has done the work of assembling a little more of what we have seen into some conjunction with the stiff-necked patterns of our mind.

These were my remarks at the symposium – these, more or
less. I ended with some vague notions paraded forward about
the possibility of existential criticism – a hint that the drama
reviewer recognize the impossibility of reviewing difficult plays
immediately, that he write for the morning daily, 'No review
today – it's too early to tell. I'll write about it in a week, and
maybe I'll even go to see it again. Maybe I won't. Let us see. In
the meantime, I suggest this play might just possibly be worth
keeping alive.'

We are asking for miracles, yes? We request the authority to
relinquish his infallibity. A faint dream. The moment is not
near. No, I was obviously making my plea with a particular play
in mind – no accident that beneath the hat of the symposiast
was the steel helmet of the playwright. I was thinking of *The
Deer Park*, and its particular strengths and weaknesses, delights
and *longueurs*, after ten stunning maniacally depressive days of
rehearsal, and I was thinking as well of the monumental
impossibility that any drama reviewer born could review this
play to his own satisfaction (or mine!) an hour after he had seen
it, when I had lived with the events, crises, and themes before
me for near to eighteen years, had worked on the play for ten,
had rewritten it four times. It was by now perhaps the dearest
work of all my work. There were times when I thought I even
cared more for it than the novel from which it was delivered; it
was certainly different from the novel, narrower, more harrow-
ing, funnier I hoped, sadder, certainly more tragic. It was also
more multilayered. If I were a novelist trying to write plays, I
was also trying to put more into this play than I had into the
novel. If the compass was obligatorily more narrow, the well
was being dug to a deeper water – I realized at one point that I
had a work with thirteen characters, and not one of these
character was unworthy of a play for himself. Indeed, it sometimes seemed to me that I had compressed ten plays into three
hours.

There was an idiom in the theatre I could not bear. It was the
one which brought all arms and aid to the lowest common
denominator of the audience. I was tired of seeing plays which
went along carefully, thoughtfully, and decently for two hours
in order to arrive at a small but perfect dramatic explosion. Any

audience which did not know all the steps from opening curtain to explosion was an audience not worth writing for, since the American public was by now finally saturated in plot, in genre, in situation, and the twenty stratagems of denouement. So why not write a play which went from explosion to explosion, or – since this is not the Fourth of July – from one moment of intensity or reality (which is to say a moment which feels more real than other moments) to the next – a play which went at full throttle all the way. Which is precisely what was done this summer when *The Deer Park*, a four-hour play, its third draft five years old, had an hour or more taken out of it, a transition which cut away all dramatic scaffolding, connective tissue, road signs, guides, and left the play stripped to its essential connections, the movement ideally from one real scene to the next, with the audience left to fill the spaces between.

I had my play then with thirteen wide-open characters and a set of one hundred blackouts or quick scenes I called changes, quick as the cuts in a movie, for it seemed right to capture the dislocation of life in Hollywood by a play which played like a movie – although not quite! Wait until you see! And I was pleased. For the play occupied a space which had been left uninhabited too long, that area between the explorations of the realistic play and that electric sense of transition which lives in the interruptions and symbols of the Theatre of the Absurd. *The Deer Park* was conceived to live in the land between. It was – could you term it so? – an existential play. A surrealistic comedy about the nature of tragedy I called it once in a fatuous moment. For I was trying to tell in this play something of what I knew about sex and love, and no theme – here comes our paradox – is more difficult to present in the theatre. None more difficult, because – dear reader – there is a no-man's-land between sex and love, and it alters in the night.

We go to sleep convinced we are in one state, we awaken in the other, and murderous emotions patrol the everchanging line of no-man's-land. You do not write a play about sex and love which is a simple play, a situation comedy, a switcheroo of slamming doors and lovers under beds, no, rather you try to induce an existence which is like an animal or a beast or a beautiful woman, a being which breathes and is mysterious and not altogether accessible and changes all the time. Ideally, it stays fascinating, then haunting, it is a play to which you go back, a play with which you fall in love, a bitch, tears of blood in her heart, the perfume of the Indies in her flanks.

We are at the core of the comic, are we not? A playwright in love with his play. It calls for Voltaire, Shaw, or our own Albee to delineate it. Stick in the needles. Bring forth the pots. Lay on the acid. This playwright is ready to burn for the love of his own dramatic work. There were too many years when he dreamed of *The Deer Park* on Broadway and the greatest first night of the decade, too many hours of rage when he declaimed to himself that his play was as good as *Death of a Salesman*, or even, and here he gulped hard, *A Streetcar Named Desire*. Yes, his play was there, so he felt. Then years went by, and experience was gained in the theatre and knowledge that a play like *Streetcar* was a miracle, and angels without dollars must also have helped it on its way. Finally the playwright learned that if he would see his play at all, and see it right, he would see it in that land below Broadway, in the terrain of a true turf, the Village, at a jewel box in red velvet (red velvet at least was there) called the Theatre DeLys, the theatre of the lily, yes, and there off-Broadway it would have a chance to live, perhaps there it could survive those opening-night reviews the playwright was certain could not be steeped in joy, and he studied the play in rehearsal and hoped *The Deer Park* was really as good as he believed, for then he could read any review, that would not be hard, for when you know the work is good there is a particular sweetness to the sad taste with which you imbibe negative opinions of yourself. But, dear readers, I let you in on a secret – there have also been moments in rehearsal when I have said to myself, 'Dear Messieurs Chapman, Kerr, Nadel, and Watts – if you do not like my play, what horror if I am obliged to agree with you.'

On the other hand, there have been moments of magic when the dialogue and the action and the set – but we have bragged enough about this theatrical baby. Here is a cigar to celebrate the birth. If you will look at the label, you will see it says: 'Theatre DeLys, eight performances a week. Be advised the actors speak so clearly you need not miss a line.'

## II

Since it is obvious from the previous part of this introduction that the playwright was in love with his play long before opening night, the question for the second part may be: what does he think of *The Deer Park* now that it breathes on the live and all but bleeding boards, and the quickest answer, madam, is that he broods but a little about his own dear play and thinks often of the life of the theatre.

But, wait! *The Deer Park* opened to a curious set of reviews, mixed in the extreme: 'Unearthly depravity,' said my old friend, *Time* magazine, kicking us in the ear. 'A blast of fresh air', was the manly word from the *Wall Street Journal*. Others cried out we were 'passionately comic', 'shocking and funny', so forth. Nonetheless, nearly every review was condescending. While it was more or less agreed that for a flamboyant and somewhat overrated novelist, the apprentice playwright had a modest flair for the theatre, it was also generally regretted that our apprentice included long soliloquies whose sentiments were sophomoric, platitudinous, and presumptively philosophical. It was further considered in meatball taste for him to pop in a speech about the war in Vietnam. That, by consensus, was regarded as an obvious attempt to modernize a ten-year-old play. Since the speech about Vietnam was lifted, however, from the novel and had therefore been written originally in 1951 and 1952 (with the Korean war on the mind), such criticism contained its unwitting ingredient for tonic – besides, excitement in the company was general. We were a hit. Not a smash hit, but a hit. So went the word in New York. When you are a hit, you are a victor. At least, you are running. You do not mind the pricks and darts.

Still the playwright was considerably confused. His play had been helped to keep running by extracting crucial nuggets from in and out reviews, phrases like 'sensational', 'soars like a skyrocket', 'dazzlingly wicked', 'endearingly wicked', 'scenes which palpitate like the hearts of a couple in the act of love'. Properly weeded, we were a full neon garden of fireworks, searchlights, explosions, comedy. 'Evil is a fun thing,' said Mr. Kerr, putting us down. We nearly put it up.

The theatre is like a marriage – you hate to lose. A marriage which goes down is like a ship which sinks; so is a play. Principles are thrown overboard to keep the living alive. You do not say, 'We will shut down *The Deer Park* because there is something disgraceful and deadening to the heart in advertising a play which is serious, as a play which is not.' You seize the quotes – ripped, often as not, all bloody from their context – you make do with what you've got. The theatre reserves her awards for those who win. It is liverish to be a loser in the theatre. The play may be a hit for the wrong reasons, but you even feel good. If the reviews have had next to nothing to do with your intent, the illusion of winning is nonetheless sweet, even as staying alive is sweet. Our apprentice, therefore, could afford to be intrigued by the reception of his play. He had a hit on the basis of quoting reviews he could not quite recognize as being related to his own work – they seemed to speak of another play. (Perhaps some work of collaboration by Céline and Saroyan). Of course he had a production where virtues were mixed with flaws – he knew the values and vices of his actors' performances to a point, or thought he did. He had a large blessing and small curse for every actor in his company and it was a fine company which had shown courage on opening night, all thirteen actors. He had a bit of love for the director, and moments when he could strike him dead. Yet the playwright's soul was in its yaws again. He felt becalmed in a nasty double-edged murmur, as if the hint of a breeze tickled first one ear, then the other, then all sails fluttered. He was annoyed. He felt he had lost his own sure sense of value. He did not know how much he liked his play, nor whether it was really any good. Was it possible that it was only boring, comic, and sensational? And he had nothing by which to measure. He had not seen anything on Broadway in several years. So to keep his critical measure, he went on a tour of the theatrical season and saw more than a dozen plays in two weeks. He was then obviously anxious to learn a little of the nature of the invisible assignation between a drama critic and his favorite girl, a fat smash hit.

But first he had the good sense to contemplate in advance the differences between book reviewing and theatre reviewing. Doubleday, or Simon & Schuster, or any publishing house which goes by some such name, may spend half a million dollars for a book by Harold Robbins or Irving Wallace, but the novels of these writers will not be reviewed on Page One of the *New York Times Book Review*. The *New York Times Book Review* is guilty of many a crime, but it does not often commit gross hierarchical adulteration. Mr. Robbins may even be put on page fifty. He will certainly hit no better than page four. Odds-on he will get a bad or facetious review. And no one except the author will suffer too much. Not even the sales.

But on Broadway! Well, we know what happens to a $500,000 musical. It is a public event more important than the Royal Shakespeare Company doing Shakespeare – the big musical runs equal in glamour and category to the opening of a major new play by Williams or Miller or Albee. And is reviewed not only with the same solemnity, but the same hyperbole. Or more. The critics are often critical of Mr. Williams, but for the book and lyrics, we can write the quotes ourself. 'An evening of magical wonder'. 'An occasion of musical splendor'. 'A heart-warming, life-giving two hours of uproarious fun'. Quick! Give us the name of this musical so that we may see it. But the name, friends, is always *Our Newest Turd Has Just Moved In*. 'Shit, señorita,' says Broadway.

Full Stop! All speed astern! Dare the playwright speak thus of *Man of La Mancha* and *Fiddler on the Roof*? Can he include *The Apple Tree* without committing sacrilege? Yes, is the answer, he can. *Fiddler on the Roof* is declared a masterpiece when it is next door to a swindle; *Man of La Mancha* is a great creation, except – don't breathe it – there are pits of monotony in the core of its charm. *Apple Tree* is celebrated for introducing a new dimension to musical comedies; in fact it has shoved together a trio of one-act plays, two poor, one good, the total saved by the impressive talents of Barbara Harris.

Well, if our apprentice critic of the drama is not merely on early foot, his thesis would seem to claim the professional reviewer has a double standard which is the reverse of the standard of the book reviewer: that the seriousness of your production – all rare exceptions admitted – is generally measured by the cost of your production. Be it understood the costly production is often a superb production with superb performances (usually by the dancers) but from the playwright's point of view, this is not so different from judging the literary merit of manuscripts by the excellence of the handwriting.

In the two weeks just past, the apprentice playwright saw a great deal of excellent handwriting. He saw *Hello, Dolly!*, and *Barefoot in the Park*, *Man of La Mancha*, *The Apple Tree*, *The Odd Couple*, *Don't Drink the Water*, *At the Drop of Another Hat*. He saw *Natural Look*, *The Homecoming*, and *Black Comedy*. He saw – he ran out of plays on Broadway. There was off-Broadway: *MacBird, Eh?*, *America Hurrah*, *Hogan's Goat*, *The Mad Show*. He saw *The Deer Park* many times. He had evidence in plenty and some new thought to masticate in detail (for what is a critic without his teeth?) Finally, he even had a critical formula. It came from his own work. It explained the mystery of the schizophrenia in the drama reviewer's heart, for the answer was simple: there were two kinds of plays. That was the beginning of what it was all about.

Would you like a metaphor to ease your way? Let the playwright tell a story he heard last night. It is perhaps apocryphal, but not grievously so, for if the story is unfair, you could change the names of the artists until you had a proper fit. This, at any rate, is how the tale was told. Some years ago, William de Kooning gave a drawing to Robert Rauschenberg, who then promptly erased the drawing and signed his own name to the smudged page. Next, the erased drawing was sold. Children, we are not discussing the final absurdity of certain terminal positions in modern art right here, no, sir, we are in on a primitive rite, the writing of money. Primitive man took a stand on a stone. He said, 'I am the leader of this tribe, and I stand on this stone, and so this stone has the value of all your tents and all your wives and all your herds and flocks.' And since no one was strong enough to kill the leader, the rock on which he stood was money. Before money can be used for barter, it is first declared – it is made into money by an act of declaration. 'I, Robert Rauschenberg, hereby make of this piece of paper a piece of money.' An erased drawing is restored in value by a signature. Emptiness plus authority equals money.

It seems we are now ready to talk of certain plays, the ones which might put the signature on the erased drawing. They are authority stamped upon emptiness, they are money. The authority of such plays is that they are known as a hit. That is their value. That is how they give value to an audience.

Look at the nightly event. A horde of the hard-working pours in from the suburbs for a night of food and playgoing. If they are tired, it is not because they have toted that bale of cotton all day, no, they are tired because their nerves are stale, flat, bored, and unendurable from the stale, flat, unprofitable work they have done as a horde of the middle and professional class all day in offices which buy and sell commodities less interesting and less well-made than they used to be, and they have stifled in modern kitchens and driven children to school and gotten caught in suburban traffic and blinked their eyes against the glare of super shopping centers. They have rushed and they have waited every day of the week – they have lived lives devoted to controlling their environment – their umbilical relation to existence is now captured in the touch of a fingertip on the plastic button of some electrical machine. They are thus a class which is devoted utterly to control, and they have lost control of everything. If we are to dwell on the Broadway theatre audience and its relation to a hit, we can only talk first of the heart of the theatre – this liberal complacent materialistic greedy pill-ridden anxiety-laden bored miserable and powerless jumble of suburban couples who jam every Broadway smash for the first few months. Later, they are joined, and still later replaced, by tourists, conventioneers, small-towners about to drown in New York, and corporation label-men with the names of the hits to drop back into the office hopper at home. There are out-of-town philosophers buried among the culls of this audience, but out-of-towners in New York are usually using all their wit to dare the subway – they cannot arrive in their seat at their critical best, for they are in New York, Fun City, they want only to be reassured they will not be mugged in the next few hours. So their synapses blend in with all the fear-ridden reflexes of all the liberal couples from the suburbs, and what you get is the middle-class horror of America (and the hint of how Vietnam finally is possible), for our people are in their seats, sprawled out, nervous, vitiated, on the giggle, dying to be manipulated for external manipulation is authority, and they can need that. But only a hit will manipulate such an audience for they do not wish to contemplate ambiguity – ambiguity is the essence of their nausea and their fatigue. Listen carefully to such an audience laugh, and you can feel the undertow which attends the manipulation, you may even hear the silent machines which make the money. The Broadway audience being an over-manipulated apathetic flesh stirs only to the intense sound of such silent machines, for those who live in the suburbs are addicted to processes which make money as simply as juvenile delinquents are hipped on marijuana. Addiction, like faith, is focus from a point of reference.

Are we too abstract? Let us take the best of examples for the other side, and think of Zero Mostel, who is curator of a rich large talent. There are many who would say he is a great actor. Some might not agree altogether, but no matter, possessed of moments of grandeur, and moments not so grand, Mostel is nonetheless a major theatrical artist, for he glides like a shark through that medium of mood we might call prime attention in the theatre, his movements slice into the center of a laugh, a roll of his eyes turns a spill of amusement through the aisle. He is a comic wind.

But the evil is this. He does not need to act any more. He can come out on stage, and the audience will laugh. If he scratches his crotch, the house breaks down. If he looks at another actor and merely turns away, the ticket-payers are instantly in delight. Let me whisper the next. If some unknown actor made up to look like Mostel came out for a minute and stood still and scratched his crotch and looked at another actor and looked away, the house might break into equal combers of hysteria provided they did not know it was not Mostel. That collective Broadway flesh wishes only to be manipulated. Mostel rat-tat-tatting his fly is pressing a button to make them laugh. It does not matter whether he is scratching these jewels in *A Funny Thing Happened on the Way to the Forum*, or in *Fiddler on the Roof*. The act of scratching is more important than the play, which is why he is not always a great actor. Audiences laugh because Mostel is the signature on that piece of paper, he is switching on the machines which make the money.

Zero is, of course, an artist of the first rank. When one gets down to the real stuff, however, down to that stretch of hits on Broadway where one ten-dollar bill is the same as the next, when you get all the way down to *Cactus Flower* and talentless technicians of high skill like Barry Nelson, then you may be in the place where the Creation is denied.

There are those who will now suspect a thesis is coming. They may be confident. The thesis is soon to be made by discussing five plays which do not deserve to be discussed separately, for they are not five plays but one play, since their internal mechanisms of manipulation are not individual but collective, and came not out of artists but computers. So specific criticism would have no real bone to bite. Besides, these plays are traitors to the stage: their secret allegiance is to television. When we discuss these plays, we will not be so foolish as to talk of their separate plots, for that would assume the original impulse had been creative rather than computed. Good. These five plays are nominally called *The Odd Couple*, *Barefoot in the Park*, *Cactus Flower*, *Don't Drink the Water*, and *Natural Look*. In fact, by existential measure, they had the duration of only two-and-one-half plays to this reviewer, since he walked out of each one at the end of the first act (which is how first he discovered their common denominator). On such a commencement one might normally have to say no more than that the basic provender of these evenings was watered oatmeal, but months and years ago, the critics had all been in like Flynn, and so the audience responded on each of our nights with a particular barking of laughter which called to mind a human tissue in a Petri dish swaying to calculated shock. A revolutionary with a sawed-off shotgun might in a rage have sprayed the critics hard enough to keep them off their seats because no humanoid tissue could have liked these plays if he had been told they were not to be liked. Subsequently, however, by a work of fierce concentration, compassion for critics was generated by the mind. Drama reviewers, all said, must have been desperately miserable in infancy, and wretched little feeders, to so enjoy watered oatmeal TV. Five pieces of Show Biz – say, nay! – five pieces of

Telev Biz – put five bowls of oatmeal down the New York drama critics' collective tummy. Five hits went up. Call it five minus one. Because *Natural Look*, a work as tasteless, empty, skillful, well acted, and well directed as the other four is a shade of a hair less satisfactory in hiding the fact that it possesses no fleshly meaning, and so it closes after opening night. Who knows where the styrene will crack? Plastic is a gas in solid form. It can only pretend to flesh.

Strike it like this: *Cactus Flower, Don't Drink the Water, The Odd Couple*, and *Barefoot in the Park* encourage underground spleen because they are the Theatre of Plastic, their content is TV, they are cooked of synthetics. Only danger is that the mode by which we perceive reality can indeed become our reality, a most elegant Marxian manner of saying that no medium is more of a message than TV – which may be why, despite the reek of the hot cigar butt, none of us can ignore McLuhan's total slogans. McLuhan has one great grip on the attention of this decade – we all know something in us slides off slowly and begins to die as we watch TV. So the medium is indubitably giving us a message. Feel the message. Salts wash out of your blood, hate and lust pass over to headache. Spook-show in the psyche, cramp in the groin. Love, tenderness, sympathy become vectors to anxious attention. Do not speak of what we see – what we see on TV can be anything – this is talk rather of lobotomizations which seep into the gray collective soul of the room after an evening of TV. Emotions are modulated (rather say: strangled, filtered, choked) while passing through the electronic valves of the transmitter and the set. Something leaves us each night we spend in attendance on the box. For the medium has one message – technological society will make certain you pass away on a bed into which national music is piped.

So these Cactus Flowers are not merely bad commercial plays called good by the bad taste of the critics, no, they are not even produced the way bad plays used to be, because back, way back then, in return for a definite waste of time, you could still get some raunchy funky little hint of theatre. But these Cactus Flowers offer preparation for nothing but the sick bed in the last ward. America has been watching television for twenty years and the style of television has transfused itself not only into the taste, but the demand, even the expectancy, of the suburban middle class – that precise compound of neurons and suet so capable of being smelted into money. Therefore, Broadway comedies now rush not only to be like television comedies, but actors are trained away from theatre in the process, and sometimes look like television sets come to life.

Television, after all, was the child of the Age of Conformity which came to America after the Second World War. Television produced a genre: moderate characters in modest situations. It offered endlessly recognizable detail, *surface* detail: supermarkets, highways, suburban streets, paste colored classrooms. However, the characters in such television dramas presented nothing which was biologically real. They bore the same relation to human beings which vinyl does to leather. And the reason was that the characters of these TV series were synthesized from incompatibles – the new documentary and the old soap opera.

Soap opera had a sentimentality which was surrealistic, but its characters – while altogether psychotic – were still real. Since they lived on your radio, their voices came out of a background much like a cave: there was no confusion in one's mind with the here and now of daily surface. The soap opera was material for your dreams. Whereas television puts forth the very latest surface of reality – it goes on hunts for real backgrounds, it is documentarily obsessed. The documentary is, it may hope, its honest buck. Since it then thrusts its own highly sophisticated mutants (hey, Ginger! hi, Flipper) of the old soap-opera characters into highly documentary situations, the dramatic product excites that same vivid sense of displacement from reality you can receive from a painted plaster hamburger by Claes Oldenburg five feet in diameter. You don't know immediately whether the object is comic, nauseating, or significant of some new reality, or even some new way of studying reality. Oldenburg's hamburger is, of course, a way to study a reality which is all before our fingers. But the housewife studying herself on a situation comedy in her electronic mirror does not know if the seemingly recognizable characters before her are in their bizarre situations because they have more wit than herself, or less; she pays for the human pleasure of recognizing some part of herself by a most indigestible psychic demand – she is plunged further into security and anxiety at the same point, and therefore further into obsession with herself. If the old radio soap opera encouraged schizophrenia by stimulating the housewife's buried secret plot (loyalty to the home vs. hots for the lover) television dulls her into nausea. Fundamental distinctions between the safe and the insecure, the reality and the dream, are marinated, dramatic oppositions are bypassed – powerful conflicts are first modulated, then mashed into one another. The side effect from such confusion is nausea.

Superb, you will say, now tell why television cannot offer stories and situations which are either frankly disturbing or honestly pacifying. Well, the medium is the message, yes, and a half-hour drama on television cannot be too pacifying or you will notice all too clearly the infernal sound of the set, feel its electronic harp, even – enter op art – see the very vibrations which erode your optic nerve. Yet one cannot go in the other direction: a story must not be too disturbing, for there is no actor's flesh and blood to warm you from a stage, nor, as in a movie, the bodies of the audience, no, you are all alone with your family and the emotional rigors of the tale, plus the psychic assault of the set. Television attacks the unconscious like a trip in a jet – you move from continent to continent or spectacle to spectacle without the accompaniment of a change in mood to prepare the flesh. (The unconscious thus becomes like that poor patient who is operated upon without warning.) So a work of deep drama on television would inspire anxiety, for one's own depths might open to what? – to the baleful electronics of which far-off God? what cold star? No, you keep it neat. The scene is recognizable to ward off any shriek, and the situations are odd and out of focus – just sufficiently unsettling to keep your mind off the flickering of the set. Estimate the difficult problems facing our Broadway Computers when they, loyal to the firm premise that all sound commercial theatre must be based on television tales (because audiences are now based on the narrative synapses of the television series), are next obliged to translate or computerize the technique from one medium to another. You now have real actors forced to imitate actors as they appear to us on a television set. You must have backgrounds which are recognizable, but situations which do not exist, you must reconstruct in the audience that hum of security and insecurity which is a television set. Since you have real actors who can be generally depended upon to give the audience a moment of true warmth at the end (since that is finally what the actors are for), the psychic payoff on all Cactus Flowers is huge – it is like watching television with a home-cooked meal at the end. The only one who can suffer in these plays is the actor, for he is thrust into a cancerous relation with his art – too much approbation too little deserved must flux his guilt, and skillful emotion skillfully applied to a situation which does not exist in the blood of his past experience must be as conducive to leukemia as kissing a plastic mask on the hour.

The medium is the message, and the message of television is electronic hum. The theatre will wash down from its old broken-down heights to the swamps of TV, the theatre – if it continues, as it will, to cohabit with TV – is close to an excruciating death by long wallowing, for the smelting operations will enlarge, and the big houses will continue to be filled with armies of pill-fed humanoids in for the night from television. The Theatre of Manipulation will swell in every joint. It will thrive like edema. And the critics will be the doctors who call this swelling, health. For it is true. To talk of Broadway is to talk not of amusement but disease.

Yes, it seems that no less a task is before us than to forgive all drama critics for invariably amputating the wrong organ – but then they are blind and ill themselves. Have pity on them. They are men who fell in love early with illusion and so cannot leave now that the lady has become an electronic ghost. Drama critics cannot see themselves as necrophiliacs. They must believe that TV's Theatre of Manipulation, watered surrealism and pistol shot gags, is still the butler to art, not its avenging ghost.

And is that all to be said for the season? These five plays which are one play and lead to no discussion of the stage, only polemics and existential analyses of the evils of television? No, the apprentice put in two weeks going to shows, and he is not likely to let anyone away without a capsule of comment for each

evening. Besides, one would not wish the rest of Broadway to
escape. Listen to more about *Man of La Mancha* and *Fiddler on
the Roof*, stay close and you will pick up criticism – we whisper
it – of *Black Comedy*, exactly where it crosses *At the Drop of
Another Hat*. But first, a word from my own play. A director and
a producer exchange dialogue:

MUNSHIN:   Extraordinary.

EITEL:   You really like it?

MUNSHIN: It's an epic study about the hole in eternity our
country is preparing for itself. It's a poem. This can make the
greatest picture in the last ten years.

EITEL:   Collie, why don't you say what you really think?

MUNSHIN  (*fingering his belly*): No audience would understand it.

EITEL:   I think it would be amazing how much this would
communicate to an audience.

MUNSHIN:   You don't communicate with an audience, you
manipulate an audience . . .


The producer is an old-fashioned producer. His type went
out ten years ago. Producers are not so full of energy any more,
and they study audiences with the aid of motivational research
and statistics on consensus. Mr. Munshin had a simpler idea.
To manipulate an audience you put on a rubber glove (although
he did not need a rubber glove) and you put your finger up as far
as it would go. Pop! That was the old-fashioned movie and the
old-fashioned smash Broadway success. Well, history is composed of layers – one is not the first to suggest it. So talk of TV's
Theatre of Manipulation must not be confused with good old
Collie Munshin's plumber's snake of a finger. No, Collie was
brought up on Zing, went the strings of my heart – emotional
sap must be there to keep happy. The old Collie Munshin
Theatre of Manipulation depended not on thin emotionless
mismarriages between surrealism and the documentary, but on

*schmaltz, shtick,* and Collie's finger maneuvering up the seat of all critical opposition.

Well, it sours the face to say this, but one can get so pleased with the fact that this abysmal old theatre of corned manipulation is not dead, that the sins of *Fiddler on the Roof* and *Man of La Mancha* could kindly be forgiven, if lunar hyperbole had not been attached to them.

But, hear! *Fiddler on the Roof* may not be the greatest musical ever made. In fact, it may be never nearly so good as *Pal Joey*. If Sholom Aleichem was almost a great writer, his particular weakness was a determined inability to confront evil in intimate forms – he preferred to present evil as some external abstract force – a catastrophe, a pogrom, a drunken peasant. With such a view, one is always close to the danger of the over-sentimental. (Look! That good man got killed for nothing.) *Fiddler on the Roof* (adaptation from a book by Maurice Samuel, *The World of Sholom Aleichem*) has added Samuel's own pervading sentimentality to Aleichem's sweet wit, and the result – surprisingly tuneless – is a hard all-out Munshin-ish manipulation of Jewish audiences. *Fiddler* plays with no quarter on emotions of self-righteousness, self-pity, ignorance, and guilt. In fact, guilt should well be mentioned first – it is so obviously felt by the audiences for that past they have evaded (no, let us say they have jettisoned) in the race to the suburb, it is the blood guilt of all the prayers which have not been said, and all the stones which have not been laid on all the graves of all the grandparents. The audience is milked like a cow, but the loss of milk feels sweet to them, for these suburbanites know next to nothing of life in the *shtetl* – it is all revelation to them – they are pleased to discover their own past is nearly so colorful as the old country life of Sicilians and Bavarians and Ukrainians. Yes, indeed, *shtetl* life is indeed colorful as presented in *Fiddler on the Roof* – but not very much more accurate than a musical about peasants and gypsies by MGM.

*Man of La Mancha* is a more exciting play and so commits a greater sin, for it manipulates one of the deepest desires of us all – which is to be noble. It plays with the joy of fulfilling this dream, and the agony of losing it: so it moves audiences to tears. But it is only a good play, and work on such a theme begs to be great. *La Mancha*'s music is thin when arias might be near, and its language is undernourished. It does not inhabit the high desires nor fill the dungeons of the emotional architecture to which it pretends. It merely gives a hint of a spark and lets the audience blow it into fire with the gale of that most curious hunger – to be noble, to be true to one's dream. But the play is not true to the demand of the theme – rather it is clever enough to see that the time has come to send Jeanette MacDonald and Nelson Eddy to college. Survey of World Literature 1 – Don Quixote!

Let us rather make a terrible confession, for that is a way to arrive at the point with a minimum of ballast and all sails high – the brute liked *Hello, Dolly!* He liked it better than *Man of La Mancha* and *Fiddler on the Roof*. It was in fact likable because it was too crude to manipulate even a ten-year-old. It had only its own gusto to offer, and the best music of all the shows, and the best dancing. So it was good the way a ball club is good. Therefore, it expressed one aspect of the theatre, only one half of the theatre, but that half it expressed altogether – that mindless half which speaks of physical health, sex, top bananas, and bazazz. Besides, it had Ginger Rogers giving what may have been the best performance she ever gave on the night the apprentice critic saw it, she did everything with a kind of stomp-it-out kick-it-up vitality, and the love of birthday cakes was in her eye, she had the rare beauty of the plump blond when the blond is concupiscent, and at the end she received bravos like a bullfighter and deserved them. And even gave a curtain speech with happy smiles and generous tears. A noisy evening ended in theatrical rainbows of love. The theatre can get away with anything when it makes a rainbow.

The theatre can also get away with anything when it is sufficiently surgical to make a brilliant incision into the nature of reality, or of desire, and do that in pure theatrical context. Witness the vast success respectively of *Black Comedy* and *At the Drop of Another Hat*. *Black Comedy* cuts right into the phenomenology of the real. It points out that if you encounter a hot hot-dog and roll in the dark, your hand will fly away as if it had encountered a turd, a dog's muzzle, or a hot set of tools. Now turn the light up for the audience, but let the actors pretend they are in the dark. Yes, we have sudden and brilliant incision into the nature of reality. Study those actors, ho! One laughs for the first twenty minutes and then waits for the moment when the play will step out to explore its premise. But *Black Comedy* has got the playwright's hand on the silent machine which makes the money and so it refuses resolutely to explore its own magic. Instead, it rushes to cash in its profits. Like a truly nasty upper-class London accent, it goes in for a witless repetitive obsessive strangling of the premise. It explores no more. Our audience having been exercised first to laugh, is then extorted to laugh, finally is tortured and at last debauched by laughs which are by now become no more than conditioned reflexes, and therefore leave the psyche as quiet and empty as the theatre ten minutes after final curtain. When the English loot a bank, they even get the pennies which roll under the carpet.

In line with this sort of robbery, absolute thoroughness is indispensable and Flanders and Swann, our next protagonists, are thorough – they mine every aspect of the muted desire to share in theatre which characterizes their most special sort of audience. The brute could say that *At the Drop of Another Hat* is prime pigeon feed for Wasps, for they are the most underfed patrons of the theatre, and he would be right. *At the Drop of Another Hat* is resolutely non-nasty, and keen as calling cards. It suggests in its assortment of songs and anecdotes (funny little ditties about the need of others to be obscene, extracts from Tolkien, etc.) the buried and doubtless not altogether bona fide memory of the best and wittiest visits of a fine British clergyman and his sexton on Sunday afternoons in June in golden British gardens there in the quiet twilight of the empire – nothing can move the heart of a Yankee banker more. *At the Drop* is indeed so resolutely non-nasty that one senses the real ugliness of the proceedings is buried in the profoundly admiring complacency of audience and performers for each other as they swell their breasts back and forth, mourning secretly for the power of empire they think has been lost, when in fact, it is the same people ultimately who fly the planes and burn the babies.

Which brings us to psychosis. In addition to *Hello, Dolly!*, there were five plays for which the brute had good words, and four of them had to do with madness, and only one, *MacBird*, was, with that, content – the three others, *America Hurrah*, *The Mad Show*, and *The Homecoming* pushed on into the most modern movements and logics of madness, on to the most advanced field of psychosis. So these three plays explored the anxiety of living on a plane and looking for a void, and because they were deeply conceived, they had no impulse to manipulate, no, rather there was some depth of mood they wished to achieve by working up the details of an obscure magic between the audience and themselves. Therefore the plays roused a presence which was like a monster or a machine or a beast. (In *The Mad Show* it was a sad sweet humor about the eye of the wacky.) But in the two others the beast lived on the stage and shared your horror and so permitted laughter, and moments occurred in *The Homecoming* and *America Hurrah* where one was in the presence of that mysterious communion of mood which can be experienced nowhere but in the theatre.

This sense of a presence was achieved in *The Homecoming* through a quiet modest exhibition of the propinquity of the commonplace and the psychotic. Its glint of genius was to demonstrate the thesis by showing what exactly was equal to what. Each character recounting the dullest details of his day was equal to the casual attention of a family group as they watched a wife and brother-in-law roll on the floor in embrace. So it was perhaps a play which was talking about the end of any world we know or perhaps it was like a street one passes in a dream, and on this street a murder is committed. In its turn, *America Hurrah* went through sometimes tedious, if always intelligent, insights into the maniacal surface of all programmed communications, and then exploded at the end with ten minutes that lived on the edge of the lip of the murder of all American life and the carnage of the psyche, and the death of the American vision.

Then, there was *MacBird. MacBird* had a truth for which the apprentice was not prepared. Beneath the parody was a wild sorrow, for suspicion flooded the heart that LBJ had more real life as MacBird than as Lyndon Johnson – one could conceive of him secretly watching MacBird with tears in his eyes: the role and the language gave him a stature life had denied.

This would be a fair quick summation of the plays one saw, and the lessons learned, and the coldest lesson came from the best plays – the future of the theatre seemed most rich where the material was most insane. A cold note. Therefore, *Hogan's Goat* was reserved for comment last, since it is out of category. A passionate and substantial work overwritten by a degree, it had another kind of sorrow, for it displayed the blood beneath the corruption and gave a feel of the muscle within the piety of the Irish in Brooklyn, New York, some generations back and that was no modest achievement.

Do you get the point? Good plays like *The Homecoming*, *MacBird*, *America Hurrah*, *The Mad Show*, *Hogan's Goat* (and you know the other) are plays which attempt to find a piece of that most mysterious and magical communion some call ceremony, some church, and some theatre. They are plays which attempt to reach a moment sufficiently magical to live in the deepest nerves and most buried caves of the memory of the people who have seen them, these plays speak of the fire at the edge of the wood and hair rising on the back of the neck when the wind becomes too intimate in its sound. The theatre lives (if it lives as anything more than a spinster aunt on allowance from movies, television, and the record business), the theatre lives on what it can do uniquely, on moods of depth and perfume and terror and exaltation and cascades of laughter which no other form can provide – it is a ceremony which takes place in a cave, and philosophers, priests, painters, tyrants, and athletes must collaborate, the bodies of some must harmonize with the minds of others. When it is really good, what it offers can be found in no other form of art, for then it is like religion for the irreligious and gives promise of something which may live forever. Its impermanence is the life of its power. But that is only true of those finest plays which never manipulate, and there are not so many. This year on Broadway the number is down to two or one, this real species of theatre has about given way to all the hybrid giants in the palaces on Broadway, those Cactus Flowers whose sins against the loving heart of the Lord are performed at the rate of a thousand a minute, for a thousand humanoid hearts are laughing at jokes which were conceived in the same place they used to package thalidomide and will package the actors tomorrow when the actors perform the benefits for themselves in the camps of concentration. 'Shit, señorita,' says Broadway.

# Film

## Some Dirt in the Talk

*Wild 90* is the name of a full-length underground movie which a few of us, soon to be cited, filmed on four consecutive nights in March this year. It was done in 16-millimeter and recorded on magnetic sound tape, and since the raw stock costs of processing 16-millimeter sound and film run about thirty cents a foot or ten dollars a minute of shooting, we shot only two and a half hours in all, or $1,500 worth of film. Obviously we couldn't afford to shoot more.

Still, for reasons one may yet be able to elucidate, the two and a half hours were not so very bad, and from them was extracted a feature film which runs for ninety minutes. It is a very odd film, indeed I know no moving picture quite like it since there are times when *Wild 90* seems close to nothing so much as the Marx Brothers doing improvisations on *Little Caesar* with the addition of a free run of obscenity equal to *Naked Lunch* or *Why Are We in Vietnam?* It has the most repetitive pervasive obscenity of any film ever made for public or even underground consumption, and so half of the ladies are fascinated because it is the first time in their life they have had an opportunity to appreciate how soldiers might talk to each other in a barracks or what big-city cowboys might find to chat about at street corners. But then the ladies are not the only sex to be polarized by *Wild 90*. While the reactions of men in the audience are more unpredictable, a rough rule of thumb presents itself – bona fide tough guys, invited for nothing, usually laugh their heads off at the film; white-collar workers and intellectual technicians of the communications industries also invited for nothing tend to regard the picture in a vault of silence. All the while we were cutting *Wild 90*, we would try to have a preview once a week. Since the projection room was small, audiences were kept to ten, twelve, or fifteen people. That is an odd number to see a film. It is a few too many to watch with the freedom to move about and talk aloud that you get from watching television; it is on the other hand a painful number too small to feel the anonymity of a movie audience. Therefore, reactions from preview night to preview night were extreme. We had banquet filmings when an audience would start to laugh in the first minute and never stop – other nights not a sound of happiness could be heard for the first forty minutes – embarrassing to a producer who thought just yesterday that he had a comedy on his hands. Finally we had a formula: get the hard guys in, get the experts out.

That makes sense. There is hardly a guy alive who is not an actor to the hilt – for the simplest of reasons. He cannot be tough all the time. There are days when he is hung over, months when he is out of condition, weeks when he is in love and soft all over. Still, his rep is to be tough. So he acts to fill the gaps. A comedy of adopted manners surrounds the probing each tough guy is forever giving his brother. *Wild 90*, which is filled with nothing so much as these vanities, bluffs, ego-supports, and downright collapses of front is therefore hilarious to such people. They thought the picture was manna. You could cool riots with it, everybody was laughing so hard.

Whereas intellectual technicians had to hate it. Because the tip of the tablecloth was being tilted, the soup was encouraged to spill. There was a self-indulgence in the smashing of Hollywood icons which spoke not only of an aesthetic rebellion (which some of the media technicians would doubtless approve) but *Wild 90* hinted also of some barbarity back of it – the Goths had come to Hollywood. Based on the gangster movies of the thirties, the movie nonetheless had a quasi-Martian flavor, a primitive pleasure in itself, as if it had discovered the wheel which made all film go round.

Testing this brand-new little American product, cutting it, shaping it, serving it to samples of audiences, made for an interesting summer. *Wild 90* was not the greatest movie ever made, no sir, and the actors would receive no Academy Awards (because they swore too much) but the picture, taken even at its worst, was a phenomenon. There was something going on in it which did not quite go on in other movies, even movies vastly superior. It had an insane intimacy, agreeable to some, odious to others. The dialogue was sensational. Where was a script-writer who wrote dialogue like this?

BUZZ CAMEO: I ain't gonna get killed here.

THE PRINCE: Look. You're gonna get killed, or you're not gonna get killed. But you don't know shit. You don't know when you're gonna get killed or how you're gonna get killed, and you just shut. Shut.

BUZZ CAMEO: The Prince. The Prince tells me.

THE PRINCE: You're nothin' but a guinea with a hard-on in your arm. That's *your* hard-on. (*A sound of disgust.*) Unhh.

BUZZ CAMEO: How about my short arm? How many guys I put away for you, daddy-o?

THE PRINCE: (*mimicking*): How many guys I put away for you, daddy-o. Unhh. Unhh. Unhh. (*Three derisive punches to his own biceps.*) I'll tell you how many guys you put away for me. One and a half! One and a half!

TWENTY YEARS: Right. The other half I had to take care of. That's how good *you* are.

THE PRINCE (*keeping up the tempo*): Punk. Unhh. (*The arm again.*) Punk.

TWENTY YEARS (*jeering*): What a mistake. What a mistake. Cameo, he says he can handle Thirty-fourth Street. (*Scream of derision.*) Hah! Thirty-fourth Street he can handle. He can't handle his own joint.

Yes, where was the scriptwriter? Who was he? And the answer – is that no hat could fit his head, for he did not exist. The dialogue had come out of the native wit of the actors: *Wild 90* was a full-length film for which not a line of dialogue was written.

Well, explanations must now be promised – we may even intimate that closet history is about to be disclosed, and of an underground film! Gather near! Listen to the subtle events which preceded the shooting.

Last winter, while the play of *The Deer Park* was having its run at the Theatre DeLys, some of the cast of *The Deer Park* used to drink together at a restaurant named Charles IV in the Village. Actors like to fill the tank after a performance. It is not only their reward, and their sedative, but it is possibly a way of accommodating their soul back to the place from which it was vacated by the more meretricious lines of their script. Now, *The Deer Park* was not signally meretricious, it was after all well-written, but perfect it was not, entirely honorable, no, it was not, lacunae of intent had collected, and since devils and demons rush to inhabit every gap, there were lines in the script the playwright could not necessarily defend to the death. Those are the sort of lines which turn actors subtly, even unconsciously, to drink. Because they have to use the best of themselves to conceal the worst of an author.

Well, drink they did then, and on any given night it was better than even you could find much of the company in their more or less civilized cups, eating a little, drinking away. We were a nice company, relatively free of jealousy, intrigue, or liaison due mainly, it might be submitted, to the fact that *The Deer Park* was full of passion, jealousy, intrigue, conniving, etc., and so the actors could be relaxed of that by the time drinks had come. (Indeed it is exactly in those wholesome family comedies the critics love so very much that you will find the actors rife in the green room, and everybody banging everybody up the back door.)

After drinking sessions went on awhile, they took a particularly modest form. Hugh Marlowe, Rosemary Tory, and Rip Torn had the longest parts, very long parts they were, so they were naturally the ones most in need of regular hours. Usually, they would be the first to leave, and Buzz Farbar, Mickey Knox, and myself would go drinking into the closing, while my wife, Beverly Bentley, and her friend and colleague, Mara Lynn, would talk at the next table on whichever subject blond sorceresses find of moment at three in the morning. Whereas Knox, Farbar, Mailer (later to be known as Supreme Mix) slipped each night into the game. We used to play at being Mafiosos. We would try to talk like Dons. We would go on so much as twenty or forty minutes at a time talking about any subject at hand in the allusive use of metaphor you can catch a hint of now and again when one or another Italian in the rackets will lay it on the line. We even picked up names. Twenty Years, Buzz Cameo, the Prince.

Of the three of us, Knox was the only real actor. He had been acting for twenty years and more, and had been in two dozen movies, half of them gangster films, he had experience on the stage and television, was a member of Actors' Studio, had worked on the production of half a hundred Italian films in Rome in the last ten years, he spoke Italian fluently. Buzz Farbar, however, had never acted but for a stretch as Don Beda, the orgiast, in *The Deer Park*, a part which began as a stunt after work for him (and remained a stunt in the sense that the part of Don Beda is one of the theatre's most difficult small parts to play). Anyway, Buzz had done his best. He was a good team man, a former Golden Gloves boxer, a football star at Dartmouth, then publisher of Legacy Books at CBS – he had not been a great Don Beda, but there was probably not an actor in New York who could have been – the part requested Porfirio Rubirosa or some Castilian with Persian silk. At any rate, Buzz Farbar may have made no immortal Don Beda, but he certainly did wing a good shtarker as Buzz Cameo in each late-nightly round of the Maf Boys, and yr author who had never acted at all in any way (except every day of his life – a quip to be examined further, close readers) did his best to hold up his end as the Prince. We played the Maf Boys. It was our answer to the Chelsea Girls.

We even got good at it. How close we came to portraying any mobsters of certified class, I do not know, but we had experiences. Drinking our booze and acting for ourselves in the restaurant, we would get good enough upon occasion that the room would seem weightless, and the air ready to spark. There was a tension afterward to judge the value of the moment. We were either getting up a mood which was more accurate and quintessentially witty than anything worked on by actors or game players before about the subject of the Mafia, or we were merely whacked up on booze and the mystery resided in the supernatural properties of grain spirits, their ability to fog all perception of creative value, and inflame the positive judgments of misperception. Say! I conceived the idea it would be fun to get a good cameraman and film a half hour with sound of the three of us sitting around a restaurant table. So we talked about that for a time. And as the winter went by, as Supreme Mix, which is to say, Farbar, Knox, and Mailer, did the Maf Boys on the unphotographed wing a couple of times a week at Charles IV, the picture got discussed with the savor of get-rich-quick schemes worked on in a Brooklyn kitchen, and so showed promise of becoming a project you talk about with too much enjoyment ever to undertake. But we had fun. Night after night. There is a dialogue in the movie which captures a little of the style we had when metaphor was in flower.

BUZZ CAMEO: I'm goin' down to the Beach.

TWENTY YEARS (*to Cameo*): Ya know there's one thing about singin' – it leaves ya hoarse.

THE PRINCE (*to Cameo*): If you leave, ya know what you are? You're the prunes.

BUZZ CAMEO: Prunes? You're the dunes.

THE PRINCE: Yeh. You're the real prunes.

BUZZ CAMEO (*a reference to burial grounds*): Ponds 'n dunes?

THE PRINCE: You're prunes. The cream's comin' out your ass.

TWENTY YEARS: You got no feels.

Farbar did not let the movie go. Calling me very early one morning, he pointed out that Mickey Knox was leaving for Rome in ten days. In the following week we had to make the movie if we were ever to make it at all. When he was reminded that we had no photographer, no lights, no set, no properties, nothing but my steadfast promise to immolate a thousand bucks (with five hundred more to burn in reserve), Farbar promised to bring together the rest of the ingredients. (That, gentlemen, presumably, was how the old two-reelers were made.) He arranged a meet with D. A. Pennebaker (of Leacock Pennebaker, inventors of portable sound-film cameras, makers of

*Don't Look Back*). Pennebaker had four nights free, and he would film us for four nights. Since Knox was still playing Collie Munshin in *The Deer Park*, we could start only after his performance each evening, which meant acting must begin at midnight. No problem. Those were our drinking hours. Acting and drinking could get together like kissing cousins. There persisted, however, the problem of locating a set. For we had taken on one more ambition. We had decided to try for more than a short film about three hoods disporting in a restaurant, we would rather take off from a contemporary piece of local history in Brooklyn. A year or more ago, the Gallo gang had undertaken a war with Joseph Profaci, by repute a *don capo* of Cosa Nostra. For self-protection the Gallos finally holed up in a little building on President Street, while the police put the block under crash surveillance to keep them from getting killed. Well, Supreme Mix knew nothing about the Gallo gang, in fact had no desire to take a page from their material, no, Supreme Mix was looking to be another gang, the three characters created before anyone was reminded of the Gallos. Yes, we would be our own three characters holed up in a loft, down by the beginning of the film from a company of twenty-one men to three men, living alone. That would give us the situation on which we could improvise. But where could we find an empty loft, and over the weekend? No, we had to settle for a big and empty room in an office building.

Monday night, we moved into the set, sat drinking very carefully for an hour or two, looking to recapture the style of Charles IV, and finally began shooting. But we could not recover that mood. Charles IV was a drinking spa with agreeable food, it had an attractive hat-check girl, moderate lights, soft booze, you slipped into *ambiente*. Now we were in the empty office, in a square room, twenty-five by twenty, with packing crates, clothes hung on pipes, fluorescent lighting, and one light bulb supported from a cord. Mood oscillated in the illumination of prison. We weren't three hoods at a restaurant. We were holed up, riding each other's nerves. It was obvious we would never find an objective correlative to the question: did we do a good imitation of three topflight hoods having drinks? No, we were in a different game – the camera on us now, and the knowledge and ten dollars a minute clicking away in film and sound. Our first dialogue was wooden, aware of itself. Action lagged. As a reaction, we weren't out at sea two minutes before the picture prematurely began. After a statement by Knox that we had been holed up in this place for twenty-one days, Farbar suddenly came back, 'Twenty-one days you been sucking my joint!'

It will be remembered we were working without a script. We were going to talk back and forth. In absolute freedom. Out of it, went our premise, would come the action. No one was necessarily ready, however, for this action. Knox is a hard self-centred man who likes to keep his dignity unruffled. People were in no hurry to go around calling him names in his daily life – suddenly he was getting it in a movie. It was wrong. Mafiosos rate themselves on their own brand of elegance. The director thought of stopping the camera, but something in the action had come alive. Next, the director reasoned – the film going on this while, of course – that if three Mafiosos were indeed holed up for twenty-one days in a loft, they might not have the use of metaphor available on happier evenings – no, they might be snarling on the bone, not kingpins of the rackets now, but rather back to adolescence, hoods on the corner. The feel of that was real. So obscenities continued – they took on love's own patina of wit. Verbal action between Mickey, Twenty Years, Buzz Cameo, and the Prince flourished. Insults winged like darts, dignities rose, vanities fell – a style came out of it. The actors had an action which carried out of that first insult and went from line to line without undue self-propulsion. This action was to carry the cast through the night and the next three nights, the visits of ten other actors, nine of whose performances were finally to be kept. 'A motion picture grew out of it,' as they say on Puffs Avenue, although in truth you could say a motion picture staggered out of it, while toe-dancing over the bottles, and then kept its balance – although the disconcerting angle at which it careened was yet to be seen.

But we have to depart from this sketch of a narrative. It does not tell the real history of what was going into *Wild 90*. That is private, personal, subterranean, and buried in the psyche of the actors and the director. Since this director is an intellectual of sorts he could not engage in a creative act without a set of major theses to support him. While he thought he was merely engaged in a $1,500 junket out to movieland for four nights in a row, he was actually delivering some old and close-to-forgotton experience which had been perhaps more obsessive than he realized, obsessive for years. He had thought he was making the movie as an exercise in a few nuances of a very special brand of Camp, gangster-movies-Camp – he was actually being more serious than he knew, although indeed he was not to discover this until he had spent months cutting the film and had begun to write about these matters. Then he realized that under the bed of the making of *Wild 90* were some dusty themes of singular complexity: themes such as Hollywood, acting, existentialism – no less – and the logic of the real disease of the film – no less. Not to mention old wounds of the ego.

BUZZ CAMEO:  Twenty years. Twenty years of shit, that's what you are. You're twenty years of nothin'. You're the prince of what?

TWENTY YEARS:  Listen, big mouth . . .

BUZZ CAMEO:  The prince of my pickle, that's what you're the prince of.

THE PRINCE:  That's what I'm the prince of, your pickle – your pickle with its dirty little warts. French tickle, Buzz Cam.

*Item: Do you know that back in World War II, a few of us used to walk those Army legs with this thought: someday I'm going to write a book and expose the fugging Army. And yea and lo, that was done, thanks to James Jones.*

*Item: Then in the postwar, we used to see movies, and flushed with the confections of new ego status, used to say to ourselves, 'Someday I'm going to make a movie and expose that fugging Hollywood.' And you know what happened? Two of one's books were made into movies,* The Naked and the Dead *and* An American Dream *were the names of these movies, and the first was one of the worst movies ever seen, and the second was inferior to it, or so I hear, because I couldn't get myself up to go and see it. And had*

*nothing to do with these movies except get paid for them, in fact both
of these movies were made without the author receiving a postcard
from the producer, and so author could plead* mea non culpa, *but for
the additional fact that Hollywood paid very well for those two
books, and nobody forced the author to sell them. So the author is
helpless when some snaggle-toothed goat-hair-bearded very late
adolescent comes up in a bar, clears his throat, and says, 'Mr.
Mailer, how could you violate your ideals by allowing* An American Dream *to be sold to the people who made the movie?' Mr.
Mailer must then button up and roll with the nausea implicit in the
rhythms of his interrogator's adenoids, because there is no right reply
left. You cannot say, 'I have become a little more corrupt than the
last time you saw me,' to every adolescent around. Besides you have
to be over forty to appreciate the good Hemingway's remark that a
man once past his own last point of terminal honor, can from there on
proceed only to lose more and more of his soul, and the trick is thus to
sell your soul dear, to fight a tough rearguard battle and take as many
of the enemy as you can. (Which presumes a God back of your soul,
and devils to slay.) Well,* An American Dream *was sold and I
didn't take any of the enemy. They took parts of me.*

*Now, what can you know, Under-Thirty, of these passions to
write a book which will expose the Army, or make a movie which
will put a light to the gas in Hollywood's leaky oven? These are
unnatural passions when you, young reader, have cut your reflexes
on Bergman, Fellini, Antonioni, and everybody can see through the
Army by now. You don't want to reform Hollywood. It has its thing,
you have yours. Let Dick Van Dyke shake hands with Debbie
Reynolds any day.*

*But for those of us who grew up in another time, and got to hate
Hollywood intimately . . . do not despair of explanations. Hollywood was like a mother-in-law's mother-in-law. Locate your time
historically. This was before Kerouac. Eisenhower was just beginning to hump the rhetoric to our respectful attention,* Life *magazine
was still confident it could show people how to live, the CIA was then
invisible but for a gleam in the secretary of state's eye, the corporations were still manufacturing products which were not wholly
inadequate to their uses, and packaging was dull. Newspaper
editorials reflected no quiver of doubt. Harlem was still a place to
visit. And Hollywood was committing hara-kiri with a blunt knife.*

*For those were the years when they got the communists out of Hollywood. All those poor writers and directors who had written all the patriotic movies in World War II – they had been the only ones who believed in Hollywood, they thought of her as a peasant queen with monumental capacities for reformation. Of course a character in a novel once said of Hollywood communists that they have the strength of big-breasted women, and these movie writers and directors were stuffniks. Which is to say they were stuffy with old platitudes which had rotted in old sentiments and they loved to try to stuff such stuff into everybody's head. Once they were exiled from Hollywood, or squeezed down into black-market work, the town lost its balance wheel. Under the pressure of television, it went all the way over to what it had promised to be at the beginning – an undifferentiated androgynous daisy chain, a victim of sexual entropy. Film power passed on to Europe. These communists had been the moral center of filmland, the bourgeois ever-living ever-loving family center, or at least in combine with the analysts they had been, and they had striven to make box-office pictures about social problems with middle-class answers. 'Maturity' was the word they loved. Cigars used to glisten like wet turds when they intoned maturity.*

*That was the Hollywood one wanted to dynamite. That silly monstrous cancerous country which ate at the best of oneself. It is just about gone now.*

*As a young man soon after the publication of* The Naked and the Dead *I tried to work in Hollywood for a spell. I did my best, I wanted to amass experience for a novel, and so wished to succeed in the movie business in order to have the richest novelistic experience. But I wasn't very good at succeeding. There was something about the process of scriptwriting which did not fit with any reflex of mine. Like most young writers I was a hint phonier than I had to be, and borrowed influences at large (where would* The Naked and the Dead *have been without John Dos Passos and James T. Farrell?), and the upper reaches of my novelistic brain were mixed with the heavier greases of the lower academic literary apparatus, to wit, I thought in terms of symbols, forms, allegorical structures, classical myths – you know like many another touted young talent I could barely write a sentence if there was no way to convince myself it was not on five levels. Nonetheless, I still sensed that under all the*

*Associated Merde and Dreck incorporated into my literary system, there was still a way to create, which was the only way to do it. And that was to keep the act of writing simple. If you wrote a thousand words on a morning and they proved later to be a good thousand words, and not a single formal thought entered your conscious mind while you were writing them, well, all the formal thought in you had gone then into the writing – none of it had been fed back into the ego-pool thinking box, there to be wasted.*

*That was the good way to write, and presumably the good way to act and direct, and conceivably to box – it took even longer to learn that it might be the way to make love. Doubtless. The nature of anything life-giving, like a good movie or a good word, must remain secret for the simplest of reasons. For every lion of our human species there is, as we all know, a trough of pigs, and the pigs root up everything good so soon as the super-highway is laid out for them. So the best stays hidden. It must be that way.*

*And out there in Hollywood, I learned what pigs do when they want to appropriate a mystery. They approach in great fear and try to exercise great control. Fear + Control = Corporate Power. Corporate Power applied to art produces a product which is on balance equal to Liberace stripped of his virility.*

*Now, readers, we have not been treated to this much language for me merely to beat old Hollywood on the head with my stick. I want rather to underline and soon try to analyze the fact that the process of commercial film-making has a natural tendency to liquidate the collective human entity of the film, and so it is a living miracle, nothing less than a miracle, when a good big-budget movie is made, once you know, as few do, how absolutely deadening is the productive machinery of the cinematic full-length feature film.*

*Consider the movie script. A man or a team of men, who have the habit of regarding themselves as writers, begin by discussing a story. It is ninety-nine to one that the story originates not with them but with a book, magazine piece, play, former movie – we can skip these steps. Working on someone else's story is like raising another man's child. The moment a writer moves away from his basic connection to that unconscious which gives original words to the pencil in his fingers, art in its turn has given up a half-life. Witness, then, these Hollywood writers singly or in team, who hobnob with producer, director, story editor, hordes of labially directed anxiety types who talk all the time. Large fear and large control – those are the protagonists who write the script. It bears the same relation to real writing, these endless discussions about form, plot, twist, and rooting interest, that a medical examination in the Army bears to the act of love.*

*Then comes the director and the producer, an ugly jealous passionate fecal marriage of bitch and stud. That overworked scenario is ignited into its first roar and flame when producer and director set out to bugger one another. Indeed that's how agreeable bad movies sometimes get made. It's art by act of war, however, and the actors get ground between them.*

*Then we have the actors who deal with existential situations like love, sex, disaster, and death, all those ultimates whose ends are by their nature indeterminable: you are in an existential situation when something important and/or unfamiliar is taking place, and you do not know how it is going to turn out. Whereas professional acting consists of getting into situations where the actor knows precisely just how everything in the plot is going to turn out. The script is there, and from it he cannot escape very far. Acting and existentialism are therefore at the poles. If existentialism is ultimately concerned with the attractions of the unknown, acting is one of the surviving rituals of invocation, repetition, and ceremony – of propitiation to the gods. Talk of ultimates, maybe the actor lays ceremonial robes on his back in order to allay our fear of the wrath which lives in the pits of metaphysics. Ceremony is designed, you can say, to mollify the gods, to safeguard us from existential situations precisely because ceremony is repetition. There is some quality primitive, powerful, and weight-free about the act of acting once you get into it, something so close to a real existential situation, yet not by real measure dangerous at all, that actors often know the delight of children, whose inner landscape you may remember is always existential, for the denouement of a situation is to a child unknown and dangerous until that moment when the outcome is perceived.*

*Actors have it well made then if they can enjoy the act of acting, for they may at once propitiate the gods of dread, feel the power of full men, and have the sensuous empyrean awareness of a child, not to mention his tact. Great popular actors are not called idols for nothing. They are revered as God, lover, and child all at once.*

*Now, of course, the model presented is too attractive. There is*

always for the stage actor the tension, horror, and most existential
moment of the opening night, and there is besides, once the actor is
not on the stage, the unspeakable insecurity of his life, the uncertainty of work, bread, love of his fellow actors, the existential
(which is to say: dangerous) privations of poverty, the manic
uprooting yaws of success which can propel him into a profound
alienation away from the most rudimentary clues to his identity. It is
not so easy to walk through life uncertain if you are god, fool, hero, or
clown, or eventually some new species of man. Rich or poor, the
likelihood is great that the actor has the most existential private life of
any artist – if nothing else, he is obliged to live closer than other
artists to the mystery of personality itself, which is – if you consider
it – related directly to the mystery of choosing one style of personality
in preference to another, provided of course one possesses the power to
exercise more than a single style well.

But we must follow this through. If I, living with a woman,
choose a style for my personality which, crudely, we may say is not
quite me, I am nonetheless in a real relationship, certainly I am if my
adopted personality is sufficiently imaginative, cohesive, and convincing, that is to say, well enough acted, to make the lady think it
is – forgive this – the real me. Because then the real emotions of my
sweet mate with their real concomitants, her very gifts and blows,
begin to rain on me, and I prosper or falter on the basis of my adopted
personality. Yet if I had adopted a different style of personality for
the same woman, the gifts and blows would have been different.
Now think of the actor who commands a choice of adopted personalities. The particular style he takes on for any role becomes as much an
existential choice as the pose of the lover – the actor is subtly
rewarded and/or punished by the real reactions he arouses and
disappoints in his audience, which audience becomes for practical
purposes the next thing to his real mate. How disagreeable then, even
brutal, is the situation of the actor when his role is not adequate to
him, when he cannot act with some subtle variations of his personal
style. But, indeed, the actor, living uncomfortably in that psychic
ground between the real and the unreal, consummate creature of
modern anxiety, can find his reality only in a role worthy of his
complex and alienated heart. What chance then has he in that
abominable industry script we have already described or in that
bucket of fecal passions swilled in by director and producer? Not to

mention our patriotic apparatus of bullies, censors, and banks which hangs like insect repellent over the making of films.

No, the actor, if he is a good talented sensitive actor, is shoveled between the maw and the mangle. For if his personality now consists of a hundred personalities, they are nonetheless like a hundred fine tools. Even if he can find some relationship to the script, and be not contradicted fatally in his work by the other actors or the director, and be not betrayed by the producer, not cheated by the cameraman, nor the film editor, nor sickened too profoundly by his publicity, he, the actor, must run nonetheless into the most unendurable trap of them all which is that the magic of the relationship he and the other actors have breathed into one another despite the script is a magic which must soon falter before the tyrannical insistence of the script that all characters and events be funneled through the narrow orifice of committee solutions to aesthetic problems. So the exceptional tools of the exceptional actor, his ten hundred antennae, his blades and springs, fine nerves and subtle heart, go all shuddering through the anesthetized fields of a commercial script: he must violate all he has learned about relationship and its thousand-footed sensitivity.

Taken even at its best in the occasional script which is first-rate, noble, fine and good – you may look long for such a script – with a director and producer who are wise, sensible in the art of interruption, illumined with those proper fires which can light a fire in the actor, and with a budget not so enormous that every scene must groan with the pomposities and platitudes of money pressing its weight upon itself, in this ideal situation, even here, with the best of honest lines to speak, the actor must still warp his art and devour his liver and/or his soul to make his exquisite sense of relationship submit to the form. At its worst, the making of films for popular consumption is a liquidation center for talent – at its best it is still a rabidly unnatural act, and everyone connected to it is, soon or late, miserable.

Well, it is hardly our aim to give comprehensive listing of the efforts directors have made to break such tyranny; so it is not our intention to talk of Rossellini and De Sica, of Ingmar Bergman, Fellini, Antonioni, of Truffaut. Nor is it part of the agenda to try for a quick run through the underground film and artists so diverse as Warhol, Brakhage, Kenneth Anger, the late Ron Rice, a dozen others – their variety is extraordinary, their research into techniques, orgies, optical extravaganzas, animation, surrealism, exquisite photography and claustrophobically inept photography have slashed out a hundred indications of new trail. Nor pertinent to talk of documentaries: no discussion will be found here of the work of Ricky Leacock, Shirley Clarke, Helen Levitt, Emile de Antonio, the Maysles brothers.

No, the point rather to be made is that with every rare exception admitted, with all honor to the five or ten good commercial films a year and the fifty other such films which will seem better in twenty-five years than they do now, and with all homage to the wit of the Camp, its triumph in 007, with all credit to the technical innovations of the underground, and the occasional epic or quiet piece of genre from the documentary, the fact remains that the contemporary film does not do enough, it does not give enough of a mirror to the complexity of our century. The production of the high-budget film is too massive to be sensitive. Of course, there are rebels in revolt upon this operation and they have explored their innovations out to insanity, but they have tended to avoid the center of the problem which remains: how to get a little of the real life – always complex – of a good actor into a film. That still remains the accident rather than the rule. The good professional actor succeeds occasionally against all odds – his eight or ten or twenty years of apprenticeship, his dedicated training, enable him to breathe a simulation of real life into the mechanical resolution of the commercial script. But at a predictable price: dead liver, soul a bit more in hock. Whereas, the greater liberty of the low-budget underground film is of necessity given to an unpaid actor who is therefore invariably an amateur, and so tends to project an agreeable, innocent, usually bizarre self-consciousness (much like the square and crazy flavor in the postures of a home movie). The underground movie tends for this among other reasons to become an inside joke, and looks for playful situations or nightmares which members of the club can appreciate out of the focus of their own games. But the average underground film is not rushing to give a mirror of the time, just an amusement-park mirror.

Now, the documentary, in contrast, is, of course, founded on our century, nowhere else, but since it substitutes legally real people for actors, the merit of the documentary still depends upon the importance of the situation, and not its subtlety or nuance. If we can *conceive of putting the camera on a man in a witness box up on real trial for his real life, the possibility, although not the certainty, is present that the man may not try to act the way he thinks he ought to act before a camera. But Heisenberg's Principle of Uncertainty probably applies. Do you remember? The particle of the atom being observed by the recording apparatus is directly (unhappy for science) affected in its movements by the presence of the apparatus. So with the documentary. There is its flaw – right in the germ plasm of the documentary. The camera, recording a real man, creates a relative unreality. If I know the camera is recording me, the real Norman Mailer, playing Norman Mailer, then I am in the unhappy position of working directly for my own product, me. Consider this for a moment: it is almost impossible not to be false at some low level, false the way the president of a small business will be unctuous when he is interviewed about an item his company is making. Is the real-life manufacturer going to say the item is sleazy? Never. In fact, he may not admit even to himself that his new commodity is anything but good; nonetheless, the knowledge that he can only say it is good, that he has no option to do otherwise, infects everyone surrounding him, interviewer, cameraman, sound man, future audience. The fact that everybody knows what he will say, before he says it, produces that characteristic woodenness which besets the documentary, the television interview, and any photographic situation where the protagonist is there in his real name. The consequences are too numerous, the traps too consequential for the man who bears his own name to reveal a real theme to the camera.*

*We have then exhausted all the alternatives but the one which went into the making of* Wild 90. *The assumption must now arise that the director has been saying all along that* Wild 90 *is his secret solution to all these ills. But it is not true. The director would swear it. He would even be forced to admit that it is worth a fight to pretend it is even a good movie. If it has its defenders, it has also its detractors and some of them would say that the first virtue of* Wild 90 *is that we get a good leisurely opportunity to see Mailer make an ass of himself.*

*Nonetheless, one will pretend that* Wild 90 *is good. In fact, the director, prejudiced, blown up with every imperative of self-interest, actually believes that his film contributes to no less than the general weal. So he will proceed to talk about its powers for uplift.*

TWENTY YEARS: There was once a guy an' he saw a little bird who was half dyin'. He was wounded. Hey, Prince, listen.

BUZZ CAMEO: Go ahead.

TWENTY YEARS: So he picked up this bird an' he said, 'This bird gotta be warm.' He looked in the field and there was a lotta cow flop – steamin' – it was warm. So he put the bird in the cow flop an' he figured that's gonna make it right. And he left – left the bird there. And the bird kinda warmed up – felt good. Started to tweet. Went tweet, tweet, tweet, tweet, tweet. . . . And . . .

BUZZ: What a long story.

TWENTY YEARS: There was a fox an' he looked over the cow flop an' said, 'Geez, never heard cow shit tweet before.' And he walked over – he trotted over – an' he saw the bird an' he gobbled it up. Now the moral is – listen – it may not always be an enemy that puts you in shit, and it may not always be a friend who's gonna take you out of the shit, but if you find yourself in cow shit, never sing. Got it? Never sing. If you ever find yourself in shit, don't sing.

What did we end up with? A picture about gangsters? Not quite. It is hardly certain there were ever three Italian gangsters like this, or three Irish gangsters, or even two and a half Jewish gangsters. Farbar, Knox, and Mailer had all grown up in Brooklyn, but they were not Italian. Still, nobody grows up in Brooklyn, without learning something about Sicily. And that is what comes through in the movie – our idea of the Mob, and that partakes of the noblest spirit of comedy, because twentieth-century reality suddenly appears on the screen. It is not social reality, nor documentary reality, certainly not historical reality, nor even the reality of the Hollywood myth, no, it is a kind of psychological reality – it is our obviously not altogether perfect idea of what this movie should be like – and that proves to be very real, for it is at least evidence on the road to reality. Whereas most movies give indications only of the road to the void.

That is the nerve which illumines the picture. To everybody's surprise, Twenty Years, Cameo, and the Prince became more complex than characters usually become in a film. The picture took on that intricacy of detail and personality which is reserved usually to the novel or the extraordinary foreign film. It did not happen because the prime players were necessarily so talented, so improvisational, nor so deep, but because they were engaged in a way of making a movie which – considerably more than the average movie – had something to do with the way people acted in life. Yet the way people act in life is so general a notion for purposes of discussion that it may provide a superior means of focus to consider instead how people live in their dream.

It seems we have come back to the making of the film only to desert the subject immediately. A further expedition remains to us: the director's most revolutionary notion about the meaning of the dream and – its country cousin – the art of the novel. Without it, he could not truly describe the critical difference between conventional professional acting and the existential variety presented in *Wild 90*, nor could he prove his case that the conceivable reason his actors are so good is that they do not have lines to remember.

THE PRINCE: You listen. How'd you get that cleft in your chin? Old lang syne, that's how you got that cleft in your chin.

BUZZ CAMEO: Ya know, I realize you guys resent me 'cause I'm the best-lookin' one here.

THE PRINCE: You're the best-lookin' guy in the what? In this filthy hole? I'd hate to the best-lookin' guy in this filthy hole. Wha' do you got to say to yourself? I'm the best-lookin' guy in a filthy hole.

*Freud saw the dream as a wish fulfillment. It is a grand theory, but it hints of the sweets and sours of middle-class life and bouts of nocturnal enuresis. For if you are in the middle class, you do not have to make out well on a given day, you can brood about a loss, indulge a fantasy on the conversion of failure to success – yes, if you are middle class, the dream is a wish fulfillment. Art comes to the middle class on that bypass called sublimation.*

*But to the saint and the psychopath, the criminal, the hipster, the activist, the athlete, the stud, the gentleman sword, the supple stick, the dream is something else – a theatrical revue which dramatizes the dangers of the day – a production in which the world of the day is dissected, exaggerated, put together again in dramatic or even surrealist intensity in order to test the power of the nervous system to pass through shocks, ambushes, tests, crises, and pleasures – future impacts of which the unconscious has received warning the day before. In the quick blink of a friend's eyes, in the psychic plumbing of an odd laugh was disclosed to the unconscious a hint of treachery. So that night the scene is replayed in its complex condensation with other scenes, and the Navigator in the mind of the hipster delineates for himself a better map, figures a little more precisely how to chart a course through the possible rapids soon to be encountered in his life.*

*The metaphor is shifting. It now seems that everyone has not only a private theatre for dreams but is possessed of a helmsman, or scout, or Navigator, who uses charts drawn from the experience of the past, maps drafted out of the emotions, education, and miseducation of childhood, the nuances, surprises, and predictable pattern of social life. These charts – submits our proposition – are altered every day of our life on the basis of what the day's experience has brought. They are kept up-to-date in order to transport us from the present into the unexpected contingencies of the future.*

*What am I saying really? Nothing more or less astounding than that every mortal (but for an occasional monster or vegetable) is elaborating somewhere in his mind the conception of a huge and great social novel. That unwritten unvoiced but nonetheless psychically real and detailed novel is precisely the map and/or chart from which the Navigator plots his course and selects his range of acts for tomorrow. (Indeed the dream may be the creative process which adds new refinements to the novel every night.) Yes, we not only possess that great novel in the map rooms of the self, but we are forever improving it, or at least altering it.*

*Let us ruminate upon this magnificent news. In the unconscious of each of us is then a detailed conception of a vast social novel greater than most of the vast social novels which have been written. In every last one of us just about lives a great novelist. Better than that. The Navigator not only dips into his fantasy or his dream for inspiration and information to serve up to the ever-evolving unwritten pages of his book, but he employs the goods he finds. He goes out the next day and walks the stage of his life as an actor. For we are not only novelists all, but we are actors all. Having a detailed conception of the world, accurate here, inaccurate there, we attempt not only to deal with the world on the basis of this conception or novel, but we push and press ourselves into styles of personality (like elegance or humility or graciousness or candor) which are not quite ourselves but will provide, or so believes our Navigator, a more effective mode for handling the events of our day. In short, we pretend to be what we are not. We are Actors. We are at least Actors a good deal of the time. Some of us are better than others, some more precise than others, or more passionate in our display of all-but-true emotion, but we are all vastly better actors than we suspect. At the least we are all more or less successful in seeming a little more or less sweet or powerful than we really are. Yet, and this is the horror of bad art, that social novel in the vaults of the unconscious, no matter how great, is nonetheless flawed in each of us by the misleading portraits of people and institutions we are fed via television and Hollywood. If the maps in this chart room of the unconscious are elaborate, they are also anchored on systematically induced misconceptions of society, and so are often as profoundly inaccurate as the maps with which Columbus set sail for Cathay. Of course a chart room with inaccurate maps is inviting its Navigator to courses of action which can plow a reef, and the actor who is serving as helmsman in the actions of the day may be psychotic in his lack of attachment to the reality of the wheel directly before him. Meretricious commercial art does not lead merely to bad taste, it pipes the nation toward psychosis. It you would look for an answer on why America — a conservative property-loving nation — is obsessed with destroying other nations' property, the answer can be found as quickly in bad movies as in bad politics. Which returns us to our quest: how does one get to the grail which blesses the making of a movie not entirely without honor?*

*Knock on door.*

THE PRINCE: Who're you? Wait. Wait. Wait. (*Picks up gun, goes to door.*) Carmela. How are ya? Carmela. Hey Mickey. Mickey, look who's here. Your wife.

*Carmela enters with a carton of milk.*

TWENTY YEARS:  Carmela. Ahhhhh. How are ya, Carmela? Why
   you come tonight? I mean, we need the milk, but you
   shouldn'ta come tonight. Carmela, you look great. Ahhh.
   How're the kids?

CARMELA:  They ask for their father.

TWENTY YEARS:  Yehhh. (*Looks her over, frowns.*) Listen, I see
   you went to the hairdresser. What do you go to the hairdresser for when I'm here? I mean, I don't like you to go to
   the hairdresser when I'm here. What do you got to get the
   nice hair for?

CARMELA:  For you.

TWENTY YEARS:  For me? I haven't seen you in a week. What is
   that crap? What's happening out there?

Follow it, now. Farbar, Knox, and Mailer had a datum – three
hoods in trouble holed up in a joint for twenty-one days. For
that much, they were in accord. For the rest, they had each their
own idea of what was going on, just as in everyday working life,
if three businessmen meet, for example, at lunch, their datum
could be that they are meeting to discuss some particular
business. Yet each man remains his own protagonist. Since
there is no written script, each of the three businessmen tends to
see his own problems and feel his own personality in the
foreground. Each of these businessmen has his own idea of how
he wants the lunch to go, what he desires for a result. To the
extent that the lunch drifts away from him, he tries to maneuver
conversation back to where he thinks it should be. While he is
working at this, he is also bluffing a bit, pretending to be
friendly one moment, disinterested another, and all the while
he is up to his ears in the lively act of shaping and trying to
improve his existence by employing adopted, or at least slightly
adapted, personalities. He is therefore acting. For – it is worth
repetition – acting is not only the preserve and torture rack of
the professional actor, but is also what we do when we enter into
new relations with man, mate, associate, or child – we start
with an idea of the situation before us and a project in our mind
(or on occasion a vision) of how this situation can or should end.

Then we work to fulfill our project. At the same time, the other man or woman is working to satisfy his plan. He is also acting. Acting in some degree at least. The result is not often geared to obey either project, but turns out willy-nilly to be the collective product, good or bad. That is about what happens at every business lunch, football game, fornication, prizefight, dinner party, and improvised performance. The product is the result, the result of the efforts, hang-ups, cooperations, and collisions of exactly as many protagonists as there are people involved. In life – let us underline the fell simplicity of this – every man is his own protagonist, he is out there acting away on his own continuing project, himself. Whereas in scripts, in written scripts, the natural tendency of any writer who might be dealing with three gangsters in a room would be to present, for purposes of clarity, no more than one protagonist and one project: the other characters would be subtly or not so subtly bent to serve the hero and his grip on the plot. So the other characters would become abstracts, stock characters. So movies remain just movies, simpler in their surface than life. That is why they are enjoyable, that is why they are also unsatisfying to our sense of existence.

In *Wild 90*, however, we had no script to reduce us – we were able to play through a situation with our own wit rather than with someone else's. Therefore we had an enormous advantage over an actor who has rehearsed his lines. For he has to pretend he is thinking of the line as he speaks, when in fact he is trying to remember it. That is indeed why most amateur actors are wooden – in their need to remember their lines, they can do nothing else for they are made uncomfortably aware by the bind of another man's words in their mouth that they are up there acting, and therefore exposing themselves. In contrast, we were forced, as in life, to speak where the moment led us. We were, consequently, forced to use only our own idea of how and where we wanted the picture to go, and this made for considerable intensity and concentration – which is exactly what actors look for. Moreover, the three of us shared, as shooting progressed, in the direct recollection of what we had already put into film. So, we were forced to draw upon that instinctively, build upon it, naturally, just as people collect their varieties of mutual or gang experience in any new operation. So we also developed an unspoken but not often dissimilar idea of how the movie should move ahead, and this idea was always in danger of being disturbed and in fact sometimes was dislocated by the new actors who paid us visits – wives, girlfriends, prizefighters, brothers, police – because they knew less about our life in that room than we did. Again we moved on some parallel to what the situation might be in life. If the three of us were constantly needling each other, fighting, setting up reconciliations, forming alliances of two against one only to shift again, forever assaulting one another's egos, or putting them back together, it was different when the Outside arrived, when the police came, or our girlfriends came, for then our three separate little visions of the film tended to become one family project, we were metaphorically now more equal to a crew, we worked with the new actors to slip them, even force them, into our idea of what and where the picture should be, and the new actors worked to slide or yank the picture back over toward our idea. Conflicts, therefore, did not show via plot, or by the camera angles of hero vs. villain, rather from that more complex opposition which is natural to every social breath of manner, that primary if subtle conflict which comes from trying to sell your idea in company when others are trying to deny you. And, note this, with the same ambiguity attached to the moment, the same comic or oppressive ambiguity. For as a scene goes its way in life, we do not always know if our plans are working, or our scheme is about to be shot down, whether we are winning in our purpose or others think us a fool, we merely work to get our way and usually have to let it go at that.

That was about how our work went. We shot for four or five hours every night for four nights, never doing retakes, *never doing retakes* – for that would have gummed the experience on which we were building. Besides, we did not have the time or money. We rocked along for four nights, and finished with something like three hours of film, much in debt to the considerable skill of the lone cameraman. Pennebaker moved his twenty-four-pound rig through our scenes like an athlete, anticipating our moves, giving us fine footage to cut into ninety minutes of comedy, ambiguity, ease, candor, vitality, barbarity. Buy a ticket! But you may never get to see it. The instincts as a director are confessed to be deep and salving; the eye for editing, novelistically acute; the talents as an actor, swell, then monumental swell; financial courage as a producer, enormous; but common sense – no, I am void of that. For the last thing I said to the actors was: use any words you wish. They bathed their tongues in the liberty: obscenity pops from every pore of *Wild 90*. It evolved into the foulest-mouthed movie ever made, and is thus vastly contemporary and profoundly underground. If you live in a small town, you will not get to see it. Not if it's like the next small town. Which is a pity. For without a sound track this film is so chaste you could invite the bishop to a screening. Of course, he would be bored. Without a sound track, there's not much film to follow. Where was common sense?

But we invoke common sense with no great respect. It is obvious most of the merit of *Wild 90* is in or right next to the obscenity itself. The obscenity loosened stores of improvisation, gave a beat to the sound, opened the actors to figures of speech – creativity is always next to the verboten – and opens all of us now to the opportunity of puzzling the subject a dangerous step further.

THE PRINCE: Ya know he's the only guy I know, does a push-up, it hurts him in the ass.

TWENTY YEARS: He's got a big ass.

THE PRINCE: I wonder how he got the big ass. How'd you get the big ass?

TWENTY YEARS: Sittin'.

THE PRINCE: No, that ass is too big to get sittin'.

BUZZ CAMEO: That's a nice suit ya got there.

THE PRINCE: Ya know how he got that big ass? He got that big 'cause he has his radar in his ass.

Obscenity is, of course, a picayune topic for those not offended by it, but it does violence to the composure of those

who are. It shatters a subtle and enjoyable balance – their sense
of good taste. Yet the right to use obscene language in a movie
(if there will come a day when the courts so decide it is a right)
has at bottom nothing to do with questions of taste. One could
show a man and woman naked in the sexual act, and yet done
well, the filming could still be said to be in good taste – the film
images might slip by as abstractly as the wash of waves against a
piling. Yet I do not have the wish to film such a scene, good taste
or poor. It is of course a problem no film director can decide in
advance, for the twentieth century, our century of technology,
the bomb, the concentration camp, the mass media, and the
mass drug addiction, may yet be the century where the orgy and
the collective replace the family. It is not necessarily a speculation to steep you in joy – in the depths of an orgy with the air
full of smog, hard-beat fornications to the sound of air con-
ditioners, nose colds, who indeed would want to film copulation
in such a bag? Still, the century rushes toward this kind of
investigation. One can easily foresee a movie which will depend
for its motivation, nay, for its story itself, on the unveiling of the
act. Still I would not wish to be the man who directed such a
scene. These days, these years, we prong into the mystery from
every angle, with scalpels, seminars, electronic probes, we
cannot bear the thought any of this mystery might escape us; yet
the nearer we come on our surreal journey toward the germ of
the creation, the further we seem removed from a life which is
collectively supportable – repeat: Vietnam, race riots, traffic,
frozen food, and smog – all these certified brats of science –
they are by-products of the technological race into the center of
the mystery. So here there is no great desire to film the sexual
act even if the camera work could be superb, the actors
delighted in themselves, and taste all secure. You could almost
say that the heart of the sexual act might be finally none of
technology's business. And work in the world of the film is
work in the fluorescent light of technology.

Yet here we have a director who makes a movie with more
obscene language than any film ever made. How allay the
contradiction?

The director would reply there is no contradiction because
obscene language has nothing to do any longer with revelations

of the sexual act, it is not even much of a sweetmeat anymore for the prurient, no, obscenity is rather become a style of speech, a code of manners, a transmission belt for humor and violence – it can shatter taste because it speaks of violence, it is probably the most ineradicable measure of the potential violence of social class upon class, for no one swears so much as the men of the proletariat when alone – that has not changed since Marx's time. Today obscene language bears about the same relation to good society that the realistic portraits of the naturalistic novel of Zola's time brought to the hypocrisies and niceties of the social world of France – the naturalistic novel came like high forceps to a difficult birth. Zola was tasteless, Zola outraged, Zola's work was raw as bile, but in its time it was essential, it gave sanity to the society of its time, it gave accuracy and deliverance for it helped to reduce the collective hypocrisy of the epoch, and so served to deliver the Victorian world from the worst of its Victorianism, and thus gave the world over to the twentieth century in slightly improved condition.

Well, one would not claim the shade of Zola's talents or merits for *Wild 90*. It is in the end a most modest pioneer work. It is indeed not even a naturalistic production, not nearly so much as it is one of the first existential movies ever made. Suffice the question in this way: we live in an American society which can remind you of nothing so much as two lobes of a brain, two hemispheres of communication themselves intact but surgically severed from one another. Between the finer nuances of High Camp and the shooting of firemen in race riots is, however, a nihilistic gulf which may never be negotiated again by living Americans. But this we may swear on: the Establishment will not begin to come its half of the distance through the national gap until its knowledge of the real social life of that isolated and – what Washington will insist on calling – deprived world is accurate, rather than liberal, condescending, and over-programmatic. Yet for that to happen, every real and subterranean language must first have its hearing, even if taste will be in the process as outraged as a vegetarian forced to watch the flushing of the entrails in the stockyards. You can ask: what point to this? The vegetarian became a vegetarian precisely because he could not bear the slaughter of animals. Yes, your director will say, but let him see how it is really done, let him know it in detail. Then perhaps he will be twice the vegetarian he was before. Or maybe by picking up a gun to defend animals, he will kill humans and end as a cannibal.

Capital, you will say, your strategy for ambushing yourself is superb. You have just done in your argument.

No, rather something may have insisted on taking us further into the argument. The vegetarian, once become a cannibal, knows at least what he has become: if the world is thus turned a shift more barbarous, it is also a click less insane. Each year, civilization gives its delineated promise of being further conterminous with schizophrenia. Good taste, we would submit, may be ultimately the jailer who keeps all good ladies and angels of civilization firmly installed in the innocence of their dungeon, that Stygian incarceration whose walls are adorned with the elegant draperies of the very best and blindest taste. All kneel! Homage to my metaphor! The aim of a robust art still remains: that it be hearty, that it be savage, that it serve to feed audiences with the marrow of its honest presence. In the end, robust art pays cash, because in return for rolling the delicacies of more than one fine and valuable nervous system, it gives in return light and definition and blasts of fresh air to the corners of the world, it is a firm presence in the world, and so helps to protect the world from its dissolution in compromise, lack of focus, and entropy, entropy, that disease of progressive formlessness, that smug, last and most poisonous exhaust of the devil's foul mouth. Yeah, and yes! Obscenity is where God and Devil meet, and so is another of the avatars in which art ferments and man distills.

## A Course in Film-Making

### 1. On the Theory
The company, jaded and exhausted, happily or unhappily sexed-out after five days and nights of movie-making and balling in midnight beds and pools, had been converted to a bunch of enforced existentialists by the making of the film.

There is no other philosophical word which will apply to the condition of being an actor who has never acted before, finding himself in a strange place with a thoroughgoing swap of strangers and familiars for bedfellows, no script, and a story which suggests that the leading man is a fit and appropriate target for assassination. Since many of the actors were not without their freaks, their kinks, or old clarion calls to violence, and since the word of the Collective Rumor was that more than one of the men was packing a piece, a real piece with bullets, these five days and nights had been the advanced course in existentialism. Nobody knew what was going to happen, but for one hundred and twenty hours the conviction had been growing that if the warning system of one's senses had been worth anything in the past, something was most certainly going to happen before the film was out. Indeed on several separate occasions, it seemed nearly to happen. A dwarf almost drowned in a pool, a fight had taken place, then a bad fight, and on the night before at a climactic party two hours of the most intense potential for violence had been filmed, yet nothing commensurate had happened. The company was now in that state of hangover, breath foul with swallowed curses and congestions of the instincts, which comes to prize-fight fans when a big night, long awaited, ends as a lackluster and lumbering waltz. Not that the party had been a failure while it was being filmed. The tension of the party was memorable in the experience of many. But finally, nothing happened.

So, at this point next day in the filming of *Maidstone*, on the lazy afternoon which followed the night of the party, the director had come to the erroneous conclusion his movie was done – even though the film was still continuing in the collective mind of some working photographers before whom the director was yet to get hit on the head by a hammer wielded by his best actor, and would respond by biting the best actor on the ear, a fight to give him a whole new conception of his movie. What a pity to remind ourselves of these violent facts, for they encourage interest in a narrative which will not be presented in a hurry and then only a little, and that after an inquiry into the director's real interest which is (less bloody and more philosophical) the possible real nature of the film – not an easy discussion since the director has already found a most special way of making movies. When he begins to discourse on the subject, he feels as if he is not so much a director as an Argument. He can literally think of himself as The Argument, some medieval wind – a Player who is there for harangue. Certainly in that precise hour of the afternoon when he took off his actor's cape and moved from Norman T. Kingsley back to Norman Mailer again, and gave an orientation on the grass of Gardiners Island, it could hardly be said that he failed to talk about his movie to the company. No, he made every effort, even went so far as to explain that his way of making films was analogous to a military operation, to a commando raid on the nature of reality – they would discover where reality was located by the attack itself, just as a company of Rangers might learn that the enemy was located not in the first town they invaded but another. Of course, even as he spoke, he felt the resumption of tension. There was still something wrong in the air. The picture, he could swear, but for some fill-in, was finished, yet the presence it created had not left.

He could, however, hardly complain if the film itself was still a *presence*. A condition of dread had been generated over the last five days which had put subtle terror and tension into the faces of people who had never acted before, lines of such delicate intent and fine signification as to draw the envy of professionals. That had been precisely the presence he wished to elicit. It was the fundament of his method, the heart of his confidence, to put untried actors into situations without a script and film them with simple or available lighting, work in the limitations of these means and unforeseen ends and exits to get the best available sound (which was not always near to superb), and yet, all limitations granted, he could by this method give a sense of the bewildering surface of his cinematic reality which was finer by far than the work of all but the very best film artists.

It was in other words, a Leviathan of a thesis, and he, with characteristic modesty, ignorant until a few years ago of nearly all to do with film-making, and still technically more ignorant than the good majority of mediocre directors, was still convinced he had wandered by easy progressions into a most complex and devilish way of working up a film. And now had the confidence he was a film maker. And the unique experience to convince himself that he was a pioneer, for he believed he had come upon a way to smash the machine which crushed every surface of cinematic reality, that organization of plot, dialogue, sets, professionals, schedules, and thundering union impedimenta which beat every effort to take a good story or a book and flesh it into movie film. No, something was wrong with that, something was dreadfully wrong with a process which wasted time, talent, and millions of dollars at a crack to produce cinematic works of the most predictable encapsulation. One could sit through such works and on rare occasion even enjoy a world of good taste and nice insight without ever a moment of sensuous discomfort, which was exactly equal to saying without a moment of aesthetic revelation.

Still it is something to skip at a leap over thirty years of movie-making apprenticeship he has not served, to propose that, all ignorance and limitations granted, he has found a novel technique, and is on the consequence ready to issue a claim that his way of putting a film together, cut by cut, is important, and conceivably closer to the nature of film than the work of other, more talented directors.

## TWO

Of course, he makes no second claim that technically, gymnastically, pyrotechnically, or by any complex measure of craft does he begin to know the secrets of the more virtuoso of the directors and the cutters, no, he would only say that the material he has filmed lends itself happily, even innocently, to whole new ways of making cuts. That is because it has captured the life it was supposed to photograph. He is unfolding no blueprint. So there tends to be less monotony to his composition, less of a necessity to have over-illumined and too simplified frames, less of a push to give a single emphasis to each scene. His lines of dramatic force are not always converging toward the same point – nobody in his frame has yet learned to look for the reaction of the hero after the villain insults him, no, his film is not diminished by supporting actors who are forever obliged to indicate what the point of the scene is supposed to be (and are thereby reminiscent of dutiful relatives at a family dinner). So, his movie is not reminiscent of other films where the scene – no matter how superb – has a hollow, not so pervasive perhaps as the cheerful hollow in the voices of visitors who have come to be cheerful to a patient in a hospital, but there, even in the best of films always there. In the worst of films it is like the cordiality at the reception desk in a mortician's manor. So it could even be said that professional movie-acting consists of the ability to reduce the hollow to an all but invisible hole, and one can measure such actors by their ability to transcend the hollow. Marlon Brando could go 'Wow' in *Waterfront* and Dustin Hoffman would limp to the kitchen sink in *Midnight Cowboy* and the lack of life in the conventional movie frame was replaced by magical life. One could speak with justice of great actors. Perhaps a thousand actors and two thousand films can be cited where the movie frame comes alive and there is no dip at the foot of consciousness because something is false at the root.

Nonetheless any such appearance of talent was close to magic. The conventional way of making most films usually guaranteed its absence. For there was an element which interfered with motion pictures as much as the blurring of print would hinder the reading of a book, and this flaw derived from the peculiar misapprehension with which the silent film was but an extension of the theatre, even as the theatre was but an extension of literature. It was assumed that movies were there to tell a story. The story might derive from the stage, or from the pages of a book, or even from an idea for a story, but the film was asked to issue from a detailed plan which would have lines of dialogue. The making of the movie would be a fulfillment of that script, that literary plan; so, each scene would be shaped like a construction unit to build the architecture of the story. It was one of those profoundly false assumptions which seem at the time absolute common sense, yet it was no more natural than to have insisted that a movie was a river and one should always experience, while watching a film, emotions analogous to an afternoon spent on the banks of a stream. That might have been seen instantly as confining, a most confining notion; but to consider the carry-over of the story from literature to the film as equally constricting – no, that was not very evident.

For few people wished to contemplate the size of the job in transporting a novelist's vision of life over to a film; indeed, who in the movie business was going to admit that once literary characters had been converted over to actors, they could not possibly produce the same relation to other actors that the characters once had to each other? Interpretations had to collide. If each actor had his own idea of the dialogue he committed to memory, be certain the director had a better idea. And the producer! Life-times of professional craft go into halving such conceptual differences. The director gives up a little of his interpretation, then a little more, then almost all of it. The actor is directed away from his favorite misconceptions (and conceptions). Both parties suffer the rigor mortis of the technical conditions – which are not so close to a brightly lit operating theatre as to a brightly lit morgue. Then the script-writer has dependably delivered the scenario with his own private – and sometimes willful – idea buried in it (and if the work is an adaptation, odd lines of the novelist are still turning over). The coherence of the original novel has been cremated and strewn. Now the film is being made with conflicting notions of those scattered ashes. Of course the director is forced back willy-nilly to his script. It is all he can finally depend upon. Given the fundamental, nay, even organic, confusion on a movie set over what everybody is really doing, the company has to pool all differences and be faithful to the script even when the script has lost any relation to the original conception, and has probably begun to constrict the real life which is beginning to emerge on the set. No wonder great novels invariably make the most disappointing movies, and modest novels (like *The Asphalt Jungle*) sometimes make very good movies. It is because the original conception in modest novels is less special and so more capable of being worked upon by any number of other writers, directors, and actors.

Still, the discussion has been too narrow. The film, after all, is fed not only by literature but by the theatre, and the theatre is a conspicuous example of how attractively a blueprint can be unfolded. In fact, the theatre is reduced to very little whenever the collaboration between the actors and script is not excellent. Yet the theatre has had to put up with many a similar difficulty.

Can it be said that something works in the theatre which only pretends to work in the film? If the first error perpetrated upon movies has been to see them as an adjunct of literature, perhaps the second is the rush to make film an auxiliary of the theatrical arts, until even movies considered classics are hardly more than pieces of filmed theatre.

Of course a film lover could counter by saying that he was not necessarily thinking only of such monuments as *Gone with the Wind* when he used the term classic. In fact, he would inquire about *A Night at the Opera* or *The Maltese Falcon*.

The difficulties had obviously begun. The Argument would be never so simple again. The Marx Brothers, for example, stampeded over every line of a script and tore off in enough directions to leave concepts fluttering like ticker tape on the mysterious nature of the movie art. Certainly, any attempt to declare *The Maltese Falcon* a piece of filmed theatre would have to confess that *The Maltese Falcon* was more, a mysterious ineffable possession of 'more' and that was precisely what one looked for in a film. It was a hint to indicate some answer to the secrets of film might begin to be found in the curious and never quite explained phenomenon of the movie star. For Humphrey Bogart was certainly an element of natural film, yes, even *the* element which made *The Maltese Falcon* more than an excellent piece of filmed theatre. Thinking of the evocative aesthetic mists of that movie, how could the question not present itself: why did every piece of good dramatic theatre have to be the enemy of the film? It was unhappily evident to The Argument that any quick and invigorating theses on the character of movie stars and the hidden nature of the movie might have to wait for a little exposition on the special qualities of theatre.

## THREE

A complex matter. You might, for instance, have to take into account why people who think it comfortable to be nicely drunk at the beginning of a play would find it no pleasure to go to a movie in the same condition. Pot was more congenial for a film. If the difference for most hard-working actors between movies and theatre seemed hardly more than a trip across a crack, the split to any philosopher of the film was an abyss, just that same existential abyss which lies between booze and the beginnings of the psychedelic.

Existentially, theatre and film were in different dominions (and literature was probably nearer to each of them than they were to each other). The theatre was a ceremony with live priests who had learned by rote to pool their aesthetic instincts for a larger purpose. So theatre partook of a near obscene ceremony: it imitated life in a living place, and it had real people as the imitators. Such imitation was either sacrilege to the roots of life, or a reinforcement of them. Certainly, sentiments called religious appeared ready to arise whenever a group of people attended a ceremony in a large and dimly lit place. But in fact anyone who has ever experienced a moment of unmistakable balance between the audience, the cast, the theatre and the *manifest* of the play, an awe usually remarked by a silence palpable as the theatrical velvet of an unvoiced echo, knows that the foundation of the theatre is in the church and in the power of kings, or at least knows (if theatre goes back to blood sacrifices performed in a cave – which is about where the most advanced theatre seems ready to go) that the more recent foundations were ecclesiastical and royal. Theatre, at all of its massive best, can be seen as equal to a ceremony, performed by noblemen who have power to chastise an audience, savage them, dignify them, warm them, marry their humors, even create a magical forest where each human on his seat is a tree and every sense is vibrating to the rustle of other leaves. One's roots return then to some lost majesty of pomp and power. Of course, theatre is seldom so good. None of us have had a night like that recently. Still, theatre has its minutes: a scene whose original concept was lost in the mixing of too many talents is recovered by the power of the actor to open relations with his audience. While he is engaged in an emotional transaction which is false by its nature (because he knows by heart the lines of apparently spontaneous passion he will say next), still he has to be true to the honest difficulty of not knowing whether the audience will believe him or not. His position on stage is existential – he cannot know in advance if his effort will succeed or not. In turn, the audience must respect him. For he is at the least brave enough to dare their displeasure. And if he is bad enough . . . well, how can he forget old nightmares where audiences kill actors? So the actor on stage is at once a fraud (because he pretends to emotion he cannot by any Method feel absolutely – *or he would be mad*) and yet is a true man engaged in a tricky venture, dangerous in its potentialities for humiliation. That is the strength of the theatre. A vision of life somewhat different each night comes into existence between the actors and the audience, and what has been lost in the playwright's vision is sometimes transcended by the mood of a high theatrical hearth.

We are speaking of course only of the best and freshest plays. Even in a good play something dies about the time an actor recognizes that he can be mediocre in his performance and survive. The reputation of the play has become so useful that the audience has become a touch mediocre as well; at this point in the season the actor inevitably becomes as interesting as a whore in a house after her favorite client has gone for the night.

Nonetheless, it is still reminiscent of orgy to have relations with two worlds, of sentience at once, and when fresh, theatre is orgy. On stage, the actor is in communion with the audience and up to his neck in relations with other actors (if they are all still working together). A world of technique supports them. There are ways and means to live and act with half-thought-out lines of dialogue and errors of placement by the director, ways to deal with sentiments which have no ring and situations one knows by heart and still must enter with a pretense of theatrical surprise. An actor's culture exists, after all, for the working up of the false into the all-but-true; actors know the audience will carry the all-but-true over into the real and emotionally stirring if given a chance. So actors develop a full organ of emotional manifests. Large vibrant voices, significant moves. It all works because the actor is literally alive on a stage and therefore can never be false altogether. His presence is the real truth: he is at once the royal center of all eyes, and a Christian up before lions. So his theatrical emotion (which bears the same relation to real emotion which veneer of walnut bears to walnut) is moved by the risk of his position into a technique which offers truth. A skillful actor with false gestures and false emotions elicits our admiration because he tries to establish a vault under which we can seize on the truth since, after all, he has told the lie so well. Why, then, must that be an emotional transaction light years of the psyche away from the same transaction carried over to film?

## FOUR

It is because the risk in film is of other varieties. No audience is present unless the actor plays his scene for the cameramen and the union grips. And that is a specific audience with the prejudices and tastes of policemen. Indeed they usually dress like cops off duty and are built like cops (with the same heavy meat in the shoulders, same bellies oiled on beer), which is not surprising for they are also in surveillance upon a criminal activity: people are forging emotions under bright lights.

But it is no longer false emotion brought by technique to a point where it can be breathed upon and given life by audiences who do not know the next line. No, now the crew is a set of skills and intelligences. They are as sophisticated to the lines of the scene as the actors themselves. Like cops they see through every fake move and hardly care. The camera must move on cue and the sound boom, the lights be shifted and the walls slid apart – the action is easily as complex as a professional football team running through the intricacies of a new play or preparing a defense against it.

In fact, the actor does not usually play for the technicians. It is the director whose intelligence he will feel first, a charged critical intelligence knowing more of the scene than himself, a center of authority altogether different from a theatrical audience's authority (which is ready to relax with every good sound the actor makes). The movie director, however, does not relax then. The good sound of the actor can turn the plot inside out. No, here, the actor must work into a focus of will. The real face he speaks to, whether a step or ten steps to the side of the director, is a circle of glass as empty of love as an empty glass. That lens is his final audience. It takes precedence over the director and even over the actors he plays with. In the moment of his profoundest passion, as he reaches forward to kiss the heroine with every tenderness, his lips to be famous for their quiver, he is of course slowly and proficiently bringing his mouth up to the erogenous zone of the lens.

On stage, an actor, after twenty years of apprenticeship, can learn to reach the depths of an audience at the moment he is employing the maximum of his technique. A film actor with equivalent technique will have developed superb skills for revealing his reaction to the circle of glass. He can fail every other way, disobey the director or appear incapable of reacting to his direction, leave the other actors isolated from him and with nothing to react to, he can even get his lines wrong, but if he has film technique he will look sensational in the rushes, he will bring life to the scene even if he was death on the set. It is not surprising. There is something sinister about film. *Film is a phenomenon whose resemblance to death has been ignored for too long.* An emotion produced from the churn of the flesh is delivered to a machine, and that machine and its connections manage to produce a flow of images which will arouse some related sentiment in those who watch. The living emotion has passed through a burial ground – and has been resurrected. The living emotion survives as a psychological reality; it continues to exist as a set of images in one's memory which are not too different, as the years go by, from the images we keep of a relative who is dead. Think of a favorite uncle who is gone. Does the apparatus of the mind which flashes his picture before us act in another fashion if we ask for a flash of Humphrey Bogart next? Perhaps it does not. Film seems part of the mechanism of memory, or at the least, a most peculiar annex to memory. For in film we remember events as if they had taken place and we were there. But we were not. The psyche has taken into itself a whole country of fantasy and made it psychologically real, made it a part of memory. We are obviously dealing with a phenomenon whose roots are less defined than the power and glory of king and church. Yes, movies are more mysterious than theatre; even a clue to the undefinable attraction of the movie star is that he remains a point of light in that measureless dark of memory where other scenes have given up their light. He has obviously become a center of meaning to millions, possessed of more meaning than the actor next to him who may be actually more attractive, more interesting – definition of the phenomenon frays as we try to touch it. But has the heart of the discussion been sounded? Does it suggest that movie stars partake of the mysterious psychic properties of film more than other actors? that something in them lends itself to the need of memory for images of the past one can refer to when the mind has need to comprehend something new before it? We have to be careful. It is perhaps not so simple as that. The movie star may also suggest obsession, that negative condition of memory, that painful place to which we return over and over because a fundamental question is still unresolved: something happened to us years ago which was important, yet we hardly know if an angel kissed us then or a witch, whether we were brave or timid. We return to the ambiguity with pain. The obsession hurts because we cannot resolve it and so are losing confidence in our ability to estimate the present.

Obsession is a wasteful fix. Memory, when it can be free of obsession is a storehouse to offer up essences of the past capable of digesting most of the problems of the present, memory is even the libido of the ego, sweetening harsh demands of the will when memory is, yes, good. But the movie star seems to serve some double function: the star feeds memory *and* obsession – one need only think back to one's feelings about Marilyn Monroe! The movie star is welcoming but mysterious, unavailable yet intimate, the movie star is the embodiment of a love which could leave us abject, yet we believe we are the only soul the movie star can love. Quintessence of the elusive nature of film, the movie star is like a guide to bring us through the adventures of a half-conscious dream. It is even possible the movie star gives focus to themes of the imagination so large, romantic, and daring that they might not encounter reality: how can an adolescent have any real idea whether he will ever have sex with a beautiful woman or fight for his life? Nonetheless, events so grand might need years of psychic preparation. It was therefore also possible that the dream life of the film existed not only to provide escape but to prepare the psyche for apocalyptic moments which would likely never come.

Some differences of film from theatre may then have been noted. Theatre works on our ideas of social life and our understanding of manners. At its most generous, theatre creates a communion of bodies and a savory of the emotions – it becomes a feast and a fuck. But film speaks to the lost islands of the mind. Film lives somewhere in that underground river of the psyche which travels from the domain of sex through the deeps of memory and the dream, on out into the possible montages of death – we need only think of any man who was rescued from drowning after he thought he was on the last trip down. Does he ever relate the experience without speaking of the sensation that his life became a film running backward? *It is as if film has an existence within the brain which may be comparable to memory and the dream,* be indeed as real as memory and the dream, be even to some degree as functional. It was as if the levels of that existential river which runs into ultimate psychic states would no longer read as perhaps once it did: sex – memory – dream – death; but now flows through a technological age and so has to be described by way of sex – memory – *film* – dream – death. Theatre has to be in the world of manners, but film is in the physiology of the psyche. For that reason, perhaps, film comes nearest to a religion as the movie houses are empty, it speaks across all the lonely traverses of the mind, it is at its most beautiful in precisely those places it is least concrete, least theatrical, most other-worldly, most ghostly, most lingering unto death – then the true experience of the film as some Atlantis of the psyche will manifest itself, and directors like Antonioni and Bergman will show us that the film inhabits a secret place where the past tense of memory and the future intimations of the dream are interchangeable, are partners in the film: there is an unmistakable quality to any film which is not made as filmed theatre but rather appears as some existence we call film. That existence runs through Chaplin and *Sunset Boulevard* and *Persona* – it runs through home movies. It was Warhol's talent to perceive that in every home movie there is a sense of Time trying to express itself as a new kind of creation, a palpability which breathes in the *being* of the film. The best of works and some of the worst of film works have this quality. One can even find it for flashes in cranky old battered films of the purest mediocrity late at night on TV, B-films without an instant of talent, yet the years have added magic to what was

once moronic – Time is winking her eye as we look at the film.
Time suddenly appears to us as a wit.

Of course, there are movies which have delivered huge
pleasures to millions and never were film at all, just celluloid
theatre convertible to cash. Some were good, some very good,
some awful, but the majority of motion pictures, particularly
the majority of expensive ones, have always labored against the
umbilical antipathy of film for theatre. They were, no matter
how good as filmed theatre, never equal to theatre at its
best – rather, scaled-down repasts for the eye and ear. They
had a kind of phlegmatic tempo and all-too-well-lit color which
rarely hindered them from reaching lists for Ten Best Pictures
of the year. They were pictures like *Oklahoma!*, *South Pacific*,
*The Sound of Music*, *Mary Poppins*, *The Best Years of Our Lives*.
They were even such critical favorites as *Marty*, *Born Yesterday*,
*Brief Encounter*, and *The Seven Year Itch*, or *Anne of the
Thousand Days*, add *Lust for Life*, *All About Eve*, *Around the
World in Eighty Days*, *West Side Story*. All that celluloid was
super-technique for audiences who had not necessarily ever
seen a play but were constantly nourished in the great cafeteria
of the American Aesthetic where the media meals were served
up as binder for the shattered nervous system of the masses. To
the owners of that cafeteria there was something obscene in the
idea that one should not be able to translate a book into a play,
film, or TV series – something arrogant, for it would say the
difference between the movies just named and films like *Zabris-
kie Point*, *M.A.S.H.*, *Naked Summer*, *Belle de Jour*, *Limelight*,
*Diabolique*, *8½*, *The Bicycle Thief*, *The Four Hundred Blows*,
*High Noon*, *Easy Rider*, and *Weekend* were as the difference
between crud and sustenance for that ghostly part of the psyche
the film was supposed to enrich.

## FIVE

Very well. He had his point at least. There was film and filmed
theatre; there were relatively pure movies, and there were
money-making motion pictures which had almost nothing to do
with movies or memory or dream, but were filmed circus for the

suckers who proceeded to enjoy them enormously (when they did – for some cost canyons of cash and brought back trickles), suckers who loved them for their binding glue, and the status of seeing them, and the easy massage such pictures gave to emotions real theatre might have satisfied more. These motion pictures, made for no motive more in focus than the desire for money, were derived from plays, or were written and directed as filmed plays, they composed three-quarters to nine-tenths of the motion pictures which were made, and they might yet be the terminal death of Hollywood for they were color television on enormous screens and so failed more often than they succeeded; the media were mixed so the messages were mixed – audiences tended to regard them with apathy.

Of course the films he loved were just as often watched in empty theatres, but if he would call upon the difference it was that they were not regarded in apathy but in subtle fear or mixed pleasure or with gloom or dread or the kind of fascination which hinted uncomfortably at future obsession. There was a quality he could almost lay his hands on in movies he admired and so would raise to the superior eminence of Film: they were experiences which were later as pure in recollection as splendid or tragic days in one's life, they were not unlike the memory of some modest love which did not survive but was tender in retrospect for now it lived with the dignity of old love. Such films changed as one remembered them since they had become part of one's psychological life. Like love, they partook a little of some miracle, they had emerged from the abominable limitations of the script, yes, they had emerged out of some mysterious but wholly agreeable lack of focus toward that script in the intent of the director and/or the actor, they were subtly attached to a creative mist, they had the ambiguity of film. For if filmed theatre could sometimes be effective, sometimes be even as perfect and deserving of admiration as *Midnight Cowboy* or *On the Waterfront*, such pictures still had their aesthetic fired by the simpler communication of the theatre where relations between actors usually produced a dramatic outcome as capable of definition as the last line of a family fight. 'Go to an analyst' turned out to be the message, or 'Lover, we'll get along', or 'God bless us, we're unhappy, but we'll stick for the kids.' If it is theatre so rich as *The Little Foxes*, it will say, 'I am prepared to kill you, and I will.' Since the need of a stage actor is to draw an audience together, his instinct is to simplify the play and concentrate it, give it a single crisp flavor. So theatre speaks. Powerfully or with banality, comically, or in the botch of hysteria, it speaks, secretly it almost always speaks vulgarly, for almost always it says, 'We're here to tell you something about life. We've got a piece of the meat for you.' Of course if it is bad theatre, conceived in advance as a television series or any other form of Cafeteria, then it is only there to tell you something about public opinion and how that works at the lowest common denominator. But good or bad, theatre functions at its simple best when every resonance of the evening can collect about a single point – that place where the actors seduced the audience to meet the play.

Film, however, is shown to audiences who do not often react together. Some laugh, while others are silent, some are bored. Few share the same time. They have come in on the movie at different places. For film always speaks of death. Theatre rouses desires between the living audience and the living actors; film stirs suicide pacts where each individual in the audience goes over the horizon alone with the star; film speaks of the ambiguity of death – is it nothingness we go to, or eternal life? Is it to peace we travel or the migrations of the soul? So the ambiguity of the movie star is essential, and it helps to understand that subtle emptiness which is usually present in the colors of their acting, that pause in the certainty of what they would say, that note of distraction and sorrows on the other side of the hill, that hint they are thinking of a late date they will meet after this guy is gone. Movie stars are caught in the complexity of the plot but they do not belong to it altogether, as stage actors do. It does not matter of whom we speak: whether it is Garbo or Harlow or Marilyn Monroe, Carole Lombard or Myrna Loy, even Dottie Lamour or Grable, the star is still one misty wink of the eye away from total absorption. Even Cagney, phallic as a column of rock, had the hint of bells ringing in his head from blows some big brother gave him in years gone by, and Gable's growling voice always seemed to hint at one big hunk of *other* business he would have to take care of in a little while. The charisma of the movie star spoke of associations with tangential thoughts, with dissipations of the story-point into ripples which went out wider and wider, out to the shores of some land only the waves of the movies could wash.

Now, much of that was gone. There were still stars, even in color film there were bona fide stars. There was Catherine Deneuve and Robert Redford and huge box-office familiars predictable as the neighbor next door and twice as vivid – Bob Hope and Lucille Ball for two. If film spoke of death, motion-pictures-for-money spoke of everything which was boring, unkillable, and bouncy, and could be stopped with a switch quick as TV, and was by couples necking in drive-in theatres. The film had also become brands of sex marked R, X, and Hard-Core, the film was epic documentaries like *Woodstock* and *Gimme Shelter*, the film was *Pound* and *Trash* and *Performance*, which some called great and some would not, the film was in transition, the film was in a place no one could name, and he was there with *Maidstone*, caught in the position of talking about a film made near to three years before. Three years was a decade in the recent history of the film. Half of the shock in his sexual scenes was nearly as comfortable by now as the lingerie ads in a fashion magazine, and his emphasis on film without script was evident in small uses everywhere, it had begun for that matter as long ago as Cassavetes' *Shadows*, a film of the fifties he did not particularly remember, but then for that matter, film without script had begun with the two-reeler and the sequence of action worked out on the director's white starched cuff. It was finally not to the point. He had had a conception of film which was more or less his own, and he did not feel the desire to argue about it, or install himself modestly in a scholar's catalogue of predecessors and contemporaries, it seemed to him naturally and without great heat that *Maidstone* was a film made more by the method by which it had been made than any film he knew, and if there were others of which it could be said that they were even more, he would cheer them for the pleasure of seeing what was done. But his film was his own, and he knew it, and he supposed he could write about it well enough to point out from time to time what was special and mysterious in the work, and therefore full of relation to that argument about cinema which has brought us this far, cinema – that river enema of the sins. Wasn't there whole appropriation of meaning in every corner of the mogul business?

## II. In the Practice

He had, of course, embarked on the making of *Maidstone* with his own money, had in fact sold a piece of his shares of *The Village Voice*, a prosperous and sentimental holding. Not wishing to undergo the neurotic bends of trying to raise funds for a film he would begin shooting in a few weeks without a line of script or the desire to put anything on paper – he looked with horror on such a move! – he had small choice. Who would give him funds on past performance? In his first picture the sound was near to muffled; the second, while ready to be shown in the fall at the New York Film Festival, was nonetheless not yet evidence at a box office, and in fact had been sold to a distributor for fifteen thousand dollars, a small sale even for a movie which had cost no more than sixty.

It was of course possible he could have raised the money. The market was full of profit that year. Risk capital ready for tax loss could have been found. He did not try. There was some marrow of satisfaction in paying for it himself. So he sold a portion of *The Voice* and did not look back. The film was calling to him with every stimulus and every fear. He had, after all, conceived the heart of his movie in the days right after the assassination of Robert Kennedy, a time when it seemed the country was getting ready to blow its separate conventions apart (and indeed he was the man least surprised when the Democratic convention in Chicago had responsible politicians talking of the Reichstag fire). Besides, he was a guilty American, guilty with the others – he felt implicated in the death of Bobby, although he could never name how (short of fornicating with a witch on the afternoon of the deed) he must therefore be so responsible; nonetheless he was, he felt, along with ten million others – perhaps a backlash from years of living with Kennedy jibes and making some of them himself, perhaps from some unconscious delinquency which amounted to more.

In any case, a film he had contemplated for a year, a modest little film to take place in a bar with pimps waiting for their whores and then dealing with them, now turned inside out. He would use that original idea for the core of a larger story, as the sketch of a film to be made by a famous film director within a larger film. This film director would be one of fifty men whom America in her bewilderment and profound demoralization might be contemplating as a possible President, a film director famous for near pornographic films would be, yes, in range of the Presidency – what a time for the country! Now the last of his elements of plot came into place: there would be an elite group of secret police debating the director's assassination. What an impulse to put this into a script! But writing such a script and managing to direct it would take three years, and call for working with executives in a studio. Others would devour his story and make it something else. He preferred to make it himself, preferred to lose the story himself.

He knew from his experience with *Beyond the Law* (a film of the greatest simplicity next to this!) that when actors were without lines and the end of a scene was undetermined, one did not control the picture. Even if he would be in the middle of the film, would play in it as he had in the two others, would in fact play the leading role of the director (indeed find another actor on earth to even believe in such a role!), that did not mean the film would proceed as he had planned. At best, making movies by his method was like being the hostess at a party with a prearranged theme – at a party, let us say, where everybody was supposed to come dressed in black or white with the understanding that those in black should pretend to be somber in mood and those in white be gay. The guests would of course rebel, first by tricks, then by open stands. A beauty would arrive in red. The party would get away from the hostess constantly – as constantly would she work to restore it to the conception with which she began, yes, she would strive until the point where the party was a success and she could put up with her rules being broken. There would be art in the relinquishing of her strength. If the party turned out to be superb it would be the product not only of her theme, nor of the attack of her guests upon it, but her compensatory efforts to bring the party back to its theme. The history of what happened at her party was bound to prove more interesting than her original plan. Indeed, something parallel to that had occurred with *Beyond the Law*. He had started with an idea of putting together police, a police station, and the interrogation of suspects. But his actors had been as rich in ideas. In trying to keep them within his conception, the picture had taken on a ferocious life.

Yet with *Maidstone* he decided to gamble by a bolder step. Given his plot, he would be obliged to separate his functions as director and actor. It would help his performance if the actor passed through situations he could not dominate because he had also as director had the privilege of laying his eyes on every scene. It was important, for example, that the secret police who would look to assassinate him be able to have their plots filmed without his knowledge. On that account he had assigned directorial powers to several of the actors. They could pick photographers to do their scenes, scenes he would not see until filming was done. So too had he assigned autonomy to Rip Torn who would play Raoul Rey O'Houlihan, his fictional half-brother, an obvious potential assassin in the film – whether Rey would actually strike was tacitly understood to be open to the pressures within the making of the movie. Since Rey would also have the Cashbox, a Praetorian Guard loyal either to Rey or to Kingsley, that must prove still another undetermined element in the film. Of necessity, therefore, would Rey have photographers he could call on. So the company as a whole had five cameras for use – four Arriflex and one Eclair – five teams composed of a cameraman and sound man who were sometimes interchangeable, each team independent, each able to work under available light conditions which might vary from splendid to absurdly difficult, five teams to be spread out on certain days as much as five miles apart, for he had managed to capture the use of four fine houses for the week of shooting the film, an exercise in diplomacy he had not been capable of on any other weekend in his life, he had the estates, and kept them by a further exercise of diplomacy through the weeks before the picture and into the shooting. There were crises every day and he was on the edge of losing more than one set of grounds on more than one day, but the torrent of preparations was on, his energy was carried with the rush – in a few weeks they began with a cast of fifty or sixty (new actors coming and leaving all the

time), a capital of seventy thousand dollars, an availability of
forty or fifty hours of sound and film, an average of eight to ten
hours for each cameraman in a week of shooting which would
begin on a light day of work for Wednesday, would pass
through the heaviest of schedules on Thursday, Friday, Saturday, Sunday, and finish with light work on Monday and
Tuesday, an impossible speed for anyone fixed to the script of a
movie as ambitious as this, but he had cards to play. They were
his cameramen.

## TWO

They had almost all taken part in the making of *Monterey Pop*,
which had some of the best cinematography he had ever seen.
They had many other credits. That was hardly the point. It was
more to the issue that the stodgy unhappy catatonia of the old
documentary, where people bearing real names sat in chairs and
explained in self-conscious voices what they were up to, had
been liberated by the invention of a *wireless* synchronizer
between camera and tape recorder. A cameraman free of the
caution that he must always move in ways the sound man could
follow (since they had once been connected by a leash to one
another) was now able to get around as he wished; he could
stand on a ladder or slide on his belly, he could walk while
filming and turn (years of technique had gone into acquiring a
flat-footed walk which might approximate the old camera move
on a dolly) but since he was not on tracks or connected to anyone
else, so the path could be free in its curve. The eye of the lens
could inquire into the scene. The cameraman could even shoot
up from the floor between the bodies of men in a dispute or
listen to a social conversation from a worm's-eye view beneath a
glass coffee table – what play of light on the ashtrays and the
highballs! Such shots went back of course to *Citizen Kane* – the
issue was that documentary could now be open to subjects
which were formerly closed. Since a camera on a man's shoulder
was not as intimidating as the old huge camera on a tripod, the
subject felt less like a prisoner booked into the stocks of
documentary record-taking. Indeed a man who actually reacted

to his voice and movements was photographing him. Animation could begin to appear in the face and voice of the subject. So the subject became more interesting. The documentary moved from the photographing of executives, engineers, and inventors to the faces of slum children playing in the street, or to the study of married couples on an evening at home (and in bed). A world of subjects too fragile in mood for the entrance of heavy equipment, high-power lights, and crews of technicians became available, and people who had formerly been as interesting in front of the camera as slabs of stone began to show a gleam in their façade. But *cinéma vérité* still had technical limits which awaited the development of high-speed film with very little grain and better portable sound equipment.

*Cinéma vérité* suffered even further from the basic flaw that people were playing themselves in real situations, and were therefore the opposite of actors. Instead of offering a well-put-together lie which had all the feel of dramatic truth, they gave off a species of fact which came out flat and wooden and like a lie. It was as if there was a law that a person could not be himself in front of a camera unless he pretended to be someone other than himself. By that logic, *cinéma vérité* would work if it photographed a performer in the midst of his performance, since a musician in the reverberating cave of his work was hardly himself, he had moved out of daily dimensions, he was a creature in a kingdom of sound. So films like *Monterey Pop* were able to explore the existence of a performer on stage as no fixed camera had been able to do. The crew was small enough to be lost in the lights and the audience. Their lens could move in, retreat, turn away and react, even swing to the beat. Film came back of Janis Joplin and Otis Redding, of Jimi Hendrix and Ravi Shankar, which went beyond any film seen before of musicians giving a performance. It was precisely because the cameraman had worked free of the stipulations of a director. They knew more of what a camera could do than any director who had not spent years as a cameraman himself, they had lived in their conscious mind and in all the aesthetic ponderings of the unconscious with the problems of composition in a fast-changing scene, their eye for the potentialities of camera expression was their own. So far as a man could take a thirty- or forty-pound camera on his shoulder and still see with the freedom of an unimpeded eye they were ready, they could interpret: critical to the matter – they could *react*. It meant musicians could play without a thought of being photographed, and so were never inhibited by the restrictions directors and cameramen working on massive tripods were obliged to impose on a performer's movement.

It had been his own idea, however, that *cinéma vérité* might also be used to photograph feature-length movies which told imaginary stories. He had come to the thought by way of his first film. Even if that had ended as a disaster (because the just-tolerable sound he heard on magnetic tape was not tolerable with an optical track), there had been a period in editing when he saw something he had never seen in other films. The actors (he was one of them) were more real, seemed more – it had to be said – more vivid than in other films. He supposed it was because people in fictional situations had never been photographed with such sensitivity before. The camera moved with the delicacy and uncertainty, the wariness before possible shock, that the human eye could feel in a strange situation. The camera had the animal awareness of a fifteen-year-old entering a room rather than a Mafia overlord promenading down a corridor. It made him realize that the movement of camera in conventional film (in filmed theatre) had none of the real movement of the eye, just the horizontal movement of vehicles, the vertical movement of elevators, and the turning movement of a door on a hinge. The eye of such cameras moved in relation to the human eye as a steam shovel moves in relation to the human body. The professional camera, however, was smooth, as indubitably smooth as the closing of a coffin lid. If it passed through space with the rigidity of a steam shovel, it did not clank. That, unhappily, was left for the *cinéma vérité* camera. The price of greater sensitivity to the unpremeditated action of actors was a set of vibrations, shudders, clunks, plus a host of missed anticipations when the camera zoomed in on the expectation of an interesting response, and the actor, whom the photographer had picked, was dull. Yet even that was cinematically curious once one recovered from the shock that not every instant on screen was shaped into significance. For now the cinematic point became the fact that the photographer could never know precisely what was coming – he was *obliged* to anticipate and he could be wrong: a story began to be told of the uncertain investigation of the eye onto each scene before us. It expanded one's notion of cinematic possibilities, and it intensified one's awareness of the moment. When significant movement was captured. It was now doubly significant because one could not take it for granted. Watching film became an act of interpretation and restoration for what was missed – much as one might look to fill the empty unpainted spaces in old canvases of Larry Rivers – it was also kin to that sense of excitement which is felt at a party when insights are arriving more quickly than one's ability to put them away neatly.

By whatever point of view, he had then a corps of cameramen, and they were equipped to photograph scenes which might veer off in any one of a dozen directions – they were ready to be surprised. It stimulated that coordination between hand, eye, and camera balance which was the dynamic of their art, surprises gave style to the rhythm and angle by which they would move in or zoom away. Once, after an impromptu free-for-all had developed in the filming of *Beyond the Law* with actors' bodies finally locked on the floor like a heap of twist-roll dough shaped for the oven, the cameraman had said, 'You know I'd like to cover the camera with a case of foam rubber.' And added wistfully, 'Then I could just get in the middle of the fight next time.' Such ideas carried to to their conclusion might slip nonstop miniaturized cameras with built-in lights up the cervix to a baby's fist so the trip through the canal could be photographed, but that was years away from its unhappy debate – for the present he had cameramen who were nimble enough to work in close to a scene and get away (most of the time) without bumping the action or photographing the sound man. Or each other, if two cameras were working different angles.

Later, comparing two men's work on the same scene, he would come to observe that each man had a mode as characteristic as a literary style. The work of one was invariably well-composed, austere, tasteful; another would be alert to the play of forces between two actors – he would have talent for capturing that body language which would most accentuate what the actors unconsciously were doing. Another had little interest in the turn of a scene, but was fascinated with visual minutiae – occasionally his minutiae were more interesting than the scene. Some were best at photographing men, others at studying women or the mood of a landscape. Some were workhorses, some were delicate. Some were delicate and still worked like horses. He came to applaud his cameramen during the week of shooting the film, for there were days when they worked for sixteen hours, bodies quivering from fatigue, yet rallying to steadiness when they worked – the love affair was to go through a turn or two when he sat in a screening room for two weeks and studied the forty-five hours they had brought back, saw the unexpected mistakes, the loss of focus on sudden shifts of action, the edge of the microphone in the frame when the unforeseen move of an actor had flushed the sound man. And wistful disappointments when scenes on which he had counted mightily had lost their emphasis because the cameraman had not seen what he, the director, had seen, had not been in the same state of psychic awareness. And there were miles of footage, filmed in his absence, where the actors had gone wandering and the cameramen had let them, idiocies piled on idiocies, wooden muddy characterless footage, the depression of the cameraman visible in his lack of desire to give visual shape to a tiresome duet. Loss was everywhere in the forty-five hours.

But there were bonuses and benefits where he had never looked. Scenes he had thought uninspired as he played them were given life by the art of the photographer, and scenes he knew were good were made even better by choices of angle he would not have had the foresight to pick himself. If he lost what he desired in one scene, he found himself compensated in another. As the months of editing went on, he would feel at times like a sculptor discovering his statue. The chisel could not go where it wished, but there was a statue to be disclosed if one would follow the veins of the stone. So *Maidstone* began to emerge, not the idea for a picture with which he had begun, but another which had come out of it, a metamorphosis for which he was prepared, since in parallel to the flaws and bonuses of his *cinéma vérité* photography the *Maidstone* emerging was as much better than the conception with which he had started, as it was inferior. If it was a movie of another sort than he had first conceived, it seemed to him finally that there were not too many movies like it, for *Maidstone* was a film which had been made out of the materials of its making, a movie which had had almost no existence in plans or on drawing boards or detailed budgets before it was begun, a movie delivered out of film material which had come to life in the heat chamber of seven days of intense improvised and scriptless film-making, so a movie which had a curious first existence which did not come from the stone but the shape of the film maker's hand. If he had arrived at six or seven hours of footage he considered suitable or agreeable or useful or tasty or splendid or fine or essential, if the smelting had reduced forty-five hours of film to a seventh of itself, there was still, he knew, a length to which the material must shrink by way of brooding, rubbing, and polishing, by elucidation then de-infatuation with pieces of film or conceits of story he had loved too much at first to relinquish. It would be a work of months, and then finally of a year (and a second year to follow) of mistakes and losses, blunders and mislaid gems of film strip, but when done, it would be his conception, he would by then have *written* a movie using strips of film rather than words, a movie different from the film anyone else would have made out of the same six or seven hours of usable film, would have written it as uniquely and differently as any one writer would have been from another writer if both were working on the same topic and had the same dictionary. It was his film. He had framed some of the language, and others had framed the rest of it for him, but by the time he began his editing, it was all part of the same dictionary; he had created *Maidstone* out of the given; so it was entirely different from films which had devoted their effort to creating the given from a script, then nailing it up according to plan.

In the act of this most particular film-writing, his pencil became the size of an editing machine,* he discovered where he

---

* With the advent of electronic editing from video tapes the notion of *writing* one's movie out of the film at one's disposal – since it promises to be quicker and easier – becomes next to inevitable.

thought the nature of the film might lie, and so tried to end with a film which would be in itself the nature of film, a metaphysical dumpling of a remark which is close to indigestible. Does it make it easier to suggest that even as an angel may be the nature of goodness and beauty, so to look at an angel is to obtain a picture of humans from heaven? By analogy he wanted a film which would live in the mind like a movie star, that is he wanted the film itself to be the movie star, some evocative, ambiguous presence which was always suggesting the ghostly but most real intrusion of the *special* existence of cinema.

## THREE

But he anticipates. He has come to the peroration before he has reached the middle. It is a natural mistake for a film maker. A novelist learns early in his career that beginning, middle, and end are a part of literary time, and cause direct notice when shifted, but in film no time exists but the order of progression. A film is made by one piece of film being stuck onto the next and that is the only scheme of time which prevails. Afloat on the full tide of a film we see an actor who looks twenty years old. In the next cut he looks sixty – we do not jump immediately to the conclusion that it is forty years later, no, we may have to recognize it is his idea of himself forty years later, or his recollection of a previous life when he was sixty. Indeed it may be a shot of his grandfather – we wait for the next cut. If it explains nothing, merely goes off to further adventures of the twenty-year-old, the isolated cut has its peculiar existence – it is a warning or a symbol or an omen, something – it sticks with its incomprehensible flash even as we have flashes in life of people we know well who are seen for an instant doing something we cannot comprehend – the town patriot sticks his tongue out at the flag: next moment he is, as always, smiling on his cigar. Did we see the tongue go out or did one crazy cell in our own head imagine it? That is a fair preparation for film. One can put anything next to anything in film – there is a correlative in some psychic state of memory, in the dream, the *déjà vu*, or the death mask, in some blink of the eye or jump of the nerve.

So one can work whole stretches of film free of any thought of the story. A piece of film can be put next to another piece of film regardless of plot – it will work or it will not work. Of course, this is exactly the place where the mystique of film begins and one starts to talk of its nature. Every beginner of a film cutter becomes willy-nilly an amateur philosopher about the time he recognizes that you cannot attach one piece of film to another simply because it makes sense for your story. If the cut is poor, the screen will jump. A virtuoso can make it jump to one side, then to the other – that, too, is a psychic state the film can offer, but it is like the dying spasms of a broken tooth – can the average film afford such pain?

No, there was a syntax to film movement. The slow sweep of a man walking to the left and out of the frame could be followed by the sweep of another man walking to the right. If the tempos were similar, the movement was restful. If the second man walked faster than the first the logical expectation was for a faster and more intense scene on the third cut. Some action would obviously be getting ready. What it was would hardly matter. A fight could follow between two men or two dogs, an airplane could dive, a train go by, or a woman could scream, then turn immobile and the freezing of her movement would go into the strictures of the scream. You could do anything in film if you could do it. Of course, some cuts were vastly better than others but led you to more exquisite troubles since several beautiful cuts in a row awakened expectations which oncoming material would have to satisfy. If there was nothing that good to follow, it was like stopping in the middle of the act.

On the other hand, mediocre cuts could follow one another, each cut more or less endurable, until suddenly a cut would go dead. The cut had seemed reasonable for the plot but it left a feeling in the lungs analogous to breathing the exhaust of a bus. Cuts were like words. You could put many an ordinary word next to another word but you could not put them all. If your last name was Klotz, you might call your son Chris, but you would not call your girl Emerald, not unless your ear and the ear of fashion were in a special little race that year. Godard made jump cuts in *Breathless* which no one had been able to endure before, did it out of all his experience as a cutter, and from his artistic insight that the verboten had moved to the edge of the virtuoso. Yet, you may be certain the twenty precise cuts before the jump cut fed subtly into it, if indeed the jump cut had not become the particular metaphysic of that film.

Still, some cuts work, some do not. Some cuts work in extraordinary fashion. One cannot understand why two pieces of film otherwise unrelated seem agreeable next to one another, even appear on screen with that same unfolding of mood the sun suggests as it works at last through a cloud. Poetry is working. A few words which had little to do with one another are now enriching each other. Peerless grapefruit peel! In color film the effect is twice to be noticed. For the syntax of good movement can be reduced by the color, or, since color film is easily as malleable to editing as black and white, an otherwise indifferent movement will be given resonance by the shift of color. It does not matter what is used. A good cutter with enough film can cut a run of images which will give pleasure to an audience. If there is no story present, no other exposition or logic than the aesthetic of color, composition, and movement, then there is a length to such a film, and it is not usually more than a quarter of an hour. Give a hint of story, however, and the interest of the audience might ride for twice as long. The good cutter is like a very good skier. He does not study the trail ahead, he sets out down the mountain, makes his turns as they come, does his checks, his drops into the fall line, his traverses into the hill, then tips around and down again. It is beauty to watch. If we add the knowledge that he is in a *race*, the beauty is hardly diminished and our tension is certainly increased. It is not unlike what happens when a hint of story is added to film montage.

Now, however, create a complexity for which film is uniquely suited. Offer a situation where the film seems to tell the audience the skier is in a race, then a minute later seems to indicate he is not in a race. All the while we are following his descent – now the race seems to be on again. To the attention and irritation of not knowing which situation is real, and to the beauty of the photography, have been added ambiguities of context. A fine slippery shiver of meaning comes over us because the situation has altered a little faster than our comprehension of it. Film can offer such sensations as no other art.

If, then, he was ready to start with a conventional, even supercharged movie plot (which he knew would be quickly warped, intensified, dissipated, and altered) and if he was equally ready to throw a Colosseum fodder of actors almost totally untrained into such maximum circus, it was because he had learned that improvised scenes with *cinéma vérité* photographers gave many more opportunities to the cutter than the choices open to a film editor who was working on a movie whose rushes came off a script. For, whether trained or untrained, actors in any improvised scene had hardly any more idea of what the final relation of their scene would be to the eventual movie than a man in a love affair may know if his woman will be with him for the rest of his life. So there was an indispensably intense air of the provisional and the real to the actors' work. They were not present to send off signals, as actors with a script must unconsciously do, that the end of the scene was near. Therefore, any improvised scenes which worked in whole or in part, which is to say had vitality or flashes of vitality, always gave some interesting ensemble of movement that could be used as the springboard for a quick or curious cut to the tempo of other actors in other improvised scenes which were also working well. Indeed, one could cut away from a continuing scene at any point – for the script was still to be put together. That was a choice which film with a script would rarely offer. With script, each scene was staged and thereby necessarily acted with its little unconscious beginning, little middle, and little end. Options for interesting cuts were on the consequence blocked. A scene which ended with a book being laid with measured finality on a table tended all too often to require an ensuing movement equally full of the slow and the stately. That was legitimate if the flow of the movie called up such a tone, but it was deadening if the next scene in the script wished to get off to a quick start. That next cut could no more ignore the last pause than a conversation could glide over the remark that a friend had passed away.

Improvisation obviously gave more freedom to the cutter, so much in fact that the logic by which one began to connect pieces of film to each other seemed at times to arise out of the very logic of film – even if the logic of film was a concept as deeply buried as the logic of language and so might have to wait for its first tentative elucidation by a semantics of film. What appeared as the immediate difference was that with improvisation and free cutting the story was not obliged to be present as the walls and foundation of a movie, but rather became a house afloat on some curious stream, a melody perhaps on which many an improvisation was winging – it was as if story now had the same rare relation to film which images bear to language. The influence of story now was partial, not whole. For even as language consists of both the concrete and the abstract, of particular images and also of concepts which have no image, so any logic of film could contain elements of natural story and elements of movement which were opposed to story or simply indifferent to story. The *resonance* of film, the *experience* of film – words were of diminishing use here – seemed to derive from some necessary tension between the two, even as language seems to require that we pass from image to concept and back.

But if *Maidstone* (as a prime example of the logic of film) is already once removed from words, it is twice dangerous to keep speaking of it without offering a little more of the particular experience which produced it. If the obvious suggestion arises that the experience resides in the nature of improvisation, one may be forgiven the excessive symmetry of next suggesting that the concealed properties of film and improvision are parallel (which is why they may belong together). We look at film, any film, and chaos is to a degree ordered. (We can, for example, photograph a wastebasket and it has become more an object of order than it was before.) We know we are looking at a life which is not quite life although it will certainly shift the way we live. So improvisation also orders chaos – gives its focus to random emotions – also becomes a life which is not quite life, and yet, even more than film, improvisation suggests it is indeed ready to become life. Ready to become life? Are we speaking of the moment when a fantasy, which is to say a psychological reality in the mind, transcends itself and becomes a fact? We are probably back to the last afternoon in the filming of *Maidstone*.

# FOUR

Given his theories on improvisation, there was a problem to filming *Maidstone*, and it was fundamental. While he took it for granted that any man or woman who could talk under stress was usually ready to burst forth with an improvised characterization (almost as if the ability to act, like the ability to make love, had been waiting for its opportunity), still one could never forget that art is art and self-expression is all too often therapy. The need therefore was to have a scheme which would keep the improvisation from flowing over into a purge. Some constraint had to be found for each scene; ideally, an overlying constraint had to be found for the entire film. In *Beyond the Law*, the problem seemed to solve itself. Being a policeman or a suspect arrested for the night was apparently one of the formal, even primeval scenes of the unconscious. None of his actors had trouble believing they were either policemen or under arrest, indeed his actors were richer in the conception of their role than the author would have been if he had written it for them. Nor had his presence as a director even been necessary in every scene. He had filmed most of *Beyond the Law* on an unrented floor in a seedy office building. It was perfect for giving the sensation that one was upstairs at a police station. Since he had set up interrogations between his detectives and suspects in separate rooms, three camera teams worked apart from one another in the different interrogation chambers. As in a police station, detectives came in and out, questioned a man, took off. Other detectives came in. After a period of filming, the floor of the office building might as well have become a police station. There was a babble of sound throughout, prisoners were arguing, weeping, protesting, going silent, detectives were bellowing or intoning charges, sounds of a beating in one room were agitating an unstable prisoner in another. Half the movie had been filmed in two nights, filmed on a sea of sound and cinematic sensations.

Now, however, he was ready to make a film of no simple premise and much complexity. Ideally, many of his scenes would be subtle. Any demonstration of the value of making a movie by this method would depend consequently on how elusive, light, and sinister, were the effects obtained. The proof that his method had resources could only be demonstrated by capturing delicate qualities which none but the most carefully prepared films had hitherto provided. Since he also wished his picture to be nothing less than comic, farcical, sexy, on the edge of horror, and with more than a hint of the ghostly, the concoction would not be automatic to obtain.

Still, he believed he could get it if he could only provide an atmosphere, some pervasive atmosphere, in which his untried actors would arrive at a working mood. For *Beyond the Law*, his police station had provided that atmosphere, provided it as forcefully as a movie being made in a coal mine. But *Maidstone* would be filmed half in open air; the other half would take place in living rooms and sitting rooms which were models of the exotic or the established. Any prevailing atmosphere could not be simply created by an ideal set – rather it would have to come from the presence of the film-making itself descended as some sort of spirit-resident upon East Hampton, a somewhat frightening film, to be certain, for its central figure was a man living in danger of assassination. Since improvisation was never dependable, far from it! the theme was uneasy to all. Murder is another of the primeval scenes of the unconscious. The impulse, however, is guarded by bulldogs in fifty restraining collars – murder was not likely to occur this week on the cheap. Nonetheless, it was only a month and a little more since Bobby Kennedy was dead. That was a thought which lay heavy. Another was the instability of fifty or sixty actors, some white, some black, all congregating and soon fornicating in two small hotels. Nor were the scenes to be played likely to reduce any tension.

He was not so paranoid as to see the venture daring more than a most risk-diminished form of Russian roulette. Surely, not more than one chance in a hundred, say at the most unlucky, one chance in ten of a real assassination attempt, but whatever the percentage, the practical working movie point was that one percent of real risk introduced a paranoid atmosphere of risk which might be put at twenty percent. And that was a percentage to work with, a percentage to keep the cast in a state of diabolical inclinations, some sensuousness, and much dread. How could legitimate fear not arise that some innocent bystander, some bit actor, would catch a maladroit effort at assassination intended for another? So a presence for the film had been created. The fear of assassination hung over the cinematic shooting like the faintest luminous evanescent arch of the ineluctable beyond, yes, some pale shade was there, some representative of the ghost-world of film there along with everything else, along with chaos, cries of love in the grass, and the physical grind of the work, the rush of scenes, the military madness of schedule. Actor and quartermaster, general, production engineer, and the only substitute for a script girl, he had himself more roles than ever before in his life, and staggered through *Maidstone* with the brain of an exhausted infantryman, his mind obliged to work as it had never before, work constantly and without respect for its age, vices, and sedentary habits. Since he also had not slept more than four hours a night for the last two weeks of preparation, keyed to a pitch which if struck could have given off a note, he was speaking slowly for the first time in his life, his brain too used-up to talk fast – the picture was later to prosper as a result since people for once could hear him! – he had nonetheless to wonder at the oddest moments (for there was an unmistakable rainbow of fear and elation in the breath of his chest and it did not leave until the film was done), had to wonder why he was taking such a peculiar chance, which if small was still unnecessary, and knew it had some murky soil of congested roots in the irrational equation that Bobby Kennedy had taken a large chance for a large goal, and he must – in some equilibration of all the underground pressure systems of guilt – now find a way to take a smaller chance for his own private goal, suspected he would never have made this movie or even conceived of it if he had not sat in a room with Bobby Kennedy a month before his death and failed to realize danger: that the man was in mortal danger. So he had a motive not far from obsession: one could return to it over many a year.

Of course his other motive was professional, even elegant in its professionalism. For the fact that he not only made a movie about a possible assassination but gave it structure as a game, even offered the fierce privilege of autonomy to actors who were scheming up plots for his possible cinematic assassination, must also mean that the presence was not being fortified. So he played his part, acting for at least half of his working day rather than directing, his own role certainly helped by that delicate baleful edge of presence which might lead to artwork, a debacle, or outright disaster. He had no idea what was being hatched about him. He knew only that a variety of large and little plots gave every indication of generating some focus, some steam, some point of a gun, and went through days with staggering schedules, his best reason for speed the instability of the situation. His actors were in for a long weekend. Any longer and the presence would explode or worse, appear absurd, dissipate. Each day in fact he was losing actors, some from frustration, some from fear, some of them good, some promising. Potentialities of story which hung on their presence would have to take a turn. He was not worried at that, not worried by any item of plot or arrival or departure. They would, as he told the company, take B if they could not take A.

So he lived on the fine fever of making the film, hardly aware of any hullabaloo but his own; he was become a powerless instrument of his own will, pleased at bottom to be out of touch with two whole sides of his film – the assassination activities of the secret police, and the possibly murderous ones of the Praetorian Guard – stayed like some animal in a zone of hunters knowing the great fatigue of a high alert, his senses an adrenalin of warnings whenever Raoul Rey O'Houlihan–Rip Torn was near, for he knew as if Torn were his true brother that the web of intriguings had Torn at the center, that if psychic biddings and curses were flying like bats through the ranks of the company, then Torn was the hole in the roof where they all came in. What pressure! What logic and what torture! What impulse! For Torn was more than an actor, he had in addition to debate his attempt to be the assassin. The vanity of a proud actor, not nearly recognized sufficiently for his talent, for the remarkable force of unholy smolderings he could always present, now had to become a vanity pushing him to take the center, to move from that secondary position of acolyte to the leading part, and pre-empt the part, be the killer who invaded the hill. Yet he was also first centurion of the guard to protect Kingsley from the point of the threat, and took his mission seriously, yes, with all the seriousness of a profound actor steeped in his improvisation. Ready to die in order to save Kingsley, he was also ready to kill him – anything but to have the quiet insistent pressure of the picture pass into nowhere, all threats stilled, his own role stilled.

So the night before the afternoon on the grass, the night of the assassination ball became O'Houlihan's high agony. Raoul Rey–Rip Torn had become the center of the film, the focus of every loyalty to the director, yet the wild card in every plot, since it had become an unspoken convention that the attempt of assassination would be on the night of the ball (as if actors in a sustained improvisation ganged naturally to the idea of a focus of plot), so in the hours of the night as the party went by, plots arose and were shattered or missed, or evaded, the director never feeling more real in the role. Uncertain of the size of the attempt, or whether the attempt was even yet to come, not knowing if he played in a game which was a real drama, or worked for a drama just so absurd as a game, he did not accept the more obvious gambits of plot which were offered him. If obvious, they seemed ridiculous, as though one gave assent to pressing a button which would release a boxing glove in one's face. No, he took up posts, or promenaded for two hours – impromptu bodyguard always about him – hung in the situation for two hours, and the time done and the party over, spoke now not to Rey but to Rip as if the movie were finished, as indeed he thought it was, for nothing but a few elements of the dream called 'The Death of the Director' would be filmed on Gardiners Island with the company next day, a day in fact for picnic and celebration that the film was over. His own danger had been as one part in one hundred or less, but he was glad it was done, and so said to his fictional brother, 'I don't know if we got anything tonight, but it's still all right,' thinking to himself of the dozen different ways he could cut the film (his security residing in a documentary on the making of an unsuccessful film since there was always footage of his own voluminous directions to the cast) and so saying, went to bed and finally to sleep, and the next day found to his horror that on Gardiners Island after the lecture of orientation was over that the presence of the dread was returned, but now shorn of elation, shorn of a rainbow. There was something heavy, then awful in the air, he knew he was in more physical danger than at any time before, and as Torn came walking toward him across the green, hammer dangling from his hand, he remembered taking off his black leather vest and holding it like a short folded cape in lieu of a better weapon, and after the fight, too furious to speak to Torn for many a month, outraged that Torn had broken the unspoken convention of their film – that violence cease with the end of the filming of the ball – was yet obliged to discover in the months of studying his forty-five hours of reels that his own blunder had been enormous in giving so much autonomy to Torn and the other assistant directors. The work they had done was by sections good, but not finally good enough. The buried half of the film he had been waiting to see would remain for the most part buried. He had been left with the most embarrassing work of all, an ego trip, for he had been the hardest-working actor in the film, and so the film was his, it was all too unhappily his, and all too much of him, since that was the part which unfortunately worked the best. Torn had therefore been right to make his attack. The hole in the film had called for that. Without it, there was not enough. And with it – he glimpsed as he worked each day with his editors that a film was emerging which he would yet be pleased to call his own for it was a mysterious film and became more mysterious as he thought on it. It was reminiscent first of the image he had held of the ski race which was on, then declared off, then put on again – the film shifted from context to context in modes as obsessive and haunting and *attached* to memory as those recollections of indefinable moments between sleep and a dream where context shifts, only to shift back again – we are in the dream . . . no, it is the edge of day. So Proust had floated his reader on a hundred-page procession of state from sleep to wakefulness into sleep.

In *Maidstone* the context moved into some other place. It was a film about the surface of reality and the less visible surface of psychological reality. For if everyday reality was a surface, or a crust, or a skin, psychological reality was a balloon which lived as a surface so long as the air of belief was within it. And since he had come to write his *Maidstone* after all the film was in, he chose the mysterious shifting character of its surface as the subject, and looked to show just how many of its realities were psychological realities which could suddenly be exploded and then where had they gone? What was left of such reality? It was a project he could never have commenced with words, nor even with the fiction of a story, but *Maidstone* had been filmed not only as an imaginary event but as a real event, and so was both a fiction and a documentary at once and then become impossible to locate so precisely, for what came nearest to the hard hide of the real? Was it Norman Mailer, the self-satisfied director, instructing his cast for the last time, or was it the suddenly real head of Norman T. Kingsley that Torn as suddenly attacked. (Yet his hammer had been held carefully on the flat to reduce the damage.) For if the attack was real, the actor upon whom it was wreaked should not be, and would not be unless the attack became fiercer still, fierce enough to kill him indeed. Then Kingsley would have become undeniably more real than Mailer.

It was a species of realization – that the hide of the real remains real only so long as the psychologically real fails to cut into its existence by an act which makes psychology real – the tongue would twist in its turnings on such a philosophical attempt faster than the film. For it was possible *Maidstone* inhabited that place where the film was supposed to live – that halfway station between the psychological and the real which helped to explain the real. As time went on, he saw that the cutting he did by newly acquired instinct was with purpose, and had a logic to reveal the topography of that halfway station. For *Maidstone* kept promising developments of plot which never quite took place, even as we travel through our lives forever anticipating the formation of plots around us which do not quite form. We are always looking for real stories to ensue which never exactly enact themselves as we expect, yet we still work at such times as actors in the real story of our life, pursuing roles which can become our life at any instant the psychological can become the real – as occasionally it will. For out of fifty stories in which we are at any instant enmeshed (fifty sets of expectations that next week we fall in love or tonight we go out and get drunk and have a terrible fight), not three times out of fifty, not two, nor one does the expected event occur. And then it does, it happens, it takes place out of the stored force of all the denouements which did not take place. So Torn attacked out of all the plots of other actors. Torn became the presence of the film, the psychological reality that became a literal reality out of the pressure of all the ones which did not. So that film about a director who would run for President became instead a photographed event of simulated plots and threats kept under high pressure by the curious curse of playing with photography of the female in the act of love, of playing with the curse of love which is gone, of playing with the curses of matrimony, yes, that film of an event which was a thousand events (of which nine hundred and ninety had small issue, or none, or were never photographed) became at last a film of the ineffable shimmer of reality, even became, as its director had wished, the star itself. Then it was that the presence of the film crystallized into the *geist* of *Maidstone*, Rip Torn. A superb actor at a pitch of intensity was there finally to reveal the premise on which a film had been built, even offer the essence of a method which might yet become the future of the film. For is it not a common premise to many a lover of movies that the hidden wealth in every strongbox of the cinematographic are those sequences of footage where the event has been innocent of script and yet resonant with life? Of course! We are talking of nothing other than movie stars in frames where the mood has been pure. Mood is our only acquaintance with the sensuous properties of time. And film is the only art which can search, cut by cut, into the mystery of moods which follow and accommodate one another; film is the only art which can study sudden shifts of mood which sever the ongoing river of time a fine film has set in flow. So we search for the pure in film as we search for the first real tear of love. We are a Faustian age determined to meet the Lord or the Devil before we are done, and the ineluctable ore of the authentic is our only key to the lock.

# PART TEN

# Hints to the Aesthetic of The Study

# One Literary Critique

## Up the Family Tree

The book was the event of the season. Not, of course, as a huge best seller, or inspirative of awe or celebration – no suggestion in publishing ranks that Princess Margaret was doing her memoirs – this was more like the fraternity initiation of the year. A medium plump, very rich, and very late Freshman, bastard son of a founding family, was actually going to submit himself to an all-out hazing, and against all the advice of his furious family, furious to the point of biting their white icy lips (accustomed for years to no kisses but the most perverted!). One kissed the devil indeed, but no member of the family submitted to a hazing conducted by yahoos and muckers with names like Richler, Fuller, Bermel, Puso, Beam, or Predictable Hicks – what a squalid yard of humpty-beaters and hard-ons. No fate could prove undeserved for Norman said the family in thin quivering late-night hisses. (For like every family which had kissed the tail of Satan's cat – say it on! – the hole! they spoke after midnight in voices like snakes and beetles and rats, hiss and titter, prick and sip.)

Yet the hazing, while brutal – coarse, intimate, snide, grasping, groping, slavering, slippery of reference, crude and naturally tasteless – was still on the side of charity if one compared the collective hooligan verdict to the earlier fulminations of the Inner Clan, yes, even if one had to face up in the reviews to such models of pig-sweat in aspic as the following: 'a career expressed as a matchless 360-page ejaculation' – Bermel, *New Leader*; 'The Egghead (I use the slightly dated term to lock Podhoretz in the persona he is so much at pains to discard)' – Raphael, *Sunday Times*; or Richler in the *Nation* – 'deplorably inbred . . . intolerable show-biz characteristics . . . grubby details . . . careerist adventures . . .' Yes, if pig-sweat, envy, anaemic sniper-hots, and spite stand out in many a review as obviously as a Watusi shaking his feathers, the fact remains that the public reception of *Making It* with all its suffocating air, since no review was ready to call the book evil, or label it great, was nonetheless – all horrors of hazing in evidence – was nonetheless kinder to Podhoretz than the first kiss of the clan.

If *Time* and *Newsweek* (career men naked in their own homeland) hated *Making It*, why the *Times* was there on daily and Sunday to give it a good respectful word, so was *Life* – grace of the guest reviewer, John Aldridge. The *Nation*, the *New Republic*, and the *New Leader* spit (no doubt to show the very balls of integrity in daring to attack the editor of *Commentary* – who was there to say they were a veritable gang of undescended testes?). The *Wall Street Journal* was mild and Waspy, avuncular in its gentle sting – so was *Sat Review*. The *Progressive* came in swell. *Book World* was bitchy and bright, the *National Observer* offered objective notes of praise, the *Washington Post* was vitriolic: 'egregiously phony', it said. The *Plain Dealer* called *Making It* fine reading. *Women's Wear* picked up its skirts and wooed with both feet in the air – 'fascinating and appalling' her verdict. If the *Los Angeles Times* was whipping the heads off flowers, 'sophomoric, humorless . . . constricted, shallow, contrived,' the *St. Louis Post-Dispatch* called *Making It* 'a book, and a good one at that.' Even the *New York Review* was left at the end of its long tether in bemusement: 'We may surely hope that successive volumes will permit us to follow the career of this remarkable, still young man. And they may be more mellow; sometimes as we age, memory softens our perceptions of reality. In *Podhoretz Returns* and *Son of Podhoretz*, the monster may turn out to have a heart of gold.' That was about the way it went. No, then it went worse! All the reviews were surpassed at the end by a draft horse of a review in *Esquire*, ten thousand words and more by the fiction editor of the *Saturday Evening Post*, America's own Rust Hills, a prodigious manynostriled neigh of a report, here fair, there foul, often full of hay, designed to prove that Podhoretz was an enemy of the novel and Hills its first defender, the whole dominated by a series of nine caricatures of Podhoretz by David Levine so connotative of old nightmares in the pages of *Der Stürmer* that one was finally obliged to wonder what occult species was Levine and how ammonia-odored was the hand which held the drawing pen of such a crotch – did the fingers stink of crap or bat or pigeon's piss?

Well, no vast joy to be found in such reviews for the writer of a book, particularly when it is his first full-length book, and was written with high ambition and in the teeth of the shaking ague of confronting the highest literary standards all packed like blood oaths and covenants in himself – one does not acquire love for literature at the feet of the Trillings and pay no price in outsize awe. Nor does one practice as an honorable literary critic for years, doing one's best by one's lights to cut the morbid anomalous tissues of ill-conceived work without starting in terror out of sleep at night at the thought of what groans and revenge are buried in the tombs of expired books – now shakes the hand of the critic-surgeon as he lifts his scalpel to – all ghouls awake – to sharpen his own creative pen for the expression of his own creative urge. Predictably, there will be New Leader Bermel to macerate the urge into 'a matchless 360-page ejaculation.' Yes, the bad breath of the future assassins can be smelled already in the wood.

Besides, the presumptive book writer is an editor, and of a magazine which if not universally well liked, is perforce everywhere respected. (Which is to say five hundred writers and spokesmen will never forgive the editor of *Commentary* for his tastes, choice, correspondence with them, exercise upon their manuscripts, or just general rejection of work, ideas, unholy passions.) The editor is a man known for the solidity of his culture, the centrality of his position in the Liberal Establishment, the depth of his sanity, sense of proportion, and independence equal to no less than the feat of resurrecting a half-dead magazine; known as well for the power of his friends, the warmth of his own personality, the charm and brilliance of his wife, the lusty wit of his children, the modesty of his own self-effacing humor – the man is endowed; wisdom and worldliness are his; he has one foot in the stirrup of all good spirit, and the other is on the kneadables of the sweet ass of success. Who but a very brave or foolhardy man would in such a fine condition sit down to write any kind of book at all, who but a demented scribbler would choose to dive through the plate-glass window of his own splendid showcase in order to allow an outside mob of hungry assassins, literary gung-hos, and assorted rhinoceri to come roaring in to examine the goods with knives, feet, and teeth. Who but a quivering whip-full of masochism would dare to end such a book with the following two paragraphs, one wretched for all of its moderate length, the other as indigestible in its brevity as a plastic peanut?

> For several years I toyed with the idea of doing a book about Mailer that would focus on the problem of success, but in the end I decided that if I ever did work up the nerve to write about this problem, I would have to do it without hiding behind him or anyone else. Such a book, I thought, ought properly to be written in the first person, and it ought in itself to constitute a frank Mailer-like bid for literary distinction, fame, and money all in one package: otherwise it would be unable to extricate itself from the locks of the dirty little secret. Writing a book like that would be a very dangerous thing to do, but someday, I told myself, I would like to try doing it.

> I just have.

Yes, who could commit such a blunder of self-assertion, self-exposure, and self-denigration but my old dear great and good friend Norman Podhoretz who brings the mind of a major engineer to elucidating the character of complex literary structures but would seek – for such is the innocence of his good heart – to climb the Matterhorn on ice skates.

Now, of course, if Podhoretz's great and good friend Norman Mailer is to say this now, it is with wisdom which comes after the fact. For *Making It*, taken on its own terms, while never possessing a chance for real fame and real literary distinction (because of flaws to be yet discussed) is, seen by a dispassionate eye in manuscript or galleys (and no eye so dispassionate as the look of an old friend) is, *Making It* is, yes, a perfectly decent and honorable book very well written for much of its length, and respectably written for the rest except for ten or twelve isolated phrases, sentences, and paragraphs so unhappy, ill-chosen, and aggressively flatulent that no reviewer with an eye to the cruel could fail to notice, and not even the kindest of critics would be ready to defend them. Small wonder that these miserable phrases crop up again and again in every review, thereby giving the impression of a graceless, malodorous, repulsive, offensive, self-aggrandizing work when in fact the overall style is – but for these scattered criminal lapses – a style restrained, cool, self-observant, modest, dispassionate, analytical and gifted with an agreeable variety of aperçus on matters such as status, class, privilege, and clan. It is an interesting book, very interesting in its way, and offensive not at all except for its precise lack of offensive threat, which irritates in about the way of any defenseless presentation. In summation its only thundering demerit is that it is not a great or major book, and it may be that nothing less was required for a literary venture by an Establishmentarian critic and editor in Podhoretz's position than to produce just such an overpowering work. Probably nothing less would have done. Instead, Podhoretz by a major effort of will against what must have been the rock-quaking tremors of his own heart, produced a minor work of much excellence, seriously flawed. It was doubtless an expensive book for the author – so much energy spent, so little fame; so much talk, so little good will; but great authors like great generals can be tempered by disastrous campaigns as well as victories; it is – wipe the old metaphor – exactly when an author begins to think not of the blow he will take to his own liver, but the shot he will deliver to the target, that he is ready for the real literary game. Podhoretz is sufficiently sturdy, honorable, clear-eyed and talented to deserve the most thorough going-over, provided the attack is clean and offers the dignity of a dispassionate critique, which of course is exactly what he did not get. So, let us go to look at *Making It*. Mysteries will confront us there, not the least being the exceptional hostility it aroused in the Establishment while the book was still in manuscript.

The Establishment has properties, not the first of which we might suggest, is its absolute detestation of any effort to classify or examine it. (Anyone doubting this last assertion is invited to recollect the outsize wrath of Jackie Kennedy at the modest inside anecdote or two of her life as told by William Manchester, a wrath whose overflow was to cost Bobby Kennedy ten points of national popularity in a year of great decision.) No, any sociologist who would attempt to analyze the Establishment would do well to begin with the assumption that it is a temple, and its members are priests and priestesses, its center of worship is a hole, a Holy of Holies, its altar undescribed. Power which is not material must dwell in mystery, its most refined codes are best left uncodified – indeed a scholar might hope to demonstrate that the Talmud could not be committed to writing until hope for the restoration of the Second Temple was lost; the intimations of such power are rarely verbal – they exist in the curve of an inhibiting eyebrow, the form of a line.

## TWO

Podhoretz, schooled as a critic at Columbia, then Cambridge, was to arrive in the pages of *Partisan Review* with a full set of preoccupations provided by Trilling, but his critical stance – solid, doughty, authoritative, and hugely egalitarian (this last to be explained in an instant) – owed much to Leavis. Leavis was, of course, a veritable monster of taste, a rabid hanging judge of the smallest literary pretense – he derived from a line who would behead the king if the king did not meet measure – but Leavis was nonetheless egalitarian: he obviously believed that the critic performing a thorough total work of scholarship, steeped in the traditions, lore, style, moral filaments, and spiritual saps of the work he considered, alert in every quiver of his senses to the nuances and defections in the fabrication of beauty or power within the poem or prose before him was, if ready to make that total effort, a work of art in himself, a living critical creation face to face on equal terms with the work; so, hugely egalitarian.

Such total commitment can come only to an Englishman or a Bolshevik, come to them, that is, and remain. A young American can be steeped in such a discipline for a time, but there is no ballast in America for joining ideological priesthoods which offer no uniform. The only invisible American priesthood with ballast is the Establishment, and that is never ideological.

But Podhoretz was ideological, ideological three times over, by Jewish Theological Seminary, Columbia, and Cambridge; any well-equipped mind passing through three such separate disciplines could hardly be expected to encounter future experience free of any set, liberated from preconceived stance.

To the contrary, Podhoretz like many an intellectual before him could use as his *cogito, ergo sum*: I cerebrate, therefore I see. No matter how sensuous the nature, sense experience in such men tends to become the raw material for the processing mills of new hypotheses. That is a superb way to do a kind of literary criticism, perhaps the best kind of literary criticism for which we can ask, since a work confronted by no critical hypothesis can merely be admired or despised, and thereby open questions of taste, but it cannot improve our mind by allowing us to consider simultaneously the work in question and the critical approach. We may enjoy the style of a critic who eschews hypotheses or we may reject it, but we cannot imbibe that deepening of context (that awareness of the work, the critic, and the world containing them both) which is the marrow, indeed the very satisfaction of reading a critic who lays siege to a work with his hypothesis. The value of a hypothesis is that it can be tested, tested by the evidence of the work, tested by how much it fails to explain, tested indeed by the fact that it will remain as the best working hypothesis until a better one comes along to replace it. That is the most energetic kind of criticism, probably the most creative, and when done well, certainly the most stimulating to any reader who like Podhoretz lives in large part for the joy of cerebration. And Podhoretz is probably as good as any critic in America at this kind of writing. Indeed his only serious competitors might be Steven Marcus, John Aldridge, and Irving Howe.

Emphasis has been put upon this kind of criticism because it is so quintessentially part of Podhoretz's way of writing, even his way of life (since *Commentary* more than any other comparable magazine attracts articles with hypotheses) that when he came to do a book it was natural for him to begin with a hypothesis. The only difficulty was that he was now dealing not with an aesthetic artifact but with himself, not with literary criticism but a species of narrative fiction which is much too quickly thought of as autobiography. That word is appropriate to use if we are considering what a man writes about himself after his career is more or less done — he is at that point less than he used to be, his possibilities are generally consumed, his externals are known, and he is probably in fair shape to see himself as others do, since his old age itself testifies to the fact that he could live with his legend much in the same manner others responded to it. By this logic, autobiography is obviously biography done by oneself, auto-biography — someone else could presumably have been as intimate with the material. But when a man writes a book about himself in the beginning or middle of his career, then his work if at all penetrating is not a biography so much as a special category of fiction, precisely because his choices for future career are still open, his possibilities remain numerous, his conflicts are as alive as his enemies, his feelings as tender as his friends, and his sense of himself is as confused, complex, even bewildered as his sense of others. So he must make that same creative abstraction from life that a novelist makes when he cooks up or conceives a character out of one or more people he partially comprehends. The character if successful comes to life, the character engages a series of events which he shapes, and fails to affect, and from his strivings the reader may draw some comprehension, even a hypothesis. If the reader is a critic he will measure the character by this hypothesis, and we as other readers will be aided in comprehending the character (let us say it is Leopold Bloom) by the critic's hypothesis, that is until a better or more fashionable hypothesis comes along.

Yet the character must first be created. If a man is writing an accurate narrative about himself with real people and their real names, and this narrative arises because some imbalance or pressure or obsession or theme persists in dogging the man through all his aesthetic or moral nature until he sets to work, then he is willy-nilly caught in the act of writing into the unexplored depths of himself, into those regions which are as mysterious to him as other people. So he can comprehend, no, rather he can deal with himself as a literary object, as the name of that man who goes through his pages, only by creating himself as a *literary* character, fully so much as any literary character in a work of undisputed fiction. That is the only way a man in mid-career can begin to approach the mysterious forces which push him to write about these matters in the first place. He is off on a search. Like Theseus he will encounter his experience on the point of his walking stick; here, his pencil. To the extent that he succeeds in making a viable character who will attract literary experience metaphorically equal to the ambiguous experience in his life which impelled him to write in the first place, so will he be able to set out on that reconnaissance into the potentialities of an overpowering work.

But it is no easy job! To the complications and hazards of creating an interesting imaginary character are now added all the real dangers of mentioning real names and real events, with all the uncharted – since works of this sort are rare – all the uncharted and spooky perils of uprooting a hundred established complacencies in a hundred real places. The perils may be no worse in reality than offending a few thousand readers by a novel, but one doesn't know, there is a point of no return implicit in such an endeavor. Moreover, one is presenting a personality which will be better or worse than one's own, and people will react to it with the same love or hate they reserve for characters in a novel. One is advancing and endangering one's career by writing the book, the book is now a protagonist in the progress of one's success. Self-interest naturally slants a word here, literary honesty bends it back there. One does not know whether to tell the little lie or shrive oneself. An overload of choices descends on the brain of any ambitious man engaged in giving a contentious portrait of himself. Yet that is not even the worst of the difficulty. The real woe is that one is forced to examine oneself existentially, perceive oneself in the act of perceiving (but worse, far worse – through the act of perceiving, perceive a Self who may manage to represent the separate warring selves by a Style). It is necessary to voyage through the fluorescent undergound of the mind, that arena of self-consciousness where Sartre grappled with the *pour-soi* and the *en-soi*; intellections consuming flesh, consciousness the negation, yes, the very consumption of being. One is digesting one's own gut in such an endeavor.

# THREE

This ulcerous claim check now stamped, let us take up an existential hypothesis: *the* Norman Podhoretz in the book called *Making It* is, we will assume, a fictional character, an editor of a well-established magazine, well regarded, etc., etc. He is not yet forty, not by several years, but is tormented out of the sum of all vectors of ambition, caution, desire, fear, honesty, horror, honor, courage, and personal dissatisfaction to write a book about himself. Why? He thinks (that is, the character thinks) it is because he has a major thesis, something new to say about success and the ambiguities of its state, the relation of others to his success. He has even a thesis in his mind as he begins his book. We can quote from it:

> For taking my career as seriously as I do in this book, I will no doubt be accused of self-inflation and therefore of tasteless-ness. So be it. There was a time when to talk candidly about sex was similarly regarded as tasteless – a betrayal of what D. H. Lawrence once called 'the dirty little secret'. For many of us, of course, this is no longer the case. But judging by the embarrassment that a frank discussion of one's feelings about one's own success, or lack of it, invariably causes in polite company today, ambition (itself a species of lustful hunger) seems to be replacing erotic lust as the prime dirty little secret of the well-educated American soul. And since the natural accompaniments of a dirty little secret are superstition, hypocrisy, and cant, it is no cause for wonder that the theme of success rarely appears in our discourse unattended by at least one of these three dismal Furies inherited from Vic-torian sex.

The thesis stated in the first pages, *Making It* then goes on to describe the adventures of the protagonist. If they are in the main intellectual, they are nonetheless novelistically interest-ing, because they partake of the most basic American tale of them all – the young man from the provinces who moves to the city and succeeds. If the trip is here only from Brooklyn to

Manhattan, the character, quite aware of his universality, remarks, 'One of the longest journeys in the world is . . . from certain neighborhoods in Brooklyn to certain parts of Manhattan. I have made that journey. . . .' Since the real, as opposed to the fictional Norman Podhoretz, is a man with a firm sense of neighborhood, he is doubtless quite aware that he has in life moved from Brownsville to West End Avenue – which is not quite up to the claims of his fictional journey; a look at his neighbors would remind him that the literal physical move is not an empire superior to jumping from Brownsville to Eastern Parkway. But this is the trouble with the book from its root. As a fictional character, Podhoretz would already be absurd – a pompous man, full of snobbery, but so blind to any true version of snobbery that he would palm off his address as superior. In life, as the real Norman Pod, he is of course speaking metaphorically. Those 'certain parts of Manhattan' are not where he lives, but rather are enclaves of society where he, unlike his West End Avenue neighbors, has entrée. But he has already, unwittingly, like a novice novelist driven a separation between the real life of the detail and its inadequate fictional manifest. His book is thus from the beginning of its first chapter two books, one for readers who know him, another for readers who don't. And the reason is simple. The art of the novel begins with a primary demand: the novel must be in its fashion literal. Since it is not life, its life depends on the scrupulous accumulation of its details. In order to make a fine phrase, Podhoretz took a shortcut with the novelist facts. That need not be fatal in criticism, but such shortcuts, particularly at the onset, distort the magnetic field of the novel. Already, to readers who do not know him, he is living in a fancier neighborhood than in fact he inhabits; to readers who do, there is a gap between the literal Normal Podhoretz and the less conscientious fictional presence in *Making It*. That is perhaps the last and most difficult demand of this special category of fiction – that one must succeed in creating a character who is not fatally separate to those who know the author and those who don't.

Nonetheless, after this opening flaw, the character Norman Podhoretz in this special-category-of-fiction continues well. We move through early chapters which have the quiet authority of good art, engaging near-tender accounts of his relation with a snobbish teacher exacerbated into 'depths of loving despair' by the contrast between his intellectual promise and his red satin Cherokees Social Athletic Club jacket. We continue, through glimpses of his family, the implicit psychic mechanics – *tastefully* delineated – of his separation from family and neighborhood, his immersion, or partial immersion, in the subtle intoxications of life at Columbia (which is to say, the life of the spirit with most intuitions plucked from the grinds of the subway wheel) and good analysis follows of the play between open and concealed scholastic ambition.

I can see now, of course, that I must have caused the 'snobs' as much pain as they caused me. If I envied them their social composure and their apparent self-assurance, they must have envied me my freedom from the scruples which governed them and the consequent torrent of unhindered energy on which I was able to call. These scruples had nothing to do with morality; they had to do only with the code of manners governing ambitiousness which seemed to bind everyone at Columbia but me. It was a code which forbade one to work too hard or to make any effort to impress a professor or to display the slightest concern over grades. Since most of the 'snobs' in question were serious students, however, the code hemmed them in, and since most of them were also ridden with ambition – quite as much, I think, as I – it forced them into secret transgressions, made them feel guilty, hypocritical and ashamed. Yet I, a flagrantly open violator, instead of being punished, was being rewarded; I would probably even wind up, a 'snob' once bitterly remarked to one of my friends, with Columbia's choicest prize, a Kellett Fellowship: 'Can you imagine *him* at Oxford or Cambridge? Sammy Glick in the *Agora*!'

Which is, in fact, exactly where he succeeds in making it, to Clare College at Cambridge. Descriptions follow – spare, comprehensive, artfully discerning of the differences in education, ambitions, class, and country. Much good analysis, modest but pertinent, so convincing in the modesty that even such large remarks as the following

> I became a Leavisian – not, perhaps, the most ardent of his young epigoni at Cambridge, but, in all truth, the others being a singularly dreary and humorless lot, the most adept . . .

are acceptable precisely because one has come to trust this detachment through the quiet severity of observation which accompanies less agreeable insights.

The novel continues well. It is an odd novel up to here, dry, almost ascetic in its details, so sparse indeed in its sensuous descriptions and so leisurely in its analyses of the protagonist's changing intellectual and social stances that one admires the courage of the novelist – he dares to push his novel in the direction of the informed sociological essay where in order to nail analysis one may even smuggle in a piece or two of carefully protected personal material. The difference, and it keens our interest, is that the tone here while close to abstract in its impersonality is never self-protective. On the contrary, it reveals, then reveals more, never guards the subject.

This tone continues for more than half the book. Podhoretz returns to America, has his first entrée into circles which are written about as if they were the equivalent to him of Versailles for Saint-Simon. There is here a gulf he does not sight completely to the bottom: there is probably a hint too little irony now in his portrait of the young literary man, extraordinarily self-made, who is feeling such vast admiration for purlieus like *Commentary* and *Partisan Review*. There was indeed a time when *Partisan Review* was the kind of duchess who could cut off more than one literary head with a stroke – it inspired fear in young authors which must have been equal to the terror of French courtiers when they first beheld the palace, but there are still differences to recognize – Philip Rahv with his mouth around a hot pastrami was not quite the novelistic equal of Louis XIV showing his knee (and if William Phillips looked like Richelieu, Richelieu was indubitably wearing his tweed jacket).

It is at about this point that the novel begins, most subtly, to falter. It has been economical, provocative, near to austere, and all readable as a narrative up to this point. If we still know little about the hero, what we do know has that tone of authority which suggests hope of a small classic in the making – we accept the hero, believe him, want to know more of him, and of his adventures. In fact, the novel continues thus good for a while – fine chapters in much the same tone carry Podhoretz through five months in New York while waiting to go into the Army, then a stretch of two years in uniform. We have at this point traversed more than half the book, and there has been but one false note – a faint hint of the stricken in describing that literary establishment of New York which Podhoretz calls The Family. There is despite all criticisms well-taken, all ongoing analyses of The Family's desires and prejudices, obsessiveness, cannibalism (of reputations, not flesh – so far as we know) there is still a hint of the one weakness which is fatal to the young novelist: flattery. The mouthful of pastrami in Rahv's mouth persists in being too small. So do all the other mouthfuls. Wherever there is a personal or professional reference to Dwight MacDonald, Mary McCarthy, F. W. Dupee, John Thompson, Lionel Trilling, Diana Trilling, Paul Goodman, Robert Warshow, Elliot Cohen, Hannah Arendt, Daniel Bell, Nathan Glazer, Irving Kristol, Steven Marcus, Rahv, Phillips, Jason Epstein, Plimpton, Mailer, Bob Silvers, Lillian Hellman, Sherry Abel, W. H. Auden, Leslie Fiedler, Alfred Kazin, Dan Moynihan, Richard Goodwin, Harold Rosenberg, Isaac Rosenfeld, Arthur Schlesinger, Delmore Schwartz, Susan Sontag, Murray Kempton, Mike Harrington, and a number of others (the index to the book suggests we are reading Main Currents of New York Thought) you may be certain the reference is invariably as attractive as the sort of remark one makes when giving a reference to a Foundation for a friend. The kindness palls. It is the one mark of timorousness in the book. Only Saul Bellow and Jimmy Baldwin are shown in any kind of unattractive light and then with care and preparation of context in order to strike no undue foul blow.

It is deadening. It saps the book, downs it not because we have been expecting an exposé of everything low, dirty, and vulpine in the New York literary establishment, nothing in the tone of the book has offered such an expectation, no, the disappointment is organic to the needs of the undeclared novel. We are being offered a restrained muted limited account of a young provincial, a local example when all is said of Julien Sorel who is making his way up in the world. Not, of course, through a judicious mixture of sexual and social audacity, but by an uncomfortable sometimes self-torturing accommodation between the power of his ambition versus his irrepressible demands for an integrity to his expression. What more fascinating event, after half a book's worth of the best preparation, to see our latter-day Sorel make it and lose it and make it again with The Family, that peculiar colony, aviary, and zoo of the most ferocious, idealistic, egotistic, narcissistic, cultivated, constipated, brilliant, sensitive, brutally insensitive, half-productive, and near-sterile gang of the best and worst literary court ever to rise right out of the immigrant ranks of a nation. The comic and tragic aspects of that gang take one's novelistic breath away – the satiric possibilities put it back.

Well, of course one may say this is merely Mailer's view of The Family, not Podhoretz's – the author of *Making It* is entitled to his own view. No argument. It is just that his view cannot be developed in any direction. What is one to make of an Establishment which is so kind and splendid in its personnel? The sum of the individual portraits Podhoretz offers of this Quality Lucifer Lit Biz Clan is so full of sugar that one cannot begin to comprehend his abstract portrait which in contrast presents The Family (in general terms so vague one cannot perceive a single figure in the fog) as no better than any other Establishment. Truth, if The Family adds up to the kind sum of the specific charitable parts Podhoretz gives them, then the demand on him is to write a novel of insuperable difficulty (or even a sociological analysis of the same difficulty) which is to say – an Establishment composed only of the kindest folk: into their ranks enters an ambitious Provincial – what a novel!

No, one does not recognize Plimpton, and Silvers, and Rahv, and Epstein, and Phillips, no, nor Mailer, and Trilling, and Sontag, and Kristol. It is not that they are despicable all, nor mean, nor even full of rapine – it is that they are complex, as unendurably complex as our century is complex, and so *Making It* ceases to be a novel just so soon as its protagonist enters the climax of his narrative; we are projected right out of that rare aesthetic vineyard where autobiography dares to become that special and most daring category of fiction which is its inner necessity, and instead we are now forced to jog along on the washboard road of a memoir. Characters come in and out, observations are made, names file through, Podhoretz suffers, becomes an editor, thrives, we do not care – the novel has disappeared – the interplay between ambitious perception and society which has been the source of its value now gives ground to the aesthetic perplexity of the author who must flounder in the now novelistically alienated remains of his hypothesis – that success is the dirty little secret. Now he has no novel on which to work it, only sketchy anecdotes, abortive essays, isolated insights, and note of the drone – repetitions. A fine even potentially marvelous book gets lost in a muddle, finally finishes itself and is done. No joy in closing the back cover.

One must wonder. How does a man who has the simple guts to begin such a work in the first place lack the nerve to hump it through to the end? And the answer, if one is to ignore such natural motives as impatience, overwork, or general anxiety, is that the instinctive fear of a sophisticated writer at attempting to explore an Establishment is even greater than the well-established fear of the ridicule he will know at presenting himself as a character. A writer as forceful and well geared for exposition as Podhoretz reveals personal anxiety in his work not through deterioration of style so much as through deterioration of intellectual connection. By the time the book is done, the hypothesis of the 'dirty little secret' and the dwindled novel have disengaged from one another, separated, we assume, by dread of invading the theme, dread of exploring the intimate play of hero and Establishment. It is no mean matter to put oneself in a real novel, but it is a nightmare to take on a true Establishment, such a nightmare that we need not wonder why Podhoretz deserted his possibilities as thoroughly as if Stendhal had presented the family of Mademoiselle de la Mole as charming.

All right, then. Let us make a quick pass at the little mystery of why Establishments provoke such vitiating fear in writers as seasoned and dedicated as Podhoretz.

## FOUR

The clue is to be found in the reception of *Making It* when the work was still in manuscript. The author's anticipatory dread was not ill-founded. Despite a $25,000 contract, the first publisher, Roger Straus, rejected the book. Publishers do not reject books in such cases because they dislike them, but because they find the long-term consequences disagreeable; the verdict of just about everyone in the Establishment who then read the manuscript was negative. Which is to say scandalized, shocked, livid, revolted, appalled, disheartened, and enraged – an excessive reaction for a book which is finally at worst a not altogether compelling memoir. What could cause so intense a reaction, so intense an overreaction?

Establishments are like banks – they release value only if it will return with interest. Podhoretz was obviously giving something away. But what was it? This is the question which remains unanswered, and has in fact attached itself to the book so closely that the reviews which followed publication were more a function of the Establishment's initial antipathy than a pristine reaction to the book itself – indeed, many reviewers expecting a work where names would be named and reputations outraged were therefore splenetic with disappointment; others, feeling the book had been killed before it saw print, were solicitous of its merits.

One could of course give the author credit for having unearthed a thesis (that success had replaced sex as the dirty little secret), a thesis sufficiently explosive to dynamite many buried Establishment furies, but the thesis while meandering in and out of the book was not organically attached to the work; rather it appeared now and again like an added starter. One could dislike the thesis and still not mind the book. Besides the thesis itself, if novel, did not seem quite accurate. It was the sort of illumination which could apply for particular Establishmentarians, but was utterly inapplicable for others: indeed, The

Family as a whole gave off the aura of all Establishments – they were obviously as interested in success as any other bank. While they did not talk a great deal about it, and were reasonably dialectical about money – resenting Mary McCarthy's modest haul, while not at all unimpressed with the size of Capote's – it would have been not impossible to defend the opposite thesis that the need for success in one's métier was so taken for granted in these salons that there was no necessity any longer to talk about it.

It is better to chase our little mystery by remembering that Establishmentarians please their peers when they write works of symbolic intensity like Trilling's *The Middle of the Journey* or memoirs of unsurpassed sweetness like Kazin's *A Walker in the City*. They charm when they write trivia about New York with agreeable tone – as in Jason Epstein's fillip for the *New York Review*, they impress when their theses are rich in reference, comprehensive, original, and assertive, as are Harold Rosenberg's on New York art. Indeed, Establishment writers displease The Family only when they fail to present themselves as critical, intelligent, superior, and *in their cool*. The only piece remotely comparable in its innocent assault on the total temper of The Family was Diana Trilling's account of going to hear Allen Ginsberg read his poetry at Columbia. That is writing with such simplicity of affect and directness of response that it may live longer in literature than anything else by the lady – it has the tone of enduring literature – yet it was loathed in its time, loathed one may suspect for the defenselessness of its approach since Diana presented herself not as a distinguished critic (which had hitherto been implicit in her style) but as a bewildered faculty wife: the Establishment reacted as if they were being thereby sucked down into a mucker's muck.

So we may as well assume that the lightnings Podhoretz aroused came not because he was revealing the dirty little secret of others, but because he was exposing himself, and this act of self-exposure was received by The Family as a treason – one simply did not go around explaining any member of the clan. To do that was to weaken all.

It is easier to comprehend if we think of the Rockefellers or the Fords, or any other gathering of wealth. Exposure by any member of such families is odious to the rest because their power – to themselves at least, as a reflection perhaps of their guilt – rests on a fragile base. Let us assume the same for our own Establishement. They came into being almost by accident for they began as left-wing militants interested in literary criticism, and attracted more or less nonradical literary scholars and critics of special stature like Trilling and Kazin and Dupee only when their politics – isolated from both the Left Wing and support of the American war effort in the forties – became so encysted, that it was politics literally of the cyst, it nourished nothing without, it was a politics without price, danger, or engagement – except for such extremes of pacifism and anarchism as provided by Lowell and MacDonald. Later, in the postwar forties and early fifties, the Establishment was to run – we may hope unwittingly – as sweepers for the CIA. From some unclassifiable brand of Trotskyism, The Family had pushed on to more or less total anti-communism as a political position. It was a position of much empty power and much empty polemic, a literary equivalent of congressional junkets, and left the Establishment on sterile ground after twenty-five years of existence – no major critic and no major novelist had developed from their influence. Of course, Trilling was quite possibly a major critic if one did not pose him too comparatively against Wilson, but he would have been that kind of major critic without The Family, he was a literary man first. Others – MacDonald, Kazin and Howe most notably – were first-rate but they did not grow over the years, no schools of criticism developed from them, no seminal ideas, no ferments – just an endless series of brilliant but tactical papers. They were guardians rather than catalysts. Any number of members of The Family were enormously impressive in fragments, and Harold Rosenberg and Meyer Schapiro and Clement Greenberg all in quite separate ways had large even commanding effect on the New York art world, Paul Goodman was later to have as much to do with the formation of the New Left as any writer about, but in the fifties he was alienated from The Family – their only poet, Robert Lowell, was a poet without them and before them; their house novelist, Mary McCarthy, had fled to Newport in search of real stimulation,

and their big novelist, Saul Bellow, who was later to justify his
reputation, had been advanced to glory in the mid-fifties on the
basis of *Augie March* which was absurd in its parts, unconvinc-
ing along its whole, overcooked, overstuffed, unfelt, heaps of
literary bull-bull. If the Establishment had been wiped out in
the late fifties by a bomb, the verdict of history might have
found them destructive of more talent than they liberated.

It was in the sixties that much began to happen. Kennedy's
desire to weld the separate establishments of America's cultural, social, and political life together, gave The Family opportunity to inherit new power – the vertices of their plots were
found now in parties at Plimpton's and forums with Schlesinger – after the birth of the *New York Review* the Establishment had real power which ran to many a connection in many a
corner of America. If the war in Vietnam had forced the
Establishment to sever its connection with the Administration,
there was still Bobby Kennedy to serve as Pope of Avignon and
an extraordinary mixture of positions everywhere from just left
of the ADA to just right of Black Power there to be taken on
every issue of the minute. This Establishment once ogreish,
fearful, arid, poisonous, proud, insular, scholarly, slavish,
tyrannical, and cold, was now hip, slick, mercurial, Camp,
evasive, treacherous, Pop, militant, and chic – yet wonder of
wonders it was the same Establishment, same not because the
people were similar (so many had gone, so many were new) but
because its essential presentation of itself to the world was the
same. The Establishment had begun as a put-on, and it was
continuing as a put-on.

Let us quote three times quickly from Jacob Brackman's
article on 'The Put-On' in the *New Yorker*, June 24, 1967.

Irony is unsuccessful when misunderstood. But the put-on,
*inherently*, cannot be understood.

Not holding any real position (the put-on) is itself invulner-
able to attack.

He (the put-on artist) doesn't deal in isolated little tricks;
rather, he has developed a pervasive style of relating to others

that perpetually casts what he says into doubt. The put-on is an *open-end* form. That is to say it is rarely climaxed by having the 'truth' set straight – when a truth, indeed, exists. 'Straight' discussion, when one of the participants is putting the others on, is soon subverted and eventually sabotaged by uncertainty. His intentions, and his opinions remain cloudy.

Who can fail to recognize what a superb description this is of the Early Establishment and the Late. The love of ambiguity in the early Establishment, the endless theses so intricately structured in the syntax of their own jargon that parodies of the old *Partisan Review* style used to deliver insights, willy-nilly, as good as the original; indeed how better than by the logic of the put-on to explain the extraordinary scholarly apparatus of the old articles which produced theses so arcane and intimately rubbed with sorcerer's garlic that no one can remember a single one of the theses today. But they were not to be remembered – the articles, the magazines, the Establishment itself existed in a way of life which would generate a kind of power and position for itself without necessity for a product which might be consumed and criticized. The old *Partisan Review* used to sit on coffee tables like a magic object, not to be examined, certainly not to be enjoyed, but to be received, an emanation.

The new Establishment, neater, niftier, swift, puts working drawings of Molotov cocktails on the cover of the *New York Review of Books* – the put-on is merely more timely. Is it revolution they are advocating with the drawing, no, it is news. Is that really news? No, but it is an attitude. What's an attitude? That's for you to define, but why are you upset by the drawing? So the new Establishment is ultra-Left, yet not very left. They will talk of going to Hanoi to sit in cafés to be bombed, but they do not sign income tax protests against the war nor are they ready to put their names to a number of causes which could land them in jail. They are indifferent to power, they are resourceful at gathering it. In fact, they have no attitude to power, goes the put-on, why do you? Where the old Establishment was often supercilious about literary values, beating every writer to death with the standard of Henry James until the moment came when the critic would say, 'I can't bear Henry James, can you?' so the new Establishment is supercilious about power, success, and money. Success is not its dirty little secret, but its ball of mercury. Do not trap the mercury, it would say – my powers of locomotion depend on its ability to keep me moving – I am a dead man once I stop!

That is the anxiety of all Establishments. Stripped of all British wickedness, their talents they believe are revealed as second-rate, they are but flowers pressed in a book. So they will play the shell game, do the dance of the veils, adore the put-on, elevate Camp, praise Pop, rush to install plastic in fashions, and avoid like demons and witches confrontation upon a point.

Can that be why *Making It* was so abominable to them? Because Podhoretz was blind to the defenses of the put-on and had the idiocy or the suicidal strength to move to the center of the stage, open his box, exhibit his tricks? If mercury is your god, then self-exposure is like sand, like sand up your ass, like bogging the armies of your friends in swamps of sand – it was with all the fury of a military betrayal that the Establishment turned on Podhoretz.

Yes. For indeed this Establishment began some thirty or thirty-five years ago when a few timid intellectuals fierce in the power of their minds took a set of uncompromising attitudes on literary standards, and discovered to their surprise that more than a few in America – that bowl of the great undefined soup – listened to them as authorities, followed them as though they might be high priests with an ear to the murmur in the void.

It had begun as a put-on. No one knew as much as they claimed to know, no one could have passed through the galaxies of experience they were ready to judge, authority was a mask they assumed as the bravest assertion of their life (the ills and the terrors of the ghetto still clinging to some of their toes) and the triumph of the assertion was in the continuing life of their put-on, their life became a put-on where a stand would never be taken, for by a stand might be judged and the mask stripped; no, they galloped and growled and huffed and puffed (nimble all the while) and stayed alive as comedians of the highest order, and were followed as their Establishment developed into another, by further newer younger practitioners of the put-on, young literary executives who would not be caught dead making a remark with their back to the wall or the ball of their foot off the ball of mercury, there was even a vaster anxiety to keep the put-on alive in this younger Establishment, for it was less well educated than the old, less seasoned, less tempered, the young were inheritors of power they had not gained by withstanding a siege. So they were somewhat appalled by their power and utterly aghast at the forces which confronted them across the gulf of America.

## FIVE

Of course, we are a severed land. We have grown too fast and never consumed our wastes. They bloat our gut, stupefy our mind, and wash the art of communication from Right Wing to Left with the St. Vitus Dance of the put-on. If the Left Establishment, now conscience of America, sits in terror before the muscle and body of that Right Wing which gained America with its fists (and its money), rest assured the Right Wing sits in its own terror before judgment, listening like Lennie to any George's speech about the rabbits, floundering in its own vast rotting cabbage of sentimental mortgages, poisoned fertilizer, ideological dustbowls, and put-ons so monumental you cannot shovel them away. The Kingfish of the put-on speaks:

> 'Sad but steady – always convinced of his cause – he stuck it out,' Mr. Johnson said of President Abraham Lincoln. 'Sad but steady, so will we,' he added.
> – *New York Times*, February 13, 1968

It's the tragedy of us all that the consummate moment of affirmation, outright confession, or sheer renunciation now appears out of a mirror whose first question becomes: Is this noble act the work of a whack or the superbest put-on of all?

# Three Prefaces

## Deaths for the Ladies

*Deaths for the Ladies* was written through a period of fifteen months, a time when my life was going through many changes including a short stretch in jail, the abrupt dissolution of one marriage, and the beginning of another. It was also a period in which I wrote very little, and so these poems and short turns of prose were my lonely connection to the one act which gave a sense of self-importance. I was drinking heavily in that period, not explosively as I had at times in the past, but steadily – most nights I went to bed with all the vats loaded, and for the first time, my hangovers in the morning were steeped in dread. Before, I had never felt weak without a drink – now I did. I felt heavy, hard on the first steps of middle age, and in need of a drink. So it occurred to me it was finally not altogether impossible that I become an alcoholic. And I hated the thought of that. My pride and my idea of myself were subject to slaughter in such a vice.

Well, this preface is not to recount the story of those years and how I may have come out of them; no, we are here to give a crack of light to the little book which follows. I used to wake up in those days, as I have just remarked, with a drear hangover, and the beasts who were ready to root in my entrails were prowling outside. To a man living on his edge, New York is a jungle, and such mornings were full of taboo. It was often directly important whether the right or left hand was crossed with water first.

One modest reality used to save such hours from dipping too quickly into too early a drink. It was the scraps of paper I would find in my jacket. There were fragments of poems on the scraps, not poems really, little groupings of lines, little crossed communications from some wistful outpost of my mind where, deep in drink the night before, it had seemed condign to record the unrecoverable nuance of a moment, a funny moment, a mean moment, a moment when something I might always have taken for granted was turned for an instant on its head.

Some of those curious little communications which came riding in on the night through an electrolyte of deep booze were fairly good, many were silly, the best were often indecipherable. Which would feel close to tragic. Almost always the sensation of writing a good poem in the dark of early morning was followed in the daylight by the knowledge I had gone so deep I could not find my eyes. My handwriting had temporarily disintegrated in the passion of putting down a few words. Somebody had obviously been down in the rapture of the depths.

It was not so very funny. In the absence of a greater faith, a professional keeps himself in shape by remaining true to his professionalism. Amateurs write when they are drunk. For a serious writer to do that is equivalent to a professional football player throwing imaginary passes in traffic when he is bombed, and smashing his body into parked cars on the mistaken impression that he is taking out the linebacker. Such a professional football player will feel like crying in the morning when he discovers his ribs are broken.

I would feel like crying too. My pride, my substance, my capital, were to be found in my clarity of mind or – since my mind is never so very clear – let us say found in the professional cool with which the brain was able to contend with the temptations and opportunities each leap of intuition offered. It was criminal to take these leaps like an amateur, steeped in drink, wasteful, wanton. To be hearing the inspirations of the angel when one is kissing the flames is a condition so implicit with agony that it took eighteen centuries of Christendom before Kierkegaard could come back alive with the knowledge that such moments not only existed but indeed were the characteristic way modern man found a knowledge of his soul – which is to say he found it by the act of perceiving that he was most certainly losing it.

I would go to work, however, on my scraps of paper. They were all I had for work. I would rewrite them carefully, printing in longhand and ink, and I would spend hours whenever there was time going over these little poems, these sharp dry crisp little instants, some of them no more and hopefully no less possessed of meaning than the little crack or clatter of an

autumn leaf underfoot. Something of the wistfulness in the fall
of the wind was in those poems for me. And since I wasn't doing
anything else very well in those days. I worked the poems over
every chance I had. Sometimes a working day would go by, and
I might put a space between two lines or remove a word. Maybe
I was mending. As the sense of work grew a little clearer and the
hangover receded, there was a happiness working mornings on
*Deaths for the Ladies* which I had not felt for years. I loved
*Deaths for the Ladies*, not because it was a big book – I knew my
gifts as a poet were determined to be small – but because I was
in love with its modesty. The modesty of *Deaths for the Ladies*
was saving me. Out of the bonfire I seemed to have made of my
life, these few embers were to be saved and set – not every last
part of one's memories would have to be consumed. Besides, I
wanted to give pleasure. It seemed to me that *Deaths for the
Ladies* would give more simple pleasure than any book I had
ever written, it was pure, it was modest, it was sad, and it was
funny – it was so very modest – how could one not like it? And
it had even one innovation to offer poets – so I thought. There
was no music or prosody or command or rush of language in the
book, no power, not much meter, not at all, much of it was
poetry only by the arbitrary insistence of the short line, but
*Deaths for the Ladies* was something else, I thought – it was a
movie in words. I set it with the greatest care. Every line was
placed on the page by me. The spaces were chosen with much
deliberation, the repetitions of phrases were like images in a
film. The music of the poem as a whole – if it had any – was like
the montage of a film. I felt that all of *Deaths for the Ladies* made
up one poem, not at all a great poem, never in any way, but still
a most modern poem about a man loose in our city, for one
cannot talk of New York without saying *our* city, there, majestic, choking in its own passions, New York, the true capital of
the twentieth century. And *Deaths for the Ladies* was like a small
sea breeze running through some of those electronic canyons
where a myriad of fine moments were forever dying in the
iridescence of foam.

Of course, if you fall in love with a book, you may be certain it
will drown, suffocate, or expire all alone on an untended bed.
*Deaths for the Ladies* came out in modest edition and sank

without a sound. It was only reviewed three or four places, and the one good review it received (the Sunday *New York Times*) was six months late. Poets, for the most part, resented it. Why should they not? I had dabbled in that life for which they were willing, if they were good enough, to starve and to lose love. They had studied their craft, I had just skipped about in it. They were dedicated to poetry. I was dedicated to climbing out of the hole I had dug for myself, and poetry was offering the first rung. Therefore, poets ignored the book, which was a pity, for a good poet might have done something with my little innovation, my movie in words.

But to end on a note less altruistic to the interests of art, let us look at one review. I had had secret hopes, I now confess, that *Deaths for the Ladies* would be a vast success at the bar of poetry. The hopes got bounced. Here is the review in *Time*, March 30, 1962:

> *Ever*
> *see*
> *a drunk*
> *come on*
> *daring*
> *I mean*
> *drunk*
> *like*
> *daring*
> *was a*
> *sloppy*
> *entrechat?*
> *Mr M*
> *comes on*
> *with fourbucks*
> *of poems*
> *about sex*
> *not love*
> *that run*
> *down*
> *like this*
> *only*
> *not*
> *lined up*

> *neat.*
> *Having less*
> *than*
> *fourbucks*
> *fun*
> *a reader*
> *counted*
> *the words*
> *and concluded*
> *Mr M*
> *is making up*
> *for his*
> *first book*
> *which had*
> *too many.*
> *You*
> *didn't*
> *score*
> *this*
> *time*
> *M*
> *a*
> *n*
> *.*
>
> *But hell you know that.*

In a fury of incalculable pains, a poem was written in reply, sent to *Time* magazine's column of letters, and printed there.

### POEM TO THE BOOK REVIEW AT *TIME*

> *You will keep hiring*
> *picadors from the back row*
> *and pic the bull back*
> *far back along his spine*
> *You will pass a wine*
> *poisoned on the vine*
> *You will saw the horns off*
> *and murmur*
> *The bulls are*
> *ah, the bulls are not*
> *what once they were*

> *Before the corrida is over*
> *    there will be Russians in the plaza*
> *Swine some of you will say*
> *What did we wrong?*
> *and go forth to kiss the conquero.*

Now, on the comfortable flank of this reminiscence, I think I may have been fortunate to get so paltry a reception on *Deaths for the Ladies*. For if I had been treated well, I might have kept floating in a still little pond, and drowned my sorrow for myself in endless wine and scraps of paper and folios of further poems. Instead, the review in *Time* put iron into my heart again, and rage, and the feeling that the enemy was more alive than ever, and dirtier in the alley, and so one had to mend, and put on the armor, and go to war, go out to war again, and try to hew huge strokes with the only broadsword God ever gave you, a glimpse of something like Almighty prose.

## The Saint and the Psychopath

Many years ago I wished to write a book called *The Saint and the Psychopath* and in time that book swelled to such proportions in my mind that I thought of a magnum opus to bear the monumental name: *A Psychology of the Orgy*. Ah, my *Psychology of the Orgy* reduced itself to the dimensions of an essay. 'The White Negro' came out of these titles and ambitions and those years of immersion in marijuana. Other years and other titles went by – I thought from time to time of *The Hip and the Square*, or *After the White Negro*, and with more time forgot all of the titles and thought of other things. I came to use the words existential and existentialism rather than Hip. Hip, I knew, would end in a box on Madison Avenue.

I, in turn, did my work. I thought, however, that many of my writings were excursions into existentialism. Now, the title comes back. It is a good fit – *The Saint and the Psychopath*. Because these are writings on two themes, violence and the mystical, writings about what is criminal and what is religious, and the root of my perception all those years ago (after marijuana first stole into the keep of my psyche and began to lower the bridges one by one) was that the saint and the psychopath were united to one another, and different from the mass of men. They were closer to existence. They shared a sense of the present so powerful that memory, caution, precedent, tradition, commonplace, project, and future enterprise were nerveless before the sense of the present in their mind and body. In their most incandescent states, they existed for their next breath, and so were indistinguishable from one another; saint and psychopath – a murderer in the moment of his murder could feel a sense of beauty and perfection as complete as the transport of the saint. (And indeed this was the root of the paradox which had driven Kierkegaard near to mad for he had the courage to see that his criminal impulses were also his most religious.)

It will be noticed that the titles to each part of this collection are not modest. 'The Psychology of the Psychopath' – it calls for a massive work. And 'The Existentialism of Death' – certainly that is a ten-volume study. But the tomes do not exist, not even the theory. To the knowledge of this author, Robert Lindner (quoted in 'The White Negro') is the only psychologist or psychoanalyst to make an imaginative pass at the first problem, and no major existentialist, not Sartre, nor Heidegger, nor Nietzsche, nor even Dostoyevsky, has advanced an inquiry into the possible existence of existential states within death (which is to say: states of dramatic purposeful change) in the dying and in one's condition after death. So the titles are novel, and the ideas arrived to the author in the purest psychopathic form – a way to tell you that they came in some degree out of that precise naïveté of the psychopath which assumes his experience is so pure in its lightning and consequent thunder that no one, not no one, has ever had an intimation before. The psychopath is insulated from history – how can he not be? He assumes in the intensity of his moment that all history is his lungs and loins, breath and sex, all is contained in that mysterious sensuous dread quite ready to disclose itself whenever we adventure nearest to life. So the titles. And an excuse for the presumption. There are worse crimes than presumption. Without it, more than one interesting action would never have begun.

## The End of Obscenity '

The book in your hand is a quiet and essentially modest account of a legal revolution led by a few determined and extraordinary publishers. When I think of Barney Rosset and Walter Minton, I am reminded on the instant of Civil War generals: Sherman and Grant race to the fore. They are men who are determined to take a hill even if it takes all summer and chews up half their resources. It was thus Minton's and Rosset's great good fortune to have one of Lee's Lieutenants for their legal counsel, a Light Horse Harry named Charles Rembar, and the purpose of this foreword is not to take up the arguments of the book, but rather to relieve its modesty with an account of the author. Like Rembar, Light Horse Harry was a great cavalryman, and his strategy and tactics were bold, luminous, witty, and exceptionally well balanced, but men endowed with the combative graces do not often write about themselves. So I will repair the lack of personal memoir and give you an introduction not to the work (which stands agreeably by itself) but to the author.

He is my cousin, Mr. Charles Rembar, the son of my mother's oldest sister, and he is the closest to an older brother I will ever come. Since he is eight years older than me (although I fear he does not look it) he was very much an older brother all through my childhood, and I worshipped him (with enormous fund of love and envy) because he was a hero. He was one of the few people I've ever known who had a happy look on his face when he came to bat in the late innings with men on base, his side behind, and the need for a homer prominent in everyone's head. Indeed he had his smile because it was slightly better than even money he was going to hit that homer. In fact, he would. This is not hyperbole. If I saw him in a hundred baseball games, there must have been fifty late inning spots of exactly the sort I describe: he probably hit thirty-six homers out of fifty. In fact, we usually didn't believe it if the ball didn't rocket over the center fielder's head. Often as not, Cy Rembar's homers would land in the tennis court at the end of our playing field, for that after all was the place where he would pull out all the winning sets from all the tennis players who were more trained than he, more devoted, more fanatical, and less humorous. Ditto for football. Ditto for getting the best-looking girls. Because of Cy Rembar, I used to believe in Jack Armstrong.

Those were Depression years. Much gloom abounded in everyone, but he was the bright spot. He was the only figure I encountered in my childhood who seemed to believe it was more natural to win than lose, and that life was therefore to be enjoyed rather than decried.

Since then, he's gotten a little older, not a great deal so far as I can see, and it's a shock to realize I'm as tall as he is today and weigh – I do not brag of this – thirty pounds more. But he's still the one man in all the world whose good opinion is gold to me, because Rembar is not only a winner, but a man with a subtle moral force. While he was never religious, probably never will be, and so far as I know evolved no elaborate set of ethics other than a profound respect for the law which served to house the architecture of his ability to reason, that particular ability in him precisely to reason has become a force which approaches the power of a mighty muscle, for in close tactical argument and debate on any subject improvised at the drop of a coin, he is doubtless one of the world's best and most brilliant quick reasoners. Which is to say he can be as bad as a boil if he beats you in a tactical brush on your favorite theme. But I have been led astray by Rembar's annoying power to reason. I was speaking of his moral force. It comes, I suppose, from a reliance on taste, a sort of implicit sense that manners, if they are excellent enough, can serve as a substitute for metaphysics. (Doubtless they so serve because exquisite manners call upon that reservoir of natural grace and animal philosophy which existentialists like myself are always trying to chart.) No matter how, he's a modest moral force in any room in which he finds himself because he's a clean man, and looks for clean issues to complex problems, and does it with good will. Consider what a recommendation is this when the man has been my lawyer for twenty years and charges solid fees. But it is true. He looks for moral issues in his activities. And still plays baseball. And still might take a girl away from me if he chose to. Although I hope the odds have closed.

And I take pleasure in this book by him because I had a little to do with the commencement of his interest in these problems, yes, back years ago with *The Deer Park*, and years before, we used to argue (since it was a matter of direct moment to me) about the defense of serious works of literature which were on the face of their language or situation obscene, and I used to fulminate against those thumbscrews of the law which required the defense to engage respectable witnesses who had then all but to perjure themselves in order to swear that the particular erotic work was moral and aroused them not at all. I would cry out, 'Why can't a novel just once be defended as erotic and valuable as well?' and Rembar would give me a short lecture, most clearly presented, about the subtle if sometimes retarded relation of the law to reality, and how perhaps the time was coming.

Well, it has come. A war has been won. Writers like myself can now in America write about any subject; if it is sexual, and we are explicit, no matter, the American writer has his freedom. Rembar has done as much as any lawyer alive to forge that freedom in several most historic cases. We can all congratulate ourselves.

He is, however, as I would remind you, a moral man, and so I was pleased to see as I read through these pages that he is troubled just a hint by the liberties won, just indeed as I am troubled. For back of the ogres of censorship and the comedies of community hypocrisy, there still rests the last defense of the censor, a sophisticated argument which might urge that sex is a mystery and men explore it and detail it and define it and examine it and eventually disembowel it of privacy at their peril. It is the argument of tradition against the power of reason. Rembar – we will repeat – personifies the positive attractions of the life of reason, but he is sufficiently instinctive as a gent to waste no time congratulating himself on heroic victories. Like the noblest (one revenges oneself on an older brother by drowning him in superlatives) yes, like the noblest of Lee's Lieutenants, he wonders privately and with concern if his cause is altogether just. So, too, do I. It is my cause as well. And like many another American writer, about to embark on a literary trip through some of the aesthetic territory Rembar's cases have given sanction to enter, I brood too about undue exposure of the mystery, and console myself with the second argument – that the inroads of science and industry, advertising, bad art,

industry, and commerce, also invade the mysteries of existence.
And thus the poet must be there as well to trim the lamp and
anoint that numbing of the flesh which serves the technician's
electrodes and probes. The novelist may help to sink the ship of
sex before all is done, but it might be even worse without a
literary exploration or two. For next to the mystery is the
disease. It is the disease of the twentieth century, that ill so
ubiquitously spawned by the anomalies of reason and the
maceration of instinct, all the promiscuous pills of all of that
labyrinthine and technological vat. So when I question the
value of the inquiry I now have real freedom to make, I lave the
edge of my doubt with the certainty that some one of us artists
must manage to be there to arrest the doctor when he also
marches into the door of the mystery. Because the doctor takes
flashbulbs into the womb, whereas we – if we are good
enough – will take the herbs of some of the good words and
balm the helpless exposure of the girl with aromatics and spice.
Perhaps life continues on a certain irreducible minimum of art.
Without that, no life. That is the *modus operandi* of the advocate
whose opinions and deeds you are now ready to encounter.
Welcome to the writing racket, Cousin Cy.

## An Imaginary Interview

INTERVIEWER: Well, here I am again.

MAILER: Nobody has seen you since *Cannibals and Christians*.

INTERVIEWER: If you want to know the truth, I'm a little annoyed about that. You feel you can call me when you want me, and then need never invite me back for a cup of coffee in between.

MAILER: I want you to learn about social life. It is built entirely on the instrumentalities we offer each other.

INTERVIEWER: Then today it seems I'm of use to you.

MAILER: On occasion, you are of use to me.

INTERVIEWER: Yes, really, you bet. Today! Why didn't you get another interviewer? Someone with a name?

MAILER: Well, you always manage to get my remarks right.

INTERVIEWER: You can also filter and select your questions.

MAILER: Leave me my pride. I am not afraid of questions. A man who can't answer questions shouldn't run for President.

INTERVIEWER: Are you really still running?

MAILER: Only for President of the literary world.

INTERVIEWER: Well, even there you've got a way to go. There's opposition, Mr. Mailer, considerable opposition.

MAILER: Still, I think I'm the best candidate around. It's a modest remark, believe me, because the best isn't necessarily that good. At any rate, I'm prepared to wait for office.

INTERVIEWER: You think you're better than Burroughs or Nabokov or Malamud?

MAILER: They have very large talents, but their nose is not on the presidency. I concentrate more than they do on that.

INTERVIEWER: What about Bellow and Algren?

MAILER: They are capital fellows. But no one from Chicago can ever become chief executive of the literary world. The East would be in insurrection.

INTERVIEWER: What about William Styron?

MAILER: He's the only Southern writer I know who's the living embodiment of the New York Yankees. I suspect the Establishment would be hopelessly lonely without him, for then they would not have much else but me. And I derive from the Brooklyn Dodgers.

INTERVIEWER: You don't think Styron is a marvelous writer?

MAILER: He has a very fragrant if slight redolent breath; but so far as I know, a dangerous idea has never infiltrated his brain. His mind is happy as a virgin oyster. Oysters taste wonderful if you like them, but they stir no foundations.

INTERVIEWER: Whereas you, sir, are a foundation shaker?

MAILER: I do my humble best.

INTERVIEWER: There are some – I am one of them – who would say that the foundation manages to shake you up considerably more than you shake it. That photograph of you, for example, on the back of your new book, with a black eye as big as a fist on your face – well, you may think it's funny, but there's low appeal concealed in it. What you are really saying is, 'Don't get too mad at me! I'm just America's No. 1 literary clown.'

MAILER: I didn't see it that way, or I wouldn't have used such a picture. No, I was trying to perform a public service. You see, people go around all the time saying, 'That Norman Mailer – I'd like to see him get punched in the nose.' Well, it's no good for Americans to walk around with so much anger bottled up. Most charitably, I was trying to relieve them.

INTERVIEWER: Or were you trying to relieve the anger a lot more Americans are going to feel for paying $4.95 for your novel *Why Are We in Vietnam?* when it's hardly two hundred pages long and has nothing to do with Vietnam?

MAILER: Do we have to rush into a discussion of my book so quickly?

INTERVIEWER: I would expect you to prefer not to talk about it too much.

MAILER: You dislike it?

INTERVIEWER: I think it's dreadful. It's the most cooked-up phony piece of I don't know what. I hated it.

MAILER: Maybe I shouldn't have called you for an interview. We're a considerable distance apart, and I was hoping I might find you in the middle. You see, there are times when I read *Why Are We in Vietnam?* and it displeases me too, but there are other times when I decide it's one of the ten funniest books written since *Huckleberry Finn.*

INTERVIEWER: You are suffering from prepublication schizophrenia with accompanying megalomania on the manic side of the moon.

MAILER: Not the first author to be so afflicted. Look, I don't know what to say of this book. Sometimes I think it's the best two hundred pages I've yet done, the most American, certainly the two hundred pages least alienated from genius.

INTERVIEWER: You are daring to say you are a genius?

MAILER: Be careful. This is one of the ways I get my terrible reputation. I didn't say I was a genius, I rather said in effect that the positive half of my prepublication schizophrenia looked now and again upon this new novel with the sentiment that my prose was here less alienated from genius than in my other works.

INTERVIEWER: What does the negative side of this schizophrenia have to say?

MAILER: That the book was written to fulfill a contract.

INTERVIEWER: You sit there and say you wrote this book to

fulfill a contract? Your cynicism would make hardened politicians walk the plank.

MAILER: I wrote the book to fulfill a contract. What's so exceptional about that? My expenses are, to me, huge. I write to make a living. That does not obligatorily inhibit the work from rising above itself. I did *An American Dream* in installments because I was in debt and had to make a small fortune in a hurry. That didn't make it a bad book. I think it's my best book. I confess I still believe sentence for sentence *An American Dream* is one of the better-written books in the language.

INTERVIEWER: And *Vietnam*, which was written in . . . ?

MAILER: Four months.

INTERVIEWER: . . . is thereby twice as good?

MAILER: I started with a cynical motive which was first burned through and then burned out by the rush of the impulse. The pages came to me faster than any book since *The Naked and the Dead*.

INTERVIEWER: But you still have a divided mind on its merit?

MAILER: Some books come to you. As *The Naked and the Dead* came to me. They are bonuses, gifts. You do not have to kill some little part of your flesh to dredge them up. This is a fatal shade mystical, but it is almost as if you are serving as agent for a book which wants to get itself written. So the author never knows what to think of such books when he is done. His real fondness – since writing books is the closest men ever come to childbearing – is more for those books he delivered out of his own flesh, torn and deadened by the process, but able at least to use all art and craft, all accumulated lore. Whereas *Why Are We in Vietnam?* came through like a storm, writing itself – I enjoyed the work, I was full of energy when I was done, but the work was by the same token impersonal. So I do not know if I love the new novel or am indifferent to it.

INTERVIEWER: Let us go back to the idea that you were serving as an agent for a book which wanted to get written. What then is this book saying?

MAILER: I'm afraid it is saying that America enters the nightmare of its destiny like a demented giant in a half-cracked canoe, bleeding from wounds top and bottom, bellowing in bewilderment, drowning with radio transmitters on the hip and radar in his ear. He has a fearful disease, this giant.

INTERVIEWER: What is it?

MAILER: Greed. Vanity.

INTERVIEWER: What else?

MAILER: The Faustian necessity to amass all knowledge, to enslave nature.

INTERVIEWER: And what is the first vice of this giant who, in your words, symbolizes America, and has now become the metaphor *pro tem* of your new novel, *Why Are We in Vietnam?*, a work – at least I can get this in – about some Texans who go off on a hunting trip in Alaska. What is the first vice of this giant who symbolizes America?

MAILER: Arrogance. Half the people in this country think they are possessed of genius. It is no accident, you see, that I run for President of the literary world. (*Sighs.*) I wish you liked my book more. Then I could open up and tell you all sorts of interesting little things about it. But as it is . . . oh, well, (*the faintest strain of self-pity appears*) they say Beethoven talked to himself.

# A One-Act Play

## A Fragment from *Vietnam*

*(The staging is obviously free. As first performed in Provincetown in the summer of 1967 with Rip Torn playing D. J., Beverly Bentley as Hallie Lee Jethroe and Dan Durning as Dr. Rothenberg, it was effective to let D. J. walk up and down the main aisle and address the audience intimately while, on stage, Hallie Lee lay on a couch and Rothenberg sat behind her, each frozen in tableau during D. J.'s long opening speech.)*

D.J.: 'He's evil,' said Mrs. Jethroe (*D. J. points to Mrs. Jethroe – he will, within quotation marks, imitate her voice*), the mother of this extraordinary late adolescent (*D. J. points to himself*), the one who calls himself D. J., who is eighteen and sometimes appears to be twice eighteen (*wink*), or thirty-six. 'Why, he's evil. What am I going to do with D. J.? The boy needs to be spanked. I would just as soon spank a puma! He's evil,' said Mrs. Jethroe to her psychiatrist (*D. J. points to the psychiatrist*), who is a Jewish fellow, nothing other, working his ass off in Dallas, which means so to speak that he must spend eight to ten clammy periods of fifty minutes each listening to Dallas matrons complain about the sexual habits of their husbands, all ex-hot rodders, hunters, cattlemen, oil riggers, corporation gears, and insurance finks, zap! Well, like every one of these bastards (as Mrs. Jeth – call her Death-row Jethroe – might say when her breath is big! like the bottom of a burnt-out bourbon barrel) well, every one of these bastards has the sexual peculiarities of red-blooded men, which is to say that one of them can't come unless he's squinting down a gunsight, and the other won't produce unless his wife sticks a pistol up his ass – that man is of course a cop. If the psychiatrist wasn't such a fink and such a nice Jewish fellow type as to be working for the general good and wheel of society, and if he wasn't afraid of drilling a little career-and-cancer piss right into the heart of Texas, he would write this book about the ejaculatory jump habits of cops, big ass Southern redneck cops all bullwhipped and bullshitted up into putteez, son, they come more ways – I froth at the mouth, said the killer, but don't think it's spit. Well, what's to say, D. J.'s mother, Death-row Jethroe, is the prettiest little blond you ever saw (looks like a draw between young Katherine Anne Porter and young Clare Booth Luce, whew) all perfume snatchy poo, appears twenty-five, is actually forty-five, airs, humors, curl to her mouth, half Texas ass accent, half London wickedness, trill and thrill, she's been traveling around the world, Heartache House in Bombay and Freedom House in Bringthatpore, shit, she's been getting cunt-tickled and fucked by all the Class 1 Dongs in Paris and London, not to mention the upper dedicated pricks of Rome and Italy while her hus, big daddy Rusty Jethroe, is holding up the corporation end all over the world including Dallas, Big D, D. J.'s father, Big Daddy, old Rusty, has got the dynamite. He don't come, he explode, he's a geyser of love, hot piss, shit, corporation pus, hate and heart, baby, he blasts, he's Texas willpower, hey yay!

Yeah, D. J.'s father, the cream of corporation corporateness, Rutherford David Jethroe Jellicoe Jethroe, came back to Dallas after spending twelve years off and on moving around the world for Central Consolidated Chemical and Plastic, CCCP being what the boys called it till they found out the Red-ass Russians had their Communist Party initials CCCP, this was a terrible day in Texas the night they found out, so they changed the name, they called it Central Consolidated *Combined* Chemical and Plastic, the new coagulation of title now being CCCCP or as the team began to say, 4C and P, which is an unhappy conjunction since how much do you have to foresee before you got – well, they say people in the Corporate life shoot their urine straighter than a '03 Springfield, y'hear Rangoon? So back came Rusty after twelve big years in the foreign ass vineyards out where the reindeer run and the flying fishes try out their flying CIA fucks past Mandalay.

Back came Rusty to Dallas to head Pew Rapports – the filter with the purest porosity of purpose – and Rusty was a_ heroic-looking figure of a Texan, six feet one-half inch, 194, red-brown lean keen of color, eyes gray-green-yellow-brown which is approved executive moderate shit hue color for eyes if you want to study corporation norms, mores, and tempos of shift and success in massive organizational configurations, and since he was big exec, what do you think he look and talk like? Well Clara, go to the rear of the line, he look like a high-breed crossing between Dwight D. Eisenhower and Henry Cabot Lodge, what the buns do you think a corporation exec is going to look like if he got the time to make his face grow the way he want it to grow during all the fifties while he's overseas, I mean what face did he ever see more of than Dwight D., and Henry C. working his ax at the U.N., these corporation eggzex are full of will, man, they're strong as bulls these hide-ass Waspy mules with their silvy-rim specs, I mean they go direction they want to go, their hair too curly they go bald, their nose too long, they sniff it up, their lips too fat, forget it, we're talking about the wrong man, they tie that nice dry-oiled West Point ramrod to their back just like they're a tomato plant on a stick, I mean they grow into a bat's ass if it help our astronauts along. Rusty can zip that corporation fly working as executive, and/or director, and/or special adviser and/or consultant and/or trouble-shooter and/or organizer and/or associate of, and/or paid employee for the 4C and P, the CIA, the C of C, the FBI, the ADA, the ADA?, the Policemen's Benevolent Society, the John Birch, natch, the Dallas Citizens Council for Infighting and Inflicting Symphonic Music, the Benevolent Order of Oilwell Riggers Drillers and Roughnecks, the Warren Commission Boosters, the President's Thousand Dollar Club, the Gridiron Club, the UIA and 4A of D, that is the Underwriters, Insurance Agents and Actuarial Agents Association of America and Dallas, the RELM Cons – the Rotary, Elks, Lambs, Masons Consolidated for corporation studs who jes ain't got the time to spread out so they put it all in one dead fuck building – and the Republican Party, not to mention the Second Congregated Anglo Episcopal and Conjoint Presbyterian Clutch and Methodist Church of Maltby Avenue, Dallas (that's St. Martin's, you faggot!) and the Gourmet

Wine and Pate Plate and Fork Society. Forget the country clubs unless you like to read lists, the Dallas Elm and Tree Club, the Dallas Cowboy Turtle Creek Cheering and Chowder, TCU Boosters, SMU Boosters, Gala Ring and Ranch, Loretta Noodlehad's Country Club, take it from D.J., forget this shit. If Rusty was to run around all year, which he does, he still couldn't get his dick in every door for which he's got a card, you know, Diners Club, Carte Blanche, American Express, Budget Rent-A-Car, Rusty's a pig! he's a real pig, man! It was all that dried-out sun-baked smoked jerkin of meat his cowboy fore-ass bears used to eat, I mean, man, they used to use that hide for everything before they'd eat it, they'd swab out their mare's dock with it, wipe their own ass with it, pick up the pus from the corner of their eye, blow their nose, mop the piss off their boots, even use that dry old piece of meat to wrap around their skinny old dick for stuffing when they want to sodomize a real big cow, why they repair holes in their chaps with it, they used to have to beat it with a hoe handle before they could even cook it and fry it in axle grease. I mean, man, they were kind of tough. So, no wonder Rusty's a pig. His cells are filled with the biological inheritance and trait transmissions of his ancestors, all such rawhide, cactus hearts, eagle eggs, and coyote. Now, Rusty rolls that Château Lafite-Mouton-Rothschild around his liver-loving lips, and he can tell '49 from '53 from '59, all the while thinking of sixty and nine. He sings the song of the swine, D.J.'s daddy, nice fellow actually. Also forgot to mention he's an unlisted agent for Luce Publications, American Airlines Overseas Division, and the IIR – the Institute for International Research – shit!, Spy Heaven they ought to call it.

Does this idyll of family life whet your curiosity, flame your balls, or sour your spit? But hush you now. Think no longer of Rusty. The real stuff is turning on. Her princess-ship. Alice Hallie Lee Jethroe is speaking to her Doc, Clam Fink, the Texas Hebe, actually his name is Leonard Levin Fichte Rothenberg, pronounced by all big-mind Texans as Linnit Live'n Fixit Rottenbug.

HALLIE: Lionhard, will you jes take a fix on what D.J. has to say. It's enough to make a mother wipe up Aunt Jemima's puke. He's out of his mind. Poor sad little fellow.

HALLIE (*with maternal pride*): He read the Marquis de Sade at the age of fifteen.

ROTHENBERG: Alice Hallie Lee Jethroe, I saw Ranald at your request, he was recalcitrant, charming, gracious, anti-Semitic, morally anesthetized, and smoldering with presumptive violence, a host of incence, I mean incest fixes, murder configurations, suicide sets, disembowelment diagrams and diabolism designs, mandalas! Face into the eye of the real, Hallelujah, he's a humdinger of a latent homosexual highly over-heterosexual with onanistic narcissistic and sodomistic overtones, a task force of libidinal cross-hybrided vectors.

HALLIE: He has high-breed vectors all right, he's got the cunningest ancestry, in fact, cause we're on my mother's side from the Norloins.

ROTHENBERG: New Orleans?

HALLIE: Yis, from Norlins, the Norlins Frenchy Montesquious and the Bat Fartsmotherers. (*Seeing that Levin Fichte is living on her word, she just knocks over a bottle of one of his urine specimens, adieu albumin!*) Mon Doo Rottenbug, you're sure full of shit for a doctor, don't y'know there are no fine Southern families called Fartsmotherer? Lord knows we ain't that fucking stupid, why even British country stock wouldn't be called Fartsmotherer, maybe Assknocking, but not the other, you can't analyze me, Living Fichte, if you don't know things like that, oh, poo, I wish you was an Italianate Jew, all earthy and Levantine and suave and had a cunt-tickler of a moustache, instead of your clammy cold Lithuanian brow, what are you, a Talmud hokum? speak up, ass, I just wish you was good enough to kiss my sweet perfumed powdered old pooty-toot, hey Linnit? am I getting out my egressions now?

ROTHENBERG: I would not call them aggressions so much as identity crises.

HALLIE: Oh, poo, let me tell you about the Montesquious. Half-Portuguese, half-French, all that hot crazy blood packed one-quarter into me, for the other half of my mother was just straight Arkansas mule, the Mulies, why they the richest family in Arkansas then, hot out of Peezer, Arkansas, and they used rat paper for tar paper on the Chic Sale, that's how benighted was their latrine, Army folk of course, the MacArthurs used to kiss their ass. And my daddy, well he was just a lover of a husband to my ma, and he must have had a dick on him like a derrick, do I shock you, Dr. Jew?

ROTHENBERG: To my cornplasters.

HALLIE: Oh, Linnit, you'll be the death of me yet. Listen to this old hen cackle. Well, Daddy was Indian for sure, and he had a personal odor like hot rocks in the sun which is in me all mixed with the fine sauces of Franco-Portuguese Montesquiou rut – I mean you should smell my armpits, noxious to some, a knockout to others, I keep them perfumed of course, we want no barmaid's fatal scent on Hallie Jethroe, so I wash, Dr. Rothenberg, three times a day, I don't want nothing but a soupçon of my good sweet crazy full-blooded woman's scent on the breeze off my knees, just enough for to keep the breed alive, talk of high-breed vectors, they're all marshals, and bastards and cowboys, and one desperado, and one railroad tycoon, and one professor at Harvard, first Texas professor they ever had in Clamsville, which is what I call Harvard, Linnit tell me straight and clear what am I going to do with Ranald, he's insane, that boy, tell me, you Talmud hokum, you clammy Have-it grit, I suppose I now have to pony up my fifty dollars for the hour.

ROTHENBERG: Madam, you owe me eleven hundred and fifty.

HALLIE: You'll have to bust a nut to get it, Rottenbug.

ROTHENBERG: I'll torture you, I love torturing Gentile females. All that white buttermilk flesh. Yum, yum. Yum, yum, yum.

DJ: Hey, hey, they really talk that way? That little blond lady, Hallie-perfume and powder on the poo – she talk that way? And Rottenbug going yum yum yum – is he out of his fucking skull? Wait and see? Nobody's got any OK patience any more, just cannibals asking for chocolate on their stick. Wait and see? You know what they're doing. They're talking about Tex, Tex Hyde, Gottfried 'Texas' Hyde Junior, that's D.J.'s best friend, and know what, get that drop of cream off your jeans before you grow hair in your hand, this is the pitch, Tex is half-German and half-Indian on his father's side, Redskin and Nazi all in one paternal blood, and his mother, well, bless his mother, Tex Hyde's mother is jes old rawhide Texas ass family running back thru fifty-two shacks, right back to the Alamo where all old saddlesore real Texas ass families run back to, why lick the scab on LBJ's knee if one-tenth of all the Dallas ass families that go back to the Alamo was really there, they'd have all drowned in shit they were so congested and Santa Anna could have thrown his marijuana seed on the top and there'd be a forest of hemp now right in the heart of Texas.

Well, Tex Hyde, he's a mother fucker, sell you pot was grown on human shit, and he nothing but D.J.'s best friend. And they are terrible together. Listen to Halleloo. Her tone is full of hell right now, Line It With Hot Bugs is shifting in horror in his seat, cause Halleloo is talking in her bitchy boozy voice which means don't come near unless you can steer your prick like a whip and French tickler all in one, worm! women know which man has got the spring and who and which is the unfortunate dead ass, here is her words:

HALLIE: Tex Hyde is the son of an *undertaker*, I mean think of that, a Montesquiou Jellicoe Jethroe a-whopping around with a Kraut mortician's offspring, and all that bastard Indian Hyde blood in the background, firewater and dirty old engine oil, Indians unless they're descended from my daddy's line, and never you mind what it was, don' ask if it's Navajo, Apache, or any of those shit questions, you anthropologist manqué, you fuckless wonder listening to the sex'l habits of all us mule-ass Texans, ought to get your ears wiped out Dr. Fink Lenin Rodzianko whateva your name is, an Indian don't tell the secret of his name in a hurry to strangers like you, Clam Grits from Harvard Square, why, honey, that Tex Hyde don't have Eenyen blood like my daddy and my Rusty's daddy's daddy, no, it's just the sort of dirty vile polluted cesspool Eenyen blood like Mexican – you know just a touch of that Latin slicky shit in it, vicious as they come, and mated up, contemplez-vous, to fatty Bavarian oonshick and poonshick jawohl furor lemme kiss your dirty socks my leader, can you imagine? the filthiest of the Indians and the slimiest of red-hot sexy-ass Nazis intercoursing each other, mating and breeding to produce Tex Hyde who grows up in his daddy's big booming business which is stuffing corpses and doing God Knows what to their little old pithy bowels and their dropped stomachs and whatever else corpses got which must be plenty or why pay thousands of dollars for a funeral unless its a fumigation, hey Tonto? and that boy growing up there comes out like a malevolent orchid in a humus pile, or a black panther, that's what he is, black panther with all his black panther piss, I'm dreaming of him, Linnit, and so is my son, the black puma, he's got my son who's just as beautiful as George Hamilton and more clean-cut swearing by him, that puma and the panther, I think they took the vow of blood, cut their thumbs and ran 'em around the rim of some debutante's pussy, after the way these kids now live there ain't much left for them but to gang-fuck tastefully wouldn't you say, speak up, Linnit?

ROTHENBERG: Now. Hallie, I know you're not going to listen to me.

HALLIE: But I am, my dear. I full intend to, Linnit?

ROTHENBERG: Yes, milady.

HALLIE: Tell me I've been ladylike. I know I haven't. I know I've been outré and spouting great clouds of baloney from inner space, I mean you might think my language was the proper vocabulary for a roughneck or a driller, but I adore you, Linnit, cause you got a kind Jewish heart and I always

said when Hitler killed the Jews, half the kindness went out
of the world.

*(He begins to laugh. He laughs so hard he cannot reply for many a
second.)*

ROTHENBERG *(gasping)*: Maybe he shoulda killed the other half.

*(They spend an apocalyptic minute laughing together. When Hallie
cools, her voice is ice.)*

HALLIE: Heh, heh, heh, heh. Gallows humor, Linnit.

D.J.: My poor old Dad. He got all the burden of one man's
family. Yeah, what poor old Rusty has to brood about.
*(Transforms himself into Rusty)*. Yeah, the time is soon coming
when fornication will be professional athletics, and everybody will watch the national eliminations on TV. Will boys
like D.J. and Tex be in the finals with a couple of Playboy
bunnies or black-ass honeys? well, shit-and-sure, fifty
thousand major league fuckers will be clawing and cutting to
get in the big time to present their open flower-petal pussy, or
hand-hewn diamond tool and testicles in happy magnification by Color Vision RCA. Only thing holding this scheme
back is the problems of integration. What if the Spades run
away with the jewels? Not to mention all the wet pussy in
America. Think of that in color TV – all the purple majesty,
if they do, America'll really be looking for a white hope, huh.

Of course, I'll be having to watch. Oh, the ignominy. Just
stick my middle-age dick against the screen. Yeah, the
twentieth century is breaking up the ball game: (1) The
women are free. They bed down with too many to believe one
man can do the job. (2) The Niggers are free, and the dues
they got to be paid is no Texas virgin's delight. (3) The
Niggers and the women are tooling each other. (4) The
Yellow races are breaking loose. (5) Africa is breaking loose.
(6) The adolescents are breaking loose including my own
son. (7) The European nations hate America's guts. (8) The
products are no fucking good anymore. (9) Communism is a
system guaranteed to collect dues from all losers. (9a) More

losers than winners in the world. (9b) and out: communism is going to defeat capitalism, unless promptly destroyed. (10) a. Sexual intercourse is king. b. Jerk-off dances are the royal road to sexual intercourse. c. I am no great jerk-off dancer. d. I am thereby disqualified from playing King Fuck. (11) Therefore, I am fucked.

ROTHENBERG: Hallie, are you saying you've got to separate those boys?

HALLIE: I know, I know. But they're stuck to each other like ranch dogs. Hunting together, playing football together, holding hands while they ride, studying karate together, I bet they can't even get their rocks off unless they're put-putting in the same vaginal slime. I hope at least D.J. has got the taste and sentiment to be putting it in the young lady's vagina rather than going up her dirt track where old Tex Hyde belongs (after all those bodies he helped his fat growing rich daddy embalm). Kiss the lint from my navel, Linnit, a mother can't even be sure of that anymore, because, I even heard of a debutante knock-up case where the boy who had to accept the onus of parenthood was the one who had ad-dressed himself to the fore, his buddy's lawyer got him to admit that cardinal fact by the following examination, 'Would you, Son, be so filthy and so foul as to address yourself to a young lady's dirt track.' 'Of course I wouldn't go near her anus,' said this idiot called Son, 'do you think I'm a pervert?' 'Well, my client *is* a pervert,' said the lawyer, 'so you are the proud papa, the Brains rest,' end of case.

ROTHENBERG: Take the undertaker out of it, that's what dis-turbs your sense of peers and social compeers. A mortician is at a social disadvantage in stable structurification of society, but it's not to be calibrated on a final scale. If Tex Hyde were the son of a normal occupation father, for instance if Gott-fried Hyde Senior was straight corporation exec like Rusty.

HALLIE: No, no, no, Rottenbug, you're thinking like a tick again.

ROTHENBERG: Tell me why, pie.

HALLIE: Because Tex grew up an undertaker's son, fool! plunging his hands into dead people's vitals, picking up through his fingertips all sorts of black occult steamy little grimes of things, swamp music and black lightning and soundless thunder – purple wonders, it's like sleeping the night in a rotten old stump – who knows what song the maggots sing, and what aromatic intuitions inflame the brain. Herbs are the nerve to a fearsome underworld – listen, baby, I didn't get fucked by Aleister Crowley for nothing, those passes at the Black Masses . . . (*putting a gloved finger up to her dear chin*)

D.J.: She is incidentally now lying her ass off because she's too young to know Aleister Crowley, but she's like her son, D.J., she's got to brag, better believe it.

Well this has gone on long enough. Cause you ought to know who had produced this material. This has been D.J. presenting to you the private scene of his mother being psychoanalyzed by that clammy little fink, with occasional odd spotlights on his father, and if the illusion has been conveyed that my mother, D.J.'s own mother, talks the way you got it here, well, dear audience, you're sick in your own drool, because my mother is a Southern lady, she's as elegant as an oyster with powder on its ass, she don't talk that way, she just thinks that way. Do we understand each other now, son? You've had fun long enough. The serious shit soon starts. You're contending with a genius, D.J. is his name, only American alive who could outtalk Cassius Clay, that's lip, duck the blip, Orlando, it's right on your radar screen. Oueep, oueep!

## A Translation from Lorca
## by Susan and Norman Mailer

## Lament for Ignacio Sánchez Mejías

### THE WOUND AND THE DEATH

At five in the afternoon
It was five on the dot of the afternoon.
A boy brought the white sheet
*at five in the afternoon.*
A basket of lime all prepared
*at five in the afternoon.*
The rest was death and death alone
*at five in the afternoon.*

The wind carried away the cottonwool
*at five in the afternoon.*
And the oxide planted crystal and nickel
*at five in the afternoon.*
The dove and the leopard were fighting
*at five in the afternoon.*
And a thigh with a desolate horn
*at five in the afternoon.*
The bass-string was plucked
*at five in the afternoon.*
Arsenic in the bells and smoke
*at five in the afternoon.*
Gangs of silence in the corners
*at five in the afternoon.*
And the bull alone, his heart held high
*at five in the afternoon.*
While the sweat of snow was coming in
*at five in the afternoon.*
while the bullring was covered with iodine
*at five in the afternoon.*
death put eggs to the wound
*at five in the afternoon.*
*At five in the afternoon.*
At five on the dot of the afternoon.

A coffin on wheels is the bed
*at five in the afternoon.*
Bones and flutes sound in his ear
*at five in the afternoon.*
The bull moans at his forehead
*at five in the afternoon.*
The room is shuddering with agony
*at five in the afternoon.*
From a distance gangrene is coming
*at five in the afternoon.*
The horn of the lily in the young groin
*at five in the afternoon.*
Wounds burned like suns
*at five in the afternoon.*
and the people were breaking the windows
*at five in the afternoon.*
At five in the afternoon.
Oh what a brutal five o'clock
It was five on all the clocks!
It was five in the shade of the afternoon.

## THE SPILLED BLOOD

*I do not want to see it!*

*Tell the moon to come
for I do not want to see the blood
of Ignacio on the sand.*

*I do not want to see it!*

*The moon is full.
Horses of the quiet clouds
and the gray bullring of sleep
with willows on the barrera.*

*I do not want to see it!
for memories burn.
Go tell the jasmines
with their delicate white, that*

*I do not want to see it!*

*The cow of the old world was passing her sad tongue*
*over a snoutful of blood*
*spilled on the sand,*
*and the bulls of Guisando*
*near to death and near to stone*
*moaned like two centuries*
*sick of stamping the earth.*

*No.*

*I do not want to see it!*

*Up by the highest bleachers goes Ignacio*
*with his death on his shoulders.*
*He was looking for the dawn*
*and the dawn was not there.*
*He was looking for his fine profile.*
*and his sleep led him away.*
*He was looking for his beautiful body*
*and found his flowing blood.*
*Do not ask me to see it!*
*I do not want to feel the spurt*

*with less force each time;*
*this spurt of blood which illumines*
*the tiers of seats and pours*
*over the corduroy and leather*
*of that thirsty mob*
*who cries out for me to look!*
*Do not ask me to see it.*

*His eyes did not close*
*when he saw the horns near,*
*but the terrible mothers*
*raised their head.*
*And across all the ranches*
*was an air of secret voices*
*who cried out to celestial bulls,*
*herders of the pale fog.*
*There was not a prince in Seville*
*who could compare to him,*
*not a sword like his sword*

nor a heart so real.
Like a river of lions
was his marvelous strength
and like a torso of marble
his fine-drawn restraint.
The air of Andalusian Rome
gilded his head
his laugh was a spikenard
of salt, a gardenia of intelligence.
What a great bullfighter in the plaza!
What a mountaineer for the hills.
How deft with the thorns!
How hard with the spurs!
How tender with the dew!
What brilliance at the fiesta!
What magnificence with the banderillas of the dusk.

Now he sleeps without end.
Now the moss and the grass
open with sure fingers
the flower of his skull.
And his blood comes singing now
singing by marshes and meadows,

slipping past numb horns
rootless and uncertain in the mist
stumbling over a herd of hooves
like a long, dark sad tongue
making a mudhole of agony
near the Guadalquivir of the stars.
Oh white wall of Spain!
Oh black bull of sorrow!
Hard blood of Ignacio!
Nightingale of his veins!
No.
I do not want to see it!
For there is no chalice to contain it,
no Swallows to drink it,
no glitter of morning frost to freeze it
no songs, no floods of white lilies
no crystal to cover the silver
No.
I do not want to see it!

## THE BODY BEFORE US

*Stone is a forehead where dreams cry out*
*never to hold the curve of water nor the ice of cypress.*
*The stone is a back to transport time*
*with arbors of tears and ribbons and planets.*

*I have seen gray rain run into the waves*
*raising its tender riddled arms*
*so it will not be imprisoned by the overhanging stone*
*who displays his bulk but never mops the blood.*

*Because the stone receives seeds and shadows*
*skeletons of larks, wolves of darkness*
*but stone gives no sound, nor crystal nor fire,*
*only bullrings and bullrings and rings without walls.*

*Already Ignacio, Ignacio of the good family, lies on the stone.*
*It is over; what is happening? Contemplate his face:*
*death has covered it with pallid sulphur*
*and has made his head from a dark minotaur.*

*It is over. The rain pours in his mouth.*
*The air like a madman in flight quits his sunken chest,*
*and Love, stepped with tears of snow*
*warms itself on the ridge of the bull ranches.*

*What do they say? A silence full of stench.*
*We are here with a body before us. That clear form*
*once made of nightingales is fading*
*and we see it is full of bottomless pits.*

*Who wrinkles the shroud? What it says is not true!*
*Here no one sings, nor cries by the corners*
*nor pricks with the spurs, nor frightens the serpent:*
*Here I want nothing but full eyes*
*to see that body without hope of repose.*

*Here I want to see the men with harsh voices.*
*Those who tame horses and rivers:*
*the men whose bones can be heard, men who sing*
*with the full mouth of sun and flint.*

*Here I want to see them. In front of the stone.*
*In front of this body with its broken reins.*
*I want them to show me the exit*
*for this captain bound by death.*

*I want them to show me a lament like a river*
*possessed of sweet mists and deep shores;*
*let them take Ignacio's body and let it be lost*
*without having to hear the quick panting of the bulls.*

*Let him disappear in the round bullring of the moon*
*which pretends in its youth to be a motionless horn:*
*let him be lost in the night without a song of the fish*
*lost in white briars of frozen smoke.*

*I do not want them to cover his face with handkerchiefs*
*so that he will make himself comfortable with death.*
*Go away Ignacio: Do not feel the hot bellow of the bull.*
*Sleep, fly, rest: the sea also dies.*

## ABSENT SOUL

*Neither the bull nor the fig tree know you,*
*nor horses, nor ants in your house.*

*The boy does not know you, nor the afternoon*
*because you have died forever.*

*The spine of the rock does not know you,*
*nor the black satin in which you fall apart,*
*Your mute memory does not know you*
*because you have died forever.*

*Autumn will come with winding staircases*
*grape of the mist and a range of hills.*
*But nobody will want to see your eyes*
*because you have died forever.*

*Because you have died forever*
*like all the dead of the Earth,*
*like all the dead who are forgotten*
*in a heap of chewed-up dogs.*

*Nobody knows you. No. But I sing of you.*
*I sing to the future of your profile and your grace.*
*Of your famous wisdom, connoisseur.*
*Your appetite for death and the taste of its mouth.*
*The sadness I had in your brave mirth.*

*It will be a long time, if ever, before there is born*
*an Andalusian so bright and rich in adventure.*
*I sing of elegance with words which weep*
*and remember a sad breeze by the olive trees.*

# An Interview

## Excerpts from *Playboy*

PLAYBOY: How do you feel about being interviewed?

MAILER: I start with a general sense of woe.

PLAYBOY: Why?

MAILER: The interviewer serves up 1 percent of himself in the questions and the man who answers has to give back 99 percent. I feel exploited the moment I step into an interview. Of course, once in a while there is such a thing as a good interview; but even then, the tape recorder eats up half the mood. It isn't the interview I really dislike so much as the tape recorder.

PLAYBOY: What do you think is the best way to conduct an interview?

MAILER: There's no good way. It's just a matter of grinding through – that's all.

PLAYBOY: If you feel so negative about being interviewed, why did you consent to this one?

MAILER: About every two or three years, I feel I have to have a psychic housecleaning, go through my ideas in general, even brutal form – the brutal form of the interview – just to see about where I stand. Because most of the time, I spend my time thinking privately. Without this kind of psychic housecleaning. I might get too infatuated with some ideas. It's a way, I suppose, of exposing ideas that are weak. After that, you can either discard them or think about them a little harder.

PLAYBOY: As you talk about housecleaning your ideas – disregarding, changing or improving them – we're reminded of your sentence in *The Deer Park* about growth: 'There was that law of life, so cruel and so just, that one must grow or else pay more for remaining the same.' Yet you've been charged by many critics with dissipating the potential growth of a major talent in American fiction by wearing so many hats. They point out that there's Mailer the politician, who once seriously considered running for mayor of New York City: there's Mailer the journalist, who writes about the maladies in American life and about the political brutalities; there's Mailer the celebrity, who grabs headlines by booze brawls and other acts of public violence. How do you answer that criticism?

MAILER: Moving from one activity to another makes sense if you do it with a hint of wit or a touch of grace – which I don't say I've always done; far from it – but I think moving from one activity to another can give momentum. If you do it well, you can increase the energy you bring to the next piece of work. Growth, in some curious way, I expect, depends on being always in motion just a little bit, one way or another. Growth is not simply going forward; it's going forward until you have to make a delicate decision either to continue in a difficult situation or to retreat and look for another way to go forward. The pattern that this creates – no, pattern is a poor word – the line of the movement reveals the nature of form.

More to the point, I've been accused of having frittered many talents away, of having taken on too many activities, of having worked too self-consciously at being a celebrity, of having performed at the edges and, indeed, at the center of my own public legend. And, of course, like any criminal in the dock, I can sing a pretty tune; I can defend myself; I'm my own best lawyer; the day when I'm not will be a sad day. The defense I'll enter today depends on my favorite notion: that an expert, by definition, is opposed to growth. Why? Because an expert is a man who works forward in one direction until he reaches that point where he has to use all his energy to maintain his advance; he cannot allow himself to look in other directions.

PLAYBOY: Is all this related to *The Naked and the Dead* and the celebrity that followed in its wake?

MAILER: Yes. Being well known at twenty-five created a chain of legend for everything I did. If I left a party early, it wasn't because I might have been sleepy; it was because I had put down the party. Every little thing I did was exaggerated. Lo! There was a feedback that had little to do with me. It was as if – if you will – every one of my actions was tuned to an amplifier.

PLAYBOY: Is this what you meant when you once remarked that your success at twenty-five was 'like a lobotomy'?

MAILER: It cut me off from my past. I felt like someone who had been dropped onto Mars.

PLAYBOY: Did you dig your sudden fame?

MAILER: Of course I dug it. I had to dig it. I mean, to be brutally frank for all our swell *Playboy* readers out there: it enabled me to get girls I would not otherwise have gotten.

PLAYBOY: You make a distinction between the legendary Mailer in the spotlight whose acts were scrutinized and gossiped about and the Mailer who wanted to grow in his own sweet time. Could you contrast the two Mailers a bit more?

MAILER: Well, contrasting two Mailers might have value in a novel, but to talk about it would end up being tiresome. This is the point I want to make: I had some instinctive sense – right or wrong – that the best way to grow was not to write one novel after another but to move from activity to activity, a notion that began with Renaissance man; it's not my idea, after all. My personal celebrity was an obstacle to any natural ability to move quickly and easily. For years, it was a tremendous obstacle; and I ended up having a very dull, dogged personality that sought to wrestle with the legend, and that tried to say, 'Look, fellows, I'm really simple, honest, hardworking; I'm as close to Abe Lincoln as Arthur Miller is.'

The hoarseness of this confession is not to enlist sympathy but to prepare the ground for my boast: I learned how to accept and live with my legend. The legend becomes your friend, the beard, a front man, a pimp, a procurer of new situations. You live with a ghost who is more real to people than yourself; every single action you take with another person is part of a triangle. Every girl you talk to is not only in love with you or disappointed in you but also is in love with or hating your legend – who, incidentally, is more real to her than you. There are times, therefore, when you beef up your legend, perform some action to support it; times when you draw credit back from your legend, like cashing in the desire of somebody else to do something nice for you. Either way, you don't pretend – as I did for years – that the legend ain't there; it *is*.

PLAYBOY: One of your celebrated experiments with growth was your experience with drugs. You were on marijuana, Benzedrine, and sleeping pills for a few years and were addicted to Seconal. Later, you said that a man on drugs will pay for it by 'a gutted and burned-out nervous system.' How do you feel about that topic today?

MAILER: Drugs are a spiritual form of gambling. This is a poetic equation that can be carried right down to the end of its metaphor, because on drugs you're even bucking the house percentage – which for a drug like marijuana is probably something like 30 to 40 percent.

PLAYBOY: Would you expand this?

MAILER: Marijuana does something with the sense of time: it accelerates you; it opens you to your unconscious. But it's as if you're calling on the reserves of the next three days. All the sweets, all the crystals, all the little decisions, all the unconscious work of the next three days – or, if the experience is deep, part of the next thirty days, or the next thirty years – is called forward. For a half hour or two hours – whatever is the high of the pot – you're better than you are normally and you get into situations you wouldn't get into normally, and generally more happens to you. You make love better, you talk better, you think better, you dig people better. The point is, you've got to get in pretty far, because you're using up three days in an hour – or whatever the particular ratio is for any particular person. So unless you come back with – let us say – seventy-two hours in one hour, you lose. Because you have to spend the next three or four days recovering. You might ask: what happens to the guy who smokes pot all the time? I don't know. But I do know something is being mortgaged; something is being drawn out of the future. If his own future has already been used up in one or another mysterious or sinister sense, then maybe the pot is drawing it out of the very substance of what I may as well confess I call God. I suspect God feeds drug addicts the way a healthy body feeds parasites.

PLAYBOY: How do you mean?

MAILER: Well, if God has great compassion, He may not be willing to cut the drug addict off from Him. During the time the addict has some of his most intense and divine experiences, it is because he is literally imbibing the very marrow and nutrient of existence. But since I do not believe that God is necessarily inexhaustible, the drug addict may end up by bleeding Him.

PLAYBOY: Do you think this happens on LSD?

MAILER: I don't think you have a mystical experience on chemicals without taking the risk of exploiting something in the creation. If you haven't paid the real wages of love or courage or abstention or discipline or sacrifice or wit in the eye of danger, then taking a psychedelic drug is living the life of a parasite; it's drawing on sweets you have not earned.

PLAYBOY: What is the danger of this parasitical self-exploitation on LSD?

MAILER: I'm not going to say that LSD is bad in every way for everyone, but I'm convinced it's bad if you keep taking it. Any drug is bad finally in the same way that being a confirmed gambler is bad. A confirmed gambler ends up losing all his friends because he blows their money and blows their trust. A gambler will tell any lie to get back into the action. By the same token, if you stay on any drug for too long, then you have a habit; you're a victim; to anticipate something, you're a totalitarian.

Let me put it this way: LSD is marvelous for experts to take when they get too frozen in their expertise. Let's suppose they've driven deep into something impenetrable, some obstacle that was bound to trap them because of the short-sighted nature of their expertise. Although they work and work manfully as experts, at this point they're similar to soldiers who have pushed far into enemy territory but are now up against a resistance they cannot get through. Their only action is to retreat, but they don't know how to, because they have no habits of retreat. They're experts; they know only how to move forward to amass more knowledge and put more concentration upon a point. When this concentration does not succeed in poking through the resistance of the problem, the expert is psychically in great trouble. He begins to live in increasing depression; he has to retreat and doesn't know how: he wasn't built to retreat.

My guess is: on LSD, you begin to die a little. That's why you get this extraordinary, even divine sense of revelation. Perhaps you taste the odor and essence of your own death in the trip: in excess, it's a deadly poison, after all. Therefore, what's given to the expert is a broader vision: dying a little, he begins to retreat from his expertise and begins to rejoin his backward brothers. Hallelujah! So that LSD taken a few times could be very good, I would imagine. But before very long, if the expert keeps taking LSD, he can become nothing but an expert on LSD.

PLAYBOY: What do you think of Timothy Leary?

MAILER: Well, I wonder who we were just talking about.

PLAYBOY: More of an answer, please.

MAILER: I never met him. Perhaps I'd like him if I did. Many of my friends like him. But I have heard him speak, and he is then nought but simple shit.

PLAYBOY: Alcohol seems to be another way by which you've tried to grow or 'move forward'. One of the characters in your stage version of *The Deer Park* declares: 'A man must drink until he locates the truth.' How does alcohol help a man do that?

MAILER: I'm going to offer one fundamental equation: A man who drinks is attempting to dissolve an obsession.

PLAYBOY: What's the obsession?

MAILER: Talk first about what an obsession *is*. I've thought about obsession a great deal, but I'm not sure I know the answer. Everybody talks about obsessions; nobody's ever really explained them. We can define them, but we don't really know what we're talking about. An obsession, I'd suggest, is not unlike a pole of magnetism, a psychic field of force. An obsession is created, I think, in the wake of some event that has altered our life profoundly, or perhaps we have passed through some relation with someone else that has altered our life drastically, yet we don't know whether we were changed for good or for bad; it's the most fundamental sort of event or relation. It has marked us, yet it's morally ambiguous.

PLAYBOY: What kind of event?

MAILER: Suppose a marriage breaks up. You don't know if it was finally your fault or your wife's fault or God's fault or the Devil's fault – four uncertainties. Let's reduce them to two: a man or his wife. Put it this way: People move forward into the future out of the way they comprehend the past. When we don't understand something in our past, we are therefore crippled. Use the metaphor of the Army here: If you move forward to attack a town and the center of this attack depends upon a road that will feed your attack, and this road passes through a town, yet you don't know if your people hold that town or someone else holds it, then, obviously, if you were a general, you'd be pretty obsessive about that town. You'd keep asking. 'Will you please find out who owns that town?' You'd send out reconnaissance parties to locate the town, enter it, patrol it. If all sorts of mysterious things occurred – if, for example, your reconnaissance platoon didn't return – you'd feel so uncertain you might not move forward to attack. The obsession is a search for a useful reality. What finally did occur? What is real?

PLAYBOY: You haven't told us yet how drink helps dissolve an obsession.

MAILER: Well, if a man's drink takes him back to an earlier, younger state of sensitivity, it is then taking him to a place back of the place where he originally got into the impasse that created the obsession. If you can return to a state just preceding the one you were in when these various ambiguous events occurred, you can say to yourself, 'Now, I'm approaching the event again. What really did happen? Who was right? Who was wrong? Let me not miss it this time.' A man must drink until he locates the truth. I think that's why it's so hard for people to give up booze. There's an artwork going on with most serious drinkers. Usually, it's a failed artwork. Once again, one's playing against the house percentage: one drinks, one wrecks one's liver, dims one's vision, burns out one's memory. Drinking is a serious activity – a serious moral and spiritual activity. We consume ourselves in order to search for a truth.

PLAYBOY: In terms of your concept of growth, you've made in *An American Dream* and other writings a brilliant, dazzling, and rather puzzling remark concerning the possibility that God Himself may be involved in a process of growth. You've said that you have an 'obsession with how God exists', and you've argued for the possibility that He may be a God whose final nature is not yet comprehended, even by Himself. Could you comment on this?

MAILER: I think I decided some time ago that if there is a God and He's all-powerful, then His relation to us is absurd. All we can see in our human condition are thundering, monumental disproportions, injustices of such dimension that even the conservative notion of existence – which might postulate that man is here on earth not to complain but to receive his just deserts and that the man who acts piggishly on earth will be repaid in hell, regardless of whether he was rich or poor – yes, even this conservative vision depends on a God who is able to run a world of reasonable proportions. If the only world we have is one of abysmal, idiotic disproportions, then it becomes too difficult to conceive of an all-powerful God who is all good. It is far easier to conceive of a God who died or who is dying or who is an imperfect God. But once I think of an imperfect God, I can begin to imagine a Being greater than ourselves, who nonetheless shares His instinctive logic with us: we as men seek to grow, so He seeks to grow; even as we each have a conception of being – my conception of being, my idea of how we should live, may triumph over yours, or yours over mine – so, in parallel, this God may be engaged in a similar war in the universe with other gods. We may even be the embodiment, the partial expression of His vision. If we fail, He fails, too. He is imperfect in the way we are imperfect. He is not always as brave or extraordinary or as graceful as He might care to be. This is my notion of God and growth. The thing about it that gives me sustenance is that it enables me to love God, if you will bear these words, rather than hate Him, because I can see Him as someone who is like other men except more noble, more tortured, more desirous of a good that He wishes to receive and give to others – a torturous ethical activity at which He may fail. Man's condition is, then, by this logic, epic or tragic – for the outcome is unknown. It is not written.

PLAYBOY: Could you talk a bit more about the relationship between a man and this God who is still involved in discovering His own nature?

MAILER: In capsule: There are times when He has to exploit us; there are times when we have to exploit Him; there are times when He has to drive us beyond our own natural depth because He needs us – those of us, at least, who are working for Him: We have yet to talk of the Devil. But a man who talks about his religion is not to be trusted. Who knows – I may be working for the Devil. In fact, I sometimes suspect every novelist is a Devil's helper. The ability to put an eye on your own heart is icy.

# A Speech

## Accepting the National Book Award

On Monday when queried by Mr. Raymont of the *Times* about my reaction to winning one of the National Book Awards, I was sufficiently ungracious to say, 'There's something obscene about a middle-aged man who wins an award. Prizes are for the young and the old.' Writers are notoriously double- and triple-layered – like color film they have their yellow base, their blue-green, their slice of sensitivity to red. Who knows what was meant? It could have been bitterness, or the growl of a curmudgeon kicking at the edge of his pleasure.

At any rate, standing on this podium, your speaker is here to state that he likes prizes, honors, and awards and will accept them. He will accept them. The honorable Jean-Paul Sartre, an author it is impossible not to esteem, refused the Nobel Prize a few years ago with the remark – let this approximate his words – that he wished the bourgeoisie to know him as Jean-Paul Sartre, not Jean-Paul Sartre, Nobel Prize Winner. Respectful of his integrity, one could nonetheless disagree with his decision. The most bourgeois elements in French society had been speaking of him for years as Jean-Paul Sartre, perverted existentialist, and would continue to do so. How much better for the final subtleties of their brain if they had been obliged instead to think of him as Jean-Paul Sartre, perverted existentialist *and* Nobel Prize Winner. An entrance might have been made into the complexity of his vision. It might have introduced that bourgeoisie to the vertiginous schizophrenia of the modern condition, a clifflike species of cultural dislocation.

We are a savagely mechanical society poised upon the lip, no, the main of a spiritual revolution which will wash the psychic roots of every national institution out to sea. We are on the brink of dreams and disasters. We are entering a world in which the value systems of the stoutest ego will spin like a turning table, the assertions of the inner voice go caroming through vales of electronic rock.

So it is nice to have awards and to accept them. They are measures of the degree to which an Establishment meets that talent it has hindered and helped. So it is a measure, an historic bench mark, as each of us, one by one, gives up his grip on the old rail of established winning procedure and proceeds to whirl down the turns into that new future, airless, insane, existential, and bright, which beats in the pulse on our neck. And as we go whirling and twisting into the future, which by God we could swear we did not make, how sweet, how charming, how comic and nice that on a given year to a given man, there came an award which was a measure of the plasticity of taste, the volatility of status, and the essential good spirit of the literary world as it readied its tools, old sweet simple pencil in hand, to meet the obliterating Armageddons of technology, the last five centuries of guilt, and the electric dread at the center, for no longer do we know where we go nor whom we fight. So three cheers for good marks, that remonstrance of devoted parents and modest schools, and bless us all as we explore the night. Thank you.

# Letters

To the *New York Review of Books*

(*April 28, 1966*)

To the Editors:

In Richard G. Stern's picaresquely written 'Report from the MLA', which included an account of the Cheever-Ellison-Mailer festivities (February 17) he also reported the following sentence about me –

> In the carful of goggling professors, sloshing his drink, he [Mailer] called out 'Nine' as the elevator hurtled from Ten, and when released at Seven, he fired genially at the uniformed auntie from his fortress of licensed clowning, 'You Jew,' and rollicked like a sailor down the mirrored corridor, leaving behind a small carnage of titillated shock.

Note: James Yuenger giving an account of the same event in the *Chicago Tribune Magazine*, February 6, 1966 –

> As the 12th floor flashed by, Mailer suddenly said, 'Stop – right – HERE.' It was on 10 already, and stopped at 7, and Mailer said: 'O, boy, you're a real pearl.'

A man I have never met happened to read these two somewhat separate versions, then told my friend, Robert Lucid, that as between pearl and Jew, I must have said to the elevator operator, 'Oh, boy, you're a jewel.' In fact, it is also my conclusion. I think Stern is wrong. I think I said, 'Sweetheart, you're a real jewel.' But I had a bit to drink (not a slosh – Stern writes like a man who has never held a glass), yes, a bit to drink in celebration, having read my paper to the ASA of the MLA, so I cannot be certain finally what I said. The elevator operator was, I recollect, one Wasp lady who could play tackle for the John Birch Society if and when they field a team, sallah! so I could indeed have said, 'You pearl, you Jew,' much as I once said, 'You Communist,' to a redneck Miami sheriff who was making us fight writers show our fight credentials in our hand as he passed us through. Which tradition encourages me to say now, 'Stern, how could you, a Jew, do this to me, a fellow son of Samuel – you Ginzo, you Mafia, you Wop.'

*Norman Mailer*

*Brooklyn, New York*

## To the *Saturday Review*

*(April 20, 1971)*

Gentlemen:

Over the years, an author collects horseflies under the tail of his self-esteem. I know the editors of the *Saturday Review* will be pleased to hear that *Time* and their own magazine are my favorite horseflies, and God willing, will go back some day to their own true natural food out in the fields.

Since it is the character of a horsefly to try its sting on every material before it, I suppose one need not be surprised at the combination of inaccuracy and unattributed reporting in the following quotation from Stuart Little's piece, 'What Happened at *Harper's*.'

> At one get-together later in Morris's apartment, Mailer, reportedly rather pleased that his article was in the center of controversy, urged resignations on the editors, but some resented his surrogation of their moral decision. 'Well, Norman,' one of them is reported to have said stormily, 'I may have done a lot of bad things, but I've never sold to *Life* for a million dollars an idea ['Of a Fire on the Moon'] Willie Morris gave me.'

Since in two sentences Little manages to make four errors, let me tell Little what he could have learned by inquiring into my version of the events.

. (1) I was not pleased that 'The Prisoner of Sex' was 'in the center of controversy.' I was sick at the thought that this piece I had written in the great editorial freedom of *Harper*'s (a climate not easy to describe to *Saturday Review* editors) had contributed to smashing that same editorial freedom. But then who reported I was pleased?

(2) I didn't urge resignations on the editors. In my outrage on first hearing the news, I blurted out, 'Well, I guess the editors will all resign now,' passing insensitively over the fact that they had families, commitments, and need for salaries, and resignation would cost them much. But I did not *urge* them. I merely spoke once, too quickly, and without the right.

(3) I didn't *sell* 'Of a Fire on the Moon' to *Life*. The *Life* editors approached me. Aware that Willie Morris had suggested the same idea two months before, he was the first man I called after accepting *Life*'s offer. It was at a time when finances were pressing, and Morris recognizing the inevitable, sighed mightily and agreed that under the circumstances I had small choice.

(4) It was not for a million dollars. This is nothing but slovenly or invidious reporting. Everybody in publishing knows by now that the true figure is $450,000, and only a small fraction of that sum was paid by *Life*. The rest, as the reporter and editors of *Saturday Review*, have to be aware, was hardcover, paperback, serial rights, and foreign rights. But a horsefly is a horsefly. Its need is to sting.

Cheers, gents, and regards to Stuart Little for getting all those facts so straight. There's nothing like reporting what a guy said he heard another guy tell him somebody said.

*Norman Mailer*


To the *New York Times Book Review*

*(June 13, 1971)*

Toward the end of Brigid Brophy's generous review of *The Prisoner of Sex* (May 23), she lights upon my phrase 'politics rendered every pride' and concludes it is a malapropism. '"Surrendered" does he mean,' asks Miss Brophy, 'or "rent"?' Well, I guess a number of us know something about the kitchen that Brigid don't. 'Render' is used to describe that process where fat heated upon a fire is returned to oil and clarified of its impurities. So too can the hot and compromising hands held in politics melt pride on occasion down to shame. But how was it ever possible that the modest manifestos of *The Prisoner of Sex* could yet have rendered Brophy's nectar into surrenders of vinegar and rents of urea's hot torrent? Brave and broiling Brigid. We must find a man good enough to kiss her hem. Ahem! Yours, and cordially.

*Norman Mailer*

# Capsule Entertainments

### An Appreciation of Henry Miller

Henry Miller was in Edinburgh for the festival in 1962, and, being present myself, I had the chance to see a bit of him for a week and never the good luck to see him again. Therefore, if I write about Miller now, it is not as an expert but an admirer. And in fact I admire not only his work, which I do, enormously (his influence has been profound on a good half of all living American writers), but I admire his personality. He has one of the best personalities I ever met. It is all of a piece, all composed, the way a fine cabinetmaker or a big-game hunter or a tightrope artist has a personality which is true to itself all the way through. No neurotic push-pull, no maggots in the smile, no envies, no nervousness. It is the kind of composure which suggested he was ready for anything which came on next – did a lion escape from the zoo and walk suddenly into the room, you had the feeling Henry Miller would say, 'Say, fellow, you look pretty big coming in here out of the zoo. How's it feel to stretch your legs?'

It is, you see, a personality which is extraordinarily gentle without being the least bit soft, and after a while you get the feeling that Miller always tells the truth, and does it as simply as possible, in a minimum of words, and tempers it only with the desire to be as kind as he can in the circumstances. In that sense, a poet without talent who has asked him to read his work would probably bother Henry Miller more than the lion, but he would tell the truth, in that slightly rough, slightly humorous voice of his, with the gutty hint of Brooklyn still in the pipes.

So there is Miller, a man of medium size, trim, jaunty in his dress (knickers and a cap in Edinburgh), with a good tough face, big nose, near bald head, looking for all the world like Marx's noble proletarian, like some bricklayer, let us say, you started talking to on a train, and then it turned out he had eighty-two kids and worked at his hobby in spare time – it was translating Sophocles. Then you wonder at the gulf which

forever exists between an artist's personality and his work –
here particularly the violent, smashing, fuck-you gusto of
*Tropic of Cancer* and the strong, benign, kindly mood of the
man today – and decide that writing is also the purge of what is
good and bad in yourself, and the writers who write sweet
books, pastorales, idylls, and hymns to the human condition,
end up snarling old beasts in their senility, whereas Henry, after
years of saying out every black thought he had in his head (and
some silver ones too), is now forced to defend himself against
the allegation that he is an angel or saint.

## An Appreciation of Cassius Clay

I'm working on something else now, so don't want to get started
writing about Muhammad Ali, because I could go on for a book.
Suffice it that the most interesting original talented and artistic
prizefighter to come along in at least a decade has been cut off by
the bully-boy mentality of the American sporting world. A
great athlete is almost always an extraordinary man, but a
mediocre athlete has a character which is usually no prettier
than the life-style of a mediocre writer. The sort of mugs and
moguls who run our amateur and professional sports and write
about them are invariably mediocrities, second-rate athletes,
rich boys – they gravitate to running sports and writing up the
canons of sports, and they ran Muhammad Ali right out of
boxing. Their basic reflex is, after all, to kiss ass (it is their
connection to the primitive) and patriotism is thus their head-
on sublimation for such kissing. Therefore we are all deprived
of an intimate spectacle which was taking place in public – the
forging of a professional artist of extraordinary dimensions.
Yes, I could write a book about Cassius: he was bringing a
revolution to the theory of boxing, and bringing it into the
monarchical spook-ridden class where every theory runs into a
bomb – the heavyweights. Those who don't know boxing don't
know the frustration one feels that he couldn't have the run of
his own true career, for the knowledge he offered was mint.

**Two Oddments from** *Esquire*

*Modern is Our Temper*

'I don't know what to do. The last time I needed some money I wrote to my parents and told them I had to have an abortion. But that was only three months ago. I wonder if it isn't too soon to tell them I need another.'

'Tell them that this time it's a Negro.'

'That's a good idea.'


*Putting Culture on to Culture*

Several years ago, visiting a friend who was sick, I was introduced to his hobby. He happened to be an actor, but his temperament was not unlike a jeweler's or a collector's. He saved quotations. Whenever he came across something he liked particularly well in a book or poem he would set it down in a notebook he kept for the purpose, a handsome notebook of good paper covered with red leather. His idea of course was not novel; most of us have started such notebooks more than once. What separated his collection from others was that he kept it going for years, and he used it. If he found himself in a profound depression he would turn to the notebook (it was of course in several volumes by now) and try to read his way out of the depression. Indeed, he would succeed as often as not. His depression encountering the precision or poetry of a good sentence would shift to sorrow or melancholy or open into anger. Conversely, he would also pick up his notebook on those nights when he could not sleep for excitement or anticipation of the day to come, and would calm himself by the contrast of one salient thought upon another.

I started to keep a notebook for myself. And I found there was a subtle, almost insidious magic to the sequence of quotations. Sometimes I would put down two or three in an hour from one book or several books, sometimes months would go by between insertions, and yet when I would open the notebook and pass through it, the collision of one thought enjoyed at a particular moment in the past situated next to another thought taken from an altogether different moment seemed to produce a shift in one's memory, a clarification of the past, and the chronology of small events took shape again so that I would remember the sequence of details in a specific episode even if the quotations I was reading bore no other relation to the event than to be near it in time.

At any rate – and I hope this is not a mistake – I thought I'd put down some of these quotations now, and see if I could induce any of you to begin your private book. In fact, if it's not too presumptuous of me, any of you are welcome to start your book with any of the quotations that follow. Be certain, however, to give credit to the correct author. Because that is the critical part of the notebook's value.

Telling the truth makes us burn with the desire to convince our audience, whereas telling a lie affords ample leisure to study the result.

– Oscar Wilde

So the blind will lead the blind and the deaf shout warnings to one another until their voices are lost.

– Herman Melville

Have you forgotten? Do you remember how the poorest of the poor used to be driven to the room where they were given death by gas?

– Albert Camus

'You ripped her kimono,' I told him.
'Yeah, I got to buy her another.'

– Mickey Spillane

Talent is in its infancy.

– G. B. Shaw

To be forced to admire what one instinctively hates, and to hate all which one would naturally love is the condition of our lives in these bad years, and so is the cause beneath other causes for our sickness and our death.

– Leo Tolstoy

Why is my brain always so alive when I'm too drunk ever to do anything about it?

– F. Scott Fitzgerald

The essence of spirit, he thought to himself, was to choose the thing which did not better one's position, but made it more perilous. That was why the world he knew was poor, for it insisted morality and caution were identical. He was so completely of that world, and she was not. She would stay with him until he wanted her no longer, and the thought of what would happen afterward ground his flesh with pain as real as a wound.

– D. H. Lawrence

He held her to him, and fondled her hair, feeling a sense of protection which bid her to stop here and ask no more; for of all the distance she had come, and he had helped her to move, and there were times like this when he felt the substance of his pride to depend upon exactly her improvement as if she were finally the only human creation in which he had taken part, he still knew that he could help her no longer, nor could anyone else, for she had come now into that domain where her problems were everyone's problems and there were no answers and no doctors, but only that high plateau where philosophy lives with despair.

– John Galsworthy

The woe of his life washed up on him at all he had not done, and all that he would never do, and he wept, he wept the harsh tears of a full-grown man.

– Ford Madox Ford

As socialists we want a socialist world not because we have the conceit that men would thereby be more happy – those claims are best left to dictators – but because we feel the moral imperative in life itself to raise the human condition even if this should ultimately mean no more than that man's suffering has been lifted to a higher level, and human history has only progressed from melodrama, farce, and monstrosity, to tragedy itself.

– Trotsky

Good style is the record of powerful emotion reaching the surface of the page through fine conscious nets of restraint, caution, tact, elegance, taste, even inhibition – if the inhibition is not without honor.

– Arthur Quiller-Couch

That many of you are frustrated in your ambitions, and undernourished in your pleasures, only makes you more venomous. Quite rightly. If I found myself in your position. I would not be charitable either.

– Thoreau

He felt the kind of merriment men know when events have ended in utter disaster.

– Jack London

Nobody could sleep . . . all through the ship, all over the convoy, was the knowledge that in a few hours some of them were going to be dead.

– Ernest Hemingway

I assure you, doctor, it is a relatively simple matter for a weathered charlatan like myself to keep up interest in so small a carnival as this.

– Nietzsche

# One Book Review

*Rush to Judgment* by Mark Lane

On May 14, 1964, when J. Edgar Hoover testified before the Warren Commission, he said about Marguerite Oswald: 'The first indication of her emotional instability was the retaining of a lawyer that anyone would not have retained if they really were serious in trying to get down to the facts.' Well, Bill Terry once asked if the Dodgers were still in the league, and J. Edgar Hoover revealed this day an even more massive incapacity to judge certain kinds of underdogs and men, for Mark Lane, the lawyer retained, has come up with four hundred pages of facts on the Warren Commission's inquiry into the murders of President John F. Kennedy, Officer J. D. Tippit, and Lee Harvey Oswald, and they are somewhat staggering facts. If one-tenth of them should prove to be significant, then the work of the Warren Commission will be judged by history to be a scandal worse than Teapot Dome.

*Rush to Judgment* is of course a defense attorney's brief, and it seeks to make its case as best it can, wherever it can. Those looking for a comprehensive explanation of the mystery of the assassination will not find it, not here. There is no single overall explanation of the unspoken possibilities, nor is one even offered. Lane is attempting to prove that Oswald most certainly could not have committed the crime alone, and that the odds are great he did not commit either murder. Lane's attempt, therefore, is to disprove the case brought in by the prosecution – it is a small continuing shock to recognize, as Lane fortifies his arguments in the most interesting detail, that the Warren Commission served as an agent of gentlemanly prosecution rather than a commission of inquiry. That this was not head-on evident when the Report came out is due to the lucidities and sweet reasonable tone of the style in which the Warren Commission Report is written. But the gentlest of men often write in a bad harsh voice, and many a quiet calculating brute has acquired the best of good tones in prose. Yes, the Warren

Commission Report convinced a majority of Americans by the reasonableness and modesty of its style – what casual study did not show, however, was that when the Commission was being most reasonable in stating that something could not be proved, it was neglecting to say that the preponderance of unexplored leads to new evidence was pointed resolutely in the opposite direction from their conclusion. The scandal of the Warren Commission was twofold – it did not look into some of the most interesting and fascinating matters before it, and it distorted its hard findings. As Hugh Trevor-Roper points out in a fine British introduction to *Rush to Judgment*, 'A pattern was made to emerge out of the evidence, and having emerged, seemed to subordinate the evidence to it.' It was not enough to read the Report; one was obliged, Trevor-Roper points out, to read the twenty-six volumes of 'Hearings'. 'To follow the same question through the three successive levels of "Hearings", "Report", and "Summary and Conclusions" is to see sometimes a quiet transformation of evidence.'

But one may ask: was the Warren Commission in conspiracy to hide the truth, all those fine, separate, august, and honorable gentlemen? And the answer is: of course not. They were not in conspiracy, they never needed to be, no more than a corporation has to be in conspiracy to push out a product which is grievously inferior to the product they are potentially equipped to make, nor the head of General Motors need hire private detectives to hound Ralph Nader. Products come from the processes, and a commission's report is a reflection of a method of inquiry. Edward Jay Epstein's book demonstrated even to Fletcher Knebel's satisfaction that the Warren Commission did not work very hard. Walter Craig, president of the American Bar Association, appointed as 'protector' of Oswald's interests, attended two out of fifty-one sessions of the Commission – he was perhaps not the kind of lawyer Mr. Hoover would have recommended to Mrs. Oswald; the only Commission member to be present much more than 50 percent of the time was Allen Dulles of the CIA – perhaps he had the most to protect.

No, for the large part, the seven members of the Commission were abstracted and often distant. The established lawyers who pursued the investigation as the Commission's professional assistants were busy in private practice, and usually absent. So the work passed on down to junior assistants, bright young lawyers with careers to make. They were forced to contend every day with agents, investigators, and detectives who knew more about criminal investigation than they did and were also presumably possessed of more physical strength, more martial arts, as well as endowed with that dead, muted, fanatical intensity which wins much in negotiation across a table. The investigation seemed to push at every turn against the likelihood of inefficiency, corruption, collusion, or direct involvement in the case by the Dallas police, and, in more complex fashion, the CIA and the FBI. The Secret Service, having done a poor job, had their own reputations to protect. In such a situation, what overworked young lawyer is going to continue to make a personal crusade of his own investigation against the revelatory somnolence of the Commission members, and the resistance of the FBI, especially when a routine performance satisfactory to the Commission gives assurance of a happy and accelerated career?

What becomes oppressively evident is that the Warren Commission from the beginning had no intention of trying to find any other assassin than Oswald. Whether from pure motives or from intentions not so clear (it will be remembered that before the Commission began to sit, the chief justice was speaking already of information which could not be divulged for seventy-five years), whether from honest bias or determined obfuscation, the evidence fitted a bed of Procrustes. Everything was enlisted to satisfy the thesis that Oswald, half mad, had done the job alone, and Ruby, half mad, had done his particular job alone. So a witness, Brennan, who had poor eyesight, was credited by the Commission with identifying Oswald in a sixth-story window – his eyes, went the unspoken assumption, could see better at one time than another; whereas a man with excellent eyesight named Rowland who saw two men in the window was considered unreliable because his wife told the Commission her young husband was prone to exaggerate the results of his report cards.

Besides, it was a game of experts. The expert always plays a game in which his side is supposed to win – the expert has a psychic structure which is umbilically opposed to finding the truth until the expert finds out first if the truth is good for his side. We have prosecuting attorneys and defense attorneys because a legal case is first a game – each side looks for its purchase of the truth, even if the search carries them into almost impossible assumptions. It is why a fact-finding commission cannot by its nature make discoveries which are as incisive as the evidence uncovered by the monomaniacal, the Ahab-like search of a dedicated attorney. In contrast to him, the totalitarians look to find their truth in consensus. You and I are more likely to find it beneath a stone.

So Lane's book provides the case for the defense. Like all lawyers' briefs, it is not wholly satisfactory as a book. One wishes that the strongest evidence of Oswald's guilt provided by the Warren Commission were presented at least in summary, if only to be demolished, or that admission were made by Lane that certain crucial damaging points cannot be refuted, but Lane's intent is to do the best for his dead client, and that is what he does. If *Rush to Judgment* accomplishes nothing else, it will live as a classic for every serious amateur detective in America. Long winter nights in the farmhouse will be spent poring over the contradictions in the twenty-six volumes of 'Hearings' with Lane's book for a guide, and plans will be made and money saved to take a trip to Dallas, which will become a shrine for all the unborn Baker Street Irregulars of the world. Because Lane's book proves once and forever that the assassination of President Kennedy is more of a mystery today than when it occurred.

Well, then – what finally does Lane produce? He presents a thousand items of clear-cut doubt in four hundred pages, material sufficient for five years of real investigation by any fair country commission. He makes it clear that most of the witnesses to the assassination thought the shots came not from the Texas Book Depository Building but from behind a fence on a knoll above and in front of the Presidential limousine. And that autopsy which could clarify whether the President was shot from the front, from behind, or from both separate positions – well, that autopsy is mired in massive confusion which the Commission did not dissolve and in fact interred, for X-rays

and photographs taken at the autopsy have not been published.
The bullet which shattered the President's skull almost certainly had to be a soft-nosed lead round to explode so large a
wound; Oswald's gun fired hard-nosed metal-jacketed rounds.
The questions raised by Edward Jay Epstein in *inquest* about the
bullet which was alleged to strike the President and Governor
Connally are explored again and point to the same conclusion –
one bullet could not have entered where it did, and come out
where it came out.

Nor has any satisfactory explanation ever been offered, Lane
shows in detail, as to how the police were able to send out a call
to apprehend Oswald fifteen minutes after the assassination,
nor why the two officers who discovered the rifle on the sixth
floor described it in careful detail as a '7.65 Mauser bolt-action
equipped with a 4/18 scope, a thick leather brownish-black
sling on it . . . gun metal color . . . blue metal . . . the rear
portion of the bolt was visibly worn. . . .' But the Mauser
turned into a pumpkin and became a 6.5 Mannlicher-Carcano.
Of course, Marina Oswald, on hearing of the assassination over
the radio, went out to the garage to see if Oswald's Mannlicher-
Carcano was in place. It was there. It was there? 'Later,' she
said, 'it turned out that the rifle was not there . . . I did not
know what to think.' The Dallas police came in soon to search
the garage and later reported that they found an empty blanket
upon a shelf. It was that empty blanket, they declared, which
Marina had mistaken for the rifle. So the rifle on the sixth floor
altered from a 7.65 Mauser bolt-action to a 6.5 Mannlicher-
Carcano carbine, a point in the shade of Sherlock Holmes, for
unless the police in Texas are such unnatural Texans as to be
innocent of rifles, they would know a 7.65 Mauser bolt-action,
since the Mauser is the most beloved and revered of bolt-
actions, whereas the 6.5 Mannlicher-Carcano rests among the
more despised of shooting irons. It is curious; one repeats: it is
curious that the Commission taking testimony from the very
same officer who discovered the original rifle which he had
declared a Mauser did not choose to show this police officer the
Mannlicher-Carcano and ask if he might be in error, or if,
horror beyond belief, the guns were switched.

Roll call of these unexplored details continues. The Mannlicher-Carcano had the same scope as the nonexistent Mauser, but Marina Oswald had never seen a scope on a rifle. (She was a woman, after all). So the suggestion intrudes itself – was the 4/18 scope on the Mauser switched in a great private frantic hurry to the Mannlicher, installed in fact so quickly that the telescopic sight was unrelated to the line of fire! Certainly we have it on record that the scope had to be reset with shims before three masters of the National Rifle Association could even aim it. This, the rifle supposed to have killed Kennedy? And when they fired for test, these three masters, six shots each in groups of two at three fixed targets, eighteen shots in total by three masters, they did not fire nearly so quickly nor so well at fixed targets as Oswald had fired at moving targets from a more difficult and certainly more extraordinary position. In fact the Mannlicher dispersed its shot group so widely (an estimated twelve inches at one hundred yards) that no one of the experts in all their collective eighteen shots succeeded in striking the head or neck of the fixed target. Nonetheless, the Commission decided that the Mannlicher-Carcano had done the job. Oswald, of course, had no great record as a rifleman, but perhaps his bad aim, the moving car, the crazy banged-up scope, the inaccurate barrel, and the very heavy trigger pull came together in the vertigo of the moment, to funnel in two hits out of three. Perhaps. Perhaps there is one chance in a thousand. But a Zen master, not a rifle expert, must be consulted for this.

Questions arise here and everywhere. The package of curtain rods in which Oswald was supposed to have concealed the Mannlicher-Carcano was too small (on the account of both witnesses who had seen it) to contain the disassembled rifle. But the size of the bag remains moot because it was ruined in the FBI labs while being examined for fingerprints. Another bag was put together – thirty-eight inches in length. The witnesses seemed to think it was about ten inches longer than the original. (The Mannlicher disassembled is almost thirty-five inches.) The Commission decided the witnesses 'could easily have been mistaken in their estimate.' So could the FBI, unless there were affidavits on the dimensions of the original bag before it had been subjected to fingerprint tests.

Move on. The only eyewitness to the murder of Tippit was a
woman named Mrs. Markham. She was certain the killing took
place at 1.06 P.M. The Commission was not able to get Oswald
to the spot before 1.16 P.M. So the Commission decided Mrs.
Markham was correct in her identification of Oswald, but
wrong in her placement of the time. Mrs. Markham, however,
in an interview with Lane, described Tippit's killer as 'a short
man, somewhat on the heavy side, with slightly bushy hair.'
The description she gave the police was 'about thirty, five feet
eight, black hair, slender.'

Tippit leads to Ruby. Among the many potential witnesses
who were not called were a variety of people who had been
associated with Ruby for years. They made a general collective
estimate that Ruby knew personally more than half the officers
on the Dallas police force. Ruby kept begging the Warren
Commission to get him out of the Dallas jail and into Washington. 'I want to tell the truth,' he said, 'and I can't tell it here.
. . . Gentlemen, unless you get me to Washington you can't get
a fair shake out of me.' Of course, many witnesses were
intimidated in mysterious ways. Two reporters who visited
Ruby's apartment just after he killed Oswald were later murdered, one in his Dallas apartment as the victim of a karate
attack (where are you, Charlie Chan?). The Commission did not
seem to explore this. Another witness, Warren Reynolds, was
shot through the head, but recovered. He had seen a man whom
he did not identify as Oswald (until many tribulations and eight
months later) fleeing the scene of the Tippit murder, pistol in
hand. Two months elapsed before Reynolds was questioned.
He then told the FBI that he could not identify the fugitive as
Oswald – although he had followed the man on foot for one
block. Two days after the interview, Reynolds was shot through
the head with a rifle and somehow survived. The prime suspect,
Darrel Wayne Garner, was arrested by Dallas police, and later
admitted he had made a call to his sister-in-law and 'advised her
he had shot Warren Reynolds,' but the charges were dropped
because Garner had an alibi in the form of a filed affidavit by
Nancy Jane Mooney, a stripteaser who had been employed once
at Jack Ruby's Carousel. Eight days later, Miss Mooney was
arrested by Dallas police for fighting with her roommate,

'disturbing the peace'. Alone in her cell – less than two hours after arrival – Miss Mooney hanged herself to death, stated the police report.

Item: In January 1964, Reynolds told the FBI that the man he saw was not Lee Harvey Oswald.

Item: In July 1964, Reynolds – who now owned a watchdog, took no walks at night, and whose house was ringed with floodlights – testified that he now believed the man was Oswald. The Commission, in reporting the changed statements, omitted to mention at that precise point the attempt on Warren Reynold's life.

Item: Information given by Nancy Perrin Rich to the Warren Commission that Jack Ruby brought money to a meeting between various agents and one U.S. Army officer for smuggling guns to Cuba, and refugees out, was stricken from the record by the Warren Commission.

Item: A communication from the CIA in response four months late to a Commission inquiry: 'An examination of Central Intelligence files has produced no information on Jack Ruby or his activities.' Indeed. Which files? The Balkan files? The Ipcress file?

Item: William Whaley, Oswald's alleged cab driver, was killed in an automobile collision on December 18, 1965.

Item: Albert G. Bogard, an automobile salesman who tried to sell a car to a man calling himself Lee Oswald, was beaten up by some men after testifying and was sent to a hospital. The Warren Commission determined that the man buying the car could not be Oswald, but it did not inquire further. That someone might be impersonating Oswald before the assassination was a matter presumably without interest to the Commission.

Item: On Wednesday, January 22, a call came to J. Lee Rankin, general counsel for the Warren Commission. It was from the attorney general of Texas who told Rankin he had learned that the FBI had an 'undercover agent' and that agent was none other than Lee Harvey Oswald. After much discussion that evening and much resolution that evening to conduct an independent investigation of this charge, the Commission nonetheless ended months later with this verdict: 'Nothing to support the speculation that Oswald was an agent, employee, or informant of the FBI,' citing as its basis the testimony of Hoover, his assistant, and three FBI agents, plus reference to some affidavits signed by various other FBI agents. That proved to be the limit of the 'independent investigation'. There is nothing to show that the attorney general of Texas was ever asked to give testimony as to how he heard the rumor.

So there we are left in this extraordinary case, and with this extraordinary Commission which looks into the psychic traumas of Oswald's childhood and Jack Ruby's mother's 'fishbone delusion', but does not find out by independent investigation which Dallas cop might have let Jack Ruby into the basement, or whether Oswald could ever have been an undercover agent for the FBI, the CIA, the MVD, MI-5, Fair Play for Cuba, JURE, Mao Tse-tung, the John Birch Society, the Nazi Renaissance Party, or whether indeed an agent for all of them. The word of Mr. Hoover is good enough for the Commission. Mr. Hoover is of course an honorable man, all kneel.

No, what we are left with, after reading this book, is an ineradicable sense of new protagonists – the Dallas police – and behind them, opposed to them, for them, beneath them, on every side of them; another protagonist or protagonists. But first, foremost, the police.

Criminals fall into two categories – good criminals and bad. A bad criminal is the simplest of people – he cannot be trusted for anything; a good criminal is not without nobility, and if he is your friend he is a rare friend. But cops! Ah, the cops are far more complex than criminals. For they contain explosive contradictions within themselves. Supposed to be law enforcers, they tend to conceive of themselves as the law. They are more responsible than the average man, they are more infantile. They are attached umbilically to the concept of honesty, they are profoundly corrupt. They possess more physical courage than the average man, they are unconscionable bullies; they serve the truth, they are psychopathic liars (no cop's testimony is ever to be trusted without corroboration); their work is authoritarian, they are cynical; and finally, if something in their heart is deeply idealistic, they are also bloated with greed. There is no human creation so contradictory, so finally enigmatic, as the character of the average cop, and these contradictions form the keel of the great American mystery – who killed President Kennedy?

Yet even that oppressive sense of the Dallas police does not satisfy all the resonance of this mystery. For the question remains: was Oswald some sort of agent? We are getting uncomfortably close to the real heart of the horror. So it is time to offer a new hypothesis (or at least offer the beginnings of a working hypothesis), even to make it out of whole cloth without a 'scintilla of evidence'. Call it a metaphor. So I will say the odds are indeed that Oswald was an undercover agent. He was too valuable not to be. How many Americans, after all, knew Soviet life in the small intimate ways Oswald had known it? And indeed how was it so possible for him to arrange his return? If you, sir, were the head of an espionage service, would you not wish to make Oswald work for you as the price of his return? If you were in Russian intelligence, would you not demand that he serve as some kind of Soviet agent in exchange for his release? A petty undercover agent for two services or three, a man without real importance or any sinister mission, he may still have been in so exposed a position that other services would have been attracted to him. Espionage services tend to collect the same particular small agents in common, for most of their operations are only serious as a game, and you need a pocket board on which to play. Oswald may have been just such a battered little pocket board.

Worked over and played over until he metamorphosed from playing board to harried rat, he may even have nibbled at the edge of twenty Dallas conspiracies. It was all comedy of the most horrible sort, but when Kennedy was assassinated, the espionage services of half the world may have discovered in the next hour that one little fellow in Dallas was – all pandemonium to the fore – a secret, useless, little undercover agent who was on their private lists. What nightmares must have ensued! What nightmares on the instant! What quiet little mind in some unknown council-of-war room, thinking of the exceptional definition of the game which might soon be given by a rat harried past the point of no return, a rat let loose in a courtroom, cried out in one or another Ivy League voice, 'Well, can't

something be done, can't we do something about this man?' and
a man getting up saying, 'See you in a while,' and a little later a
phone call made and another and finally a voice saying to our
friend Ruby, 'Jack, I got good news. There's a little job . . .' Is
it so unreasonable that the tiny metaphorical center of a host of
espionage games should be killed by that precise intersection of
the Mafia, the police, the invisible government, and the strip-
tease business which Jack Ruby personified to the point.

No, there may have been no formal master plan to murdering
Kennedy, just coincidences beyond repair and beyond tolerance, as if all things came together in a blaze of one huge
existential moment, and nothing left but wreckage, paranoia,
and the secret bewildered sense in every cop, criminal, and
agent of the western hemisphere that something beyond anyone's ken had occurred; now the evidence had to be covered. So
Kennedy may have been killed by a conspiracy which was petty
to its root; certainly he must have been killed by a very petty
conspiracy with a few good Texas marksmen in it, but the
power of several master conspiracies may then have been
aroused to protect every last one of us against the possibility of
discovery, against the truth, for no one in power in America
knew what the truth was. Not any longer. So the case was
fertilized and refertilized – it grew into a thicket. And the
Commission was obliged to cut a tidy path through the thicket
and this laid the ground for future scandals and disasters out of
measure.

If in the next few years some new kind of commission does
not establish in hard and satisfactory fashion the known and
unknown boundaries of the case, then the way is open to a series
of surrealistic political machinations. On that unhappy – let us
hope impossible – day when America becomes a totalitarian
government of Left, Center, or Right, the materials are now at
hand for a series of trials of high government figures which will
make the Moscow trials of 1936 to 1938, following upon the
assassination of Kirov, seem like modest exercises in domination, for the wealth of contradictory evidence now upon us from
the rot-pile of Dallas permits any interpretation, any neat little
path, to be cut through the thicket. From any direction to any
direction. The Right may now convict the Left. The Left may

now stifle the Right. The Center may eat them both. The cannibal's pure totalitarianism is near.

So one would propose one last new commission, one real commission – a literary commission supported by public subscription to spend a few years on the case. There are major intellectuals in this country who are old now and have never been able to serve in American life. Not ever. It is time for that. Time for the best of intellectuals to serve. I would trust a commission headed by Edmund Wilson before I trusted another by Earl Warren. Wouldn't you? Would you not estimate that Dwight MacDonald, working alone, could nose out more facts and real contradictions than could twenty crack FBI investigators working together? Laugh, angels, pass the drinks, make this the game for the week. Pick your members of the new commission. It is very funny. And yet the small persisting national need is for a few men who can induce, from contradictory evidence, a synthesis. The solution to President Kennedy's murder will come not from legal or government commissions, but from minds deeply grounded first and last in the mysteries of hypothesis, uncorrupted, logic, tragedy, and metaphor. In the meanwhile, waiting for such a literary commission, three cheers for Mark Lane. His work is not without a trace of that stature we call heroic. Three cheers. Because the game is not yet over. Nor the echo of muffled drums. Nor the memory of the riderless horse.

## PART ELEVEN

# Grips on the Aesthetic of The Street

# Black Power

## Looking for the Meat and Potatoes –
## Thoughts on Black Power

'You don't even know who you are,' Reginald had said. 'You don't even know, the white devil has hidden it from you, that you are of a race of people of ancient civilizations, and riches in gold and kings. You don't even know your true family name, you wouldn't recognize your true language if you heard it. You have been cut off by the devil white man from all true knowledge of your own kind. You have been a victim of the evil of the devil white man ever since he murdered and raped and stole you from your native land in the seeds of your forefathers. . . .'

*– The Autobiography of Malcolm X*

In not too many years, we will travel to the moon, and on the trip, the language will be familiar. We have not had our education for nothing – all those sanitized hours of orientation via high school, commercials, corporations and mass media have given us one expectation: no matter how beautiful, insane, dangerous, sacrilegious, explosive, holy or damned a new venture may be, count on it, fellow Americans, the language will be familiar. Are you going in for a serious operation, voting on the political future of the country, buying insurance, discussing nuclear disarmament, or taking a trip to the moon? You can depend on the one great American certainty – the public vocabulary of the discussion will suggest the same relation to the resources of the English language that a loaf of big-bakery bread in plastic bag and wax bears to the secret heart of wheat and butter and eggs and yeast.

Your trip to the moon will not deal needlessly with the vibrations of the heavens (now that man dares to enter eschatology) nor the metaphysical rifts in the philosophical firmament; no poets will pluck a stringed instrument to conjure with the pale shades of the white lady as you move along toward the lunar space. Rather, a voice will emerge from the loudspeaker. 'This is your pilot. On our starboard bow at four o'clock directly below, you can pick out a little doojigger of land down there like a vermiform appendix, and that, as we say good-bye to the Pacific Coast, is Baja California. The spot of light at the nub, that little bitty illumination like the probe bulb in a cystoscope or comparable medical instrument is Ensenada, which the guidebooks called a jeweled resort.'

Good-bye to earth, hello the moon! We will skip the technological dividend in the navigator's voice as he delivers us to that space station which will probably look like a breeding between a modern convention hall and the computer room at CBS. Plus the packaged air in the space suits when the tourists, after two days of acclimation in air-sealed moon motels, take their first reconnoiter outside in the white moon dust while their good American bowels accommodate to relative weightlessness.

All right, bright fellow, the reader may now say – what does all this have to do with Black Power? And the author, while adept at dancing in the interstices of a metaphor, is going to come back straight and fast with this remark – our American language is not any more equipped to get into a discussion of Black Power than it is ready to serve as interpreter en route to the moon. The American language has become a conveyor belt to carry each new American generation into its ordained position in the American scene, which is to say the corporate technological world. It can deal with external descriptions of everything which enters or leaves a man, it can measure the movements of that man, it can predict until such moment as it is wrong what the man will do next, but it cannot give a spiritual preparation for our trip to the moon any more than it can talk to us about death, or the inner experiences of real sex, real danger, real dread. Or Black Power.

If the preface has not been amusing, cease at once to read. What follows will be worse: the technological American is programmed to live with answers, which is why his trip to the moon will be needlessly God-awful; the subject of Black Power opens nothing but questions, precisely those unendurable questions which speak of premature awakenings and the hour of the wolf. But let us start with something comfortable, something we all know, and may encounter with relaxation, for the matter is familiar:

> . . . think of that black slave man filled with fear and dread, hearing the screams of his wife, his mother, his daughter being *taken* – in the barn, the kitchen, in the bushes! . . . *Think* of hearing wives, mothers, daughters, being *raped*! And you were too filled with *fear* of the rapist to do anything about it! . . . Turn around and look at each other, brothers and sisters, and *think* of this! You and me, polluted all these colors – and this devil has the arrogance and the gall to think we, his victims, should *love* him!
>
>           – *The Autobiography of Malcom X*

'Okay,' you say, 'I know that, I know that already. I didn't do it. My great-grandfather didn't even do it. He was a crazy Swede. He never even saw a black skin. And now for Crysake, the girls in Sweden are crazy about Floyd Patterson. I don't care, I say more power to him. All right,' goes the dialogue of this splendid American now holding up a hand, 'all right, I know about collective responsibility. If some Scotch-Irish planter wanted to tomcat in the magnolias, then I'll agree it's easier for me than for the victim to discern subtle differences between one kind of Wasp and another, I'll buy my part of the ancestral curse for that Scotch-Irish stud's particular night of pleasure, maybe I'm guilty of something myself, but there are limits, man. All right, we never gave the Negro a fair chance, and now we want to, we're willing to put up with a reasonable amount of disadvantage, in fact, discomfort, outright inequality and efficiency. I'll hire Negroes who are not as equipped in the productive scheme of things as whites; that doesn't mean we have to pay iota for iota on every endless misdemeanor of the past and suffer a vomit bag of bad manners to boot. Look, every student of revolution can tell you that the danger comes from giving the oppressed their first liberties. A poor man who wins a crazy bet always squanders it. The point, buddy, is that the present must forgive the past, there must be forgiveness for old sins, or else progress is impossible.' And there is the key to the first door: progress depends upon anesthetizing the past. 'What if,' says Black Power, 'we are not interested in progress, not your progress with packaged food for soul food, smog for air, hypodermics for roots, air conditioning for breeze – what if we think we have gotten strong by living without progress and your social engineering, what if we think that an insult to the blood is never to be forgotten because it keeps your life alive and reminds you to meditate before you urinate. Who are you to say that spooks don't live behind the left ear and ha'nts behind the right? Whitey, you smoke so much you can't smell, taste, or kiss – your breath is too bad. If you don't have a gun, I can poke you and run – you'll never catch me. I'm alive 'cause I keep alive the curse you put in my blood. Primitive people don't forget. If they do, they turn out no better than the civilized and the sick. Who are you, Whitey, to tell me to drop my curse, and join your line of traffic going to work? I'd rather keep myself in shape and work out the curse, natural style. There's always white women, ahem! Unless we decide they're too full of your devil's disease, hypocritical pus-filled old white blood, and so we stay black with black, and repay the curse by drawing blood. That's the life-giving way to repay a curse.'

'Why must you talk this way?' says the splendid American. 'Can't you see that there are whites and whites, whites I do not begin to control? They wish to destroy you. They agree with your values. They are primitive whites. They think in blood for blood. In a war, they will kill you, and they will kill me.'

'Well, daddy, I'm just putting you on. Didn't you ever hear of the hereafter? That's where it will all work out, there where us Blacks are the angels and honkies is the flunky. Now, let me take you by the tail, white cat, long enough to see that I want some more of these handouts, see, these homey horseballs and government aid.'

The splendid American has just been left in the mire of a put-on and throwaway. How is he to know if this is spring mud or the muck of the worst Negro Hades?

The native's relaxation takes precisely the form of a muscular orgy in which the most acute aggressivity and the most impelling violence are canalised, transformed and con-

jured away. . . . At certain times on certain days, men and
women come together at a given place, and there, under the
solemn eye of the tribe, fling themselves into a seemingly
unorganized pantomime, which is in reality extremely systematic, in which by various means – shakes of the head,
bending of the spinal column, throwing of the whole body
backwards – may be deciphered as in an open book the huge
effort of a community to exorcise itself, to liberate itself . . .
in reality your purpose in coming together is to allow the
accumulated libido, the hampered aggressivity to dissolve as
in a volcanic eruption. Symbolical killings, fantastic rites,
imaginary mass murders – all must be brought out. The evil
humours are undammed, and flow away with a din as of
molten lava. . . .

> – Frantz Fanon, *The Wretched of the Earth*

Here is the lesson learned by the struggles of present-day
colonial countries to obtain their independence: a war of liberation converts the energies of criminality, assassination, religious orgy, voodoo, and the dance into the determined artful
phalanxes of bold guerrilla armies. A sense of brotherhood
comes to replace the hitherto murderous clan relations of the
natives. Once, that propensity to murder each other had proved
effective in keeping the peace – for the settler. Now, these
violent sentiments turn against the whites who constrain them.
Just as the natives upon a time made good servants and workers
for the whites, while reserving the worst of their characters for
each other, now they looked to serve each other, to cleanse the
furies of their exploited lives in open rude defiance against the
authority.

This is the conventional explanation offered by any revolutionary spokesman for the Third World – that new world
which may or may not emerge triumphant in Latin America,
Asia, and Africa. It is a powerful argument, an uplifting
argument, it stirs the blood of anyone who has ever had a
revolutionary passion, for the faith of the revolutionary (if he is
revolutionary enough to have faith) is that the repressed blood
of mankind is ultimately good and noble blood. Its goodness
may be glimpsed in the emotions of its release. If a sense of

brotherhood animates the inner life of guerrilla armies, then it does not matter how violent they are to their foe. That violence safeguards the sanctity of their new family relations.

If this is the holy paradigm of the colonial revolutionary, its beauty has been confirmed in places, denied in others. While the struggles of the NLF and the North Vietnamese finally proved impressive even to the most gung-ho Marine officers in Southeast Asia, the horrors of the war in Biafra go far toward proving the opposite. The suspicion remains that beneath the rhetoric of revolution, another war, quite separate from a revolutionary war, is also being waged, and the forces of revolution in the world are as divided by this concealed war as the civilized powers who would restrain them. It is as if one war goes on between the privileged and the oppressed to determine how the productive wealth of civilization will be divided; the other war, the seed contained within this first war, derives from a notion that the wealth of civilization is not wealth but a corporate productive poisoning of the well-springs, avatars, and conduits of nature; the power of civilization is therefore equal to the destruction of life itself. It is, of course, a perspective open to the wealthy as well as to the poor – not every millowner who kills the fish in his local rivers with the wastes from his factory is opposed to protecting our wilderness preserve, not at all, some even serve on the State Conservation Committee. And our First Lady would try to keep billboards from defacing those new highways which amputate the ecology through which they pass. Of course, her husband helped to build those highways. But then the rich, unless altogether elegant, are inevitably comic. It is in the worldwide militancy of the underprivileged, undernourished, and exploited that the potential horror of this future war (concealed beneath the present war) will make itself most evident. For the armies of the impoverished, unknown to themselves, are already divided. Once victorious over the wealthy West – if ever! – they could only have a new war. It would take place between those forces on their side who are programmatic, scientific, more or less socialist, and near maniac in their desire to bring technological culture at the fastest possible rate into every backward land, and those more traditional and/or primitive forces in the revolution of the Third World who reject not only the exploitation of the Western world but reject the West as well, in toto, as a philosophy, a culture, a technique, as a way indeed of even attempting to solve the problems of man himself.

Of these colonial forces, black, brown, and yellow, which look to overthrow the economic and social tyrannies of the white man, there is no force in Africa, Asia, or Latin America which we need think of as being any more essentially colonial in stance than the American Negro. Consider these remarks in *The Wretched of the Earth* about the situation of colonials:

'The colonial world is a world cut in two. The dividing line, the frontiers are shown by barracks and police stations.' (Of this, it may be said that Harlem is as separate from New York as East Berlin from West Berlin.)

' . . . if, in fact, my life is worth as much as the settler's, his glance no longer shrivels me up nor freezes me, and his voice no longer turns me into stone. I am no longer on tenterhooks in his presence; in fact, I don't give a damn for him. Not only does his presence no longer trouble me, but I am already preparing such efficient ambushes for him that soon there will be no way out but that of flight.' (Now, whites flee the subways in New York.)

' . . . There is no colonial power today which is capable of adopting the only form of contest which has a chance of succeeding, namely, the prolonged establishment of large forces of occupation.' (How many divisions of paratroops would it take to occupy Chicago's South Side?)

The American Negro is of course not synonymous with Black Power. For every Black militant, there are ten Negroes who live quietly beside him in the slums, resigned for the most part to the lessons, the action, and the treadmill of the slums. As many again have chosen to integrate. They live now like Negroid Whites in mixed neighborhoods, suburbs, factories, obtaining their partial peace within the white dream. But no American Negro is contemptuous of Black Power. Like the accusing finger in the dream, it is the rarest nerve in their head, the frightening pulse in their heart, equal in emotional weight to that passion which many a noble nun sought to conquer on a cold stone floor. Black Power obviously derives from a heritage of anger which makes the American Negro one man finally with the African, the Algerian, and even the Vietcong – he would become schizophrenic if he tried to suppress his fury over the mutilations of the past.

The confrontation of Black Power with American life gives us then not only an opportunity to comprehend some of the forces and some of the style of that war now smoldering between the global rich and the global poor, between the culture of the past and the intuitions of the future, but – since Black Power has more intimate, everyday knowledge of what it is like to live in an advanced technological society than any other guerrilla force on earth – the division of attitudes within Black Power has more to tell us about the shape of future wars and revolutions than any other militant force in the world. Technological man in his terminal diseases, dying of air he can no longer breathe, of packaged food he can just about digest, of plastic clothing his skin can hardly bear, and of static before which his spirit has near expired, stands at one end of revolutionary ambition – at the other is an inchoate glimpse of a world now visited only by the primitive and the drug-ridden, a world where technology shatters before magic and electronic communication is surpassed by the psychic telegraphy of animal mood.

Most of the literature of Black Power is interested entirely, or so it would seem, in immediate political objectives of the most concrete sort. Back in 1923, Marcus Garvey, father of the Back-to-Africa movement, might have written, 'When Europe was inhabited by a race of cannibals, a race of savages, naked men, heathens and pagans, Africa was peopled with a race of cultured black men, who were masters in art, science, and literature, men who were cultured and refined; men who, it was said, were like the gods,' but the present leaders of Black Power are concerned with political mandate and economic clout right here. Floyd McKissick of CORE: the Black Power Movement seeks to win power in a half-dozen ways. These are:

'1. The growth of Black *political* power.
'2. The building of Black *economic* power.
'3. The improvement of the *self-image* of Black people.
'4. The development of Black *leadership*.
'5. The attainment of *Federal law enforcement*.
'6. The mobilization of Black *consumer power*.'

These demands present nothing exceptional. On their face, they are not so different from manifestos by the NAACP or planks by the Democratic Party. A debater with the skill of William F. Buckley or Richard Nixon could stay afloat for hours on the lifesaving claim that there is nothing in these six points antithetical to conservatives. Indeed, there is not. Not on the face. For example, here is Adam Clayton Powell, a politician most respected by Black Power militants, on some of these points. Political power: 'Where we are 20 percent of the voters, we should command 20 percent of the jobs, judgeships, commissionerships, and all political appointments.' Economic power: 'Rather than a race primarily of consumers and stock boys, we must become a race of producers and stockbrokers.' Leadership: 'Black communities . . . must neither tolerate nor accept outside leadership – black or white.' Federal law enforcement: 'The battle against segregation in America's public-school systems must become a national effort, instead of the present regional skirmish that now exists.' Even consumer protest groups to stand watch on the quality of goods sold in a slum neighborhood are hardly revolutionary, more an implementation of good conservative buying practices. *Consumers Digest* is not yet at the barricades.

Indeed, which American institution of power is already to argue with these six points? They are so rational! The power of the technological society is shared by the corporations, the military, the mass media, the trade unions, and the Government. It is to the interest of each to have a society which is rational even as a machine is rational. When a machine breaks down, the cause can be discovered; in fact, the cause must be capable of being discovered or we are not dealing with a machine. So the pleasure of working with machines is that malfunctions are correctable; satisfaction is guaranteed by the application of work, knowledge, and reason. Hence, any race problem is anathema to power groups in the technological society, because the subject of race is irrational. At the very least, race problems seem to have the property of repelling reason. Still, the tendency of modern society to shape men for function in society like parts of a machine grows more powerful all the time. So we have the paradox of a conservative capitalistic democracy, profoundly entrenched in racial prejudice (and hitherto profoundly attracted to racial exploitation) now transformed into the most developed technological society in the world. The old prejudices of the men who wield power have become therefore inefficient before the needs of the social machine – so inefficient, in fact, that prejudiced as many of them still are, they consider it a measure of their responsibility to shed prejudice. (We must by now move outside the center of power before we can even find General Curtis LeMay.)

So the question may well be posed: if the demands formally presented by Black Power advocates like McKissick and Powell are thus rational, and indeed finally fit the requirements of the technological society, why then does Black Power inspire so much fear, distrust, terror, horror, and even outright revulsion among the best liberal descendants of the beautiful old Eleanor Roosevelt bag and portmanteau? And the answer is that an intellectual shell game has been played up to here. We have not covered McKissick's six points, only five. The sixth (point number three) was 'the improvement of the *self-image* of Black people.' It is here that Black hell busts loose. A technological society can deal comfortably with people who are mature, integrated, goal-oriented, flexible, responsive, group-responsive, etc., etc. – the word we cannot leave out is white or white-oriented. The technological society is not able to deal with the self-image of separate peoples and races if the development of their self-image produces personalities of an explosive individuality. We do not substitute sticks of dynamite for the teeth of a gear and assume we still have an automotive transmission.

McKissick covers his third point, of course: 'Negro history, art, music and other aspects of Black culture . . . make Black people aware of their contributions to the American heritage and to world civilization.' Powell bastes the goose with orotundities of rhetorical gravy: 'We must give our children a sense of pride in being black. The glory of our past and the dignity of our present must lead the way to the power of our future.' Amen. We have been conducted around the point.

Perhaps the clue is that political Right and political Left are meaningless terms when applied conventionally to Black Power. If we are to use them at all (and it is a matter of real convenience), then we might call the more or less rational, programmatic, and recognizably political arm of Black Power, presented by McKissick and Powell, as the Right Wing, since their program can conceivably be attached to the programs of the technological society, whether Democrat or Republican. The straight-out political demands of this kind of Black Power not only can be integrated (at least on paper) into the needs of the technological society, but must be, because – we would repeat – an exploited class creates disruption and therefore irrationality in a social machine; efforts to solve exploitation and disruption become mandatory for the power groups. If this last sentence sounds vaguely Marxist in cadence, the accident is near. What characterizes technological societies is that they tend to become more and more like one another. So America and the Soviet Union will yet have interchangeable parts, or at least be no more different than a four-door Ford from a two-door Chevrolet. It may thus be noticed that what we are calling the Right Wing of Black Power – the technological wing – is in the conventional sense interested in moving to the left. Indeed, after the Blacks attain equality – so goes the unspoken assumption – America will be able to progress toward a rational society of racial participation, etc., etc. What then is the Left Wing of Black Power? Say, let us go back to Africa, back to Garvey.

> We must understand that we are replacing a *dying* culture, and we must be prepared to do this, and be absolutely conscious of what we are replacing it with. We are sons and daughters of the most ancient societies on this planet. . . . No movement shaped or contained by Western culture will ever benefit Black people. Black power must be the actual force and beauty and wisdom of Blackness . . . reordering the world.
>
> – LeRoi Jones

Are you ready to enter the vision of the Black Left? It is profoundly anti-technological. Here are a few remarks by Ron Karenga:

'The fact that we are Black is our ultimate reality. We were Black before we were born.

'The white boy is engaged in the worship of technology; we must not sell our souls for money and machines. We must free ourselves culturally before we proceed politically.

'Revolution to us is the creation of an alternative . . . we are not here to be taught by the world, but to teach the world.'

We have left the splendid American far behind. He believes in speaking his mind; but if LeRoi Jones – insults, absolute rejection, and consummate bad-mouthing – is not too much for him, then Karenga will be his finish. Karenga obviously believes that in the root is the answer to where the last growth went wrong – so he believes in the wisdom of the blood, and blood-wisdom went out for the splendid American after reading *Lady Chatterley's Lover* in sophomore year. Life is hard enough to see straight without founding your philosophy on a metaphor.

Nonetheless the mystique of Black Power remains. Any mystique which has men ready to die for it is never without political force. The Left Wing of Black Power speaks across the void to the most powerful conservative passions – for any real conservatism is founded on regard for the animal, the oak and the field; it has instinctive detestation of science, of the creation-by-machine. Conservatism is a body of traditions which once served as the philosophical home of society. If the traditions are now withered in the hum of electronics; if the traditions have become almost hopelessly inadequate to meet the computed moves of the technological society; if conservatism has become the grumbling of the epicure at bad food, bad air, bad manners; if conservatism lost the future because it enjoyed the greed of its privileged position to that point where the exploited depths stirred in righteous rage; if the conservatives and their traditions failed because they violated the balance of society, exploited the poor too savagely and searched for justice not nearly enough; if finally the balance between property rights and the rights of men gave too much to the land and too little to the living blood, still conservatism and tradition had one last Herculean strength: they were of the marrow, they partook of primitive wisdom. The tradition had been founded on some half-remembered sense of primitive perception, and so was close to life and the sense of life. Tradition had appropriated the graceful movements with which primitive strangers and friends might meet in the depth of a mood, all animal in their awareness: lo! the stranger bows before the intense presence of the monarch or the chief, and the movement is later engraved upon a code of ceremony. So tradition was once a key to the primitive life still breathing within us, a key too large, idiosyncratic, and unmanageable for the quick shuttles of the electronic. Standing before technology, tradition began to die, and air turned to smog. But the black man, living a life on the fringe of technological society, exploited by it, poisoned by it, half rejected by it, gulping prison air in the fluorescent nightmare of shabby garish electric ghettos, uprooted centuries ago from his native Africa, his instincts living ergo like nerves in the limbo of an amputated limb, had thereby an experience unique to modern man – he was forced to live at one and the same time in the old primitive jungle of the slums, and the hygienic surrealistic landscape of the technological society. And as he began to arise from his exploitation, he discovered that the culture which had saved him owed more to the wit and telepathy of the jungle than the value and programs of the West. His dance had taught him more than writs and torts, his music was sweeter than Shakespeare or Bach (since music had never been a luxury to him but a need), prison had given him a culture deeper than libraries in the grove, and violence had produced an economy of personal relations as negotiable as money. The American Black had survived – of all the peoples of the Western world, he was the only one in the near seven decades of the twentieth century to have undergone the cruel weeding of real survival. So it was possible his manhood had improved while the manhood of others was being leached. He had at any rate a vision. It was that he was black, beautiful, and secretly superior – he had therefore the potentiality to conceive and create a new culture (perchance a new civilization), richer, wiser, deeper, more beautiful and profound than any he had seen. (And conceivably more demanding, more torrential, more tyrannical.) But he would not know until he had power for himself. He would not know if he could provide a wiser science, subtler schooling, deeper medicine, richer victual, and deeper view of creation until he had the power. So while some (the ones the Blacks called Negroes) looked to integrate into the super-suburbs of technology land (and find, was their hope, a little peace for the kids), so others dreamed of a future world which their primitive lore and sophisticated attainments might now bring. And because they were proud and loved their vision, they were warriors as well, and had a mystique which saw the cooking of food as good or bad for the soul. And taste gave the hint. That was the Left of Black Power, a movement as mysterious, dedicated, instinctive, and conceivably bewitched as a gathering of Templars for the next Crusade. Soon their public fury might fall upon the fact that civilization was a trap, and therefore their wrath might be double, for they had been employed to build civilization, had received none of its gains, and yet, being allowed to enter now, now, this late, could be doomed with the rest. What a thought!

When the *canaille roturière* took the liberty of beheading the high *noblesse*, it was done less, perhaps, to inherit their goods than to inherit their ancestors.

– Heinrich Heine

But I am a white American, more or less, and writing for an audience of Americans, white and Negro in the main. So the splendid American would remind me that my thoughts are romantic projections, hypotheses unverifiable by any discipline, no more legitimate for discussion than melody. What, he might ask, would you do with the concrete problem before us. . . .

You mean: not jobs, not schools, not votes, not production, not consumption. . . .

No, he said hoarsely, law and order.

Well, the man who sings the melody is not normally consulted for the bylaws of the Arrangers' Union.

Crap and craparola, said the splendid American, what it all comes down to is: how do you keep the peace?

I do not know. If they try to keep it by force – we will not have to wait so very long before there are Vietnams in our own cities. A race which arrives at a vision must test that vision by deeds.

Then what would you do?

If I were king?

We are a republic and will never support a king.

Ah, if I were a man who had a simple audience with Richard Milhous Nixon, I would try to say, 'Remember when all else has failed, that honest hatred searches for responsibility. I would look to encourage not merely new funding for businessmen who are Black, but Black schools with their own teachers and their own texts, Black solutions to Black housing where the opportunity might be given to rebuild one's own slum room by room, personal idiosyncrasy next to mad neighbor's style, floor by floor, not block by block; I would try to recognize that an area of a city where whites fear to go at night belongs by all existential – which is to say natural – law to the Blacks, and would respect the fact, and so would encourage Black local self-government as in a separate city with a Black sanitation department run by themselves, a Black fire department, a funding for a Black concert hall, and most of all a Black police force responsible only to this city within our city and Black courts of justice for their own. There will be no peace short of the point where the Black man can measure his new superiorities and inferiorities against our own.'

You are absolutely right but for one detail, said the splendid American. What will you do when they complain about the smog our factories push into their air?

Oh, I said, the Blacks are so evil their factories will push worse air back. And thus we went on arguing into the night. Yes, the times are that atrocious you can hardly catch your breath. 'Confronted by outstanding merit in another, there is no way of saving one's ego except by love.'

Goethe is not the worse way to say good-night.

## Contribution to a *Partisan Review* Symposium

Allow a symposiast to quote from himself. The following is out of *The Armies of the Night*.

Not for little humor had Negroes developed that odd humorless crack in their personality which cracked each other into laughter, playing on one side an odd mad practical black man who could be anything, wise chauffeur, drunken butler, young moneymad Pullman porter, Negro college graduate selling insurance – the other half was sheer psychopath, rocks in the ice-cube, pocket oiled for the switchblade, I'll kill you, Whitey, burn baby, all turned to a cool. These Blacks moved through the New Left with a physical indifference to the bodies about them, as if ten Blacks could handle any hundred of these flaccid Whites, and they signaled to each other across the aisles, and talked in quick idioms and out, an English not comprehensible to any ear which knew nothing of the separate meanings of the same word at separate pitch (Maoists not for nothing these Blacks!) their hair carefully brushed out in every direction like African guerrillas or huge radar stations on some lonely isle, they seemed to communicate with one another in ten dozen modes, with fingers like deaf and dumb, with feet, with their stance, by the flick of their long wrist, with the radar of their hair, the smoke of their will, the glide of their passage, by a laugh, a nod, a disembodied gesture, through mediums, seeming to speak through silent mediums among them who never gave hint to a sign. In the apathy which had begun to lie over the crowd as the speeches went on and on (and the huge army gathered by music, now was ground down by words, and the hollow absurd imprecatory thunder of the loudspeakers with their reductive echo – you must FIGHT . . . *fight* . . . fight . . . fite . . . ite . . . , in the soul-killing repetition of political jargon which reminded people that the day was well past one o'clock and they still had not started) the Blacks in the roped-in area about the speaker's stand were the only sign of active conspiracy, they were up to some collective expression of disdain, something to symbolize their detestation of the White Left – yes, the observer was to brood on it much of the next day when he learned without great surprise that almost all of the Negroes had left to make their own demonstration in another part of Washington, their announcement to the press underlying their reluctance to use their bodies in

a White War. That was comprehensible enough. If the Negroes were at the Pentagon and did not preempt the front rank, they would lose face as fighters; if they were too numerous on the line, they would be beaten half to death. That was the ostensible reason they did not go, but the observer wondered if he saw a better.

There is an old tendency among writers of the Left when apologists for one indigestible new convulsion or another – they go in for a species of calculated reduction which attempts to introduce comfortable proportions into historic phenomena which are barbaric, heroic, monstrous, epic, and/or apocalyptic. (*New Republic* and *Nation* writers please stand!) So we may remember there was never much of a famine in the Ukraine, just various local dislocations of distribution; never real Moscow trials, rather the sort of predictable changing of the guard which accompanies virile epochs of history. The American labor unions were never really in danger of leaving the Left, just being led down the garden path by unscrupulous but limited leadership. Et cetera. So forth.

Now, Black Power. We are bound to hear before we are done that Black Power is merely a long-due corrective for premature and administratively betrayed efforts at integration – an indispensable period of self-development which will result in future integrations at a real level.

Like all such Left perspectives, it is wishful, pretty, programmatic, manipulable by jargon, and utterly stripped of that existential content which is indispensable to comprehending the first thing about Black Power.

The first thing to say, pretty or no, is that the Negro (that is the active volatile cadres of every militant Negro movement, SNCC, Black Muslims, etc., plus those millions of latently rebellious black masses behind them – which is what we will refer to when we speak of the Negro), yes, this Negro does not want equality any longer, he wants superiority, and wants it because he feels he is in fact superior. And there is some justice on his side for believing it. Sufficiently fortunate to be alienated from the benefits of American civilization, the Negro seems to have been better able to keep his health. It would take a liberal with a psychotic sense of moderation to claim that whites and Negroes have equally healthy bodies; the Negroes know they have become on the average physically superior, and this *against all the logic of America's medical civilization* – the Negroes get less good food ostensibly, no vitamins, a paucity of antibiotics, less medical care, less fresh air, less light and sanitation in living quarters. Let us quit the list – it is parallel to another list one could make of educational opportunities vs. actual culture (which is to say – real awareness of one's milieu). The Negro's relatively low rate of literacy seems to be in inverse relation to his philosophical capacity to have a comprehensive vision of his life, a large remark whose only support is existential – let us brood, brothers, on the superior cool of the Negro in public places. For the cool comes from a comprehensive vision, a relaxation before the dangers of life, a readiness to meet death, philosophy, or amusement at any turn.

Commend us, while we are on lists, to the ability of the Negro to police himself, as opposed to the ability of the White to police others. At the civil rights march on Washington in 1963 with over a hundred thousand Negroes in town, no episodes of violence were reported – in the riots in the years which followed, fascinating patterns of cooperation among the rioters emerge. One may look, as government commissions do, for patterns of a plot; or one may do better to entertain the real possibility that the Negroes have psychic powers of mass impromptu collaboration which are mysterious, and by that measure, superior to the White.

What the Negro may have decided at this point, as Black Power emerges, is that he has gotten the worst and the least of civilization, and yet has been able to engage life more intensely. It is as if the cells of his body now know more than the white man – so his future potentiality is greater. Whether this is true, half-true, or a species of madness is beyond anyone's capacity to know in this year, but the psychological reality is that breaking through his feelings of vast inferiority, a feeling of vast superiority is beginning to arise in the black man, and the antennae of this superiority lead not to developing the Negro to a point where he can live effectively as an equal in white society, but rather toward developing a viable modern culture of his own, a new kind of civilization. This is the real and natural intent of Black Power; not to get better schools, but to find a way to educate their own out of textbooks not yet written; not to get fair treatment from the police, but grapple instead with the incommensurable problem of policing one's own society – what will Black justice be? Ergo, not to get a fair share of hospitals, but an opportunity to explore Black medicine, herbs in place of antibiotics, witchcraft for cancer cures, surgical grace with the knife in preference to heart transfers. In parallel: not to get into unions, but to discover – it is far off in the distance – Black notions of labor, cooperation, and the viability of hip in production methods; not housing projects, but a new way to build houses; not shuttle planes, but gliders; not computers – rather psychic inductions.

Black Power moves then, obviously, against the technological society. Since the Negro has never been able to absorb a technological culture with success, even reacting against it with instinctive pain and distrust, he is now in this oncoming epoch of automation going to be removed from the technological society anyway. His only salvation, short of becoming a city brigand or a government beggar, is to build his own society out of his own culture, own means, own horror, own genius. Or own heroic, tragic, or evil possibilities. For there is no need to assume that the black man will prove morally superior to the white man. Schooled in treachery, steeped in centuries of white bile, there are avalanches and cataracts of violence, destruction, inchoate rage, and promiscuous waste to be encountered – there is well a question whether he can build his own society at all, so perverse are the conduits of his crossed emotions by now. But the irony is that the White would be well to hope the Black can build a world, for those well-ordered epochs of capitalism which flushed the white wastes down into the Black heart are gone – the pipes of civilization are backing up. The irony is that we may even yet need a Black vision of existence if civilization is to survive the death chamber it has built for itself. So let us at least recognize the real ground of Black Power – it is ambitious, beautiful, awesome, terrifying, and has to do with nothing so much as the most important questions of us all – what is man? why are we here? will we survive?

## A Consequent Exchange: Letters

Sirs:

In your Spring 1968 issue Norman Mailer writes:

Sufficiently fortunate to be alienated from the benefits of American civilization, the Negro seems to have been better able to keep his health. It would take a liberal with a psychotic sense of moderation to claim that whites and Negroes have equally healthy bodies; the Negroes know they have become on the average physically superior, and this *against all the logic of America's medical civilization.* . . .

In the *New York Times*, May 19, 1968, there appears the following:

Poor Americans are four times as likely to die before the age of 35 as the average citizen. Negro women in Mississippi die six times as often in childbirth as white women and in some urban ghettos of the North one child in ten dies in infancy. The life expectancy of an American Negro at birth is 61 years, that of a white American is 68.

In citing these figures Dr. H. Jack Geiger of Tufts– New England Medical Center said recently that the health of the poor in this country 'is an ongoing national disaster.'

The effects of racial discrimination and economic disadvantage begin before birth, Dr. Geiger said. . . . Poor women obtain prenatal care less often than others. In the maternity wards of public hospitals 45 percent of the mothers have had no such care. This increases three-fold their likelihood of bearing children prematurely. Mental retardation occurs ten times more often in very small premature babies than in those born at full term. . . .

The health gap between rich and poor is growing. In 1940 the infant mortality rate for nonwhites was 70 percent higher than that for whites. In 1962 the rate was 90 percent greater.

We all know that 'the poor' includes a vast number of Negroes and often is used as a euphemism for Negroes. Now then, who is right – Dr. Geiger or Mr. Mailer?

*Irving Howe*

Mr. Mailer replies:

I was not aware of Dr. Geiger's figures when I wrote the piece from which Irving Howe quotes, or I would have attempted to use his statistics to fortify my case, particularly the relation of the following two sentences: 'The life expectancy of an American Negro at birth is 61 years, . . . of a white American . . . 68' and 'in 1962 the [infant mortality rate for nonwhites] was 90 percent higher.'

Now a few figures from a book by J. I. Rodale, *Are We Really Living Longer?* (Emmaus, Pa., 1955). In 1850, the life expectancy of a white male at birth was 38.3 years; in 1947 it was 65.16 years. But 'in 1850, white men who lived to be forty years old could expect on the average to live 27.9 years longer or to a total age of 67.9 . . . in 1947 it [life expectancy] had only increased to 30.6 (total age 70.6). In 100 years, therefore, the life expectancy had only increased 2.7 years *after forty years of age* [italics mine].' In fact, a man reaching the age of 60 in the year 1850 had a slightly longer life expectancy than a man of 60 in 1947.

Evidently, the medical gains are to be found in infant mortality rates. Infants and children who would have died one hundred years ago are kept alive today by medical science.

Now, Negro infants obviously receive inferior medical care. So their mortality rate by the Geiger figures is 90 percent higher. Yet note that every time an infant dies, someone else must live to the age of seventy in order to have an average life expectancy for the two of 35 years. If, then, the American Negro's life expectancy at birth is *so high* as 61 years (after incorporating an infant mortality rate 90 percent higher than the white man's) and the white American's life expectancy (after the advantage of his reduced infant mortality rate) is still *so low* at birth as 68 years, the inference can hardly be ignored that if the American Negro can manage to get through the rigors of his infancy, his future life expectancy – poor medical care and all – is going to be higher than the white's. And indeed after the age of 65, the contemporary Negro, despite all early obstacles, has a greater life expectancy than the white man.

Perhaps the logic of America's white medical civilization is to keep the babies alive and debilitate the men.

Regards to Mr. Howe.

Sirs:

Your readers may recall the exchange between Norman Mailer and myself in the last *Partisan Review* concerning health, physical condition, etc., among Negroes and whites in America. Since my letter was based on a report by Dr. H. Jack Geiger, I thought it might be useful to submit the Howe-Mailer exchange to him and see what he thought. Which I did. Dr. Geiger then wrote me the following letter, asking that it be submitted to *Partisan Review* for publication. Which I do.

*Irving Howe*

Dear Mr. Howe:

Your letter of August 5 has just been forwarded to me in Mississippi, where most of my work is now focused. I am pleased at your thoughtfulness in sending me the exchange of correspondence between yourself and Norman Mailer in the *Partisan Review*. I think the issue is a most important one.

First of all, I have to point out an error which occurred either in your letter, or in the *Times* of May 19. The quote should have said 'and in some urban ghettos of the North one child in ten dies in infancy.'

With regard to Mr. Mailer's reply, it is inaccurate. I do not want to bore you, or him, or the readers of *Partisan Review*, with a long and statistical analysis, but the fundamental error is in the application to whole populations of the idea that 'every time an infant dies someone else must live to the age of 70 in order to have an average life expectancy for the two of 35 years.' In a sample of two people, life may be divided between 0 and 70 years to reach an average of 35; but in the large Negro population of the United States it is not 50 percent that dies under one year of age but approximately 4 per cent – even though this is a rate 90 percent higher than the white rate. The fact of the matter is that most but not all of the seven-year differential in life expectancy between Negroes and whites in the United States is accounted for by infant mortality. It is worth emphasizing the 'not all'. While it is quite true as Mr Mailer points out, that there has been very little progress for life expectancy beyond age 40 (regardless of race) in the last 50 years, the fact is that at *almost every age* from o to 65, including the ages past 40, the Negro has a lower life expectancy in the United States than the white. Put more bluntly, a Negro in the United States at any age is likelier to die sooner than a white man of the same age. The death rates for virtually every major grouping of diseases, at any age, is higher for Negroes than for whites in the United States.

This is obviously in very large measure – if not entirely – due to the circumstances of life for the Black American – that is, miserable housing, overcrowding, inadequate nutrition, greater exposure to infectious disease, discrimination, social and psychological stress, and all the rest of the dreary litany that is so familiar to us.

It is just not true in the United States that Negroes and whites have equally healthy bodies; at any age, the Negro is likelier to suffer illness – or at least to die from the illnesses he suffers. I do not know what Mr. Mailer means by 'the Negroes have become on the average physically superior. . . .' What is the criterion of physical superiority? It cannot be in growth and development; inadequate nutrition and faulty medical care have seen to that. It cannot be in life expectancy. The implication is that there is some sort of intrinsic or genetic physical superiority in Negroes, however obscured it may be by the effects of environment and faulty medical care. On the basis of our present knowledge, this is as ridiculous as the contention that Negroes are intrinsically inferior and whites superior. There is just no scientific support for claims of racial superiority and inferiority, no matter which race we are talking about.

The most profound admiration for American Negroes – for the ability to survive, somehow, to some extent, in the face of brutalizing, bitter, discriminatory biological, social, and physical environment – does not require statistical manipulation nor genetic mythology. It would be tragic if we let anything obscure our confrontation of the slow and systematic damage our social order wreaks on Black Americans, just as it would be foolish if we made longevity the test of the quality of a social order. After all, whites in North Dakota live longer than anybody in the United States, and I doubt that Mr. Mailer would be interested in the thesis that rural North Dakota represents the epitome of Western civilization.

Finally, I do not know what Mr. Mailer means by 'America's medical civilization.' Discrimination and injustice in medical care are a significant and disgusting feature of American life, but the basic harm that is done to Blacks in the United States has nothing to do with medicine; it has to do with the social order of which medicine is only a part.

*H. Jack Geiger, M.D.*
*Tufts University School of Medicine*

Mr. Mailer replies:

One point I wished to make in my answer to Irving Howe: With the exception of infant care, our medical civilization (by which I mean techniques, pharmacopia, hospitals, etc.) deprive people of more health than they furnish. Dr. Geiger's letter with its corrected statistics – statistics, mind you, which had to be corrected after passing through three reliable sources, Dr. Geiger, the *New York Times* and Irving Howe – admits that even with the corrected statistics, Negro life expectancy is almost as great as white. The Negro's greater mortality, as Dr. Geiger points out quite justly, is due to leading lives of such abysmal economic misery that Black health is affected. Obviously their slightly greater rate of adult mortality is due not to insufficiency of medical care, but to a lack of the most basic requirements of life, food, and shelter. It seems to me that the true test of the argument might be to study Negro communities which have decent food and shelter but not enough income to afford any expensive medical care against prosperous white samples who receive all the medical care in the world. Then we might see whose body was voting for longevity. I do not wish to make a fetish of longevity in and of itself. It was the others, after all, who first brought it up. I would rather point out that my attack was made upon the conditioned reflexes of the liberal stance which rushes to claim that he who does without professional medical care is automatically damned, and damned unhealthy, whereas I would rush to assume that one of the roots of the twentieth-century disease is the over-proliferation of medical techniques and medical drugs without in some – by now is it in most? – cases rudimentary studies of their ultimate effects.

In none of this have I mentioned once that the physical superiority of the Negro appears most evident in the extraordinary number of Negroes who make superb athletes. Let Irving Howe say that the reason for athletic eminence is because nothing else is open to the talented Negro – I would suggest he watch a few of their moves. The resources of an emerging culture can sometimes be glimpsed in the passage of a figure. (Or is that what modern dance has been trying to tell me all these years?)

# White Politics

## An Open Letter to Richard Nixon

Dear Mr. President-Elect:

Years ago, talented sportswriters like Jimmy Cannon used to write columns which began: 'You're Ray Robinson and you used to be the greatest welterweight in the world. Now, you're older, and trying to make it back as a middleweight.' Mr. Cannon was employing a subtle literary form: exhortation by the insinuation of the second person. It is a style of literary address used for speaking to children, monarchs, champions, union workers, and chiefs, so it is hardly a routine tense to employ for open correspondence with a President. We are a republic, after all, and it is incumbent on us to venerate the Presidency. Only a fool, fanatic, lout, or very wicked fellow would presume to speak in the Insinuative Exhortative to his Commander-in-Chief.

Yet, as you have been the first to remark, we live in times so divisive that the most affecting moment of your campaign was the sight of a sign, BRING US TOGETHER, which a young girl held up at the edge of the crowd as evening came on. We are all hungry for honest sentiment to nourish the marrow of our raddled psychology, so hungry one would feel demonic to suggest that we cannot be certain of the precise occasion of any fact. Yet it is impossible in the age of the Avenue of the Madison not to suspect that the girl and the sign could have been the bright idea of a bright young executive with horn-rimmed glasses who simply set out to design that scene, and converted the meaning of the sign, therefore, from sentiment to a computation of the techno-structure.

Well, we could never know. In the horror of our modern times, there is nothing more difficult to verify than the root of a fact. It may be incumbent on us, therefore, to trust your Presidency until that day we are certain you do not mean what you say. It is happier to believe that you do, that you are a man who has made a remarkable return from an abysmal political defeat, and that your passion is to bring peace and justice to this country, to unite us, drain our running wounds, and flesh us a vision of some creative future. Nothing less would entitle you to be called a great President; nothing less than a great President might be ready to satisfy our need.

Of course your detractors in the Democratic Party, even writers so elegant as Mr. Schlesinger and Mr. Galbraith, expect you to entertain policies they think detestable: a search for nuclear superiority, a program of law and order with increments of local police force too large for democratic balance, even a certain cynicism about the rate of unemployment, a flirtation with depression rather than inflation, a bending of the tax structure to cushion the corporations and the rich; they are blunt to fear that you are a man of paranoid disposition, unstable temperament in crisis, and not above striking a low blow. Of course these two gentlemen might today admit that the same description of personality could fit Lyndon Johnson. Yet if any writer had suggested such a syndrome in 1964, Schlesinger and Galbraith would have wished to dispatch him to an institution. So we do not have to accept their view of your character, especially since they have already certified themselves as fine fellows, but abominably off the point on occasion in their judgments of men. Of course, they are Democrats, and the Democratic Party has much to bewilder it today. It is a party of the people which lately does not find a candidate the people desire. Dump the Hump! It is a party which has become all program and no coherent philosophy. Its approach to every social, moral, and spiritual ill of man is to inject money; so it has the psychology of the pusher: in trouble? – take a fix! People, in fact, are so addicted to voting for the Democratic Party that many pulled the lever for its last nominee even if the thought of him offered nausea.

Of course, many voted for you without enthusiasm either. It is conceivably part of your strength that you are well aware of this. One would hope so. For in that case, it could prove an attractive and powerful passion to demonstrate to America that it was wrong and that there are funds of imagination, decency, and creative politics open to you which will yet astound the nation. That is why one may hope the liberal intellectuals of the

Democratic Party are mistaken in their assumption that you will look for nuclear superiority, massive dragoonings of law and order, policies of repression in the ghetto, and the engineering of all oxygen out of one's breath. There is a crisis in the world today which comes out of the massive over-development of the machine before we have comprehended its excesses, or even how to dispose of its wastes. This super-employment of machines is accelerated every instant by the promiscuities of electronic communication which strip the husk of new ideas as pervasively as paper money once uprooted the yeoman from his field and the craftsman from his bench. Now a new generation of rulers has entered our century. We are governed no longer by chieftains, statesmen, or princes – now managers, experts, and executives, members of what some have come to call the techno-structure, seem to rule society. You are a respectable member of that techno-structure, as was your Democratic opponent. Your political differences seemed no more separated philosophically than the discussion of two mechanics (with different religious affiliations) about the best way to repair a machine which had become hopelessly inefficient, if not downright sinister, since its fumes brought death to every breath of air, its wastes gave promise of destroying the fields and glutting the rivers, its plastic residue proved insoluble to departments of sanitation all over the world, and its ferocious coupling of new ideas thrust nihilism into every pore of intellectual and academic life.

Since it is obvious that you are still full of belief in the power of the techno-structure to solve the problems of society, one anticipates your Administration with heavy foreboding. Yet this sense of gloom might have been greater if either of your opponents had won, since the man to your Right could have brought on a civil war in the cities, and the man to your Left would have looked like nothing so much as a third-string tailback scurrying from sideline to sideline, first Left, then Right, never gaining a yard. Hysteria is the wild gallop of unleashed horses who never move, and if your opponents claim that you are unstable, any common witness would know that the candidate on your Left was hysterical.

Let us hope then, sir, that you are precisely unstable enough to move in ways unforeseen by any of your critics or supporters. If you are on the one hand a believer in the techno-structure, you are on the other a conservative, you believe or pretend to believe in the immanence of God, the nourishment of tradition, and the sanctity of nature. The technological society which you now begin to administer proceeds to destroy all three at a rate far greater than the worst Communism of your nightmares; you, like every other American, must look into the eye of a dilemma no smaller than the agony of the twentieth century. Nothing less than the artful balance of old dialogues and new, of revolutionary approaches to particular problems and the delicate restoration of tradition within other kinds of crisis can begin to awaken our world from the chimeras of destruction which now surround us. Once, on television, in a show called 'Firing Line', the writer of this letter said to William F. Buckley that he thought Fidel Castro and Charles de Gaulle were the two greatest political figures alive today. It is the only time he ever saw Mr. Buckley's jaw fly open in a debate. If you feel a clue to the impact of that remark, then there is cause for optimism that you as President will be able to contribute an unforeseen thought or two to the political theatre of America and our dramatic sense of the democratic art. If, on the other hand, praise for two such existential leaders leaves you perplexed, one is forced to suggest that the health of a good society in evil times may come from the grace to recognize a merit in the most unlikely man. But here I am, sir, working for myself again, or is it tooling the trick for you?

Yours for an interesting and prosperous Administration,
*Norman Mailer*

## An Instrument for the City

*The* New York Times *Magazine, May 18, 1969*
How is one to speak of the illness of a city? A clear day can come, a morning in early May like the pride of June. The streets are cool, the buildings have come out of shadow, and silences are

broken by the voices of children. It is as if the neighborhood has slept in the winding-sheet of the past. Forty years go by – one can recollect the milkman and the clop of a horse. It is a great day. Everyone speaks of the delight of the day on the way to work. It is hard on such mornings to believe that New York is the victim 'etherized upon a table'.

Yet by afternoon the city is incarcerated once more. Haze covers the sky, a grim, formless glare blazes back from the horizon. The city has become unbalanced again. By the time work is done, New Yorkers push through the acrid, lung-rotting air and work their way home, avoiding each other's eyes on the subway. Later, near midnight, thinking of a walk to buy the *Times*, they hesitate – in the darkness a familiar sense of dread returns, the streets are not quite safe, the sense of waiting for some apocalyptic fire, some night of long knives, hangs over the city. We recognize one more time that the city is ill, that our own New York, the Empire City, is not too far from death.

Recollect: When we were children, we were told air was invisible, and it was. Now we see it shift and thicken, move in gray depression over a stricken sky. Now we grow used to living with colds all year, and viruses suggestive of the plague. Tempers shorten in our hideous air. The sick get sicker, the violent more violent. The frayed tissue of New York manners seems ready to splatter on every city street. It is the first problem of the city, our atrocious air. People do not die dramatically like the one-day victims of Donora, rather they dwindle imperceptibly, die five years before their time, ten years before, cough or sneeze helplessly into the middle of someone else's good mood, stroll about with the hot iron of future asthma manacled to their lungs. The air pollution in New York is so bad, and gives so much promise of getting worse, that there is no solution to any other problem until the air is relieved of its poisonous ingestions. New York has conceivably the worst air of any city in the universe today – certainly it is the worst air in the most technologically developed nation in the world, which is to say it is the air of the future if the future is not shifted from its program. Once Los Angeles was famous for the liver-yellow of her smog: we have surpassed her.

That is our pervasive ill. It is fed by a host of tributary ills which flow into the air, fed first by our traffic, renowned through the world for its incapacity to move. Midtown Manhattan is next to impenetrable by vehicle from midday to evening – the average rate of advance is, in fact, six miles an hour, about the speed of a horse at a walk. Once free of the center, there is the threat of hour-long tie-ups at every bridge, tunnel, and expressway if even a single car breaks down in a lane. In the course of a year, people lose weeks of working time through the sum of minutes and quarter hours of waiting to crawl forward in traffic. Tempers blow with lost schedules, work suffers everywhere. All the while stalled cars gun their motors while waiting in place, pumping carbon monoxide into air already laden with caustic sulphur dioxide from fuel oil we burn to make electricity.

Given this daily burden, this air pollution, noise pollution, stagnant transport, all but crippled subways, routes of new transportation twenty years unbuilt – every New Yorker sallies forth into an environment which strips him before noon of his good cheer, his charity, his calm nerve, and his ability to discipline his anger.

Yet, beneath that mood of pestilential clangor, something worse is ticking away – our deeper sense of a concealed and continuing human horror. If there are eight million people in New York, one million live on welfare, no, the figure is higher now, it will be one million two hundred thousand by the end of the year. Not a tenth of these welfare cases will ever be available for work; they are women and children first, then too old, too sick, too addicted, too illiterate, too unskilled, too ignorant of English. Fatherless families and motherless families live at the end of an umbilical financial cord which perpetuates them in an embryonic economic state. Welfare is the single largest item in the city budget – two years ago it surpassed the figure we reserve for education, yet it comes down to payments of no more than $3,800 a year for a family of four. Each member of that family is able to spend a dollar a day for food, at most $1.25 a day.

Still it is worse than that. If one of eight people in New York is on welfare, half as many again might just as well be on welfare because their minimum wage brings in no more than such a check. So the natural incentive is to cease working. Close to $1.5 billion is spent on welfare now. The figure will go up. Manpower Training, in contrast, spends about a twenty-fifth as much. Looking to skill the poor for work, it will train as many as 4,000 men a year, and place perhaps 10,000 men out of 100,000 applicants in bad jobs without foreseeable future, the only jobs indeed available for the untrained. Sometimes in the Job Corps it cost $13,000 to train a man for a job where he might be able to make $6,000 a year if he could find a job, but the skills he had learned were not related to the jobs he might return to at home. Poverty lies upon the city like a layer of smog.

Our housing offers its unhappy figures. If we have calculated that it is necessary to build 7,500 new low-income apartments a year, merely to keep on the same terms with the problem, we end in fact with 4,000 units constructed. Never mind how most of it looks – those grim, high-rise, new-slum prisons on every city horizon. Face rather the fact that we lose near to the same number of units a year as old buildings which could have been saved run down into a state requiring condemnation. Of the $100,000,000 the city spends each budget year for new housing, $20,000,000 goes into demolition. If four times as much were spent by present methods on low- and middle-income housing, 36,000 new and rehabilitated units could be provided a year, but housing needs would still be huge and unmet – the average family could wait twenty-five years to benefit from the program.

Our finances are intolerable. If New York State delivers $17 billion in income tax and $5 billion in corporate taxes to the federal government, it is conservative to assume that $14 billion of the total of $22 billion has come from the people of New York City. But our city budget is about $7.5 billion: of that sum only $3 billion derives from the state and from Washington. New York must find another $4.5 billion in real estate and other local taxes. Consider then: We pay $14 billion in income tax to the federal government and to Albany: back comes $3 billion. We put out five dollars for every dollar which returns. So we live in vistas of ironbound civic poverty. Four of those lost five dollars are going to places like Vietnam and Malmstrom in North Dakota where the ABM will find a site, or dollars are going to interstate highways which pass through regions we probably will never visit. In relation to the federal government, the city is like a sharecropper who lives forever in debt at the company store.

Yes, everything is wrong. The vocations of the past disintegrate. Jewish teachers who went into the education system twenty years ago to have security for themselves and to disseminate enlightenment among the children of the poor, now feel no security in their work, and are rejected in their liberal sociological style of teaching. The collective ego of their life-style is shattered. They are forced to comprehend that there are black people who would rather be taught by other black people than by experts. The need for authenticity has become the real desire in education. 'Who am I? What is the meaning of my skin, my passion, my dread, my fury, my dream of glories undreamed, my very need for bread?' – these questions are now become so powerful they bring the pumps of blood up to pressure and leave murder in the heart. What can education be in the womb of a dying city but a fury to discover for oneself whether one is victim or potential hero, stupid or too bright for old pedagogical ways? Rage at the frustration of the effort to find a style became the rage at the root of the uproar in the schools last year, and the rage will be there until the schools are free to discover a new way to learn. Let us not be arrogant toward the ignorant – their sensitivity is often too deep to dare the knowledge of numbers or the curlicue within a letter. Picasso, age of eleven, could still not do arithmetic because the figure 7 looked like a nose upside down to him.

Among the poor, genius may stay buried behind the mask of the most implacable stupidity, for if genius can have no issue in a man's life, he must conceal it, and protect it, reserve it for his seed, or his blessing, or, all else gone, for his curse. No wonder we live with dread in our heart, and the nicest of the middle class still padlock their doors against the curse. We are like a Biblical city which has fallen from grace. Our parks deteriorate, and after duty our police go home to suburbs beyond the city – they come back to govern us from without. And municipal employees drift in the endless administrative bogs of Wagnerian systems of apathy and attrition. Work gets done at the rate of work accomplished by a draft army in peacetime at a

sullen out-of-the-way post. The Poverty Program staggers from
the brilliance of its embezzlements. But, of course, if you were a
bright young black man, might you not want to steal a million
from the feds?

Here, let us take ourselves to the problem. It goes beyond the
Durham gang. Our first problem is that no one alive in New
York can answer with honesty the question: can New York be
saved? None of us can know. It is possible people will emigrate
from New York in greater and greater numbers, and administration will collapse under insufferable weights, order will be
restored from without. Then, everyone who can afford it will
redouble his efforts to go, and New York will end as the first
asylum of the megacity of the technological future. We who
leave will carry with us the infection of the cowardice and
apathy, the sense of defeat of the terminal years. We will move
into other cities similarly affected or into a countryside wary of
us, for we are then packers and peddlers from an expiring social
world. So our first problem is to find whether we can find a way
to rally our morale.

Part of the tragedy, part of the unbelievable oncoming
demise of New York is that none of us can simply believe it. We
were always the best and the strongest of cities, and our people
were vital to the teeth. Knock them down eight times and they
would get up with that look in the eye which suggests the fight
has barely begun. We were the city of optimists. It is probably
why we settled so deep into our mistakes. We simply couldn't
believe that we weren't inexhaustible as a race – an unspoken
race of New Yorkers.

Now all of our problems have the magnitude of junkie
problems – they are so coexistent with our life that New Yorkers do not try to solve them but escape them. Our fix is to put the
blame on the Blacks and Puerto Ricans. But everybody knows
that nobody can really know where the blame resides. Nobody
but a candidate for mayor. It is the only way he can have the
optimism to run. So the prospective candidate writing these
words has the heart to consider entering the Democratic primary on June 17 because he thinks he sees a way out of the
swamp: better, he believes he glimpses a royal road.

The face of the solution may reside in the notion that the Left has been absolutely right on some critical problems of our time, and the conservatives have been altogether correct about one enormous matter – which is that the federal government has no business whatever in local affairs. The style of New York life has shifted since the Second World War (along with the rest of the American cities) from a scene of local neighborhoods and personalities to a large dull impersonal style of life which deadens us with its architecture, its highways, its abstract welfare, and its bureaucratic reflex to look for government solutions which come into the city from without (and do not work). So the old confidence that the problems of our life were roughly equal to our abilities has been lost. Our authority has been handed over to the federal power. We expect our economic solutions, our habitats, yes, even our entertainments, to derive from that remote abstract power, remote as the other end of a television tube. We are like wards in an orphan asylum. The shaping of the style of our lives is removed from us – we pay for huge military adventures and social experiments so separated from our direct control that we do not even know where to begin to look to criticize the lack of our power to criticize. We cannot – the words are now a cliché, the life has gone out of them – we cannot forge our destiny. So our condition is spiritless. We wait for abstract impersonal powers to save us, we despise the abstractness of those powers, we loathe ourselves for our own apathy. Orphans.

Who is to say that the religious heart is not right to think the need of every man and woman alive may be to die in a state of grace, a grace which for atheists and agnostics may reside in the basic art of having done one's best, of having found some part of a destiny to approach, and having worked for the view of it? New York will not begin to be saved until its men and women begin to believe that it must become the greatest city in the world, the most magnificent, most creative, most extraordinary, most just, dazzling, bewildering, and balanced of cities. The demand upon us has come down to nothing less than that.

How can we begin? By the most brutal view, New York City is today a legislative pail of dismembered organs strewn from

Washington to Albany. We are without a comprehensive function or a skin. We cannot begin until we find a function which will become our skin. It is simple: our city must become a state. We must look to become a state of the United States separate from New York State; the fifty-first, in fact, of the United States. New York City State, or the State of New York City. It is strange on the tongue, but not so strange.

Think on the problem of this separation. People across the state are oriented toward Buffalo or Albany or Rochester or Montreal or Toronto or Boston or Cleveland. They do not think in great numbers of coming to New York City to make their life. In fact the good farmers and small-town workers of New York State rather detest us. They hear of the evils of our city with quiet thin-lipped glee; in the state legislature they rush to compound those evils. Every time the city needs a program which the state must approve, the city returns with a part of its package – the rest has been lost in deals, compromises, and imposts. The connection of New York City to New York State is a marriage of misery, incompatibility, and abominable old quarrels.

While the separation could hardly be as advantageous to New York State as it would be for the city, it might nonetheless begin the development of what has been hitherto a culturally undernourished hinterland, a typically colorless national tract.

But we will not weep for New York State – look, rather, to the direct advantages to ourselves. We have, for example, received no money so far for improving our city transit lines, yet the highway program for America in 1968 was $5 billion. Of this, New York State received at least $350 million for its roads. New York City received not a dollar from Washington or Albany for reconstruction of its six thousand miles of streets and avenues.

As a city-state we could speak to the federal government in the unmistakable tones of a state. If so many hundreds of millions go to Pennsylvania and Oklahoma and Colorado and Maine for their highway programs, then we could claim that a comparable amount is required for our transportation problems, which can better be resolved by the construction of new rapid transit. Add the money attainable by an increased ability as the fifty-first state to press for more equitable return on our taxes. Repeat: we give to Washington and Albany almost five tax dollars for every dollar which returns; Mississippi, while declaiming the virtues and inviolability of states' rights, still gets four federal dollars for every income-tax dollar she pays up.

As the center of the financial and communications industries, as the first victim of a nuclear war, the new state of the City of New York would not have the influence of one state in fifty-one, but rather would exist as one of the two or three states whose force and influence could be felt upon every change in the country's policy. With the power implicit in this grip, it may not be excessive to assume that divorce from Albany would produce an extra billion in real savings and natural efficiency, and still another billion (not to mention massive allocations for transit problems) could derive from our direct relation with the federal government: the first shift in our ability to solve our problems might have begun.

It would not, however, be nearly enough. The ills of New York cannot be solved by money. New York will be ill until it is magnificent. For New York must be ready to show the way to the rest of Western civilization. Until it does, it will be no more than the first victim of the technological revolution no matter how much money it receives in its budget. Money bears the same relation to social solutions that water does to blood.

Yet the beginning of a city-state and the tonic of a potential budget of eight or nine or ten billion dollars would offer a base on which to build. Where then could we take it? How would we build?

We could direct our effort first against the present thickets of the City Charter. The Charter is a formidable document. There are some who would say it is a hideous document. Taken in combination with the laws of New York State, it is a legal mat guaranteed to deaden the nerve of every living inquiry. The Charter in combination with the institutional and municipal baggage surrounding it is guaranteed to inhibit any honest man from erecting a building, beginning an enterprise, organizing a new union, searching for a sensible variety of living zone, or speaking up for local control in education. It would strangle any honest mayor who approached the suffocations of air pollution

or traffic, tried to build workable on-the-job training, faced the
most immediate problems of law and order, attacked our
shortage of housing or in general even tried to conceive of a new
breath of civic effort. There is no way at present to circumvent
the thicket without looking to power brokers in the trade
unions, the Mafia, and real estate.

Only if the people of New York City were to deliver an
overwhelming mandate for a city-state could anything be done
about the thicket. Then the legal charter of the new state
could rewrite the means by which men and women could
work to make changes in the intimate details of their neighborhoods and their lives.

Such a new document would most happily be built upon one
concept so fundamental that all others would depend upon it.
This concept might state that power would return to the
neighborhoods.

Power to the neighborhoods! In the new city-state, every
opportunity would be offered to neighborhoods to vote to
become townships, villages, hamlets, subboroughs, tracts, or
small cities, at which legal point they would be funded directly
by the fifty-first state. Many of these neighborhoods would
manage their own municipal services, their police, sanitation,
fire protection, education, parks, or like very small towns, they
could, if they wished, combine services with other neighborhoods. Each neighborhood would thus begin to outline the style
of its local government by the choice of its services.

It may be recognized that we are at this point not yet vastly
different from a patch of suburbs and townships in Westchester
or Jersey. The real significance of power to the neighborhoods is
that people could come together and constitute themselves
upon any principle. Neighborhoods which once existed as
separate towns or districts, like Jamaica or New Utrecht or
Gravesend, might wish to become towns again upon just such a
historic base. Other neighborhoods with a sense of unity provided by their geography like Bay Ridge, Park Slope, Washington Heights, Yorkville, Fordham Road, Riverdale, Jackson
Heights, Canarsie, or Corona might be able without undue
discussion to draw their natural lines.

Poorer neighborhoods would obviously look to establish

themselves upon their immediate problems, rather than upon historical or geographical tradition. So Harlem, Bedford-Stuyvesant, and the Barrio in East Harlem might be the first to vote for power to their own neighborhoods so that they might be in position to administer their own poverty program, own welfare, their own education systems, and their own – if they so voted –police and sanitation and fire protection for which they would proceed to pay out their funds. They would then be able to hire their own people for their own neighborhood jobs and services. Their own teachers and communities would, if they desired, control their own schools. Their own union could rebuild their own slums. Black Power would be a political reality for Harlem and Bedford-Stuyvesant. Black people and, to the extent they desired, Puerto Rican people, could make separate but thoroughgoing attacks upon their economic problems, since direct neighborhoods funding would be available to begin every variety of economic enterprise. Black militants interested in such communal forms of economic activity as running their own factories could begin to build economies, new unions, and new trades in their neighborhoods.

Power to the neighborhoods would mean that any neighborhood could constitute itself on any principle, whether spiritual, emotional, economical, idealogical, or idealistic. Even prejudicial principles could serve as the base – if one were willing to pay. It could, for example, be established in the charter of the city-state that no principle of exclusion by race or religion would be tolerated in the neighborhoods unless each such neighborhood was willing to offer a stiff and proper premium for this desire in their taxes.

In reaction to this, each and every liberal, Negro and white, who would detest the relinquishment of the principle that no prejudice was allowed by law, might also consider the loss of the dream of integration as the greatest loss in the work of their lives. They would now be free to create neighborhoods which would incorporate on the very base of integration itself – Integration City might be the name of the first neighborhood to stand on the recapture of the old dream. Perhaps it might even exist where now is Stuyvesant Town.

On the other hand, people who wished anonymity or isolation from their neighbor could always choose large anonymous areas, neighborhoods only in name, or indeed could live in those undifferentiated parts of the city which chose no neighborhood for themselves at all. The critical point to conceive is that no neighborhood would come into existence because the mayoralty so dictated. To the extent that they had been conditioned for years by the notion that the government was the only agency large enough and therefore effective enough to solve their problems, so to that extent would many people be reluctant to move to solutions which came from themselves.

To the degree, however, that we have lost faith in the power of the government to conduct our lives, so too would the principle of power to the neighborhoods begin to thrive, so too would the first spiritual problem of the twentieth century – alienation from the self – be given a tool by which to rediscover oneself.

In New York, which is to say, in the twentieth century, one can never know whether the world is vastly more or less violent than it seems. Nor can we discover which actions in our lives are authentic or which belong to the art of the put-on. Conceive that society has come to the point where tolerance of others' ideas has no meaning unless there is benumbed acceptance of the fact that we must accept their lives. If there are young people who believe that human liberty is blockaded until they have the right to take off their clothes in the street – and more! and more! – make love on the hood of an automobile – there are others who think it is a sin against the eyes of the Lord to even contemplate the act in one's mind. Both could now begin to build communities on their separate faiths – a spectrum which might run from Compulsory Free Love to Mandatory Attendance in Church on Sunday! Grant us to recognize that wherever there is a common desire among people vital enough to keep a community alive, then there must be also the presence of a clue that some kind of real life resides in the desire. Others may eventually discern how.

Contained beneath the surface of the notion is a recognition that the twentieth century has lost its way – the religious do not know if they believe in God, or even if God is not dead; the materialist works through the gloomy evidence of socialism and bureaucracy; the traditionalist is hardly aware any longer of a battlefield where the past may be defended; the technician – if sensitive – must wonder if the world he fashions is evil, insane, or rational; the student rebellion stares into the philosophical gulf of such questions as the nature of culture and the student's responsibility to it; the Blacks cannot be certain if they are fundamentally deprived, or a people of genius, or both. The answers are unknown because the questions all collide in the vast empty arena of the mass media where no price has ever to be paid for your opinion. So nobody can be certain of his value – one cannot even explore the validity of one's smallest belief. To wake up in New York with a new idea is to be plunged into impotence by noon, plunged into that baleful sense of boredom which hints of dread and future violence.

So the cry of 'Power to the Neighborhoods!' may yet be heard. For even as marriage reveals the balance between one's dream of pleasure and one's small real purchase upon it, even as marriage is the mirror of one's habits, and the immersion of the ego into the acid of the critic, so life in the kind of neighborhood which contains one's belief of a possible society is a form of marriage between one's social philosophy and one's private contract with the world. The need is deeper than we could expect, for we are modern, which is to say we can never locate our roots without a voyage of discovery.

Perhaps then it can be recognized that power to the neighborhoods is a most peculiar relocation of the old political directions. It speaks from the Left across the divide to conservatism. Speaking from the Left, it says that a city cannot survive unless the poor are recognized, until their problems are underlined as not directly of their own making; so their recovery must be based upon more than their own private efforts, must be based in fact upon their being capitalized by the city-state in order that the initial construction of their community economics, whether socialist or capitalist or both, can begin.

Yet with power in the neighborhoods, so also could there be on-the-job training in carpentry, stonemasonry, plumbing, plastering, electrical work, and painting. With a pool of such newly skilled workers, paid by the neighborhood, the possibility is present to rebuild a slum area *room by room*.

Better! The occupant of an apartment who desires better housing could go to work himself on his own apartment, using neighborhood labor and funds, patching, plastering, painting, installing new wiring and plumbing – as the tenant made progress he could be given funds to continue, could own the pride of having improved his housing in part through his own efforts.

So power to these poor neighborhoods still speaks to conservative principles, for it recognizes that a man must have the opportunity to work out his own destiny, or he will never know the dimensions of himself, he will be alienated from any sense of whether he is acting for good or evil. It goes further. Power to all neighborhoods recognizes that we cannot work at our destiny without a contest – that most specific neighborhood which welcomes or rejects our effort, and so gives a mirror to the value of our striving, and the distortion of our prejudice. Perhaps it even recognizes the deepest of conservative principles – that a man has a right to live his life in such a way that he may know if he is dying in a state of grace. Our lives, directed by abstract outside forces, have lost that possibility most of all. It is a notion on which to hit the campaign trail.

Which is where we go now – into the campaign: to talk in the days ahead of what power to the neighborhoods will mean. We will go down the steps of the position papers and talk of jobs and housing and welfare, of education, municipal unions, and law and order, finance, the names of laws, the statistics of the budget, the problems of traffic and transportation. There will be a paucity of metaphor and a taste of stale saliva to the debates, for voters are hardworking people who trust the plain more than the poetic. How then can Mailer and Breslin, two writers with reputations notorious enough for four, ever hope to convince the voting hand of the electorate? What would they do if, miracle of political explosions, they were to win?

Well, they might cry like Mario Procaccino, for they would never have a good time again; but they would serve, they would learn on the job, they would conduct their education in public. They would be obliged to. And indeed the supposition could remain that they might even do well, better than the men before them. How else could they have the confidence to run. They might either have supposed that the Lord was not dead but behind them or they must have felt such guilt about the years of their lives that only the long running duties of office could satisfy the list of their dues.

As for the fact that they were literary men – that might be the first asset of all. They would know how to talk to the people – they would be forced to govern by the fine art of the voice. Exposed by their own confession as amateurs they might even attract the skill of the city to their service, for the community would be forced to swim in full recognition of the depth of the soup. And best of all, what a tentative confidence would reign in the eye of New York that her literary men, used to dealing with the proportions of worlds hitherto created only in the mind, might now have a sensitive nose for the balances and the battles, the tugs, the pushing, the heaves of that city whose declaration of new birth was implicit in the extraordinary fact that *him*, Mailer! and *him*, Breslin! had been voted in.

Sweet Sunday, dear friends, and take a chance. We are out on the lottery of the years.


## Two Mayoralty Speeches


### At the Village Gate

*(May 7, 1969)*

Now, look, let me talk, because it's my evening and you know it. I listened to you a long time, and I'll tell you why I listened to you. I'll tell you why there are no Black people here tonight – it's a simple reason. It's because Adam Clayton Powell has not decided whether he's going to declare yet or not, and the Black people know they would be foolish to declare for a maverick candidate until Adam Clayton Powell has made up his mind. It's as simple as that.

All right, now look, let me have your attention, really. Let me try something. Can you hear me without the mike? All right now, let's get into a couple of very simple small bags, which is – one, we're in the Village Gate, which has the worst psychedelic acoustics in the whole world. The acoustics in this place are hooked, (yea, fuck you)* are hooked out of Art D'Lugoff's beard. And I love Art, because he is an ogre just like me, and Art decided a long time ago that he was expendable, but he said to the whole world and New York, 'To hell with you; shove it up your screw. I'm here, I'm running the Village Gate. You cannot stop me unless you come in here and wipe me out.' And they never came in, and Art created a neighborhood.

Now the reason I hate talking into this mike is because it sets up a hypnotic trance which is full of the weaker bullshit in our continuing relationship. Now get away from me, everybody. Now look, look, let's be sensible for a little while. You're just nothing but a bunch of spoiled pigs -- and there ain't a cop in the house! And yesterday I went up to the Police Academy and talked not to the cops first, but to the students at the John Jay Criminal Justice Academy or whatever it is called. (Please get away from me, and stop all this dull bullshit. I'm onto it -- I'm onto it. Don't interrupt me when I'm talking, I'll be interrupted soon enough.)

(From audience: Norman, talk about the fifty-first state, you're among friends.) Hey, I'll tell you something. Shut up. You're not my friend if you interrupt me when I'm talking 'cause it just breaks into the mood in my mind. So fuck you, too. All right, I said you're all a bunch of spoiled pigs. You're more spoiled than the cops. I'll tell you that, I'll tell you that. You've been sittin' around jerkin' off, havin' your jokes for twenty-two years. Yeah! And more than that -- more than that. You all want to work for us? You get in there, and you do your discipline, and you do your devotion. You get in there, and you do some dull work. Don't come in there and help us because 'we're gonna give Norm a little help.' Fuck you! You help us or don't come near us. I'll tell you why -- 'cause we can win this thing. We can win it, if we're very good. We can win it with all of you angels and devils. But we can't win it, we can't win it if you come in here with your dull little vanities. The cops I talked to yesterday were a more impressive group of people than all of you. I'll tell you that.

* Parentheses are response to audience heckling.

Now is there anybody here who is not familiar with our program by now? No one? All right, then this I say to you. This I say to you. You are all gonna go through a tremendous hour of horror, panic, and vomit if you start to work seriously for us, because you know I'm not the only nearsighted crazy man in America, and some of you could get hit. Get it straight. If you're gonna come in and work for us then work, but leave your ego at the door. If you think I'm in this for fun, then I feel sorry for you, 'cause I might have to pass on you after I have gone through. Got it? Got it? All right. Then fuck you. Got it? If you're gonna help me, then help me. But I don't want any of those dull mother-tired ego trips. Work.

Now, to prove to you how good this mayoralty is gonna be . . . I didn't quit while I was ahead, I'm about to reinvest my winnings and see if I can capture some of the more delicate spirits in the house. The point to what we're up to is that we are either running in fun or not. Since the neighborhood assembled here has only one thing in common, which is that they have a ticklish little liver and anus on the notion of who is putting who on, they think, they think that we are running in fun. Some of our own people put out campaign buttons like 'Mailer-Breslin Seriously.' Let me point out to you one quick little notion. Anybody who is runnin' in fun in the mayoralty election in New York deserves to run in fun.

Now I wanna finish with a small story, which you can shove down your throats. Years ago, I went out with the distinguished novelist, Mr. Ralph Ellison, to Iowa for a schlock magazine called *Esquire* run by a martinet and tyrant named Harold Hayes, who wouldn't know a good piece of writing until the Pulitzer Prize kicks him in the back of the ear. One of my dearest friends! And he went out there. A little fellow named Mark Harris – he's a little Jewish fellow with a big cigar which he blew in everyone's face, he's a tiny version of Groucho Marx, and Dwight MacDonald looking as though he was gonna die of asthma and apoplexy twenty-two years ago, and Ellison, and myself. And we went out there to Iowa and we said – this is back in 1959 – over and over again that the country is in a terrible time. It is full of the worst disease. You don't begin to know how bad this country has become. You people in Iowa have to recognize this is a marvelous state, Iowa, but it really doesn't begin to know how awful things are outside. And we got this marvelous applause, and we kept saying people in Iowa – we didn't know the word 'turned on' – we kept saying people in Iowa are marvelous, until we found out they all were graduate students from Michigan and, ah, places like, ah, Philadelphia. So when it was over, like a high-school team that fought a very good game and finally lost in the last quarter, I turned to Ellison in the dressing room – we were having some drinks with some marvelous-looking Republican women – and I said, 'Ralph, what the hell do we do it for? Why do we work so hard?' And he said, 'Well, we're expendable.'

So get that into your head. There's a very simple little notion going on, which is, we're all going to run and we're gonna do our best, and we'll go on for eighty-two years or more. But the notion to get through your heads is to get over your silly little ego-tired trips. If you have a lot of money, and that's the way that you turn on to workin' for us, then thank you very much. We can use that money if you give it to us, and you can give it to us any way you want – publicly, privately, quietly, at large or small. If you have other ways of working for us, work for us.

What we really want is to get out into the nieghborhoods. I want to go out and talk in every neighborhood before I'm done. I'll talk in the sweetest neighborhoods and the worst neighborhoods. But I'm running on the notion that New York can't begin to become the incredibly absolute and magnificent city that it is until there is power to the neighborhoods. Two weeks ago at the end of a long evening of campaigning, speaking at a marvelous, to me, Irish Club in Park Slope – overcome with happiness, I said, 'I am running on everything from Black Power to Irish Self-Righteousness,' and the good Irishmen in that place laughed and applauded, and I thought I had a victory until I read in the *Village Voice* that the smell of political death was upon us. I know what the fellow was up to. He was saying – 'Get out of this campaign. You're just a little Jewish fellow from Brooklyn, and you don't know what's up.' Well, let me tell you something. I know what's up because the greatest Jewish paper in New York, the despicable *New York Post*, won't print a word of what we're up to. And let me tell you what that means – let me tell you this – I am proud of my people. Very few people understand the Jews, but I do, 'cause I'm one of them. Fuck you, let me talk. The Jews are an incredible people at their best. At their worst they are swine. Like every Wasp I ever met, at their worst they are awful. All people are awful at their worst. Some are worse than others. But the Jews are sensational at their best, which is rare enough, given Miami and a fur coat. No, don't laugh, because you don't know what you're laughing at. Think about it. Whenever a people loses its highest race, there's nothing funnier going on in the world.

What we're running on is this: that this town has come to the point where this town, that many of us grew up in, the greatest city in the history of the world conceivably, is now some sort of paralytic victim in an orphan asylum. This city must be saved by vigorous activity by everybody within it, and I'm not just talking in my cups. But as the people of New York turn on and become fantastic, which we all are because I've met more interesting people in New York, per capita, than anywhere else in the world . . . Come on, let's not spend any time on applause, let's get to the point. The point is simple. Unless this city turns on and becomes fantastic, it'll become the first victim of the technological society – you know what that means? That means that the smog, the dead, dull air of oppression will be upon us first, and we will destroy each other first, because we all have too much within us to be able to bear the unendurable dullness of our days in New York when we all know we're capable of so much more.

So this I say to you. If we don't save our city, our city will become that little ward, that ward of eight million. There'll be a fifty-mile bypass around us, and they'll say, 'We understand there are three divisions of Marines in there to keep the populace down.' (No, keep quiet! Let me finish 'cause I'm talkin' very hard. Look – don't come here to be entertained), we're into somethin' that's deep. Don't kid yourself on this. We're running on the notion of power to the neighborhoods. What we're saying is very simple. We're saying – (Shut up and fuck you! Let me talk) – we're here on something very simple, which is that nobody knows any longer which idea has more validity than another, because there's no ground, there's no content, there's no situation for an idea. We're running on one notion – let the Left and the Right have their neighborhoods. Let them each see what kind of society they can create and then decide on the basis of a thousand contests and a hundred bloody encounters which particular neighborhood, or style, or conception of life is more interesting than another. Let people at least be ready to begin to put their notion of existence behind themselves, in front of themselves, within themselves. Let them begin to work for something they believe in. Nobody in this city can begin to work for anything they believe in, 'cause it just isn't there, it just doesn't exist.

This city is controlled from without. That's why everybody is going crazy in this city, because they have no objective correlative, which I remind you literary people is a remark first coined in twentieth-century cultural history by Mr. T. S. Eliot, of all people. There is no objective correlative in this city, but we say power to the neighborhoods would give an objective correlative that would give a notion of where everybody is. We are running on one profound notion. Free Huey Newton, end fluoridation. We're running on another profound notion – compulsory free love in those neighborhoods which vote for it along with compulsory church attendance on Sunday for those neighborhoods who vote for that. What we are running on is one basic, simple notion – which is that till people see where their ideas lead they know nothing; and that, my fine friends, is why I am running. I want to see where my own ideas lead. Thank you very much.

*To the Time – Life Staff*

(*June 3, 1969*)

If I win the primary on June 17, I am – as Breslin always says – in trouble. I'm in terrible trouble. I will then have to go on and work in the mayoralty campaign all summer and earn not a sou. And after that point, if I win, I'll be in the paltry position of entering the mayoralty a tremendous number of bucks in debt. How will I ever keep from becoming corrupt? So you have to assume my candidacy is a prima facie case of seriousness. No man runs to win in such a way as to pauperize himself, unless he is either the victim of a *grande idée* or paying his debt to society. I submit that I'm paying my debt to society, and that is why I'm running for mayor.

Since I have brought the mood of this audience down to zero in my feisty* little way, let me present the simple campaign notions upon which we're running. They are several. One, that New York has become a city so sick, so wracked with pain, so torporous, feverish, edemic, pandemic, and miserable that, as my running mate, James Breslin, says: 'To run frivolously in a city as mortally ill as New York would be a sin.' The city is suffering from every disease that sets upon America, including the disease of bad reportage. None of us, by now, has an accurate notion of what is going on anywhere at all. We have the most extraordinary network of communications in the history of Western civilization, and we have less sense of where reality resides than perhaps at any time in our history. And the reason is that we are a divided nation. But we are a nation divided within the soul of each man and woman alive in the country, because we are racing forward, on the one hand, at a great rate toward the most extraordinary adventures in the history of man, and on the other hand, we find ourselves each year, each season, virtually each month, more and more unable to solve our most fundamental social problems. And in New York the diseases of America settle, and develop, and fester, and finally begin to burn and suggest that eventually they may even explode. We live in a city which has an enormous welfare roll. We have more than a million people on welfare in this city. The figure is actually one million two hundred thousand people. The moneys that we spend for welfare are over a billion and a half dollars a year now – they're larger than the amount we spend for education. Yet that welfare roll we support in this city – not through direct payments – although more than directly we support it, as I will try to suggest a little later, that welfare roll is not even of our own creation.

There have been extraordinary developments made by the kind of corporations who produce farm machinery. They have

* There had been a reference to the candidate as 'feisty' in the preceding issue of *Time*.

discovered ways to mine the bottom lands of great cotton states like Mississippi. And in the course of that, whole hordes of tenant farmers who'd been buried in a miserable existence but nonetheless a cultivated one, because they at least partook of a culture down South, were uprooted and came here to the North, where they immediately were drawn by the fact that New York was a city with a mildly liberal tradition, a city which sought to pay people on welfare a little more than people were being paid in other cities. So a disproportionate number of dispossessed farm workers came to New York, and our welfare rolls began to grow, and grew at a huge rate.

We had, at the same time, a series of powerful unions in this city, who would not let Black or Puerto Rican people into those unions. So the people who came here went on welfare and stayed on welfare, and their condition deepened until it became a way of life. And as it became a way of life, so it became a way of criminal life; and criminality became attached to the edges of welfare so that many a hardworking woman lived on her welfare check and brought up her children, legitimate or illegitimate, and the young boys who grew up in this environment began to look more and more for purposes in crime. Because crime, for a man who is poor and landless and disenfranchised and living on a government dole, is finally a witty activity. It is the one way in which he may express himself.

So the crisis of the city deepened. It was like a boat waterlogged with welfare. On the other hand, all sorts – to use the worst word for crime – all sorts of rats were feeding on the cargo. This ship has been staggering along and getting into worse condition year after year after year, until now there's grave question whether it can really be saved, short of a federal takeover of the economic necessities of this city. Now in this situation, any man who runs for mayor has good cause to examine his motives, if he's interested in attacking the problem on the old basis. To wit, running for mayor in such a way that he would be elected: making the old deals in the old ways, coming into power with an administration and a bureaucracy and a set of municipal unions who are all waterlogged themselves, all corrupt themselves, all full of crime themselves. Trying to work and accomplish anything in such a city – no matter how brave or honorable or worthwhile or even noble he may be in his own mind and to others – his hands are tied, he is manacled to the oppression of his condition because he too is oppressed. He has to deal with an administrative system which is impenetrable. So, at that point, he may be a man as well-intentioned as our honorable John V. Lindsay and still fail. He can work like a Trojan for four years and go down to abysmal defeat after defeat. The dificulty in the situation is that there is no way to solve the problems of New York, because the most fundamental problems of New York are not only aggravated by the farm machinery, but by the legislative morass of the north in Albany.

So over the last year, as must have been suggested to a thousand men in this city, many people came to me time and again to say, 'Well, why don't you run for mayor? If Bill Buckley could run for mayor, you certainly can run for mayor.' And I kept saying it was impossible. It was hopeless. One would not even begin to think of running for mayor. It is too terrible a job to contemplate if you ever won.

Until that marvelous day, and I blush to admit this, when a magazine editor talking to me said: 'Norman, have you ever thought of the fifty-first state, of New York becoming a separate state?' And at that moment I said, 'Good Lord, I've now found a way to pay my enormous account to you. I can work, I can campaign, I can serve. I can run on a notion that makes sense to me, which is that if New York can become the fifty-first state, it can begin to attack its incredible problems.' Because if I run, and win a primary, and go on from there to win a mayoralty election against the extraordinary opposition of forces by stealing a primary election, then indeed a small miracle would have happened in this city; and the people of this city would have voted for a set of ideas which would be unheralded in previous political history. To wit, they would not have voted for their immediate security, but for setting out on an adventure whose end could not be foreseen. Because at that moment when the people would vote to become the fifty-first state, which as I say would be embodied in our candidacy, at that moment the city would have declared that it had lost faith in the old ways of solving political problems, that it wished to embark on a new conception for politics.

Now this new conception would revolve around the second point in our platform, which is power to the neighborhoods. And what indeed could that possibly mean? It means something unheralded in American politics. It means that, because a state had been declared by majority vote of the citizens of this city and I can say in parenthesis that if the mayoralty election were won in a three- to four-cornered race, and one did not have a majority, there would be no recourse but to throw the city open to a referendum, where the people of the city would vote on whether they wished to have a fifty-first state or not, because one could not begin to proceed without a majority of the people in the city voting to become the fifty-first state – one could not steal or trick such an election. At that point, having won such a majority, one could then call into being a constitutional convention, which might be one of the most remarkable moments in the history of this city or of any city, because the talent and the dedication and the hard consciousness of people in this city is remarkable. There's more talent waiting on line in this city, there's more energy bottled up and pent waiting to express itself in this city than perhaps in any city in America – and that's possibly a way of saying any city in the world. The people in this city have been disenfranchised from any kind of power, any kind of approach to the problems before them which could have political issue for twenty years. It is impossible for any man, even a man of power, to get anything done in this city, and it has been impossible for many, many years. So, at this moment, we might assume that an extraordinary amount of intelligence and experience might collect to write a constitution which would be a remarkable document, because it would have to contend with the age-old problems – no, the two-centuries-old problems of the constitution. It would have to deal with checks and balances, the proportion of power. It would have to contend primarily with the notion, upon the one hand of power to the neighborhoods, and on the other hand that power which is due in respect to the Constitution of the United States to the Supreme Court, the decisions of the Supreme Court, and to the power of the new state. Under the umbrellas of the Constitution of the United States, the Supreme Court, and the powers allocated to the new state, power to the neighborhoods could have its expression. It would begin by neighborhoods voting themselves into existence in the new state, declaring that they wish to become neighborhoods incorporated, small towns, small cities, hamlets, villages – whatever. These neighborhoods would have powers to deal with their own immediate problems in a way they cannot deal with them now. And so a great variety of neighborhoods would soon begin to flourish, one might hope, in this city. At the very least, if the acrimony, if the sense of combat and strife in these neighborhoods was fierce, people living in these neighborhoods would have a sense of whether they adhered to the principles of the neighborhood, or if they really, literally, wished to move out and move on. But the one virtue of this, it seems to me, is that the energies of the people of New York, which at present have no purchase or power – no purchase on their own natural wit or intelligence – no purchase other than to watch with a certain grim humor, a gallows humor, the progressive deterioration of this city, those energies could now be attached to working for their deepest and most private and most passionate ideas about the nature of government, the nature of politics, the nature of man's relation to his own immediate society. And it's possible that out of this interaction of these neighborhoods – which would be like small towns only in one sense, which is that they be small – these people might produce extraordinary results. So I present to you this notion: that we might begin to discover the nature of our reality as men and women in this seventh decade of the twentieth century. We might begin to discover which political ideas had validity, the power to continue themselves, and nourish themselves, and those ideas which, finally, were surrealistic, nihilistic, excessive, and destructive to the ultimate aims of society, which finally is to find some balance in the lives of men and women.

Now, on this notion, I would like to throw some time open to you for questions and I will do my best to answer them, and then proceed with a peroration, if that still remains within our possibility. Thank you.

*What makes you think you could get the fifty-first state?*

I would ask you to use your imagination. We are not talking
about the city as it exists today. We're talking about the city
after Mailer and Breslin – forgive me for talking like a conventional politician – after Mailer and Breslin succeed in stealing a
primary election in the Democratic Party from Meade Esposito,
Mario Procaccino, and a few other people. Now, at that point,
that is an extraordinary moment in the history of the city,
nothing less. If we then go on, but I would submit that is easier
to do than win the mayoralty election, because at that point the
time is so surrealistic that people might just say, 'Oh, the hell
with everyone. Let's just vote them in. Vote them in, so we'll
have some amusement.' Well, at that point, we then have four
months to run through a hot summer through September and
October, working under the long shadow of John Lindsay, who
will seem more viable to leftists, liberals, conservatives, and
reactionaries alike each day that they come face to face with the
fact that if they vote for us, they are voting for an embarkation
upon an unknown journey, which may end with the city of New
York being cut loose from the mainland of America and being
shipped out to sea. So I say to you, at that point, when we win
the mayoralty election, this city will have gone through a
transformation so extraordinary that the questions with which
we engage ourselves today are not likely to be nearly so alive and
pressing.

*If you were mayor or governor of New York would you be able to
continue writing?*

I think, since I pay great attention to my betters, that would be a
small sacrifice to make. I would merely have confirmed the fond
opinion that *Time* magazine has of me, which is 'this fella better
stop writing or none of us will benefit.' Seriously, I would not be
able to continue writing, dear lady.

*What are the legal steps necessary to achieve statehood?*

There are three steps. A constitutional convention would have
to be called; it would doubtless take months for a constitution to

be written. At that point, it would be submitted to the state legislature in Albany for ratification; once Albany had ratified it, it would go to the Congress of the United States for ratification, and on that happy day we would be a state. Now, if you say how is that possible, how would Albany ever begin to pass it, let me point out to you, sir, that something like forty-two or forty-three percent of the legislators, I think it's actually more than that, forty-four percent of the legislators in Albany come from New York City. And one would assume that the large majority of those men and women would be prepared to vote for statehood about the time we had gotten in, for that would be the shock from which no one could recover. It would mean that people who felt they really understood the political game would have to recognize they didn't understand it at all, and so they would be inclined to go along with the winner. Politicians keep that as their last resort. If you can't figure out what else to do, go along with the winner. I think we could find another five or ten or fifteen percent in the upstaters who are proud and feel that we in New York City have been dragging them down for one hundred and eighty-two years. On top of that, I think that President Nixon might go to the phone and talk to Rockefeller and say, 'Now look, there's not much else you can do. Are you going to put on your tin hat? Are you going to go at the head of the state militia and cross at Yonkers?' He'll be worse than that; he'll say, 'Will you defile through the hills of the Bronx? Cross the Harlem River? Move south? You will never reach Central Park!'

*Do you have political ambitions beyond becoming the mayor of New York City?*

It's precisely because I have the stature I have that my ambitions are limited. I wish to be mayor of New York. Lindsay, who's a tall fellow, looks further.

*You've put forward a very provocative idea, the fifty-first state. Do you feel anyone is listening to this at all?*

When we go down the street, we find that more people have heard of this idea than have heard of us, when we get out in the neighborhoods. They say, 'Oh yeah, you're the fellows who are running with the ah – what is it – the fifty-first state.' And I get the feeling, maybe, that I have nothing but candidatitis; but I also get the feeling that people are particularly excited by this idea. Of course, I have an interest in thinking that way.

*Why did you support the dual admissions policy for CCNY?*

Well, I was the only candidate who supported the dual admissions plan, and I was pleased to find myself in such a position because it meant that I was living well, since it's almost impossible in a mayoral primary in which you have five men running in one election and two in another to find yourself on one side of an issue . . . well, you're all very serious about CCNY, aren't you? All right, I'll talk particularly straight about CCNY. It gives no one any pleasure, who has grown up in this city as I have, in Brooklyn, to enjoy seeing the pearl of the free higher educational system in New York having its standards adulterated. But the fact of the matter is simply this: we really don't know. One, we have no idea at all what's going to happen after two or three years; in other words, the students who succeed in being admitted without academic standards to CCNY will have much more life experience, presumably, than the students whose marks are a little better, because they've grown up in an environment which is near criminal for many of them. So I would just suggest that a great many of the people – among them the candidates who have been bleating about law and order and getting the crime off the streets – are acting like unconscionable hypocrites. Would they rather have those young people out on the streets, unemployed, living on welfare and looking for extraordinary varieties of mischief or would they rather have some of them going through the Draconian steps of trying to reorient themselves into an educational system, and conceivably some of them even wrestling with books at night to catch up? So to begin with, what was marvelous about the dual admissions system is that it would have opened the system to the kids who are presently wrecking and sacking the high schools and running through them with only one sort of expertise, which is, whoever is most adept at disrupting the educational system in the high school because there is no future past these high schools. They know their marks are so poor that they can't begin to contemplate getting into a university. Having them now being able to contemplate the fact that, yes, they can get into universities, they will feel that first moment of fear – of what happens if I go to a university and I'm completely ill-equipped? Some of them might even begin to start studying in high school, which opens up the possibility that the high schools may be seeded by this first seeding and may begin to improve a little bit, so that the morale of the teachers may begin to improve at that point also. Now, all these matters, I think, are more substantial than the fact that the educational standards at CCNY may be lowered for a period. It's my optimism and my hope that Black and Puerto Rican students who enter CCNY will end up being fine students, and the academic standards of CCNY, after a few years, will become as high as they are now or even higher. But even if that does not happen, we have to recognize that we are merely paying our dues, because the history of the treatment of Black people in this city is not an honorable history or an agreeable one. They've been kept from getting into any of the powerful unions of this city, so they have not been able to enter the working class and the middle class in any numbers. And now that they've been shut out from all other opportunities, now that they are pushing into the colleges, we bleat when we discover that white boys who are qualified are not going to get into these colleges. Well, I say fine, because that's the point when you're going to begin to have community colleges in this city built to fulfill precisely that need. The moment white boys can't get a free education, then you're going to get the community colleges, not before. So long as Black boys can't get it, you're going to keep having the same buck-passing and the same complaining about expenses, and so that was why I supported the dual admissions system.

*Wouldn't communities set up along geographical lines tend to freeze in present racial and economic distinctions very poor cities or very poor mini-cities that couldn't afford the police, the sanitation, and the fire departments that they would need . . . ?*

I think you'd have to begin with the notion that the fifty-first state would be able to command more moneys than New York City. We've had people working on it, and they can't come up with any figure that's really sufficiently satisfactory to present to a technical audience or even a critical audience, because there are too many fluctuations in too many of the figures. We estimate that, immediately, it would be worth between two and three billion dollars more a year to New York City, if it were a state. For instance, there are all sorts of taxes that we would be able to collect directly, like the cigarette tax, the gasoline tax, the tax on registered automobiles, the take on parimutuels – and if off-track betting were legalized, there would be a tremendous amount of money there. There would be any number of funds available that we don't have now, so we would have more money to deal with immediately. It seems to me that you would have to make some sort of estimate of the funds that are going into each neighbourhood now. For example, when you take poor neighborhoods you would have to estimate how much of the money that goes into those poor neighborhoods is spent on police. After the neighborhoods were constituted block to block, you could figure out what the administration of those neighborhoods had cost in the past, and these moneys would be passed over to the neighborhoods so they could elaborate their own forms of administration. They might wish to save money on one service or another in order to have more money available for other purposes. But on top of that, this could be any place in the city, and this is why I call myself a left-conservative, we would have to recognize that the history of these communities is not a fair nor an equitable history, and they are not capable of solving their problems through their own human agency nearly so well as we are in more fortunate communities. And so a majority of the new moneys in the new state would have to go toward economic funding in these communities. Now the difference between that and federal funding, which is going to happen anyway, is a great one, I think – because these particular poor neighborhoods would now be administering the funds themselves. So when people working in these programs began to cheat and swindle the programs they'd be cheating and might give even greater pause. So I think that would make swindling their own people rather than the federal government, and that I think would make a noticeable difference. I don't mean that all crime and all corruption and all embezzlement would stop; but I do think that it would make a big difference, because not only would they be cheating their own people, which might give great pause, but also they would have to face their own people, which might give even greater pause. So I think that would make for a more lively basis for economic funding for economic self-development in the poor communities.

*Even more than financial problems you might have the freezing of racial enclaves and the polarization of communities which I think we've got to try to correct in New York.*

Well, I think what you'd find is that you'd have a certain freezing into racial enclaves, as you put it, although I would suggest that that's exactly what we have today in the city, because there are few white people, for instance, who are going to just travel on the loose through Harlem after dark – just as a small example. So, as a practical matter, Harlem and the rest of Manhattan are more separated, I'd say, than East Berlin and West Berlin. But apart from that, what you also could recognize is to the extent that certain neighborhoods declared themselves for this sort of separation, other people who had been rather tolerant, fairly noncommittal liberals up to that point might say, 'This is a disgrace, now we've really got to work for integration because we're about to really lose it.' They might recognize that integration is something that has been given to us from above, and if they really wish to work for it, they now have to work for it directly. So I think you would have communities that would form themselves on principles of integration and collaboration and tolerance. And on top of that, you've also got to recognize that New York is a particularly curious city, and there are any number of blocks in this city and small neighborhoods in this city where you have a mix of six, eight, ten minority groups, and they all get along together reasonably well. Sometimes there's a historic tradition for it. There's one neighborhood, Park Slope in Brooklyn, that's marvelous, and I think one of the reasons for it is that architecturally it's a superb neighborhood. So even though people live there who are rich, poor, of all minority groups and races, the architecture – the character of the neighborhood – is lovely. So there's a certain possibility for getting and living together.

*Are you worried about hurting Badillo's chances in the primary?*

Let's take it head on. One, I don't think Herman Badillo has the chance of a snowball in hell of winning the primary, whether I'm in it or not. That's because I don't think he's a winner. I think he's a congressman, and I'm prepared to support him for Congress on that happy day he runs. Two, if Herman Badillo ever did win the primary he would hurt Mr. Lindsay's chances, because you would then have Lindsay running against Badillo, and you could be certain that you would have Marchi or Procaccino running on some other ticket. In fact, you certainly would have Marchi running against them, and you would have two liberals running against a conservative at that point. You would have an unhappy situation for yourself if you were a liberal. So I don't think I'm hurting anyone's chances because, since I'm running as a left-conservative, I'm to the left and right of every man in the race.

*If elected to the Harvard Board of Overseers, would you undermine Nathan Pusey's position as president?*

I think Nathan Pusey undermined his position on the campus many years ago when he put up that building on Mount Auburn Street, that Medical Health Center which is fourteen stories high and expresses a style in architecture known as brutalism, which is unfinished gray concrete. That building is one of the six ugliest buildings in the United States. And the campus at Harvard, no matter what you might have said about it in the past, was not a disagreeable campus, and Mount Auburn Street was one of the pleasanter streets in our vast vanishing Western world. I think on that day that Dr. Pusey permitted that building to be put in, one could read the future. He would do something precisely so idiotic as calling up the Cambridge cops to get the kids out of University Hall. So whether I'm elected to the Board of Overseers or not, I can't say that I have a high opinion of the ongoing potentialities of Dr. Pusey's presidency.

*Primary odds?*

Breslin figures he's an odds-on two-to-three favorite. I think I'm running as a twenty-to-one shot. But in the handicap, the mayoral handicap we set up the other day at Aqueduct, we did say that while I was by Amateur out of Statehood and it was my first start, I was out of a good barn. So the handicapper put stars after my entry and said 'Best Bet'. Of course, the handicapper was my campaign manager. Would you like to hear the rest of the handicapping? Well, it was the mayoral handicap, and in post position one was Wagner, a twelve-year-old gelding by Meade Esposito out of Machine. The handicapper's comment on him was 'Knows the track'. The odds were eight to five. In the second post position was Procaccino, a Bronx ridgling. Now a ridgling, for the ladies I must say to you, is a horse of evil disposition. In fact, the Italian word *vellano* is the only way to describe the disposition of a horse – what you do with a horse or a man who's *vellano* – I'll leave the man out of it – but in any case what you do with a horse who's *vellano* is you're obliged to perform a curious testicular operation – ah – which leaves the fellow with one nut. A ridgling. There was Procaccino, a Bronx ridgling. This is the one argument I had with my handicapper, who wrote this particular sheet. He had 'By Fear out of Law and Order.' I said to him after, 'You should have had "By Prunes out of Law and Order."' Anyway, the comment on him was 'Moves up on a sloppy track.' Then there was Badillo and Scheuer. They were an entry. They were both 'By Liberal out of Loser', eleven to one. And finally there was our own entry. 'Best Bet'.

So the notion that we're running on, finally, is that everybody in this city suffers from the same disease that everyone in America suffers from – that we suffer from it doubly, triply, and in exaggerated form, which is, we do not have a proper sense of our own identity. So, we argue that statehood, the quality of statehood, once achieved would perform several wonders for this city. Not because we would get more money, although I think we would, and I think that money would be terribly necessary, but because the citizens of this city would have embarked upon an adventure in voting for that statehood particularly since we're the candidates, at the moment, who embodied that desire. So to get to statehood at that point, they would have to vote for us, which means they would be voting for amateurs, which means they would be deserting their belief in expertise because we run on one notion over and over again, which is that the experts have driven this city right into the ground. And we run on the notion, finally, that politics is philosophy and that one cannot begin to solve the problems of a city without engaging in philosophical arrangements with oneself and with one's neighbor.

And the particular small continuing event which gives me most pleasure since I've been campaigning is I find that I can give my speeches at the level at which I wish to give them, I never try to talk down, I say what I wish to say to an audience, trying to pick up the mood of that audience, talking at my best to reach that audience, and I find that the philosophical density of the argument never bothers them one bit. I've talked to left-wing audiences, to right-wing audiences, to all sorts of audiences, and they all listen. The right-wing audiences listen even more carefully than the left-wing audiences because, perhaps, our words are fresher to them. At any rate, the powerful notion in it, which I think is appealing to all people in degree, is that if each group of people, each interest, each force in this city can begin to think in terms of neighborhoods, then it can begin to think in terms of discovering whether its own ideas have validity, have savor, give energy to others, give energy to oneself, or don't.

The tragedy of this city and the tragedy of this country is that we all live in a situation where none of us know what the reality is, and we explore for it and we explore for it – we spend our lives exploring for it – and we never find an objective ground where we can begin to locate whether some pet idea of ours or some profound idea of ours is partially true or partially untrue.

To talk about the situation, even briefly, people on the right wing feel that the Black people are lazy, spoiled, ungrateful, and incapable of managing their own society. Black people feel, I would guess on the one hand, that they have extraordinary possibilities and that they are great people. On the other hand, they have to feel that they can't possibly know, because they never had an opportunity to express that desire. So, if nothing else, Black communities working with their own power in their own neighborhoods could show to other neighborhoods one of two things, which is either that Black people were right about their potentiality for the future or that they were wrong and that, finally, they are incapable of making those extraordinary steps. And so that even right-wing people would have, at the end of that time, the confidence of knowing that they were seriously right or seriously wrong about some extraordinary matter. In turn, right-wing neighborhoods would discover in living with their principles whether their principles were nourishing and could maintain a society against all of the nihilistic tides of the twentieth century, or whether, finally, their principles were not sufficiently flexible to meet the extraordinary quality of the age. And on top of that, we would have the marvelous, if somewhat comic, alternatives of considering all those magical LSD communities where you would have children living on LSD for five years. At the end of that time they would either be creating castles, or they might be two-thirds dead of liver disease.

The notion that we're running on, then, is that until we begin to know a little more about each other – not through the old-fashioned New Deal governmental methods of tolerance – but through the quality of human experience in societies, small societies and somewhat larger societies, founded upon various principles – philosophical, spiritual, economic, geographical, territorial, historical, or whatever – we know nothing at all. And that's why I feel a certain optimism about this candidacy.

Because what I think it offers to all the people of the city of New York is a chance to turn this city around and make it what it once was – the leader of the world. Thank you.